The
Treasury *of*
English
Short Stories

The
Treasury *of*
English
Short Stories

Selected and with an Introduction by
Nancy Sullivan

BARNES
&NOBLE
BOOKS
NEW YORK

This edition published by Barnes & Noble, Inc.,
by arrangement with Doubleday Book and Music Clubs, Inc.

1993 Barnes & Noble Books

ISBN 1-56619-125-4
Printed and bound in the United States of America

M 9 8 7 6 5 4 3

ACKNOWLEDGMENTS

Grateful acknowledgment is made to the following for permission to reprint their copyrighted material. Every reasonable effort has been made to trace the ownership of all copyrighted stories included in this volume. Any errors which may have occurred are inadvertent and will be corrected in subsequent editions, provided notification is sent to the publisher.

"Rape Fantasies" by Margaret Atwood first appeared in *The Fiddlehead* (Winter 1975). Copyright © 1975 by Margaret Atwood. Reprinted by permission of the author.

"The Spring Hat" by H. E. Bates, copyright © 1961 by Evensford Productions, Ltd. Reprinted from *The Enchantress and Other Stories* by permission of Little, Brown and Company in association with The Atlantic Monthly Press; Laurence Pollinger Ltd. and the Estate of H. E. Bates.

"The Confirmation Suit" by Brendan Behan reprinted from *Brendan Behan's Island*, copyright © 1962 by Brendan Behan. Reprinted by permission of The Hutchinson Publishing Group, London.

"Hand in Glove" from *The Collected Stories of Elizabeth Bowen*, copyright 1952 by Curtis Brown, Ltd., Literary Executors of the Estate of Elizabeth Bowen. Reprinted by permission of Alfred A. Knopf, Inc. and Curtis Brown, Ltd.

"A Wedding-Dress" by Morley Callaghan from *Morley Callaghan's Short Stories*, copyright © 1959 by Morley Callaghan. Reprinted by permission of Don Congdon Associates, Inc. and Macmillan of Canada, Ltd.

"The Courtship of Mr. Lyon" from *The Bloody Chamber and Other Adult Tales* by Angela Carter. Copyright © 1979 by Angela Carter. Reprinted by permission of Harper & Row Publishers, Inc. and International Creative Management.

"New Women" copyright © 1958 by Joyce Cary. Reprinted from *Spring Song and Other Stories* by permission of Curtis Brown Group Limited.

Prolog and "The Reeve's Tale" from *The Canterbury Tales of Geoffrey Chaucer* translated by R. M. Lumiansky, copyright © 1948, 1975 by Simon & Schuster, Inc. Reprinted by permission of the publisher.

"Il Conde" from *A Set of Six* by Joseph Conrad. Copyright 1909 by Jessie Conrad. Reprinted by permission of Doubleday & Company, Inc. and Withers, Trustees of the Joseph Conrad Estate.

"Arabesque—The Mouse" from *The Collected Tales of A. E. Coppard*, reprinted by permission of David Higham Associates, Ltd.

"Timoshenko" from *The Hermit and Other Stories* by Iain Crichton Smith. Copyright © 1977 by Iain Crichton Smith. Reprinted by permission of Victor Gollancz Ltd.

"Royal Jelly" copyright © 1959 by Roald Dahl. Reprinted from *Kiss Kiss* by Roald Dahl, by permission of Alfred A. Knopf, Inc.

"The Creatures" by Walter de la Mare, reprinted by permission of the Literary Trustees of Walter de la Mare and The Society of Authors as their representatives.

"The Old Man" copyright 1952, 1953 by Daphne du Maurier. Reprinted from *Kiss Me Again, Stranger* by permission of Doubleday & Company, Inc. and Curtis Brown Ltd. on behalf of Daphne du Maurier.

"Prizes" from *The Reservoir* by Janet Frame, reprinted by permission of George Braziller, Inc.

"The Broken Boot" by John Galsworthy from *Captures*. Copyright 1923 by Charles Scribner's Sons; copyright renewed 1951 by Ada Galsworthy. Reprinted with the permission of Charles Scribner's Sons.

"Native Country" from *Not for Publication and Other Stories* by Nadine Gordimer. Copyright © 1965 by Nadine Gordimer. Reprinted by permission of Viking Penguin, Inc.

"Mortmain" from *Collected Stories* by Graham Greene. Copyright © 1963 by Graham Greene. Reprinted by permission of Viking Penguin, Inc. and Laurence Pollinger, Ltd.

"Weekend" from *Cliff of Fall and Other Stories* by Shirley Hazzard. Copyright © 1962 by Shirley Hazzard. First published in *The New Yorker*. Reprinted by permission of McIntosh & Otis, Inc.

"The Story of a Piebald Horse" from *Tales of the Pampas* by W. H. Hudson. Copyright 1916, 1939 and renewed 1967 by Alfred A. Knopf, Inc. Reprinted by permission of Alfred A. Knopf, Inc.

"Fard" from *Collected Short Stories* by Aldous Huxley. Copyright © 1922, 1957 by Aldous Huxley. Reprinted by permission of Mrs. Laura Huxley, Chatto & Windus and Harper & Row Publishers, Inc.

"A Day in the Country" from *A Long Way from London* by Dan Jacobson. Reprinted by permission of A. M. Heath & Co. Ltd. on behalf of the author.

"Night in Tunisia" from *Night in Tunisia* by Neil Jordan. Copyright © 1980 by Neil Jordan. Reprinted by permission of George Braziller, Inc.

"The Boarding House" from *The Dubliners* by James Joyce. Copyright 1916 by B. W. Huebsch. Definitive text copyright © 1967 by The Estate of James Joyce. Reprinted by permission of Viking Penguin, Inc.

"Mary Postgate" copyright 1915 by Rudyard Kipling, from *Best Short Stories of Rudyard Kipling*. Reprinted by permission of Doubleday & Company, Inc. and A. P. Watt Ltd., The National Trust and Macmillan London, Ltd.

"Eterna" from *The Shrine and Other Stories* by Mary Lavin. Reprinted by permission of Wallace & Sheil Agency, Inc. and Anthony Sheil Assoc. Ltd.

"The Prussian Officer" from *The Complete Short Stories of D. H. Lawrence*, Vol. I. Copy-

"The Ballroom of Romance" from *The Ballroom of Romance* by William Trevor. Copyright © 1972 by William Trevor. Reprinted by permission of Viking Penguin, Inc.

"Bachelors" by Hugh Walpole. Reprinted by permission of Sir Rupert Hart-Davis.

"Idenborough" from *Winter in the Air and Other Stories* by Sylvia Townsend Warner. Reprinted by permission of the Author's Literary Estate and Chatto & Windus.

"Threnody" from *Watching You Watching Me* by Fay Weldon. Copyright © 1981 by Fay Weldon. Reprinted by permission of Sterling Lord Agency, Inc. and Hodder & Stoughton Ltd.

"Willy-Wagtails by Moonlight" from *The Burnt Ones* by Patrick White. Copyright © by Patrick White. Permission granted by Curtis Brown (Australia) Pty. Ltd.

"The Duchess and the Jeweller" from *A Haunted House and Other Stories* by Virginia Woolf. Copyright 1944, 1972 by Harcourt Brace Jovanovich, Inc. Reprinted by permission of the publisher, the author's Literary Estate and The Hogarth Press.

For
Dorothy and Stanley Murphy
and
Charles Sullivan

CONTENTS

INTRODUCTION

The main function of this anthology of short stories by authors writing in English from countries other than the United States is to delight and enlighten readers of imaginative fiction. Included are stories by writers from England, Scotland, Ireland, Wales, New Zealand, Australia, India, Canada, and South Africa which represent a cross section of some of the most brilliant short fiction ever assembled between the covers of a single book.

The selections in this anthology are not arbitrary; they are both personal and historical in the sense that they reflect the heritage of the genre from a British perspective. As the dictionary states, an anthology is a bouquet, but as Randall Jarrell added, "A bouquet that leaves out most of the world's flowers." What he probably meant is that no matter how thick an anthology is it's only so thick, and like a small garden it can accommodate only so many selections from among the vast assortment of worthy and fascinating candidates eager for a space in the sun. The sixty-five stories in this *Treasury* provide a rich sample of the scope, variety, and quality of the English short story since Chaucer, as well as a survey of the evolution of the genre.

The English short story is difficult to classify; in the case of this anthology, the word *English* is used to designate short stories written in the English language as well as to classify certain writers geographically. The technique used in English short stories can be apparently spontaneous as in the case of Katherine Mansfield or noticeably crafted and arch as in the work of Virginia Woolf. Its language may be economically casual or sensuously lyrical. Its setting may be recognizable and faintly nostalgic as in Charles Dickens or chilling and surreal as in the stories of Angela Carter and Roald Dahl. The conclusion may shock and take the reader by surprise as in Saki's stories or the basic conflict may be revealed immediately, shifting the reader's concern to details in the story or to characterization and dialogue as in the work of Frank O'Connor.

Attempts to define the short story, especially the modern short story, have been numerous and perplexing. Poe's obvious, somewhat pedestrian but accurate observation that the genre is "the short prose narrative, requiring from a half-hour to one or two hours in its perusal" may be the wisest definition of the form, because, as the eminent British critic and writer Walter Allen has commented, "any definition of the short story must be tentative, allowing for many apparent contradictions and some genuine ones." The short story, as a result of the form's elusive nature, guarantees its readers diversity, spontaneity, and the kind of immediate pleasure not possible with the novel but long associated with the poem. As Walter Allen puts it, "I seem trembling on the verge of saying that the modern short-story writer is a lyric poet in prose; and indeed, the effect on the reader of many short stories . . . is nearer to that of lyric poetry than to that of the novel or of older stories . . ."

One might ponder the causes for this theory. The American critic Brander Matthews has pointed out that "There were nine muses in Greece of old, and no one of these daughters of Apollo was expected to inspire the writer of prose fiction . . . prose seemed to the Greeks, and even to the Latins who followed in their footsteps, as fit only for pedestrian purposes." It seems that epic poems have described nations in their golden eras. Prose tales, fables, and short stories have come later in quieter times.

Chaucer, because he knew both the poetry and the prose-fiction of Boccaccio, had the opportunity to tell his tales in either poetry or prose. For the most part, he chose poetry; in only two instances in *The Canterbury Tales* does he revert to prose and those tales are among his least successful. "The Reeve's Tale," included in this anthology, was originally written in poetry by Chaucer and was later translated into modern prose by R. M. Lumiansky. This is the one instance in this *Treasury* where a story is not printed in its original version. Curiously enough, "The Reeve's Tale" was borrowed by Chaucer from the prose version of Boccaccio's *Decameron*.

The short story told in prose experienced a hibernation period of almost a century and a half before emerging as a hybrid some classified as the sketch or tale. Not until Daniel Defoe and the rise of the newspaper do we note any advance in technique. In "The Apparition of Mrs. Veal," Defoe is greatly in advance of his time in that he has written an almost perfect example of the modern method of handling a ghost tale. Most of the English short stories prior to those written by James Hogg, also known as the Ettrick Shepherd, in the late eighteenth and early nineteenth centuries leave very little to the imagination. Even into the late nineteenth and early twentieth centuries when the short story had come to be recognized in America as a distinct branch of literature, the efforts of British writers were too often little more than compressed novels.

In his classic study of the form, *The Lonely Voice,* Frank O'Connor speculates that while the novel encourages the identification of its reader with a recognizable hero, "the short story has never had a hero." Instead, O'Connor maintains that the story celebrates "the submerged population," the individuals who have been defeated by oppression or wander at the fringe of society. He includes within that submerged population "Gogol's officials, Turgenev's serfs, Maupassant's prostitutes, Chekhov's doctors and teachers, Sherwood Anderson's provincials." O'Connor also speculates that the novel and the short story tend not to flourish simultaneously; he suggests that Czarist Russia and twentieth-century Ireland were golden periods for the story.

Since its earliest form as the spoken tale, the story has been concerned with its audience; the storyteller has been aware of the listener or reader. Chaucer's Canterbury pilgrims, for example, had a captive audience as each was called upon to tell his tale and thus entertain or instruct his fellow travelers. As evidenced in *The Canterbury Tales,* the ancestors of the modern English short story lie in self-contained episodes of longer works, the recounting of romance or tragedy in ballads or in allegories, parables, anecdotes, homilies, and sketches all often written in verse rather than in prose. The public act of listening to a story being told by someone—sometimes to a musical accompaniment and enhanced with gestures and melodramatic facial expressions—yielded eventually to a silent and solitary reading of the work in a magazine or a collection. To trace the history of the English story is to review the history of five or six centuries of publishing and how that history reflects radical developments in technology and education.

The story, like any lively work of art, is dependent upon flexibility and restraint, tradition and innovation. Like the novel, the story is paradoxical in that it depends upon some basic credibility in voice, situation, or details but must provide, simultaneously, some novelty or fantasy. It must disclose something new about an often familiar situation or aspect of life.

Of all the conflicting definitions and explications of the story form, probably the only one that most critics and readers would agree upon is that it must be short. How short? The short story depends upon concentrated episodes and scenes and upon economy and selection. It must be completed within a shorter measure than the novella or the novel, but the exact number of words in a short story has always varied according to the marketplace, custom, and tradition. The episodes within George Eliot's *Scenes from Clerical Life* and Conrad's tales such as *Youth* and *Typhoon,* for instance, are considerably longer than typical stories by Katherine Mansfield, Saki or Frank O'Connor. Nadine Gordimer, among others, has suggested that the story's comparative brevity explains its enduring popularity when she says, "The short story is a fragmented and restless form, a matter of hit or miss, and it is perhaps for this reason that it suits modern consciousness—which seems best expressed as flashes of fearful insight alternating with near hypnotic states of indifference."

George Eliot's *Scenes from Clerical Life* are really short novels and not short stories, and are read as such. While they might deal with what Walter Allen labels "the ordinary traffic of life," they are not concerned with the single incident or perception that is so revered by modern short story writers. This might also help to explain the absence of fiction by George Eliot from this anthology. Similar reasons, coupled with space limitations, might help to rationalize the absence of prose by Jane Austen, Emily Brontë, and Charlotte Brontë, whose shorter fiction must, for better or worse, be classified as fragmentary. This does not imply a value judgment on its quality; it is merely an observation on its uniqueness. Not every novelist is adept at writing what we have come to define as the short story, nor is every novelist interested in writing in that genre.

In *The Treasury of English Short Stories* the reader will discover remarkable stories by writers equally or best known as novelists: Somerset Maugham, John Galsworthy, H. G. Wells, Rudyard Kipling, for example, as well as Thomas Hardy, James Joyce, D. H. Lawrence, and Charles Dickens. Authors better known for their poetry or drama are represented by Robert Louis Stevenson, Oscar Wilde, Dylan Thomas, and Brendan Behan. A significant group of stories by authors known primarily or only for their short stories includes Saki, A. E. Coppard, Katherine Mansfield, H. E. Bates, Frank O'Connor, V. S. Pritchett, and William Trevor.

Superficially at least, there are some distinctions between the American and the English short story. The story form was encouraged in nineteenth-century America by the number of publishing markets and by the diverse examples of Nathaniel Hawthorne and Herman Melville, as well as by Edgar Allan Poe and Mark Twain. Tall stories, gothic tales, domestic romances, and local-color narratives were published in newspapers and magazines and then collected in volumes for wider distribution. It could be argued that nineteenth-century England fostered the writing and reading of novels which often had been serialized in popular magazines before publication. Fortunately, some of these novelists—Scott, Thackeray, Dickens, Trollope, Collins, and Hardy—published short stories as well.

By the middle of the twentieth century the development of the English short story was considerably enriched not only by such extremely popular writers as Hardy, Kipling, Galsworthy, and Maugham but by specialists in the genre like A. E. Coppard, Saki, and Bates. Probably the greatest enrichment, however, came from Irish, Scottish, Welsh, and other Commonwealth writers who renewed the traditional style and language with fresh insights and a dazzling reach of landscape from Belfast and Dublin to Manitoba, Sidney, Wellington, and Johannesburg. Among the Commonwealth writers, new themes, such as the examination of political injustices in South Africa in Nadine Gordimer's work or the sense of a fading heritage in Canada in Alice Munro's stories and of a similar demise in New Zealand as reflected in Janet Frame's work, contribute an electricity and vigor to the short fiction from these areas, while the early tension between the young American colonies and the British Empire is reflected in Patrick White's fictional analyses of his native Australia.

The contemporary political and religious struggles in Ireland between the British-controlled North and the Republic of Ireland in the South, between Protestant and Catholic, between tradition and emancipation, have been a haunting element in Irish short stories since James Joyce. Notable examples in this *Treasury* of contemporary Irish stories which overtly or covertly examine these conflicts can be found in the work of Edna O'Brien, Mary Lavin, William Trevor, and Bernard MacLaverty, to mention just a few. The nationalism reflected in their work is tempered, however, by an awareness of the vagaries of the human condition. They know, as do all good writers and certainly those included in this collection, that human experience is universal and that the measure of a story's impact is defined by that truth.

My chief debt, of course, in compiling this anthology is to the authors represented in it. Without them the durable population of wise tellers of sad and happy tales would be greatly diminished. I hail them, each and every one. I also wish to thank Nancy Potter for her kind encouragement and suggestions; my editor, Mary Sherwin, for her patience and tact; and Florence Eichin in the permissions department at Doubleday for her wisdom and efficiency.

NANCY SULLIVAN

The
Treasury *of*
English
Short Stories

The Reeve's Tale

❦

GEOFFREY CHAUCER
(English, 1340?–1400)

Translated into modern prose by
R. M. Lumiansky

THE PROLOGUE OF THE REEVE'S TALE: When the people had laughed at
this silly adventure of Absalom and clever Nicholas, different ones gave
different opinions, but for the most part they laughed and joked about it.
The only one I saw who was distressed by this tale was Oswald, the
Reeve. Since he was a carpenter by trade, a little irritation lingered in his
heart, and he began to grumble and find fault.

"So help me," he said, "I could very well pay you back with an account of the hoodwinking of a proud miller, if I chose to speak in a
vulgar way. But I am old; my age has overcome my desire to joke. My
grass time is over; my fodder is now forage. This white top bears witness
to my advanced years; my passion is as moldy as my hair, unless I turn
out to be like the medlar, that fruit which grows worse as it grows older,
until it rots in muck and straw, and then becomes edible. With us old
men, I'm afraid it's like this: we cannot rot until we are thoroughly ripe.
We continue to dance as long as the world will pipe for us. There is
always some stumbling block to our desire to have a white head and a
green tail, like a leek. For, though our virility is gone, we still desire folly.
That which we cannot do, we want to talk about. The fire still smolders
in our burnt-out ashes.

"Four coals burn us, by my count—boasting, lying, anger, and covetousness. These four sparks belong to old age. Though our old limbs may be unwieldy, our desire still remains with us, that's the truth. I still have a colt's tooth, though many a year has passed since my tap began to run. Truly, when I was born, death immediately opened the tap of life and let it run, and it has run ever since, until the barrel is now almost empty. The stream of life now drips upon the rim. The poor old tongue may well chatter about misery which occurred long ago; for old folk, nothing remains except dotage!"

When the Host heard this discourse, he began to speak as pompously as a king. "What is the good of all this wisdom?" he said. "Why should we speak all day of Holy Writ? The Devil made a preacher out of a reeve, just as he made a shipman or a doctor of a cobbler. Tell your tale; don't waste time. Look there's Deptford, and it's half-past seven! Look, there's Greenwich, where there's many a shrew. It's high time for you to begin your tale."

"Now, sirs," said Oswald, the Reeve, "I ask all of you not to be grieved, when I answer this Miller and to some extent make a fool of him; it is quite legal to repulse attack with counterattack.

"This drunken Miller has told us here how a carpenter was deceived; perhaps he told his tale in mockery, for I am a carpenter. By your leave, I shall at once repay him; I will speak in his own vulgar terms. I hope to God he breaks his neck. He can very well observe a stick in my eye, but he can't see a beam in his own."

HERE BEGINS THE REEVE'S TALE: At Trumpington, not far from Cambridge, there runs a brook with a bridge over it, and by this brook stands a mill. Everything that I am telling you is the exact truth. For many years a miller lived there, and he was as proud and gay as a peacock. He could play the pipes, fish, mend nets, turn cups on a lathe, and wrestle and shoot well. In his belt he always carried a long knife and a sword with a sharp blade. He carried a pretty dagger in his pouch, and no man, on peril of his life, dared touch him. In his hose he wore another knife from Sheffield. This miller's face was round, his nose flat, and his skull was as hairy as an ape's. In fact, he was a full-fledged market-bully. No one dared lay a hand on him, for the miller swore he would at once repay him. He was a thief of grain and meal, truly a sly one, who made a habit of stealing. He was called Scornful Simkin. He had a wife with relatives among the nobility; her father was parson of the town. For her dowry he gave many a brass piece, so that Simkin would marry into the family. She had been brought up in a nunnery. Simkin had often said that he would not have a wife who was not well reared and a virgin, worthy of his position as a yeoman. She was proud and as pert as a magpie. Truly, these two made a fine sight on holy days. He would walk in front of her with the tail of his hood wound about his head, and she came behind in a red dress. Simkin's hose were of the same color. No one dared call her anything but "madam" then. No man in the vicinity once dared to trifle or play with her, unless he wished to be killed by Simkin with a knife or dagger or bodkin. Jealous folk are always dangerous; at least they want their wives to think so. And she, because she was of a somewhat dubious reputation, was as standoffish as water in a ditch, and full of scorn and mockery. She thought all ladies should treat her respectfully because of her family and the education she had gained in the nunnery.

These two had a daughter who was twenty years old, and no other children except a baby of six months which lay in its cradle and was a fine-looking child. The daughter was stout and well developed, with a pug nose, blue eyes, broad buttocks, and round, high breasts. Her hair was very pretty; I do not lie.

Because she was pretty, the town parson planned to make her his heir, both of his movable property and of his house, and he made difficulties about her marriage. His purpose was to marry her well into some noble family. Holy Church's goods must be kept in a family descended from Holy Church; therefore, he wanted to dignify his holy blood even though he harmed Holy Church.

This miller got large profits, without a doubt, in wheat and malt all over the district. Especially, the great college which is called King's Hall at Cambridge had its wheat and malt ground at his mill. One day it happened that the manciple suffered an attack of illness and was sick in bed; it was thought that he would surely die. Because of this, the miller stole a hundred times more meal and grain than usual. Before he had stolen sparingly, but now he stole outrageously. For this the warden scolded and made a fuss, but the miller didn't care a straw. He made loud boasts and swore it was not so.

There were two young, poor students who lived in the college of which I speak. They were high-spirited and eager for any kind of sport. In the hope of having some fun, they eagerly begged permission from the warden to be absent a short while in order to go to the mill and watch the grain being ground. They boldly wagered their necks that the miller would not rob them of so much as a half-peck of grain, either by cunning or by force. At last the warden gave his assent. One student was named John and the other Allan. They were both born in the same place—a town called Strother, far in the north; I don't know where it is.

This student, Allan, got everything ready and put the sack on a horse's back. Then he and John started out, with swords and shields by their sides. John knew the way—they needed no guide—and upon arriving at the mill they threw down the sack. Allan spoke first. "Hail, Simon! How is your fair daughter and your wife?"

"Welcome, Allan," said Simkin, "and you also John; what are you two doing here?"

"Simon," answered John, "by God, necessity knows no law. As the clerks say, he who has no servant must serve himself or else he is a fool. I fear our manciple is going to die, judging from the way he gnashes his teeth. Therefore Allan and I have come to bring the college's grain to be ground and to carry it back home. Please help us to get back as quickly as possible."

"It shall be done," said Simkin, "by my faith! What would you like to do while the work is in progress?"

"By God, I want to stand next to the hopper," said John, "and watch how the grain goes in. I never yet have understood, by my father's cows, how the hopper goes back and forth."

"John, do you want to do that?" asked Allan. "Then by my father's head, I'll go down below and watch how the meal falls down into the trough; I'll pass the time that way. John, you know I'm just like you: I don't know any more than you about the job of a miller."

The miller smiled at their naïveté and thought: "All this is just a trick. They think no one can outwit them, but, by my soul, I'll hoodwink them, in spite of all the cunning in their philosophy. The more sly tricks they play, the more I will steal from them. Instead of flour, I'll give them bran. 'The greatest clerks are not the wisest men,' as the wolf said to the mare. I don't care a straw for all their book learning."

When he saw his opportunity, he slipped quietly out of the door. He looked up and down till he spied the students' horse where it stood tied behind the, mill under an arbor. He went softly up to the horse and quickly took off the bridle. As soon as the horse was free, he started through the underbrush with loud whinnies, heading for the marsh, where there were wild mares running loose.

The miller went back inside and, without a word about the horse, attended to his work, joking meanwhile with the students, until all the grain was completely ground. When the meal was sacked and tied, John went outside and found their horse gone. He began to shout "Help!" and "Alas! Our horse is lost, Allan; for God's sake, get a move on. Come here at once, man. The warden's saddle horse is lost." Allan forgot all about the meal and the flour; his thrifty intentions went clear out of his mind. "What? Which way did he go?" he cried.

The wife came running out. She said, "Alas, your horse has gone to the marsh as fast as he can, to join the wild mares. Curses on whoever tied him; the bridle should have been tied better!"

"Alas," said John. "Allan, for the pain of Christ, put down your sword and I'll do the same. I can run as fast as a deer, God knows; the horse won't get away from us. Why didn't you put the nag in the barn? Bad luck to you, Allan; by God, you're a fool!"

And both poor students, Allan and John, ran quickly into the marsh.

When the miller saw that they were gone, he took a half-bushel of their flour and bade his wife make a cake with it. He said: "I believe these students were afraid of what might happen. But a miller can get the best of clerks, in spite of their learning. Let them go ahead now. Look where they've gone! Yes, let those children play; they won't catch that horse so easily, by my crown."

The poor clerks ran up and down, shouting, "Stop, stop! Whoa, whoa! Here; look out behind; you whistle; I'll catch him here!" But, in brief, in spite of their efforts, their horse ran so fast that it was black night before they at last caught him in a ditch.

Weary, and as wet as beasts in the rain, poor John and Allan started back. "Curse the day that I was born!" said John. "Now we will have to put up with mockery and jokes. Our meal is stolen; people will call us fools—the warden and our friends, and particularly the miller. Alas!"

Thus John complained as he and Allan proceeded to the mill, leading Bayard. They found the miller sitting by the fire. It was night, and they could go no farther. They begged the miller, for the love of God, to furnish them food and lodging, for which they would pay.

The miller replied, "If there is anything to eat you shall have a share, such as it is. My house is small, but you two have book learning: by logic, you can create a space a mile wide where there are only twenty feet. Let's see if this place will do; otherwise, make it larger by talking, as is your custom."

"Now, Simon," said John, "by St. Cuthbert, you are a great joker and that was a good answer. I have heard it said, 'A man must choose one of two things: that which he finds or that which he brings.' But I beg you especially, dear host, bring us some food and drink and make us comfortable; we will pay you generously. Men with empty hands catch no hawks; look, here is our money, ready to be spent."

The miller sent his daughter to the village for bread and ale, roasted a goose for them, and tied their horse so that it could not run away again. He also prepared a bed for them himself, with sheets and blankets carefully arranged, not more than ten or twelve feet away from his own bed. His daughter had a bed all to herself near by in the same room. The students could do no better; there was no more spacious lodging in the place. They ate supper and talked, trying to comfort themselves, and steadily drank the best strong ale. About midnight they all went to bed.

The miller was extremely well oiled. He was so drunk that he was pale, not red. He hiccoughed, and he spoke through his nose as if he were hoarse or had a cold. He went to bed, and his wife went with him. She was gay and frisky as a jay bird, so well was her jolly whistle wet. The baby's cradle was placed at the foot of their bed, so that the mother could rock and suckle the child. When all that was in the jug had been drunk, the daughter at once went to bed. Allan and John also went to bed; there was no more to drink—no one needed a sleeping potion. The miller had drunk so much that in his sleep he snorted like a horse and unconcernedly broke wind. His wife accompanied him with a full strong bass; one could hear her snoring a quarter of a mile away. The daughter snored also, to keep them company.

Allan, hearing this music, poked John, and said, "Are you asleep? Did you ever hear such a song before? A plague on people who make such harmony! Whoever heard such a fantastic thing? Yes, they must come to the worst of bad ends. I won't be able to sleep this whole night long. But, nevertheless, things will turn out for the best, for, John, as I hope to prosper, I'm going to sleep with that wench. Surely, John, we are legally entitled to some compensation. There is a law which says that if a man suffers a grievance in one way he shall be repaid in another. Our grain is stolen, there's no doubt about that; and we've had a bad time all day.

Since we are not going to be repaid for our loss, I will arrange my own compensation. By God's soul, it shall not be otherwise!"

John answered, "Allan, listen; the miller is a dangerous man. If he wakes up, he may do us both harm."

Allan replied, "I don't care a fly for him." And he got up and crept into bed with the daughter. She lay fast asleep on her back and didn't know what was happening until it was too late to call for help. In brief, they were soon hard at it. Now play, Allan, for I want to speak of John.

John lay still a few minutes, feeling very sorry for himself. "Alas," he said. "This is a cruel joke; I see clearly that I am nothing but a fool. My friend now has something for the harm he suffered: he is in bed with the miller's daughter. He took a risk and has got what he wanted, while I lie like a sack of straw in my bed. In the future, when this adventure is told, I'll look like a fool, a sissy! I will get up and try my chances too, by my faith! 'Nothing ventured, nothing gained,' they say." He got up and went quietly to the cradle, and, taking it in his hands, moved it softly to the foot of his own bed.

A bit later, the wife stopped her snoring, woke up, went to make water, and, upon returning, missed the cradle. She groped here and there without finding it. "Alas," she said, "I almost made a mistake—I almost got into bed with the students. Oh! bless me, then I would have been in a bad spot." She groped about until she found the cradle, and from the cradle she felt her way to John's bed, which she thought was her own because the cradle stood at its foot. She didn't know where she was because it was pitch-dark. She crept softly into bed with John, lay still, and would have gone to sleep. Soon John jumped up and began to make love most vigorously with the good woman. She had not had so much fun in many a year! John penetrated hard and deep, as though he were mad. These two students continued their jolly sport until about dawn.

Allan, who had worked hard all night, grew weary shortly before dawn and said, "Farewell, Molly, sweet one! Daylight is here; I can stay no longer. But in the future, wherever I go, I am your own scholar, as long as the soul is in my body!"

"Now, dear lover," she said, "go, farewell! But before you go I want to tell you one thing: when you pass by the mill on the way home, if you look behind the front door you will find a cake made from a half-bushel of your own flour which I helped my father steal. And, beloved, God save you and guard you!" With these words she almost began to cry.

Allan got up and thought, "Before dawn comes I'll slip into bed with John." He soon found the cradle with his hand. "By God," he thought, "I'm completely lost. My head is dizzy from my night's work; that's what's making me go wrong. I know by the cradle that I have gone astray. The miller and his wife are in this bed." Accordingly, he made his way—twenty devils' luck!—to the bed in which the miller slept. He thought the miller, whom he got in next to, was John and grabbed him by the neck and whispered, "John, you hog's head, wake up for Christ's soul, and hear a great joke. By St. James, three times during this short night, I have laid the miller's daughter flat on her back, while you have stayed here like a coward."

"Oh, have you, false knave?" cried the miller. "False traitor, false scholar! You shall die, by God's worth! How dare you brazenly insult my daughter, who comes of such a noble family?" He grabbed Allan by the Adam's apple, and he, in return, roughly grabbed the miller and hit him on the nose with his fist. The blood streamed down on the miller's breast while the two wallowed on the floor, their noses and mouths crushed, like two pigs in a poke. First they were up and then they were down again, until the miller stumbled on a stone and fell backwards upon his wife, who had heard nothing of this ridiculous fight. She had fallen into a short doze, after making love with John all night. When the miller fell on her, she started up out of her sleep and shouted, "Help! Holy cross of Bromholm, I'm in your hands! Lord, I call to you! Wake up, Simon, the devil has fallen on me! My heart is crushed; help, I'm as good as killed! Somebody is lying on my stomach and my head. Help, Simon, the false scholars are fighting!"

John jumped up as quickly as he could and groped back and forth around the walls in search of a stick. She got up also and, since she knew the interior of the house better than John, she soon found a stick by the wall. She saw a ray of light, where the moon shone in through a hole in the wall, and by this light she saw the two on the floor, but she couldn't tell for certain who was who; they appeared to her as a white something. When she caught sight of this white thing, she supposed it was a nightcap which one of the students wore, and drew nearer with the stick, thinking to hit Allan squarely. Actually she beat the miller on his hairy skull. He fell flat and cried, "Help, I die!" The two students beat him thoroughly and let him lie there. They dressed themselves, took their horse and meal, and went on their way. At the mill they picked up the cake baked with the half-bushel of their meal.

In this way, the proud miller was well beaten; he lost the money for grinding the wheat and he paid for every bit of supper for Allan and John, who beat him thoroughly and who slept with his wife and daughter. See what happens to a miller who is false! Therefore the proverb is true which says: 'He who does evil must not expect good.' A cheat himself will be outwitted. And God, who sits on high in majesty, save all this company, great and small! Now I have repaid the Miller with my tale. HERE ENDS THE REEVE'S TALE.

The Apparition of Mrs. Veal

❧✦❧

DANIEL DEFOE
(English, 1660?–1731)

This thing is so rare in all its circumstances, and on so good authority, that my reading and conversation have not given me anything like it. It is fit to gratify the most ingenious and serious inquirer. Mrs. Bargrave is the person to whom Mrs. Veal appeared after her death; she is my intimate friend, and I can avouch for her reputation for these fifteen or sixteen years, on my own knowledge; and I can confirm the good character she had from her youth to the time of my acquaintance. Though, since this relation, she is calumniated by some people that are friends to the brother of Mrs. Veal who appeared, who think the relation of this appearance to be a reflection, and endeavor what they can to blast Mrs. Bargrave's reputation and to laugh the story out of countenance. But by the circumstances thereof, and the cheerful disposition of Mrs. Bargrave, notwithstanding the ill usage of a very wicked husband, there is not yet the least sign of dejection in her face; nor did I ever hear her let fall a desponding or murmuring expression; nay, not when actually under her husband's barbarity, which I have been a witness to, and several other persons of undoubted reputation.

Now you must know Mrs. Veal was a maiden gentlewoman of about thirty years of age, and for some years past had been troubled with fits, which were perceived coming on her by her going off from her discourse very abruptly to some impertinence. She was maintained by an only brother, and kept his house in Dover. She was a very pious woman, and her brother a very sober man to all appearance; but now he does all he can to null and quash the story. Mrs. Veal was intimately acquainted with Mrs. Bargrave from her childhood. Mrs. Veal's circumstances were then mean; her father did not take care of his children as he ought, so that they were exposed to hardships. And Mrs. Bargrave in those days had as unkind a father, though she wanted neither for food nor clothing; while Mrs. Veal wanted for both, insomuch that she would often say, "Mrs. Bargrave, you are not only the best, but the only friend I have in the world; and no circumstance of life shall over dissolve my friendship." They would often condole each other's adverse fortunes, and read together *Drelincourt upon Death,* and other good books; and so, like two Christian friends, they comforted each other under their sorrow.

Some time after, Mr. Veal's friends got him a place in the custom-house at Dover, which occasioned Mrs. Veal, by little and little, to fall off from her intimacy with Mrs. Bargrave, though there was never any such thing as a quarrel; but an indifferency came on by degrees, till at last Mrs. Bargrave had not seen her in two years and a half, though above a twelvemonth of the time Mrs. Bargrave hath been absent from Dover, and this last half-year has been in Canterbury about two months of the time, dwelling in a house of her own.

In this house, on the eighth of September, one thousand seven hundred and five, she was sitting alone in the forenoon, thinking over her unfortunate life, and arguing herself into a due resignation to Providence, though her condition seemed hard: "And," said she, "I have been provided for hitherto, and doubt not but I shall be still, and am well satisfied that my afflictions shall end when it is most fit for me." And then took up her sewing work, which she had no sooner done but she hears a knocking at the door; she went to see who was there, and this proved to be Mrs. Veal, her old friend, who was in a riding-habit. At that moment of time the clock struck twelve at noon.

"Madam," says Mrs. Bargrave, "I am surprised to see you, you have been so long a stranger"; but told her she was glad to see her, and offered to salute her, which Mrs. Veal complied with, till their lips almost touched, and then Mrs. Veal drew her hand across her own eyes, and said, "I am not very well," and so waived it. She told Mrs. Bargrave she was going a journey, and had a great mind to see her first. "But," says Mrs. Bargrave, "how can you take a journey alone? I am amazed at it, because I know you have a fond brother." "Oh," says Mrs. Veal, "I gave my brother the slip, and came away, because I had so great a desire to see you before I took my journey." So Mrs. Bargrave went in with her into another room within the first, and Mrs. Veal sat her down in an elbow-chair, in which Mrs. Bargrave was sitting when she heard Mrs. Veal knock. "Then," says Mrs. Veal, "my dear friend, I am come to renew our old friendship again, and beg your pardon for my breach of it; and if you can forgive me, you are the best of women." "Oh," says Mrs. Bargrave, "do not mention such a thing; I have not had an uneasy thought about it." "What did you think of me?" says Mrs. Veal. Says Mrs. Bargrave, "I thought you were like the rest of the world, and that prosperity had made you forget yourself and me." Then Mrs. Veal reminded Mrs. Bargrave of the many friendly offices she did her in former days, and much of the conversation they had with each other in the times of their adversity; what books they read, and what comfort in particular they received from Drelincourt's *Book of Death,* which was the best, she said, on the subject ever wrote. She also mentioned Doctor Sherlock, and two Dutch books, which were translated, wrote upon death, and several others. But Drelincourt, she said, had the clearest notions of death and of the future state of any who had handled that subject. Then she asked Mrs. Bargrave whether she had Drelincourt. She said, "Yes." Says Mrs. Veal, "Fetch it." And so Mrs. Bargrave goes up-stairs and brings it down. Says Mrs. Veal, "Dear Mrs. Bargrave, if the eyes of our faith were as open as the eyes of our body, we should see numbers of angels about us for our guard. The notions we have of Heaven now are nothing like what it is, as Drelincourt says; therefore be comforted under your afflictions, and believe that the Almighty has a particular regard to you, and that your afflictions are marks of God's favor; and when they have done the business they are sent for, they shall be removed from you. And believe me, my dear friend, believe what I say to you, one minute of future happiness will infinitely reward you for all your sufferings. For I can never believe" (and claps her hand upon her knee with great earnestness, which, indeed, ran through most of her discourse) "that ever God will suffer you to spend all your days in this afflicted state. But be assured that your afflictions shall leave you, or you them, in a short time." She spake in that pathetical and heavenly manner that Mrs. Bargrave wept several times, she was so deeply affected with it.

Then Mrs. Veal mentioned Doctor Kendrick's *Ascetic,* at the end of which he gives an account of the lives of the primitive Christians. Their pattern she recommended to our imitation, and said, "Their conversation was not like this of our age. For now," says she, "there is nothing but vain, frothy discourse, which is far different from theirs. Theirs was to edification, and to build one another up in faith, so that they were not as we are, nor are we as they were. But," said she, "we ought to do as they did; there was a hearty friendship among them; but where is it now to be found?" Says Mrs. Bargrave, "It is hard indeed to find a true friend in these days." Says Mrs. Veal, "Mr. Norris has a fine copy of verses, called *Friendship in Perfection,* which I wonderfully admire. Have you seen the book?" says Mrs. Veal. "No," says Mrs. Bargrave, "but I have the verses of my own writing out." "Have you?" says Mrs. Veal; "then fetch them"; which she did from above stairs, and offered them to Mrs. Veal to read, who refused, and waived the thing, saying, "holding down her head would make it ache"; and then desiring Mrs. Bargrave to read them to her, which she did. As they were admiring *Friendship,* Mrs. Veal said, "Dear Mrs. Bargrave, I shall love you forever." In these verses there is twice used the word "Elysian." "Ah!" says Mrs. Veal, "these poets have such names for Heaven." She would often draw her hand across her own eyes, and say, "Mrs. Bargrave, do not you think I am mightily impaired by my fits?" "No," says Mrs. Bargrave; "I think you look as well as ever I knew you."

After this discourse, which the apparition put in much finer words than Mrs. Bargrave said she could pretend to, and as much more than she can remember—for it cannot be thought that an hour and three quarters' conversation could all be retained, though the main of it she thinks she does—she said to Mrs. Bargrave she would have her write a letter to her brother, and tell him she would have him give rings to such and such; and that there was a purse of gold in her cabinet, and that she would have two broad pieces given to her cousin Watson.

Talking at this rate, Mrs. Bargrave thought that a fit was coming upon her, and so placed herself on a chair just before her knees, to keep her from falling to the ground, if her fits should occasion it; for the elbow-chair, she thought, would keep her from falling on either side. And to divert Mrs. Veal, as she thought, took hold of her gown-sleeve several times, and commended it. Mrs. Veal told her it was a scoured silk, and newly made up. But, for all this, Mrs. Veal persisted in her request, and told Mrs. Bargrave she must not deny her. And she would have her tell her brother all their conversation when she had the opportunity. "Dear Mrs. Veal," says Mrs. Bargrave, "this seems so impertinent that I cannot tell how to comply with it; and what a mortifying story will our conversation be to a young gentleman. Why," says Mrs. Bargrave, "it is much better, methinks, to do it yourself." "No," says Mrs. Veal; "though it seems impertinent to you now, you will see more reasons for it hereafter." Mrs. Bargrave, then, to satisfy her importunity, was going to fetch a pen and ink, but Mrs. Veal said, "Let it alone now, but do it when I am gone; but you must be sure to do it"; which was one of the last things she enjoined her at parting, and so she promised her.

Then Mrs. Veal asked for Mrs. Bargrave's daughter. She said she was not at home. "But if you have a mind to see her," says Mrs. Bargrave, "I'll send for her." "Do," says Mrs. Veal; on which she left her, and went to a neighbor's to see her; and by the time Mrs. Bargrave was returning, Mrs. Veal was got without the door in the street, in the face of the beast-market, on a Saturday (which is market-day), and stood ready to part as soon as Mrs. Bargrave came to her. She asked her why she was in such haste. She said she must be going, though perhaps she might not go her journey till Monday; and told Mrs. Bargrave she hoped she should see her again at her cousin Watson's before she went whither she was going. Then she said she would take her leave of her, and walked from Mrs. Bargrave, in her view, till a turning interrupted the sight of her, which was three-quarters after one in the afternoon.

Mrs. Veal died the seventh of September, at twelve o'clock at noon, of her fits, and had not above four hours' senses before her death, in which time she received the sacrament. The next day after Mrs. Veal's appearance, being Sunday, Mrs. Bargrave was mightily indisposed with a cold and sore throat, that she could not go out that day; but on Monday morning she sends a person to Captain Watson's to know if Mrs. Veal was there. They wondered at Mrs. Bargrave's inquiry, and sent her word she was not there, nor was expected. At this answer, Mrs. Bargrave told the maid she had certainly mistook the name or made some blunder. And though she was ill, she put on her hood and went herself to Captain Watson's, though she knew none of the family, to see if Mrs. Veal was there or not. They said they wondered at her asking, for that she had not been in town; they were sure, if she had, she would have been there. Says Mrs. Bargrave, "I am sure she was with me on Saturday almost two hours." They said it was impossible, for they must have seen her if she had. In comes Captain Watson, while they were in dispute, and said that Mrs. Veal was certainly dead, and the escutcheons were making. This strangely surprised Mrs. Bargrave, when she sent to the person immediately who had the care of them, and found it true. Then she related the whole story to Captain Watson's family; and what gown she had on, and how striped; and that Mrs. Veal told her that it was scoured. Then Mrs. Watson cried out, "You have seen her indeed, for none knew but Mrs. Veal and myself that the gown was scoured." And Mrs. Watson owned that she described the gown exactly; "for," said she, "I helped her to make it up." This Mrs. Watson blazed all about the town, and avouched the demonstration of truth of Mrs. Bargrave's seeing Mrs. Veal's apparition. And Captain Watson carried two gentlemen immediately to Mrs. Bargrave's house to hear the relation from her own mouth. And when it spread so fast that gentlemen and persons of quality, the judicious and sceptical part of the world, flocked in upon her, it at last became such a task that she was forced to go out of the way; for they were in general extremely satisfied of the truth of the thing, and plainly saw that Mrs. Bargrave was no hypochondriac, for she always appears with such a cheerful air and pleasing mien that she has gained the favor and esteem of all the gentry, and it is thought a great favor if they can but get the relation from her own mouth. I should have told you before that Mrs. Veal told Mrs. Bargrave that her sister and brother-in-law were just come down from London to see her. Says Mrs. Bargrave, "How came you to order matters so strangely?" "It could not be helped," said Mrs. Veal. And her brother and sister did come to see her, and entered the town of Dover just as Mrs. Veal was expiring. Mrs. Bargrave asked her whether she would drink some tea. Says Mrs. Veal, "I do not care if I do; but I'll warrant you this mad fellow"—meaning Mrs. Bargrave's husband—"has broke all your trinkets." "But," says Mrs. Bargrave, "I'll get something to drink in for all that"; but Mrs. Veal waived it, and said, "It is no matter; let it alone"; and so it passed.

All the time I sat with Mrs. Bargrave, which was some hours, she recollected fresh sayings of Mrs. Veal. And one material thing more she told Mrs. Bargrave, that old Mr. Bretton allowed Mrs. Veal ten pounds a year, which was a secret, and unknown to Mrs. Bargrave till Mrs. Veal told her.

Mrs. Bargrave never varies in her story, which puzzles those who doubt of the truth, or are unwilling to believe it. A servant in the neighbor's yard adjoining to Mrs. Bargrave's house heard her talking to somebody an hour of the time Mrs. Veal was with her. Mrs. Bargrave went out to her next neighbor's the very moment she parted with Mrs. Veal, and told her what ravishing conversation she had had with an old friend, and told the whole of it. Drelincourt's *Book of Death* is, since this happened, bought up strangely. And it is to be observed that, notwithstanding all the trouble and fatigue Mrs. Bargrave has undergone upon this account, she never took the value of a farthing, nor suffered her daughter to take anything of anybody, and therefore can have no interest in telling the story.

But Mr. Veal does what he can to stifle the matter, and said he would see Mrs. Bargrave; but yet it is certain matter of fact that he has been at Captain Watson's since the death of his sister, and yet never went near Mrs. Bargrave; and some of his friends report her to be a liar, and that she knew of Mr. Bretton's ten pounds a year. But the person who pretends to say so has the reputation to be a notorious liar among persons whom I know to be of undoubted credit. Now, Mr. Veal is more of a gentleman than to say she lies, but says a bad husband has crazed her; but she needs only present herself, and it will effectually confute that pretence. Mr. Veal says he asked his sister on her death-bed whether she had a mind to dispose of anything. And she said no. Now the things which Mrs. Veal's apparition would have disposed of were so trifling, and nothing of justice aimed at in the disposal, that the design of it appears to me to be only in order to make Mrs. Bargrave satisfy the world of the reality thereof as to what she had seen and heard, and to secure her reputation among the reasonable and understanding part of mankind. And then, again, Mr. Veal owns that there was a purse of gold; but it was not found in her cabinet, but in a comb-box. This looks improbable; for that Mrs. Watson owned that Mrs. Veal was so very careful of the key of her cabinet that she would trust nobody with it; and if so, no doubt she would not trust her gold out of it. And Mrs. Veal's often drawing her hands over her eyes, and asking Mrs. Bargrave whether her fits had not impaired her, looks to me as if she did it on purpose to remind Mrs. Bargrave of her fits, to prepare her not to think it strange that she should put her upon writing to her brother, to dispose of rings and gold, which look so much like a dying person's request; and it took accordingly with Mrs. Bargrave as the effect of her fits coming upon her, and was one of the many instances of her wonderful love to her and care of her, that she should not be affrighted, which, indeed, appears in her whole management, particularly in her coming to her in the daytime, waiving the salutation, and when she was alone; and then the manner of her parting, to prevent a second attempt to salute her.

Now, why Mr. Veal should think this relation a reflection—as it is plain he does, by his endeavoring to stifle it—I cannot imagine; because the generality believe her to be a good spirit, her discourse was so heavenly. Her two great errands were, to comfort Mrs. Bargrave in her affliction, and to ask her forgiveness for her breach of friendship, and with a pious discourse to encourage her. So that, after all, to suppose that Mrs. Bargrave could hatch such an invention as this, from Friday noon to Saturday noon—supposing that she knew of Mrs. Veal's death the very first moment—without jumbling circumstances, and without any interest, too, she must be more witty, fortunate, and wicked, too, than any indifferent person, I dare say, will allow. I asked Mrs. Bargrave several times if she was sure she felt the gown. She answered, modestly, "If my senses be to be relied on, I am sure of it." I asked her if she heard a sound when she clapped her hand upon her knee. She said she did not remember she did, but said she appeared to be as much a substance as I did who talked with her. "And I may," said she, "be as soon persuaded that your apparition is talking to me now as that I did not really see her; for I was under no manner of fear, and received her as a friend, and parted with her as such. I would not," says she, "give one farthing to make any one believe it; I have no interest in it; nothing but trouble is entailed upon me for a long time, for aught I know; and, had it not come to light by accident, it would never have been made public." But now she says she will make her own private use of it, and keep herself out of the way as much as she can; and so she has done since. She says she had a gentleman who came thirty miles to her to hear the relation; and that she had told it to a roomful of people at the time. Several particular gentlemen have had the story from Mrs. Bargrave's own mouth.

This thing has very much affected me, and I am as well satisfied as I am of the best-grounded matter of fact. And why we should dispute matter of fact, because we cannot solve things of which we can have no certain or demonstrative notions, seems strange to me; Mrs. Bargrave's authority and sincerity alone would have been undoubted in any other case.

The Wedding of Jenny Distaff

RICHARD STEELE
(English, 1672–1729)

Felices ter, et amplius,
  Quos irrupta tenet copula; nec malis
Divulsus querimoniis,
  Suprema citius solvet amor die.
                                HOR. *Od.* i. 13, 17.

My sister Jenny's lover, the honest Tranquillus, for that shall be his name, has been impatient with me to despatch the necessary direction for his marriage; that while I am taken up with imaginary schemes, as he calls them, he might not burn with real desire, and the torture of expectation. When I had reprimanded him for the ardour wherein he expressed himself, which I thought had not enough of that veneration with which the marriage-bed is to be ascended, I told him, "the day of his nuptials should be on the Saturday following, which was the eighth instant." On the seventh in the evening, poor Jenny came into my chamber, and, having her heart full of the great change of life from a virgin condition to that of a wife, she long sat silent. I saw she expected me to entertain her on this important subject, which was too delicate a circumstance for herself to touch upon; whereupon I relieved her modesty in the following manner: "Sister," said I, "you are now going from me: and be contented, that you leave the company of a talkative old man, for that of a sober young one: but take this along with you, that there is no mean in the state you are entering into, but you are to be exquisitely happy or miserable, and your fortune in this way of life will be wholly of your own making. In all the marriages I have ever seen, most of which have been unhappy ones, the great cause of evil has proceeded from slight occasions; but I take it to be the first maxim in a married condition, that you are to be above trifles. When two persons have so good an opinion of each other as to come together for life, they will not differ in matters of importance, because they think of each other with respect, in regard to all things of consideration that may affect them, and are prepared for mutual assistance and relief in such occurrences; but for less occasions, they have formed no resolutions, but leave their minds unprepared.

"This, dear Jenny, is the reason that the quarrel between Sir Harry Willit and his lady, which began about her squirrel, is irreconcilable. Sir Harry was reading a grave author; she runs into his study, and in a playing humour, claps the squirrel upon the folio: he threw the animal in a rage upon the floor; she snatches it up again, calls Sir Harry a sour pedant, without good nature or good manners. This cast him into such a rage, that he threw down the table before him, kicked the book round the room; then recollected himself: 'Lord, madam,' said he, 'why did you run into such expressions? I was,' said he, 'in the highest delight with that author, when you clapped your squirrel upon my book'; and, smiling, added upon recollection, 'I have a great respect for your favourite, and pray let us all be friends.' My lady was so far from accepting this apology, that she immediately conceived a resolution to keep him under for ever: and with a serious air replied, 'There is no regard to be had to what a man says, who can fall into so indecent a rage, and such an abject submission, in the same moment, for which I absolutely despise you.' Upon which she rushed out of the room. Sir Harry staid some minutes behind, to think and command himself; after which he followed her into her bed-chamber, where she was prostrate upon the bed, tearing her hair, and naming twenty coxcombs who would have used her otherwise. This provoked him to so high a degree, that he forbore nothing but beating her; and all the servants in their family were at their several stations listening, whilst the best man and woman, the best master and mistress, defamed each other in a way that is not to be repeated even at Billingsgate. You know this ended in an immediate separation: she longs to return home, but knows not how to do it: he invites her home every day. Her husband requires no submission of her; but she thinks her very return will argue she is to blame, which she is resolved to be for ever, rather than acknowledge it. Thus, dear Jenny, my great advice to you is, be guarded against giving or receiving little provocations. Great matters of offence I have not reason to fear either from you or your husband."

After this, we turned our discourse into a more gay style, and parted: but before we did so, I made her resign her snuff-box for ever, and half-drown herself with washing away the stench of the musty.

But the wedding morning arrived, and our family being very numerous, there was no avoiding the inconvenience of making the ceremony and festival more public, than the modern way of celebrating them makes me approve of. The bride next morning came out of her chamber, dressed with all the art and care that Mrs. Toilet, the tire-woman, could bestow on her. She was on her wedding-day three-and-twenty; her person is far from what we call a regular beauty; but a certain sweetness in her countenance, an ease in her shape and motion, with an unaffected modesty in her looks, had attractions beyond what symmetry and exactness can inspire, without the addition of these endowments. When her lover entered the room, her features flushed with shame and joy; and the ingenuous manner, so full of passion and of awe, with which Tranquillus approached to salute her, gave me good omens of his future behaviour towards her. The wedding was wholly under my care. After the ceremony at church, I was resolved to entertain the company with a dinner suitable to the occasion, and pitched upon the Apollo at the Old-Devil at Temple Bar, as a place sacred to mirth tempered with discretion, where Ben Jonson and his sons used to make their liberal meetings. Here the chief of the Staffian race appeared; and as soon as the company were come into that ample room, Lepidus Wagstaff began to make me compliments for choosing that place, and fell into a discourse upon the subject of pleasure and entertainment, drawn from the rules of Ben's club, which are in gold letters over the chimney. Lepidus has a way very uncommon, and speaks on subjects on which any man else would certainly offend, with great dexterity. He gave us a large account of the public meetings of all the well-turned minds who had passed through this life in ages past, and closed his pleasing narrative with a discourse on marriage, and a repetition of the following verses out of Milton:

> Hail, wedded love! mysterious law! true source
> Of human offspring, sole propriety
> In Paradise, of all things common else.
> By thee adulterous lust was driven from men
> Among the bestial herds to range; by thee
> Founded in reason, loyal, just, and pure,
> Relations dear, and all the charities
> Of father, son, and brother, first were known . . .
> Perpetual fountain of domestic sweets
> Whose bed is undefiled and chaste pronounced,
> Present or past, as saints and patriarchs used.
> Here Love his golden shafts employs; here lights
> His constant lamp, and waves his purple wings:
> Reigns here and revels; not in the bought smile
> Of harlots, loveless, joyless, unendeared,
> Casual fruition; nor in court amours,
> Mixed dance, or wanton mask, or midnight ball,
> Or serenade, which the starved lover sings
> To his proud fair, best quitted with disdain.

In these verses, all the images that can come into a young woman's head on such an occasion are raised; but that in so chaste and elegant a manner, that the bride thanked him for his agreeable talk, and we sat down to dinner. . . .

A Story of an Heir

JOSEPH ADDISON
(English, 1672–1719)

Doctrina sed vim promovet insitam,
Rectique cultus pectora roborant:
Utcunque defecere mores,
Dedecorant bene nata culpae.—HOR.

As I was yesterday taking the air with my friend Sir Roger, we were met by a fresh-coloured ruddy young man who rid by us full speed, with a couple of servants behind him. Upon my inquiry who he was, Sir Roger told me that he was a young gentleman of a considerable estate, who had been educated by a tender mother that lived not many miles from the place where we were. She is a very good lady, says my friend, but took so much care of her son's health that she has made him good for nothing. She quickly found that reading was bad for his eyes, and that writing made his head ake. He was let loose among the woods as soon as he was able to ride on horseback, or to carry a gun upon his shoulder. To be brief, I found, by my friend's account of him, that he had got a great stock of health, but nothing else; and that if it were a man's business only to live, there would not be a more accomplished young fellow in the whole country.

The truth of it is, since my residing in these parts I have seen and heard innumerable instances of young heirs and elder brothers who either from their own reflecting upon the estates they are born to, and therefore thinking all other accomplishments unnecessary, or from hearing these notions frequently inculcated to them by the flattery of their servants and domesticks, or from the same foolish thought prevailing in those who have the care of their education, are of no manner of use but to keep up their families, and transmit their lands and houses in a line to posterity.

This makes me often think on a story I have heard of two friends, which I shall give my reader at large, under feigned names. The moral of it may, I hope, be useful, though there are some circumstances which make it rather appear like a novel, than a true story.

Eudoxus and Leontine began the world with small estates. They were both of them men of good sense and great virtue. They prosecuted their studies together in their earlier years, and entered into such a friendship as lasted to the end of their lives. Eudoxus, at his first setting out in the world, threw himself into a court, where by his natural endowments and his acquired abilities he made his way from one post to another, till at length he had raised a very considerable fortune. Leontine on the contrary sought all opportunities of improving his mind by study, conversation and travel. He was not only acquainted with all the sciences, but with the most eminent professors of them throughout Europe. He knew perfectly well the interests of its princes, with the customs and fashions of their courts, and could scarce meet with the name of an extraordinary person in the *Gazette* whom he had not either talked to or seen. In short, he had so well mixt and digested his knowledge of men and books, that he made one of the most accomplished persons of his age. During the whole course of his studies and travels he kept up a punctual correspondence with Eudoxus, who often made himself acceptable to the principal men about court by the intelligence which he received from Leontine. When they were both turned of forty (an age in which, according to Mr. Cowley, *there is no dallying with life)* they determined, pursuant to the resolution they had taken in the beginning of their lives, to retire, and pass the remainder of their days in the country. In order to this, they both of them married much about the same time. Leontine, with his own and his wife's fortune, bought a farm of three hundred a year, which lay within the neighbourhood of his friend Eudoxus, who had purchased an estate of as many thousands. They were both of them fathers about the same time, Eudoxus having a son born to him, and Leontine a daughter; but to the unspeakable grief of the latter, his young wife (in whom all his happiness was wrapt up) died in a few days after the birth of her daughter. His affliction would have been insupportable, had not he been comforted by the daily visits and conversations of his friend. As they were one day talking together with their usual intimacy, Leontine, considering how incapable he was of giving his daughter a proper education in his own house, and Eudoxus, reflecting on the ordinary behaviour of a son who knows himself to be the heir of a great estate, they both agreed upon an exchange of children, namely that the boy should be bred up with Leontine as his son, and that the girl should live with Eudoxus as his daughter, till they were each of them arrived at years of discretion. The wife of Eudoxus, knowing that her son could not be so advantageously brought up as under the care of Leontine, and considering at the same time that he would be perpetually under her own eye, was by degrees prevailed upon to fall in with the project. She therefore took Leonilla, for that was the name of the girl, and educated her as her own daughter. The two friends on each side had wrought themselves to such an habitual tenderness for the children who were under their direction, that each of them had the real passion of a father, where the title was but imaginary. Florio, the name of the young heir that lived with Leontine, though he had all the duty and affection imaginable for his supposed parent, was taught to rejoice at the sight of Eudoxus, who visited his friend very frequently, and was dictated by his natural affection, as well as by the rules of prudence, to make himself esteemed and beloved by Florio. The boy was now old enough to know his supposed father's circumstances, and that therefore he was to make his way in the world by his own industry. This consideration grew stronger in him every day, and produced so good an effect, that he applied himself with more than ordinary attention to the pursuit of every thing which Leontine recommended to him. His natural abilities, which were very good, assisted by the directions of so excellent a counsellor, enabled him to make a quicker progress than ordinary through all the parts of his education. Before he was twenty years of age, having finished his studies and exercises with great applause, he was removed from the university to the Inns of Court, where there are very few that make themselves considerable proficients in the studies of the place, who know they shall arrive at great estates without them. This was not Florio's case; he found that three hundred a year was but a poor estate for Leontine and himself to live upon, so that he studied without intermission till he gained a very good insight into the constitution and laws of his country.

I should have told my reader, that whilst Florio lived at the house of his foster-father he was always an acceptable guest in the family of Eudoxus, where he became acquainted with Leonilla from her infancy. His acquaintance with her by degrees grew into love, which in a mind trained up in all the sentiments of honour and virtue became a very uneasy passion. He despaired of gaining an heiress of so great a fortune, and would rather have died than attempted it by any indirect methods. Leonilla, who was a woman of the greatest beauty joined with the greatest modesty, entertained at the same time a secret passion for Florio, but conducted herself with so much prudence that she never gave him the least intimation of it. Florio was now engaged in all those arts and improvements that are proper to raise a man's private fortune, and give him a figure in his country, but secretly tormented with that passion which burns with the greatest fury in a virtuous and noble heart, when he received a sudden summons from Leontine to repair to him in the country the next day. For it seems Eudoxus was so filled with the report of his son's reputation, that he could no longer withhold making himself known to him. The morning after his arrival at the house of his supposed father, Leontine told him that Eudoxus had something of great importance to communicate to him; upon which the good man embraced him and wept. Florio was no sooner arrived at the great house that stood in his neighbourhood, but Eudoxus took him by the hand, after the first salutes were over, and conducted him into his closet. He there opened to him the whole secret of his parentage and education, concluding after this manner: *I have no other way left of acknowledging my gratitude to Leontine, than by marrying you to his daughter. He shall not lose the pleasure of being your father by the discovery I have made to you. Leonilla too shall be still my daughter; her filial piety, though misplaced, has been so exemplary that it deserves the greatest reward I can confer upon it. You shall have the pleasure of seeing a great estate fall to you, which you would have lost the relish of had you known yourself born to it. Continue only to deserve it in the same manner you did before you were possessed of it. I have left your mother in the next room. Her heart yearns towards you. She is making the same discoveries to Leonilla which I have made to yourself.* Florio was so overwhelmed with this profusion of happiness, that he was not able to make a reply, but threw himself down at his father's feet, and amidst a flood of tears, kissed and embraced his knees, asking his blessing, and expressing in dumb show those sentiments of love, duty, and gratitude that were too big for utterance. To conclude, the happy pair were married, and half Eudoxus's estate settled upon them. Leontine and Eudoxus passed the remainder of their lives together; and received in the dutiful and affectionate behaviour of Florio and Leonilla the just recompence, as well as the natural effects, of that care which they had bestowed upon them in their education.

The Mysterious Bride

JAMES HOGG

(Scottish, 1770–1835)

A great number of people nowadays are beginning broadly to insinuate that there are no such things as ghosts, or spiritual beings visible to mortal sight. Even Sir Walter Scott is turned renegade, and, with his stories made up of half-and-half, like Nathaniel Gow's toddy, is trying to throw cold water on the most certain, though most impalpable, phenomena of human nature. The bodies are daft. Heaven mend their wits! Before they had ventured to assert such things, I wish they had been where I have often been; or, in particular, where the Laird of Birkendelly was on St. Lawrence's Eve, in the year 1777, and sundry times subsequent to that.

Be it known, then, to every reader of this relation of facts that happened in my own remembrance that the road from Birkendelly to the great muckle village of Balmawhapple (commonly called the muckle town, in opposition to the little town that stood on the other side of the burn)—that road, I say, lay between two thorn-hedges, so well kept by the Laird's hedger, so close, and so high, that a rabbit could not have escaped from the highway into any of the adjoining fields. Along this road was the Laird riding on the Eve of St. Lawrence, in a careless, indifferent manner, with his hat to one side, and his cane dancing a hornpipe before him. He was, moreover, chanting a song to himself, and I have heard people tell what song it was too. There was once a certain, or rather uncertain, bard, ycleped Robert Burns, who made a number of good songs; but this that the Laird sang was an amorous song of great antiquity, which, like all the said bard's best songs, was sung one hundred and fifty years before he was born. It began thus:

> "I am the Laird of Windy-wa's,
> I cam nae here without a cause,
> An' I hae gotten forty fa's
>   In coming o'er the knowe, joe.
> The night it is baith wind and weet;
> The morn it will be snaw and sleet;
> My shoon are frozen to my feet;
>   O, rise an' let me in, joe!
>   Let me in this ae night," etc.

This song was the Laird singing, while, at the same time, he was smudging and laughing at the catastrophe, when, ere ever aware, he beheld, a short way before him, an uncommonly elegant and beautiful girl walking in the same direction with him. "Aye," said the Laird to himself, "here is something very attractive indeed! Where the deuce can she have sprung from? She must have risen out of the earth, for I never saw her till this breath. Well, I declare I have not seen such a female figure—I wish I had such an assignation with her as the Laird of Windy-wa's had with his sweetheart."

As the Laird was half-thinking, half-speaking this to himself, the enchanting creature looked back at him with a motion of intelligence that she knew what he was half-saying, half-thinking, and then vanished over the summit of the rising ground before him, called the Birky Brow. "Aye, go your ways!" said the Laird; "I see by you, you'll not be very hard to overtake. You cannot get off the road, and I'll have a chat with you before you make the Deer's Den."

The Laird jogged on. He did not sing the *Laird of Windy-wa's* any more, for he felt a stifling about his heart; but he often repeated to himself, "She's a very fine woman!—a very fine woman indeed!—and to be walking here by herself! I cannot comprehend it."

When he reached the summit of the Birky Brow he did not see her, although he had a longer view of the road than before. He thought this very singular, and began to suspect that she wanted to escape him, although apparently rather lingering on him before. "I shall have another look at her, however," thought the Laird, and off he set at a flying trot. No. He came first to one turn, then another. There was nothing of the young lady to be seen. "Unless she take wings and fly away, I shall be up with her," quoth the Laird, and off he set at the full gallop.

In the middle of his career he met with Mr. M'Murdie, of Aulton, who hailed him with, "Hilloa, Birkendelly! Where the deuce are you flying at that rate?"

"I was riding after a woman," said the Laird, with great simplicity, reining in his steed.

"Then I am sure no woman on earth can long escape you, unless she be in an air balloon."

"I don't know that. Is she far gone?"

"In which way do you mean?"

"In this."

"Aha-ha-ha! Hee-hee-hee!" nichered M'Murdie, misconstruing the Laird's meaning.

"What do you laugh at, my dear sir? Do you know her, then?"

"Ho-ho-ho! Hee-hee-hee! How should I, or how can I, know her, Birkendelly, unless you inform me who she is?"

"Why, that is the very thing I want to know of you. I mean the young lady whom you met just now."

"You are raving, Birkendelly. I met no young lady, nor is there a single person on the road I have come by, while you know that for a mile and a half forward your way she could not get out of it."

"I know that," said the Laird, biting his lip and looking greatly puzzled; "but confound me if I understand this; for I was within speech of her just now on the top of the Birky Brow there, and, when I think of it, she could not have been even thus far as yet. She had on a pure white gauze frock, a small green bonnet and feathers, and a green veil, which, flung back over her left shoulder, hung below her waist, and was altogether such an engaging figure that no man could have passed her on the road without taking some note of her. Are you not making game of me? Did you not really meet with her?"

"On my word of truth and honor, I did not. Come, ride back with me, and we shall meet her still, depend on it. She has given you the go-by on the road. Let us go; I am only to call at the mill about some barley for the distillery, and will return with you to the big town."

Birkendelly returned with his friend. The sun was not yet set, yet M'Murdie could not help observing that the Laird looked thoughtful and confused, and not a word could he speak about anything save this lovely apparition with the white frock and the green veil; and lo! when they reached the top of Birky Brow there was the maiden again before them, and exactly at the same spot where the Laird first saw her before, only walking in the contrary direction.

"Well, this is the most extraordinary thing that I ever knew!" exclaimed the Laird.

"What is it, sir?" said M'Murdie.

"How that young lady could have eluded me," returned the Laird. "See, here she is still!"

"I beg your pardon, sir, I don't see her. Where is she?"

"There, on the other side of the angle; but you are shortsighted. See, there she is ascending the other eminence in her white frock and green veil, as I told you. What a lovely creature!"

"Well, well, we have her fairly before us now, and shall see what she is like at all events," said M'Murdie.

Between the Birky Brow and this other slight eminence there is an obtuse angle of the road at the part where it is lowest, and, in passing this, the two friends necessarily lost sight of the object of their curiosity. They pushed on at a quick pace, cleared the low angle—the maiden was not there! They rode full speed to the top of the eminence from whence a long extent of road was visible before them—there was no human creature in view. M'Murdie laughed aloud, but the Laird turned pale as death and bit his lip. His friend asked him good-humoredly why he was so much affected. He said, because he could not comprehend the meaning of this singular apparition or illusion, and it troubled him the more as he now remembered a dream of the same nature which he had, and which terminated in a dreadful manner.

"Why, man, you are dreaming still," said M'Murdie. "But never mind; it is quite common for men of your complexion to dream of beautiful maidens with white frocks, and green veils, bonnets, feathers, and slender waists. It is a lovely image, the creation of your own sanguine imagination, and you may worship it without any blame. Were her shoes black or green? And her stockings—did you note them? The symmetry of the limbs, I am sure you did! Good-bye; I see you are not disposed to leave the spot. Perhaps she will appear to you again."

So saying, M'Murdie rode on toward the mill, and Birkendelly, after musing for some time, turned his beast's head slowly round, and began to move toward the great muckle village.

The Laird's feelings were now in terrible commotion. He was taken beyond measure with the beauty and elegance of the figure he had seen, but he remembered, with a mixture of admiration and horror, that a dream of the same enchanting object had haunted his slumbers all the days of his life; yet, how singular that he should never have recollected the circumstance till now! But farther, with the dream there were connected some painful circumstances which, though terrible in their issue, he could not recollect so as to form them into any degree of arrangement.

As he was considering deeply of these things and riding slowly down the declivity, neither dancing his cane nor singing the *Laird of Windywa's,* he lifted up his eyes, and there was the girl on the same spot where he saw her first, walking deliberately up the Birky Brow. The sun was down, but it was the month of August and a fine evening, and the Laird, seized with an unconquerable desire to see and speak with that incomparable creature, could restrain himself no longer, but shouted out to her to stop till he came up. She beckoned acquiescence, and slackened her pace into a slow movement. The Laird turned the corner quickly, but when he had rounded it the maiden was still there, though on the summit of the brow. She turned round, and, with an ineffable smile and curtsy, saluted him, and again moved slowly on. She vanished gradually beyond the summit, and while the green feathers were still nodding in view, and so nigh that the Laird could have touched them with a fishing-rod, he reached the top of the brow himself. There was no living soul there, nor onward, as far as his view reached. He now trembled in every limb, and, without knowing what he did, rode straight on to the big town, not daring well to return and see what he had seen for three several times; and certain he would see it again when the shades of evening were deepening, he deemed it proper and prudent to decline the pursuit of such a phantom any farther.

He alighted at the Queen's Head, called for some brandy and water, quite forgot what was his errand to the great muckle town that afternoon, there being nothing visible to his mental sight but lovely images, with white gauze frocks and green veils. His friend M'Murdie joined him; they drank deep, bantered, reasoned, got angry, reasoned themselves calm again, and still all would not do. The Laird was conscious that he had seen the beautiful apparition, and, moreover, that she was the very maiden, or the resemblance of her, who, in the irrevocable decrees of Providence, was destined to be his. It was in vain that M'Murdie reasoned of impressions on the imagination, and

> "Of fancy moulding in the mind,
> Light visions on the passing wind."

Vain also was a story that he told him of a relation of his own, who was greatly harassed by the apparition of an officer in a red uniform that haunted him day and night, and had very nigh put him quite distracted several times, till at length his physician found out the nature of this illusion so well that he knew, from the state of his pulse, to an hour when the ghost of the officer would appear, and by bleeding, low diet, and emollients contrived to keep the apparition away altogether.

The Laird admitted the singularity of this incident, but not that it was one in point; for the one, he said, was imaginary, the other real, and that no conclusions could convince him in opposition to the authority of his own senses. He accepted of an invitation to spend a few days with M'Murdie and his family, but they all acknowledged afterward that the Laird was very much like one bewitched.

As soon as he reached home he went straight to the Birky Brow, certain of seeing once more the angelic phantom, but she was not there. He took each of his former positions again and again, but the desired vision would in no wise make its appearance. He tried every day and every hour of the day, all with the same effect, till he grew absolutely desperate, and had the audacity to kneel on the spot and entreat of Heaven to see her. Yes, he called on Heaven to see her once more, whatever she was, whether a being of earth, heaven, or hell.

He was now in such a state of excitement that he could not exist; he grew listless, impatient, and sickly, took to his bed, and sent for M'Murdie and the doctor; and the issue of the consultation was that

Birkendelly consented to leave the country for a season, on a visit to his only sister in Ireland, whither we must accompany him for a short space.

His sister was married to Captain Bryan, younger, of Scoresby, and they two lived in a cottage on the estate, and the Captain's parents and sisters at Scoresby Hall. Great was the stir and preparation when the gallant young Laird of Birkendelly arrived at the cottage, it never being doubted that he came to forward a second bond of connection with the family, which still contained seven dashing sisters, all unmarried, and all alike willing to change that solitary and helpless state for the envied one of matrimony—a state highly popular among the young women of Ireland. Some of the Misses Bryan had now reached the years of womanhood, several of them scarcely, but these small disqualifications made no difference in the estimation of the young ladies themselves; each and all of them brushed up for the competition with high hopes and unflinching resolutions. True, the elder ones tried to check the younger in their good-natured, forthright Irish way; but they retorted, and persisted in their superior pretensions. Then there was such shopping in the county town! It was so boundless that the credit of the Hall was finally exhausted, and the old Squire was driven to remark that "Och, and to be sure it was a dreadful and tirrabell concussion, to be put upon the equipment of seven daughters all at the same moment, as if the young gentleman could marry them all! Och, then, poor dear shoul, he would be after finding that one was sufficient, if not one too many. And therefore there was no occasion, none at all, at all, and that there was not, for any of them to rig out more than one."

It was hinted that the Laird had some reason for complaint at this time, but as the lady sided with her daughters, he had no chance. One of the items of his account was thirty-seven buckling-combs, then greatly in vogue. There were black combs, pale combs, yellow combs, and gilt ones, all to suit or set off various complexions; and if other articles bore any proportion at all to these, it had been better for the Laird and all his family that Birkendelly had never set foot in Ireland.

The plan was all concocted. There was to be a grand dinner at the Hall, at which the damsels were to appear in all their finery. A ball to follow, and note be taken which of the young ladies was their guest's choice, and measures taken accordingly. The dinner and the ball took place; and what a pity I may not describe that entertainment, the dresses, and the dancers, for they were all exquisite in their way, and *outré* beyond measure. But such details only serve to derange a winter evening's tale such as this.

Birkendelly having at this time but one model for his choice among womankind, all that ever he did while in the presence of ladies was to look out for some resemblance to her, the angel of his fancy; and it so happened that in one of old Bryan's daughters named Luna, or, more familiarly, Loony, he perceived, or thought he perceived, some imaginary similarity in form and air to the lovely apparition. This was the sole reason why he was incapable of taking his eyes off from her the whole of that night; and this incident settled the point, not only with the old people, but even the young ladies were forced, after every exertion on their own parts, to "yild the p'int to their sister Loony, who certainly was not the mist genteelest nor mist handsomest of that guid-lucking fimily."

The next day Lady Luna was dispatched off to the cottage in grand style, there to live hand in glove with her supposed lover. There was no standing all this. There were the two parrocked together, like a ewe and a lamb, early and late; and though the Laird really appeared to have, and probably had, some delight in her company, it was only in contemplating that certain indefinable air of resemblance which she bore to the sole image impressed on his heart. He bought her a white gauze frock, a green bonnet and feather, with a veil, which she was obliged to wear thrown over her left shoulder, and every day after, six times a day, was she obliged to walk over a certain eminence at a certain distance before her lover. She was delighted to oblige him; but still, when he came up, he looked disappointed, and never said, "Luna, I love you; when are we to be married?" No, he never said any such thing, for all her looks and expressions of fondest love; for, alas! in all this dalliance he was only feeding a mysterious flame that preyed upon his vitals, and proved too severe for the powers either of reason or religion to extinguish. Still, time flew lighter and lighter by, his health was restored, the bloom of his cheek returned, and the frank and simple confidence of Luna had a certain charm with it that reconciled him to his sister's Irish economy. But a strange incident now happened to him which deranged all his immediate plans.

He was returning from angling one evening, a little before sunset, when he saw Lady Luna awaiting him on his way home. But instead of brushing up to meet him as usual, she turned, and walked up the rising ground before him. "Poor sweet girl! how condescending she is," said he to himself, "and how like she is in reality to the angelic being whose form and features are so deeply impressed on my heart! I now see it is no fond or fancied resemblance. It is real! real! real! How I long to clasp her in my arms, and tell her how I love her; for, after all, that is the girl that is to be mine, and the former a vision to impress this the more on my heart."

He posted up the ascent to overtake her. When at the top she turned, smiled, and curtsied. Good heavens! it was the identical lady of his fondest adoration herself, but lovelier, far lovelier, than ever. He expected every moment that she would vanish, as was her wont; but she did not— she awaited him, and received his embraces with open arms. She was a being of real flesh and blood, courteous, elegant, and affectionate. He kissed her hand, he kissed her glowing cheek, and blessed all the powers of love who had thus restored her to him again, after undergoing pangs of love such as man never suffered.

"But, dearest heart, here we are standing in the middle of the highway," said he; "suffer me to conduct you to my sister's house, where you shall have an apartment with a child of nature having some slight resemblance to yourself." She smiled, and said, "No, I will not sleep with Lady Luna to-night. Will you please to look round you, and see where you are." He did so, and behold they were standing on the Birky Brow, on the only spot where he had ever seen her. She smiled at his embarrassed look, and asked if he did not remember aught of his coming over from Ireland. He said he thought he did remember something of it, but love with him had long absorbed every other sense. He then asked her to his own house, which she declined, saying she could only meet him on that spot till after their marriage, which could not be before St. Lawrence's Eve come three years. "And now," said she, "we must part. My name is Jane Ogilvie, and you were betrothed to me before you were born. But I am come to release you this evening, if you have the slightest objection."

He declared he had none; and kneeling, swore the most solemn oath to be hers forever, and to meet her there on St. Lawrence's Eve next, and every St. Lawrence's Eve until that blessed day on which she had consented to make him happy by becoming his own forever. She then asked him affectionately to change rings with her, in pledge of their faith and troth, in which he joyfully acquiesced; for she could not have then asked any conditions which, in the fulness of his heart's love, he would not have granted; and after one fond and affectionate kiss, and repeating all their engagements over again, they parted.

Birkendelly's heart was now melted within him, and all his senses overpowered by one overwhelming passion. On leaving his fair and kind one, he got bewildered, and could not find the road to his own house, believing sometimes that he was going there, and sometimes to his sister's, till at length he came, as he thought, upon the Liffey, at its junction with Loch Allan; and there, in attempting to call for a boat, he awoke from a profound sleep, and found himself lying in his bed within his sister's house, and the day sky just breaking.

If he was puzzled to account for some things in the course of his dream, he was much more puzzled to account for them now that he was wide awake. He was sensible that he had met his love, had embraced, kissed, and exchanged vows and rings with her, and, in token of the truth and reality of all these, her emerald ring was on his finger, and his own away; so there was no doubt that they had met—by what means it was beyond the power of man to calculate.

There was then living with Mrs. Bryan an old Scotswoman, commonly styled Lucky Black. She had nursed Birkendelly's mother, and been dry-nurse to himself and sister; and having more than a mother's attachment for the latter, when she was married, old Lucky left her country to spend the last of her days in the house of her beloved young lady. When the Laird entered the breakfast-parlor that morning she was sitting in her black velvet hood, as usual, reading *The Fourfold State of Man,* and, being paralytic and somewhat deaf, she seldom regarded those who went or came. But chancing to hear him say something about the 9th of August, she quitted reading, turned round her head to listen, and then asked, in a hoarse, tremulous voice: "What's that he's saying? What's the unlucky callant saying about the 9th of August? Aih? To be sure it is St. Lawrence's Eve, although the 10th be his day. It's ower true, ower true, ower true for him an' a' his kin, poor man! Aih? What was he saying then?"

The men smiled at her incoherent earnestness, but the lady, with true feminine condescension, informed her, in a loud voice, that Allan had an engagement in Scotland on St. Lawrence's Eve. She then started up, extended her shrivelled hands, that shook like the aspen, and panted out: "Aih, aih? Lord preserve us! Whaten an engagement has he on St. Lawrence's Eve? Bind him! bind him! Shackle him wi' bands of steel, and of brass, and of iron! O may He whose blessed will was pleased to leave him an orphan sae soon, preserve him from the fate which I tremble to think on!"

She then tottered round the table, as with supernatural energy, and seizing the Laird's right hand, she drew it close to her unstable eyes, and then perceiving the emerald ring chased in blood, she threw up her arms with a jerk, opened her skinny jaws with a fearful gape, and uttering a shriek that made all the house yell, and every one within it to tremble, she fell back lifeless and rigid on the floor. The gentlemen both fled, out of sheer terror; but a woman never deserts her friends in extremity. The lady called her maids about her, had her old nurse conveyed to bed, where every means were used to restore animation. But, alas, life was extinct! The vital spark had fled forever, which filled all their hearts with grief, disappointment, and horror, as some dreadful tale of mystery was now sealed up from their knowledge which, in all likelihood, no other could reveal. But to say the truth, the Laird did not seem greatly disposed to probe it to the bottom.

Not all the arguments of Captain Bryan and his lady, nor the simple entreaties of Lady Luna, could induce Birkendelly to put off his engagement to meet his love on the Birky Brow on the evening of the 9th of August; but he promised soon to return, pretending that some business of the utmost importance called him away. Before he went, however, he asked his sister if ever she had heard of such a lady in Scotland as Jane Ogilvie. Mrs. Bryan repeated the name many times to herself, and said that name undoubtedly was once familiar to her, although she thought not for good, but at that moment she did not recollect one single individual of the name. He then showed her the emerald ring that had been the death of Lucky Black; but the moment the lady looked at it, she made a grasp at it to take it off by force, which she had very nearly effected. "Oh, burn it! burn it!" cried she; "it is not a right ring! Burn it!"

"My dear sister, what fault is in the ring?" said he. "It is a very pretty ring, and one that I set great value by."

"Oh, for Heaven's sake, burn it, and renounce the giver!" cried she. "If you have any regard for your peace here or your soul's welfare hereafter, burn that ring! If you saw with your own eyes, you would easily perceive that that is not a ring befitting a Christian to wear."

This speech confounded Birkendelly a good deal. He retired by himself and examined the ring, and could see nothing in it unbecoming a Christian to wear. It was a chased gold ring, with a bright emerald, which last had a red foil, in some lights giving it a purple gleam, and inside was engraven *"Elegit,"* much defaced, but that his sister could not see; therefore he could not comprehend her vehement injunctions concerning it. But that it might no more give her offence, or any other, he sewed it within his vest, opposite his heart, judging that there was something in it which his eyes were withholden from discerning.

Thus he left Ireland with his mind in great confusion, groping his way, as it were, in a hole of mystery, yet with the passion that preyed on his heart and vitals more intense than ever. He seems to have had an impression all his life that some mysterious fate awaited him, which the correspondence of his dreams and day visions tended to confirm. And though he gave himself wholly up to the sway of one overpowering passion, it was not without some yearnings of soul, manifestations of terror, and so much earthly shame, that he never more mentioned his love, or his engagements, to any human being, not even to his friend M'Murdie, whose company he forthwith shunned.

It is on this account that I am unable to relate what passed between the lovers thenceforward. It is certain they met at the Birky Brow that St. Lawrence's Eve, for they were seen in company together; but of the engagements, vows, or dalliance that passed between them I can say nothing; nor of all their future meetings, until the beginning of August, 1781, when the Laird began decidedly to make preparations for his approaching marriage; yet not as if he and his betrothed had been to reside at Birkendelly, all his provisions rather bespeaking a meditated journey.

On the morning of the 9th he wrote to his sister, and then arraying himself in his new wedding suit, and putting the emerald ring on his finger, he appeared all impatience, until toward evening, when he sallied out on horseback to his appointment. It seems that his mysterious inamorata had met him, for he was seen riding through the big town before sunset, with a young lady behind him, dressed in white and green, and the villagers affirmed that they were riding at the rate of fifty miles an hour! They were seen to pass a cottage called Mosskilt, ten miles farther on, where there was no highway, at the same tremendous speed; and I could never hear that they were any more seen, until the following morning, when Birkendelly's fine bay horse was found lying dead at his own stable door; and shortly after his master was likewise discovered lying, a blackened corpse, on the Birky Brow at the very spot where the mysterious but lovely dame had always appeared to him. There was neither wound, bruise, nor dislocation in his whole frame; but his skin was of a livid color, and his features terribly distorted.

This woful catastrophe struck the neighborhood with great consternation, so that nothing else was talked of. Every ancient tradition and modern incident were raked together, compared, and combined; and certainly a most rare concatenation of misfortunes was elicited. It was authenticated that his father had died on the same spot that day twenty years, and his grandfather that day forty years, the former, as was supposed, by a fall from his horse when in liquor, and the latter, nobody knew how; and now this Allan was the last of his race, for Mrs. Bryan had no children.

It was, moreover, now remembered by many, and among the rest by the Rev. Joseph Taylor, that he had frequently observed a young lady, in white and green, sauntering about the spot on a St. Lawrence's Eve.

When Captain Bryan and his lady arrived to take possession of the premises, they instituted a strict inquiry into every circumstance; but nothing further than what was related to them by Mr. M'Murdie could be learned of this Mysterious Bride, besides what the Laird's own letter bore. It ran thus:

"Dearest Sister,—I shall before this time to-morrow be the most happy, or most miserable, of mankind, having solemnly engaged myself this night to wed a young and beautiful lady, named Jane Ogilvie, to whom it seems I was betrothed before I was born. Our correspondence has been of a most private and mysterious nature; but my troth is pledged, and my resolution fixed. We set out on a far journey to the place of her abode on the nuptial eve, so that it will be long before I see you again. Yours till death,

"Allan George Sandison.

"Birkendelly, August 8, 1781."

That very same year, an old woman, named Marion Haw, was returned upon that, her native parish, from Glasgow. She had led a migratory life with her son—who was what he called a bell-hanger, but in fact a tinker of the worst grade—for many years, and was at last returned to the muckle town in a state of great destitution. She gave the parishioners a history of the Mysterious Bride, so plausibly correct, but withal so romantic, that everybody said of it (as is often said of my narratives, with the same narrow-minded prejudice and injustice) that it was a *made story*. There were, however, some strong testimonies of its veracity.

She said the first Allan Sandison, who married the great heiress of Birkendelly, was previously engaged to a beautiful young lady named Jane Ogilvie, to whom he gave anything but fair play; and, as she believed, either murdered her, or caused her to be murdered, in the midst of a thicket of birch and broom, at a spot which she mentioned; and she had good reason for believing so, as she had seen the red blood and the new grave, when she was a little girl, and ran home and mentioned it to her grandfather, who charged her as she valued her life never to mention that again, as it was only the nombles and hide of a deer which he himself had buried there. But when, twenty years subsequent to that, the wicked and unhappy Allan Sandison was found dead on that very spot, and lying across the green mound, then nearly level with the surface, which she had once seen a new grave, she then for the first time ever thought of a Divine Providence; and she added, "For my grandfather, Neddy Haw, he dee'd too; there's naebody kens how, nor ever shall."

As they were quite incapable of conceiving from Marion's description anything of the spot, Mr. M'Murdie caused her to be taken out to the Birky Brow in a cart, accompanied by Mr. Taylor and some hundreds of the town's folks; but whenever she saw it, she said, "Aha, birkies! the haill kintra's altered now. There was nae road here then; it gaed straight ower the tap o' the hill. An' let me see—there's the thorn where the cushats biggit; an' there's the auld birk that I ance fell aff an' left my shoe sticking i' the cleft. I can tell ye, birkies, either the deer's grave or bonny Jane Ogilvie's is no twa yards aff the place where that horse's hind-feet are standin'; sae ye may howk, an' see if there be ony remains."

The minister and M'Murdie and all the people stared at one another, for they had purposely caused the horse to stand still on the very spot where both the father and son had been found dead. They digged, and deep, deep below the road they found part of the slender bones and skull of a young female, which they deposited decently in the church-yard. The family of the Sandisons is extinct, the Mysterious Bride appears no more on the Eve of St. Lawrence, and the wicked people of the great muckle village have got a lesson on divine justice written to them in lines of blood.

The Tapestried Chamber
or
The Lady in The Sacque

⟡⟡⟡

SIR WALTER SCOTT
(Scottish, 1771–1832)

The following narrative is given from the pen, so far as memory permits, in the same character in which it was presented to the author's ear; nor has he claim to further praise, or to be more deeply censured, than in proportion to the good or bad judgment which he has employed in selecting his materials, as he has studiously avoided any attempt at ornament which might interfere with the simplicity of the tale.

At the same time, it must be admitted that the particular class of stories which turns on the marvellous, possesses a stronger influence when told than when committed to print. The volume taken up at noonday, though rehearsing the same incidents, conveys a much more feeble impression than is achieved by the voice of the speaker on a circle of fireside auditors, who hang upon the narrative as the narrator details the minute incidents which serve to give it authenticity, and lowers his voice with an affectation of mystery while he approaches the fearful and wonderful part. It was with such advantages that the present writer heard the following events related, more than twenty years since, by the celebrated Miss Seward, of Litchfield, who, to her numerous accomplishments, added, in a remarkable degree, the power of narrative in private conversation. In its present form the tale must necessarily lose all the interest which was attached to it, by the flexible voice and intelligent features of the gifted narrator. Yet still, read aloud, to an undoubting audience by the doubtful light of the closing evening, or, in silence, by a decaying taper, and amidst the solitude of a half-lighted apartment, it may redeem its character as a good ghost story. Miss Seward always affirmed that she had derived her information from an authentic source, although she suppressed the names of the two persons chiefly concerned. I will not avail myself of any particulars I may have since received concerning the localities of the detail, but suffer them to rest under the same general description in which they were first related to me; and, for the same reason, I will not add to or diminish the narrative, by any circumstance, whether more or less material, but simply rehearse, as I heard it, a story of supernatural terror.

About the end of the American war, when the officers of Lord Cornwallis's army, which surrendered at Yorktown, and others, who had been made prisoners during the impolitic and ill-fated controversy, were returning to their own country, to relate their adventures, and repose themselves after their fatigues, there was amongst them a general officer, to whom Miss S. gave the name of Browne, but merely, as I understood, to save the inconvenience of introducing a nameless agent in the narrative. He was an officer of merit, as well as a gentleman of high consideration for family and attainments.

Some business had carried General Browne upon a tour through the western counties, when, in the conclusion of a morning stage, he found himself in the vicinity of a small country town, which presented a scene of uncommon beauty, and of a character peculiarly English.

The little town, with its stately old church, whose tower bore testimony to the devotion of ages long past, lay amidst pastures and cornfields of small extent, but bounded and divided with hedgerow timber of great age and size. There were few marks of modern improvement. The environs of the place intimated neither the solitude of decay nor the bustle of novelty; the houses were old, but in good repair; and the beautiful little river murmured freely on its way to the left of the town, neither restrained by a dam, nor bordered by a towing-path.

Upon a gentle eminence, nearly a mile to the southward of the town, were seen, amongst many venerable oaks and tangled thickets, the turrets of a castle, as old as the wars of York and Lancaster, but which seemed to have received important alterations during the age of Elizabeth and her successor. It had not been a place of great size; but whatever accommodation it formerly afforded was, it must be supposed, still to be obtained within its walls; at least such was the inference which General Browne drew from observing the smoke arise merrily from several of the ancient chimney-stacks. The wall of the park ran alongside of the highway for two or three hundred yards; and through the different points by which the eye found glimpses into the woodland scenery, it seemed to be well stocked. Other points of view opened in succession; now a full one, of the front of the old castle, and now a side glimpse at its particular towers; the former rich in all the bizarrerie of the Elizabethan school, while the simple and solid strength of other parts of the building seemed to show that they had been raised more for defence than ostentation.

Delighted with the partial glimpses which he obtained of the castle through the woods and glades by which this ancient feudal fortress was surrounded, our military traveller was determined to inquire whether it might not deserve a nearer view, and whether it contained family pictures or other objects of curiosity worthy of a stranger's visit; when, leaving the vicinity of the park, he rolled through a clean and well-paved street, and stopped at the door of a well-frequented inn.

Before ordering horses to proceed on his journey, General Browne made inquiries concerning the proprietor of the château which had so attracted his admiration; and was equally surprised and pleased at hearing in reply a nobleman named, whom we shall call Lord Woodville. How fortunate! Much of Browne's early recollections, both at school and at college, had been connected with young Woodville, whom, by a few questions, he now ascertained to be the same with the owner of this fair domain. He had been raised to the peerage by the decease of his father a few months before, and, as the General learned from the landlord, the term of mourning being ended, was now taking possession of his paternal estate, in the jovial season of merry autumn, accompanied by a select party of friends to enjoy the sports of a country famous for game.

This was delightful news to our traveller. Frank Woodville had been Richard Browne's fag at Eton, and his chosen intimate at Christ Church; their pleasures and their tasks had been the same; and the honest soldier's heart warmed to find his early friend in possession of so delightful a residence, and of an estate, as the landlord assured him with a nod and a wink, fully adequate to maintain and add to his dignity. Nothing was more natural than that the traveller should suspend a journey, which there was nothing to render hurried, to pay a visit to an old friend under such agreeable circumstances.

The fresh horses, therefore, had only the brief task of conveying the General's travelling carriage to Woodville Castle. A porter admitted them at a modern Gothic lodge, built in that style to correspond with the castle itself, and at the same time rang a bell to give warning of the approach of visitors. Apparently the sound of the bell had suspended the separation of the company, bent on the various amusements of the morning; for, on entering the court of the château, several young men were lounging about in their sporting dresses, looking at and criticising the dogs which the keepers held in readiness to attend their pastime. As General Browne alighted, the young lord came to the gate of the hall, and for an instant gazed, as at a stranger, upon the countenance of his friend, on which war, with its fatigues and its wounds, had made a great alteration. But the uncertainty lasted no longer than till the visitor had spoken, and the hearty greeting which followed was such as can only be exchanged betwixt those who have passed together the merry days of careless boyhood or early youth.

"If I could have formed a wish, my dear Browne," said Lord Woodville, "it would have been to have you here, of all men, upon this occasion, which my friends are good enough to hold as a sort of holiday. Do not think you have been unwatched during the years you have been absent from us. I have traced you through your dangers, your triumphs, your misfortunes, and was delighted to see that, whether in victory or defeat, the name of my old friend was always distinguished with applause."

The General made a suitable reply, and congratulated his friend on his new dignities, and the possession of a place and domain so beautiful.

"Nay, you have seen nothing of it as yet," said Lord Woodville, "and I trust you do not mean to leave us till you are better acquainted with it. It is true, I confess, that my present party is pretty large, and the old house, like other places of the kind, does not possess so much accommodation as the extent of the outward walls appears to promise. But we can give you a comfortable old-fashioned room, and I venture to suppose that your campaigns have taught you to be glad of worse quarters."

The General shrugged his shoulders, and laughed. "I presume," he said, "the worst apartment in your château is considerably superior to the old tobacco-cask, in which I was fain to take up my night's lodging when I was in the bush, as the Virginians call it, with the light corps. There I lay, like Diogenes himself, so delighted with my covering from the elements, that I made a vain attempt to have it rolled on to my next quarters; but my commander for the time would give way to no such luxurious provision, and I took farewell of my beloved cask with tears in my eyes."

"Well, then, since you do not fear your quarters," said Lord Woodville, "you will stay with me a week at least. Of guns, dogs, fishing-rods, flies, and means of sport by sea and land, we have enough and to spare: you cannot pitch on an amusement but we will find the means of pursuing it. But if you prefer the gun and pointers, I will go with you myself, and see whether you have mended your shooting since you have been amongst the Indians of the back settlements."

The General gladly accepted his friendly host's proposal in all its points. After a morning of manly exercise, the company met at dinner, where it was the delight of Lord Woodville to conduce to the display of the high properties of his recovered friend, so as to recommend him to his guests, most of whom were persons of distinction. He led General Browne to speak of the scenes he had witnessed; and as every word marked alike the brave officer and the sensible man, who retained possession of his cool judgment under the most imminent dangers, the company looked upon the soldier with general respect, as on one who had proved himself possessed of an uncommon portion of personal courage— that attribute, of all others, of which everybody desires to be thought possessed.

The day at Woodville Castle ended as usual in such mansions. The hospitality stopped within the limits of good order. Music, in which the young lord was a proficient, succeeded to the circulation of the bottle; cards and billiards, for those who preferred such amusements, were in readiness; but the exercise of the morning required early hours, and not long after eleven o'clock the guests began to retire to their several apartments.

The young lord himself conducted his friend, General Browne, to the chamber destined for him, which answered the description he had given of it, being comfortable, but old-fashioned. The bed was of the massive form used in the end of the seventeenth century, and the curtains of faded silk, heavily trimmed with tarnished gold. But then the sheets, pillows, and blankets looked delightful to the campaigner, when he thought of his "mansion, the cask." There was an air of gloom in the tapestry hangings, which, with their worn-out graces, curtained the walls of the little chamber, and gently undulated as the autumnal breeze found its way through the ancient lattice-window, which pattered and whistled as the air gained entrance. The toilet, too, with its mirror, turbaned, after the manner of the beginning of the century, with a coiffure of murrey-coloured silk, and its hundred strange-shaped boxes, providing for arrangements which had been obsolete for more than fifty years, had an antique, and in so far a melancholy, aspect. But nothing could blaze more brightly and cheerfully than the two large wax candles; or if aught could rival them, it was the flaming bickering fagots in the chimney that sent at once their gleam and their warmth through the snug apartment, which, notwithstanding the general antiquity of its appearance, was not wanting in the least convenience that modern habits rendered either necessary or desirable.

"This is an old-fashioned sleeping apartment, General," said the young lord; "but I hope you find nothing that makes you envy your old tobacco-cask."

"I am not particular respecting my lodgings," replied the General; "yet were I to make any choice, I would prefer this chamber by many degrees to the gayer and more modern rooms of your family mansion. Believe me, that when I unite its modern air of comfort with its venerable antiquity, and recollect that it is your lordship's property, I shall feel in better quarters here, than if I were in the best hotel London could afford."

"I trust—I have no doubt—that you will find yourself as comfortable as I wish you, my dear General," said the young nobleman; and once more bidding his guest good-night, he shook him by the hand, and withdrew.

The General once more looked around him, and internally congratulating himself on his return to peaceful life, the comforts of which were endeared by the recollection of the hardships and dangers he had lately sustained, undressed himself, and prepared for a luxurious night's rest.

Here, contrary to the custom of this species of tale, we leave the General in possession of his apartment until the next morning.

The company assembled for breakfast at an early hour, but without the appearance of General Browne, who seemed the guest that Lord Woodville was desirous of honouring above all whom his hospitality had assembled around him. He more than once expressed himself surprised at the General's absence, and at length sent a servant to make inquiry after him. The man brought back information that General Browne had been walking abroad since an early hour of the morning, in defiance of the weather, which was misty and ungenial.

"The custom of a soldier," said the young nobleman to his friends; "many of them acquire habitual vigilance, and cannot sleep after the early hour at which their duty usually commands them to be alert."

Yet the explanation which Lord Woodville thus offered to the company seemed hardly satisfactory to his own mind, and it was in a fit of silence and abstraction that he awaited the return of the General. It took place near an hour after the breakfast bell had rung. He looked fatigued and feverish. His hair—the powdering and arrangement of which was at this time one of the most important occupations of a man's whole day, and marked his fashion as much as, in the present time, the tying of a cravat, or the want of one—was dishevelled, uncurled, void of powder, and dank with dew. His clothes were huddled on with a careless negligence, remarkable in a military man, whose real or supposed duties are usually held to include some attention to the toilet; and his looks were haggard and ghastly in a peculiar degree.

"So you have stolen a march upon us this morning, my dear General," said Lord Woodville; "or you have not found your bed so much to your mind as I had hoped and you seemed to expect. How did you rest last night?"

"Oh, excellently well! remarkably well! never better in my life," said General Browne rapidly, and yet with an air of embarrassment which was obvious to his friend. He then hastily swallowed a cup of tea, and, neglecting or refusing whatever else was offered, seemed to fall into a fit of abstraction.

"You will take the gun to-day, General?" said his friend and host, but had to repeat the question twice ere he received the abrupt answer, "No, my lord; I am sorry I cannot have the opportunity of spending another day with your lordship: my post horses are ordered, and will be here directly."

All who were present showed surprise, and Lord Woodville immediately replied, "Post horses, my good friend! what can you possibly want with them, when you promised to stay with me quietly for at least a week?"

"I believe," said the General, obviously much embarrassed, "that I might, in the pleasure of my first meeting with your lordship, have said something about stopping here a few days; but I have since found it altogether impossible."

"This is very extraordinary," answered the young nobleman. "You seemed quite disengaged yesterday, and you cannot have had a summons to-day; for our post has not come up from the town, and therefore you cannot have received any letters."

General Browne, without giving any further explanation, muttered something about indispensable business, and insisted on the absolute necessity of his departure in a manner which silenced all opposition on the part of his host, who saw that his resolution was taken, and forbore all further importunity.

"At least, however," he said, "permit me, my dear Browne, since go you will or must, to show you the view from the terrace, which the mist, that is now rising, will soon display."

He threw open a sash window, and stepped down upon the terrace as he spoke. The General followed him mechanically, but seemed little to attend to what his host was saying, as, looking across an extended and rich prospect, he pointed out the different objects worthy of observation. Thus they moved on till Lord Woodville had attained his purpose of drawing his guest entirely apart from the rest of the company, when, turning round upon him with an air of great solemnity, he addressed him thus:

"Richard Browne, my old and very dear friend, we are now alone. Let me conjure you to answer me, upon the word of a friend, and the honour of a soldier. How did you in reality rest during last night?"

"Most wretchedly indeed, my lord," answered the General, in the same tone of solemnity; "so miserably, that I would not run the risk of such a second night, not only for all the lands belonging to this castle, but for all the country which I see from this elevated point of view."

"This is most extraordinary," said the young lord, as if speaking to himself; "then there must be something in the reports concerning that apartment." Again turning to the General, he said, "For God's sake, my dear friend, be candid with me, and let me know the disagreeable particulars which have befallen you under a roof where, with consent of the owner, you should have met nothing save comfort."

The General seemed distressed by this appeal, and paused a moment before he replied. "My dear lord," he at length said, "what happened to me last night is of a nature so peculiar and so unpleasant, that I could hardly bring myself to detail it even to your lordship, were it not that, independent of my wish to gratify any request of yours, I think that sincerity on my part may lead to some explanation about a circumstance equally painful and mysterious. To others, the communication I am about to make might place me in the light of a weak-minded, superstitious fool, who suffered his own imagination to delude and bewilder him; but you have known me in childhood and youth, and will not suspect me of having adopted in manhood the feelings and frailties from which my early years were free." Here he paused, and his friend replied:

"Do not doubt my perfect confidence in the truth of your communication, however strange it may be," replied Lord Woodville; "I know your firmness of disposition too well to suspect you could be made the object of imposition, and am aware that your honour and your friendship will equally deter you from exaggerating whatever you may have witnessed."

"Well, then," said the General, "I will proceed with my story as well as I can, relying upon your candour, and yet distinctly feeling that I would rather face a battery than recall to my mind the odious recollections of last night."

He paused a second time, and then perceiving that Lord Woodville remained silent and in an attitude of attention, he commenced, though not without obvious reluctance, the history of his night adventures in the Tapestried Chamber.

"I undressed and went to bed so soon as your lordship left me yesterday evening; but the wood in the chimney, which nearly fronted my bed, blazed brightly and cheerfully, and, aided by a hundred exciting recollections of my childhood and youth, which had been recalled by the unexpected pleasure of meeting your lordship, prevented me from falling immediately asleep. I ought, however, to say that these reflections were all of a pleasant and agreeable kind, grounded on a sense of having for a time exchanged the labour, fatigues, and dangers of my profession, for the enjoyments of a peaceful life, and the reunion of those friendly and affectionate ties, which I had torn asunder at the rude summons of war.

"While such pleasing reflections were stealing over my mind, and gradually lulling me to slumber, I was suddenly aroused by a sound like that of the rustling of a silken gown, and the tapping of a pair of high-heeled shoes, as if a woman were walking in the apartment. Ere I could draw the curtain to see what the matter was, the figure of a little woman passed between the bed and the fire. The back of this form was turned to me, and I could observe, from the shoulders and neck, it was that of an old woman, whose dress was an old-fashioned gown, which, I think, ladies call a sacque; that is, a sort of robe completely loose in the body, but gathered into broad plaits upon the neck and shoulders, which fall down to the ground, and terminate in a species of train.

"I thought the intrusion singular enough, but never harboured for a moment the idea that what I saw was anything more than the mortal form of some old woman about the establishment, who had a fancy to dress like her grandmother, and who, having perhaps (as your lordship mentioned that you were rather straitened for room) been dislodged from her chamber for my accommodation, had forgotten the circumstance, and returned by twelve to her old haunt. Under this persuasion, I moved myself in bed and coughed a little, to make the intruder sensible of my being in possession of the premises. She turned slowly round, but, gracious Heaven, my lord, what a countenance did she display to me! There was no longer any question what she was, or any thought of her being a living being. Upon a face which wore the fixed features of a corpse were imprinted the traces of the vilest and most hideous passions which had animated her while she lived. The body of some atrocious criminal seemed to have been given up from the grave, and the soul restored from the penal fire, in order to form, for a space, an union with the ancient accomplice of its guilt. I started up in bed, and sat upright, supporting myself on my palms, as I gazed on this horrible spectre. The hag made, as it seemed, a single and swift stride to the bed where I lay, and squatted herself down upon it in precisely the same attitude which I had assumed in the extremity of horror, advancing her diabolical countenance within half a yard of mine, with a grin that seemed to intimate the malice and the derision of an incarnate fiend."

Here General Browne stopped, and wiped from his brow the cold perspiration with which the recollection of his horrible vision had covered it.

"My Lord," he said, "I am no coward. I have been in all the mortal dangers incidental to my profession, and I may truly boast, that no man ever knew Richard Browne dishonour the sword he wears; but in these horrible circumstances, under the eyes, and, as it seemed, almost in the grasp of an incarnation of an evil spirit, all firmness forsook me, all manhood melted from me like wax in the furnace, and I felt my hair individually bristle. The current of my life-blood ceased to flow, and I sank back in a swoon, as very a victim to panic terror as ever was a village girl, or a child of ten years old. How long I lay in this condition I cannot pretend to guess.

"But I was roused by the castle clock striking one, so loud that it seemed as if it were in the very room. It was some time before I dared open my eyes, lest they should again encounter the horrible spectacle. When, however, I summoned courage to look up, she was no longer visible. My first idea was to pull my bell, wake the servants, and remove to a garret or a hay-loft, to be ensured against a second visitation. Nay, I will confess the truth, that my resolution was altered, not by the shame of exposing myself, but by the fear that, as the bell cord hung by the chimney, I might, in making my way to it, be again crossed by the fiendish hag, who, I figured to myself, might be still lurking about some corner of the apartment.

"I will not pretend to describe what hot and cold fever-fits tormented me for the rest of the night, through broken sleep, weary vigils, and that dubious state which forms the neutral ground between them. An hundred terrible objects appeared to haunt me; but there was the great difference betwixt the vision which I have described, and those which followed, that I knew the last to be deceptions of my own fancy and overexcited nerves.

"Day at last appeared, and I rose from my bed ill in health and humiliated in mind. I was ashamed of myself as a man and a soldier, and still more so, at feeling my own extreme desire to escape from the haunted apartment, which, however, conquered all other considerations; so that, huddling on my clothes with the most careless haste, I made my escape from your lordship's mansion, to seek in the open air some relief to my nervous system, shaken as it was by this horrible encounter with a visitant, for such I must believe her, from the other world. Your lordship has now heard the cause of my discomposure, and of my sudden desire to leave your hospitable castle. In other places I trust we may often meet; but God protect me from ever spending a second night under that roof!"

Strange as the General's tale was, he spoke with such a deep air of conviction, that it cut short all the usual commentaries which are made on such stories. Lord Woodville never once asked him if he was sure he did not dream of the apparition, or suggested any of the possibilities by which it is fashionable to explain supernatural appearances, as wild vagaries of the fancy, or deceptions of the optic nerves. On the contrary, he seemed deeply impressed with the truth and reality of what he had heard; and after a considerable pause, regretted, with much appearance of sincerity, that his early friend should in his house have suffered so severely.

"I am the more sorry for your pain, my dear Browne," he continued, "that it is the unhappy, though most unexpected, result of an experiment of my own. You must know that, for my father and grandfather's time at least, the apartment which was assigned to you last night had been shut on account of reports that it was disturbed by supernatural sights and noises. When I came, a few weeks since, into possession of the estate, I thought the accommodation which the castle afforded for my friends was not extensive enough to permit the inhabitants of the invisible world to retain possession of a comfortable sleeping apartment. I therefore caused the Tapestried Chamber, as we call it, to be opened; and, without destroying its air of antiquity, I had such new articles of furniture placed in it as became the modern times. Yet as the opinion that the room was haunted very strongly prevailed among the domestics, and was also known in the neighbourhood and to many of my friends, I feared some prejudice might be entertained by the first occupant of the Tapestried Chamber, which might tend to revive the evil report which it had laboured under, and so disappoint my purpose of rendering it an useful part of the house. I must confess, my dear Browne, that your arrival yesterday, agreeable to me for a thousand reasons besides, seemed the most favourable opportunity of removing the unpleasant rumours which attached to the room, since your courage was indubitable, and your mind free of any preoccupation on the subject. I could not, therefore, have chosen a more fitting subject for my experiment."

"Upon my life," said General Browne, somewhat hastily, "I am infinitely obliged to your lordship—very particularly indebted indeed. I am likely to remember for some time the consequences of the experiment, as your lordship is pleased to call it."

"Nay, now you are unjust, my dear friend," said Lord Woodville. "You have only to reflect for a single moment, in order to be convinced that I could not augur the possibility of the pain to which you have been so unhappily exposed. I was yesterday morning a complete sceptic on the subject of supernatural appearances. Nay, I am sure that had I told you what was said about that room, those very reports would have induced you, by your own choice, to select it for your accommodation. It was my misfortune, perhaps my error, but really cannot be termed my fault, that you have been afflicted so strangely."

"Strangely indeed!" said the General, resuming his good temper; "and I acknowledge that I have no right to be offended with your lordship for treating me like what I used to think myself—a man of some firmness and courage. But I see my post horses are arrived, and I must not detain your lordship from your amusement."

"Nay, my old friend," said Lord Woodville, "since you cannot stay with us another day, which, indeed, I can no longer urge, give me at least half an hour more. You used to love pictures and I have a gallery of portraits, some of them by Vandyke, representing ancestry to whom this property and castle formerly belonged. I think that several of them will strike you as possessing merit."

General Browne accepted the invitation, though somewhat unwillingly. It was evident he was not to breathe freely or at ease till he left Woodville Castle far behind him. He could not refuse his friend's invitation, however; and the less so, that he was a little ashamed of the peevishness which he had displayed towards his well-meaning entertainer.

The General, therefore, followed Lord Woodville through several rooms, into a long gallery hung with pictures, which the latter pointed out to his guest, telling the names, and giving some account of the personages whose portraits presented themselves in progression. General Browne was but little interested in the details which these accounts conveyed to him. They were, indeed, of the kind which are usually found in an old family gallery. Here, was a cavalier who had ruined the estate in the royal cause; there, a fine lady who had reinstated it by contracting a match with a wealthy Roundhead. There, hung a gallant who had been in danger for corresponding with the exiled Court at Saint Germain's; here, one who had taken arms for William at the Revolution; and there, a third that had thrown his weight alternately into the scale of whig and tory.

While Lord Woodville was cramming these words into his guest's ear, "against the stomach of his sense," they gained the middle of the gallery, when he beheld General Browne suddenly start, and assume an attitude of the utmost surprise, not unmixed with fear, as his eyes were caught and suddenly riveted by a portrait of an old, old lady in a sacque, the fashionable dress of the end of the seventeenth century.

"There she is!" he exclaimed; "there she is, in form and features, though inferior in demoniac expression, to the accursed hag who visited me last night!"

"If that be the case," said the young nobleman, "there can remain no longer any doubt of the horrible reality of your apparition. That is the picture of a wretched ancestress of mine, of whose crimes a black and fearful catalogue is recorded in a family history in my charter-chest. The recital of them would be too horrible; it is enough to say, that in yon fatal apartment incest and unnatural murder were committed. I will restore it to the solitude to which the better judgment of those who preceded me had consigned it; and never shall any one, so long as I can prevent it, be exposed to a repetition of the supernatural horrors which could shake such courage as yours."

Thus the friends, who had met with such glee, parted in a very different mood; Lord Woodville to command the Tapestried Chamber to be unmantled, and the door built up; and General Browne to seek in some less beautiful country, and with some less dignified friend, forgetfulness of the painful night which he had passed in Woodville Castle.

The Half-Brothers

ELIZABETH GASKELL
(English, 1810–1865)

My mother was twice married. She never spoke of her first husband, and it is only from other people that I have learnt what little I know about him. I believe she was scarcely seventeen when she was married to him: and he was barely one-and-twenty. He rented a small farm up in Cumberland, somewhere towards the sea-coast; but he was perhaps too young and inexperienced to have the charge of land and cattle: anyhow, his affairs did not prosper, and he fell into ill health, and died of consumption before they had been three years man and wife, leaving my mother a young widow of twenty, with a little child only just able to walk, and the farm on her hands for four years more by the lease, with half the stock on it dead, or sold off one by one to pay the more pressing debts, and with no money to purchase more, or even to buy the provisions needed for the small consumption of every day. There was another child coming, too; and sad and sorry, I believe, she was to think of it. A dreary winter she must have had in her lonesome dwelling with never another near it for miles around; her sister came to bear her company, and they two planned and plotted how to make every penny they could raise go as far as possible. I can't tell you how it happened that my little sister, whom I never saw, came to sicken and die; but, as if my poor mother's cup was not full enough, only a fortnight before Gregory was born the little girl took ill of scarlet fever, and in a week she lay dead. My mother was, I believe, just stunned with this last blow. My aunt has told me that she did not cry; Aunt Fanny would have been thankful if she had; but she sat holding the poor wee lassie's hand, and looking in her pretty, pale, dead face, without so much as shedding a tear. And it was all the same, when they had to take her away to be buried. She just kissed the child, and sat her down in the window-seat to watch the little black train of people (neighbours—my aunt, and one far-off cousin, who were all the friends they could muster) go winding away amongst the snow, which had fallen thinly over the country the night before. When my aunt came back from the funeral, she found my mother in the same place, and as dry-eyed as ever. So she continued until after Gregory was born; and, somehow, his coming seemed to loosen the tears, and she cried day and night, till my aunt and the other watcher looked at each other in dismay, and would fain have stopped her if they had but known how. But she bade them let her alone, and not be over-anxious, for every drop she shed eased her brain, which had been in a terrible state before for want of the power to cry. She seemed after that to think of nothing but her new little baby; she had hardly appeared to remember either her husband or her little daughter that lay dead in Brigham churchyard—at least so Aunt Fanny said; but she was a great talker, and my mother was very silent by nature, and I think Aunt Fanny may have been mistaken in believing that my mother never thought of her husband and child just because she never spoke about them. Aunt Fanny was older than my mother, and had a way of treating her like a child; but, for all that, she was a kind, warmhearted creature, who thought more of her sister's welfare than she did of her own; and it was on her bit of money that they principally lived, and on what the two could earn by working for the great Glasgow sewing-merchants. But by-and-by my mother's eyesight began to fail. It was not that she was exactly blind, for she could see well enough to guide herself about the house, and to do a good deal of domestic work; but she could no longer do fine sewing and earn money. It must have been with the heavy crying she had had in her day, for she was but a young creature at this time, and as pretty a young woman, I have heard people say, as any on the country side. She took it sadly to heart that she could no longer gain anything towards the keep of herself and her child. My Aunt Fanny would fain have persuaded her that she had enough to do in managing their cottage and minding Gregory; but my mother knew that they were pinched, and that Aunt Fanny herself had not as much to eat, even of the commonest kind of food, as she could have done with; and as for Gregory, he was not a strong lad, and needed, not more food—for he always had enough, whoever went short—but better nourishment, and more flesh meat. One day—it was Aunt Fanny who told me all this about my poor mother, long after her death—as the sisters were sitting together, Aunt Fanny working, and my mother hushing Gregory to sleep, William Preston, who was afterwards my father, came in. He was reckoned an old bachelor; I suppose he was long past forty, and he was one of the wealthiest farmers thereabouts, and had known my grandfather well, and my mother and my aunt in their more prosperous days. He sat down, and began to twirl his hat by way of being agreeable; my Aunt Fanny talked, and he listened and looked at my mother. But he said very little, either on that visit, or on many another that he paid before he spoke out what had been the real purpose of his calling so often all along, and from the very first time he came to their house. One Sunday, however, my Aunt Fanny stayed away from church, and took care of the child, and my mother went alone. When she came back, she ran straight upstairs, without going into the kitchen to look at Gregory or speak any word to her sister, and Aunt Fanny heard her cry as if her heart was breaking; so she went up and scolded her right well through the bolted door, till at last she got her to open it. And then she threw herself on my aunt's neck, and told her that William Preston had asked her to marry him, and had promised to take good charge of her boy, and to let him want for nothing, neither in the way of keep nor of education, and that she had consented. Aunt Fanny was a good deal shocked at this; for, as I have said, she had often thought that my mother had forgotten her first husband very quickly, and now here was proof positive of it, if she could so soon think of marrying again. Besides, as Aunt Fanny used to say, she herself would have been a far more suitable match for a man of William Preston's age than Helen, who, though she was a widow, had not seen her four-and-twentieth summer. However, as Aunt Fanny said, they had not asked her advice; and there was much to be said on the other side of the question. Helen's eyesight would never be good for much again, and as William Preston's wife she would never need to do anything, if she chose to sit with her hand before her; and a boy was a great charge to a widowed mother, and now there would be a decent steady man to see after him. So, by-and-by, Aunt Fanny seemed to take a brighter view of the marriage than did my mother herself, who hardly ever looked up, and never smiled after the day when she promised William Preston to be his wife. But much as she had loved Gregory before, she seemed to love him more now. She was continually talking to him when they were alone, though he was far too young to understand her moaning words, or give her any comfort, except by his caresses.

At last William Preston and she were wed; and she went to be mistress of a well-stocked house, not above half-an-hour's walk from where Aunt Fanny lived. I believe she did all that she could to please my father; and a more dutiful wife, I have heard him himself say, could never have been. But she did not love him, and he soon found it out. She loved Gregory, and she did not love him. Perhaps, love would have come in time, if he had been patient enough to wait; but it just turned him sour to see how her eye brightened and her colour came at the sight of that little child, while for him who had given her so much she had only gentle words as cold as ice. He got to taunt her with the difference in her manner, as if that would bring love: and he took a positive dislike to Gregory,—he was so jealous of the ready love that always gushed out like a spring of fresh water when he came near. He wanted her to love him more, and perhaps that was all well and good; but he wanted her to love her child less, and that was an evil wish. One day, he gave way to his temper, and cursed and swore at Gregory, who had got into some mischief, as children will; my mother made some excuse for him; my father said it was hard enough to have to keep another man's child, without having it perpetually held up in its naughtiness by his wife, who ought to be always in the same mind as he was; and so from little they got to more; and the end of it was, that my mother took to her bed before her time, and I was born that very day. My father was glad, and proud, and sorry, all in a breath; glad and proud that a son was born to him; and sorry for his poor wife's state, and to think how his angry words had brought it on. But he was a man who liked better to be angry than sorry, so he soon found out that it was all Gregory's fault, and owed him an additional grudge for having hastened my birth. He had another grudge against him before long. My mother began to sink the day after I was born. My father sent to Carlisle for doctors, and would have coined his heart's blood into gold to save her, if that could have been; but it could not. My Aunt Fanny used to say sometimes, that she thought that Helen did not wish to live, and so just let herself die away without trying to take hold on life; but when I questioned her, she owned that my mother did all the doctors bade her do, with the same sort of uncomplaining patience with which she had acted through life. One of her last requests was to have Gregory laid in her bed by my side, and then she made him take hold of my little hand. Her husband came in while she was looking at us so, and when he bent tenderly over her to ask her how she felt now, and seemed to gaze on us two little half-brothers, with a grave sort of kindliness, she looked up in his face and smiled, almost her first smile at him; and such a sweet smile! as more besides Aunt Fanny have said. In an hour she was dead. Aunt Fanny came to live with us. It was the best thing that could be done. My father would have been glad to return to his old mode of bachelor life, but what could he do with two little children? He needed a woman to take care of him, and who so fitting as his wife's elder sister? So she had the charge of me from my birth; and for a time I was weakly, as was but natural, and she was always beside me, night and day watching over me, and my father nearly as anxious as she. For his land had come down from father to son for more than three hundred years, and he would have cared for me merely as his flesh and blood that was to inherit the land after him. But he needed something to love, for all that, to most people, he was a stern, hard man, and he took to me as, I fancy, he had taken to no human being before, as he might have taken to my mother, if she had had no former life for him to be jealous of. I loved him back again right heartily. I loved all around me, I believe, for everybody was kind to me. After a time, I overcame my original weakliness of constitution, and was just a bonny, strong-looking lad whom every passer-by noticed, when my father took me with him to the nearest town.

At home I was the darling of my aunt, the tenderly-beloved of my father, the pet and plaything of the old domestics, the "young master" of the farm-labourers, before whom I played many a lordly antic, assuming a sort of authority which sat oddly enough, I doubt not, on such a baby as I was.

Gregory was three years older than I. Aunt Fanny was always kind to him in deed and in action, but she did not often think about him, she had fallen so completely into the habit of being engrossed by me, from the fact of my having come into her charge as a delicate baby. My father never got over his grudging dislike to his step-son, who had so innocently wrestled with him for the possession of my mother's heart. I mistrust me, too, that my father always considered him as the cause of my mother's death and my early delicacy; and utterly unreasonable as this may seem, I believe my father rather cherished his feeling of alienation to my brother as a duty, than strove to repress it. Yet not for the world would my father have grudged him anything that money could purchase. That was, as it were, in the bond when he had wedded my mother. Gregory was lumpish and loutish, awkward and ungainly, marring whatever he meddled in, and many a hard word and sharp scolding did he get from the people about the farm, who hardly waited till my father's back was turned before they rated the step-son. I am ashamed—my heart is sore to think how I fell into the fashion of the family, and slighted my poor orphan step-brother. I don't think I ever scouted him, or was wilfully ill-natured to him; but the habit of being considered in all things, and being treated as something uncommon and superior, made me insolent in my prosperity, and I exacted more than Gregory was always willing to grant, and then, irritated, I sometimes repeated the disparaging words I had heard others use with regard to him, without fully understanding their meaning. Whether he did or not I cannot tell. I am afraid he did. He used to turn silent and quiet—sullen and sulky, my father thought it: stupid, Aunt Fanny used to call it. But every one said he was stupid and dull, and this stupidity and dulness grew upon him. He would sit without speaking a word, sometimes, for hours; then my father would bid him rise and do some piece of work, may be, about the farm. And he would take three or four tellings before he would go. When we were sent to school, it was all the same. He could never be made to remember his lessons; the schoolmaster grew weary of scolding and flogging, and at last advised my father just to take him away, and set him to some farm-work that might not be above his comprehension. I think he was more gloomy and stupid than ever after this, yet he was not a cross lad; he was patient and good-natured, and would try to do a kind turn for any one, even if they had been scolding or cuffing him not a minute before. But very often his attempts at kindness ended in some mischief to the very people he was trying to serve, owing to his awkward, ungainly ways. I suppose I was a clever lad; at any rate, I always got plenty of praise; and was, as we called it, the cock of the school. The schoolmaster said I could learn anything I chose, but my father, who had no great learning himself, saw little use in much for me, and took me away betimes, and kept me with him about the farm. Gregory was made into a kind of shepherd, receiving his training under old Adam, who was nearly past his work. I think old Adam was almost the first person who had a good opinion of Gregory. He stood to it that my brother had good parts, though he did not rightly know how to bring them out; and, for knowing the bearings of the Fells, he said he had never seen a lad like him. My father would try to bring Adam round to speak of Gregory's faults and shortcomings; but, instead of that, he would praise him twice as much, as soon as he found out what was my father's object.

One winter-time, when I was about sixteen, and Gregory nineteen, I was sent by my father on an errand to a place about seven miles distant by the road, but only about four by the Fells. He bade me return by the road whichever way I took in going, for the evenings closed in early, and were often thick and misty; besides which, old Adam, now paralytic and bed-ridden, foretold a downfall of snow before long. I soon got to my journey's end, and soon had done my business; earlier by an hour, I thought, than my father had expected, so I took the decision of the way by which I would return into my own hands, and set off back again over the Fells, just as the first shades of evening began to fall. It looked dark and gloomy enough; but everything was so still that I thought I should have plenty of time to get home before the snow came down. Off I set at a pretty quick pace. But night came on quicker. The right path was clear enough in the daytime, although at several points two or three exactly similar diverged from the same place; but when there was a good light, the traveller was guided by the sight of distant objects,—a piece of rock, —a fall in the ground—which were quite invisible to me now. I plucked up a brave heart, however, and took what seemed to me the right road. It was wrong, nevertheless, and led me whither I knew not, but to some wild boggy moor where the solitude seemed painful, intense, as if never footfall of man had come thither to break the silence. I tried to shout— with the dimmest possible hope of being heard—rather to reassure myself by the sound of my own voice; but my voice came husky and short, and yet it dismayed me; it seemed so weird and strange, in that noiseless expanse of black darkness. Suddenly the air was filled thick with dusky flakes, my face and hands were wet with snow. It cut me off from the slightest knowledge of where I was, for I lost every idea of the direction from which I had come, so that I could even retrace my steps; it hemmed me in, thicker, thicker, with a darkness that might be felt. The boggy soil on which I stood quaked under me if I remained long in one place, and yet I dared not move far. All my youthful hardiness seemed to leave me at once. I was on the point of crying, and only very shame seemed to keep it down. To save myself from shedding tears, I shouted—terrible, wild shouts for bare life they were. I turned sick as I paused to listen; no answering sound came but the unfeeling echoes. Only the noiseless, pitiless snow kept falling thicker, thicker—faster, faster! I was growing numb and sleepy. I tried to move about, but I dared not go far, for fear of the precipices which, I knew, abounded in certain places on the Fells. Now and then, I stood still and shouted again; but my voice was getting choked with tears, as I thought of the desolate helpless death I was to die, and how little they at home, sitting round the warm, red, bright fire, wotted what was become of me,—and how my poor father would grieve for me—it would surely kill him—it would break his heart, poor old man! Aunt Fanny too—was this to be the end of all her cares for me? I began to review my life in a strange kind of vivid dream, in which the various scenes of my few boyish years passed before me like visions. In a pang of agony, caused by such remembrance of my short life, I gathered up my strength and called out once more, a long, despairing, wailing cry, to which I had no hope of obtaining any answer, save from the echoes around, dulled as the sound might be by the thickened air. To my surprise I heard a cry—almost as long, as wild as mine—so wild, that it seemed unearthly, and I almost thought it must be the voice of some of the mocking spirits of the Fells, about whom I had heard so many tales. My heart suddenly began to beat fast and loud. I could not reply for a minute or two. I nearly fancied I had lost the power of utterance. Just at this moment a dog barked. Was it Lassie's bark—my brother's collie?— an ugly enough brute, with a white, ill-looking face, that my father always kicked whenever he saw it, partly for its own demerits, partly because it belonged to my brother. On such occasions, Gregory would whistle Lassie away, and go off and sit with her in some outhouse. My father had once or twice been ashamed of himself, when the poor collie had yowled out with the suddenness of the pain, and had relieved himself of his self-reproach by blaming my brother, who, he said, had no notion of training a dog, and was enough to ruin any collie in Christendom with his stupid way of allowing them to lie by the kitchen fire. To all which Gregory would answer nothing, nor even seem to hear, but go on looking absent and moody.

Yes! there again! It was Lassie's bark! Now or never! I lifted up my voice and shouted "Lassie! Lassie! For God's sake, Lassie!" Another moment, and the great white-faced Lassie was curving and gambolling with delight round my feet and legs, looking, however, up in my face with her intelligent, apprehensive eyes, as if fearing lest I might greet her with a blow, as I had done oftentimes before. But I cried with gladness, as I stooped down and patted her. My mind was sharing in my body's weakness, and I could not reason, but I knew that help was at hand. A grey figure came more and more distinctly out of the thick, close-pressing darkness. It was Gregory wrapped in his maud.

"Oh, Gregory!" said I, and I fell upon his neck, unable to speak another word. He never spoke much, and made me no answer for some little time. Then he told me we must move, we must walk for the dear life —we must find our road home, if possible; but we must move, or we should be frozen to death.

"Don't you know the way home?" asked I.

"I thought I did when I set out, but I am doubtful now. The snow blinds me, and I am feared that in moving about just now, I have lost the right gait homewards."

He had his shepherd's staff with him, and by dint of plunging it before us at every step we took—clinging close to each other, we went on safely enough, as far as not falling down any of the steep rocks, but it was slow, dreary work. My brother, I saw, was more guided by Lassie and the way she took than anything else, trusting to her instinct. It was too dark to see far before us; but he called her back continually, and noted from what quarter she returned, and shaped our slow steps accordingly. But the tedious motion scarcely kept my very blood from freezing. Every bone, every fibre in my body seemed first to ache, and then to swell, and then to turn numb with the intense cold. My brother bore it better than I, from having been more out upon the hills. He did not speak, except to call Lassie. I strove to be brave, and not complain; but now I felt the deadly fatal sleep stealing over me.

"I can go no farther," I said, in a drowsy tone. I remember I suddenly became dogged and resolved. Sleep I would, were it only for five minutes. If death were to be the consequence, sleep I would. Gregory stood still. I suppose, he recognized the peculiar phase of suffering to which I had been brought by the cold.

"It is of no use," said he, as if to himself. "We are no nearer home than we were when we started, as far as I can tell. Our only chance is in Lassie. Here! roll thee in my maud, lad, and lay thee down on this sheltered side of this bit of rock. Creep close under it, lad, and I'll lie by thee, and strive to keep the warmth in us. Stay! hast gotten aught about thee they'll know at home?"

I felt him unkind thus to keep me from slumber, but on his repeating the question, I pulled out my pocket-handkerchief, of some showy pattern, which Aunt Fanny had hemmed for me—Gregory took it, and tied it round Lassie's neck.

"Hie thee, Lassie, hie thee home!" And the white-faced ill-favoured brute was off like a shot in the darkness. Now I might lie down—now I might sleep. In my drowsy stupor, I felt that I was being tenderly covered up by my brother; but what with I neither knew nor cared—I was too dull, too selfish, too numb to think and reason, or I might have known that in that bleak bare place there was naught to wrap me in, save what was taken off another. I was glad enough when he ceased his cares and lay down by me. I took his hand.

"Thou canst not remember, lad, how we lay together thus by our dying mother. She put thy small, wee hand in mine—I reckon she sees us now; and belike we shall soon be with her. Anyhow, God's will be done."

"Dear Gregory," I muttered, and crept nearer to him for warmth. He was talking still, and again about our mother, when I fell asleep. In an instant—or so it seemed—there were many voices about me—many faces hovering round me—the sweet luxury of warmth was stealing into every part of me. I was in my own little bed at home. I am thankful to say, my first word was "Gregory?"

A look passed from one to another—my father's stern old face strove in vain to keep its sternness; his mouth quivered, his eyes filled with unwonted tears.

"I would have given him half my land—I would have blessed him as my son,—Oh God! I would have knelt at his feet, and asked him to forgive my hardness of heart."

I heard no more. A whirl came through my brain, catching me back to death.

I came slowly to my consciousness, weeks afterwards. My father's hair was white when I recovered, and his hands shook as he looked into my face.

We spoke no more of Gregory. We could not speak of him; but he was strangely in our thoughts. Lassie came and went with never a word of blame; nay, my father would try to stroke her, but she shrank away; and he, as if reproved by the poor dumb beast, would sigh, and be silent and abstracted for a time.

Aunt Fanny—always a talker—told me all. How, on that fatal night, my father, irritated by my prolonged absence, and probably more anxious than he cared to show, had been fierce and imperious, even beyond his wont, to Gregory; had upbraided him with his father's poverty, his own stupidity which made his services good for nothing—for so, in spite of the old shepherd, my father always chose to consider them. At last, Gregory had risen up, and whistled Lassie out with him—poor Lassie, crouching underneath his chair for fear of a kick or a blow. Some time before, there had been some talk between my father and my aunt respecting my return; and when Aunt Fanny told me all this, she said she fancied that Gregory might have noticed the coming storm, and gone out silently to meet me. Three hours afterwards, when all were running about in wild alarm, not knowing whither to go in search of me, not even missing Gregory, or heeding his absence, poor fellow—poor, poor fellow! —Lassie came home, with my handkerchief tied round her neck. They knew and understood, and the whole strength of the farm was turned out to follow her, with wraps, and blankets, and brandy, and everything that could be thought of. I lay in chilly sleep, but still alive, beneath the rock that Lassie guided them to. I was covered over with my brother's plaid, and his thick shepherd's coat was carefully wrapped round my feet. He was in his shirt-sleeves—his arm thrown over me—a quiet smile (he had hardly ever smiled in life) upon his still, cold face.

My father's last words were, "God forgive me my hardness of heart towards the fatherless child!"

And what marked the depth of his feeling of repentance, perhaps more than all, considering the passionate love he bore my mother, was this; we found a paper of directions after his death, in which he desired that he might lie at the foot of the grave, in which, by his desire, poor Gregory had been laid with OUR MOTHER.

Snobs and Marriage
⸙⸙⸙

WILLIAM MAKEPEACE THACKERAY
(English, 1811–1863)

In that noble romance called *Ten Thousand a Year,* I remember a profoundly pathetic description of the hero, MR. AUBREY'S, Christian manner of bearing his misfortunes. After making a display of the most florid and grandiloquent resignation, and quitting his country mansion, the delightful writer supposes AUBREY to come to town in a post-chaise and pair sitting bodkin probably between his wife and sister. It is at about seven o'clock, carriages are rattling about, knockers are thundering, and tears bedim the fine eyes of KATE and MRS. AUBREY as they think that in happier times at this hour—their AUBREY used formerly to go out to dinner to the houses of the aristocracy his friends. This is the gist of the passage—the elegant words I forget. But the noble, noble sentiment I shall always cherish and remember. What can be more sublime than the notion of a great man's relatives in tears about—his dinner? With a few unconscious touches, what author ever so happily described a SNOB?

We were reading the passage lately at the house of my friend RAYMOND GRAY, ESQUIRE, BARRISTER-AT-LAW, an ingenuous youth without the least practice, but who has luckily a great share of good spirits, which enables him to bide his time, and bear laughingly his humble position in the world. Meanwhile, until it is altered, the stern laws of necessity and the expenses of the Northern Circuit oblige MR. GRAY to live in a very tiny mansion in a very queer small square in the airy neighbourhood of Gray's Inn.

What is the more remarkable is, that GRAY has a wife there. MRS.

GRAY was a MISS HARLEY BAKER: and I suppose I need not say *that* is a respectable family. Allied to the CAVENDISHES, the OXFORDS, the MAR-RYBONES, they still, though rather *déchus* from their original splendour, hold their heads as high as any. MRS. HARLEY BAKER, I know, never goes to church without JOHN behind to carry her prayer-book; nor will MISS WELBECK, her sister, walk twenty yards a shopping without the protection of FIGBY, her sugar-loaf page; though the old lady is as ugly as any woman in the parish, and as tall and whiskery as a Grenadier. The astonishment is, how EMILY HARLEY BAKER could have stooped to marry RAYMOND GRAY. She, who was the prettiest and proudest of the family; she, who refused SIR COCKLE BYLES, of the Bengal Service; she, who turned up her little nose at ESSEX TEMPLE, Q.C., and connected with the noble house of Albyn; she, who had but 4000 *pour tout potage,* to marry a man who had scarcely as much more. A scream of wrath and indignation was uttered by the whole family when they heard of this *mésalliance.* MRS. HARLEY BAKER never speaks of her daughter now but with tears in her eyes, and as a ruined creature. MISS WELBECK says, 'I consider that man a villain;'—and has denounced poor good-natured MRS. PERKINS as a swindler, at whose ball the young people met for the first time.

MR. and MRS. GRAY, meanwhile, live in Gray's Inn, aforesaid, with a maid-servant and a nurse, whose hands are very full, and in a most provoking and unnatural state of happiness. They have never once thought of crying about their dinner, like the wretchedly puling and Snobbish womankind of my favourite Snob AUBREY, of *Ten Thousand a Year;* but, on the contrary, accept such humble victuals as Fate awards them with a most perfect and thankful good grace—nay, actually have a portion for a hungry friend at times—as the present writer can gratefully testify.

I was mentioning these dinners, and some admirable lemon puddings which MRS. GRAY makes, to our mutual friend the great MR. GOLDMORE, the East India Director, when that gentleman's face assumed an expression of almost apoplectic terror, and he gasped out, 'What! Do they give dinners?' He seemed to think it a crime and a wonder that such people should dine at all; or that it was their custom to huddle round their kitchen fire over a bone and a crust. Whenever he meets them in society, it is a matter of wonder to him (and he always expresses his surprise very loud) how the lady can appear decently dressed, and the man have an unpatched coat to his back. I have heard him enlarge upon this poverty before the whole room at the Conflagrative Club, to which he and I and GRAY have the honour to belong.

We meet at the Club on most days. At half-past four, GOLDMORE arrives in St. James's Street, from the City, and you may see him reading the evening papers in the bow window of the Club which enfilades Pall Mall—a large plethoric man, with a bunch of seals in a large bow-windowed light waistcoat. He has large coat-tails, stuffed with agents' letters and papers about companies of which he is a Director. His seals jingle as he walks. I wish I had such a man for an uncle, and that he himself were childless. I would love and cherish him, and be kind to him.

At six o'clock in the full season, when all the world is in St. James's Street, and the carriages are cutting in and out among the cabs on the stand, and the tufted dandies are showing their listless faces out of WHITE'S; and you see respectable grey-headed gentlemen waggling their heads to each other through the plate-glass windows of ARTHUR'S; and the red-coats wish to be Briarean, so as to hold all the gentlemen's horses; and that wonderful red-coated royal porter is sunning himself before Marlborough House at the noon of London time: you see a light-yellow carriage with black horses, and a coachman in a tight floss-silk wig, and two footmen in powder and white and yellow liveries, and a large woman inside in shot silk, a poodle, and a pink parasol, which drives up to the gate of the Conflagrative, and the page goes and says to MR. GOLDMORE (who is perfectly aware of the fact, as he is looking out of the windows with about forty other Conflagrative bucks), 'Your carriage, sir.' G. wags his head. 'Remember, eight o'clock precisely,' says he to MULLI-GATAWNEY, the other East India Director, and ascending the carriage, plumps down by the side of MRS. GOLDMORE for a drive in the Park, and then home to Portland Place. As the carriage whirls off, all the young bucks in the Club feel a secret elation. It is a part of their establishment as it were. That carriage belongs to their Club, and their Club belongs to them. They follow the equipage with interest; they eye it knowingly as they see it in the Park. But halt! we are not come to the CLUB SNOBS yet. O my brave Snobs, what a flurry there will be among you when those papers appear!

Well, you may judge, from the above description, what sort of a man GOLDMORE is. A dull and pompous Leadenhall Street CROESUS, good-natured withal, and affable—cruelly affable. 'MR. GOLDMORE can never forget,' his lady used to say, 'that it was MRS. GRAY's grandfather who sent him to India; and though that young woman has made the most imprudent marriage in the world, and has left her station in society, her husband seems an ingenious and laborious young man, and we shall do everything in our power to be of use to him.' So they used to ask the GRAYS to dinner twice or thrice in a season, when, by way of increasing the kindness, BUFF, the butler, is ordered to hire a fly to convey them to and from Portland Place.

Of course I am much too good-natured a friend of both parties not to tell GRAY of GOLDMORE's opinion regarding him, and the Nabob's astonishment at the idea of the briefless barrister having any dinner at all. Indeed GOLDMORE's saying became a joke against GRAY amongst us wags at the Club, and we used to ask him when he tasted meat last? whether we should bring him home something from dinner? and cut a thousand other mad pranks with him in our facetious way.

One day, then, coming home from the Club, MR. GRAY conveyed to his wife the astounding information that he had asked GOLDMORE to dinner.

'My love,' says MRS. GRAY, in a tremor, 'how could you be so cruel? Why, the dining-room won't hold MRS. GOLDMORE.'

'Make your mind easy, MRS. GRAY, her ladyship is in Paris. It is only CROESUS that's coming, and we are going to the play afterwards—to Sadler's Wells. GOLDMORE said at the Club that he thought SHAKSPEARE was a great dramatist poet and ought to be patronised; whereupon, fired with enthusiasm, I invited him to our banquet.'

'Goodness gracious! what *can* we give him for dinner? He has two French cooks; you know MRS. GOLDMORE is always telling us about them; and he dines with Aldermen every day.'

> 'A plain leg of mutton, my LUCY,
>   I prythee get ready at three;
> Have it tender, and smoking, and juicy,
>   And what better meat can there be?'

says GRAY, quoting my favourite poet.

'But the cook is ill; and you know that horrible PATTYPAN, the pastry-cook's. . . .'

'Silence, Frau!' says GRAY, in a deep-tragedy voice. 'I will have the

ordaining of this repast. Do all things as I bid thee. Invite our friend
SNOB here to partake of the feast. Be mine the task of procuring it.'

'Don't be expensive, RAYMOND,' says his wife.

'Peace, thou timid partner of the briefless one. GOLDMORE's dinner
shall be suited to our narrow means. Only do thou do in all things my
commands.' And seeing, by the peculiar expression of the rogue's countenance, that some mad waggery was in preparation, I awaited the morrow
with anxiety.

The Boots at the
Holly-Tree Inn

CHARLES DICKENS
(English, 1812–1870)

Where had he been in his time? he repeated, when I asked him the
question. Lord, he had been everywhere! And what had he been? Bless
you, he had been everything you could mention, a'most!

Seen a good deal? Why, of course he had. I should say so, he could
assure me, if I only knew about a twentieth part of what had come in *his*
way. Why, it would be easier for him, he expected, to tell what he hadn't
seen than what he had. Ah! a deal, it would.

What was the curiousest thing he had seen? Well! He didn't know. He
couldn't momently name what was the curiousest thing he had seen—
unless it was a Unicorn—and he saw *him* once at a fair. But supposing a
young gentleman not eight year old was to run away with a fine young
woman of seven, might I think *that* a queer start? Certainly. Then that

was a start as he himself had had his blessed eyes on, and he had cleaned the shoes they run away in—and they was so little he couldn't get his hand into 'em.

Master Harry Walmers' father, you see, he lived at the Elmses, down away by Shooter's Hill there, six or seven miles from Lunnon. He was a gentleman of spirit, and good-looking, and held his head up when he walked, and had what you call Fire about him. He wrote poetry, and he rode, and he ran, and he cricketed, and he danced, and he acted, and he done it all equally beautiful. He was uncommon proud of Master Harry as was his only child; but he didn't spoil him neither. He was a gentleman that had a will of his own and a eye of his own, and that would be minded. Consequently, though he made quite a companion of the fine bright boy, and was delighted to see him so fond of reading his fairy-books, and was never tired of hearing him say my name is Norval, or hearing him sing his songs about Young May Moons is beaming love, and when he as adores thee has left but the name, and that; still he kept the command over the child, and the child *was* a child, and it's to be wished more of 'em was.

How did Boots happen to know all this? Why, through being under-gardener. Of course he couldn't be under-gardener, and he always about, in the summer-time, near the windows on the lawn, a-mowing, and sweeping, and weeding, and pruning, and this and that, without getting acquainted with the ways of the family. Even supposing Master Harry hadn't come to him one morning early, and said, "Cobbs, how should you spell Norah, if you was asked?" and then began cutting it in print all over the fence.

He couldn't say that he had taken particular notice of children before that; but really it was pretty to see them two mites a-going about the place together, deep in love. And the courage of the boy! Bless your soul, he'd have throwed off his little hat, and tucked up his little sleeves, and gone in at a lion, he would, if they had happened to meet one, and she had been frightened of him. One day he stops, along with her, where Boots was hoeing weeds in the gravel, and says, speaking up, "Cobbs," he says, "I like *you.*" "Do you, sir? I'm proud to hear it." "Yes, I do, Cobbs. Why do I like you, do you think, Cobbs?" "Don't know, Master Harry, I am sure." "Because Norah likes you, Cobbs." "Indeed, sir? That's very gratifying." "Gratifying, Cobbs? It's better than millions of the brightest diamonds to be liked by Norah." "Certainly, sir." "Would you like another situation, Cobbs?" "Well, sir, I shouldn't object if it was a good 'un." "Then, Cobbs," says he, "you shall be our Head Gardener when we are married." And he tucks her, in her little sky-blue mantle, under his arm, and walks away.

Boots could assure me that it was better than a picter, and equal to a play, to see them babies, with their long, bright, curling hair, their sparkling eyes, and their beautiful light tread, a-rambling about the garden, deep in love. Boots was of opinion that the birds believed they was birds, and kept up with 'em, singing to please 'em. Sometimes they would creep under the tulip-tree, and would sit there with their arms round one another's necks, and their soft cheeks touching, a-reading about the Prince and the Dragon, and the good and bad enchanters, and the king's fair daughter. Sometimes he would hear them planning about a house in a forest, keeping bees and a cow, and living entirely on milk and honey. Once he came upon them by the pond, and heard Master Harry say, "Adorable Norah, kiss me, and say you love me to distraction, or I'll jump in head foremost." And Boots made no question he would have done it if she hadn't complied. On the whole, Boots said it had a tendency to make him feel he was in love himself—only he didn't exactly know who with.

"Cobbs," said Master Harry, one evening, when Cobbs was watering the flowers, "I am going on a visit, this present midsummer, to my grandmamma's at York."

"Are you, indeed, sir? I hope you'll have a pleasant time. I am going into Yorkshire, myself, when I leave here."

"Are you going to your grandmamma's, Cobbs?"

"No, sir. I haven't got such a thing."

"Not as a grandmamma, Cobbs?"

"No, sir."

The boy looked on at the watering of the flowers for a little while, and then said, "I shall be very glad indeed to go, Cobbs—Norah's going."

"You'll be all right, then, sir," says Cobbs, "with your beautiful sweetheart by your side."

"Cobbs," returned the boy, flushing, "I never let anybody joke about it when I can prevent them."

"It wasn't a joke, sir," says Cobbs, with humility—"wasn't so meant."

"I am glad of that, Cobbs, because I like you, you know, and you're going to live with us. Cobbs!"

"Sir."

"What do you think my grandmamma gives me when I go down there?"

"I couldn't so much as make a guess, sir."

"A Bank-of-England five-pound note, Cobbs."

"Whew!" says Cobbs, "that's a spanking sum of money, Master Harry."

"A person could do a great deal with such a sum of money as that—couldn't a person, Cobbs?"

"I believe you, sir!"

"Cobbs," said the boy, "I'll tell you a secret. At Norah's house they have been joking her about me, and pretending to laugh at our being engaged—pretending to make game of it, Cobbs!"

"Such, sir," says Cobbs, "is the depravity of human natur'."

The boy, looking exactly like his father, stood for a few minutes with his glowing face toward the sunset, and then departed with, "Good-night, Cobbs. I'm going in."

If I was to ask Boots how it happened that he was a-going to leave that place just at that present time, well, he couldn't rightly answer me. He did suppose he might have stayed there till now if he had been anyways inclined. But you see, he was younger then, and he wanted change. That's what he wanted—change. Mr. Walmers, he said to him when he gave him notice of his intentions to leave, "Cobbs," he says, "have you anythink to complain of? I make the inquiry, because if I find that any of my people really has anythink to complain of, I wish to make it right if I can." "No, sir," says Cobbs; "thanking you, sir, I find myself as well sitiwated here as I could hope to be anywheres. The truth is, sir, that I'm a-going to seek my fortun'." "Oh, indeed, Cobbs!" he says; "I hope you may find it." And Boots could assure me—which he did, touching his hair with his bootjack, as a salute in the way of his present calling—that he hadn't found it yet.

Well, sir! Boots left the Elmses when his time was up, and Master Harry, he went down to the old lady's at York, which old lady would have given that child the teeth out of her head (if she had had any), she was so wrapped up in him. What does that Infant do—for Infant you may call him, and be within the mark—but cut away from that old lady's with his Norah, on a expedition to go to Gretna Green and be married!

Sir, Boots was at this identical Holly-Tree Inn (having left it several times to better himself, but always come back through one thing or another), when, one summer afternoon, the coach drives up, and out of the coach gets them two children. The Guard says to our Governor, "I don't quite make out these little passengers, but the young gentleman's words was, that they was to be brought here." The young gentleman gets out; hands his lady out; gives the Guard something for himself; says to our Governor, "We're to stop here to-night, please. Sitting-room and two bedrooms will be required. Chops and cherry-pudding for two!" and tucks her in her little sky-blue mantle, under his arm, and walks into the house much bolder than Brass.

Boots leaves me to judge what the amazement of that establishment was, when these two tiny creatures all alone by themselves was marched into the Angel—much more so when he, who had seen them without their seeing him, give the Governor his views upon the expedition they was upon. "Cobbs," says the Governor, "if this is so, I must set off myself to York, and quiet their friends' minds. In which case you must keep your eye upon 'em, and humor 'em till I come back. But before I take these measures, Cobbs, I should wish you to find from themselves whether your opinions is correct." "Sir, to you," says Cobbs, "that shall be done directly."

So Boots goes up-stairs to the Angel, and there he finds Master Harry, on a e'normous sofa—immense at any time, but looking like the Great Bed of Ware, compared with him—a-drying the eyes of Miss Norah with his pocket-hankecher. Their little legs was entirely off the ground, of course, and it really is not possible for Boots to express to me how small them children looked.

"It's Cobbs! It's Cobbs!" cries Master Harry, and comes running to him on t'other side, and catching hold of his t'other hand, and they both jump for joy.

"I see you a-getting out, sir," says Cobbs. "I thought it was you. I thought I couldn't be mistaken in your height and figure. What's the object of your journey, sir? Matrimonial?"

"We're going to be married, Cobbs, at Gretna Green," returned the boy. "We have run away on purpose. Norah has been in rather low spirits, Cobbs; but she'll be happy, now we have found you to be our friend."

"Thank you, sir, and thank *you,* miss," says Cobbs, "for your good opinion. *Did* you bring any luggage with you, sir?"

If I will believe Boots when he gives me his word and honor upon it, the lady had got a parasol, a smelling-bottle, a round and a half of cold buttered toast, eight peppermint drops, and a hair-brush—seemingly a doll's. The gentleman had got about half a dozen yards of string, a knife, three or four sheets of writing-paper, folded up surprising small, a orange, and a Chaney mug with his name upon it.

"What may be the exact nature of your plans, sir?" says Cobbs.

"To go on," replied the boy—which the courage of that boy was something wonderful!—"in the morning, and be married to-morrow."

"Just so, sir," says Cobbs. "Would it meet your views, sir, if I was to accompany you?"

When Cobbs said this, they both jumped for joy again, and cried out, "Oh yes, yes, Cobbs! Yes!"

"Well, sir!" says Cobbs. "If you will excuse me having the freedom to give an opinion, what I should recommend would be this. I am acquainted with a pony, sir, which, put in a pheayton that I could borrow, would take you and Mrs. Harry Walmers, Junior (myself driving, if you approved), to the end of your journey in a very short space of time. I am not altogether sure, sir, that this pony will be at liberty to-morrow, but even if you had to wait over to-morrow for him, it might be worth your while. As to the small account here, sir, in case you was to find yourself running at all short, that don't signify; because I am a part proprietor of this inn, and it could stand over."

Boots assures me that when they clapped their hands, and jumped for joy again, and called him "Good Cobbs!" and "Dear Cobbs!" and bent across him to kiss one another in the delight of their confiding hearts, he felt himself the meanest rascal for deceiving 'em that ever was born.

"Is there anything you want just at present, sir?" says Cobbs, mortally ashamed of himself.

"We should like some cakes after dinner," answered Master Harry, folding his arms, putting out one leg, and looking straight at him, "and two apples and jam. With dinner we should like to have toast and water. But Norah has always been accustomed to half a glass of currant wine at dessert. And so have I."

"It shall be ordered at the bar, sir," says Cobbs; and away he went.

Boots has the feeling as fresh upon him this moment of speaking as he had then, that he would far rather have had it out in half a dozen rounds with the Governor than have combined with him; and that he wished with all his heart there was any impossible place where two babies could make an impossible marriage, and live impossibly happy ever afterward. However, as it couldn't be, he went into the Governor's plans, and the Governor set off for York in half an hour.

The way in which the women of that house—without exception—every one of 'em—married *and* single—took to that boy when they heard the story, Boots considers surprising. It was as much as he could do to keep 'em from dashing into the room and kissing him. They climbed up all sorts of places, at the risk of their lives, to look at him through a pane of glass. They was seven deep at the keyhole. They was out of their minds about him and his bold spirit.

In the evening, Boots went into the room to see how the runaway couple was getting on. The gentleman was on the window-seat, supporting the lady in his arms. She had tears upon her face, and was lying, very tired and half asleep, with her head upon his shoulder.

"Mrs. Harry Walmers, Junior, fatigued, sir?" says Cobbs.

"Yes, she is tired, Cobbs; but she is not used to be away from home, and she has been in low spirits again. Cobbs, do you think you could bring a biffin, please?"

"I ask your pardon, sir," says Cobbs. "What was it you—"

"I think a Norfolk biffin would rouse her, Cobbs. She is very fond of them."

Boots withdrew in search of the required restorative, and, when he brought it in, the gentleman handed it to the lady, and fed her with a spoon, and took a little himself; the lady being heavy with sleep, and rather cross. "What should you think, sir," says Cobbs, "of a chamber candlestick?" The gentleman approved; the chambermaid went first, up the great staircase; the lady, in her sky-blue mantle, followed, gallantly escorted by the gentleman; the gentleman embraced her at her door, and retired to his own apartment, where Boots softly locked him in.

Boots couldn't but feel with increased acuteness what a base deceiver he was, when they consulted him at breakfast (they had ordered sweet milk-and-water, and toast and currant jelly, over-night) about the pony. It really was as much as he could do, he don't mind confessing to me, to look them two young things in the face, and think what a wicked old father of lies he had grown up to be. Howsomever, he went on a-lying like a Trojan about the pony. He told 'em that it did so unfortunately happen that the pony was half clipped, you see, and that he couldn't be taken out in that state, for fear it should strike to his inside. But that he'd be finished clipping in the course of the day, and that to-morrow morning at eight o'clock the pheayton would be ready. Boots' view of the whole case, looking back on it in my room, is, that Mrs. Harry Walmers, Junior, was beginning to give in. She hadn't had her hair curled when she went to bed, and she didn't seem quite up to brushing it herself, and its getting in her eyes put her out. But nothing put out Master Harry. He sat behind his breakfast-cup, a-tearing away at the jelly, as if he had been his own father.

After breakfast Boots is inclined to consider they drawed soldiers—at least he knows that many such was found in the fireplace, all on horseback. In the course of the morning Master Harry rang the bell—it was surprising how that there boy did carry on—and said, in a sprightly way, "Cobbs, is there any good walks in this neighborhood?"

"Yes, sir," says Cobbs. "There's Love Lane."

"Get out with you, Cobbs!"—that was that there boy's expression—"you're joking."

"Begging your pardon, sir," says Cobbs, "there *really is* Love Lane. And a pleasant walk it is, and proud shall I be to show it to yourself and Mrs. Harry Walmers, Junior."

"Norah, dear," says Master Harry, "this is curious. We really ought to see Love Lane. Put on your bonnet, my sweetest darling, and we will go there with Cobbs."

Boots leaves me to judge what a Beast he felt himself to be, when that young pair told him, as they all three jogged along together, that they had made up their minds to give him two thousand guineas a year as Head Gardener, on account of his being so true a friend to 'em. Boots could have wished at the moment that the earth would have opened and swallowed him up, he felt so mean, with their beaming eyes a-looking at him, and believing him. Well, sir, he turned the conversation as well as he could, and he took 'em down Love Lane to the water-meadows, and there Master Harry would have drowned himself in half a moment more, a-getting out a water-lily for her—but nothing daunted that boy. Well, sir, they was tired out. All being so new and strange to 'em, they was tired as tired could be. And they laid down on a bank of daisies, like the children in the wood, leastways meadows, and fell asleep.

Boots don't know—perhaps I do—but never mind, it don't signify either way—why it made a man fit to make a fool of himself to see them two pretty babies a-lying there in the clear, still day, not dreaming half so hard when they was asleep as they done when they was awake. But, Lord! when you come to think of yourself, you know, and what a game you have been up to ever since you was in your own cradle, and what a poor sort of chap you are, and how it's always either Yesterday with you, or To-morrow, and never To-day, that's where it is!

Well, sir, they woke up at last, and then one thing was getting pretty clear to Boots—namely, that Mrs. Harry Walmerses, Junior's, temper was on the move. When Master Harry took her round the waist, she said he "teased her so"; and when he says, "Norah, my young May Moon, your Harry tease you?" she tells him, "Yes; and I want to go home."

A biled fowl and baked bread-and-butter pudding brought Mrs. Walmers up a little; but Boots could have wished, he must privately own to me, to have seen her more sensible of the voice of love, and less abandoning of herself to currants. However, Master Harry, he kept up, and his noble heart was as fond as ever. Mrs. Walmers turned very sleepy about dusk, and began to cry. Therefore, Mrs. Walmers went off to bed as per yesterday; and Master Harry ditto repeated.

About eleven or twelve at night comes back the Governor in a chaise, along with Mr. Walmers and a elderly lady. Mr. Walmers looks amused and very serious, both at once, and says to our Missis: "We are much indebted to you, ma'am, for your kind care of our little children, which we can never sufficiently acknowledge. Pray, ma'am, where is my boy?" Our Missis says: "Cobbs has the dear child in charge, sir. Cobbs, show Forty!" Then he says to Cobbs: "Ah, Cobbs, I am glad to see *you!* I understood you was here!" And Cobbs says: "Yes, sir. Your most obedient, sir."

I may be surprised to hear Boots say it, perhaps; but Boots assures me that his heart beat like a hammer, going up-stairs. "I beg your pardon, sir," says he, while unlocking the door; "I do hope you are not angry with Master Harry. For Master Harry is a fine boy, sir, and will do you credit and honor." And Boots signifies to me that, if the fine boy's father had contradicted him in the daring state of mind in which he then was, he thinks he should have "fetched him a crack," and taken the consequences.

But Mr. Walmers only says: "No, Cobbs. No, my good fellow. Thank you!" And, the door being opened, goes in.

Boots goes in, too, holding the light, and he sees Mr. Walmers go up to the bedside, bend gently down, and kiss the little sleeping face. Then he stands looking at it for a minute, looking wonderfully like it (they do say he ran away with Mrs. Walmers); and then he gently shakes the little shoulder.

"Harry, my dear boy! Harry!"

Master Harry starts up and looks at him. Looks at Cobbs, too. Such is the honor of that mite, that he looks at Cobbs, to see whether he has brought him into trouble.

"I'm not angry, my child. I only want you to dress yourself and come home."

"Yes, pa."

Master Harry dresses himself quickly. His breast begins to swell when he has nearly finished, and it swells more and more as he stands, at last, a-looking at his father; his father standing a-looking at him, the quiet image of him.

"Please may I"—the spirit of that little creatur', and the way he kept his rising tears down!—"please, dear pa—may I—kiss Norah before I go?"

"You may, my child."

So he takes Master Harry in his hand, and Boots leads the way with the candle, and they come to that other bedroom, where the elderly lady is seated by the bed, and poor little Mrs. Harry Walmers, Junior, is fast asleep. There the father lifts the child up to the pillow, and he lays his little face down for an instant by the little warm face of poor unconscious little Mrs. Harry Walmers, Junior, and gently draws it to him—a sight so touching to the chambermaids, who are peeping through the door, that one of them called out, "It's a shame to part 'em!" But this chambermaid was always, as Boots informs us, a soft-hearted one. Not that there was any harm in that girl. Far from it.

Finally, Boots says, that's all about it. Mr. Walmers drove away in the chaise, having hold of Master Harry's hand. The elderly lady and Mrs. Walmers, Junior, that was never to be (she married a Captain long afterward, and died in India), went off next day. In conclusion, Boots puts it to me whether I hold with him in two opinions: firstly, that there are not many couples on their way to be married who are half as innocent of guile as those two children; secondly, that it would be a jolly good thing for a great many couples on their way to be married, if they could only be stopped in time, and brought back separately.

The White Cat of Drumgunniol

J. S. LE FANU
(Irish, 1814–1873)

There is a famous story of a white cat, with which we all become acquainted in the nursery. I am going to tell a story of a white cat very different from the amiable and enchanted princess who took that disguise for a season. The white cat of which I speak was a more sinister animal.

The traveller from Limerick toward Dublin, after passing the hills of Killaloe upon the left, as Keeper Mountain rises high in view, finds himself gradually hemmed in, up the right, by a range of lower hills. An undulating plain that dips gradually to a lower level than that of the road interposes, and some scattered hedgerows relieve its somewhat wild and melancholy character.

One of the few human habitations that send up their films of turf-smoke from that lonely plain, is the loosely-thatched, earth-built dwelling of a "strong farmer," as the more prosperous of the tenant-farming classes are termed in Munster. It stands in a clump of trees near the edge of a wandering stream, about half-way between the mountains and the Dublin road, and had been for generations tenanted by people named Donovan.

In a distant place, desirous of studying some Irish records which had fallen into my hands, and inquiring for a teacher capable of instructing me in the Irish language, a Mr. Donovan, dreamy, harmless, and learned, was recommended to me for the purpose.

I found that he had been educated as a Sizar in Trinity College, Dublin. He now supported himself by teaching, and the special direction of my studies, I suppose, flattered his national partialities, for he unbosomed himself of much of his long-reserved thoughts, and recollections about his country and his early days. It was he who told me this story, and I mean to repeat it, as nearly as I can, in his own words.

I have myself seen the old farm-house, with its orchard of huge moss-grown apple trees. I have looked round on the peculiar landscape; the roofless, ivied tower, that two hundred years before had afforded a refuge from raid and rapparee, and which still occupies its old place in the angle of the haggard; the bush-grown "liss," that scarcely a hundred and fifty steps away records the labours of a bygone race; the dark and towering outline of old Keeper in the background; and the lonely range of furze and heath-clad hills that form a nearer barrier, with many a line of grey rock and clump of dwarf oak or birch. The pervading sense of loneliness made it a scene not unsuited for a wild and unearthly story. And I could quite fancy how, seen in the grey of a wintry morning, shrouded far and wide in snow, or in the melancholy glory of an autumnal sunset, or in the chill splendour of a moonlight night, it might have helped to tone a dreamy mind like honest Dan Donovan's to superstition and a proneness to the illusions of fancy. It is certain, however, that I never anywhere met with a more simple-minded creature, or one on whose good faith I could more entirely rely.

When I was a boy, said he, living at home at Drumgunniol, I used to take my Goldsmith's *Roman History* in my hand and go down to my favourite seat, the flat stone, sheltered by a hawthorn tree beside the little lough, a large and deep pool, such as I have heard called a tarn in England. It lay in the gentle hollow of a field that is overhung toward the north by the old orchard, and being a deserted place was favourable to my studious quietude.

One day reading here, as usual, I wearied at last, and began to look about me, thinking of the heroic scenes I had just been reading of. I was as wide awake as I am at this moment, and I saw a woman appear at the corner of the orchard and walk down the slope. She wore a long, light grey dress, so long that it seemed to sweep the grass behind her, and so singular was her appearance in a part of the world where female attire is so inflexibly fixed by custom, that I could not take my eyes off her. Her course lay diagonally from corner to corner of the field, which was a large one, and she pursued it without swerving.

When she came near I could see that her feet were bare, and that she seemed to be looking steadfastly upon some remote object for guidance. Her route would have crossed me—had the tarn not interposed—about ten or twelve yards below the point at which I was sitting. But instead of arresting her course at the margin of the lough, as I had expected, she went on without seeming conscious of its existence, and I saw her, as plainly as I see you, sir, walk across the surface of the water, and pass, without seeming to see me, at about the distance I had calculated.

I was ready to faint from sheer terror. I was only thirteen years old then, and I remember every particular as if it had happened this hour.

The figure passed through the gap at the far corner of the field, and there I lost sight of it. I had hardly strength to walk home, and was so nervous, and ultimately so ill, that for three weeks I was confined to the house, and could not bear to be alone for a moment. I never entered that field again, such was the horror with which from that moment every object in it was clothed. Even at this distance of time I should not like to pass through it.

This apparition I connected with a mysterious event; and, also, with a singular liability, that has for nearly eight years distinguished, or rather afflicted, our family. It is no fancy. Everybody in that part of the country knows all about it. Everybody connected what I had seen with it.

I will tell it all to you as well as I can.

When I was about fourteen years old—that is about a year after the sight I had seen in the lough field—we were one night expecting my father home from the fair of Killaloe. My mother sat up to welcome him home, and I with her, for I liked nothing better than such a vigil. My brothers and sisters, and the farm servants, except the men who were driving home the cattle from the fair, were asleep in their beds. My mother and I were sitting in the chimney corner chatting together, and watching my father's supper, which was kept hot over the fire. We knew that he would return before the men who were driving home the cattle, for he was riding, and told us that he would only wait to see them fairly on the road, and then push homeward.

At length we heard his voice and the knocking of his loaded whip at the door, and my mother let him in. I don't think I ever saw my father drunk, which is more than most men of my age, from the same part of the country, could say of theirs. But he could drink his glass of whisky as well as another, and he usually came home from fair or market a little merry and mellow, and with a jolly flush in his cheeks.

To-night he looked sunken, pale and sad. He entered with the saddle and bridle in his hand, and he dropped them against the wall, near the door, and put his arms round his wife's neck, and kissed her kindly.

"Welcome home, Meehal," said she, kissing him heartily.

"God bless you, mavourneen," he answered.

And hugging her again, he turned to me, who was plucking him by the hand, jealous of his notice. I was little, and light of my age, and he lifted me up in his arms, and kissed me, and my arms being about his neck, he said to my mother:

"Draw the bolt, acuishla."

She did so, and setting me down very dejectedly, he walked to the fire and sat down on a stool, and stretched his feet toward the glowing turf, leaning with his hands on his knees.

"Rouse up, Mick, darlin'," said my mother, who was growing anxious, "and tell me how did the cattle sell, and did everything go lucky at the fair, or is there anything wrong with the landlord, or what in the world is it that ails you, Mick, jewel?"

"Nothin', Molly. The cows sould well, thank God, and there's nothin' fell out between me an' the landlord, an' everything's the same way. There's no fault to find anywhere."

"Well, then, Mickey, since so it is, turn round to your hot supper, and ate it, and tell us is there anything new."

"I got my supper, Molly, on the way, and I can't ate a bit," he answered.

"Got your supper on the way, an' you knowin' 'twas waiting for you at home, an' your wife sittin' up an' all!" cried my mother, reproachfully.

"You're takin' a wrong meanin' out of what I say," said my father. "There's something happened that leaves me that I can't ate a mouthful, and I'll not be dark with you, Molly, for, maybe, it ain't very long I have to be here, an' I'll tell you what it was. It's what I've seen, the white cat."

"The Lord between us and harm!" exclaimed my mother, in a moment as pale and as chap-fallen as my father; and then, trying to rally, with a laugh, she said: "Ha! 'tis only funnin' me you are. Sure a white rabbit was snared a Sunday last, in Grady's wood; an' Teigue seen a big white rat in the haggard yesterday."

" 'Twas neither rat nor rabbit was in it. Don't ye think but I'd know a rat or a rabbit from a big white cat, with green eyes as big as halfpennies, and its back riz up like a bridge, trottin' on and across me, and ready, if I dar' stop, to rub its sides against my shins, and maybe to make a jump and seize my throat, if that it's a cat, at all, an' not something worse?"

As he ended his description in a low tone, looking straight at the fire, my father drew his big hand across his forehead once or twice, his face being damp and shining with the moisture of fear, and he sighed, or rather groaned, heavily.

My mother had relapsed into panic, and was praying again in her fear. I, too, was terribly frightened, and on the point of crying, for I knew all about the white cat.

Clapping my father on the shoulder, by way of encouragement, my mother leaned over him, kissing him, and at last began to cry. He was wringing her hands in his, and seemed in great trouble.

"There was nothin' came into the house with me?" he asked, in a very low tone, turning to me.

"There was nothin', father," I said, "but the saddle and bridle that was in your hand."

"Nothin' white kem in at the doore wid me," he repeated.

"Nothin' at all," I answered.

"So best," said my father, and making the sign of the cross, he began mumbling to himself, and I knew he was saying his prayers.

Waiting for a while, to give him time for this exercise, my mother asked him where he first saw it.

"When I was riding up the bohereen,"—the Irish term meaning a little road, such as leads up to a farm-house—"I bethought myself that the men was on the road with the cattle, and no one to look to the horse barrin' myself, so I thought I might as well leave him in the crooked field below, an' I tuck him there, he bein' cool, and not a hair turned, for I rode him aisy all the way. It was when I turned, after lettin' him go—the saddle and bridle bein' in my hand—that I saw it, pushin' out o' the long grass at the side o' the path, an' it walked across it, in front of me, an' then back again, before me, the same way, an' sometimes at one side, an' then at the other, lookin' at me wid them shinin' eyes; and I consayted I heard it growlin' as it kep' beside me—as close as ever you see—till I kem up to the doore, here, an' knocked an' called, as ye heerd me."

Now, what was it, in so simple an incident, that agitated my father, my mother, myself, and finally, every member of this rustic household, with a terrible foreboding? It was this that we, one and all, believed that my father had received, in thus encountering the white cat, a warning of his approaching death.

The omen had never failed hitherto. It did not fail now. In a week after my father took the fever that was going, and before a month he was dead.

My honest friend, Dan Donovan, paused here; I could perceive that he was praying, for his lips were busy, and I concluded that it was for the repose of that departed soul.

In a little while he resumed.

It is eighty years now since that omen first attached to my family. Eighty years? Ay, is it. Ninety is nearer the mark. And I have spoken to many old people, in those earlier times, who had a distinct recollection of everything connected with it.

It happened in this way.

My grand-uncle, Connor Donovan, had the old farm of Drumgunniol in his day. He was richer than ever my father was, or my father's father either, for he took a short lease of Balraghan, and made money of it. But money won't soften a hard heart, and I'm afraid my grand-uncle was a cruel man—a profligate man he was, surely, and that is mostly a cruel man at heart. He drank his share, too, and cursed and swore, when he was vexed, more than was good for his soul, I'm afraid.

At that time there was a beautiful girl of the Colemans, up in the mountains, not far from Capper Cullen. I'm told that there are no Colemans there now at all, and that family has passed away. The famine years made great changes.

Ellen Coleman was her name. The Colemans were not rich. But, being such a beauty, she might have made a good match. Worse than she did for herself, poor thing, she could not.

Con Donovan—my grand-uncle, God forgive him!—sometimes in his rambles saw her at fairs or patterns, and he fell in love with her, as who might not?

He used her ill. He promised her marriage, and persuaded her to come away with him; and, after all, he broke his word. It was just the old story. He tired of her, and he wanted to push himself in the world; and he married a girl of the Collopys, that had a great fortune—twenty-four cows, seventy sheep, and a hundred and twenty goats.

He married this Mary Collopy, and grew richer than before; and Ellen Coleman died broken-hearted. But that did not trouble the strong farmer much.

He would have liked to have children, but he had none, and this was the only cross he had to bear, for everything else went much as he wished.

One night he was returning from the fair of Nenagh. A shallow stream at that time crossed the road—they have thrown a bridge over it, I am told, some time since—and its channel was often dry in summer weather. When it was so, as it passes close by the old farm-house of Drumgunniol, without a great deal of winding, it makes a sort of road, which people then used as a short cut to reach the house by. Into this dry channel, as there was plenty of light from the moon, my grand-uncle turned his horse, and when he had reached the two ash-trees at the meering of the farm he turned his horse short into the river-field, intending to ride through the gap at the other end, under the oak-tree, and so he would have been within a few hundred yards of his door.

As he approached the "gap" he saw, or thought he saw, with a slow motion, gliding along the ground toward the same point, and now and then with a soft bound, a white object, which he described as being no bigger than his hat, but what it was he could not see, as it moved along the hedge and disappeared at the point to which he was himself tending.

When he reached the gap the horse stopped short. He urged and coaxed it in vain. He got down to lead it through, but it recoiled, snorted, and fell into a wild trembling fit. He mounted it again. But its terror continued, and it obstinately resisted his caresses and his whip. It was bright moonlight, and my grand-uncle was chafed by the horse's resistance, and, seeing nothing to account for it, and being so near home, what little patience he possessed forsook him, and, plying his whip and spur in earnest, he broke into oaths and curses.

All on a sudden the horse sprang through, and Con Donovan, as he passed under the broad branch of the oak, saw clearly a woman standing on the bank beside him, her arm extended, with the hand of which, as he flew by, she struck him a blow upon the shoulders. It threw him forward upon the neck of the horse, which, in wild terror, reached the door at a gallop, and stood there quivering and steaming all over.

Less alive than dead, my grand-uncle got in. He told his story, at least, so much as he chose. His wife did not quite know what to think. But that something very bad had happened she could not doubt. He was very faint and ill, and begged that the priest should be sent for forthwith. When they were getting him to his bed they saw distinctly the marks of five fingerpoints on the flesh of his shoulder, where the spectral blow had fallen. These singular marks—which they said resembled in tint the hue of a body struck by lightning—remained imprinted on his flesh, and were buried with him.

When he had recovered sufficiently to talk with the people about him —speaking, like a man at his last hour, from a burdened heart, and troubled conscience—he repeated his story, but said he did not see, or, at all events, know, the face of the figure that stood in the gap. No one believed him. He told more about it to the priest than to others. He certainly had a secret to tell. He might as well have divulged it frankly, for the neighbours all knew well enough that it was the face of dead Ellen Coleman that he had seen.

From that moment my grand-uncle never raised his head. He was a scared, silent, broken-spirited man. It was early summer then, and at the fall of the leaf in the same year he died.

Of course there was a wake, such as beseemed a strong farmer so rich as he. For some reason the arrangements of this ceremonial were a little different from the usual routine.

The usual practice is to place the body in the great room, or kitchen, as it is called, of the house. In this particular case there was, as I told you, for some reason, an unusual arrangement. The body was placed in a small room that opened upon the greater one. The door of this, during the wake, stood open. There were candles about the bed, and pipes and tobacco on the table, and stools for such guests as chose to enter, the door standing open for their reception.

The body, having been laid out, was left alone, in this smaller room, during the preparations for the wake. After nightfall one of the women, approaching the bed to get a chair which she had left near it, rushed from the room with a scream, and, having recovered her speech at the further end of the "kitchen," and surrounded by a gaping audience, she said, at last:

"May I never sin, if his face bain't riz up again the back o' the bed, and he starin' down to the doore, wid eyes as big as pewter plates, that id be shinin' in the moon!"

"Arra, woman! Is it cracked you are?" said one of the farm boys as they are termed, being men of any age you please.

"Agh, Molly, don't be talkin', woman! 'Tis what ye consayted it, goin' into the dark room, out o' the light. Why didn't ye take a candle in your fingers, ye aumadhaun?" said one of her female companions.

"Candle, or no candle; I seen it," insisted Molly. "An' what's more, I could a'most tak' my oath I seen his arum, too, stretchin' out o' the bed along the flure, three times as long as it should be, to take hould o' me be the fut."

"Nansinse, ye fool, what id he want o' yer fut?" exclaimed one scornfully.

"Gi' me the candle, some o' yez—in the name o' God," said old Sal Doolan, that was straight and lean, and a woman that could pray like a priest almost.

"Give her a candle," agreed all.

But whatever they might say, there wasn't one among them that did not look pale and stern enough as they followed Mrs. Doolan, who was praying as fast as her lips could patter, and leading the van with a tallow candle, held like a taper, in her fingers.

The door was half open, as the panic-stricken girl had left it; and holding the candle on high the better to examine the room, she made a step or so into it.

If my grand-uncle's hand had been stretched along the floor, in the unnatural way described, he had drawn it back again under the sheet that covered him. And tall Mrs. Doolan was in no danger of tripping over his arm as she entered. But she had not gone more than a step or two with her candle aloft, when, with a drowning face, she suddenly stopped short, staring at the bed which was now fully in view.

"Lord, bless us, Mrs. Doolan, ma'am, come back," said the woman next her, who had fast hold of her dress, or her 'coat,' as they call it, and drawing her backwards with a frightened pluck, while a general recoil among her followers betokened the alarm which her hesitation had inspired.

"Whisht, will yez?" said the leader, peremptorily, "I can't hear my own ears wid the noise ye're makin', an' which iv yez let the cat in here, an' whose cat is it?" she asked, peering suspiciously at a white cat that was sitting on the breast of the corpse.

"Put it away, will yez?" she resumed, with horror at the profanation. "Many a corpse as I sthretched and crossed in the bed, the likes o' that I never seen yet. The man o' the house, wid a brute baste like that mounted on him, like a phooka, Lord forgi' me for namin' the like in this room. Dhrive it away, some o' yez! out o' that, this minute, I tell ye."

Each repeated the order, but no one seemed inclined to execute it. They were crossing themselves, and whispering their conjectures and misgivings as to the nature of the beast, which was no cat of that house, nor one that they had ever seen before. On a sudden, the white cat placed itself on the pillow over the head of the body, and having from that place glared for a time at them over the features of the corpse, it crept softly along the body towards them, growling low and fiercely as it drew near.

Out of the room they bounced, in dreadful confusion, shutting the door fast after them, and not for a good while did the hardiest venture to peep in again.

The white cat was sitting in its old place, on the dead man's breast, but this time it crept quietly down the side of the bed, and disappeared under it, the sheet which was spread like a coverlet, and hung down nearly to the floor, concealing it from view.

Praying, crossing themselves, and not forgetting a sprinkling of holy water, they peeped, and finally searched, poking spades, "wattles," pitchforks and such implements under the bed. But the cat was not to be found, and they concluded that it had made its escape among their feet as they stood near the threshold. So they secured the door carefully, with hasp and padlock.

But when the door was opened next morning they found the white cat sitting, as if it had never been disturbed, upon the breast of the dead man.

Again occurred very nearly the same scene with a like result, only that some said they saw the cat afterwards lurking under a big box in a corner of the outer-room, where my grand-uncle kept his leases and papers, and his prayer-book and beads.

Mrs. Doolan heard it growling at her heels wherever she went; and although she could not see it, she could hear it spring on the back of her chair when she sat down, and growl in her ear, so that she would bounce up with a scream and a prayer, fancying that it was on the point of taking her by the throat.

And the priest's boy, looking round the corner, under the branches of the old orchard, saw a white cat sitting under the little window of the room where my grand-uncle was laid out and looking up at the four small panes of glass as a cat will watch a bird.

The end of it was that the cat was found on the corpse again, when the room was visited, and do what they might, whenever the body was left alone, the cat was found again in the same ill-omened contiguity with the dead man. And this continued, to the scandal and fear of the neighbourhood, until the door was opened finally for the wake.

My grand-uncle being dead, and, with all due solemnities, buried, I have done with him. But not quite yet with the white cat. No banshee ever yet was more inalienably attached to a family than this ominous apparition is to mine. But there is this difference. The banshee seems to be animated with an affectionate sympathy with the bereaved family to whom it is hereditarily attached, whereas this thing has about it a suspicion of malice. It is the messenger simply of death. And its taking the shape of a cat—the coldest, and they say, the most vindictive of brutes—is indicative of the spirit of its visit.

When my grandfather's death was near, although he seemed quite well at the time, it appeared not exactly, but very nearly in the same way in which I told you it showed itself to my father.

The day before my Uncle Teigue was killed by the bursting of his gun, it appeared to him in the evening, at twilight, by the lough, in the field where I saw the woman who walked across the water, as I told you. My uncle was washing the barrel of his gun in the lough. The grass is short there, and there is no cover near it. He did not know how it approached but the first he saw of it, the white cat was walking close round his feet, in the twilight, with an angry twist of its tail, and a green glare in its eyes, and do what he would, it continued walking round and round him, in larger or smaller circles, till he reached the orchard, and there he lost it.

My poor Aunt Peg—she married one of the O'Brians, near Oolah—came to Drumgunniol to go to the funeral of a cousin who died about a mile away. She died herself, poor woman, only a month after.

Coming from the wake, at two or three o'clock in the morning, as she got over the stile into the farm of Drumgunniol, she saw the white cat at her side, and it kept close beside her, she ready to faint all the time, till she reached the door of the house, where it made a spring up into the white-thorn tree that grows close by, and so it parted from her. And my

little brother Jim saw it also, just three weeks before he died. Every
member of our family who dies, or takes his death-sickness, at Drumgunniol, is sure to see the white cat, and no one of us who sees it need hope
for long life after.

Returning Home

ANTHONY TROLLOPE
(English, 1815–1882)

It is generally supposed that people who live at home—good domestic
people who love tea and their armchairs, and who keep the parlour
hearthrug ever warm—it is generally supposed that these are the people
who value home the most, and best appreciate all the comforts of that
cherished institution. I am inclined to doubt this. It is, I think, to those
who live farthest away from home, to those who find the greatest difficulty in visiting home, that the word conveys the sweetest idea. In some
distant parts of the world it may be that an Englishman acknowledges his
permanent restingplace, but there are many others in which he will not
call his daily house his home. He would, in his own idea, desecrate the
word by doing so. His home is across the blue waters, in the little northern island, which, perhaps, he may visit no more; which he has left at any
rate for half his life; from which circumstances, and the necessity of
living, have banished him. His home is still in England; and when he
speaks of home his thoughts are there.

No one can understand the intensity of this feeling, who has not seen
or felt the absence of interest in life, which falls to the lot of many who
have to eat their bread on distant soils. We are all apt to think that a life
in strange countries will be a life of excitement, of stirring enterprise and

varied scenes; that, in abandoning the comforts of home, we shall receive in exchange more of movement and of adventure than would come in our way in our own tame country; and this feeling has, I am sure, sent many a young man roaming. Take any spirited fellow of twenty, and ask him whether he would like to go to Mexico for the next ten years. Prudence and his father may ultimately save him from such banishment, but he will not refuse without a pang of regret.

Alas! it is a mistake. Bread may be earned, and fortunes, perhaps, made in such countries; and as it is the destiny of our race to spread itself over the wide face of the globe, it is well that there should be something to gild and paint the outward face of that lot which so many are called upon to choose. But for a life of daily excitement, there is no life like life in England; and the farther that one goes from England, the more stagnant, I think, do the waters of existence become.

But if it be so for men, it is ten times more so for women. An Englishman, if he be at Guatemala or at Belise, must work for his bread, and that work will find him in thought and excitement. But what of his wife? where will she find excitement? by what pursuit will she repay herself for all that she has left behind her at her mother's fireside? She will love her husband, yes, that at least. If there be not that, there will be a hell indeed. Then she will nurse her children, and talk of her home. When the time shall come that her promised return thither is within a year or two of its accomplishment, her thoughts will all be fixed on that coming pleasure, as are the thoughts of a young girl on her first ball for the fortnight before that event comes off.

On the central plain of that portion of Central America which is called Costa Rica, stands the city of San José. It is the capital of the Republic— for Costa Rica is a Republic, and, for Central America, is a town of some importance. It is in the middle of the coffee district, surrounded by rich soil, on which the sugar-cane is produced; is blessed with a climate only moderately hot, and the native inhabitants are neither cut-throats nor cannibals. It may be said, therefore, that by comparison with some other spots to which Englishmen and others are congregated for the gathering together of money, San José may be considered as a happy region; but, nevertheless, a life there is not in every way desirable. It is a dull place, with little to interest either the eye or the ear. Although the heat of the tropics is but little felt there, on account of its altitude, men and women become too listless for much enterprise. There is no society. There are a few Germans and a few Englishmen in the place, who see each other on matters of business during the day, but, sombre as life generally is, they seem to care little for each other's company on any other footing. I know not to what point the aspirations of the Germans may stretch themselves, but to the English the one idea that gives salt to life is the idea of home. On some day, however distant it may be, they will once more turn their faces towards the little northern island, and then all will be well with them.

To a certain Englishman then, and to his dear little wife, this prospect came some few years since somewhat suddenly. Events and tidings, it matters not which or what, brought it about that they resolved between themselves that they would start immediately—almost immediately. They would pack up and leave San José within four months of the day on which their purpose was first formed. At San José, a period of only four months for such a purpose was immediately. It created a feeling of instant excitement, a necessity for instant doing, a consciousness that there was in those few weeks ample work both for the hands and thoughts, work almost more than ample. The dear little wife who, for the last two years, had been so listless, felt herself flurried.

"Harry," she said to her husband, "how shall we ever be ready?" and her pretty face was lighted up with unusual brightness, at the happy thought of so much haste with such an object. "And baby's things, too?" she said, as she thought of all the various little articles of dress that would be needed.

A journey from San José to Southampton cannot in truth be made as easily as one from London to Liverpool. Let us think of a month to be passed without any aid from the washerwoman, and the greatest part of that month amidst the sweltering heats of the West Indian tropics!

For the first month of her hurry and flurry Mrs. Arkwright was a happy woman. She would see her mother again, and her sisters. It was now four years since she had left them on the quays at Southampton, while all their hearts were broken at the parting. She was a young bride then going forth with her new lord, to meet the stern world. He had then been home to look for a wife, and he had found what he looked for in the youngest sister of his partner. For he, Henry Arkwright, and his wife's brother, Abel Ring, had established themselves together in San José. And now she thought how there should be another meeting on those quays, at which there should be no broken hearts—at which there should be love without sorrow, and kisses sweet with the sweetness of welcome, not bitter with the bitterness of parting. And people told her—the few neighbours around her—how happy, how fortunate she was to get home thus early in her life. They had been out some ten, some twenty years, and still the day of their return was distant. And then she pressed her living baby to her breast, and wiped away a tear as she thought of the other darling, whom she would leave beneath that distant sod.

And then came the question as to the route home. San José stands in the middle of the high plain of Costa Rica, half-way between the Pacific and the Atlantic. The journey thence down to the Pacific is by comparison easy. There is a road, and the mules on which the travellers must ride go steadily and easily down to Puntas Arenas, the port in that ocean. There are inns, too, on the way—places of public entertainment, at which refreshment may be obtained, and beds, or fair substitutes for beds. But then, by this route, the traveller must take a long additional sea voyage. He must convey himself and his baggage down to that wretched place on the Pacific, there wait for a steamer to take him to Panama, cross the isthmus, and reship himself in the other waters for his long journey home. That terrible unshipping and reshipping is a sore burden to the unaccustomed traveller. When it is absolutely necessary, then, indeed, it is done without much thought; but in the case of the Arkwrights it was not absolutely necessary. And there was another reason which turned Mrs. Arkwright's heart against that journey by Puntas Arenas. The place is unhealthy, having at certain seasons a very bad name; and here, on their outward journey, her husband had been taken ill. She had never ceased to think of the fortnight she had spent there among uncouth strangers, during a portion of which his life had trembled in the balance. Early, therefore, in those four months she begged that she might not be taken round by Puntas Arenas. There was another route.

"Harry, if you love me, let us go by the Serapiqui."

As to Harry's loving her, there was no doubt about that, as she well knew.

There was this other route by the Serapiqui river, and by Greytown. Greytown, it is true, is quite as unhealthy as Puntas Arenas, and by that route one's baggage must be shipped and unshipped into small boats. There are all manner of difficulties attached to it; perhaps no direct road to or from any city on the world's surface is subject to sharper fatigue while it lasts. Journeying by this route also, the traveller leaves San José mounted on his mule, and so mounted he makes his way through the vast primeval forests down to the banks of the Serapiqui river. That there is a track for him is of course true, but it is simply a track, and during nine months out of the twelve is so deep in mud that the mules sink in it to their bellies. Then, when the river has been reached, the traveller seats him in his canoe, and for two days is paddled down—down along the Serapiqui, into the San Juan river, and down along the San Juan till he reaches Greytown, passing one night at some hut on the river side. At Greytown he waits for the steamer, which will carry him his first stage on his road towards Southampton. He must be a connoisseur in disagreeables of every kind who can say with any precision whether Greytown or Puntas Arenas is the better place for a week's sojourn.

For a full month Mr. Arkwright would not give way to his wife. At first he all but conquered her by declaring that the Serapiqui journey would be dangerous for the baby; but she heard from someone that it could be made less fatiguing for the baby than the other route. A baby had been carried down in a litter, strapped on to a mule's back. A guide at the mule's head would be necessary, and that was all. When once in her boat the baby would be as well as in her cradle. What purpose cannot a woman gain by perseverance? Her purpose in this instance Mrs. Arkwright did at last gain by persevering.

And then their preparations for the journey went on with much flurrying and hot haste. To us at home, who live and feel our life every day, the manufacture of endless baby-linen, and the packing of mountains of clothes, does not give an idea of much pleasurable excitement; but at San José, when there was scarcely motion enough in existence to prevent its water from becoming foul with stagnation, this packing of baby-linen was delightful, and for a month or so the days went by with happy wings.

But by degrees reports began to reach both Arkwright and his wife as to this new route, which made them uneasy. The wet season had been prolonged, and even though they might not be deluged by rain themselves, the path would be in such a state of mud as to render the labour incessant. One or two people declared that the road was unfit, at any time, for a woman; and then the river would be much swollen. These tidings did not reach Arkwright and his wife together, or at any rate not till late amidst their preparations, or a change might still have been made. As it was, after all her entreaties, Mrs. Arkwright did not like to ask him now again to alter his plans, and he, having altered them once, was averse to change them again. So things went on till the mules and the boats had been hired, and things had gone so far that no change could then be made without much cost and trouble.

During the last ten days of their sojourn in San José, Mrs. Arkwright had lost all that appearance of joy which had cheered up her sweet face during the last few months. Terror at that terrible journey obliterated in her mind all the happiness which had arisen from the hope of being soon at home. She was thoroughly cowed by the dangers to be encountered, and would gladly have gone down to Puntas Arenas, had it been now possible that she could so arrange it. It rained and rained, and still rained when there was now only a week's further time before they started. Oh! if they could only wait for another month! But this she said to no one. After what had passed between her and her husband, she had not the heart to say such words to him. Arkwright himself was a man not given to much talking—a silent, thoughtful man, stern withal in his outward bearing, but tender-hearted and loving in his nature. The sweet young wife, who had left all and come with him out to that dull, distant place, was very dear to him, dearer than she herself was aware; and in these days he was thinking much of her coming troubles. Why had he given way to her foolish prayers? Ah, why indeed?

And thus the last few days of their sojourn in San José passed away from them. Once or twice during these days she did speak out, expressing her fears. Her feelings were too much for her, and she could not restrain herself. "Poor mama," she said, "I shall never see her!" And then again —"Harry, I know I shall never reach home alive!"

"Fanny, my darling, that is nonsense." But in order that his spoken word might not sound stern to her, he took her in his arms and kissed her.

"You must behave well, Fanny," he said to her the day before they started. Though her heart was then very low within her, she promised him that she would do her best, and then she made a great resolution. Though she should be dying on the road, she would not complain beyond the absolute necessity of her nature. She fully recognised his thoughtful, tender kindness; for though he thus cautioned her, he never told her that the dangers which she feared were the result of her own choice. He never threw in her teeth those prayers which she had made, in yielding to which he knew that he had been weak.

Then came the morning of their departure. The party of travellers consisted of four, besides the baby. There was Mr. Arkwright, his wife, and an English nurse who was going home to England with them, and her brother, Abel Ring, who was to accompany them as far as the Serapiqui river. When they had reached that, the real labour of the journey would be over. They had eight mules—four for the four travellers, one for the baby, a spare mule, laden simply with blankets, so that Mrs. Arkwright might change, in order that she should not be fatigued by the fatigue of her beast, and two for their luggage. The heavier portion of the baggage had already been sent off by Puntas Arenas, and would meet them at the other side of the isthmus of Panama.

For the last four days the rain had ceased—had ceased, at any rate, at San José. Those who knew the country well would know that it might still be raining over those vast forests; but now, as the matter was settled, they would all hope for the best. On that morning on which they started, the sun shone fairly, and they accepted this as an omen of good. Baby seemed to lie comfortably on her pile of blankets on the mule's back, and the face of the tall Indian guide who took his place at that mule's head pleased the anxious mother. "Not leave him ever," he said, in Spanish, laying his hand on the cord which was fastened to the beast's head; and not for one moment did he leave his charge, though the labour of sticking close to him was very great.

They had four attendants, or guides, all of whom made the journey on foot. That they were all men of mixed race was probable; but three of them would have been called Spaniards—Spaniards, that is, of Costa Rica—and the other would be called an Indian. One of the Spaniards was the leader, or chief man of the party; but the others seemed to stand on an equal footing with each other, and, indeed, the place of greatest care had been given to the Indian.

In the first four or five miles their route lay along the high road which leads from San José to Puntas Arenas, and so far a group of acquaintances followed them, all mounted on mules. Here, where the ways forked, their road leading away through the great forests to the Atlantic, they all separated, and many tears were shed on each side. What might be the future life of the Arkwrights had not been absolutely fixed, but there was a strong hope on their part that they might never be forced to return to Costa Rica. Those from whom they now parted had not seemed to be dear to them in any especial degree, while they all lived together in the same small town, seeing each other day by day; but now—now that they might never meet again, a certain love sprang up for the old familiar faces, and women kissed each other who hitherto had hardly cared to enter each other's houses.

And then the party of the Arkwrights again started, and its steady work began. For the whole of the first day the way beneath their feet was tolerably good, and the weather continued fine. It was one long gradual ascent from the place where the roads parted, but there was no real labour in travelling. Mrs. Arkwright rode beside her baby's mule, at the head of which the Indian always walked, and the two men went together in front. The husband had found that his wife would prefer this, as long as the road allowed of such an arrangement. Her heart was too full to admit of much speaking, and so they went on in silence.

The first night was passed in a hut by the road-side, which seemed to have been deserted—a hut or "rancho," as it is called in that country. Their food they had of course brought with them; and here, by common consent, they endeavoured in some sort to make themselves merry.

"Fanny," Arkwright said to her, "it is not so bad, after all; eh, my darling?"

"No," she answered; "only that the mule tires one so. Will all the days be as long as that?"

He had not the heart to tell her that, as regarded hours of work, that first day must of necessity be the shortest. They had risen to a considerable altitude, and the night was very cold; but baby was enveloped among a pile of coloured blankets, and things did not go very badly with them; only this—that when Fanny Arkwright rose from her hard bed, her limbs were more weary and much more stiff than they had been when Arkwright had lifted her from her mule.

On the second morning they mounted before the day had quite broken, in order that they might breakfast on the summit of the ridge which separates the two oceans. At this spot the good road comes to an end, and the forest track begins; and here also they would in truth enter the forest, though their path had for some time been among straggling trees and bushes. And now again they rode two and two up to this place of halting, Arkwright and Ring well knowing that from hence their labours would in truth commence.

Poor Mrs. Arkwright, when she reached this resting-place, would fain have remained there for the rest of the day. One word in her low plaintive voice she said, asking whether they might not sleep in the large shed which stands there. But this was manifestly impossible; at such a pace they would never reach Greytown; and she spoke no further word when he told her that they must go on.

At about noon that day the file of travellers formed itself into the line which it afterwards kept during the whole of the journey, and then started by the narrow path into the forest. First walked the leader of the guides; then another man following him; Abel Ring came next, and behind him the maid-servant; then the baby's mule, with the Indian ever at its head; close at his heels followed Mrs. Arkwright, so that the mother's eye might be always on her child; and after her her husband. Then another guide on foot completed the number of the travellers. In this way they went on and on, day after day, till they reached the banks of the Serapiqui, never once varying their places in the procession. As they started in the morning so they went on till their noon-day's rest; and so again they made their evening march. In that journey there was no idea of variety, no searching after the pleasures of scenery, no attempts at conversation with any object of interest or amusement. What words were spoken were those simply needful, or produced by sympathy for suffering. So they journeyed, always in the same places, with one exception— they began their work with two guides leading them; but before the first day was over, one of them had fallen back to the side of Mrs. Arkwright, for she was unable to sit on her mule without support.

Their daily work was divided into two stages, so as to give some time for rest in the middle of the day. It had been arranged that the distance for each day should not be long—should be very short, as was thought by them all when they talked it over up at San José; but now the hours which they passed in the saddle seemed to be endless. Their descent began from that ridge of which I have spoken; and they had no sooner turned their faces down upon the mountain slopes looking towards the Atlantic, than that passage of mud began to which there was no cessation till they found themselves on the banks of the Serapiqui river. I doubt whether it be possible to convey in words an adequate idea of the labour of riding over such a path. It is not that any active exertion is necessary— that there is anything which requires doing. The traveller has before him the simple task of sitting on his mule from hour to hour, and of seeing that his knees do not get themselves jammed against the trees. But at every step the beast he rides has to drag his legs out from the deep clinging mud, and the body of the rider never knows one moment of ease.

Why the mules do not die on the road, I cannot say; they live through it, and do not appear to suffer. They have their own way in everything, for no exertion on the rider's part will make them walk either faster or slower than is their wont.

On the day on which they entered the forest, that being the second of their journey, Mrs. Arkwright had asked for mercy—for permission to escape that second stage. On the next she allowed herself to be lifted into her saddle, after her midday rest, without a word. She had tried to sleep, but in vain, and had sat within a little hut, looking out upon the desolate scene before her, with her baby in her lap. She had this one comfort, that of all the travellers she and the baby suffered the least. They had now left the high grounds, and the heat was becoming great, though not as yet intense. And then the Indian guide, looking out slowly over the forest, saw that the rain was not yet over. He spoke a word or two to one of his companions in a low voice, and in a *patois* which Mrs. Arkwright did not understand; and then, going after her husband, told him that the heavens were threatening.

"We have only two leagues," said Arkwright, "and it may perhaps hold up."

"It will begin in an hour," said the Indian, "and the two leagues are four hours."

"And to-morrow?" asked Arkwright.

"To-morrow, and to-morrow, and to-morrow it will still rain," said the guide, looking, as he spoke, up over the huge primeval forest.

"Then we had better start at once," said Arkwright, "before the first falling drops frighten the woman."

So the mules were brought out, and he lifted his uncomplaining wife on to the blankets which formed her pillow. The file again formed itself, and slowly they wound their way out upon the small enclosure by which the hut was surrounded—out from the enclosure on to a rough scrap of undrained pasture ground, from which the trees had been cleared. In a few minutes they were once more struggling through the mud.

The name of the spot which our travellers had just left is Careblanco. There they had found a woman living, all alone. Her husband was away, she told them, at San José, but would be back to her when the dry weather came, to look up the young cattle which were straying in the forest. What a life for a woman! Nevertheless, in talking with Mrs. Arkwright she made no complaint of her own lot, but had done what little she could to comfort the poor lady who was so little able to bear the fatigues of her journey.

"Is the road very bad?" Mrs. Arkwright asked her in a whisper.

"Ah, yes, it is a bad road."

"And when shall we be at the river?"

"It took me four days," said the woman.

"Then I shall never see my mother again;" and as she spoke Mrs. Arkwright pressed her baby to her bosom. Immediately after that her husband came in, and then they started.

Their path now led away across the slope of a mountain, which seemed to fall from the very top of that central ridge in an unbroken descent, down to the valley at its foot. Hitherto, since they had entered the forest, they had had nothing before their eyes but the trees and bushes which grew close around them. But now a prospect of unrivalled grandeur was opened before them, if only they had been able to enjoy it. At the bottom of the valley ran a river which, so great was the depth, looked like a moving silver cord; and on the other side of this there arose another mountain, steep, but unbroken, like that which they were passing—unbroken, so that the eye could stretch from the river up to the very summit. Not a spot on that mountain side, or on their side either, was left uncovered by thick forest, which had stood there, untouched by man, since nature first produced it.

But all this was nothing to our travellers; nor was the clang of the macaws anything, or the roaring of the little congo ape. Nothing was gained by them from beautiful scenery, nor was there any fear from beasts of prey. The immediate pain of each step of the journey drove all other feelings from them, and their thoughts were bounded by an intense longing for the evening halt.

And then, as the guide had prophesied, the rain began. At first it came in such small soft drops that it was found to be refreshing, but the clouds soon gathered, and poured forth their collected waters as though it had not rained for months among those mountains. Not that they came in big drops, or with the violence which wind can give them, beating hither and thither, breaking branches from the trees, and rising up again as they pattered against the ground. There was no violence in the rain. It fell softly in a long continuous noiseless stream, sinking into everything that it touched, converting the deep rich earth on all sides into mud.

Not a word was said by any of them as it came on. The Indian covered the baby with her blanket, closer than she was covered before, and the guide who walked by Mrs. Arkwright's side drew her cloak around her knees. But such efforts were in vain. There is a rain that will penetrate everything, and such was the rain which fell upon them now. Nevertheless, as I have said, hardly a word was spoken. The poor woman, finding that the heat of her cloak increased her sufferings, threw it open again.

"Fanny," said her husband, "you had better let him protect you as well as he can."

She answered him merely by an impatient wave of the hand, intending to signify that she could not speak, but that in this matter she must have her way.

After that her husband made no further attempt to control her. He could see, however, that ever and again she would have slipped forward from her mule and fallen, had not the man by her side steadied her with his hand. At every tree he protected her knees and feet, though there was hardly room for him to move between the beast and the bank against which he was thrust.

And then, at last, that day's work was also over, and Fanny Arkwright slipped from her pillow down into her husband's arms, at the door of another rancho in the forest. Here there lived a large family, adding from year to year to the patch of ground which they had rescued from the wood, and valiantly doing their part in the extension of civilisation.

Our party was but a few steps from the door when they left their mules, but Mrs. Arkwright did not now as heretofore hasten to receive her baby in her arms. When placed upon the ground she still leaned against the mule, and her husband saw that he must carry her into the hut. This he did, and then, wet, mud-laden, dishevelled as she was, she laid herself down upon the planks that were to form her bed, and then stretched out her arms for her infant. On that evening they undressed and tended her like a child, and then, when she was alone with her husband, she repeated to him her sad foreboding.

"Harry," she said, "I shall never see my mother again."

"Oh, yes, Fanny. You will see her and talk over all these troubles with pleasure. It is very bad, I know; but we shall win through it yet."

"You will, of course; and you will take baby home to her."

"And face her without you! No, my darling. Three more days' riding, or rather two-and-a-half, will bring us to the river, and then your trouble will be over. All will be easy after that."

"Ah! Harry, you do not know."

"I do know that it is very bad, my girl, but you must cheer up. We shall be laughing at all this in a month's time."

On the following morning she allowed herself again to be lifted up, speaking no word of remonstrance. Indeed, she was like a child in their hands, having dropped all the dignity and authority of a woman's demeanour. It rained again during the whole of this day, and the heat was becoming oppressive, as every hour they were descending nearer and nearer to the sea-level. During this first stage hardly a word was spoken by anyone, but when she was again taken from her mule she was in tears. The poor servant-girl, too, was almost prostrate with fatigue, and absolutely unable to wait upon her mistress, or even to do anything for herself. Nevertheless they did make the second stage, seeing that their midday resting-place had been under the trees of the forest. Had there been any but these, they would have remained for the night.

On the following day they rested altogether, though the place at which they remained had but few attractions. It was another forest hut, inhabited by an old Spanish couple, who were by no means willing to give them room, although they paid for their accommodation at exorbitant rates. It is one singularity of places, strange and out of the way like such forest tracks as these, that money in small sums is hardly valued. Dollars there were not appreciated as sixpences are in this rich country. But there they stayed for a day, and the guides employed themselves in making a litter with long poles, so that they might carry Mrs. Arkwright over a portion of the ground. Poor fellows! When once she had thus changed her mode of conveyance, she never again was lifted on to the mule.

There was strong reason against this day's delay. They were to go down the Serapiqui, along with the post, which would overtake them on its banks; but if the post should pass them before they got there, it could not wait, and then they would be deprived of the best canoe on the water. Then also it was possible, if they encountered further delay, that the steamer might sail from Greytown without them, and a month's residence at that frightening place be thus made necessary. That would indeed be a finish to their misfortunes!

The day's rest apparently did little to relieve Mrs. Arkwright's sufferings. On the following day she allowed herself to be put upon the mule, but after the first hour the beasts were stopped, and she was taken off it. During that hour they had travelled hardly over half a league. At that time she so sobbed and moaned that Arkwright absolutely feared that she would perish in the forest, and he implored the guides to use the poles which they had prepared. She had declared to him over and over again that she felt sure that she should die, and, half delirious with weariness and suffering had begged him to leave her at the last hut. They had not yet come to the flat ground, over which a litter might be carried with comparative ease; but nevertheless, the men yielded, and she was placed in a recumbent position upon blankets supported by boughs of trees. In this way she went through that day, with somewhat less of suffering than before, and without that necessity for self-exertion, which had been worse to her than any suffering.

There were places between that and the river at which one could have said it was impossible that a litter should be carried, or even impossible that a mule should work with a load on his back. But still they went on, and the men carried their burdens without complaining. Not a word was said about extra pay—not a word, at least by them; and when Arkwright was profuse in his offer, their leader told him that they would not have done it for money. But for the poor suffering Senora they would make exertions which no money would have bought from them.

On the next day, about noon, the post did pass them, consisting of three strong men, carrying great weights on their backs, suspended by bands from their foreheads. They travelled much quicker than our friends, and would reach the banks of the river that evening. In their ordinary course they would start down the river close after daybreak the following day; but after some consultation with the guides they agreed to wait till noon. Poor Mrs. Arkwright knew nothing of hours, or of any such arrangements now, but her husband greatly doubted their power of catching this mail dispatch. However, it did not much depend on their exertions that afternoon. Their resting-place was marked out for them, and they would not go beyond it, unless, indeed, they could make the whole journey, which was impossible.

But towards evening matters seemed to improve with them. They had now got on to ground which was more open, and the men who carried the litter could walk with greater ease. Mrs. Arkwright also complained less, and when they reached their resting-place on that night, said nothing of a wish to be left there to her fate. This was a place called Padregal, a cacao plantation, which had been cleared in the forest with much labour. There was a house here, containing three rooms, and some forty or

fifty acres around it had been stripped of the forest trees. But, nevertheless, the adventure had not been a prosperous one, for the place was at
that time deserted. There were the cacao plants, but there was no one to
pick the cocoa. There was a certain melancholy beauty about the place. A
few grand trees had been left standing near the house, and the grass
around was rich and park-like. But it was deserted, and nothing was to be
heard but the roaring of the congos. Ah me! Indeed, it was a melancholy
place as it was seen by some of them afterwards.

On the following morning they were astir very early, and Mrs. Arkwright was so much better that she offered to ride again upon her mule.
The men, however, declared that they would finish their task, and she
was placed again upon the litter, and thus, with slow and weary steps,
they did make their way to the river bank. It was not yet noon when they
saw the mud fort which stands there, and as they drew into the enclosure,
round a small house which stands close by the river side, they saw the
three postmen still busy about their packages.

"Thank God!" said Arkwright.

"Thank God, indeed," said his brother. "All will be right with you
now."

"Well, Fanny," said her husband, as he took her gently from the litter
and seated her on a bench which stood outside the door, "it is all over
now, is it not?"

She answered by a shower of tears, but they were tears which brought
her relief. He was aware of this, and therefore stood by her, still holding
her by both her hands, while her head rested against his side.

"You will find the motion of the boat very gentle," he said; "indeed,
there will be no motion, and you and baby will sleep all the way down to
Greytown."

She did not answer him in words, but she looked up into his face, and
he could see that her spirit was recovering itself.

There was almost a crowd of people collected on the spot, preparatory
to the departure of the canoes. In the first place there was the commandant of the fort, to whom the small house belonged. He was looking to
the passports of our friends, and with due diligence endeavouring to
make something of the occasion by discovering fatal legal impediments to
the further prosecution of their voyage, which impediments would disappear on the payment of certain dollars. And then there were half-a-dozen
Costa Rica soldiers, men with coloured caps and old muskets, ready to

support the dignity and authority of the commandant. There were the guides taking payment from Abel Ring for their past work, and the postmen preparing their boats for the further journey. And then there was a certain German there, with a German servant, to whom the boats belonged; he also was very busy preparing for the river voyage. He was not going down with them, but it was his business to see them well started. A singular-looking man was he, with a huge shaggy beard and shaggy uncombed hair, but with bright blue eyes, which gave to his face a remarkable look of sweetness. He was an uncouth man to the eye, and yet a child would have trusted herself with him in a forest.

At this place they remained some two hours. Coffee was prepared here, and Mrs. Arkwright refreshed herself and her child. They washed and arranged their clothes, and when she stepped down the steep bank, clinging to her husband's arm as she made her way towards the boat, she smiled upon him as he looked at her.

"It is all over now—is it not, my girl?" he said, encouraging her.

"Oh, Harry, do not talk about it!" she answered, shuddering.

"But I want you to say a word to me to let me know that you are better."

"I am better—much better."

"And you will see your mother again, will you not; and give baby to her yourself?"

To this she made no immediate answer, for she was on a level with the river, and the canoe was close at her feet. And then she had to bid farewell to her brother. He now was the unfortunate one of the party, for his destiny required that he should go back to San José alone,—go back and remain there, perhaps, some ten years longer before he might look for the happiness of home.

"God bless you, dearest Abel!" she said, kissing him and sobbing as she spoke.

"Good-bye, Fanny!" he said, "and do not let them forget me in England. It is a great comfort to think that the worst of your troubles are over."

"Oh, she's all right now," said Arkwright. "Good-bye, old boy," and the two brothers-in-law grasped each other's hands heartily; "keep up your spirits, and we'll have you home before long."

"Oh, I am all right," said the other. But from the tone of their voices it was clear that poor Ring was despondent at the thoughts of his coming solitude, and that Arkwright was already triumphing at his emancipation.

And then, with much care, Fanny Arkwright was stowed away in her boat. There was a great contest about the baby, but at last it was arranged, that at any rate, for the first few hours she should be placed in the same boat with the servant. The mother was told that by this plan she would feel herself at liberty to sleep during the heat of the day, and then she might hope to have strength to look to the child when they should be on shore during the night. In this way, therefore, they prepared to start, while Abel Ring stood on the bank looking at them with wishful eyes. In the first boat were two Indians paddling, and a third man steering with another paddle. In the middle there was much luggage, and near the luggage, so as to be under shade, was the baby's soft bed. If nothing evil happened to the boat, the child could not be more safe in the best cradle that was ever rocked. With her was the maid servant and some stranger who was also going down to Greytown.

In the second boat there was the same number of men to paddle, the Indian guide being one of them, and there were the mails placed. Then there was a seat arranged with blankets, cloaks, and cushions, for Mrs. Arkwright, so that she might lean back and sleep without fatigue, and immediately opposite to her her husband placed himself.

"You all look very comfortable," said poor Abel from the bank.

"We shall do very well now," said Arkwright.

"And I do think I shall see mama again," said his wife.

"That's right, old girl; of course you will see her. Now then, we are all ready!" and with some little assistance from the German on the bank, the first boat was pushed off into the stream.

The river in this place is rapid, because the full course of the water is somewhat impeded by a bank of earth jutting out from the opposite side of the river into the stream; but it is not so rapid as to make any recognized danger in the embarcation. Below this bank, which is opposite to the spot at which the boats were entered, there were four or five broken trees in the water, some of the shattered boughs of which showed themselves above the surface. These are called snags, and are very dangerous if met with in the course of the stream; but in this instance no danger was apprehended from them, as they lay considerably to the left of the passage which the boats would take. The first canoe was pushed off by the German, and went rapidly away. The waters were strong with the rain, and it was pretty to see with what velocity the boat was carried on some hundred of yards in advance of the other, by the force of the first efforts of the paddles. The German, however, from the bank, hallooed to the first men in Spanish, bidding them relax their efforts for a while; and then he said a word or two of caution to those who were now on the point of starting.

The boat then was pushed steadily forward, the man at the stern keeping it with his paddle a little further away from the bank at which they had embarked. It was close under the land that the stream ran the fastest, and in obedience to the directions given to him, he made his course somewhat nearer the sunken trees. It was but one turn of his hand that gave the light boat its direction, but that turn of the hand was too strong. Had the anxious master of the canoes been but a thought less anxious all might have been well; but, as it was, the prow of the boat was caught by some slight hidden branch which impeded its course, and turned it round in the rapid river. The whole length of the canoe was thus brought against the sunken tree, and in half a minute the five occupants of the boat were struggling in the stream.

Abel Ring and the German were both standing on the bank close to the water when this happened, and each for a moment looked into the other's face.

"Stand where you are," shouted the German, "so that you may assist them from the shore. I will go in." And then, throwing from him his boots and coat, he plunged into the river.

The canoe had been swept round so as to be brought by the force of the waters absolutely in among the upturned roots and broken stumps of the trees which impeded the river, and thus when the party was upset they were, at first, to be seen scrambling among the branches. But, unfortunately, there was much more wood below the water than above it, and the force of the stream was so great that those who caught hold of the timber were not able to support themselves above the surface. Arkwright was soon to be seen some fifty yards down, having been carried clear of the trees, and here he got out of the river on the further bank. The distance to him was not above forty yards, but, from the nature of the ground, he could not get up towards his wife unless he could have forced his way against the stream.

The Indian who had had charge of the baby rose quickly to the surface, was carried once round in the eddy with his head high above the water, and then was seen to throw himself among the broken wood. He had seen the dress of the poor woman, and made his efforts to save her. The other two men were so caught by the fragments of the boughs, that they could not extricate themselves, so as to make any exertions; ultimately, however, they also got out on the further bank.

Mrs. Arkwright had sunk at once on being precipitated into the water, but the buoyancy of her clothes had brought her for a moment again to the surface. She had risen for a moment, and then had again gone down, immediately below the forked trunk of a huge tree—had gone down, alas, alas! never to rise again with life within her bosom. The poor Indian made two attempts to save her, and then came up himself, incapable of further effort.

It was then that the German, the owner of the canoes, who had fought his way with great efforts across the violence of the waters, and, indeed, up against the stream, for some few yards, made his effort to save the life of that poor frail creature. He had watched the spot at which she had gone down, and, even while struggling across the river, had seen how the Indian had followed her and had failed. It was now his turn. His life was in his hand, and he was prepared to throw it away in that attempt. Having succeeded in placing himself a little above the large tree, he turned his face towards the bottom of the river, and dived down among the branches. And he also, after that, was never again seen with the life blood flowing round his heart.

When the sun set that night the two swollen corpses were lying in the commandant's hut, and Abel Ring and Arkwright were sitting beside them. Arkwright had his baby sleeping in his arms, but he sat there for hours—into the middle of the long night—without speaking a word to anyone.

"Harry," said his brother at last, "come away and lie down; it will be good for you to sleep."

"Nothing ever will be good for me again," said he.

"You must bear up against your sorrow as other men do," said Ring.

"Why am I not sleeping with her as the poor German sleeps? Why did I let another man take my place in dying for her?" And then he walked away that the other might not see the tears on his face.

It was a sad night—that at the commandant's hut, and a sad morning followed upon it. It must be remembered that they had there none of those appurtenances which are so necessary to make woe decent and misfortune comfortable. They sat through the night in the small hut, and in the morning they came forth with their clothes still wet and dirty, with their haggard faces and weary, stiff limbs, encumbered with the horrid task of burying that loved body among the forest trees. And then, to keep life in them till it was done, the brandy flask passed from hand to hand; and after that, with slow but resolute efforts, they re-formed the litter on which the living woman had been carried thither, and took her body back to the wild plantation at Padregal. There they dug for her her grave, and repeating over her some portions of the service for the dead, left her to sleep the sleep of death. But before they left her they erected a palisade of timber round the grave, so that the beasts of the forest should not tear the body from its resting-place.

When that was done Arkwright and his brother made their slow journey back to San José. The widowed husband could not face his darling's mother with such a tale upon his tongue as that!

The Dead Hand

WILKIE COLLINS
(English, 1824–1889)

When this present nineteenth century was younger by a good many years than it is now, a certain friend of mine, named Arthur Holliday, happened to arrive in the town of Doncaster exactly in the middle of the race-week, or, in other words, in the middle of the month of September.

He was one of those reckless, rattle-pated, open-hearted and open-mouthed young gentlemen who possess the gift of familiarity in its highest perfection, and who scramble carelessly along the journey of life, making friends, as the phrase is, wherever they go. His father was a rich manufacturer, and had bought landed property enough in one of the midland counties to make all the born squires in his neighborhood thoroughly envious of him. Arthur was his only son, possessor in prospect of the great business after his father's death; well supplied with money, and not too rigidly looked after during his father's lifetime. Report, or scandal, whichever you please, said that the old gentleman had been rather wild in his youthful days, and that, unlike most parents, he was not disposed to be violently indignant when he found that his son took after him. This may be true or not. I myself only knew the elder Mr. Holliday when he was getting on in years, and then he was as quiet and as respectable a gentleman as ever I met with.

Well, one September, as I told you, young Arthur comes to Doncaster, having decided all of a sudden, in his hare-brained way, that he would go to the races. He did not reach the town till towards the close of evening, and he went at once to see about his dinner and bed at the principal hotel. Dinner they were ready enough to give him, but as for a bed, they laughed when he mentioned it. In the race-week at Doncaster it is no uncommon thing for visitors who have not bespoken apartments to pass the night in their carriages at the inn doors. As for the lower sort of strangers, I myself have often seen them, at that full time, sleeping out on the door-steps for want of a covered place to creep under. Rich as he was, Arthur's chance of getting a night's lodging (seeing that he had not written beforehand to secure one) was more than doubtful. He tried the second hotel, and the third hotel, and two of the inferior inns after that, and was met everywhere with the same form of answer. No accommodation for the night of any sort was left. All the bright golden sovereigns in his pocket would not buy him a bed at Doncaster in the race week.

To a young fellow of Arthur's temperament, the novelty of being turned away into the street like a penniless vagabond, at every house where he asked for a lodging, presented itself in the light of a new and highly amusing experience. He went on with his carpet-bag in his hand, applying for a bed at every place of entertainment for travellers that he could find in Doncaster, until he wandered into the outskirts of the town.

By this time the last glimmer of twilight had faded out, the moon was rising dimly in a mist, the wind was getting cold, the clouds were gathering heavily, and there was every prospect that it was soon going to rain!

The look of the night had rather a lowering effect on young Holliday's good spirits. He began to contemplate the houseless situation in which he

was placed from the serious rather than the humorous point of view, and
he looked about him for another public house to inquire at with something very like downright anxiety in his mind on the subject of a lodging
for the night.

The suburban part of the town towards which he had now strayed was
hardly lighted at all, and he could see nothing of the houses as he passed
them, except that they got progressively smaller and dirtier the farther he
went. Down the winding road before him shone the dull gleam of an oil
lamp, the one faint lonely light that struggled ineffectually with the foggy
darkness all round him. He resolved to go on as far as this lamp, and
then, if it showed him nothing in the shape of an inn, to return to the
central part of the town, and to try if he could not at least secure a chair
to sit down on through the night at one of the principal hotels.

As he got near the lamp he heard voices, and, walking close under it,
found that it lighted the entrance to a narrow court, on the wall of which
was painted a long hand in a faded flesh color, pointing with a lean
forefinger to this inscription: THE TWO ROBINS.

Arthur turned into the court without hesitation to see what The Two
Robins could do for him. Four or five men were standing together round
the door of the house, which was at the bottom of the court, facing the
entrance from the street. The men were all listening to one other man,
better dressed than the rest, who was telling his audience something, in a
low voice, in which they were apparently very much interested.

On entering the passage, Arthur was passed by a stranger with a knapsack in his hand, who was evidently leaving the house.

"No," said the traveller with the knapsack, turning round and addressing himself cheerfully to a fat, sly-looking bald-headed man, with a dirty
white apron, who had followed him down the passage, "no, Mr. Landlord, I am not easily scared by trifles; but I don't mind confessing that I
can't stand that."

It occurred to young Holliday, the moment he heard these words, that
the stranger had been asked an exorbitant price for a bed at The Two
Robins, and that he was unable or unwilling to pay it. The moment his
back was turned, Arthur, comfortably conscious of his own well-filled
pockets, addressed himself in a great hurry, for fear any other benighted
traveller should slip in and forestall him, to the sly-looking landlord with
the dirty apron and the bald head.

"If you have got a bed to let," he said, "and if that gentleman who has just gone out won't pay your price for it, I will."

The sly landlord looked hard at Arthur.

"Will you, sir?" he asked, in a meditative, doubtful way.

"Name your price," said young Holliday, thinking that the landlord's hesitation sprang from some boorish distrust of him. "Name your price, and I'll give you the money at once, if you like."

"Are you game for five shillings?" inquired the landlord, rubbing his stubby double chin, and looking up thoughtfully at the ceiling above him.

Arthur nearly laughed in the man's face; but, thinking it prudent to control himself, offered the five shillings as seriously as he could. The sly landlord held out his hand, then suddenly drew it back again.

"You're acting all fair and aboveboard by me," he said, "and, before I take your money, I'll do the same by you. Look here, this is how it stands. You can have a bed all for yourself for five shillings, but you can't have more than a half share of the room it stands in. Do you see what I mean, young gentleman?"

"Of course I do," returned Arthur, a little irritably. "You mean that it is a double-bedded room, and that one of the beds is occupied?"

The landlord nodded his head, and rubbed his double chin harder than ever. Arthur hesitated, and mechanically moved back a step or two towards the door. The idea of sleeping in the same room with a total stranger did not present an attractive prospect to him. He felt more than inclined to drop his five shillings into his pocket, and go out into the street once more.

"Is it yes or no?" asked the landlord. "Settle it as quick as you can, because there's lots of people wanting a bed at Doncaster tonight, besides you."

Arthur looked towards the court, and heard the rain falling heavily in the street outside. He thought he would ask a question or two before he rashly decided on leaving the shelter of The Two Robins.

"What sort of a man is it who has got the other bed?" he inquired. "Is he a gentleman? I mean, is he a quiet, well-behaved person?"

"The quietest man I ever came across," said the landlord, rubbing his fat hands stealthily one over the other. "As sober as a judge, and as regular as clock-work in his habits. It hasn't struck nine not ten minutes ago, and he's in his bed already. I don't know whether that comes up to your notion of a quiet man: it does a long way ahead of mine, I can tell you."

"Is he asleep, do you think?" asked Arthur.

"I know he's asleep," returned the landlord; "and what's more, he's gone off so fast that I'll warrant you don't wake him. This way, sir," said the landlord, speaking over young Holliday's shoulder, as if he was addressing some new guest who was approaching the house.

"Here you are," said Arthur, determined to be beforehand with the stranger, whoever he might be. "I'll take the bed." And he handed the five shillings to the landlord, who nodded, dropped the money carelessly into his waistcoat pocket, and lighted a candle.

"Come up and see the room," said the host of the Two Robins, leading the way to the staircase quite briskly, considering how fat he was.

They mounted to the second floor of the house. The landlord half opened a door fronting the landing, then stopped, and turned round to Arthur.

"It's a fair bargain, mind, on my side as well as on yours," he said. "You give me five shillings, and I give you in return a clean, comfortable bed; and I warrant, beforehand, that you won't be interfered with, or annoyed in any way, by the man who sleeps in the room with you." Saying those words, he looked hard, for a moment, in young Holliday's face, and then led the way into the room.

It was larger and cleaner than Arthur had expected it would be. The two beds stood parallel with each other, a space of about six feet intervening between them. They were both of the same medium size, and both had the same plain white curtains, made to draw, if necessary, all round them.

The occupied bed was the bed nearest the window. The curtains were all drawn round it except the half curtain at the bottom, on the side of the bed farthest from the window.

Arthur saw the feet of the sleeping man raising the scanty clothes into a sharp little eminence, as if he was lying flat on his back. He took the candle, and advanced softly to draw the curtain; he stopped half way, and listened for a moment; then he turned to the landlord.

"He is a very quiet sleeper," said Arthur.

"Yes," said the landlord, "very quiet."

Young Holliday advanced with the candle, and looked in at the man cautiously.

"How pale he is," said Arthur.

"Yes," returned the landlord, "pale enough, isn't he?"

Arthur looked closer at the man. The bed-clothes were drawn up to his chin, and they lay perfectly still over the region of his chest. Surprised and vaguely startled as he noticed this, Arthur stooped down closer over the stranger, looked at his ashy, parted lips, listened breathlessly for an instant; looked again at the strangely still face, and the motionless lips and chest, and turned round suddenly on the landlord with his own cheek as pale for the moment as the hollow cheeks of the man on the bed.

"Come here," he whispered, under his breath. "Come, for God's sake! The man's not asleep. He is dead."

"You have found that out sooner than I thought you would," said the landlord, composedly. "Yes, he's dead, sure enough. He died at five o'clock today."

"How did he die? Who is he?" asked Arthur, staggered for the moment by the audacious coolness of the answer.

"As to who is he?" rejoined the landlord, "I know no more about him than you do. There are his books, and letter, and things all sealed up in that brown paper parcel for the coroner's inquest to open tomorrow or next day. He's been here a week, paying his way fairly enough, and stopping indoors, for the most part, as he was ailing. My girl brought him up his tea at five today, and as he was pouring of it out, he fell down in a faint, or a fit, or a compound of both, for anything I know. We couldn't bring him to, and I said he was dead. And the doctor couldn't bring him to, and the doctor said he was dead. And there he is. And the coroner's inquest's coming as soon as it can. And that's as much as I know about it."

Arthur held the candle close to the man's lips. The flame still burned straight up as steadily as ever. There was a moment of silence, and the rain pattered drearily through it against the panes of the window.

"If you haven't got nothing more to say to me," continued the landlord, "I suppose I may go. You don't expect your five shillings back, do you? There's the bed I promised you, clean and comfortable. There's the man I warranted not to disturb you, quiet in this world forever. If you're frightened to stop alone with him, that's not my lookout. I've kept my part of the bargain and I mean to keep the money. I'm not Yorkshire myself, young gentleman, but I've lived long enough in these parts to have my wits sharpened, and I shouldn't wonder if you found out the way to brighten up yours next time you come among us."

With these words the landlord turned towards the door, and laughed to himself softly, in high satisfaction at his own sharpness.

Startled and shocked as he was, Arthur had by this time sufficiently recovered himself to feel indignant at the trick that had been played on him, and at the insolent manner in which the landlord exulted in it.

"Don't laugh," he said, sharply, "till you are sure you have got the laugh against me. You shan't have the five shillings for nothing, my man. I'll keep the bed."

"Will you?" said the landlord. "Then I wish you a good night's rest." With that brief farewell he went out and shut the door after him.

A good night's rest! The words had hardly been spoken, the door had hardly been closed, before Arthur half repented the hasty words that had just escaped him. Though not naturally over-sensitive, and not wanting in courage of the moral as well as the physical sort, the presence of the dead man had an instantaneously chilling effect on his mind when he found himself alone in the room; alone, and bound by his own rash words to stay there till the next morning, an older man would have thought nothing of those words, and would have acted, without reference to them, as his calmer sense suggested. But Arthur was too young to treat the ridicule even of his inferiors with contempt; too young not to fear the momentary humiliation of falsifying his own foolish boast more than he feared the trial of watching out the long night in the same chamber with the dead.

"It's but a few hours," he thought to himself, "and I can get away the first thing in the morning."

He was looking towards the occupied bed as that idea passed through his mind, and the sharp angular eminence made in the clothes by the dead man's upturned feet again caught his eye. He advanced and drew the curtains, purposely abstaining, as he did so, from looking at the face of the corpse, lest he might unnerve himself at the outset by fastening some ghastly impression of it on his mind. He drew the curtain very gently, and sighed involuntarily as he closed it.

"Poor fellow," he said, almost as sadly as if he had known the man. "Ah! poor fellow!"

He went next to the window. The night was black, and he could see nothing from it. The rain still pattered heavily against the glass. He inferred, from hearing it, that the window was at the back of the house, remembering that the front was sheltered from the weather by the court and the buildings over it.

While he was still standing at the window, for even the dreary rain was a relief, because of the sound it made; a relief, also, because it moved, and had some faint suggestion, in consequence, of life and companionship in it; while he was standing at the window, and looking vacantly into the black darkness outside, he heard a distant church clock strike ten. Only ten! How was he to pass the time till the house was astir the next morning?

Under any other circumstances he would have gone down to the public-house parlour, would have called for his grog, and would have laughed and talked with the company, assembled as familiarly as if he had known them all his life. But the very thought of whiling away the time in this manner was now distasteful to him. The new situation in which he was placed seemed to have altered him to himself already. Thus far his life had been the common, trifling, prosaic, surface-life of a prosperous young man, with no troubles to conquer and no trials to face. He had lost no relation whom he loved, no friend whom he treasured. Till this night, what share he had of the immortal inheritance that is divided among us all had lain dormant within him. Till this night, Death and he had not once met, even in thought.

He took a few turns up and down the room, then stopped. The noise made by his boots on the poorly carpeted floor jarred on his ear. He hesitated a little, and ended by taking his boots off, and walking backwards and forwards noiselessly.

All desire to sleep or to rest had left him. The bare thought of lying down on the unoccupied bed instantly drew the picture on his mind of a dreadful mimicry of the position of the dead man. Who was he? What was the story of his past life? Poor he must have been, or he would not have stopped at such a place as the Two Robins Inn; and weakened, probably, by long illness, or he could hardly have died in the manner which the landlord had described. Poor, ill, lonely, dead in a strange place, dead, with nobody but a stranger to pity him. A sad story; truly, on the mere face of it, a very sad story.

While these thoughts were passing through his mind, he had stopped insensibly at the window, close to which stood the foot of the bed with the closed curtains. At first he looked at it absently, then he became conscious that his eyes were fixed on it; and then a perverse desire took possession of him to do the very thing which he had resolved not to do up to this time: to look at the dead man.

He stretched out his hand towards the curtains, but checked himself in the very act of undrawing them, turned his back sharply on the bed, and walked towards the chimney-piece, to see what things were placed on it, and to try if he could keep the dead man out of his mind in that way.

There was a pewter inkstand on the chimney-piece, with some mildewed remains of ink in the bottle. There were two coarse china ornaments of the commonest kind; and there was a square of embossed card, dirty and fly-blown, with a collection of wretched riddles printed on it, in all sorts of zigzag directions, and in variously colored inks. He took the card, and went away to read it at the table on which the candle was placed, sitting down with his back turned to the curtained bed.

He read the first riddle, the second, the third, all in one corner of the card, then turned it round impatiently to look at another. Before he could begin reading the riddles printed here the sound of the church clock stopped him.

Eleven.

He had got through an hour of the time in the room with the dead man.

Once more he looked at the card. It was not easy to make out the letters printed on it in consequence of the dimness of the light which the landlord had left him: a common tallow candle, furnished with a pair of heavy old-fashioned steel snuffers. Up to this time his mind had been too much occupied to think of the light. He had left the wick of the candle unsnuffed till it had risen higher than the flame, and had burned into an odd pent-house shape at the top, from which morsels of the charred cotton fell off from time to time in little flakes. He took up the snuffers now and trimmed the wick. The light brightened directly, and the room became less dismal.

Again he turned to the riddles, reading them doggedly and resolutely, now in one corner of the card, now in another. All his efforts, however, could not fix his attention on them. He pursued his occupation mechanically, deriving no sort of impression from what he was reading. It was as if a shadow from the curtained bed had got between his mind and the gaily-printed letters: a shadow that nothing could dispel. At last, he gave up the struggle, threw the card from him impatiently, and took to walking softly up and down the room again.

The dead man, the dead man, the hidden dead man on the bed!

There was the one persistent idea still haunting him. Hidden! Was it only the body being there, or was it the body being there, concealed, that was preying on his mind? He stopped at the window with that doubt in him, once more listening to the pattering rain, once more looking out into the black darkness.

Still the dead man!

The darkness forced his mind back upon itself, and set his memory at work, reviving with a painfully-vivid distinctness the momentary impression it had received from his first sight of the corpse. Before long the face seemed to be hovering out in the middle of the darkness, confronting him through the window, with the paleness whiter, with the dreadful dull line of light between the imperfectly closed eyelids broader than he had seen it, with the parted lips slowly dropping farther and farther away from each other, with the features growing larger and moving closer, till they seemed to fill the window, and to silence the rain, and to shut out the night.

The sound of a voice shouting below stairs woke him suddenly from the dream of his own distempered fancy. He recognized it as the voice of the landlord.

'Shut up at twelve, Ben,' he heard it say. 'I'm off to bed.'

He wiped away the damp that had gathered on his forehead, reasoned with himself for a little while, and resolved to shake his mind free of the ghastly counterfeit which still clung to it by forcing himself to confront, if it was only for a moment, the solemn reality. Without allowing himself an instant to hesitate, he parted the curtains at the foot of the bed, and looked through.

There was the sad, peaceful, white face, with the awful mystery of stillness on it, laid back upon the pillow. No stir, no change there! He only looked at it for a moment before he closed the curtains again, but that moment steadied him, calmed him, restored him, mind and body, to himself. He returned to his old occupation of walking up and down the room, persevering in it this time till the clock struck again.

Twelve.

As the sound of the clock-bell died away, it was succeeded by the confused noise downstairs of the drinkers in the taproom leaving the house. The next sound, after an interval of silence, was caused by the barring of the door and the closing of the shutters at the back of the inn. Then the silence followed again, and was disturbed no more.

He was alone now: absolutely, hopelessly alone with the dead man till the next morning.

The wick of the candle wanted trimming again. He took up the snuffers, but paused suddenly on the very point of using them, and looking attentively at the candle, then back, over his shoulder, at the curtained bed, then again at the candle. It had been lighted for the first time to show him the way up stairs, and three parts of it, at least, were already consumed. In another hour it would be burned out. In another hour, unless he called at once to the man who had shut up the inn for a fresh candle, he would be left in the dark.

Strongly as his mind had been affected since he had entered the room, his unreasonable dread of encountering ridicule and of exposing his courage to suspicion had not altogether lost its influence over him even yet.

He lingered irresolutely by the table, waiting till he could prevail on himself to open the door, and call from the landing to the man who had shut up the inn. In his present hesitating frame of mind, it was a kind of relief to gain a few moments only by engaging in the trifling occupation of snuffing the candle. His hand trembled a little, and the snuffers were heavy and awkward to use. When he closed them on the wick, he closed them a hair's breadth too low. In an instant the candle was out, and the room was plunged in pitch darkness.

The one impression which the absence of light immediately produced on his mind was distrust of the curtained bed, distrust which shaped itself into no distinct idea, but which was powerful enough, in its very vagueness, to bind him down to his chair, to make his heart beat fast, and to set him listening intently. No sound stirred in the room, but the familiar sound of the rain against the window, louder and sharper now than he had heard it yet.

Still the vague distrust, the inexpressible dread possessed him, and kept him in his chair. He had put his carpet-bag on the table when he first entered the room, and he now took the key from his pocket, reached out his hand softly, opened the bag, and groped in it for his travelling writing-case, in which he knew that there was a small store of matches. When he had got one of the matches, he waited before he struck it on the coarse wooden table, and listened intently again without knowing why. Still there was no sound in the room but the steady, ceaseless rattling sound of the rain.

He lighted the candle again without another moment of delay, and, on the instant of its burning up, the first object in the room that his eyes sought for was the curtained bed.

Just before the light had been put out he had looked in that direction, and had seen no change, no disarrangement of any sort in the folds of the closely-drawn curtains.

When he looked at the bed now, he saw hanging over the side of it a long white hand.

It lay perfectly motionless midway on the side of the bed, where the curtain at the head and the curtain at the foot met. Nothing more was visible. The clinging curtains hid everything but the long white hand.

He stood looking at it, unable to stir, unable to call out, feeling nothing, knowing nothing, every faculty he possessed gathered up and lost in the one seeing faculty. How long that first panic held him he never could tell afterwards. It might have been only for a moment; it might have been for many minutes together. How he got to the bed; whether he ran to it headlong, or whether he approached it slowly: how he wrought himself up to unclose the curtains and look in, he never has remembered, and never will remember to his dying day. It is enough that he did go to the bed, and that he did look inside the curtains.

The man had moved. One of his arms was outside the clothes; his face was turned a little on the pillow; his eyelids were wide open. Changed as to position and as to one of the features, the face was otherwise fearfully and wonderfully unaltered. The dead paleness and the dead quiet were on it still.

One glance showed Arthur this; one glance before he flew breathlessly to the door and alarmed the house.

The man whom the landlord called 'Ben' was the first to appear on the stairs. In three words Arthur told him what had happened, and sent him for the nearest doctor.

I, who tell you this story, was then staying with a medical friend of mine, in practice at Doncaster, taking care of his patients for him during his absence in London; and I, for the time being, was the nearest doctor. They had sent for me from the inn when the stranger was taken ill in the afternoon but I was not at home, and medical assistance was sought for elsewhere. When the man from The Two Robins rang the night-bell, I was just thinking of going to bed. Naturally enough, I did not believe a word of his story about a dead man who had come to life again. However, I put on my hat, armed myself with one or two bottles of restorative medicine, and ran to the inn, expecting to find nothing more remarkable, when I got there, than a patient in a fit.

My surprise at finding that the man had spoken the literal truth was almost, if not quite, equaled by my astonishment at finding myself face to face with Arthur Holliday as soon as I entered the bedroom. It was no time then for giving or seeking explanations. We just shook hands amazedly, and then I ordered everybody but Arthur out of the room, and hurried to the man on the bed.

The kitchen fire had not been long out. There was plenty of hot water in the boiler, and plenty of flannel to be had. With these, with my medicines, and with such help as Arthur could render under my direction, I dragged the man literally out of the jaws of death. In less than an hour from the time when I had been called in, he was alive and talking in the bed on which he had been laid out to wait for the coroner's inquest.

You will naturally ask me what had been the matter with him, and I might treat you, in reply, to a long theory, plentifully sprinkled with what the children call hard words. I prefer telling you that, in this case, cause and effect could not be satisfactorily joined together by any theory whatever. There are mysteries in life and the conditions of it which human science has not fathomed yet; and I candidly confess to you that, in bringing that man back to existence, I was morally speaking, groping haphazard in the dark. I know (from the testimony of the doctor who attended him in the afternoon) that the vital machinery, so far as its action is appreciable by our senses, had, in this case, unquestionably stopped, and I am equally certain (seeing that I recovered him) that the vital principle was not extinct. When I add that he had suffered from a long and complicated illness, and that his whole nervous system was utterly deranged, I have told you all I really know of the condition of my dead-alive patient at The Two Robins Inn.

When he 'came to', as the phrase goes, he was a startling object to look at, with his colorless face, his sunken cheeks, his wild black eyes, and his long black hair. The first question he asked me about himself when he could speak made me suspect that I had been called in to a man in my own profession. I mentioned to him my surmise, and he told me that I was right.

He said he had come last from Paris, where he had been attached to a hospital; that he had lately returned to England, on his way to Edinburgh, to continue his studies; that he had been taken ill on the journey; and that he had stopped to rest and recover himself at Doncaster. He did not add a word about his name, or who he was, and of course I did not question him on the subject. All I inquired when he ceased speaking was what branch of the profession he intended to follow.

"Any branch," he said, bitterly, "which will put bread into the mouth of a poor man."

At this, Arthur, who had been hitherto watching him in silent curiosity, burst out impetuously in his usual good-humored way.

"My dear fellow" (everybody was "my dear fellow" with Arthur), "now you have come to life again, don't begin by being downhearted about your prospects. I'll answer for it I can help you to some capital thing in the medical line, or, if I can't, I know my father can."

The medical student looked at him steadily.

"Thank you," he said, coldly; then added, "May I ask who your father is?"

"He's well enough known all about this part of the country; he is a great manufacturer, and his name is Holliday," replied Arthur.

My hand was on the man's wrist during this brief conversation. The instant the name of Holliday was pronounced I felt the pulse under my fingers flutter, stop, go on suddenly with a bound, and beat afterwards for a minute or two at the fever rate.

"How did you come here?" asked the stranger, quickly, excitably, passionately almost.

Arthur related briefly what had happened from the time of his first taking the bed at the inn.

"I am indebted to Mr. Holliday's son, then, for the help that has saved my life," said the medical student, speaking to himself, with a singular sarcasm in his voice. "Come here!"

He held out, as he spoke, his long, white, bony right hand.

"With all my heart," said Arthur, taking his hand cordially. "I may confess it now," he continued, laughing, "upon my honor, you almost frightened me out of my wits."

The stranger did not seem to listen. His wild black eyes were fixed with a look of eager interest on Arthur's face, and his long bony fingers kept tight hold of Arthur's hand. Young Holliday, on his side, returned the gaze, amazed and puzzled by the medical student's odd language and manners. The two faces were close together; I looked at them, and, to my amazement I was suddenly impressed by the sense of likeness between them: not in features or complexion, but solely in expression. It must have been a strong likeness, or I should certainly not have found it out, for I am naturally slow at detecting resemblances between faces.

"You have saved my life," said the strange man, still looking hard in Arthur's face, still holding tightly by his hand. "If you had been my own brother, you could not have done more for me than that."

He laid a singularly strong emphasis on those three words "my own brother," and a change passed over his face as he pronounced them; a change that no language of mind is competent to describe.

"I hope I have not done being of service to you yet," said Arthur. "I'll speak to my father as soon as I get home."

"You seem to be fond and proud of your father," said the medical student. "I suppose, in return, he is fond and proud of you?"

"Of course, he is," answered Arthur, laughing, "is there anything wonderful in that? Isn't your father fond . . ."

The stranger suddenly dropped Holliday's hand and turned his face away.

"I beg your pardon," said Arthur. "I hope I have not unintentionally pained you. I hope you have not lost your father?"

"I can't well lose what I have never had," retorted the medical student, with a harsh mocking laugh.

"What you have never had!"

The strange man suddenly caught Arthur's hand again, suddenly looked once more hard in his face.

"Yes," he said, with a repetition of the bitter laugh. "You have brought a poor devil back into the world who has no business there. Do I astonish you? Well, I have a fancy of my own for telling you what men in my situation generally keep a secret. I have no name and no father. The merciful law of society tells me I am nobody's son! Ask your father if he will be my father too, and help me on in life with the family name."

Arthur looked at me more puzzled than ever.

I signed to him to say nothing, and laid my fingers again on the man's wrist. No. In spite of the extraordinary speech that he had just made, he was not, as I have been disposed to suspect, beginning to get light-headed. His pulse, by this time, had fallen back to a quiet, slow beat, and his skin was moist and cool. Not a symptom of fever or agitation about him.

Finding that neither of us answered him, he turned to me, and began talking of the extraordinary nature of his case, and asking my advice about the future course of medical treatment to which he ought to subject himself. I said the matter required a careful thinking over, and suggested that I should send him a prescription a little later. He told me to write it at once, as he would most likely be leaving Doncaster in the morning before I was up. It was quite useless to represent to him the folly and danger of such a proceeding as this. He heard me politely and patiently, but held to his resolution, without offering any reason or explanations, and repeated to me that, if I wished to give him a chance of seeing my prescription, I must write it at once.

Hearing this, Arthur volunteered the loan of a travelling writing-case which he said he had with him, and, bringing it to the bed, shook the note-paper out of the pocket of the case forthwith in his usual careless way. With the paper there fell out on the counterpane of the bed a small packet of sticking-plaster, and a little water-color drawing of a landscape.

The medical student took up the drawing and looked at it. His eye fell on some initials neatly written in cipher in one corner. He started and trembled; his pale face grew whiter than ever; his wild black eyes turned on Arthur, and looked through and through him.

"A pretty drawing," he said, in a remarkably quiet voice.

"Ah! and done by such a pretty girl," said Arthur. "Oh, such a pretty girl! I wish it was not a landscape; I wish it was a portrait of her!"

"You admire her very much?"

Arthur, half in jest, half in earnest, kissed his hand for answer.

"Love at first sight," said young Holliday, putting the drawing away again. "But the course of it doesn't run smooth. It's the old story. She's monopolized, as usual; trammelled by a rash engagement to some poor man who is never likely to get money enough to marry her. It was lucky I heard of it in time, or I should certainly have risked a declaration when she gave me that drawing. Here, doctor, here is pen, ink, and paper all ready for you."

"When she gave you that drawing? Gave it? gave it?"

He repeated the words slowly to himself, and suddenly closed his eyes. A momentary distortion passed across his face, and I saw one of his hands clutch up the bedclothes and squeeze them hard. I thought he was going to be ill again, and begged that there might be no more talking. He opened his eyes when I spoke, fixed them once more searchingly on Arthur, and said, slowly and distinctly,

"You like her, and she likes you. The poor man may die out of your way. Who can tell that she may not give you herself as well as her drawing, after all?"

Before young Holliday could answer, he turned to me, and said in a whisper, "Now for the prescription." From that time, though he spoke to Arthur again, he never looked at him more.

When I had written the prescription, he examined it, approved of it, and then astonished us both by abruptly wishing us good night. I offered to sit up with him, and he shook his head, Arthur offered to sit up with him, and he said, shortly, with his face turned away, "No." I insisted on having somebody left to watch him. He gave way when he found I was determined, and said he would accept the services of the waiter at the inn.

"Thank you both," he said, as we rose to go. "I have one last favor to ask: not of you, doctor, for I leave you to exercise your professional discretion, but of Mr. Holliday." His eyes, while he spoke, still rested steadily on me, and never once turned towards Arthur. "I beg that Mr. Holliday will not mention to anyone, least of all his father, the events that have occurred and the words that have passed in this room. I entreat him to bury me in his memory as, but for him, I might have been buried in my grave. I cannot give my reason for making this strange request. I can only implore him to grant it."

His voice faltered for the first time, and he hid his face on the pillow. Arthur, completely bewildered, gave the required pledge. I took young Holliday away with me immediately afterwards to the house of my friend, determined to go back to the inn and to see the medical student again before he had left in the morning.

I returned to the inn at eight o'clock, purposely abstaining from waking Arthur, who was sleeping off the past night's excitement on one of my friend's sofas. A suspicion had occurred to me, as soon as I was alone in my bedroom, which made me resolve that Holliday and the stranger whose life he had saved should not meet again, if I could prevent it.

I have already alluded to certain reports or scandals which I knew of relating to the early life of Arthur's father. While I was thinking, in my bed, of what had passed at the inn; of the change in the student's pulse when he heard the name of Holliday; of the resemblance of expression that I had discovered between his face and Arthur's; of the emphasis he had laid on those three words, "my own brother"; and of his incomprehensible acknowledgement of his own illegitimacy; while I was thinking of these things, the reports I have mentioned suddenly flew into my mind, and linked themselves fast to the chain of my previous reflections. Something within me whispered, "It is best that those two men should not meet again." I felt it before I slept; I felt it when I woke; and I went, as I told you, alone to the inn the next morning.

I had missed my only opportunity of seeing my nameless patient again. He had been gone nearly an hour when I inquired for him.

I have now told you everything that I know for certain in relation to the man whom I brought back to life in the double-bedded room of the inn at Doncaster. What I have next to add is matter of inference and surmise, and is not, strictly speaking, matter of fact.

I have to tell you, first, that the medical student turned out to be strangely and unaccountably right in assuming it as more than probable that Arthur Holliday would marry the young lady who had given him the water-color drawing of the landscape. That marriage took place a little more than a year after the events occurred which I have just been relating.

The young couple came to live in the neighborhood in which I was then established in practice. I was present at the wedding and was rather surprised to find that Arthur was singularly reserved with me, both before and after his marriage, on the subject of the young lady's prior engagement. He only referred to it once when we were alone, merely telling me, on that occasion, that his wife had done all that honor and duty required of her in the matter, and that the engagement had been broken off with the full approval of her parents. I never heard more from him than this. For three years he and his wife lived together happily. At the expiration of that time the symptoms of a serious illness first declared themselves in Mrs. Arthur Holliday. It turned out to be a long, lingering, hopeless malady. I attended her throughout. We had been great friends when she was well, and we became more attached to each other than ever when she was ill. I had many long and interesting conversations with her in the intervals when she suffered least. The result of one of those conversations I may briefly relate, leaving you to draw any inferences from it that you please.

The interview to which I refer occurred shortly before her death.

I called one evening, as usual, and found her alone, with a look in her eyes which told me she had been crying. She only informed me at first that she had been depressed in spirits, but by little and little she became more communicative, and confessed to me that she had been looking over some old letter which had been addressed to her, before she had seen Arthur, by a man to whom she had been engaged to be married. I asked her how the engagement came to be broken. She replied that it had not been broken off, but that it had died out in a very mysterious way. The person to whom she was engaged, her first love, she called him, was very poor and there was no immediate prospect of their being married. He followed my profession, and went abroad to study. They had corresponded regularly until the time when, as she believed, he had returned to England. From that period she heard no more of him. He was of a fretful, sensitive temperament, and she feared that she might have inadvertently done or said something to offend him. However that might be, he had never written to her again, and after waiting a year she had married Arthur. I asked when the first estrangement had begun, and found that the time at which she ceased to hear anything of her first lover exactly corresponded with the time at which I had been called in to my mysterious patient at The Two Robins Inn.

A fortnight after that conversation she died. In course of time Arthur married again. Of late years he has lived principally in London, and I have seen little or nothing of him.

I have some years to pass before I can approach to anything like a conclusion of this fragmentary narrative. And even when that later period is reached, the little that I have to say will not occupy your attention for more than a few minutes.

One rainy evening, while I was still practising as a country doctor, I was sitting alone, thinking over a case then under my charge, which sorely perplexed me, when I heard a low knock at the door of my room.

"Come in," I cried, looking up curiously to see who wanted me.

After a momentary delay, the lock moved, and a long, white, bony hand stole round the door as it opened, gently pushing it over a fold in the carpet which hindered it from working freely on the hinges. The hand was followed by a man whose face instantly struck me with a very strange sensation. There was something familiar to me in the look of him, and yet it was also something that suggested the idea of change.

He quietly introduced himself as Mr. "Lorn", presented to me some excellent professional recommendations, and proposed to fill the place, then vacant, of my assistant. While he was speaking, I noticed it as singular that we did not appear to be meeting each other like strangers, and that, while I was certainly startled at seeing him, he did not appear to be at all startled at seeing me.

It was on the tip of my tongue to say that I thought I had met with him before. But there was something in his face, and something in my own recollections, I can hardly say what, which unaccountably restrained me from speaking, and which as unaccountably attracted me to him at once, and made me feel ready and glad to accept his proposal.

He took his assistant's place on that very day. We got on together as if we had been old friends from the first; but, throughout the whole time of his residence in my house, he never volunteered any confidences on the subject of his past life, and I never approached the forbidden topic except by hints, which he resolutely refused to understand.

I had long had a notion that my patient at the inn might have been a natural son of the elder Mr. Holliday's, and that he might also have been the man who was engaged to Arthur's first wife. And now another idea occurred to me, that Mr. Lorn was the only person in existence who could, if he chose, enlighten me on both those doubtful points. But he never did choose, and I was never enlightened. He remained with me till I removed to London to try my fortune there as a physician for the second time, and then he went his way and I went mine, and we have never seen each other since.

I can add no more. I may have been right in my suspicion, or I may have been wrong. All I know is that, in those days of my country practice, when I came home late, and found my assistant asleep, and woke him, he used to look, in coming to, wonderfully like the stranger at Doncaster as he raised himself in the bed on that memorable night.

A Tradition of Eighteen
Hundred and Four

THOMAS HARDY
(English, 1840–1928)

The widely discussed possibility of an invasion of England through a Channel tunnel has more than once recalled old Solomon Selby's story to my mind.

The occasion on which I numbered myself among his audience was one evening when he was sitting in the yawning chimney-corner of the inn-kitchen, with some others who had gathered there, and I entered for shelter from the rain. Withdrawing the stem of his pipe from the dental notch in which it habitually rested, he leaned back in the recess behind him and smiled into the fire. The smile was neither mirthful nor sad, not precisely humorous nor altogether thoughtful. We who knew him recognized it in a moment: it was his narrative smile. Breaking off our few desultory remarks we drew up closer, and he thus began:—

'My father, as you mid know, was a shepherd all his life, and lived out by the Cove four miles yonder, where I was born and lived likewise, till I moved here shortly afore I was married. The cottage that first knew me stood on the top of the down, near the sea; there was no house within a mile and a half of it; it was built o' purpose for the farm-shepherd, and had no other use. They tell me that it is now pulled down, but that you can see where it stood by the mounds of earth and a few broken bricks that are still lying about. It was a bleak and dreary place in winter-time, but in summer it was well enough, though the garden never came to much, because we could not get up a good shelter for the vegetables and currant bushes; and where there is much wind they don't thrive.

'Of all the years of my growing up the ones that bide clearest in my mind were eighteen hundred and three, four, and five. This was for two reasons: I had just then grown to an age when a child's eyes and ears take in and note down everything about him, and there was more at that date to bear in mind than there ever has been since with me. It was, as I need hardly tell ye, the time after the first peace, when Bonaparte was scheming his descent upon England. He had crossed the great Alp mountains, fought in Egypt, drubbed the Turks, the Austrians, and the Proossians, and now thought he'd have a slap at us. On the other side of the Channel, scarce out of sight and hail of a man standing on our English shore, the French army of a hundred and sixty thousand men and fifteen thousand horses had been brought together from all parts, and were drilling every day. Bonaparte had been three years a-making his preparations; and to ferry these soldiers and cannon and horses across he had contrived a couple of thousand flat-bottomed boats. These boats were small things, but wonderfully built. A good few of 'em were so made as to have a little stable on board each for the two horses that were to haul the cannon carried at the stern. To get in order all these, and other things required, he had assembled there five or six thousand fellows that worked at trades —carpenters, blacksmiths, wheelwrights, saddlers, and what not. O 'twas a curious time!

'Every morning Neighbour Boney would muster his multitude of soldiers on the beach, draw 'em up in line, practise 'em in the manoeuvre of embarking, horses and all, till they could do it without a single hitch. My father drove a flock of ewes up into Sussex that year, and as he went along the drover's track over the high downs thereabout he could see this drilling actually going on—the accoutrements of the rank and file glittering in the sun like silver. It was thought and always said by my uncle Job, sergeant of foot (who used to know all about these matters), that Bonaparte meant to cross with oars on a calm night. The grand query with us was, Where would my gentleman land? Many of the common people thought it would be at Dover; others, who knew how unlikely it was that any skilful general would make a business of landing just where he was expected, said he'd go either east into the River Thames, or west'ard to some convenient place, most likely one of the little bays inside the Isle of Portland, between the Beal and St. Alban's Head—and for choice the three-quarter-round Cove, screened from every mortal eye, that seemed made o' purpose, out by where we lived, and which I've climmed up with two tubs of brandy across my shoulders on scores o' dark nights in my younger days. Some had heard that a part o' the French fleet would sail right round Scotland, and come up the Channel to a suitable haven. However, there was much doubt upon the matter; and no wonder, for after-years proved that Bonaparte himself could hardly make up his mind upon that great and very particular point, where to land. His uncertainty came about in this wise, that he could get no news as to where and how our troops lay in waiting, and that his knowledge of possible places where flat-bottomed boats might be quietly run ashore, and the men they brought marshalled in order, was dim to the last degree. Being flat-bottomed, they didn't require a harbour for unshipping their cargo of men, but a good shelving beach away from sight, and with a fair open road toward London. How the question posed that great Corsican tyrant (as we used to call him), what pains he took to settle it, and, above all, what a risk he ran on one particular night in trying to do so, were known only to one man here and there; and certainly to no maker of newspapers or printer of books, or my account o't would not have had so many heads shaken over it as it has by gentry who only believe what they see in printed lines.

'The flocks my father had charge of fed all about the downs near our house, overlooking the sea and shore each way for miles. In winter and early spring father was up a deal at nights, watching and tending the lambing. Often he'd go to bed early, and turn out at twelve or one; and on the other hand, he'd sometimes stay up till twelve or one, and then turn in to bed. As soon as I was old enough I used to help him, mostly in the way of keeping an eye upon the ewes while he was gone home to rest. This is what I was doing in a particular month in either the year four or five—I can't certainly fix which, but it was long before I was took away from the sheepkeeping to be bound prentice to a trade. Every night at that time I was at the fold, about half a mile, or it may be a little more, from our cottage, and no living thing at all with me but the ewes and young lambs. Afeard? No; I was never afeard of being alone at these times; for I had been reared in such an out-step place that the lack o' human beings at night made me less fearful than the sight of 'em. Directly I saw a man's shape after dark in a lonely place I was frightened out of my senses.

'One day in that month we were surprised by a visit from my uncle Job, the sergeant in the Sixty-first foot, then in camp on the downs above King George's watering-place, several miles to the west yonder. Uncle Job dropped in about dusk, and went up with my father to the fold for an hour or two. Then he came home, had a drop to drink from the tub of sperrits that the smugglers kept us in for housing their liquor when they'd made a run, and for burning 'em off when there was danger. After that he stretched himself out on the settle to sleep. I went to bed: at one o'clock father came home, and waking me to go and take his place, according to custom, went to bed himself. On my way out of the house I passed Uncle Job on the settle. He opened his eyes, and upon my telling him where I was going he said it was a shame that such a youngster as I should go up there all alone; and when he had fastened up his stock and waist-belt he set off along with me, taking a drop from the sperrit-tub in a little flat bottle that stood in the corner-cupboard.

'By and by we drew up to the fold, saw that all was right, and then, to keep ourselves warm, curled up in a heap of straw that lay inside the thatched hurdles we had set up to break the stroke of the wind when there was any. To-night, however, there was none. It was one of those very still nights when, if you stand on the high hills anywhere within two or three miles of the sea, you can hear the rise and fall of the tide along the shore, coming and going every few moments like a sort of great snore of the sleeping world. Over the lower ground there was a bit of a mist, but on the hill where we lay the air was clear, and the moon, then in her last quarter, flung a fairly good light on the grass and scattered straw.

'While we lay there Uncle Job amused me by telling me strange stories of the wars he had served in and the wounds he had got. He had already fought the French in the Low Countries, and hoped to fight 'em again. His stories lasted so long that at last I was hardly sure that I was not a soldier myself, and had seen such service as he told of. The wonders of his tales quite bewildered my mind, till I fell asleep and dreamed of battle, smoke, and flying soldiers, all of a kind with the doings he had been bringing up to me.

'How long my nap lasted I am not prepared to say. But some faint sounds over and above the rustle of the ewes in the straw, the bleat of the lambs, and the tinkle of the sheep-bell brought me to my waking senses.

Uncle Job was still beside me; but he too had fallen asleep. I looked out from the straw, and saw what it was that had aroused me. Two men, in boat-cloaks, cocked hats, and swords, stood by the hurdles about twenty yards off.

'I turned my ear thitherward to catch what they were saying, but though I heard every word o't, not one did I understand. They spoke in a tongue that was not ours—in French, as I afterward found. But if I could not gain the meaning of a word, I was shrewd boy enough to find out a deal of the talkers' business. By the light o' the moon I could see that one of 'em carried a roll of paper in his hand, while every moment he spoke quick to his comrade, and pointed right and left with the other hand to spots along the shore. There was no doubt that he was explaining to the second gentleman the shapes and features of the coast. What happened soon after made this still clearer to me.

'All this time I had not waked Uncle Job, but now I began to be afeard that they might light upon us, because uncle breathed so heavily through's nose. I put my mouth to his ear and whispered, "Uncle Job."

' "What is it, my boy?" he said, just as if he hadn't been asleep at all.

' "Hush!" says I. "Two French generals—"

' "French?" says he.

' "Yes," says I. "Come to see where to land their army!"

'I pointed 'em out; but I could say no more, for the pair were coming at that moment much nearer to where we lay. As soon as they got as near as eight or ten yards, the officer with a roll in his hand stooped down to a slanting hurdle, unfastened his roll upon it, and spread it out. Then suddenly he sprung a dark lantern open on the paper, and showed it to be a map.

' "What be they looking at?" I whispered to Uncle Job.

' "A chart of the Channel," says the sergeant (knowing about such things).

'The other French officer now stooped likewise, and over the map they had a long consultation, as they pointed here and there on the paper, and then hither and thither at places along the shore beneath us. I noticed that the manner of one officer was very respectful toward the other, who seemed much his superior, the second in rank calling him by a sort of title that I did not know the sense of. The head one, on the other hand, was quite familiar with his friend, and more than once clapped him on the shoulder.

'Uncle Job had watched as well as I, but though the map had been in the lantern-light, their faces had always been in shade. But when they rose from stooping over the chart the light flashed upward, and fell smart upon one of 'em's features. No sooner had this happened than Uncle Job gasped, and sank down as if he'd been in a fit.

' "What is it—what is it, Uncle Job?" said I.

' "O good God!" says he, under the straw.

' "What?" says I.

' "Boney!" he groaned out.

' "Who?" says I.

' "Bonaparty," he said. "The Corsican ogre. O that I had got but my new-flinted firelock, that there man should die! But I haven't got my new-flinted firelock, and that there man must live. So lie low, as you value your life!"

'I did lie low, as you mid suppose. But I couldn't help peeping. And then I too, lad as I was, knew that it was the face of Bonaparte. Not know Boney? I should think I did know Boney. I should have known him by half the light o' that lantern. If I had seen a picture of his features once, I had seen it a hundred times. There was his bullet head, his short neck, his round yaller cheeks and chin, his gloomy face, and his great glowing eyes. He took off his hat to blow himself a bit, and there was the forelock in the middle of his forehead, as in all the draughts of him. In moving, his cloak fell a little open, and I could see for a moment his white-fronted jacket and one of his epaulets.

'But none of this lasted long. In a minute he and his general had rolled up the map, shut the lantern, and turned to go down toward the shore.

'Then Uncle Job came to himself a bit. "Slipped across in the night-time to see how to put his men ashore," he said. "The like o' that man's coolness eyes will never again see! Nephew, I must act in this, and immediate, or England's lost!"

'When they were over the brow, we crope out, and went some little way to look after them. Halfway down they were joined by two others, and six or seven minutes brought them to the shore. Then, from behind a rock, a boat came out into the weak moonlight of the Cove, and they jumped in; it put off instantly, and vanished in a few minutes between the two rocks that stand at the mouth of the Cove as we all know. We climmed back to where we had been before, and I could see, a short way out, a larger vessel, though still not very large. The little boat drew up alongside, was made fast at the stern as I suppose, for the largest sailed away, and we saw no more.

'My uncle Job told his officers as soon as he got back to camp; but what they thought of it I never heard—neither did he. Boney's army never came, and a good job for me; for the Cove below my father's house was where he meant to land, as this secret visit showed. We coast-folk should have been cut down one and all, and I should not have sat here to tell this tale.'

We who listened to old Selby that night have been familiar with his simple grave-stone for these ten years past. Thanks to the incredulity of the age his tale has been seldom repeated. But if anything short of the direct testimony of his own eyes could persuade an auditor that Bonaparte had examined these shores for himself with a view to a practicable landing-place, it would have been Solomon Selby's manner of narrating the adventure which befell him on the down.

The Story of a Piebald Horse

W. H. HUDSON
(English, 1841–1922)

This is all about a piebald. People there are like birds that come down in flocks, hop about chattering, gobble up their seed, then fly away, forgetting what they have swallowed. I love not to scatter grain for such as these. With you, friend, it is different. Others may laugh if they like at the old man of many stories, who puts all things into his copper memory. I can laugh, too, knowing that all things are ordered by destiny; otherwise I might sit down and cry.

The things I have seen! There was the piebald that died long ago; I could take you to the very spot where his bones used to lie bleaching in the sun. There is a nettle growing on the spot. I saw it yesterday. What important things are these to remember and talk about! Bones of a dead horse and a nettle; a young bird that falls from its nest in the night and is found dead in the morning: puffballs blown about by the wind: a little lamb left behind by the flock bleating at night amongst the thorns and thistles, where only the fox or wild dog can hear it! Small matters are these, and our lives, what are they? And the people we have known, the men and women who have spoken to us and touched us with warm hands —the bright eyes and red lips! Can we cast these things like dead leaves on the fire? Can we lie down full of heaviness because of them, and sleep and rise in the morning without them? Ah, friend!

Let us to the story of the piebald. There was a cattle-marking at neighbour Sotelo's estancia, and out of a herd of three thousand head we had to part all the yearlings to be branded. After that, dinner and a dance. At sunrise we gathered, about thirty of us; all friends and neighbours to do the work. Only with us came one person nobody knew. He joined us when we were on our way to the cattle; a young man, slender, well-formed, of pleasing countenance and dressed as few could dress in those days. His horse also shone with silver trappings. And what an animal! Many horses have I seen in this life, but never one with such a presence as this young stranger's piebald.

Arrived at the herd, we began to separate the young animals, the men riding in couples through the cattle, so that each calf when singled out could be driven by two horsemen, one on each side, to prevent it from doubling back. I happened to be mounted on a demon with a fiery mouth —there was no making him work, so I had to leave the parters and stand with little to do, watching the yearlings already parted, to keep them from returning to the herd.

Presently neighbour Chapaco rode up to me. He was a good-hearted man, well-spoken, half Indian and half Christian; but he also had another half, and that was devil.

"What! neighbour Lucero, are you riding on a donkey or a goat, that you remain here doing boy's work?"

I began telling him about my horse, but he did not listen; he was looking at the parters.

"Who is that young stranger?" he asked.

"I see him to-day," I replied, "and if I see him again to-morrow then I shall have seen him twice."

"And in what country of which I have never heard did he learn cattle-parting?" said he.

"He rides," I answered, "like one presuming on a good horse. But he is safe, his fellow-worker has all the danger."

"I believe you," said Chapaco. "He charges furiously and hurls the heifer before his comrade, who has all the work to keep it from doubling, and all the danger, for at any moment his horse may go over it and fall. This our young stranger does knowingly, thinking that no one here will resent it. No, Lucero, he is presuming more on his long knife than on his good horse."

Even while we spoke, the two we were watching rode up to us. Chapaco saluted the young man, taking off his hat, and said: "Will you take me for a partner, friend?"

"Yes; why not, friend?" returned the other; and together the two rode back to the herd.

Now I shall watch them, said I to myself, to see what this Indian devil intends doing. Soon they came out of the herd driving a very small animal. Then I knew what was coming. "May your guardian angel be with you to avert a calamity, young stranger!" I exclaimed. Whip and spur those two came towards me like men riding a race and not parting cattle. Chapaco kept close to the calf, so that he had the advantage, for his horse was well trained. At length he got a little ahead, then, quick as lightning, he forced the calf round square before the other. The piebald struck it full in the middle, and fell because it had to fall. But, Saints in Heaven! why did not the rider save himself? Those who were watching saw him throw up his feet to tread his horse's neck and leap away; nevertheless man, horse, and calf came down together. They ploughed the ground for some distance, so great had been their speed, and the man was under. When we picked him up he was senseless, the blood flowing from his mouth. Next morning, when the sun rose and God's light fell on the earth, he expired.

Of course, there was no dancing that night. Some of the people, after eating, went away; others remained sitting about all night, talking in low tones, waiting for the end. A few of us were at his bedside watching his white face and closed eyes. He breathed, and that was all. When the sunlight came over the world he opened his eyes, and Sotelo asked him how he did. He took no notice, but presently his lips began to move, though they seemed to utter no sound. Sotelo bent his ear down to listen. "Where does she live?" he asked. He could not answer—he was dead.

"He seemed to be saying many things," Sotelo told us, "but I understood only this—'Tell her to forgive me . . . I was wrong. She loved him from the first. . . . I was jealous and hated him. . . . Tell Elaria not to grieve—Anacleto will be good to her.' Alas! my friends, where shall I find his relations to deliver this dying message to them?"

The Alcalde came that day and made a list of the dead man's possessions, and bade Sotelo take charge of them till the relations could be found. Then, calling all the people together, he bade each person cut on his whip-handle and on the sheath of his knife the mark branded on the flank of the piebald, which was in shape like a horse-shoe with a cross inside, so that it might be shown to all strangers, and made known through the country until the dead man's relations should hear of it.

When a year had gone by, the Alcalde told Sotelo that, all inquiries having failed, he could now take the piebald and the silver trappings for himself. Sotelo would not listen to this, for he was a devout man and coveted no person's property, dead or alive. The horse and things, however, still remained in his charge.

Three years later I was one afternoon sitting with Sotelo, taking maté, when his herd of dun mares were driven up. They came galloping and neighing to the corral and ahead of them, looking like a wild horse, was the piebald, for no person ever mounted him.

"Never do I look on that horse," I remarked, "without remembering the fatal marking, when its master met his death."

"Now you speak of it," said he, "let me inform you that I am about to try a new plan. That noble piebald and all those silver trappings hanging in my room are always reproaching my conscience. Let us not forget the young stranger we put under ground. I have had many masses said for his soul's repose, but that does not quite satisfy me. Somewhere there is a place where he is not forgotten. Hands there are, perhaps, that gather wild flowers to place them with lighted candles before the image of the Blessed Virgin; eyes there are that weep and watch for his coming. You know how many travellers and cattle-drovers going to Buenos Ayres from the south call for refreshment at the *pulperia.* I intend taking the piebald and trying him every day at the gate there. No person calling will fail to notice the horse, and some day perhaps some traveller will recognise the brand on its flank and will be able to tell us what department and what estancia it comes from."

I did not believe anything would result from this, but said nothing, not wishing to discourage him.

Next morning the piebald was tied up at the gate of the *pulperia,* at the road side, only to be released again when night came, and this was repeated every day for a long time. So fine an animal did not fail to attract the attention of all strangers passing that way, still several weeks went by and nothing was discovered. At length, one evening, just when the sun was setting, there appeared a troop of cattle driven by eight men. It had come a great distance, for the troop was a large one—about nine hundred head—and they moved slowly, like cattle that had been many days on the road. Some of the men came in for refreshments; then the store-keeper noticed that one remained outside leaning on the gate.

"What is the capatas doing that he remains outside?" said one of the men.

"Evidently he has fallen in love with that piebald," said another, "for he cannot take his eyes off it."

At length the capatas, a young man of good presence, came in and sat down on a bench. The others were talking and laughing about the strange things they had all been doing the day before; for they had been many days and nights on the road, only nodding a little in their saddles, and at length becoming delirious from want of sleep, they had begun to act like men that are half-crazed.

"Enough of the delusions of yesterday," said the capatas, who had been silently listening to them, "but tell me, boys, am I in the same condition to-day?"

"Surely not!" they replied. "Thanks to those horned devils being so tried and footsore, we all had some sleep last night."

"Very well then," said he, "now you have finished eating and drinking, go back to the troop, but before you leave look well at that piebald tied at the gate. He that is not a cattle-drover may ask, 'How can my eyes deceive me?' but I know that a crazy brain makes us see many strange things when the drowsy eyes can only be held open with the fingers."

The men did as they were told, and when they had looked well at the piebald, they all shouted out, "He has the brand of the estancia de Silva on his flank, and no counter-brand—claim the horse, capatas, for he is yours." And after that they rode away to the herd.

"My friend," said the capatas to the storekeeper, "will you explain how you came possessed of this piebald horse?"

Then the other told him everything, even the dying words of the young stranger, for he knew all.

The capatas bent down his head, and covering his face shed tears. Then he said, "And you died thus, Torcuato, amongst strangers! From my heart I have forgiven you the wrong you did me. Heaven rest your soul, Torcuato; I cannot forget that we were once brothers. I, friend, am that Anacleto of whom he spoke with his last breath."

Sotelo was then sent for, and when he arrived and the *pulperia* was closed for the night, the capatas told his story, which I will give you in his own words, for I was also present to hear him. This is what he told us:

I was born on the southern frontier. My parents died when I was very small, but Heaven had compassion on me and raised up one to shelter me in my orphanhood. Don Loreto Silva took me to his estancia on the Sarandi, a stream half a day's journey from Tandil, towards the setting sun. He treated me like one of his own children, and I took the name of Silva. He had two other children, Torcuato, who was about the same age as myself, and his daughter, Elaria, who was younger. He was a widower when he took charge of me, and died when I was still a youth. After his death we moved to Tandil, where we had a house close to the little town; for we were all minors, and the property had been left to be equally divided between us when we should be of age. For four years we lived happily together; then when we were of age we preferred to keep the property undivided. I proposed that we should go and live on the estancia, but Torcuato would not consent, liking the place where we were living best. Finally, not being able to persuade him, I resolved to go and attend to the estancia myself. He said that I could please myself and that he should stay where he was with Elaria. It was only when I told Elaria of these things that I knew how much I loved her. She wept and implored me not to leave her.

"Why do you shed tears, Elaria?" I said; "is it because you love me? Know, then, that I also love you with all my heart, and if you will be mine, nothing can ever make us unhappy. Do not think that my absence at the estancia will deprive me of this feeling which has ever been growing up in me."

"I do love you, Anacleto," she replied, "and I have also known of your love for a long time. But there is something in my heart which I cannot impart to you; only I ask you, for the love you bear me, do not leave me, and do not ask me why I say this to you."

After this appeal I could not leave her, nor did I ask her to tell me her secret. Torcuato and I were friendly, but not as we had been before this difference. I had no evil thoughts of him; I loved him and was with him continually; but from the moment I announced to him that I had changed my mind about going to the estancia, and was silent when he demanded the reason, there was a something in him which made it different between us. I could not open my heart to him about Elaria, and sometimes I thought that he also had a secret which he had no intention of sharing with me. This coldness did not, however, distress me very much, so great was the happiness I now experienced, knowing that I possessed Elaria's love. He was much away from the house, being fond of amusements, and he had also begun to gamble. About three months passed in this way, when one morning Torcuato, who was saddling his horse to go out, said, "Will you come with me, to-day, Anacleto?"

"I do not care to go," I answered.

"Look, Anacleto," said he; "once you were always ready to accompany me to a race or dance or cattle-marking. Why have you ceased to care for these things? Are you growing devout before your time, or does my company no longer please you?"

"It is best to tell him everything and done with secrets," said I to myself, and so replied:

"Since you ask me, Torcuato, I will answer you frankly. It is true that I now take less pleasure than formerly in these pastimes; but you have not guessed the reason rightly."

"What then is this reason of which you speak?"

"Since you cannot guess it," I replied, "know that it is love."

"Love for whom?" he asked quickly, and turning very pale.

"Do you need ask? Elaria," I replied.

I had scarcely uttered the name before he turned on me full of rage.

"Elaria!" he exclaimed. "Do you dare tell me of love for Elaria! But you are only a blind fool, and do not know that I am going to marry her myself."

"Are you mad, Torcuato, to talk of marrying your sister?"

"She is no more my sister than you are my brother," he returned. "I," he continued, striking his breast passionately, "am the only child of my father, Loreto Silva. Elaria, whose mother died in giving her birth, was adopted by my parents. And because she is going to be my wife, I am willing that she should have a share of the property; but you, a miserable foundling, why were you lifted up so high? Was it not enough that you were clothed and fed till you came to man's estate? Not a hand's-breadth of the estancia land should be yours by right, and now you presume to speak of love for Elaria."

My blood was on fire with so many insults, but I remembered all the benefits I had received from his father, and did not raise my hand against him. Without more words he left me. I then hastened to Elaria and told her what had passed.

"This," I said, "is the secret you would not impart to me. Why, when you knew these things, was I kept in ignorance?"

"Have pity on me, Anacleto," she replied, crying. "Did I not see that you two were no longer friends and brothers, and this without knowing of each other's love? I dared not open my lips to you or to him. It is always a woman's part to suffer in silence. God intended us to be poor, Anacleto, for we were both born of poor parents, and had this property never come to us, how happy we might have been!"

"Why do you say such things, Elaria? Since we love each other, we cannot be unhappy, rich or poor."

"Is it a little matter," she replied, "that Torcuato must be our bitter enemy? But you do not know everything. Before Torcuato's father died, he said he wished his son to marry me when we came of age. When he spoke about it we were sitting together by his bed."

"And what did you say, Elaria?" I asked, full of concern.

"Torcuato promised to marry me. I only covered my face, and was silent, for I loved you best even then, though I was almost a child, and my heart was filled with grief at his words. After we came here, Torcuato reminded me of his father's words. I answered that I did not wish to marry him, that he was only a brother to me. Then he said that we were young and he could wait until I was of another mind. This is all I have to say; but how shall we three live together any longer? I cannot bear to part from you, and every moment I tremble to think what may happen when you two are together."

"Fear nothing," I said. "To-morrow morning you can go to spend a week at some friend's house in the town; then I will speak to Torcuato, and tell him that since we cannot live in peace together we must separate.

Even if he answers with insults I shall do nothing to grieve you, and if he refuses to listen to me, I shall send some person we both respect to arrange all things between us."

This satisfied her, but as evening approached she grew paler, and I knew she feared Torcuato's return. He did not, however, come back that night. Early next morning she was ready to leave. It was an easy walk to the town, but the dew was heavy on the grass, and I saddled a horse for her to ride. I had just lifted her to the saddle when Torcuato appeared. He came at great speed, and throwing himself off his horse, advanced to us. Elaria trembled and seemed ready to sink upon the earth to hide herself like a partridge that has seen the hawk. I prepared myself for insults and perhaps violence. He never looked at me; he only spoke to her.

"Elaria," he said, "something has happened—something that obliges me to leave this house and neighbourhood at once. Remember when I am away that my father, who cherished you and enriched you with his bounty, and who also cherished and enriched this ingrate, spoke to us from his dying bed and made me promise to marry you. Think what his love was; do not forget that his last wish is sacred, and that Anacleto has acted a base, treacherous part in trying to steal you from me. He was lifted out of the mire to be my brother and equal in everything except this. He has got a third part of my inheritance—let that satisfy him; your own heart, Elaria, will tell you that a marriage with him would be a crime before God and man. Look not for my return to-morrow nor for many days. But if you two begin to laugh at my father's dying wishes, look for me, for then I shall not delay to come back to you, Elaria, and to you, Anacleto. I have spoken."

He then mounted his horse and rode away. Very soon we learned the cause of his sudden departure. He had quarrelled over his cards and in a struggle that followed had stabbed his adversary to the heart. He had fled to escape the penalty. We did not believe that he would remain long absent; for Torcuato was very young, well off, and much liked, and this was, moreover, his first offence against the law. But time went on and he did not return, nor did any message from him reach us, and we at last concluded that he had left the country. Only now after four years have I accidentally discovered his fate through seeing his piebald horse.

After he had been absent over a year, I asked Elaria to become my wife. "We cannot marry till Torcuato returns," she said. "For if we take the property that ought to have been all his, and at the same time disobey his father's dying wish, we shall be doing an evil thing. Let us take care of the property till he returns to receive it all back from us; then, Anacleto, we shall be free to marry."

I consented, for she was more to me than lands and cattle. I put the estancia in order and leaving a trustworthy person in charge of everything I invested my money in fat bullocks to resell in Buenos Ayres, and in this business I have been employed ever since. From the estancia I have taken nothing, and now it must all come back to us—his inheritance and ours. This is a bitter thing and will give Elaria great grief.

Thus ended Anacleto's story, and when he had finished speaking and still seemed greatly troubled in his mind, Sotelo said to him, "Friend, let me advise you what to do. You will now shortly be married to the woman you love and probably some day a son will be born to you. Let him be named Torcuato, and let Torcuato's inheritance be kept for him. And if God gives you no son, remember what was done for you and for the girl you are going to marry, when you were orphans and friendless, and look out for some unhappy child in the same condition, to protect and enrich him as you were enriched."

"You have spoken well," said Anacleto. "I will report your words to Elaria, and whatever she wishes done that will I do."

So ends my story, friend. The cattle-drover left us that night and we saw no more of him. Only before going he gave the piebald and the silver trappings to Sotelo. Six months after his visit, Sotelo also received a letter from him to say that his marriage with Elaria had taken place; and the letter was accompanied with a present of seven cream-coloured horses with black manes and hoofs.

A Lodging for the Night

ROBERT LOUIS STEVENSON
(English, 1850–1894)

It was late in November 1456. The snow fell over Paris with rigorous, relentless persistence; sometimes the wind made a sally and scattered it in flying vortices; sometimes there was a lull, and flake after flake descended out of the black night air, silent, circuitous, interminable. To poor people, looking up under moist eyebrows, it seemed a wonder where it all came from. Master Francis Villon had propounded an alternative that afternoon, at a tavern window: was it only Pagan Jupiter plucking geese upon Olympus, or were the holy angels moulting? He was only a poor Master of Arts, he went on; and as the question somewhat touched upon divinity, he durst not venture to conclude. A silly old priest from Montargis, who was among the company, treated the young rascal to a bottle of wine in honor of the jest and the grimaces with which it was accompanied, and swore on his own white beard that he had been just such another irreverent dog when he was Villon's age.

The air was raw and pointed, but not far below freezing; and the flakes were large, damp, and adhesive. The whole city was sheeted up. An army might have marched from end to end and not a footfall given the alarm. If there were any belated birds in heaven, they saw the island like a large white patch, and the bridges like slim white spars, on the black ground of the river. High up overhead the snow settled among the tracery of the cathedral towers. Many a niche was drifted full; many a statue wore a long white bonnet on its grotesque or sainted head. The gargoyles had been transformed into great false noses, drooping toward the point. The crockets were like upright pillows swollen on one side. In the intervals of the wind there was a dull sound of dripping about the precincts of the church.

The cemetery of St. John had taken its own share of the snow. All the graves were decently covered; tall, white housetops stood around in grave array; worthy burghers were long ago in bed, benightcapped like their domiciles; there was no light in all the neighborhood but a little peep from a lamp that hung swinging in the church choir, and tossed the shadows to and fro in time to its oscillations. The clock was hard on ten when the patrol went by with halberds and a lantern, beating their hands; and they saw nothing suspicious about the cemetery of St. John.

Yet there was a small house, backed up against the cemetery wall, which was still awake, and awake to evil purpose, in that snoring district. There was not much to betray it from without; only a stream of warm vapor from the chimney-top, a patch where the snow melted on the roof, and a few half-obliterated footprints at the door. But within, behind the shuttered windows, Master Francis Villon, the poet, and some of the thievish crew with whom he consorted, were keeping the night alive and passing round the bottle.

A great pile of living embers diffused a strong and ruddy glow from the arched chimney. Before this straddled Dom Nicolas, the Picardy monk, with his skirts picked up and his fat legs bared to the comfortable warmth. His dilated shadow cut the room in half; and the firelight only escaped on either side of his broad person, and in a little pool between his outspread feet. His face had the beery, bruised appearance of the continual drinker's; it was covered with a network of congested veins, purple in ordinary circumstances, but now pale violet, for even with his back to the fire the cold pinched him on the other side. His cowl had half fallen back, and made a strange excrescence on either side of his bull neck. So he straddled, grumbling, and cut the room in half with the shadow of his portly frame.

On the right, Villon and Guy Tabary were huddled together over a scrap of parchment; Villon making a ballade which he was to call the *Ballade of Roast Fish,* and Tabary spluttering admiration at his shoulder. The poet was a rag of a man, dark, little, and lean, with hollow cheeks and thin black locks. He carried his four-and-twenty years with feverish animation. Greed had made folds about his eyes, evil smiles had puckered his mouth. The wolf and pig struggled together in his face. It was an eloquent, sharp, ugly, earthly countenance. His hands were small and prehensile, with fingers knotted like a cord; and they were continually flickering in front of him in violent and expressive pantomime. As for Tabary, a broad, complacent, admiring imbecility breathed from his squash nose and slobbering lips: he had become a thief, just as he might have become the most decent of burgesses, by the imperious chance that rules the lives of human geese and human donkeys.

At the monk's other hand, Montigny and Thevenin Pensete played a game of chance. About the first there clung some flavor of good birth and training, as about a fallen angel; something long, lithe, and courtly in the person; something aquiline and darkling in the face. Thevenin, poor soul, was in great feather: he had done a good stroke of knavery that afternoon in the Faubourg St. Jacques, and all night he had been gaining from Montigny. A flat smile illuminated his face; his bald head shone rosily in a garland of red curls; his little protuberant stomach shook with silent chucklings as he swept in his gains.

"Doubles or quits?" said Thevenin.

Montigny nodded grimly.

"Some may prefer to dine in state," wrote Villon, *"On bread and cheese on silver plate.* Or—or—help me out, Guido!"

Tabary giggled.

"Or parsley on a silver dish," scribbled the poet.

The wind was freshening without; it drove the snow before it, and sometimes raised its voice in a victorious whoop, and made sepulchral grumblings in the chimney. The cold was growing sharper as the night went on. Villon, protruding his lips, imitated the gust with something between a whistle and a groan. It was an eerie, uncomfortable talent of the poet's, much detested by the Picardy monk.

"Can't you hear it rattle in the gibbet?" said Villon. "They are all dancing the devil's jig on nothing, up there. You may dance, my gallants, you'll be none the warmer! Whew, what a gust! Down went somebody just now! A medlar the fewer on the three-legged medlar-tree!—I say, Dom Nicolas, it'll be cold to-night on the St. Denis Road?" he asked.

Dom Nicolas winked both his big eyes, and seemed to choke upon his Adam's apple. Montfaucon, the great grisly Paris gibbet, stood hard by the St. Denis Road, and the pleasantry touched him on the raw. As for Tabary, he laughed immoderately over the medlars; he had never heard anything more light-hearted; and he held his sides and crowed. Villon fetched him a fillip on the nose, which turned his mirth into an attack of coughing.

"Oh, stop that row," said Villon, "and think of rhymes to 'fish.' "

"Doubles or quits," said Montigny doggedly.

"With all my heart," quoth Thevenin.

"Is there any more in that bottle?" asked the monk.

"Open another," said Villon. "How do you ever hope to fill that big hogshead, your body, with little things like bottles? And how do you expect to get to heaven? How many angels, do you fancy, can be spared to carry up a single monk from Picardy? Or do you think yourself another Elias—and they'll send the coach for you?"

"Hominibus impossibile," replied the monk, as he filled his glass.

Tabary was in ecstasies.

Villon filliped his nose again.

"Laugh at my jokes, if you like," he said.

"It was very good," objected Tabary.

Villon made a face at him. "Think of rhymes to 'fish,' " he said. "What have you to do with Latin? You'll wish you knew none of it at the great assizes, when the devil calls for Guido Tabary, clericus—the devil with the humpback and red-hot finger-nails. Talking of the devil," he added, in a whisper, "look at Montigny!"

All three peered covertly at the gamester. He did not seem to be enjoying his luck. His mouth was a little to a side; one nostril nearly shut, and the other much inflated. The black dog was on his back, as people say, in terrifying nursery metaphor; and he breathed hard under the gruesome burden.

"He looks as if he could knife him," whispered Tabary, with round eyes.

The monk shuddered, and turned his face and spread his open hands to the red embers. It was the cold that thus affected Dom Nicolas, and not any excess of moral sensibility.

"Come now," said Villon—"about this ballade. How does it run so far?" And beating time with his hand, he read it aloud to Tabary.

They were interrupted at the fourth rhyme by a brief and fatal movement among the gamesters. The round was completed, and Thevenin was just opening his mouth to claim another victory, when Montigny leaped up, swift as an adder, and stabbed him to the heart. The blow took effect before he had time to utter a cry, before he had time to move. A tremor or two convulsed his frame; his hands opened and shut, his heels rattled on the floor; then his head rolled backward over one shoulder with the eyes open, and Thevenin Pensete's spirit had returned to Him who made it.

Every one sprang to his feet; but the business was over in two twos. The four living fellows looked at each other in rather a ghastly fashion; the dead man contemplating a corner of the roof with a singular and ugly leer.

"My God!" said Tabary, and he began to pray in Latin.

Villon broke out into hysterical laughter. He came a step forward and ducked a ridiculous bow at Thevenin, and laughed still louder. Then he sat down suddenly, all of a heap, upon a stool, and continued laughing bitterly as though he would shake himself to pieces.

Montigny recovered his composure first.

"Let's see what he has about him," he remarked; and he picked the dead man's pockets with a practised hand, and divided the money into four equal portions on the table. "There's for you," he said.

The monk received his share with a deep sigh, and a single stealthy glance at the dead Thevenin, who was beginning to sink into himself and topple sideways off the chair.

"We're all in for it," cried Villon, swallowing his mirth. "It's a hanging job for every man jack of us that's here—not to speak of those who aren't." He made a shocking gesture in the air with his raised right hand, and put out his tongue and threw his head on one side, so as to counterfeit the appearance of one who has been hanged. Then he pocketed his share of the spoil, and executed a shuffle with his feet as if to restore the circulation.

Tabary was the last to help himself; he made a dash at the money, and retired to the other end of the apartment.

Montigny stuck Thevenin upright in the chair, and drew out the dagger, which was followed by a jet of blood.

"You fellows had better be moving," he said, as he wiped the blade on his victim's doublet.

"I think we had," returned Villon with a gulp. "Damn his fat head!" he broke out. "It sticks in my throat like phlegm. What right has a man to have red hair when he is dead?" And he fell all of a heap again upon the stool, and fairly covered his face with his hands.

Montigny and Dom Nicolas laughed aloud, even Tabary feebly chiming in.

"Cry baby," said the monk.

"I always said he was a woman," added Montigny with a sneer. "Sit up, can't you?" he went on, giving another shake to the murdered body. "Tread out that fire, Nick."

But Nick was better employed; he was quietly taking Villon's purse, as the poet sat, limp and trembling, on the stool where he had been making a ballade not three minutes before. Montigny and Tabary dumbly demanded a share of the booty, which the monk silently promised as he passed the little bag into the bosom of his gown. In many ways an artistic nature unfits a man for practical existence.

No sooner had the theft been accomplished than Villon shook himself, jumped to his feet, and began helping to scatter and extinguish the embers. Meanwhile Montigny opened the door and cautiously peered into the street. The coast was clear; there was no meddlesome patrol in sight. Still it was judged wiser to slip out severally; and as Villon was himself in a hurry to escape from the neighborhood of the dead Thevenin, and the rest were in a still greater hurry to get rid of him before he should discover the loss of his money, he was the first by general consent to issue forth into the street.

The wind had triumphed and swept all the clouds from heaven. Only a few vapors, as thin as moonlight, fleeted rapidly across the stars. It was bitter cold; and by a common optical effect, things seemed almost more definite than in the broadest daylight. The sleeping city was absolutely still: a company of white hoods, a field full of little Alps, below the twinkling stars. Villon cursed his fortune. Would it were still snowing! Now, wherever he went he left an indelible trail behind him on the glittering streets; wherever he went he was still tethered to the house by the cemetery of St. John; wherever he went he must weave, with his own plodding feet, the rope that bound him to the crime and would bind him to the gallows. The leer of the dead man came back to him with a new significance. He snapped his fingers as if to pluck up his own spirits, and choosing a street at random, stepped boldly forward in the snow.

Two things preoccupied him as he went: the aspect of the gallows at Montfaucon in this bright windy phase of the night's existence, for one; and for another, the look of the dead man with his bald head and garland of red curls. Both struck cold upon his heart, and he kept quickening his pace as if he could escape from unpleasant thoughts by mere fleetness of foot. Sometimes he looked back over his shoulder with a sudden nervous jerk; but he was the only moving thing in the white streets, except when the wind swooped round a corner and threw up the snow, which was beginning to freeze, in spouts of glittering dust.

Suddenly he saw, a long way before him, a black clump and a couple of lanterns. The clump was in motion, and the lanterns swung as though carried by men walking. It was a patrol. And though it was merely crossing his line of march, he judged it wiser to get out of eyeshot as speedily as he could. He was not in the humor to be challenged, and he was conscious of making a very conspicuous mark upon the snow. Just on his left hand there stood a great hotel, with some turrets and a large porch before the door; it was half-ruinous, he remembered, and had long stood empty; and so he made three steps of it and jumped inside the shelter of the porch. It was pretty dark inside, after the glimmer of the snowy streets, and he was groping forward with outspread hands, when he stumbled over some substance which offered an indescribable mixture of resistances, hard and soft, firm and loose. His heart gave a leap, and he sprang two steps back and stared dreadfully at the obstacle. Then he gave a little laugh of relief. It was only a woman, and she dead. He knelt beside her to make sure upon this latter point. She was freezing cold, and rigid like a stick. A little ragged finery fluttered in the wind about her hair, and her cheeks had been heavily rouged that same afternoon. Her pockets were quite empty; but in her stocking, underneath the garter, Villon found two of the small coins that went by the name of whites. It was little enough; but it was always something; and the poet was moved with a deep sense of pathos that she should have died before she had spent her money. That seemed to him a dark and pitiable mystery; and he looked from the coins in his hand to the dead woman, and back again to the coins, shaking his head over the riddle of man's life. Henry V. of England, dying at Vincennes just after he had conquered France, and this poor jade cut off by a cold draught in a great man's doorway, before she had time to spend her couple of whites—it seemed a cruel way to carry on the world. Two whites would have taken such a little while to squander; and yet it would have been one more good taste in the mouth, one more smack of the lips, before the devil got the soul, and the body was left to birds and vermin. He would like to use all his tallow before the light was blown out and the lantern broken.

While these thoughts were passing through his mind, he was feeling, half-mechanically, for his purse. Suddenly his heart stopped beating; a feeling of cold scales passed up the back of his legs, and a cold blow seemed to fall upon his scalp. He stood petrified for a moment; then he felt again with one feverish movement; and then his loss burst upon him, and he was covered with perspiration. To spendthrifts money is so living and actual—it is such a thin veil between them and their pleasures! There is only one limit to their fortune—that of time; and a spendthrift with only a few crowns is the Emperor of Rome until they are spent. For such a person to lose his money is to suffer the most shocking reverse, and fall from heaven to hell, from all to nothing, in a breath. And all the more if he has put his head in the halter for it; if he may be hanged to-morrow for that same purse, so dearly earned, so foolishly departed. Villon stood and cursed; he threw the two whites into the street; he shook his fist at heaven; he stamped, and was not horrified to find himself trampling the poor corpse. Then he began rapidly to retrace his steps toward the house beside the cemetery. He had forgotten all fear of the patrol, which was long gone by at any rate, and had no idea but that of his lost purse. It was in vain that he looked right and left upon the snow; nothing was to be seen. He had not dropped it in the streets. Had it fallen in the house? He would have liked dearly to go in and see; but the idea of the grisly occupant unmanned him. And he saw besides, as he drew near, that their efforts to put out the fire had been unsuccessful; on the contrary, it had broken into a blaze, and a changeful light played in the chinks of the door and window, and revived his terror for the authorities and Paris gibbet.

He returned to the hotel with the porch, and groped about upon the snow for the money he had thrown away in his childish passion. But he could only find one white; the other had probably struck sideways and sunk deeply in. With a single white in his pocket, all his projects for a rousing night in some wild tavern vanished utterly away. And it was not only pleasure that fled laughing from his grasp; positive discomfort, positive pain, attacked him as he stood ruefully before the porch. His perspiration had dried upon him; and though the wind had now fallen, a binding frost was setting in stronger with every hour, and he felt benumbed and sick at heart. What was to be done? Late as was the hour, improbable as was success, he would try the house of his adopted father, the chaplain of St. Benoît.

He ran there all the way, and knocked timidly. There was no answer. He knocked again and again, taking heart with every stroke; and at last steps were heard approaching from within. A barred wicket fell open in the iron-studded door, and emitted a gush of yellow light.

"Hold up your face to the wicket," said the chaplain from within.

"It's only me," whimpered Villon.

"Oh, it's only you, is it?" returned the chaplain; and he cursed him with foul unpriestly oaths for disturbing him at such an hour, and bade him be off to hell, where he came from.

"My hands are blue to the wrists," pleaded Villon; "my feet are dead and full of twinges; my nose aches with the sharp air; the cold lies at my heart. I may be dead before morning. Only this once, father, and before God I will never ask again."

"You should have come earlier," said the ecclesiastic, coolly. "Young men require a lesson now and then." He shut the wicket and retired deliberately into the interior of the house.

Villon was beside himself; he beat upon the door with his hands and feet, and shouted hoarsely after the chaplain.

"Wormy old fox," he cried. "If I had my hand under your twist, I would send you flying headlong into the bottomless pit."

A door shut in the interior, faintly audible to the poet down long passages. He passed his hand over his mouth with an oath. And then the humor of the situation struck him, and he laughed and looked lightly up to heaven, where the stars seemed to be winking over his discomfiture.

What was to be done? It looked very like a night in the frosty streets. The idea of the dead woman popped into his imagination, and gave him a hearty fright; what had happened to her in the early night might very well happen to him before morning. And he so young! and with such immense possibilities of disorderly amusement before him! He felt quite pathetic over the notion of his own fate, as if it had been some one else's, and made a little imaginative vignette of the scene in the morning when they should find his body.

He passed all his chances under review, turning the white between his thumb and forefinger. Unfortunately he was on bad terms with some old friends who would once have taken pity on him in such a plight. He had lampooned them in verses, he had beaten and cheated them; and yet now, when he was in so close a pinch, he thought there was at least one who might perhaps relent. It was a chance. It was worth trying at least, and he would go and see.

On the way, two little accidents happened to him which colored his musings in a very different manner. For, first, he fell in with the track of a patrol, and walked in it for some yards, although it lay out of his direction. And this spirited him up; at least he had confused his trail; for he was still possessed with the idea of people tracking him all about Paris over the snow, and collaring him next morning before he was awake. The other matter affected him very differently. He passed a street corner, where, not so long before, a woman and her child had been devoured by wolves. This was just the kind of weather, he reflected, when wolves might take it into their heads to enter Paris again; and a lone man in these deserted streets would run the chance of something worse than a mere scare. He stopped and looked upon the place with unpleasant interest—it was a centre where several lanes intersected each other; and he looked down them all one after another, and held his breath to listen, lest he should detect some galloping black things on the snow or hear the sound of howling between him and the river. He remembered his mother telling him the story and pointing out the spot, while he was yet a child. His mother! If he only knew where she lived, he might make sure at least of shelter. He determined he would inquire upon the morrow: nay, he would go and see her, too, poor old girl! So thinking, he arrived at his destination—his last hope for the night.

The house was quite dark, like its neighbors, and yet after a few taps, he heard a movement overhead, a door opening, and a cautious voice asking who was there. The poet named himself in a loud whisper, and waited, not without some trepidation, the result. Nor had he to wait long. A window was suddenly opened, and a pailful of slops splashed down upon the doorstep. Villon had not been unprepared for something of the sort, and had put himself as much in shelter as the nature of the porch admitted; but for all that, he was deplorably drenched below the waist. His hose began to freeze almost at once. Death from cold and exposure stared him in the face; he remembered he was of phthisical tendency, and began coughing tentatively. But the gravity of the danger steadied his nerves. He stopped a few hundred yards from the door where he had been so rudely used, and reflected with his finger to his nose. He could only see one way of getting a lodging, and that was to take it. He had noticed a house not far away which looked as if it might be easily broken into, and thither he betook himself promptly, entertaining himself on the way with the idea of a room still hot, with a table still loaded with the remains of supper, where he might pass the rest of the black hours, and whence he should issue, on the morrow, with an armful of valuable plate. He even considered on what viands and what wines he should prefer; and as he was calling the roll of his favorite dainties, roast fish presented itself to his mind with an odd mixture of amusement and horror.

"I shall never finish that ballade," he thought to himself; and then, with another shudder at the recollection, "Oh, damn his fat head!" he repeated fervently, and spat upon the snow.

The house in question looked dark at first sight; but as Villon made a preliminary inspection in search of the handiest point of attack, a little twinkle of light caught his eye from behind a curtained window.

"The devil!" he thought. "People awake! Some student or some saint, confound the crew! Can't they get drunk and lie in bed snoring like their neighbors! What's the good of curfew, and poor devils of bell-ringers jumping at a rope's-end in bell-towers? What's the use of day, if people sit up all night? The gripes to them!" He grinned as he saw where his logic was leading him. "Every man to his business, after all," added he, "and if they're awake, by the Lord, I may come by a supper honestly for this once, and cheat the devil."

He went boldly to the door, and knocked with an assured hand. On both previous occasions he had knocked timidly and with some dread of attracting notice; but now, when he had just discarded the thought of a burglarious entry, knocking at a door seemed a mighty simple and innocent proceeding. The sound of his blows echoed through the house with thin, phantasmal reverberations, as though it were quite empty; but these had scarcely died away before a measured tread drew near, a couple of bolts were withdrawn, and one wing was opened broadly, as though no guile or fear of guile were known to those within. A tall figure of a man, muscular and spare, but a little bent, confronted Villon. The head was massive in bulk, but finely sculptured; the nose blunt at the bottom but refining upward to where it joined a pair of strong and honest eyebrows; the mouth and eyes surrounded with delicate markings, and the whole face based upon a thick white beard, boldly and squarely trimmed. Seen as it was by the light of a flickering hand-lamp, it looked perhaps nobler than it had a right to do; but it was a fine face, honorable rather than intelligent, strong, simple, and righteous.

"You knock late, sir," said the old man in resonant, courteous tones.

Villon cringed, and brought up many servile words of apology; at a crisis of this sort, the beggar was uppermost in him, and the man of genius hid his head with confusion.

"You are cold," repeated the old man, "and hungry? Well, step in." And he ordered him into the house with a noble enough gesture.

"Some great seigneur," thought Villon, as his host, setting down the lamp on the flagged pavement of the entry, shot the bolts once more into their places.

"You will pardon me if I go in front," he said, when this was done; and he preceded the poet up-stairs into a large apartment, warmed with a pan of charcoal and lit by a great lamp hanging from the roof. It was very bare of furniture; only some gold plate on a sideboard; some folios; and a stand of armor between the windows. Some smart tapestry hung upon the walls, representing the crucifixion of our Lord in one piece, and in another a scene of shepherds and shepherdesses by a running stream. Over the chimney was a shield of arms.

"Will you seat yourself," said the old man, "and forgive me if I leave you? I am alone in my house to-night, and if you are to eat I must forage for you myself."

No sooner was his host gone than Villon leaped from the chair on which he just seated himself, and began examining the room, with the stealth and passion of a cat. He weighed the gold flagons in his hand, opened all the folios, and investigated the arms upon the shield, and the stuff with which the seats were lined. He raised the window-curtains, and saw that the windows were set with rich stained glass in figures, so far as he could see, of martial import. Then he stood in the middle of the room, drew a long breath, and retaining it with puffed cheeks, looked round and round him, turning on his heels, as if to impress every feature of the apartment on his memory.

"Seven pieces of plate," he said. "If there had been ten I would have risked it. A fine house, and a fine old master, so help me all the saints."

And just then, hearing the old man's tread returning along the corridor, he stole back to his chair, and began toasting his wet legs before the charcoal pan.

His entertainer had a plate of meat in one hand and a jug of wine in the other. He set down the plate upon the table, motioning Villon to draw in his chair, and going to the sideboard, brought back two goblets, which he filled.

"I drink to your better fortune," he said, gravely touching Villon's cup with his own.

"To our better acquaintance," said the poet, growing bold. A mere man of the people would have been awed by the courtesy of the old seigneur, but Villon was hardened in that matter; he had made mirth for great lords before now, and found them as black rascals as himself. And so he devoted himself to the viands with a ravenous gusto, while the old man, leaning backward, watched him with steady, curious eyes.

"You have blood on your shoulder, my man," he said.

Montigny must have laid his wet right hand upon him as he left the house. He cursed Montigny in his heart.

"It was none of my shedding," he stammered.

"I had not supposed so," returned his host quietly. "A brawl?"

"Well, something of that sort," Villon admitted with a quaver.

"Perhaps a fellow murdered?"

"Oh, no, not murdered," said the poet, more and more confused. "It was all fair play—murdered by accident. I had no hand in it, God strike me dead!" he added fervently.

"One rogue the fewer, I dare say," observed the master of the house.

"You may dare to say that," agreed Villon, infinitely relieved. "As big a rogue as there is between here and Jerusalem. He turned up his toes like a lamb. But it was a nasty thing to look at. I dare say you've seen dead men in your time, my lord?" he added, glancing at the armor.

"Many," said the old man. "I have followed the wars, as you imagine."

Villon laid down his knife and fork, which he had just taken up again.

"Were any of them bald?" he asked.

"Oh, yes, and with hair as white as mine."

"I don't think I would mind the white so much," said Villon. "His was red." And he had a return of his shuddering and tendency to laughter, which he drowned with a great draught of wine. "I'm a little put out when I think of it," he went on. "I knew him—damn him! And the cold gives a man fancies—or the fancies give a man cold, I don't know which."

"Have you any money?" asked the old man.

"I have one white," returned the poet, laughing. "I got it out of a dead jade's stocking in a porch. She was as dead as Caesar, poor wench, and as cold as a church, with bits of ribbon sticking in her hair. This is a hard world in winter for wolves and wenches and poor rogues like me."

"I," said the old man, "am Enguerrand de la Feuillée, seigneur se Brisetout, bailly du Patatrac. Who and what may you be?"

Villon rose and made a suitable reverence. "I am called Francis Villon," he said, "a poor Master of Arts of this university. I know some Latin, and a deal of vice. I can make chansons, ballades, lais, virelais, and roundels, and I am very fond of wine. I was born in a garret, and I shall not improbably die upon the gallows. I may add, my lord, that from this night forward I am your lordship's very obsequious servant to command."

"No servant of mine," said the knight; "my guest for this evening, and no more."

"A very grateful guest," said Villon, politely; and he drank in dumb show to his entertainer.

"You are shrewd," began the old man, tapping his forehead, "very shrewd; you have learning; you are a clerk; and yet you take a small piece of money off a dead woman in the street. Is it not a kind of theft?"

"It is a kind of theft much practised in the wars, my lord."

"The wars are the field of honor," returned the old man proudly. "There a man plays his life upon the cast; he fights in the name of his lord the king, his Lord God, and all their lordships the holy saints and angels."

"Put it," said Villon, "that I were really a thief, should I not play my life also, and against heavier odds?"

"For gain, and not for honor."

"Gain?" repeated Villon with a shrug. "Gain! The poor fellow wants supper, and takes it. So does the soldier in a campaign. Why, what are all these requisitions we hear so much about? If they are not gain to those who take them, they are loss enough to the others. The men-at-arms drink by a good fire, while the burgher bites his nails to buy them wine and wood. I have seen a good many ploughmen swinging on trees about the country; ay, I have seen thirty on one elm, and a very poor figure they made; and when I asked some one how all these came to be hanged, I was told it was because they could not scrape together enough crowns to satisfy the men-at-arms."

"These things are a necessity of war, which the low-born must endure with constancy. It is true that some captains drive overhard; there are spirits in every rank not easily moved by pity; and, indeed, many follow arms who are no better than brigands."

"You see," said the poet, "you cannot separate the soldier from the brigand; and what is a thief but an isolated brigand with circumspect manners? I steal a couple of mutton chops, without so much as disturbing the farmer's sheep; the farmer grumbles a bit, but sups none the less wholesomely on what remains. You come up blowing gloriously on a trumpet, take away the whole sheep, and beat the farmer pitifully into the bargain. I have no trumpet; I am only Tom, Dick, or Harry; I am a rogue and a dog, and hanging's too good for me—with all my heart—but just you ask the farmer which of us he prefers, just find out which of us he lies awake to curse on cold nights."

"Look at us two," said his lordship. "I am old, strong, and honored. If I were turned from my house to-morrow, hundreds would be proud to shelter me. Poor people would go out and pass the night in the streets with their children, if I merely hinted that I wished to be alone. And I find you up, wandering homeless, and picking farthings off dead women by the wayside! I fear no man and nothing; I have seen you tremble and lose countenance at a word. I wait God's summons contentedly in my own house, or, if it please the king to call me out again, upon the field of battle. You look for the gallows; a rough, swift death, without hope or honor. Is there no difference between these two?"

"As far as to the moon," Villon acquiesced. "But if I had been born lord of Brisetout, and you had been the poor scholar Francis, would the difference have been any the less? Should not I have been warming my knees at this charcoal pan, and would not you have been groping for farthings in the snow? Should not I have been the soldier, and you the thief?"

"A thief!" cried the old man. "I a thief! If you understood your words, you would repent them."

Villon turned out his hands with a gesture of inimitable impudence. "If your lordship had done me the honor to follow my argument!" he said.

"I do you too much honor in submitting to your presence," said the knight. "Learn to curb your tongue when you speak with old and honorable men, or some one hastier than I may reprove you in a sharper fashion." And he rose and paced the lower end of the apartment, struggling with anger and antipathy. Villon surreptitiously refilled his cup, and settled himself more comfortably in the chair, crossing his knees and leaning his head upon one hand and the elbow against the back of the chair. He was now replete and warm; and he was in nowise frightened for his host, having gauged him as justly as was possible between two such different characters. The night was far spent, and in a very comfortable fashion after all; and he felt morally certain of a safe departure on the morrow.

"Tell me one thing," said the old man, pausing in his walk. "Are you really a thief?"

"I claim the sacred rights of hospitality," returned the poet. "My lord, I am."

"You are very young," the knight continued.

"I should never have been so old," replied Villon, showing his fingers, "if I had not helped myself with these ten talents. They have been my nursing mothers and my nursing fathers."

"You may still repent and change."

"I repent daily," said the poet. "There are few people more given to repentance than poor Francis. As for change, let somebody change my circumstances. A man must continue to eat, if it were only that he may continue to repent."

"The change must begin in the heart," returned the old man solemnly.

"My dear lord," answered Villon, "do you really fancy that I steal for pleasure? I hate stealing, like any other piece of work or danger. My teeth chatter when I see a gallows. But I must eat, I must drink, I must mix in society of some sort. What the devil! Man is not a solitary animal—*Cui Deus foeminam tradit.* Make me king's pantler—make me abbot of St. Denis; make me bailly of the Patatrac; and then I shall be changed indeed. But as long as you leave me the poor scholar Francis Villon, without a farthing, why, of course, I remain the same."

"The grace of God is all-powerful."

"I should be a heretic to question it," said Francis. "It has made you lord of Brisetout, and bailly of the Patatrac; it has given me nothing but the quick wits under my hat and these ten toes upon my hands. May I help myself to wine? I thank you respectfully. By God's grace, you have a very superior vintage."

The lord of Brisetout walked to and fro with his hands behind his back. Perhaps he was not yet quite settled in his mind about the parallel between thieves and soldiers; perhaps Villon had interested him by some cross-thread of sympathy; perhaps his wits were simply muddled by so much unfamiliar reasoning; but whatever the cause, he somehow yearned to convert the young man to a better way of thinking, and could not make up his mind to drive him forth again into the street.

"There is something more than I can understand in this," he said, at length. "Your mouth is full of subtleties, and the devil has led you very far astray; but the devil is only a very weak spirit before God's truth, and all his subtleties vanish at a word of true honor, like darkness at morning. Listen to me once more. I learned long ago that a gentleman should live chivalrously and lovingly to God, and the king, and his lady; and though I have seen many strange things done, I have still striven to command my ways upon that rule. It is not only written in all noble histories, but in every man's heart, if he will take care to read. You speak of food and wine, and I know very well that hunger is a difficult trial to endure; but you do not speak of other wants; you say nothing of honor, of faith to God and other men, of courtesy, of love without reproach. It may be that I am not very wise—and yet I think I am—but you seem to me like one who has lost his way and made a great error in life. You are attending to the little wants, and you have totally forgotten the great and only real ones, like a man who should be doctoring a toothache on the Judgment Day. For such things as honor and love and faith are not only nobler than food and drink, but, indeed, I think that we desire them more, and suffer more sharply for their absence. I speak to you as I think you will most easily understand me. Are you not, while careful to fill your belly, disregarding another appetite in your heart, which spoils the pleasure of your life and keeps you continually wretched?"

Villon was sensibly nettled under all this sermonizing. "You think I have no sense of honor!" he cried. "I'm poor enough, God knows! It's hard to see rich people with their gloves, and you blowing your hands. An empty belly is a bitter thing, although you speak so lightly of it. If you had had as many as I, perhaps you would change your tune. Anyway, I'm a thief—make the most of that—but I'm not a devil from hell, God strike me dead. I would have you to know I've an honor of my own, as good as yours, though I don't prate about it all day long, as if it were a God's miracle to have any. It seems quite natural to me; I keep it in its box till it's wanted. Why now, look you here, how long have I been in this room with you? Did you not tell me you were alone in the house? Look at your gold plate! You're strong, if you like, but you're old and unarmed, and I have my knife. What did I want but a jerk of the elbow, and here would have been you with the cold steel in your bowels, and there would have been me, linking in the streets, with an armful of gold cups! Did you suppose I hadn't wit enough to see that? And I scorned the action. There are your damned goblets, as safe as in a church; there are you, with your heart ticking as good as new; and here am I, ready to go out again as poor as I came in, with my one white that you threw in my teeth! And you think I have no sense of honor—God strike me dead!"

The old man stretched out his right arm. "I will tell you what you are," he said. "You are a rogue, my man, an impudent and a black-hearted rogue and vagabond. I have passed an hour with you. Oh! believe me, I feel myself disgraced! And you have eaten and drank at my table. But now I am sick at your presence; the day has come, and the night-bird should be off to his roost. Will you go before, or after?"

"Which you please," returned the poet, rising. "I believe you to be strictly honorable." He thoughtfully emptied his cup. "I wish I could add you were intelligent," he went on, knocking on his head with his knuckles. "Age, age! the brains stiff and rheumatic."

The old man preceded him from a point of self-respect; Villon followed, whistling, with his thumbs in his girdle.

"God pity you," said the lord of Brisetout at the door.

"Good-bye, papa," returned Villon, with a yawn. "Many thanks for the cold mutton."

The door closed behind him. The dawn was breaking over the white roofs. A chill, uncomfortable morning ushered in the day. Villon stood and heartily stretched himself in the middle of the road.

"A very dull old gentleman," he thought. "I wonder what his goblets may be worth."

The Birthday of the Infanta

OSCAR WILDE
(Irish, 1854–1900)

It was the birthday of the Infanta. She was just twelve years of age, and the sun was shining brightly in the gardens of the palace.

Although she was a real Princess and the Infanta of Spain, she had only one birthday every year, just like the children of quite poor people, so it was naturally a matter of great importance to the whole country that she should have a really fine day for the occasion. And a really fine day it certainly was. The tall striped tulips stood straight up upon their stalks, like long rows of soldiers, and looked defiantly across the grass at the roses, and said: 'We are quite as splendid as you are now.' The purple butterflies fluttered about with gold dust on their wings, visiting each flower in turn; the little lizards crept out of the crevices of the wall, and lay basking in the white glare; and the pomegranates split and cracked with the heat, and showed their bleeding red hearts. Even the pale yellow lemons, that hung in such profusion from the mouldering trellis and along the dim arcades, seemed to have caught a richer colour from the wonderful sunlight, and the magnolia trees opened their great globe-like blossoms of folded ivory, and filled the air with a sweet heavy perfume.

The little Princess herself walked up and down the terrace with her companions, and played at hide and seek round the stone vases and the old moss-grown statues. On ordinary days she was only allowed to play with children of her own rank, so she had always to play alone, but her birthday was an exception, and the King had given orders that she was to invite any of her young friends whom she liked to come and amuse themselves with her. There was a stately grace about these slim Spanish children as they glided about, the boys with their large-plumed hats and short fluttering cloaks, the girls holding up the trains of their long brocaded gowns, and shielding the sun from their eyes with huge fans of black and silver. But the Infanta was the most graceful of all, and the most tastefully attired, after the somewhat cumbrous fashion of the day. Her robe was of grey satin, the skirt and the wide puffed sleeves heavily embroidered with silver, and the stiff corset studded with rows of fine pearls. Two tiny slippers with big pink rosettes peeped out beneath her dress as she walked. Pink and pearl was her great gauze fan, and in her hair, which like an aureole of faded gold stood out stiffly round her pale little face, she had a beautiful white rose.

From a window in the palace the sad melancholy King watched them. Behind him stood his brother, Don Pedro of Aragon, whom he hated, and his confessor, the Grand Inquisitor of Granada, sat by his side. Sadder even than usual was the King, for as he looked at the Infanta bowing with childish gravity to the assembling courtiers, or laughing behind her fan at the grim Duchess of Albuquerque who always accompanied her, he thought of the young Queen, her mother, who but a short time before—so it seemed to him—had come from the gay country of France, and had withered away in the sombre splendour of the Spanish court, dying just six months after the birth of her child, and before she had seen the almonds blossom twice in the orchard, or plucked the second year's fruit from the old gnarled fig-tree that stood in the centre of the now grass-grown courtyard. So great had been his love for her that he had not suffered even the grave to hide her from him. She had been embalmed by a Moorish physician, who in return for this service had been granted his life, which for heresy and suspicion of magical practices had been already forfeited, men said, to the Holy Office, and her body was still lying on its tapestried bier in the black marble chapel of the Palace, just as the monks had borne her in on that windy March day nearly twelve years before. Once every month the King, wrapped in a dark cloak and with a muffled lantern in his hand, went in and knelt by her side, calling out, '*Mi reina! Mi reina!*' and sometimes breaking through the formal etiquette that in Spain governs every separate action of life, and sets limits even to the sorrow of a King, he would clutch at the pale jewelled hands in a wild agony of grief, and try to wake by his mad kisses the cold painted face.

To-day he seemed to see her again, as he had seen her first at the Castle of Fontainebleau, when he was but fifteen years of age, and she still younger. They had been formally betrothed on that occasion by the Papal Nuncio in the presence of the French King and all the Court, and he had returned to the Escurial bearing with him a little ringlet of yellow hair, and the memory of two childish lips bending down to kiss his hand as he stepped into his carriage. Later on had followed the marriage, hastily performed at Burgos, a small town on the frontier between the two countries, and the grand public entry into Madrid with the customary celebration of high mass at the Church of La Atocha, and a more than usually solemn *auto-da-fé*, in which nearly three hundred heretics, amongst whom were many Englishmen, had been delivered over to the secular arm to be burned.

Certainly he had loved her madly, and to the ruin, many thought, of his country, then at war with England for the possession of the empire of the New World. He had hardly ever permitted her to be out of his sight; for her, he had forgotten, or seemed to have forgotten, all grave affairs of State; and, with that terrible blindness that passion brings upon its servants, he had failed to notice that the elaborate ceremonies by which he sought to please her did but aggravate the strange malady from which she suffered. When she died he was, for a time, like one bereft of reason. Indeed, there is no doubt but that he would have formally abdicated and retired to the great Trappist monastery at Granada, of which he was already titular Prior, had he not been afraid to leave the little Infanta at the mercy of his brother, whose cruelty, even in Spain, was notorious, and who was suspected by many of having caused the Queen's death by means of a pair of poisoned gloves that he had presented to her on the occasion of her visiting his castle in Aragon. Even after the expiration of the three years of public mourning that he had ordained throughout his whole dominions by royal edict, he would never suffer his ministers to speak about any new alliance, and when the Emperor himself sent to him, and offered him the hand of the lovely Archduchess of Bohemia, his niece, in marriage, he bade the ambassadors tell their master that the King of Spain was already wedded to Sorrow, and that though she was but a barren bride he loved her better than Beauty; an answer that cost his crown the rich provinces of the Netherlands, which soon after, at the Emperor's instigation, revolted against him under the leadership of some fanatics of the Reformed Church.

His whole married life, with its fierce, fiery-coloured joys and the terrible agony of its sudden ending, seemed to come back to him to-day as he watched the Infanta playing on the terrace. She had all the Queen's pretty petulance of manner, the same wilful way of tossing her head, the same proud curved beautiful mouth, the same wonderful smile—*vrai sourire de France* indeed—as she glanced up now and then at the window, or stretched out her little hand for the stately Spanish gentlemen to kiss. But the shrill laughter of the children grated on his ears, and the bright pitiless sunlight mocked his sorrow, and a dull odour of strange spices, spices such as embalmers use, seemed to taint—or was it fancy?—the clear morning air. He buried his face in his hands, and when the Infanta looked up again the curtains had been drawn, and the King had retired.

She made a little *moue* of disappointment, and shrugged her shoulders. Surely he might have stayed with her on her birthday. What did the stupid State-affairs matter? Or had he gone to that gloomy chapel, where the candles were always burning, and where she was never allowed to enter? How silly of him, when the sun was shining so brightly, and everybody was so happy! Besides, he would miss the sham bull-fight for which the trumpet was already sounding, to say nothing of the puppet show and the other wonderful things. Her uncle and the Grand Inquisitor were much more sensible. They had come out on the terrace, and paid her nice compliments. So she tossed her pretty head, and taking Don Pedro by the hand, she walked slowly down the steps towards a long pavilion of purple silk that had been erected at the end of the garden, the other children following in strict order of precedence, those who had the longest names going first.

A procession of noble boys, fantastically dressed as *toreadors,* came out to meet her, and the young Count of Tierra-Nueva, a wonderfully handsome lad of about fourteen years of age, uncovering his head with all the grace of a born hidalgo and grandee of Spain, led her solemnly in to a little gilt and ivory chair that was placed on a raised daïs above the arena. The children grouped themselves all round, fluttering their big fans and whispering to each other, and Don Pedro and the Grand Inquisitor stood laughing at the entrance. Even the Duchess—the Camerera-Mayor as she was called—a thin, hard-featured woman with a yellow ruff, did not look quite so bad-tempered as usual, and something like a chill smile flitted across her wrinkled face and twitched her thin bloodless lips.

It certainly was a marvellous bull-fight, and much nicer, the Infanta thought, than the real bull-fight that she had been brought to see at Seville, on the occasion of the visit of the Duke of Parma to her father. Some of the boys pranced about on richly-caparisoned hobby-horses brandishing long javelins with gay streamers of bright ribands attached to them; others went on foot waving their scarlet cloaks before the bull, and vaulting lightly over the barrier when he charged them; and as for the bull himself he was just like a live bull, though he was only made of wicker-work and stretched hide, and sometimes insisted on running round the arena on his hind legs, which no live bull ever dreams of doing. He made a splendid fight of it too, and the children got so excited that they stood up upon the benches, and waved their lace handkerchiefs and cried out: *Bravo toro! Bravo toro!* just as sensibly as if they had been grown-up people. At last, however, after a prolonged combat, during which several of the hobby-horses were gored through and through, and their riders dismounted, the young Count of Tierra-Nueva brought the bull to his knees, and having obtained permission from the Infanta to give the *coup de grâce,* he plunged his wooden sword into the neck of the animal with such violence that the head came right off, and disclosed the laughing face of little Monsieur de Lorraine, the son of the French Ambassador at Madrid.

The arena was then cleared amidst much applause, and the dead hobby-horses dragged solemnly away by two Moorish pages in yellow and black liveries, and after a short interlude, during which a French posture-master performed upon the tight rope, some Italian puppets appeared in the semi-classical tragedy of *Sophonisba* on the stage of a small theatre that had been built up for the purpose. They acted so well, and their gestures were so extremely natural, that at the close of the play the eyes of the Infanta were quite dim with tears. Indeed some of the children really cried, and had to be comforted with sweetmeats, and the Grand Inquisitor himself was so affected that he could not help saying to Don Pedro that it seemed to him intolerable that things made simply out of wood and coloured wax, and worked mechanically by wires, should be so unhappy and meet with such terrible misfortunes.

An African juggler followed, who brought in a large flat basket covered with a red cloth, and having placed it in the centre of the arena, he took from his turban a curious reed pipe, and blew through it. In a few moments the cloth began to move, and as the pipe grew shriller and shriller two green and gold snakes put out their strange wedge-shaped heads and rose slowly up, swaying to and fro with the music as a plant sways in the water. The children, however, were rather frightened at their spotted hoods and quick darting tongues, and were much more pleased when the juggler made a tiny orange-tree grow out of the sand and bear pretty white blossoms and clusters of real fruit; and when he took the fan of the little daughter of the Marquess de Las-Torres, and changed it into a blue bird that flew all round the pavilion and sang, their delight and amazement knew no bounds. The solemn minuet, too, performed by the dancing boys from the church of Nuestra Señora Del Pilar, was charming. The Infanta had never before seen this wonderful ceremony which takes place every year at May-time in front of the high altar of the Virgin, and in her honour; and indeed none of the royal family of Spain had entered the great cathedral of Saragossa since a mad priest, supposed by many to have been in the pay of Elizabeth of England, had tried to administer a poisoned wafer to the Prince of the Asturias. So she had known only by hearsay of 'Our Lady's Dance,' as it was called, and it certainly was a beautiful sight. The boys wore old-fashioned court dresses of white velvet, and their curious three-cornered hats were fringed with silver and surmounted with huge plumes of ostrich feathers, the dazzling whiteness of their costumes, as they moved about in the sunlight, being still more accentuated by their swarthy faces and long black hair. Everybody was fascinated by the grave dignity with which they moved through the intricate figures of the dance, and by the elaborate grace of their slow gestures, and stately bows, and when they had finished their performance and doffed their great plumed hats to the Infanta, she acknowledged their reverence with much courtesy, and made a vow that she would send a large wax candle to the shrine of Our Lady of Pilar in return for the pleasure that she had given her.

A troop of handsome Egyptians—as the gipsies were termed in those days—then advanced into the arena, and sitting down cross-legs, in a circle, began to play softly upon their zithers, moving their bodies to the tune, and humming, almost below their breath, a low dreamy air. When they caught sight of Don Pedro they scowled at him, and some of them looked terrified, for only a few weeks before he had had two of their tribe hanged for sorcery in the market-place at Seville, but the pretty Infanta charmed them as she leaned back peeping over her fan with her great blue eyes, and they felt sure that one so lovely as she was could never be cruel to anybody. So they played on very gently and just touching the cords of the zithers with their long pointed nails, and their heads began to nod as though they were falling asleep. Suddenly, with a cry so shrill that all the children were startled and Don Pedro's hand clutched at the agate pommel of his dagger, they leapt to their feet and whirled madly round the enclosure beating their tambourines, and chaunting some wild love-song in their strange guttural language. Then at another signal they all flung themselves again to the ground and lay there quite still, the dull strumming of the zithers being the only sound that broke the silence. After that they had done this several times, they disappeared for a moment and came back leading a brown shaggy bear by a chain, and carrying on their shoulders some little Barbary apes. The bear stood upon his head with the utmost gravity, and the wizened apes played all kinds of amusing tricks with two gipsy boys who seemed to be their masters, and fought with tiny swords, and fired off guns, and went through a regular soldier's drill just like the King's own bodyguard. In fact the gipsies were a great success.

But the funniest part of the whole morning's entertainment, was undoubtedly the dancing of the little Dwarf. When he stumbled into the arena, waddling on his crooked legs and wagging his huge misshapen head from side to side, the children went off into a loud shout of delight, and the Infanta herself laughed so much that the Camerera was obliged to remind her that although there were many precedents in Spain for a King's daughter weeping before her equals, there were none for a Princess of the blood royal making so merry before those who were her inferiors in birth. The Dwarf, however, was really quite irresistible, and even at the Spanish Court, always noted for its cultivated passion for the horrible, so fantastic a little monster had never been seen. It was his first appearance, too. He had been discovered only the day before, running wild through the forest, by two of the nobles who happened to have been hunting in a remote part of the great cork-wood that surrounded the town, and had been carried off by them to the Palace as a surprise for the Infanta, his father, who was a poor charcoal-burner, being but too well pleased to get rid of so ugly and useless a child. Perhaps the most amusing thing about him was his complete unconsciousness of his own grotesque appearance. Indeed he seemed quite happy and full of the highest spirits. When the children laughed, he laughed as freely and as joyously as any of them, and at the close of each dance he made them each the funniest of bows, smiling and nodding at them just as if he was really one of themselves, and not a little misshapen thing that Nature, in some humourous mood, had fashioned for others to mock at. As for the Infanta, she absolutely fascinated him. He could not keep his eyes off her, and seemed to dance for her alone, and when at the close of the performance, remembering how she had seen the great ladies of the Court throw bouquets to Caffarelli the famous Italian treble, whom the Pope had sent from his own chapel to Madrid that he might cure the King's melancholy by the sweetness of his voice, she took out of her hair the beautiful white rose, and partly for a jest and partly to tease the Camerera, threw it to him across the arena with her sweetest smile, he took the whole matter quite seriously, and pressing the flower to his rough coarse lips he put his hand upon his heart, and sank on one knee before her, grinning from ear to ear, and with his little bright eyes sparkling with pleasure.

This so upset the gravity of the Infanta that she kept on laughing long after the little Dwarf had run out of the arena, and expressed a desire to her uncle that the dance should be immediately repeated. The Camerera, however, on the plea that the sun was too hot, decided that it would be better that her Highness should return without delay to the Palace, where a wonderful feast had been already prepared for her, including a real birthday cake with her own initials worked all over it in painted sugar and a lovely silver flag waving from the top. The Infanta accordingly rose up with much dignity, and having given orders that the little dwarf was to dance again for her after the hour of siesta, and conveyed her thanks to the young Count of Tierra-Nueva for his charming reception, she went back to her apartments, the children following in the same order in which they had entered.

Now when the little Dwarf heard that he was to dance a second time before the Infanta, and by her own express command, he was so proud that he ran out into the garden, kissing the white rose in an absurd ecstasy of pleasure, and making the most uncouth and clumsy gestures of delight.

The Flowers were quite indignant at his daring to intrude into their beautiful home, and when they saw him capering up and down the walks, and waving his arms above his head in such a ridiculous manner, they could not restrain their feelings any longer.

'He is really far too ugly to be allowed to play in any place where we are,' cried the Tulips.

'He should drink poppy-juice, and go to sleep for a thousand years,' said the great scarlet Lilies, and they grew quite hot and angry.

'He is a perfect horror!' screamed the Cactus. 'Why, he is twisted and stumpy, and his head is completely out of proportion with his legs. Really he makes me feel prickly all over, and if he comes near me I will sting him with my thorns.'

'And he has actually got one of my best blooms,' exclaimed the White Rose-Tree. 'I gave it to the Infanta this morning myself, as a birthday present, and he has stolen it from her.' And she called out: 'Thief, thief, thief!' at the top of her voice.

Even the red Geraniums, who did not usually give themselves airs, and were known to have a great many poor relations themselves, curled up in disgust when they saw him, and when the Violets meekly remarked that though he was certainly extremely plain, still he could not help it, they retorted with a good deal of justice that that was his chief defect, and that there was no reason why one should admire a person because he was incurable; and, indeed, some of the Violets themselves felt that the ugliness of the little Dwarf was almost ostentatious, and that he would have shown much better taste if he had looked sad, or at least pensive, instead of jumping about merrily, and throwing himself into such grotesque and silly attitudes.

As for the old Sundial, who was an extremely remarkable individual, and had once told the time of day to no less a person than the Emperor Charles V himself, he was so taken aback by the little Dwarf's appearance, that he almost forgot to mark two whole minutes with his long shadowy finger, and could not help saying to the great milk-white Peacock, who was sunning herself on the balustrade, that everyone knew that the children of Kings were Kings, and that the children of charcoal-burners were charcoal-burners, and that it was absurd to pretend that it wasn't so; a statement with which the Peacock entirely agreed, and indeed screamed out, 'Certainly, certainly,' in such a loud, harsh voice, that the gold-fish who lived in the basin of the cool splashing fountain put their heads out of the water, and asked the huge stone Tritons what on earth was the matter.

But somehow the Birds liked him. They had seen him often in the forest, dancing about like an elf after the eddying leaves, or crouched up in the hollow of some old oak-tree, sharing his nuts with the squirrels. They did not mind his being ugly, a bit. Why, even the nightingale herself, who sang so sweetly in the orange groves at night that sometimes the Moon leaned down to listen, was not much to look at after all; and, besides, he had been kind to them, and during that terribly bitter winter, when there were no berries on the trees, and the ground was as hard as iron, and the wolves had come down to the very gates of the city to look for food, he had never once forgotten them, but had always given them crumbs out of his little hunch of black bread, and divided with them whatever poor breakfast he had.

So they flew round and round him, just touching his cheek with their wings as they passed, and chattered to each other, and the little Dwarf was so pleased that he could not help showing them the beautiful white rose, and telling them that the Infanta herself had given it to him because she loved him.

They did not understand a single word of what he was saying, but that made no matter, for they put their heads on one side, and looked wise, which is quite as good as understanding a thing, and very much easier.

The Lizards also took an immense fancy to him, and when he grew tired of running about and flung himself down on the grass to rest, they played and romped all over him, and tried to amuse him in the best way they could. 'Every one cannot be as beautiful as a lizard,' they cried; 'that would be too much to expect. And, though it sounds absurd to say so, he is really not so ugly after all, provided, of course, that one shuts one's eyes, and does not look at him.' The Lizards were extremely philosophical by nature, and often sat thinking for hours and hours together, when there was nothing else to do, or when the weather was too rainy for them to go out.

The Flowers, however, were excessively annoyed at their behaviour, and at the behaviour of the birds. 'It only shows,' they said, 'what a vulgarising effect this incessant rushing and flying about has. Well-bred people always stay exactly in the same place, as we do. No one ever saw us hopping up and down the walks, or galloping madly through the grass after dragon-flies. When we do want change of air, we send for the gardener, and he carries us to another bed. This is dignified, and as it should be. But birds and lizards have no sense of repose, and indeed birds have not even a permanent address. They are mere vagrants like the gipsies, and should be treated in exactly the same manner.' So they put their noses in the air, and looked very haughty, and were quite delighted when after some time they saw the little Dwarf scramble up from the grass, and make his way across the terrace to the palace.

'He should certainly be kept indoors for the rest of his natural life,' they said. 'Look at his hunched back, and his crooked legs,' and they began to titter.

But the little Dwarf knew nothing of all this. He liked the birds and the lizards immensely, and thought that the flowers were the most marvellous things in the whole world, except of course the Infanta, but then she had given him the beautiful white rose, and she loved him, and that made a great difference. How he wished that he had gone back with her! She would have put him on her right hand, and smiled at him, and he would have never left her side, but would have made her his playmate, and taught her all kinds of delightful tricks. For though he had never been in a palace before, he knew a great many wonderful things. He could make little cages out of rushes for the grasshoppers to sing in, and fashion the long-jointed bamboo into the pipe that Pan loves to hear. He knew the cry of every bird, and could call the starlings from the tree-top, or the heron from the mere. He knew the trail of every animal, and could track the hare by its delicate footprints, and the boar by the trampled leaves. All the wind-dances he knew, the mad dance in red raiment with the autumn, the light dance in blue sandals over the corn, the dance with white snow-wreaths in winter, and the blossom-dance through the orchards in spring. He knew where the wood-pigeons built their nests, and once when a fowler had snared the parent birds, he had brought up the young ones himself, and had built a little dovecot for them in the cleft of a pollard elm. They were quite tame, and used to feed out of his hands every morning. She would like them, and the rabbits that scurried about in the long fern, and the jays with their steely feathers and black bills, and the hedgehogs that could curl themselves up into prickly balls, and the great wise tortoises that crawled slowly about, shaking their heads and nibbling at the young leaves. Yes, she must certainly come to the forest and play with him. He would give her his own little bed, and would watch outside the window till dawn, to see that the wild horned cattle did not harm her, nor the gaunt wolves creep too near the hut. And at dawn he would tap at the shutters and wake her, and they would go out and dance together all the day long. It was really not a bit lonely in the forest. Sometimes a Bishop rode through on his white mule, reading out of a painted book. Sometimes in their green velvet caps, and their jerkins of tanned deerskin, the falconers passed by, with hooded hawks on their wrists. At vintage time came the grape-treaders, with purple hands and feet, wreathed with glossy ivy and carrying dripping skins of wine; and the charcoal-burners sat round their huge braziers at night, watching the dry logs charring slowly in the fire, and roasting chestnuts in the ashes, and the robbers came out of their caves and made merry with them. Once, too, he had seen a beautiful procession winding up the long dusty road to Toledo. The monks went in front singing sweetly, and carrying bright banners and crosses of gold, and then, in silver armour, with matchlocks and pikes, came the soldiers, and in their midst walked three barefooted men, in strange yellow dresses painted all over with wonderful figures, and carrying lighted candles in their hands. Certainly there was a great deal to look at in the forest, and when she was tired he would find a soft bank of moss for her, or carry her in his arms, for he was very strong, though he knew that he was not tall. He would make her a necklace of red bryony berries, that would be quite as pretty as the white berries that she wore on her dress, and when she was tired of them, she could throw them away, and he would find her others. He would bring her acorn-cups and dew-drenched anemones, and tiny glow-worms to be stars in the pale gold of her hair.

But where was she? He asked the white rose, and it made him no answer. The whole palace seemed asleep, and even where the shutters had not been closed, heavy curtains had been drawn across the windows to keep out the glare. He wandered all round looking for some place through which he might gain an entrance, and at last he caught sight of a little private door that was lying open. He slipped through, and found himself in a splendid hall, far more splendid, he feared, than the forest, there was so much more gilding everywhere, and even the floor was made of great coloured stones, fitted together into a sort of geometrical pattern. But the little Infanta was not there, only some wonderful white statues that looked down on him from their jasper pedestals, with sad blank eyes and strangely smiling lips.

At the end of the hall hung a richly embroidered curtain of black velvet, powdered with suns and stars, the King's favourite devices, and broidered on the colour he loved best. Perhaps she was hiding behind that? He would try at any rate.

So he stole quietly across, and drew it aside. No; there was only another room, though a prettier room, he thought, than the one he had just left. The walls were hung with a many-figured green arras of needle-wrought tapestry representing a hunt, the work of some Flemish artists who had spent more than seven years in its composition. It had once been the chamber of *Jean le Fou,* as he was called, that mad King who was so enamoured of the chase, that he had often tried in his delirium to mount the huge rearing horses, and to drag down the stag on which the great hounds were leaping, sounding his hunting horn, and stabbing with his dagger at the pale flying deer. It was now used as the council-room, and on the centre table were lying the red portfolios of the ministers, stamped with the gold tulips of Spain, and with the arms and emblems of the house of Hapsburg.

The little Dwarf looked in wonder all round him, and was half-afraid to go on. The strange silent horsemen that galloped so swiftly through the long glades without making any noise, seemed to him like those terrible phantoms of whom he had heard the charcoal-burners speaking —the Comprachos, who hunt only at night, and if they meet a man, turn him into a hind, and chase him. But he thought of the pretty Infanta, and took courage. He wanted to find her alone, and to tell her that he too loved her. Perhaps she was in the room beyond.

He ran across the soft Moorish carpets, and opened the door. No! She was not here either. The room was quite empty.

It was a throne-room, used for the reception of foreign ambassadors, when the King, which of late had not been often, consented to give them a personal audience; the same room in which, many years before, envoys had appeared from England to make arrangements for the marriage of their Queen, then one of the Catholic sovereigns of Europe, with the Emperor's eldest son. The hangings were of gilt Cordovan leather, and a heavy gilt chandelier with branches for three hundred wax lights hung down from the black and white ceiling. Underneath a great canopy of gold cloth, on which the lions and towers of Castile were broidered in seed pearls, stood the throne itself, covered with a rich pall of black velvet studded with silver tulips and elaborately fringed with silver and pearls. On the second step of the throne was placed the kneeling-stool of the Infanta, with its cushion of cloth of silver tissue, and below that again, and beyond the limit of the canopy, stood the chair for the Papal Nuncio, who alone had the right to be seated in the King's presence on the occasion of any public ceremonial, and whose Cardinal's hat, with its tangled scarlet tassels, lay on a purple *tabouret* in front. On the wall, facing the throne, hung a life-sized portrait of Charles V in hunting dress, with a great mastiff by his side, and a picture of Philip II receiving the homage of the Netherlands occupied the centre of the other wall. Between the windows stood a black ebony cabinet, inlaid with plates of ivory, on which the figures from Holbein's Dance of Death had been graved—by the hand, some said, of that famous master himself.

But the little Dwarf cared nothing for all this magnificence. He would not have given his rose for all the pearls on the canopy, nor one white petal of his rose for the throne itself. What he wanted was to see the Infanta before she went down to the pavilion, and to ask her to come away with him when he had finished his dance. Here, in the Palace, the air was close and heavy, but in the forest the wind blew free, and the sunlight with wandering hands of gold moved the tremulous leaves aside. There were flowers, too, in the forest, not so splendid, perhaps, as the flowers in the garden, but more sweetly scented for all that; hyacinths in early spring that flooded with waving purple the cool glens, and grassy knolls; yellow primroses that nestled in little clumps round the gnarled roots of the oak-trees; bright celandine, and blue speedwell, and irises lilac and gold. There were grey catkins on the hazels, and the foxgloves drooped with the weight of their dappled bee-haunted cells. The chestnut had its spires of white stars, and the hawthorn its pallid moons of beauty. Yes: surely she would come if he could only find her! She would come with him to the fair forest, and all day long he would dance for her delight. A smile lit up his eyes at the thought, and he passed into the next room.

Of all the rooms this was the brightest and the most beautiful. The walls were covered with a pink-flowered Lucca damask, patterned with birds and dotted with dainty blossoms of silver; the furniture was of massive silver, festooned with florid wreaths, and swinging Cupids; in front of the two large fire-places stood great screens broidered with parrots and peacocks, and the floor, which was of sea-green onyx, seemed to stretch far away into the distance. Nor was he alone. Standing under the shadow of the doorway, at the extreme end of the room, he saw a little figure watching him. His heart trembled, a cry of joy broke from his lips, and he moved out into the sunlight. As he did so, the figure moved out also, and he saw it plainly.

The Infanta! It was a monster, the most grotesque monster he had ever beheld. Not properly shaped, as all other people were, but hunchbacked, and crooked-limbed, with huge lolling head and mane of black hair. The little Dwarf frowned, and the monster frowned also. He laughed, and it laughed with him, and held its hands to its sides, just as he himself was doing. He made it a mocking bow, and it returned him a low reverence. He went towards it, and it came to meet him, copying each step that he made, and stopping when he stopped himself. He shouted with amusement, and ran forward, and reached out his hand, and the hand of the monster touched his, and it was as cold as ice. He grew afraid, and moved his hand across, and the monster's hand followed it quickly. He tried to press on, but something smooth and hard stopped him. The face of the monster was now close to his own, and seemed full of terror. He brushed his hair off his eyes. It imitated him. He struck at it, and it returned blow for blow. He loathed it, and it made hideous faces at him. He drew back, and it retreated.

What is it? He thought for a moment, and looked round at the rest of the room. It was strange, but everything seemed to have its double in this invisible wall of clear water. Yes, picture for picture was repeated, and couch for couch. The sleeping Faun that lay in the alcove by the doorway had its twin brother that slumbered, and the silver Venus that stood in the sunlight held out her arms to a Venus as lovely as herself.

Was it Echo? He had called to her once in the valley, and she had answered him word for word. Could she mock the eye, as she mocked the voice? Could she make a mimic world just like the real world? Could the shadow of things have colour and life and movement? Could it be that—?

He started, and taking from his breast the beautiful white rose, he turned round, and kissed it. The monster had a rose of its own, petal for petal the same! It kissed it with like kisses, and pressed it to its heart with horrible gestures.

When the truth dawned upon him, he gave a wild cry of despair, and fell sobbing to the ground. So it was he who was misshapen and hunchbacked, foul to look at and grotesque. He himself was the monster, and it was at him that all the children had been laughing, and the little Princess who he had thought loved him—she too had been merely mocking at his ugliness, and making merry over his twisted limbs. Why had they not left him in the forest, where there was no mirror to tell him how loathsome he was? Why had his father not killed him, rather than sell him to his shame? The hot tears poured down his cheeks, and he tore the white rose to pieces. The sprawling monster did the same, and scattered the faint petals in the air. It grovelled on the ground, and, when he looked at it, it watched him with a face drawn with pain. He crept away, lest he should see it, and covered his eyes with his hands. He crawled, like some wounded thing, into the shadow, and lay there moaning.

And at that moment the Infanta herself came in with her companions through the open window, and when they saw the ugly little dwarf lying on the ground and beating the floor with his clenched hands, in the most fantastic and exaggerated manner, they went off into shouts of happy laughter, and stood all round him and watched him.

'His dancing was funny,' said the Infanta; 'but his acting is funnier still. Indeed he is almost as good as the puppets, only of course not quite so natural.' And she fluttered her big fan, and applauded.

But the little Dwarf never looked up, and his sobs grew fainter and fainter, and suddenly he gave a curious gasp, and clutched his side. And then he fell back again, and lay quite still.

'That is capital,' said the Infanta, after a pause; 'but now you must dance for me.'

'Yes,' cried all the children, 'you must get up and dance, for you are as clever as the Barbary apes, and much more ridiculous.'

But the little Dwarf never moved.

And the Infanta stamped her foot, and called out to her uncle, who was walking on the terrace with the Chamberlain, reading some despatches that had just arrived from Mexico where the Holy Office had recently been established. 'My funny little dwarf is sulking,' she cried, 'you must wake him up, and tell him to dance for me.'

They smiled at each other, and sauntered in, and Don Pedro stooped down, and slapped the Dwarf on the cheek with his embroidered glove. 'You must dance,' he said, *'petit monstre.* You must dance. The Infanta of Spain and the Indies wishes to be amused.'

But the little Dwarf never moved.

'A whipping master should be sent for,' said Don Pedro wearily, and he went back to the terrace. But the Chamberlain looked grave, and he knelt beside the little dwarf, and put his hand upon his heart. And after a few moments he shrugged his shoulders, and rose up, and having made a low bow to the Infanta, he said:

'*Mi bella Princesa,* your funny little dwarf will never dance again. It is a pity, for he is so ugly that he might have made the King smile.'

'But why will he not dance again?' asked the Infanta, laughing.

'Because his heart is broken,' answered the Chamberlain.

And the Infanta frowned, and her dainty rose-leaf lips curled in pretty disdain. 'For the future let those who come to play with me have no hearts,' she cried, and she ran out into the garden.

Il Conde
"Vedi Napoli e poi mori."

$\backsim\!\!\!\curvearrowright\!\!\!\sim$

JOSEPH CONRAD
(Polish/English, 1857–1924)

The first time we got into conversation was in the National Museum in Naples, in the rooms on the ground floor containing the famous collection of bronzes from Herculaneum and Pompeii: that marvelous legacy of antique art whose delicate perfection has been preserved for us by the catastrophic fury of a volcano.

He addressed me first, over the celebrated Resting Hermes which we had been looking at side by side. He said the right things about that wholly admirable piece. Nothing profound. His taste was natural rather than cultivated. He had obviously seen many fine things in his life and appreciated them; but he had no jargon of a dilettante or the connoisseur. A hateful tribe. He spoke like a fairly intelligent man of the world, a perfectly unaffected gentleman.

We had known each other by sight for some few days past. Staying in the same hotel—good, but not extravagantly up to date—I had noticed him in the vestibule going in and out. I judged he was an old and valued client. The bow of the hotelkeeper was cordial in its deference, and he acknowledged it with familiar courtesy. For the servants he was *Il Conde*. There was some squabble over a man's parasol—yellow silk with white lining sort of thing—the waiters had discovered abandoned outside the dining-room door. Our gold-laced doorkeeper recognized it and I heard him directing one of the lift boys to run after *Il Conde* with it. Perhaps he was the only count staying in the hotel, or perhaps he had the distinction of being *the* Count *par excellence,* conferred upon him because of his tried fidelity to the house.

Having conversed at the Museo—(and by the by he had expressed his dislike of the busts and statues of Roman emperors in the gallery of marbles: their faces were too vigorous, too pronounced for him)—having conversed already in the morning I did not think I was intruding when in the evening, finding the dining room very full, I proposed to share his little table. Judging by the quiet urbanity of his consent he did not think so either. His smile was very attractive.

He dined in an evening waistcoat and a "smoking" (he called it so) with a black tie. All this of very good cut, not new—just as these things should be. He was, morning or evening, very correct in his dress. I have no doubt that his whole existence had been correct, well ordered and conventional, undisturbed by startling events. His white hair brushed upwards off a lofty forehead gave him the air of an idealist, of an imaginative man. His white mustache, heavy but carefully trimmed and arranged, was not unpleasantly tinted a golden yellow in the middle. The faint scent of some very good perfume, and of good cigars (that last an odor quite remarkable to come upon in Italy) reached me across the table. It was in his eyes that his age showed most. They were a little weary with creased eyelids. He must have been sixty or a couple of years more. And he was communicative. I would not go so far as to call it garrulous—but distinctly communicative.

He had tried various climates, of Abbazia, of the Riviera, of other places, too, he told me, but the only one which suited him was the climate of the Gulf of Naples. The ancient Romans, who, he pointed out to me, were men expert in the art of living, knew very well what they were doing when they built their villas on these shores, in Baiae, in Vico, in Capri. They came down to this seaside in search of health, bringing with them their trains of mimes and flute-players to amuse their leisure. He thought it extremely probable that the Romans of the higher classes were specially predisposed to painful rheumatic affections.

This was the only personal opinion I heard him express. It was based on no special erudition. He knew no more of the Romans than an average informed man of the world is expected to know. He argued from personal experience. He had suffered himself from a painful and dangerous rheumatic affection till he found relief in this particular spot of Southern Europe.

This was three years ago, and ever since he had taken up his quarters on the shores of the gulf, either in one of the hotels in Sorrento or hiring a small villa in Capri. He had a piano, a few books; picked up transient acquaintances of a day, week, or month in the stream of travelers from all Europe. One can imagine him going out for his walks in the streets and lanes, becoming known to beggars, shopkeepers, children, country people; talking amiably over the walls to the *contadini*—and coming back to his rooms or his villa to sit before the piano, with his white hair brushed up and his thick orderly mustache, "to make a little music for myself." And, of course, for a change there was Naples near by—life, movement, animation, opera. A little amusement, as he said, is necessary for health. Mimes and flute-players, in fact. Only unlike the magnates of ancient Rome, he had no affairs of the city to call him away from these moderate delights. He had no affairs at all. Probably he had never had any grave affairs to attend to in his life. It was a kindly existence, with its joys and sorrows regulated by the course of Nature—marriages, births, deaths— ruled by the prescribed usages of good society and protected by the State.

He was a widower; but in the months of July and August he ventured to cross the Alps for six weeks on a visit to his married daughter. He told me her name. It was that of a very aristocratic family. She had a castle— in Bohemia, I think. This is as near as I ever came to ascertaining his nationality. His own name, strangely enough, he never mentioned. Perhaps he thought I had seen it on the published list. Truth to say, I never looked. At any rate, he was a good European—he spoke four languages to my certain knowledge—and a man of fortune. Not of great fortune evidently and appropriately. I imagine that to be extremely rich would have appeared to him improper, *outré*—too blatant altogether. And obviously, too, the fortune was not of his making. The making of a fortune cannot be achieved without some roughness. It is a matter of temperament. His nature was too kindly for strife. In the course of conversation he mentioned his estate quite by the way, in reference to that painful and alarming rheumatic affection. One year, staying incautiously beyond the Alps as late as the middle of September, he had been laid up for three months in that lonely country house with no one but his valet and the caretaking couple to attend to him. Because, as he expressed it, he "kept no establishment there." He had only gone for a couple of days to confer with his land agent. He promised himself never to be so imprudent in the future. The first weeks of September would find him on the shores of his beloved gulf.

Sometimes in traveling one comes upon such lonely men, whose only business is to wait for the unavoidable. Deaths and marriages have made a solitude round them, and one really cannot blame their endeavors to make the waiting as easy as possible. As he remarked to me, "At my time of life freedom from physical pain is a very important matter."

It must not be imagined that he was a wearisome hypochondriac. He was really much too well bred to be a nuisance. He had an eye for the small weaknesses of humanity. But it was a good-natured eye. He made a restful, easy, pleasant companion for the hours between dinner and bedtime. We spent three evenings together, and then I had to leave Naples in a hurry to look after a friend who had fallen seriously ill in Taormina. Having nothing to do, *Il Conde* came to see me off at the station. I was somewhat upset, and his idleness was always ready to take a kindly form. He was by no means an indolent man.

He went along the train peering into the carriages for a good seat for me, and then remained talking cheerily from below. He declared he would miss me that evening very much and announced his intention of going after dinner to listen to the band in the public garden, the Villa Nazionale. He would amuse himself by hearing excellent music and looking at the best society. There would be a lot of people, as usual.

I seem to see him yet—his raised face with a friendly smile under the thick mustaches, and his kind, fatigued eyes. As the train began to move, he addressed me in two languages: first in French, saying, *"Bon voyage";* then, in his very good, somewhat emphatic English, encouragingly, because he could see my concern: "All will—be—well—yet!"

My friend's illness having taken a decidedly favorable turn, I returned to Naples on the tenth day. I cannot say I had given much thought to *Il Conde* during my absence, but entering the dining room I looked for him

in his habitual place. I had an idea he might have gone back to Sorrento
to his piano and his books and his fishing. He was great friends with all
the boatmen, and fished a good deal with lines from a boat. But I made
out his white head in the crowd of heads, and even from a distance
noticed something unusual in his attitude. Instead of sitting erect, gazing
all round with alert urbanity, he drooped over his plate. I stood opposite
him for some time before he looked up, a little wildly, if such a strong
word can be used in connection with his correct appearance.

"Ah, my dear sir! Is it you?" he greeted me. "I hope all is well."

He was very nice about my friend. Indeed, he was always nice, with
the niceness of people whose hearts are genuinely humane. But this time
it cost him an effort. His attempts at general conversation broke down
into dullness. It occurred to me he might have been indisposed. But
before I could frame the inquiry he muttered:

"You find me here very sad."

"I am sorry for that," I said. "You haven't had bad news, I hope?"

It was very kind of me to take an interest. No. It was not that. No bad
news, thank God. And he became very still as if holding his breath.
Then, leaning forward a little, and in an odd tone of awed embarrassment, he took me into his confidence.

"The truth is that I have had a very—a very—how shall I say?—
abominable adventure happen to me."

The energy of the epithet was sufficiently startling in that man of
moderate feelings and toned-down vocabulary. The word unpleasant I
should have thought would have fitted amply the worst experience likely
to befall a man of his stamp. And an adventure, too. Incredible! But it is
in human nature to believe the worst; and I confess I eyed him stealthily,
wondering what he had been up to. In a moment, however, my unworthy
suspicions vanished. There was a fundamental refinement of nature about
the man which made me dismiss all idea of some more or less disreputable scrape.

"It is very serious. Very serious." He went on, nervously. "I will tell
you after dinner, if you will allow me."

I expressed my perfect acquiescence by a little bow, nothing more. I
wished him to understand that I was not likely to hold him to that offer,
if he thought better of it later on. We talked of indifferent things, but with
a sense of difficulty quite unlike our former easy, gossipy intercourse. The

hand raising a piece of bread to his lips, I noticed, trembled slightly. This symptom, in regard to my reading of the man, was no less than startling. In the smoking room he did not hang back at all. Directly we had taken our usual seats he leaned sideways over the arm of his chair and looked straight into my eyes earnestly.

"You remember," he began, "that day you went away? I told you then I would go to the Villa Nazionale to hear some music in the evening."

I remembered. His handsome old face, so fresh for his age, unmarked by any trying experience, appeared haggard for an instant. It was like the passing of a shadow. Returning his steadfast gaze, I took a sip of my black coffee. He was systematically minute in his narrative, simply in order, I think, not to let his excitement get the better of him.

After leaving the railway station, he had an ice, and read the paper in a café. Then he went back to the hotel, dressed for dinner, and dined with a good appetite. After dinner he lingered in the hall (there were chairs and tables there) smoking his cigar; talked to the little girl of the Primo Tenore of the San Carlo Theater, and exchanged a few words with that "amiable lady," the wife of the Primo Tenore. There was no performance that evening, and these people were going to the Villa also. They went out of the hotel. Very well.

At the moment of following their example—it was half-past nine already—he remembered he had a rather large sum of money in his pocket-book. He entered, therefore, the office and deposited the greater part of it with the bookkeeper of the hotel. This done, he took a *carozella* and drove to the seashore. He got out of the cab and entered the Villa on foot from the Largo di Vittoria end.

He stared at me very hard. And I understood then how really impressionable he was. Every small fact and event of that evening stood out in his memory as if endowed with mystic significance. If he did not mention to me the color of the pony which drew the *carozella,* and the aspect of the man who drove, it was a mere oversight arising from his agitation, which he repressed manfully.

He had then entered the Villa Nazionale from the Largo di Vittoria end. The Villa Nazionale is a public pleasure-ground laid out in grass plots, bushes, and flowerbeds between the houses of the Riviera di Chiaja and the waters of the bay. Alleys of trees, more or less parallel, stretch its whole length—which is considerable. On the Riviera di Chiaja side the electric tramcars run close to the railings. Between the garden and the sea is the fashionable drive, a broad road bordered by a low wall, beyond which the Mediterranean splashes with gentle murmurs when the weather is fine.

As life goes on late at night in Naples, the broad drive was all astir with a brilliant swarm of carriage lamps moving in pairs, some creeping slowly, others running rapidly under the thin, motionless line of electric lamps defining the shore. And a brilliant swarm of stars hung above the land humming with voices, piled up with houses, glittering with lights—and over the silent flat shadows of the sea.

The gardens themselves are not very well lit. Our friend went forward in the warm gloom, his eyes fixed upon a distant luminous region extending nearly across the whole width of the Villa, as if the air had glowed there with its own cold, bluish, and dazzling light. This magic spot, behind the black trunks of trees and masses of inky foliage, breathed out sweet sounds mingled with bursts of brassy roar, sudden clashes of metal, and grave, vibrating thuds.

As he walked on, all these noises combined together into a piece of elaborate music whose harmonious phrases came persuasively through a great disorderly murmur of voices and shuffling of feet on the gravel of that open space. An enormous crowd immersed in the electric light, as if in a bath of some radiant and tenuous fluid shed upon their heads by luminous globes, drifted in hundreds round the band. Hundreds more sat on chairs in more or less concentric circles, receiving unflinchingly the great waves of sonority that ebbed out into the darkness. The Count penetrated the throng, drifted with it in tranquil enjoyment, listening and looking at the faces. All people of good society: mothers with their daughters, parents and children, young men and young women all talking, smiling, nodding to each other. Very many pretty faces, and very many pretty toilettes. There was, of course, a quantity of diverse types: showy old fellows with white mustaches, fat men, thin men, officers in uniform; but what predominated, he told me, was the South Italian type of young man, with a colorless, clear complexion, red lips, jet-black little mustache and liquid black eyes so wonderfully effective in leering or scowling.

Withdrawing from the throng, the Count shared a little table in front of the café with a young man of just such a type. Our friend had some lemonade. The young man was sitting moodily before an empty glass. He looked up once, and then looked down again. He also tilted his hat forward. Like this—

The Count made the gesture of a man pulling his hat down over his brow, and went on:

"I think to myself: he is sad; something is wrong with him; young men have their troubles. I take no notice of him, of course. I pay for my lemonade, and go away."

Strolling about in the neighborhood of the band, the Count thinks he saw twice that young man wandering alone in the crowd. Once their eyes met. It must have been the same young man, but there were so many there of that type that he could not be certain. Moreover, he was not very much concerned except in so far that he had been struck by the marked, peevish discontent of that face.

Presently, tired of the feeling of confinement one experiences in a crowd, the Count edged away from the band. An alley, very somber by contrast, presented itself invitingly with its promise of solitude and coolness. He entered it, walking slowly on till the sound of the orchestra became distinctly deadened. Then he walked back and turned about once more. He did this several times before he noticed that there was somebody occupying one of the benches.

The spot being midway between two lampposts the light was faint.

The man lolled back in the corner of the seat, his legs stretched out, his arms folded and his head drooping on his breast. He never stirred, as though he had fallen asleep there, but when the Count passed by next time he had changed his attitude. He sat leaning forward. His elbows were propped on his knees, and his hands were rolling a cigarette. He never looked up from that occupation.

The Count continued his stroll away from the band. He returned slowly, he said. I can imagine him enjoying to the full, but with his usual tranquility, the balminess of this southern night and the sounds of music softened delightfully by the distance.

Presently, he approached for the third time the man on the garden seat, still leaning forward with his elbows on his knees. It was a dejected pose. In the semiobscurity of the alley his high shirt collar and his cuffs made small patches of vivid whiteness. The Count said that he had noticed him getting up brusquely as if to walk away, but almost before he was aware of it the man stood before him asking in a low, gentle tone whether the signore would have the kindness to oblige him with a light.

The Count answered this request by a polite "Certainly," and dropped his hands with the intention of exploring both pockets of his trousers for the matches.

"I dropped my hands," he said, "but I never put them in my pockets. I felt a pressure there—"

He put the tip of his finger on a spot close under his breastbone, the very spot of the human body where a Japanese gentleman begins the operations of the hara-kiri, which is a form of suicide following upon dishonor, upon an intolerable outrage to the delicacy of one's feelings.

"I glance down," the Count continued in an awestruck voice, "and what do I see? A knife! A long knife—"

"You don't mean to say," I exclaimed, amazed, "that you have been held up like this in the Villa at half-past ten o'clock, within a stone's throw of a thousand people!"

He nodded several times, staring at me with all his might.

"The clarinet," he declared, solemnly, "was finishing its solo, and I assure you I could hear every note. Then the band crashed *fortissimo,* and that creature rolled its eyes and gnashed its teeth hissing at me with the greatest ferocity. 'Be silent! No noise or—' "

I could not get over my astonishment.

"What sort of knife was it?" I asked, stupidly.

"A long blade. A stiletto—perhaps a kitchen knife. A long narrow blade. It gleamed. And his eyes gleamed. His white teeth, too. I could see them. He was very ferocious. I thought to myself: 'If I hit him he will kill me.' How could I fight with him? He had the knife and I had nothing. I am nearly seventy, you know, and that was a young man. I seemed even to recognize him. The moody young man of the café. The young man I met in the crowd. But I could not tell. There are so many like him in this country."

The distress of that moment was reflected in his face. I should think that physically he must have been paralyzed by surprise. His thoughts, however, remained extremely active. They ranged over every alarming possibility. The idea of setting up a vigorous shouting for help occurred to him, too. But he did nothing of the kind, and the reason why he refrained gave me a good opinion of his mental self-possession. He saw in a flash that nothing prevented the other from shouting, too.

"That young man might in an instant have thrown away his knife and pretended I was the aggressor. Why not? He might have said I attacked him. Why not? It was one incredible story against another! He might have said anything—bring some dishonoring charge against me—what do I know? By his dress he was no common robber. He seemed to belong to the better classes. What could I say? He was an Italian—I am a foreigner. Of course, I have my passport, and there is our consul—but to be arrested, dragged at night to the police office like a criminal!"

He shuddered. It was in his character to shrink from scandal, much more than from mere death. And certainly for many people this would have always remained—considering certain peculiarities of Neapolitan manners—a deucedly queer story. The Count was no fool. His belief in the respectable placidity of life having received this rude shock, he thought that now anything might happen. But also a notion came into his head that this young man was perhaps merely an infuriated lunatic.

This was for me the first hint of his attitude towards this adventure. In his exaggerated delicacy of sentiment he felt that nobody's self-esteem need be affected by what a madman may choose to do to one. It became apparent, however, that the Count was to be denied that consolation. He enlarged upon the abominably savage way in which that young man rolled his glistening eyes and gnashed his white teeth. The band was going now through a slow movement of solemn braying by all the trombones, with deliberately repeated bangs of the big drum.

"But what did you do?" I asked, greatly excited.

"Nothing," answered the Count. "I let my hands hang down very still. I told him quietly I did not intend making a noise. He snarled like a dog, then said in an ordinary voice:

" 'Vostro portofolio.' "

"So I naturally," continued the Count—and from this point acted the whole thing in pantomime. Holding me with his eyes, he went through all the motions of reaching into his inside breast pocket, taking out a pocketbook, and handing it over. But that young man, still bearing steadily on the knife, refused to touch it.

He directed the Count to take the money out himself, received it into his left hand, motioned the pocketbook to be returned to the pocket, all this being done to the sweet trilling of flutes and clarinets sustained by the emotional drone of the hautboys. And the "young man," as the Count called him, said: "This seems very little."

"It was, indeed, only 340 or 360 lire," the Count pursued. "I had left my money in the hotel, as you know. I told him this was all I had on me. He shook his head impatiently and said:

" *'Vostro orologio.'* "

The Count gave me the dumb show of pulling out his watch, detaching it. But, as it happened, the valuable gold half-chronometer he possessed had been left at a watchmaker's for cleaning. He wore that evening (on a leather guard) the Waterbury fifty-franc thing he used to take with him on his fishing expeditions. Perceiving the nature of this booty, the well-dressed robber made a contemptuous clicking sound with his tongue like this, "Tse-Ah!" and waved it away hastily. Then, as the Count was returning the disdained object to his pocket, he demanded with a threateningly increased pressure of the knife on the epigastrium, by way of reminder:

"Vostri anelli."

"One of the rings," went on the Count, "was given me many years ago by my wife; the other is the signet ring of my father. I said, 'No. *That* you shall not have!' "

Here the Count reproduced the gesture corresponding to that declaration by clapping one hand upon the other, and pressing both thus against his chest. It was touching in its resignation. "That you shall not have," he repeated, firmly, and closed his eyes, fully expecting—I don't know whether I am right in recording that such an unpleasant word had passed his lips—fully expecting to feel himself being—I really hesitate to say—being disemboweled by the push of the long, sharp blade resting murderously against the pit of his stomach—the very seat, in all human beings, of anguishing sensations.

Great waves of harmony went on flowing from the band.

Suddenly the Count felt the nightmarish pressure removed from the sensitive spot. He opened his eyes. He was alone. He had heard nothing. It is probable that "the young man" had departed, with light steps, some time before, but the sense of the horrid pressure had lingered even after the knife had gone. A feeling of weakness came over him. He had just time to stagger to the garden seat. He felt as though he had held his breath for a long time. He sat all in a heap, panting with the shock of the reaction.

The band was executing, with immense bravura, the complicated finale. It ended with a tremendous crash. He heard it, unreal and remote, as if his ears had been stopped, and then the hard clapping of a thousand, more or less, pairs of hands, like a sudden hail shower passing away. The profound silence which succeeded recalled him to himself.

A tramcar resembling a long glass box wherein people sat with their heads strongly lighted, ran along swiftly within sixty yards of the spot where he had been robbed. Then another rustled by, and yet another going the other way. The audience about the band had broken up, and were entering the alley in small conversing groups. The Count sat up straight and tried to think calmly of what had happened to him. The vileness of it took his breath away again. As far as I can make it out he was disgusted with himself. I do not mean to say with his behavior. Indeed, if his pantomimic rendering of it for my information was to be trusted, it was simply perfect. No, it was not that. He was not ashamed. He was shocked at being the selected victim, not of robbery so much as of contempt. His tranquillity had been wantonly desecrated. His lifelong, kindly nicety of outlook had been defaced.

Nevertheless, at that stage, before the iron had time to sink deep, he was able to argue himself into comparative equanimity. As his agitation calmed down somewhat, he became aware that he was frightfully hungry. Yes, hungry. The sheer emotion had made him simply ravenous. He left the seat and, after walking for some time, found himself outside the gardens and before an arrested tramcar, without knowing very well how he came there. He got in as if in a dream, by a sort of instinct. Fortunately he found in his trouser pocket a copper to satisfy the conductor. Then the car stopped, and as everybody was getting out he got out, too. He recognized the Piazza San Ferdinando, but apparently it did not occur to him to take a cab and drive to the hotel. He remained in distress on the Piazza like a lost dog, thinking vaguely of the best way of getting something to eat at once.

Suddenly he remembered his twenty-franc piece. He explained to me that he had that piece of French gold for something like three years. He used to carry it about with him as a sort of reserve in case of accident. Anybody is liable to have his pocket picked—a quite different thing from a brazen and insulting robbery.

The monumental arch of the Galleria Umberto faced him at the top of a noble flight of stairs. He climbed these without loss of time, and directed his steps towards the Café Umberto. All the tables outside were occupied by a lot of people who were drinking. But as he wanted something to eat, he went inside into the café, which is divided into aisles by square pillars set all round with long looking glasses. The Count sat down on a red plush bench against one of these pillars, waiting for his *risotto*. And his mind reverted to his abominable adventure.

He thought of the moody, well-dressed young man, with whom he had exchanged glances in the crowd around the bandstand, and who, he felt confident, was the robber. Would he recognize him again? Doubtless. But he did not want ever to see him again. The best thing was to forget this humiliating episode.

The Count looked round anxiously for the coming of his *risotto*, and, behold! to the left against the wall—there sat the young man. He was alone at a table, with a bottle of some sort of wine or syrup and a carafe of iced water before him. The smooth olive cheeks, the red lips, the little jet-black mustache turned up gallantly, the fine black eyes a little heavy and shaded by long eyelashes, that peculiar expression of cruel discontent to be seen only in the busts of some Roman emperors—it was he, no doubt at all. But that was a type. The Count looked away hastily. The young officer over there reading a paper was like that, too. Same type. Two young men farther away playing checkers also resembled—

The Count lowered his head with the fear in his heart of being everlastingly haunted by the vision of that young man. He began to eat his *risotto*. Presently he heard the young man on his left call the waiter in a bad-tempered tone.

At the call, not only his own waiter, but two other idle waiters belonging to a quite different row of tables, rushed towards him with obsequious alacrity, which is not the general characteristic of the waiters in the Café Umberto. The young man muttered something and one of the waiters walking rapidly to the nearest door called out into the Galleria: "Pasquale! O! Pasquale!"

Everybody knows Pasquale, the shabby old fellow who, shuffling between the tables, offers for sale cigars, cigarettes, picture postcards, and matches to the clients of the café. He is in many respects an engaging scoundrel. The Count saw the gray-haired, unshaven ruffian enter the café, the glass case hanging from his neck by a leather strap, and, at a word from the waiter, make his shuffling way with a sudden spurt to the young man's table. The young man was in need of a cigar with which Pasquale served him fawningly. The old peddler was going out, when the Count, on a sudden impulse, beckoned to him.

Pasquale approached, the smile of deferential recognition combining oddly with the cynical searching expression of his eyes. Leaning his case on the table, he lifted the glass lid without a word. The Count took a box of cigarettes and urged by a fearful curiosity, asked as casually as he could—

"Tell me, Pasquale, who is that young signore sitting over there?"

The other bent over his box confidentially.

"That, *Signor Conde,*" he said, beginning to rearrange his wares busily and without looking up, "that is a young *Cavaliere* of a very good family from Bari. He studies in the University here, and is the chief, *capo,* of an association of young men—of very nice young men."

He paused, and then, with mingled discretion and pride of knowledge, murmured the explanatory word *"Camorra"* and shut down the lid. "A very powerful *Camorra,*" he breathed out. "The professors themselves respect it greatly . . . *una lira e cinquanti centesimi, Signor Conde.*"

Our friend paid with the gold piece. While Pasquale was making up the change, he observed that the young man, of whom he had heard so much in a few words, was watching the transaction covertly. After the old vagabond had withdrawn with a bow, the Count settled with the waiter and sat still. A numbness, he told me, had come over him.

The young man paid, too, got up, and crossed over, apparently for the purpose of looking at himself in the mirror set in the pillar nearest to the Count's seat. He was dressed all in black with a dark green bow tie. The Count looked round, and was startled by meeting a vicious glance out of the corners of the other's eyes. The young *Cavaliere* from Bari (according to Pasquale; but Pasquale is, of course, an accomplished liar) went on arranging his tie, settling his hat before the glass, and meantime he spoke just loud enough to be heard by the Count. He spoke through his teeth with the most insulting venom of contempt and gazing straight into the mirror.

"Ah! So you had some gold on you—you old liar—you old *birba*—you *furfante!* But you are not done with me yet."

The fiendishness of his expression vanished like lightning, and he lounged out of the café with a moody, impassive face.

The poor Count, after telling me this last episode, fell back trembling in his chair. His forehead broke into perspiration. There was a wanton insolence in the spirit of this outrage which appalled even me. What it was to the Count's delicacy I won't attempt to guess. I am sure that if he had been not too refined to do such a blatantly vulgar thing as dying from apoplexy in a café, he would have had a fatal stroke there and then. All irony apart, my difficulty was to keep him from seeing the full extent of my commiseration. He shrank from every excessive sentiment, and my commiseration was practically unbounded. It did not surprise me to hear that he had been in bed a week. He had got up to make his arrangements for leaving Southern Italy for good and all.

And the man was convinced that he could not live through a whole year in any other climate!

No argument of mine had any effect. It was not timidity, though he did say to me once: "You do not know what a *Camorra* is, my dear sir. I am a marked man." He was not afraid of what could be done to him. His delicate conception of his dignity was defiled by a degrading experience. He couldn't stand that. No Japanese gentleman, outraged in his exaggerated sense of honor, could have gone about his preparations for hara-kiri with greater resolution. To go home really amounted to suicide for the poor Count.

There is a saying of Neapolitan patriotism, intended for the information of foreigners, I presume: "See Naples and then die." *Vedi Napoli e poi mori.* It is a saying of excessive vanity, and everything excessive was abhorrent to the nice moderation of the poor Count. Yet, as I was seeing him off at the railway station, I thought he was behaving with singular fidelity to its conceited spirit. *Vedi Napoli!* . . . He had seen it! He had seen it with startling thoroughness—and now he was going to his grave. He was going to it by the *train de luxe* of the International Sleeping Car Company, via Trieste and Vienna. As the four long, somber coaches pulled out of the station I raised my hat with the solemn feeling of paying the last tribute of respect to a funeral cortège. *Il Conde's* profile, much aged already, glided away from me in stony immobility, behind the lighted pane of glass—*Vedi Napoli e poi mori!*

The New Catacomb

SIR ARTHUR CONAN DOYLE
(English, 1859–1930)

"Look here, Burger," said Kennedy, "I do wish that you would confide in me."

The two famous students of Roman remains sat together in Kennedy's comfortable room overlooking the Corso. The night was cold, and they had both pulled up their chairs to the unsatisfactory Italian stove which threw out a zone of stuffiness rather than of warmth. Outside under the bright winter stars lay the modern Rome, the long, double chain of the electric lamps, the brilliantly lighted cafés, the rushing carriages, and the dense throng upon the footpaths. But inside, in the sumptuous chamber of the rich young English archaeologist, there was only old Rome to be seen. Cracked and timeworn friezes hung upon the walls, grey old busts of senators and soldiers with their fighting heads and their hard, cruel faces peered out from the corners. On the centre table, amidst a litter of inscriptions, fragments, and ornaments, there stood the famous reconstruction by Kennedy of the Baths of Caracalla, which excited such interest and admiration when it was exhibited in Berlin. Amphorae hung from the ceiling, and a litter of curiosities strewed the rich red Turkey carpet. And of them all there was not one which was not of the most unimpeachable authenticity, and of the utmost rarity and value; for Kennedy, though little more than thirty, had a European reputation in this particular branch of research, and was, moreover, provided with that long purse which either proves to be a fatal handicap to the student's energies, or, if his mind is still true to its purpose, gives him an enormous advantage in the race for fame. Kennedy had often been seduced by whim and pleasure from his studies, but his mind was an incisive one, capable of long and concentrated efforts which ended in sharp reactions of sensuous languor. His handsome face, with its high, white forehead, its aggressive nose, and its somewhat loose and sensual mouth, was a fair index of the compromise between strength and weakness in his nature.

Of a very different type was his companion, Julius Burger. He came of a curious blend, a German father and an Italian mother, with the robust qualities of the North mingling strangely with the softer graces of the South. Blue Teutonic eyes lightened his sun-browned face, and above them rose a square, massive forehead, with a fringe of close yellow curls lying round it. His strong, firm jaw was clean-shaven, and his companion had frequently remarked how much it suggested those old Roman busts which peered out from the shadows in the corners of his chamber. Under its bluff German strength there lay always a suggestion of Italian subtlety, but the smile was so honest, and the eyes so frank, that one understood that this was only an indication of his ancestry, with no actual bearing upon his character. In age and in reputation, he was on the same level as his English companion, but his life and his work had both been far more arduous. Twelve years before, he had come as a poor student to Rome, and had lived ever since upon some small endowment for research which had been awarded to him by the University of Bonn. Painfully, slowly, and doggedly, with extraordinary tenacity and single-mindedness, he had climbed from rung to rung of the ladder of fame, until now he was a member of the Berlin Academy, and there was every reason to believe that he would shortly be promoted to the Chair of the greatest of German Universities. But the singleness of purpose which had brought him to the same high level as the rich and brilliant Englishman, had caused him in everything outside their work to stand infinitely below him. He had never found a pause in his studies in which to cultivate the social graces. It was only when he spoke of his own subject that his face was filled with life and soul. At other times he was silent and embarrassed, too conscious of his own limitations in larger subjects, and impatient of that small talk which is the conventional refuge of those who have no thoughts to express.

And yet for some years there had been an acquaintanceship which appeared to be slowly ripening into a friendship between these two very different rivals. The base and origin of this lay in the fact that in their own studies each was the only one of the younger men who had knowledge and enthusiasm enough to properly appreciate the other. Their common interests and pursuits had brought them together, and each had been attracted by the other's knowledge. And then gradually something had been added to this. Kennedy had been amused by the frankness and simplicity of his rival, while Burger in turn had been fascinated by the brilliancy and vivacity which had made Kennedy such a favourite in Roman society. I say "had," because just at the moment the young Englishman was somewhat under a cloud. A love-affair, the details of which had never quite come out, had indicated a heartlessness and callousness upon his part which shocked many of his friends. But in the bachelor circles of students and artists in which he preferred to move there is no very rigid code of honour in such matters, and though a head might be shaken or a pair of shoulders shrugged over the flight of two and the return of one, the general sentiment was probably one of curiosity and perhaps of envy rather than of reprobation.

"Look here, Burger," said Kennedy, looking hard at the placid face of his companion, "I do wish that you would confide in me."

As he spoke he waved his hand in the direction of a rug which lay upon the floor. On the rug stood a long, shallow fruit-basket of the light wicker-work which is used in the Campagna, and this was heaped with a litter of objects, inscribed tiles, broken inscriptions, cracked mosaics, torn papyri, rusty metal ornaments, which to the uninitiated might have seemed to have come straight from a dustman's bin, but which a specialist would have speedily recognized as unique of their kind. The pile of odds and ends in the flat wicker-work basket supplied exactly one of those missing links of social development which are of such interest to the student. It was the German who had brought them in, and the Englishman's eyes were hungry as he looked at them.

"I won't interfere with your treasure-trove, but I should very much like to hear about it," he continued, while Burger very deliberately lit a cigar. "It is evidently a discovery of the first importance. These inscriptions will make a sensation throughout Europe."

"For every one here there are a million there!" said the German. "There are so many that a dozen savants might spend a lifetime over them, and build up a reputation as solid as the Castle of St. Angelo."

Kennedy sat thinking with his fine forehead wrinkled and his fingers playing with his long, fair moustache.

"You have given yourself away, Burger!" said he at last. "Your words can only apply to one thing. You have discovered a new catacomb."

"I had no doubt that you had already come to that conclusion from an examination of these objects."

"Well, they certainly appeared to indicate it, but your last remarks make it certain. There is no place except a catacomb which could contain so vast a store of relics as you describe."

"Quite so. There is no mystery about that. I *have* discovered a new catacomb."

"Where?"

"Ah, that is my secret, my dear Kennedy. Suffice it that it is so situated that there is not one chance in a million of anyone else coming upon it. Its date is different from that of any known catacomb, and it has been reserved for the burial of the highest Christians, so that the remains and the relics are quite different from anything which has ever been seen before. If I was not aware of your knowledge and of your energy, my friend, I would not hesitate, under the pledge of secrecy, to tell you everything about it. But as it is I think that I must certainly prepare my own report of the matter before I expose myself to such formidable competition."

Kennedy loved his subject with a love which was almost a mania—a love which held him true to it, amidst all the distractions which come to a wealthy and dissipated young man. He had ambition, but his ambition was secondary to his mere abstract joy and interest in everything which concerned the old life and history of the city. He yearned to see this new underworld which his companion had discovered.

"Look here, Burger," said he, earnestly, "I assure you that you can trust me most implicitly in the matter. Nothing would induce me to put pen to paper about anything which I see until I have your express permission. I quite understand your feeling and I think it is most natural, but you have really nothing whatever to fear from me. On the other hand, if you don't tell me I shall make a systematic search, and I shall most certainly discover it. In that case, of course, I should make what use I liked of it, since I should be under no obligation to you."

Burger smiled thoughtfully over his cigar.

"I have noticed, friend Kennedy," said he, "that when I want information over any point you are not always so ready to supply it."

"When did you ever ask me anything that I did not tell you? You remember, for example, my giving you the material for your paper about the temple of the Vestals."

"Ah, well, that was not a matter of much importance. If I were to question you upon some intimate thing would you give me an answer, I wonder! This new catacomb is a very intimate thing to me, and I should certainly expect some sign of confidence in return."

"What you are driving at I cannot imagine," said the Englishman, "but if you mean that you will answer my question about the catacomb if I answer any question which you may put to me I can assure you that I will certainly do so."

"Well, then," said Burger, leaning luxuriously back in his settee, and puffing a blue tree of cigar-smoke into the air, "tell me all about your relations with Miss Mary Saunderson."

Kennedy sprang up in his chair and glared angrily at his impassive companion.

"What the devil do you mean?" he cried. "What sort of a question is this? You may mean it as a joke, but you never made a worse one."

"No, I don't mean it as a joke," said Burger, simply. "I am really rather interested in the details of the matter. I don't know much about the world and women and social life and that sort of thing, and such an incident has the fascination of the unknown for me. I know you, and I knew her by sight—I had even spoken to her once or twice. I should very much like to hear from your own lips exactly what it was which occurred between you."

"I won't tell you a word."

"That's all right. It was only my whim to see if you would give up a secret as easily as you expected me to give up my secret of the new catacomb. You wouldn't, and I didn't expect you to. But why should you expect otherwise of me? There's Saint John's clock striking ten. It is quite time that I was going home."

"No; wait a bit, Burger," said Kennedy; "this is really a ridiculous caprice of yours to wish to know about an old love-affair which has burned out months ago. You know we look upon a man who kisses and tells as the greatest coward and villain possible."

"Certainly," said the German, gathering up his basket of curiosities, "when he tells anything about a girl which is previously unknown he must be so. But in this case, as you must be aware, it was a public matter which was the common talk of Rome, so that you are not really doing

Miss Mary Saunderson any injury by discussing her case with me. But still, I respect your scruples, and so good night!"

"Wait a bit, Burger," said Kennedy, laying his hand upon the other's arm; "I am very keen upon this catacomb business, and I can't let it drop quite so easily. Would you mind asking me something else in return—something not quite so eccentric this time?"

"No, no; you have refused, and there is an end of it," said Burger, with his basket on his arm. "No doubt you are quite right not to answer, and no doubt I am quite right also—and so again, my dear Kennedy, good night!"

The Englishman watched Burger cross the room, and he had his hand on the handle of the door before his host sprang up with the air of a man who is making the best of that which cannot be helped.

"Hold on, old fellow," said he; "I think you are behaving in a most ridiculous fashion; but still; if this is your condition, I suppose that I must submit to it. I hate saying anything about a girl, but, as you say, it is all over Rome, and I don't suppose I can tell you anything which you do not know already. What was it you wanted to know?"

The German came back to the stove, and, laying down his basket, he sank into his chair once more.

"May I have another cigar?" said he. "Thank you very much! I never smoke when I work, but I enjoy a chat much more when I am under the influence of tobacco. Now, as regards this young lady, with whom you had this little adventure. What in the world has become of her?"

"She is at home with her own people."

"Oh, really—in England?"

"Yes."

"What part of England—London?"

"No, Twickenham."

"You must excuse my curiosity, my dear Kennedy, and you must put it down to my ignorance of the world. No doubt it is quite a simple thing to persuade a young lady to go off with you for three weeks or so, and then to hand her over to her own family at—what did you call the place?"

"Twickenham."

"Quite so—at Twickenham. But it is something so entirely outside my own experience that I cannot even imagine how you set about it. For example, if you had loved this girl your love could hardly disappear in three weeks, so I presume that you could not have loved her at all. But if you did not love her why should you make this great scandal which has damaged you and ruined her?"

Kennedy looked moodily into the red eye of the stove.

"That's a logical way of looking at it, certainly," said he. "Love is a big word, and it represents a good many different shades of feeling. I liked her, and—well, you say you've seen her—you know how charming she could look. But still I am willing to admit, looking back, that I could never have really loved her."

"Then, my dear Kennedy, why did you do it?"

"The adventure of the thing had a great deal to do with it."

"What! You are so fond of adventures!"

"Where would the variety of life be without them? It was for an adventure that I first began to pay my attentions to her. I've chased a good deal of game in my time, but there's no chase like that of a pretty woman. There was the piquant difficulty of it also, for, as she was the companion of Lady Emily Rood, it was almost impossible to see her alone. On the top of all the other obstacles which attracted me, I learned from her own lips very early in the proceedings that she was engaged."

"Mein Gott! To whom?"

"She mentioned no names."

"I do not think that anyone knows that. So that made the adventure more alluring, did it?"

"Well, it did certainly give a spice to it. Don't you think so?"

"I tell you that I am very ignorant about these things."

"My dear fellow, you can remember that the apple you stole from your neighbour's tree was always sweeter than that which fell from your own. And then I found that she cared for me."

"What—at once?"

"Oh, no, it took about three months of sapping and mining. But at last I won her over. She understood that my judicial separation from my wife made it impossible for me to do the right thing by her—but she came all the same, and we had a delightful time, as long as it lasted."

"But how about the other man?"

Kennedy shrugged his shoulders.

"I suppose it is the survival of the fittest," said he. "If he had been the better man she would not have deserted him. Let's drop the subject, for I have had enough of it!"

"Only one other thing. How did you get rid of her in three weeks?"

"Well, we had both cooled down a bit, you understand. She absolutely refused, under any circumstances, to come back to face the people she had known in Rome. Now, of course, Rome is necessary to me, and I was already pining to be back at my work—so there was one obvious cause of separation. Then, again, her old father turned up at the hotel in London, and there was a scene, and the whole thing became so unpleasant that really—though I missed her dreadfully at first—I was very glad to slip out of it. Now, I rely upon you not to repeat anything of what I have said."

"My dear Kennedy, I should not dream of repeating it. But all that you say interests me very much, for it gives me an insight into your way of looking at things, which is entirely different from mine, for I have seen so little of life. And now you want to know about my new catacomb. There's no use my trying to describe it, for you would never find it by that. There is only one thing, and that is for me to take you there."

"That would be splendid."

"When would you like to come?"

"The sooner the better. I am all impatience to see it."

"Well, it is a beautiful night—though a trifle cold. Suppose we start in an hour. We must be very careful to keep the matter to ourselves. If anyone saw us hunting in couples they would suspect that there was something going on."

"We can't be too cautious," said Kennedy. "Is it far?"

"Some miles."

"Not too far to walk?"

"Oh, no, we could walk there easily."

"We had better do so, then. A cabman's suspicions would be aroused if he dropped us both at some lonely spot in the dead of the night."

"Quite so. I think it would be best for us to meet at the Gate of the Appian Way at midnight. I must go back to my lodgings for the matches and candles and things."

"All right, Burger! I think it is very kind of you to let me into this secret, and I promise you that I will write nothing about it until you have published your report. Good-bye for the present! You will find me at the Gate at twelve."

The cold, clear air was filled with the musical chimes from that city of clocks as Burger, wrapped in an Italian overcoat, with a lantern hanging from his hand, walked up to the rendezvous. Kennedy stepped out of the shadow to meet him.

"You are ardent in work as well as in love!" said the German, laughing.

"Yes; I have been waiting here for nearly half an hour."

"I hope you left no clue as to where we were going."

"Not such a fool! By Jove, I am chilled to the bone! Come on, Burger, let us warm ourselves by a spurt of hard walking."

Their footsteps sounded loud and crisp upon the rough stone paving of the disappointing road which is all that is left of the most famous highway of the world. A peasant or two going home from the wine-shop, and a few carts of country produce coming up to Rome, were the only things which they met. They swung along, with the huge tombs looming up through the darkness upon each side of them, until they had come as far as the Catacombs of St. Calistus, and saw against a rising moon the great circular bastion of Cecilia Metella in front of them. Then Burger stopped with his hand to his side.

"Your legs are longer than mine, and you are more accustomed to walking," said he, laughing. "I think that the place where we turn off is somewhere here. Yes, this is it, round the corner of the trattoria. Now, it is a very narrow path, so perhaps I had better go in front and you can follow."

He had lit his lantern, and by its light they were enabled to follow a narrow and devious track which wound across the marshes of the Campagna. The great Aqueduct of old Rome lay like a monstrous caterpillar across the moonlit landscape, and their road led them under one of its huge arches, and past the circle of crumbling bricks which marks the old arena. At last Burger stopped at a solitary wooden cow-house, and he drew a key from his pocket.

"Surely your catacomb is not inside a house!" cried Kennedy.

"The entrance to it is. That is just the safeguard which we have against anyone else discovering it."

"Does the proprietor know of it?"

"Not he. He had found one or two objects which made me almost certain that his house was built on the entrance to such a place. So I rented it from him, and did my excavations for myself. Come in, and shut the door behind you."

It was a long, empty building, with the mangers of the cows along one wall. Burger put his lantern down on the ground, and shaded its light in all directions save one by draping his overcoat round it.

"It might excite remark if anyone saw a light in this lonely place," said he. "Just help me to move this boarding."

The flooring was loose in the corner, and plank by plank the two savants raised it and leaned it against the wall. Below there was a square aperture and a stair of old stone steps which led away down into the bowels of the earth.

"Be careful!" cried Burger, as Kennedy, in his impatience, hurried down them. "It is a perfect rabbits'-warren below, and if you were once to lose your way there the chances would be a hundred to one against your ever coming out again. Wait until I bring the light."

"How do you find your own way if it is so complicated?"

"I had some very narrow escapes at first, but I have gradually learned to go about. There is a certain system to it, but it is one which a lost man, if he were in the dark, could not possibly find out. Even now I always spin out a ball of string behind me when I am going far into the catacomb. You can see for yourself that it is difficult, but every one of these passages divides and subdivides a dozen times before you go a hundred yards."

They had descended some twenty feet from the level of the byre, and they were standing now in a square chamber cut out of the soft tufa. The lantern cast a flickering light, bright below and dim above, over the cracked brown walls. In every direction were the black openings of passages which radiated from this common centre.

"I want you to follow me closely, my friend," said Burger. "Do not loiter to look at anything upon the way, for the place to which I will take you contains all that you can see, and more. It will save time for us to go there direct."

He led the way down one of the corridors, and the Englishman followed closely at his heels. Every now and then the passage bifurcated, but Burger was evidently following some secret marks of his own, for he neither stopped nor hesitated. Everywhere along the walls, packed like the berths upon an emigrant ship, lay the Christians of old Rome. The yellow light flickered over the shrivelled features of the mummies, and gleamed upon rounded skulls and long, white armbones crossed over fleshless chests. And everywhere as he passed Kennedy looked with wistful eyes upon inscriptions, funeral vessels, pictures, vestments, utensils, all lying as pious hands had placed them so many centuries ago. It was apparent to him, even in those hurried, passing glances, that this was the earliest and finest of the catacombs, containing such a storehouse of Roman remains as had never before come at one time under the observation of the student.

"What would happen if the light went out?" he asked, as they hurried onwards.

"I have a spare candle and a box of matches in my pocket. By the way, Kennedy, have you any matches?"

"No; you had better give me some."

"Oh, that is all right. There is no chance of our separating."

"How far are we going? It seems to me that we have walked at least a quarter of a mile."

"More than that, I think. There is really no limit to the tombs—at least, I have never been able to find any. This is a very difficult place, so I think that I will use our ball of string."

He fastened one end of it to a projecting stone and he carried the coil in the breast of his coat, paying it out as he advanced. Kennedy saw that it was no unnecessary precaution, for the passages had become more complex and tortuous than ever, with a perfect network of intersecting corridors. But these all ended in one large circular hall with a square pedestal of tufa topped with a slab of marble at one end of it.

"By Jove!" cried Kennedy in an ecstasy, as Burger swung his lantern over the marble. "It is a Christian altar—probably the first one in existence. Here is the little consecration cross cut upon the corner of it. No doubt this circular space was used as a church."

"Precisely," said Burger. "If I had more time I should like to show you all the bodies which are buried in these niches upon the walls, for they are the early popes and bishops of the Church, with their mitres, their croziers, and full canonicals. Go over to that one and look at it!"

Kennedy went across, and stared at the ghastly head which lay loosely on the shredded and mouldering mitre.

"This is most interesting," said he, and his voice seemed to boom against the concave vault. "As far as my experience goes, it is unique. Bring the lantern over, Burger, for I want to see them all."

But the German had strolled away, and was standing in the middle of a yellow circle of light at the other side of the hall.

"Do you know how many wrong turnings there are between this and the stairs?" he asked. "There are over two thousand. No doubt it was one of the means of protection which the Christians adopted. The odds are two thousand to one against a man getting out, even if he had a light; but if he were in the dark it would, of course, be far more difficult."

"So I should think."

"And the darkness is something dreadful. I tried it once for an experiment. Let us try it again!" He stooped to the lantern, and in an instant it was as if an invisible hand was squeezed tightly over each of Kennedy's eyes. Never had he known what such darkness was. It seemed to press upon him and to smother him. It was a solid obstacle against which the body shrank from advancing. He put his hands out to push it back from him.

"That will do, Burger," said he, "let's have the light again."

But his companion began to laugh, and in that circular room the sound seemed to come from every side at once.

"You seem uneasy, friend Kennedy," said he.

"Go on, man, light the candle!" said Kennedy impatiently.

"It's very strange, Kennedy, but I could not in the least tell by the sound in which direction you stand. Could you tell where I am?"

"No; you seem to be on every side of me."

"If it were not for this string which I hold in my hand I should not have a notion which way to go."

"I dare say not. Strike a light, man, and have an end of this nonsense."

"Well, Kennedy, there are two things which I understand that you are very fond of. The one is an adventure, and the other is an obstacle to surmount. The adventure must be the finding of your way out of this catacomb. The obstacle will be the darkness and the two thousand wrong turns which make the way a little difficult to find. But you need not hurry, for you have plenty of time, and when you halt for a rest now and then, I should like you just to think of Miss Mary Saunderson, and whether you treated her quite fairly."

"You devil, what do you mean?" roared Kennedy. He was running about in little circles and clasping at the solid blackness with both hands.

"Good-bye," said the mocking voice, and it was already at some distance. "I really do not think, Kennedy, even by your own showing that you did the right thing by that girl. There was only one little thing which you appeared not to know, and I can supply it. Miss Saunderson was engaged to a poor ungainly devil of a student, and his name was Julius Burger."

There was a rustle somewhere, the vague sound of a foot striking a stone, and then there fell silence upon that old Christian church—a stagnant, heavy silence which closed round Kennedy and shut him in like water round a drowning man.

Some two months afterwards the following paragraph made the round of the European Press:

"One of the most interesting discoveries of recent years is that of the new catacomb in Rome, which lies some distance to the east of the well-known vaults of St. Calixtus. The finding of this important burial-place, which is exceeding rich in most interesting early Christian remains, is due to the energy and sagacity of Dr. Julius Burger, the young German specialist, who is rapidly taking the first place as an authority upon ancient Rome. Although the first to publish his discovery, it appears that a less fortunate adventurer had anticipated Dr. Burger. Some months ago Mr. Kennedy, the well-known English student, disappeared suddenly from his rooms in the Corso, and it was conjectured that his association with a recent scandal had driven him to leave Rome. It appears now that he had in reality fallen a victim to that fervid love of archaeology which had raised him to a distinguished place among living scholars. His body was discovered in the heart of the new catacomb, and it was evident from the condition of his feet and boots that he had tramped for days through the tortuous corridors which make these subterranean tombs so dangerous to explorers. The deceased gentleman had, with inexplicable rashness, made his way into this labyrinth without, as far as can be discovered, taking with him either candles or matches, so that his sad fate was the natural result of his own temerity. What makes the matter more painful is that Dr. Julius Burger was an intimate friend of the deceased. His joy at the extraordinary find which he has been so fortunate as to make has been greatly marred by the terrible fate of his comrade and fellow-worker."

Mary Postgate

RUDYARD KIPLING
(English, 1865–1936)

Of Miss Mary Postgate, Lady McCausland wrote that she was "thoroughly conscientious, tidy, companionable, and ladylike. I am very sorry to part with her, and shall always be interested in her welfare."

Miss Fowler engaged her on this recommendation, and to her surprise, for she had had experience of companions, found that it was true. Miss Fowler was nearer sixty than fifty at the time, but though she needed care she did not exhaust her attendant's vitality. On the contrary, she gave out, stimulatingly and with reminiscences. Her father had been a minor Court official in the days when the Great Exhibition of 1851 had just set its seal on Civilisation made perfect. Some of Miss Fowler's tales, none the less, were not always for the young. Mary was not young, and though her speech was as colourless as her eyes or her hair, she was never shocked. She listened unflinchingly to every one; said at the end, "How interesting!" or "How shocking!" as the case might be, and never again referred to it, for she prided herself on a trained mind, which "did not dwell on these things." She was, too, a treasure at domestic accounts, for which the village tradesmen, with their weekly books, loved her not. Otherwise she had no enemies; provoked no jealousy even among the plainest; neither gossip nor slander had ever been traced to her; she supplied the odd place at the Rector's or the Doctor's table at half an hour's notice; she was a sort of public aunt to very many small children of the village street, whose parents, while accepting everything, would have been swift to resent what they called "patronage"; she served on the

Village Nursing Committee as Miss Fowler's nominee when Miss Fowler was crippled by rheumatoid arthritis, and came out of six months' fortnightly meetings equally respected by all the cliques.

And when Fate threw Miss Fowler's nephew, an unlovely orphan of eleven, on Miss Fowler's hands, Mary Postgate stood to her share of the business of education as practised in private and public schools. She checked printed clothes-lists, and unitemised bills of extras; wrote to Head and House masters, matrons, nurses and doctors, and grieved or rejoiced over half-term reports. Young Wyndham Fowler repaid her in his holidays by calling her "Gatepost," "Postey," or "Packthread," by thumping her between her narrow shoulders, or by chasing her bleating, round the garden, her large mouth open, her large nose high in air, at a stiff-necked shamble very like a camel's. Later on he filled the house with clamour, argument, and harangues as to his personal needs, likes and dislikes, and the limitations of "you women," reducing Mary to tears of physical fatigue, or, when he chose to be humorous, of helpless laughter. At crises, which multiplied as he grew older, she was his ambassadress and his interpretress to Miss Fowler, who had no large sympathy with the young; a vote in his interest at the councils on his future; his sewing-woman, strictly accountable for mislaid boots and garments; always his butt and his slave.

And when he decided to become a solicitor, and had entered an office in London; when his greeting had changed from "Hullo, Postey, you old beast," to "Mornin' Packthread," there came a war which, unlike all wars that Mary could remember, did not stay decently outside England and in the newspapers, but intruded on the lives of people whom she knew. As she said to Miss Fowler, it was "most vexatious." It took the Rector's son who was going into business with his elder brother; it took the Colonel's nephew on the eve of fruit-farming in Canada; it took Mrs. Grant's son who, his mother said, was devoted to the ministry; and, very early indeed, it took Wynn Fowler, who announced on a postcard that he had joined the Flying Corps and wanted a cardigan waistcoat.

"He must go, and he must have the waistcoat," said Miss Fowler. So Mary got the proper-sized needles and wool, while Miss Fowler told the men of her establishment—two gardeners and an odd man, aged sixty—that those who could join the Army had better do so. The gardeners left. Cheape, the odd man, stayed on, and was promoted to the gardener's cottage. The cook, scorning to be limited in luxuries, also left, after a spirited scene with Miss Fowler, and took the house-maid with her. Miss Fowler gazetted Nellie, Cheape's seventeen-year-old daughter, to the vacant post; Mrs. Cheape to the rank of cook with occasional cleaning bouts; and the reduced establishment moved forward smoothly.

Wynn demanded an increase in his allowance. Miss Fowler, who always looked facts in the face, said, "He must have it. The chances are he won't live long to draw it, and if three hundred makes him happy——"

Wynn was grateful, and came over, in his tight-buttoned uniform, to say so. His training centre was not thirty miles away, and his talk was so technical that it had to be explained by charts of the various types of machines. He gave Mary such a chart.

"And you'd better study it, Postey," he said. "You'll be seeing a lot of 'em soon." So Mary studied the chart, but when Wynn next arrived to swell and exalt himself before his womenfolk, she failed badly in crossexamination, and he rated her as in the old days.

"You *look* more or less like a human being," he said in his new Service voice. "You *must* have had a brain at some time in your past. What have you done with it? Where d'you keep it? A sheep would know more than you do, Postey. You're lamentable. You are less use than an empty tin can, you dowey old cassowary."

"I suppose that's how your superior officer talks to *you?*" said Miss Fowler from her chair.

"But Postey doesn't mind," Wynn replied. "Do you, Packthread?"

"Why? Was Wynn saying anything? I shall get this right next time you come," she muttered, and knitted her pale brows again over the diagrams of Taubes, Farmans, and Zeppelins.

In a few weeks the mere land and sea battles which she read to Miss Fowler after breakfast passed her like idle breath. Her heart and her interest were high in the air with Wynn, who had finished "rolling" (whatever that might be) and had gone on from a "taxi" to a machine more or less his own. One morning it circled over their very chimneys, alighted on Vegg's Heath, almost outside the garden gate, and Wynn came in, blue with cold, shouting for food. He and she drew Miss Fowler's bath-chair, as they had often done, along the Heath foot-path to look at the biplane. Mary observed that "it smelt very badly."

"Postey, I believe you think with your nose," said Wynn. "I know you don't with your mind. Now, what type's that?"

"I'll go and get the chart," said Mary.

"You're hopeless! You haven't the mental capacity of a white mouse," he cried, and explained the dials and the sockets for bomb-dropping till it was time to mount and ride the wet clouds once more.

"Ah!" said Mary, as the stinking thing flared upward. "Wait till our Flying Corps gets to work! Wynn says it's much safer than in the trenches."

"I wonder," said Miss Fowler. "Tell Cheape to come and tow me home again."

"It's all downhill. I can do it," said Mary, "if you put the brake on." She laid her lean self against the pushing-bar and home they trundled.

"Now, be careful you aren't heated and catch a chill," said overdressed Miss Fowler.

"Nothing makes me perspire," said Mary. As she bumped the chair under the porch she straightened her long back. The exertion had given her a colour, and the wind had loosened a wisp of hair across her forehead. Miss Fowler glanced at her.

"What do you ever think of, Mary?" she demanded suddenly.

"Oh, Wynn says he wants another three pairs of stockings—as thick as we can make them."

"Yes. But I mean the things that women think about. Here you are, more than forty——"

"Forty-four," said truthful Mary.

"Well?"

"Well?" Mary offered Miss Fowler her shoulder as usual.

"And you've been with me ten years now."

"Let's see," said Mary. "Wynn was eleven when he came. He's twenty now, and I came two years before that. It must be eleven."

"Eleven! And you've never told me anything that matters in all that while. Looking back, it seems to me that *I've* done all the talking."

"I'm afraid I'm not much of a conversationalist. As Wynn says, I haven't the mind. Let me take your hat."

Miss Fowler, moving stiffly from the hip, stamped her rubber-tipped stick on the tiled hall floor. "Mary, aren't you *anything* except a companion? Would you *ever* have been anything except a companion?"

Mary hung up the garden hat on its proper peg. "No," she said after consideration. "I don't imagine I ever should. But I've no imagination, I'm afraid."

She fetched Miss Fowler her eleven-o'clock glass of Contrexeville.

That was the wet December when it rained six inches to the month, and the women went abroad as little as might be. Wynn's flying chariot visited them several times, and for two mornings (he had warned her by postcard) Mary heard the thresh of his propellers at dawn. The second time she ran to the window, and stared at the whitening sky. A little blur passed overhead. She lifted her lean arms towards it.

That evening at six o'clock there came an announcement in an official envelope that Second Lieutenant W. Fowler had been killed during a trial flight. Death was instantaneous. She read it and carried it to Miss Fowler.

"I never expected anything else," said Miss Fowler; "but I'm sorry it happened before he had done anything."

The room was whirling round Mary Postgate, but she found herself quite steady in the midst of it.

"Yes," she said. "It's a great pity he didn't die in action after he had killed somebody."

"He was killed instantly. That's one comfort," Miss Fowler went on.

"But Wynn says the shock of a fall kills a man at once—whatever happens to the tanks," quoted Mary.

The room was coming to rest now. She heard Miss Fowler say impatiently, "But why can't we cry, Mary?" and herself replying, "There's nothing to cry for. He has done his duty as much as Mrs. Grant's son did."

"And when he died, *she* came and cried all the morning," said Miss Fowler. "This only makes me feel tired—terribly tired. Will you help me to bed, please, Mary?—And I think I'd like the hot-water bottle."

So Mary helped her and sat beside, talking of Wynn in his riotous youth.

"I believe," said Miss Fowler suddenly, "that old people and young people slip from under a stroke like this. The middle-aged feel it most."

"I expect that's true," said Mary, rising. "I'm going to put away the things in his room now. Shall we wear mourning?"

"Certainly not," said Miss Fowler. "Except, of course, at the funeral. I can't go. You will. I want you to arrange about his being buried here. What a blessing it didn't happen at Salisbury!"

Every one, from the Authorities of the Flying Corps to the Rector, was most kind and sympathetic. Mary found herself for the moment in a world where bodies were in the habit of being despatched by all sorts of conveyances to all sorts of places. And at the funeral two young men in buttoned-up uniforms stood beside the grave and spoke to her afterwards.

"You're Miss Postgate, aren't you?" said one. "Fowler told me about you. He was a good chap—a first-class fellow—a great loss."

"Great loss!" growled his companion. "We're all awfully sorry."

"How high did he fall from?" Mary whispered.

"Pretty nearly four thousand feet, I should think, didn't he? You were up that day, Monkey?"

"All of that," the other child replied. "My bar made three thousand, and I wasn't as high as him by a lot."

"Then *that's* all right," said Mary. "Thank you very much."

They moved away as Mrs. Grant flung herself weeping on Mary's flat chest, under the lych-gate, and cried, *"I* know how it feels! *I* know how it feels!"

"But both his parents are dead," Mary returned, as she fended her off. "Perhaps they've all met by now," she added vaguely as she escaped towards the coach.

"I've thought of that too," wailed Mrs. Grant; "but then he'll be practically a stranger to them. Quite embarrassing!"

Mary faithfully reported every detail of the ceremony to Miss Fowler, who, when she described Mrs. Grant's outburst, laughed aloud.

"Oh, how Wynn would have enjoyed it! He was always utterly unreliable at funerals. D'you remember——" And they talked of him again, each piecing out the other's gaps. "And now," said Miss Fowler, "we'll pull up the blinds and we'll have a general tidy. That always does us good. Have you seen to Wynn's things?"

"Everything—since he first came," said Mary. "He was never destructive—even with his toys."

They faced that neat room.

"It can't be natural not to cry," Mary said at last. "I'm *so* afraid you'll have a reaction."

"As I told you, we old people slip from under the stroke. It's you I'm afraid for. Have you cried yet?"

"I can't. It only makes me angry with the Germans."

"That's sheer waste of vitality," said Miss Fowler. "We must live till the war's finished." She opened a full wardrobe. "Now, I've been thinking things over. This is my plan. All his civilian clothes can be given away—Belgian refugees, and so on."

Mary nodded. "Boots, collars, and gloves?"

"Yes. We don't need to keep anything except his cap and belt."

"They came back yesterday with his Flying Corps clothes"—Mary pointed to a roll on the little iron bed.

"Ah, but keep his Service things. Some one may be glad of them later. Do you remember his sizes?"

"Five feet eight and a half; thirty-six inches round the chest. But he told me he's just put on an inch and a half. I'll mark it on a label and tie it on his sleeping-bag."

"So that disposes of *that,*" said Miss Fowler, tapping the palm of one hand with the ringed third finger of the other. "What waste it all is! We'll get his old school trunk to-morrow and pack his civilian clothes."

"And the rest?" said Mary. "His books and pictures and the games and the toys—and—and the rest?"

"My plan is to burn every single thing," said Miss Fowler. "Then we shall know where they are and no one can handle them afterwards. What do you think?"

"I think that would be much the best," said Mary. "But there's such a lot of them."

"We'll burn them in the destructor," said Miss Fowler.

This was an open-air furnace for the consumption of refuse; a little circular four-foot tower of pierced brick over an iron grating. Miss Fowler had noticed the design in a gardening journal years ago, and had had it built at the bottom of the garden. It suited her tidy soul, for it saved unsightly rubbish-heaps, and the ashes lightened the stiff clay soil.

Mary considered for a moment, saw her way clear, and nodded again. They spent the evening putting away well-remembered civilian suits, underclothes that Mary had marked, and the regiments of very gaudy socks and ties. A second trunk was needed, and, after that, a little packing-case, and it was late next day when Cheape and the local carrier lifted them to the cart. The Rector luckily knew of a friend's son, about five feet eight and a half inches high, to whom a complete Flying Corps outfit would be most acceptable, and sent his gardener's son down with a barrow to take delivery of it. The cap was hung up in Miss Fowler's bedroom, the belt in Miss Postgate's; for, as Miss Fowler said, they had no desire to make tea-party talk of them.

"That disposes of *that,*" said Miss Fowler. "I'll leave the rest to you,

Mary. I can't run up and down the garden. You'd better take the big clothes-basket and get Nellie to help you."

"I shall take the wheel-barrow and do it myself," said Mary, and for once in her life closed her mouth.

Miss Fowler, in moments of irritation, had called Mary deadly methodical. She put on her oldest water-proof and gardening-hat and her ever-slipping goloshes, for the weather was on the edge of more rain. She gathered fire-lighters from the kitchen, a half-scuttle of coals, and a faggot of brushwood. These she wheeled in the barrow down the mossed paths to the dank little laurel shrubbery where the destructor stood under the drip of three oaks. She climbed the wire fence into the Rector's glebe just behind, and from his tenant's rick pulled two large armfuls of good hay, which she spread neatly on the fire-bars. Next, journey by journey, passing Miss Fowler's white face at the morning-room window each time, she brought down in the towel-covered clothes-basket, on the wheel-barrow, thumbed and used Hentys, Marryats, Levers, Stevensons, Baroness Orczys, Garvices, schoolbooks, and atlases, unrelated piles of the *Motor Cyclist,* the *Light Car,* and catalogues of Olympia Exhibitions; the remnants of a fleet of sailing-ships from nine-penny cutters to a three-guinea yacht; a prep.-school dressing-gown; bats from three-and-sixpence to twenty-four shillings; cricket and tennis balls; disintegrated steam and clockwork locomotives with their twisted rails; a grey and red tin model of a submarine; a dumb gramophone and cracked records; golf-clubs that had to be broken across the knee, like his walking-sticks, and an assegai; photographs of private and public school cricket and football elevens, and his O.T.C. on the line of march; kodaks, and film-rolls; some pewters, and one real silver cup, for boxing competitions and Junior Hurdles; sheaves of school photographs; Miss Fowler's photograph; her own which he had borne off in fun and (good care she took not to ask!) had never returned; a playbox with a secret drawer; a load of flannels, belts, and jerseys, and a pair of spiked shoes unearthed in the attic; a packet of all the letters that Miss Fowler and she had ever written to him, kept for some absurd reason through all these years; a five-day attempt at a diary; framed pictures of racing motors in full Brooklands career, and load upon load of undistinguishable wreckage of tool-boxes, rabbit-hutches, electric batteries, tin soldiers, fret-saw outfits, and jig-saw puzzles.

Miss Fowler at the window watched her come and go, and said to herself, "Mary's an old woman. I never realised it before."

After lunch she recommended her to rest.

"I'm not in the least tired," said Mary. "I've got it all arranged. I'm going to the village at two o'clock for some paraffin. Nellie hasn't enough, and the walk will do me good."

She made one last quest round the house before she started, and found that she had overlooked nothing. It began to mist as soon as she had skirted Vegg's Heath, where Wynn used to descend—it seemed to her that she could almost hear the beat of his propellers overhead, but there was nothing to see. She hoisted her umbrella and lunged into the blind wet till she had reached the shelter of the empty village. As she came out of Mr. Kidd's shop with a bottle full of paraffin in her string shopping-bag, she met Nurse Eden, the village nurse, and fell into talk with her, as usual, about the village children. They were just parting opposite the "Royal Oak," when a gun, they fancied, was fired immediately behind the house. It was followed by a child's shriek dying into a wail.

"Accident!" said Nurse Eden promptly, and dashed through the empty bar, followed by Mary. They found Mrs. Gerritt, the publican's wife, who could only gasp and point to the yard, where a little cart-lodge was sliding sideways amid a clatter of tiles. Nurse Eden snatched up a sheet drying before the fire, ran out, lifted something from the ground, and flung the sheet round it. The sheet turned scarlet and half her uniform too, as she bore the load into the kitchen. It was little Edna Gerritt, aged nine, whom Mary had known since her perambulator days.

"Am I hurted bad?" Edna asked, and died between Nurse Eden's dripping hands. The sheet fell aside and for an instant, before she could shut her eyes, Mary saw the ripped and shredded body.

"It's a wonder she spoke at all" said Nurse Eden. "What in God's name was it?"

"A bomb," said Mary.

"One o' the Zeppelins?"

"No. An aeroplane. I thought I heard it on the Heath but I fancied it was one of ours. It must have shut off its engines as it came down. That's why we didn't notice it."

"The filthy pigs!" said Nurse Eden, all white and shaken. "See the pickle I'm in! Go and tell Dr. Hennis, Miss Postgate." Nurse looked at the mother, who had dropped face down on the floor. "She's only in a fit. Turn her over."

Mary heaved Mrs. Gerritt right side up, and hurried off for the doctor.

When she told her tale, he asked her to sit down in the surgery till he got her something.

"But I don't need it, I assure you," said she. "I don't think it would be wise to tell Miss Fowler about it, do you? Her heart is so irritable in this weather."

Dr. Hennis looked at her admiringly as he packed up his bag.

"No. Don't tell anybody till we're sure," he said, and hastened to the "Royal Oak," while Mary went on with the paraffin. The village behind her was as quiet as usual, for the news had not yet spread. She frowned a little to herself her large nostrils expanded uglily and from time to time she muttered a phrase which Wynn who never restrained himself before his women-folk, had applied to the enemy. "Bloody pagans! They *are* bloody pagans. But," she continued, falling back on the teaching that had made her what she was, "one mustn't let one's mind dwell on these things."

Before she reached the house Dr. Hennis, who was also a special constable, overtook her in his car.

"Oh, Miss Postgate," he said, "I wanted to tell you that that accident at the 'Royal Oak' was due to Gerritt's stable tumbling down. It's been dangerous for a long time. It ought to have been condemned."

"I thought I heard an explosion too," said Mary.

"You might have been misled by the beams snapping. I've been looking at 'em. They were dry-rotted through and through. Of course, as they broke, they would make a noise just like a gun."

"Yes?" said Mary politely.

"Poor little Edna was playing underneath it," he went on, still holding her with his eyes, "and that and the tiles cut her to pieces, you see?"

"I saw it," said Mary, shaking her head. "I heard it too."

"Well, we cannot be sure." Dr. Hennis changed his tone completely. "I know both you and Nurse Eden (I've been speaking to her) are perfectly trustworthy, and I can rely on you not to say anything—yet at least. It is no good to stir up people unless——"

"Oh, I never do—anyhow," said Mary, and Dr. Hennis went on to the county town.

After all, she told herself, it might, just possibly, have been the collapse of the old stable that had done all those things to poor little Edna. She was sorry she had even hinted at other things, but Nurse Eden was discretion itself. By the time she reached home the affair seemed increasingly remote by its very monstrosity. As she came in, Miss Fowler told her that a couple of aeroplanes had passed half an hour ago.

"I thought I heard them," she replied, "I'm going down to the garden now. I've got the paraffin."

"Yes, but—what *have* you got on your boots? They're soaking wet. Change them at once."

Not only did Mary obey but she wrapped the boots in a newspaper, and put them into the string bag with the bottle. So, armed with the longest kitchen poker, she left.

"It's raining again," was Miss Fowler's last word, "but—I know you won't be happy till that's disposed of."

"It won't take long. I've got everything down there, and I've put the lid on the destructor to keep the wet out."

The shrubbery was filling with twilight by the time she had completed her arrangements and sprinkled the sacrificial oil. As she lit the match that would burn her heart to ashes, she heard a groan or a grunt behind the dense Portugal laurels.

"Cheape?" she called impatiently, but Cheape, with his ancient lumbago, in his comfortable cottage would be the last man to profane the sanctuary. "Sheep," she concluded, and threw in the fusee. The pyre went up in a roar, and the immediate flame hastened night around her.

"How Wynn would have loved this!" she thought, stepping back from the blaze.

By its light she saw, half hidden behind a laurel not five paces away, a bareheaded man sitting very stiffly at the foot of one of the oaks. A broken branch lay across his lap—one booted leg protruding from beneath it. His head moved ceaselessly from side to side, but his body was as still as the tree's trunk. He was dressed—she moved sideways to look more closely—in a uniform something like Wynn's, with a flap buttoned across the chest. For an instant she had some idea that it might be one of the young flying men she had met at the funeral. But their heads were dark and glossy. This man's was as pale as a baby's, and so closely cropped that she could see the disgusting pinky skin beneath. His lips moved.

"What do you say?" Mary moved towards him and stooped.

"Laty! Laty! Laty!" he muttered, while his hands picked at the dead wet leaves. There was no doubt as to his nationality. It made her so angry that she strode back to the destructor, though it was still too hot to use the poker there. Wynn's books seemed to be catching well. She looked up at the oak behind the man; several of the light upper and two or three rotten lower branches had broken and scattered their rubbish on the shrubbery path. On the lowest fork a helmet with dependent strings, showed like a bird's-nest in the light of a long-tongued flame. Evidently this person had fallen through the tree. Wynn had told her that it was quite possible for people to fall out of aeroplanes. Wynn told her too, that trees were useful things to break an aviator's fall, but in this case the aviator must have been broken or he would have moved from his queer position. He seemed helpless except for his horrible rolling head. On the other hand, she could see a pistol case at his belt—and Mary loathed pistols. Months ago, after reading certain Belgian reports together, she and Miss Fowler had had dealings with one—a huge revolver with flat-nosed bullets, which latter, Wynn said, were forbidden by the rules of war to be used against civilised enemies. "They're good enough for us," Miss Fowler had replied. "Show Mary how it works." And Wynn, laughing at the mere possibility of any such need, had led the craven winking Mary into the Rector's disused quarry, and had shown her how to fire the terrible machine. It lay now in the top-left-hand drawer of her toilet-table —a memento not included in the burning. Wynn would be pleased to see how she was not afraid.

She slipped up to the house to get it. When she came through the rain, the eyes in the head were alive with expectation. The mouth even tried to smile. But at sight of the revolver its corners went down just like Edna Gerritt's. A tear trickled from one eye, and the head rolled from shoulder to shoulder as though trying to point out something.

"Cassée. Tout cassée," it whimpered.

"What do you say?" said Mary disgustedly, keeping well to one side, though only the head moved.

"Cassée," it repeated. "Che me rends. Le médicin! Toctor!"

"Nein!" said she, bringing all her small German to bear with the big pistol. "Ich haben der todt Kinder gesehn."

The head was still. Mary's hand dropped. She had been careful to keep her finger off the trigger for fear of accidents. After a few moments' waiting, she returned to the destructor, where the flames were falling, and churned up Wynn's charring books with the poker. Again the head groaned for the doctor.

"Stop that!" said Mary, and stamped her foot. "Stop that, you bloody pagan!"

The words came quite smoothly and naturally. They were Wynn's own words, and Wynn was a gentleman who for no consideration on earth would have torn little Edna into those vividly coloured strips and strings. But this thing hunched under the oak-tree had done that thing. It was no question of reading horrors out of newspapers to Miss Fowler. Mary had seen it with her own eyes on the "Royal Oak" kitchen table. She must not allow her mind to dwell upon it. Now Wynn was dead, and everything connected with him was lumping and rustling and tinkling under her busy poker into red black dust and grey leaves of ash. The thing beneath the oak would die too. Mary had seen death more than once. She came of a family that had a knack of dying under, as she told Miss Fowler, "most distressing circumstances." She would stay where she was till she was entirely satisfied that It was dead—dead as dear papa in the late 'eighties; aunt Mary in 'eighty-nine; mamma in 'ninety-one; cousin Dick in 'ninety-five; Lady McCausland's housemaid in 'ninety-nine; Lady McCausland's sister in nineteen hundred and one; Wynn buried five days ago; and Edna Gerritt still waiting for decent earth to hide her. As she thought—her underlip caught up by one faded canine, brows knit and nostrils wide—she wielded the poker with lunges that jarred the grating at the bottom, and careful scrapes round the brick-work above. She looked at her wrist-watch. It was getting on to half-past four, and the rain was coming down in earnest. Tea would be at five. If It did not die before that time, she would be soaked and would have to change. Meantime, and this occupied her, Wynn's things were burning well in spite of the hissing wet though now and again a book-back with a quite distinguishable title would be heaved up out of the mass. The exercise of stoking had given her a glow which seemed to reach to the marrow of her bones. She hummed—Mary never had a voice—to herself. She had never believed in all those advanced views—though Miss Fowler herself leaned a little that way—of woman's work in the world; but now she saw there was much to be said for them. This, for instance, was her work—work which no man, least of all Dr. Hennis, would ever have done. A man, at such a crisis, would be what Wynn called a "sportsman"; would leave everything to fetch help, and would certainly bring It into the house. Now a woman's business was to make a happy home for—for a husband and children. Failing these—it was not a thing one should allow one's mind to dwell upon—but——

"Stop it!" Mary cried once more across the shadows. "Nein, I tell you! Ich haben der todt Kinder gesehn."

But it was a fact. A woman who had missed these things could still be useful—more useful than a man in certain respects. She thumped like a pavior through the settling ashes at the secret thrill of it. The rain was damping the fire, but she could feel—it was too dark to see—that her work was done. There was a dull red glow at the bottom of the destructor, not enough to char the wooden lid if she slipped it half over against the driving wet. This arranged, she leaned on the poker and waited, while an increasing rapture laid hold on her. She ceased to think. She gave herself up to feel. Her long pleasure was broken by a sound that she had waited for in agony several times in her life. She leaned forward and listened, smiling. There could be no mistake. She closed her eyes and drank it in. Once it ceased abruptly.

"Go on," she murmured, half aloud. "That isn't the end."

Then the end came very distinctly in a lull between two rain-gusts.

Mary Postgate drew her breath short between her teeth and shivered from head to foot. *"That's* all right," said she contentedly, and went up to the house, where she scandalised the whole routine by taking a luxurious hot bath before tea, and came down looking, as Miss Fowler said when she saw her lying all relaxed on the other sofa, "quite handsome!"

Mr. Brisher's Treasure

⚭‿ᴧᴧ‿☙

H. G. Wells
(English, 1866–1946)

"You can't be *too* careful *who* you marry," said Mr. Brisher, and pulled thoughtfully with a fat-wristed hand at the lank moustache that hides his want of chin.

"That's why——" I ventured.

"Yes," said Mr. Brisher, with a solemn light in his bleary, blue-grey eyes, moving his head expressively and breathing alcohol intimately at me. "There's lots as 'ave 'ad a try at me—many as I could name in *this* town—but none 'ave done it—none."

I surveyed the flushed countenance, the equatorial expansion, the masterly carelessness of his attire, and heaved a sigh to think that by reason of the unworthiness of women he must needs be the last of his race.

"I was a smart young chap when I was younger," said Mr. Brisher. "I 'ad my work cut out. But I was very careful—very. And I got through . . ."

He leant over the taproom table and thought visibly on the subject of my trustworthiness. I was relieved at last by his confidence.

"I was engaged once," he said at last, with a reminiscent eye on the shuv-a'penny board.

"So near as that?"

He looked at me. "So near as that. Fact is——" He looked about him, brought his face close to mine, lowered his voice, and fenced off an unsympathetic world with a grimy hand. "If she ain't dead or married to some one else or anything—I'm engaged still. Now." He confirmed this statement with nods and facial contortions. *"Still,"* he said, ending the pantomime, and broke into a reckless smile at my surprise. *"Me!*

"Run away," he explained further, with coruscating eyebrows. "Come 'ome.

"That ain't all.

"You'd 'ardly believe it," he said, "but I found a treasure. Found a regular treasure."

I fancied this was irony, and did not, perhaps, greet it with proper surprise. "Yes," he said, "I found a treasure. And come 'ome. I tell you I could surprise you with things that has happened to me." And for some time he was content to repeat that he had found a treasure—and left it.

I made no vulgar clamour for a story, but I became attentive to Mr. Brisher's bodily needs, and presently I led him back to the deserted lady.

"She was a nice girl," he said—a little sadly, I thought. *"And* respectable."

He raised his eyebrows and tightened his mouth to express extreme respectability—beyond the likes of us elderly men.

"It was a long way from 'ere. Essex, in fact. Near Colchester. It was when I was up in London—in the buildin' trade. I was a smart young chap then, I can tell you. Slim. 'Ad best clo'es 's good as anybody. 'At— *silk* 'at, mind you." Mr. Brisher's hand shot above his head towards the infinite to indicate a silk hat of the highest. "Umbrella—nice umbrella with a 'orn 'andle. Savin's. Very careful I was. . . ."

He was pensive for a little while, thinking, as we must all come to think sooner or later, of the vanished brightness of youth. But he refrained, as one may do in taprooms, from the obvious moral.

"I got to know 'er through a chap what was engaged to 'er sister. She was stopping in London for a bit with a naunt that 'ad a 'am an' beef shop. This aunt was very particular—they was all very particular people, all 'er people was—and wouldn't let 'er sister go out with this feller except 'er other sister, *my* girl that is, went with them. So 'e brought me into it, sort of to ease the crowding. We used to go walks in Battersea Park of a Sunday afternoon. Me in my topper, and 'im in 'is; and the girls —well—stylish. There wasn't many in Battersea Park 'ad the larf of us. She wasn't what you'd call pretty, but a nicer girl I never met. *I* liked 'er from the start, and, well—though I say it who shouldn't—she liked me. You know 'ow it is, I dessay?"

I pretended I did.

"And when this chap married 'er sister—'im and me was great friends —what must 'e do but arst me down to Colchester, close by where She lived. Naturally I was introjuced to 'er people, and well, very soon, her and me was engaged."

He repeated "engaged."

"She lived at 'ome with 'er father and mother, quite the lady, in a very nice little 'ouse with a garden—and remarkable respectable people they was. Rich you might call 'em a'most. They owned their own 'ouse—got it out of the Building Society, and cheap because the chap who had it before was a burglar and in prison—and they 'ad a bit of free'old land, and some cottages and money 'nvested—all nice and tight: they was what you'd call snug and warm. I tell you, I was On. Furniture too. Why! They 'ad a pianner. Jane—'er name was Jane—used to play it Sundays, and very nice she played too. There wasn't 'ardly a 'im toon in the book she *couldn't* play . . .

"Many's the evenin' we've met and sung 'ims there, me and 'er and the family.

" 'Er father was quite a leadin' man in chapel. You should ha' seen him Sundays, interruptin' the minister and givin' out 'ims. He had gold spectacles, I remember, and used to look over 'em at you while he sang hearty —he was always great on singing 'earty to the Lord—and when *he* got out o' toon 'arf the people went after 'im—always. 'E was that sort of man. And to walk be'ind 'im in 'is nice black clo'es—'is 'at was a brimmer—made one regular proud to be engaged to such a father-in-law. And when the summer came I went down there and stopped a fortnight.

"Now, you know there was a sort of Itch," said Mr. Brisher. "We wanted to marry, me and Jane did, and get things settled. But 'E said I 'ad to get a proper position first. Consequently there was a Itch. Consequently, when I went down there, I was anxious to show that I was a good useful sort of chap like. Show I could do pretty nearly everything like. See?"

I made a sympathetic noise.

"And down at the bottom of their garden was a bit of wild part like. So I says to 'im, 'Why don't you 'ave a rockery 'ere?' I says. 'It 'ud look nice.'

" 'Too much expense,' he says.

" 'Not a penny,' says I. 'I'm a dab at rockeries. Lemme make you one.' You see, I'd 'elped my brother make a rockery in the beer garden be'ind 'is tap, so I knew 'ow to do it to rights. 'Lemme make you one,' I says. 'It's 'olidays, but I'm that sort of chap, I 'ate doing nothing,' I says. 'I'll make you one to rights.' And the long and the short of it was, he said I might.

"And that's 'ow I come on the treasure."

"What treasure?" I asked.

"Why!" said Mr. Brisher, "the treasure I'm telling you about, what's the reason why I never married."

"What!—a treasure—dug up?"

"Yes—buried wealth—treasure trove. Come out of the ground. What I kept on saying—regular treasure. . . ." He looked at me with unusual disrespect.

"It wasn't more than a foot deep, not the top of it," he said. "I'd 'ardly got thirsty like, before I come on the corner."

"Go on," I said. "I didn't understand."

"Why! Directly I 'it the box I knew it was treasure. A sort of instinct told me. Something seemed to shout inside of me—'Now's your chance—lie low.' It's lucky I knew the laws of treasure trove or I'd 'ave been shoutin' there and then. I daresay you know——"

"Crown bags it," I said, "all but one per cent. Go on. It's a shame. What did you do?"

"Uncovered the top of the box. There wasn't anybody in the garden or about like. Jane was 'elping 'er mother do the 'ouse. I *was* excited—I tell you. I tried the lock and then gave a whack at the hinges. Open it came. Silver coins—full! Shining. It made me tremble to see 'em. And jest then —I'm blessed if the dustman didn't come round the back of the 'ouse. It pretty nearly gave me 'eart disease to think what a fool I was to 'ave that money showing. And directly after I 'eard the chap next door—'e was 'olidaying, too—I 'eard him watering 'is beans. If only 'e'd looked over the fence!"

"What did you do?"

"Kicked the lid on again and covered it up like a shot, and went on digging about a yard away from it—like mad. And my face, so to speak, was laughing on its own account till I had it hid. I tell you I was regular scared like at my luck. I jest thought that it 'ad to be kep' close and that was all. 'Treasure,' I kep' whisperin' to myself, 'Treasure' and ' 'undreds of pounds, 'undreds, 'undreds of pounds.' Whispering to myself like, and digging like blazes. It seemed to me the box was regular sticking out and showing, like your legs do under the sheets in bed, and I went and put all the earth I'd got out of my 'ole for the rockery slap on top of it. I *was* in a sweat. And in the midst of it all out toddles 'er father. He didn't say anything to me, jest stood behind me and stared, but Jane tole me afterwards when he went indoors, 'e says, 'That there jackanapes of yours, Jane'—he always called me a jackanapes some'ow—'knows 'ow to put 'is back into it after all.' Seemed quite impressed by it, 'e did."

"How long was the box?" I asked, suddenly.

" 'Ow long?" said Mr. Brisher.

"Yes—in length?"

"Oh! 'bout so—by so." Mr. Brisher indicated a moderate-sized trunk.

"*Full?*" said I.

"Full up of silver coins—'arf-crowns, I believe."

"Why!" I cried, "that would mean—hundreds of pounds."

"Thousands," said Mr. Brisher, in a sort of sad calm. "I calc'lated it out."

"But how did they get there?"

"All I know is what I found. What I thought at the time was this. The chap who'd owned the 'ouse before 'er father 'd been a regular slap-up burglar. What you'd call a 'igh-class criminal. Used to drive 'is trap—like Peace did." Mr. Brisher meditated on the difficulties of narration and embarked on a complicated parenthesis. "I don't know if I told you it'd been a burglar's 'ouse before it was my girl's father's, and I knew 'e'd robbed a mail train once, I did know that. It seemed to me——"

"That's very likely," I said. "But what did you do?"

"Sweated," said Mr. Brisher. "Regular run orf me. All that morning," said Mr. Brisher, "I was at it, pretending to make that rockery and wondering what I should do. I'd 'ave told 'er father p'r'aps, only I was doubtful of 'is honesty—I was afraid he might rob me of it like, and give it up to the authorities—and besides, considering I was marrying into the family, I thought it would be nicer like if it came through me. Put me on a better footing, so to speak. Well, I 'ad three days before me left of my 'olidays, so there wasn't no hurry, so I covered it up and went on digging, and tried to puzzle out 'ow I was to make sure of it. Only I couldn't.

"I thought," said Mr. Brisher, "*and* I thought. Once I got regular doubtful whether I'd seen it or not, and went down to it and 'ad it uncovered again, just as her ma came out to 'ang up a bit of washin' she'd done. Jumps again! Afterwards I was just thinking I'd 'ave another go at it, when Jane comes to tell me dinner was ready. 'You'll want it,' she said, 'seeing all the 'ole you've dug.'

"I was in a regular daze all dinner, wondering whether that chap next door wasn't over the fence and filling 'is pockets. But in the afternoon I got easier in my mind—it seemed to me it must 'ave been there so long it was pretty sure to stop a bit longer—and I tried to get up a bit of a discussion to dror out the old man and see what 'e thought of treasure trove."

Mr. Brisher paused, and affected amusement at the memory.

"The old man was a scorcher," he said; "a regular scorcher."

"What!" said I; "did he——?"

"It was like this," explained Mr. Brisher, laying a friendly hand on my arm and breathing into my face to calm me. "Just to dror 'im out, I told a story of a chap I said I knew—pretendin', you know—who'd found a sovring in a novercoat 'e'd borrowed. I said 'e stuck to it, but I said I wasn't sure whether that was right or not. And then the old man began. Lor'! 'e *did* let me 'ave it!" Mr. Brisher affected an insincere amusement. " 'E was, well——what you might call a rare 'and at Snacks. Said that was the sort of friend 'e'd naturally expect me to 'ave. Said 'e'd naturally expect that from the friend of a out-of-work loafer who took up with daughters who didn't belong to 'im. There! I couldn't tell you *'arf* 'e said. 'E went on most outrageous. I stood up to 'im about it, just to dror 'im out. 'Wouldn't you stick to a 'arf-sov', not if you found it in the street?' I says. 'Certainly not,' 'e says; 'certainly I wouldn't.' 'What! not if you found it as a sort of treasure?' 'Young man,' 'e says, 'there's 'i'er 'thority than mine—Render unto Caesar'—what is it? Yes. Well, he fetched up that. A rare 'and at 'itting you over the 'ed with the Bible, was the old man. And so he went on. 'E got to such Snacks about me at last I couldn't stand it. I'd promised Jane not to answer 'im back, but it got a bit *too* thick. I—I give it 'im . . ."

Mr. Brisher, by means of enigmatical facework, tried to make me think he had had the best of that argument, but I knew better.

"I went out in a 'uff at last. But not before I was pretty sure I 'ad to lift that treasure by myself. The only thing that kep' me up was thinking 'ow I'd take it out of 'im when I 'ad the cash. . . ."

There was a lengthy pause.

"Now, you'd 'ardly believe it, but all them three days I never 'ad a chance at the blessed treasure, never got out not even a 'arf-crown. There was always a Somethink—always.

" 'Stonishing thing it isn't thought of more," said Mr. Brisher. "Finding treasure's no great shakes. It's gettin' it. I don't suppose I slep' a wink any of those nights, thinking where I was to take it, what I was to do with it, 'ow I was to explain it. It made me regular ill. And days I was that dull, it made Jane regular 'uffy. 'You ain't the same chap you was in London,' she says, several times. I tried to lay it on 'er father and 'is Snacks, but bless you, she knew better. What must she 'ave but that I'd got another girl on my mind! Said I wasn't True. Well, we had a bit of a row. But I was that set on the Treasure, I didn't seem to mind a bit Anything she said.

"Well, at last I got a sort of plan. I was always a bit good at planning, though carrying out isn't so much in my line. I thought it all out and settled on a plan. First, I was going to take all my pockets full of these 'ere 'arf-crowns—see?—and afterwards——as I shall tell.

"Well, I got to that state I couldn't think of getting at the Treasure again in the daytime, so I waited until the night before I had to go, and then, when everything was still, up I gets and slips down to the back door, meaning to get my pockets full. What must I do in the scullery but fall over a pail! Up gets 'er father with a gun—'e was a light sleeper was 'er father, and very suspicious—and there was me: 'ad to explain I'd come down to the pump for a drink because my water-bottle was bad. 'E didn't let me off a Snack or two over that bit, you lay a bob."

"And you mean to say——" I began.

"Wait a bit," said Mr. Brisher. "I say, I'd made my plan. That put the kybosh on one bit, but it didn't 'urt the general scheme not a bit. I went and I finished that rockery next day, as though there wasn't a Snack in the world; cemented over the stones, I did, dabbed it green and everythink. I put a dab of green just to show where the box was. They all came and looked at it, and said 'ow nice it was—even 'e was a bit softer like to see it, and all he said was, "It's a pity you can't always work like that, then you might get something definite to do," he says.

" 'Yes,' I says—I couldn't 'elp it—'I put a lot in that rockery,' I says, like that. See? 'I put a lot in that rockery'—meaning——"

"I see," said I—for Mr. Brisher is apt to over-elaborate his jokes.

" 'E didn't," said Mr. Brisher. "Not then, anyhow.

"Ar'ever—after all that was over, off I set for London. . . . Orf I set for London. . . ."

Pause.

"On'y I wasn't going to no London," said Mr. Brisher, with sudden animation, and thrusting his face into mine. "No fear! What do *you* think?

"I didn't go no further than Colchester—not a yard.

"I'd left the spade just where I could find it. I'd got everything planned and right. I 'ired a little trap in Colchester, and pretended I wanted to go to Ipswich and stop the night, and come back next day, and the chap I 'ired it from made me leave two sovrings on it right away, and off I set.

"I didn't go to no Ipswich neither.

"Midnight the 'orse and trap was 'itched by the little road that ran by the cottage where 'e lived—not sixty yards off, it wasn't—and I was at it like a good 'un. It was jest the night for such games—overcast—but a trifle too 'ot, and all round the sky there was summer lightning and presently a thunderstorm. Down it came. First big drops in a sort of fizzle, then 'ail. I kep' on. I whacked at it—I didn't dream the old man would 'ear. I didn't even trouble to go quiet with the spade, and the thunder and lightning and 'ail seemed to excite me like. I shouldn't wonder if I was singing. I got so 'ard at it I clean forgot the thunder and the 'orse and trap. I precious soon got the box showing, and started to lift it. . . ."

"Heavy?" I said.

"I couldn't no more lift it than fly. I *was* sick. I'd never thought of that! I got regular wild—I tell you, I cursed. I got sort of outrageous. I didn't think of dividing it like for the minute, and even then I couldn't 'ave took money about loose in a trap. I hoisted one end sort of wild like, and over the whole show went with a tremenjous noise. Perfeck smash of silver. And then right on the heels of that, Flash! Lightning like the day! and there was the back door open and the old man coming down the garden with 'is blooming old gun. He wasn't not a 'undred yards away!

"I tell you I was that upset—I didn't think what I was doing. I never stopped—not even to fill my pockets. I went over the fence like a shot, and ran like one o'clock for the trap, cussing and swearing as I went. I *was* in a state. . . .

"And will you believe me, when I got to the place where I'd left the 'orse and trap, they'd gone. Orf! When I saw that I 'adn't a cuss left for it. I jest danced on the grass, and when I'd danced enough I started off to London. . . . I was done."

Mr. Brisher was pensive for an interval. "I was done," he repeated, very bitterly.

"Well?" I said.

"That's all," said Mr. Brisher.

"You didn't go back?"

"No fear. I'd 'ad enough of *that* blooming treasure, any'ow for a bit. Besides, I didn't know what was done to chaps who tried to collar a treasure trove. I started off for London there and then. . . ."

"And you never went back?"

"Never."

"But about Jane? Did you write?"

"Three times, fishing like. And no answer. We'd parted in a bit of a 'uff on account of 'er being jealous. So that I couldn't make out for certain what it meant.

"I didn't know what to do. I didn't even know whether the old man knew it was me. I sort of kep' an eye open on papers to see when he'd give up that treasure to the Crown, as I hadn't a doubt 'e would, considering 'ow respectable he'd always been."

"And did he?"

Mr. Brisher pursed his mouth and moved his head slowly from side to side. "Not *'im,*" he said.

"Jane was a nice girl," he said, "a thorough nice girl mind you, *if* jealous, and there's no knowing I mightn't 'ave gone back to 'er after a bit. I thought if he didn't give up the treasure I might 'ave a sort of 'old on 'im. . . . Well, one day I looks as usual under Colchester—and there I saw 'is name. What for, d'yer think?"

I could not guess.

Mr. Brisher's voice sank to a whisper, and once more he spoke behind his hand. His manner was suddenly suffused with a positive joy. "Issuing counterfeit coins," he said. "Counterfeit coins!"

"You don't mean to say——?"

"Yes—It. Bad. Quite a long case they made of it. But they got 'im, though he dodged tremenjous. Traced 'is 'aving passed, oh!—nearly a dozen bad 'arf-crowns."

"And you didn't——?"

"No fear. And it didn't do 'im much good to say it was treasure trove."

The Broken Boot

❦

JOHN GALSWORTHY

(English, 1867–1933)

The actor, Gilbert Caister, who had been 'out' for six months, emerged from his East Coast seaside lodging about noon in the day, after the opening of 'Shooting the Rapids,' on tour, in which he was playing Dr. Dominick in the last act. A salary of four pounds a week would not, he was conscious, remake his fortunes, but a certain jauntiness had returned to the gait and manner of one employed again at last.

Fixing his monocle, he stopped before a fishmonger's and, with a faint smile on his face, regarded a lobster. Ages since he had eaten a lobster! One could long for a lobster without paying, but the pleasure was not solid enough to detain him. He moved upstreet and stopped again, before a tailor's window. Together with the actual tweeds, in which he could so easily fancy himself refitted, he could see a reflection of himself, in the faded brown suit wangled out of the production of 'Marmaduke Mandeville' the year before the war. The sunlight in this damned town was very strong, very hard on seams and buttonholes, on knees and elbows! Yet he received the ghost of aesthetic pleasure from the reflected elegance of a man long fed only twice a day, of an eyeglass well rimmed out from a soft brown eye, of a velour hat salved from the production of 'Educating Simon' in 1912; and, in front of the window he removed that hat, for under it was his new phenomenon, not yet quite evaluated, his *mêche blanche.* Was it an asset, or the beginning of the end? It reclined backwards on the right side, conspicuous in his dark hair, above that shadowy face always interesting to Gilbert Caister. They said it came from atrophy of the—er—something nerve, an effect of the war, or of under-nourished tissue. Rather distinguished, perhaps, but——!

He walked on, and became conscious that he had passed a face he knew. Turning, he saw it also turned on a short and dapper figure—a face rosy, bright, round, with an air of cherubic knowledge, as of a getter-up of amateur theatricals.

Bryce-Green, by George!

"Caister? It is! Haven't seen you since you left the old camp. Remember what sport we had over 'Gotta Grampus'? By Jove! I am glad to see you. Doing anything with yourself? Come and have lunch with me."

Bryce-Green, the wealthy patron, the moving spirit of entertainment in that South Coast convalescent camp. And, drawling slightly, Caister answered:

"Shall be delighted." But within him something did not drawl: 'By God, you're going to have a feed, my boy!'

And—elegantly threadbare, roundabout and dapper—the two walked side by side.

"Know this place? Let's go in here! Phyllis, cocktails for my friend Mr. Caister and myself, and caviare on biscuits. Mr. Caister is playing here! you must go and see him."

The girl who served the cocktails and the caviare looked up at Caister with interested blue eyes. Precious! He had been 'out' for six months!

"Nothing of a part," he drawled; "took it to fill a gap." And below his waistcoat the gap echoed: 'Yes, and it'll take some filling.'

"Bring your cocktail along, Caister; we'll go into the little further room, there'll be nobody there. What shall we have—a lobstah?"

And Caister murmured: "I love lobstahs."

"Very fine and large here. And how are you, Caister? So awfully glad to see you—only real actor we had."

"Thanks," said Caister, "I'm all right." And he thought: 'He's a damned amateur, but a nice little man.'

"Sit here. Waiter, bring us a good big lobstah and a salad; and then—er —a small fillet of beef with potatoes fried crisp, and a bottle of my special hock. Ah! and a rum omelette—plenty of rum and sugah. Twig?"

And Caister thought: 'Thank God, I do.'

They had sat down opposite each other at one of two small tables in the little recessed room.

"Luck!" said Bryce-Green.

"Luck!" replied Caister; and the cocktail trickling down him echoed: 'Luck!'

"And what do you think of the state of the drama?" Oh! ho! A question after his own heart. Balancing his monocle by a sweetish smile on the opposite side of his mouth, Caister drawled his answer: "Quite too bally awful!"

"H'm! Yes," said Bryce-Green; "nobody with any genius, is there?" And Caister thought: 'Nobody with any money.'

"Have you been playing anything great? You were so awfully good in 'Gotta Grampus'!"

"Nothing particular. I've been—er—rather slack." And with their feel around his waist his trousers seemed to echo: 'Slack!'

"Ah!" said Bryce-Green. "Here we are! Do you like claws?"

"Tha-a-nks. Anything!" To eat—until warned by the pressure of his waist against his trousers! Huh! What a feast! And what a flow of his own tongue suddenly released—on drama, music, art; mellow and critical, stimulated by the round eyes and interjections of his little provincial host.

"By Jove, Caister! You've got a *mêche blanche*. Never noticed. I'm awfully interested in *mêches blanches*. Don't think me too frightfully rude—but did it come suddenly?"

"No, gradually."

"And how do you account for it?"

'Try starvation,' trembled on Caister's lips.

"I don't."

"I think it's ripping. Have some more omelette? I often wish I'd gone on the regular stage myself. Must be a topping life, if one has talent, like you."

Topping?

"Have a cigar. Waiter! Coffee and cigars. I shall come and see you tonight. Suppose you'll be here a week?"

Topping! The laughter and applause—"Mr. Caister's rendering left nothing to be desired; its —— and its —— are in the true spirit of ——!"

Silence recalled him from his rings of smoke. Bryce-Green was sitting, with cigar held out and mouth a little open, and bright eyes round as pebbles, fixed—fixed on some object near the floor, past the corner of the

tablecloth. Had he burnt his mouth? The eyelids fluttered; he looked at
Caister, licked his lips like a dog, nervously, and said:

"I say, old chap, don't think me a beast, but are you at all—er—er—
rocky? I mean—if I can be of any service, don't hesitate! Old acquaintance, don't you know, and all that——"

His eyes rolled out again towards the object, and Caister followed
them. Out there above the carpet he saw it—his own boot. It dangled,
because his knees were crossed, six inches off the ground—split—right
across, twice, between lace and toecap. Quite! He knew it. A boot left him
from the rôle of Bertie Carstairs, in 'The Dupe,' just before the war.
Good boots. His only pair, except the boots of Dr. Dominick, which he
was nursing. And from the boot he looked back at Bryce-Green, sleek
and concerned. A drop, black when it left his heart, suffused his eye
behind the monocle; his smile curled bitterly; he said:

"Not at all, thanks! Why?"

"Oh! n-n-nothing. It just occurred to me." His eyes—but Caister had
withdrawn the boot. Bryce-Green paid the bill and rose.

"Old chap, if you'll excuse me; engagement at half-past two. So awf'ly
glad to have seen you. Good-bye!"

"Good-bye!" said Caister. "And thanks!"

He was alone. And, chin on hand, he stared through his monocle into
an empty coffee cup. Alone with his heart, his boot, his life to come. . . .
'And what have you been in lately, Mr. Caister?' 'Nothing very much
lately. Of course I've played almost everything.' 'Quite so. Perhaps you'll
leave your address; can't say anything definite, I'm afraid.' 'I—I should
—er—be willing to rehearse on approval; or—if I could read the part?'
'Thank you, afraid we haven't got as far as that.' 'No? Quite! Well, I shall
hear from you, perhaps.' And Caister could see his own eyes looking at
the manager. God! What a look. . . . A topping life! A dog's life! Cadging—cadging—cadging for work! A life of draughty waiting, of concealed
beggary, of terrible depressions, of want of food!

The waiter came skating round as if he desired to clear. Must go! Two
young women had come in and were sitting at the other table between
him and the door. He saw them look at him, and his sharpened senses
caught the whisper:

"Sure—in the last act. Don't you see his *mèche blanche?*"

"Oh! yes—of course! Isn't it—wasn't he——!"

Caister straightened his back; his smile crept out, he fixed his monocle.
They had spotted his Dr. Dominick!

"If you've quite finished, sir, may I clear?"

"Certainly. I'm going." He gathered himself and rose. The young
women were gazing up. Elegant, with faint smile, he passed them close,
managing—so that they could not see—his broken boot.

Tobermory

❦

SAKI (H. H. MUNRO)
(English, 1870–1916)

It was a chill, rain-washed afternoon of a late August day, that indefinite
season when partridges are still in security or cold storage, and there is
nothing to hunt—unless one is bounded on the north by the Bristol
Channel, in which case one may lawfully gallop after fat red stags. Lady
Blemley's house-party was not bounded on the north by the Bristol
Channel, hence there was a full gathering of her guests round the tea-
table on this particular afternoon. And, in spite of the blankness of the
season and the triteness of the occasion, there was no trace in the company of that fatigued restlessness which means a dread of the pianola and
a subdued hankering for auction bridge. The undisguised open-mouthed
attention of the entire party was fixed on the homely negative personality
of Mr. Cornelius Appin. Of all her guests, he was the one who had come
to Lady Blemley with the vaguest reputation. Some one had said he was
"clever," and he had got his invitation in the moderate expectation, on
the part of his hostess, that some portion at least of his cleverness would
be contributed to the general entertainment. Until tea-time that day she
had been unable to discover in what direction, if any, his cleverness lay.

He was neither a wit nor a croquet champion, a hypnotic force nor a begetter of amateur theatricals. Neither did his exterior suggest the sort of man in whom women are willing to pardon a generous measure of mental deficiency. He had subsided into mere Mr. Appin, and the Cornelius seemed a piece of transparent baptismal bluff. And now he was claiming to have launched on the world a discovery beside which the invention of gunpowder, of the printing-press, and of steam locomotion were inconsiderable trifles. Science had made bewildering strides in many directions during recent decades, but this thing seemed to belong to the domain of miracle rather than to scientific achievement.

"And do you really ask us to believe," Sir Wilfrid was saying, "that you have discovered a means for instructing animals in the art of human speech, and that dear old Tobermory has proved your first successful pupil?"

"It is a problem at which I have worked for the last seventeen years," said Mr. Appin, "but only during the last eight or nine months have I been rewarded with glimmerings of success. Of course I have experimented with thousands of animals, but latterly only with cats, those wonderful creatures which have assimilated themselves so marvellously with our civilization while retaining all their highly developed feral instincts. Here and there among cats one comes across an outstanding superior intellect, just as one does among the ruck of human beings, and when I made the acquaintance of Tobermory a week ago I saw at once that I was in contact with a 'Beyond-cat' of extraordinary intelligence. I had gone far along the road to success in recent experiments; with Tobermory, as you call him, I have reached the goal."

Mr. Appin concluded his remarkable statement in a voice which he strove to divest of a triumphant inflection. No one said "Rats," though Clovis's lips moved in a monosyllabic contortion which probably invoked those rodents of disbelief.

"And do you mean to say," asked Miss Resker, after a slight pause, "that you have taught Tobermory to say and understand easy sentences of one syllable?"

"My dear Miss Resker," said the wonder-worker patiently, "one teaches little children and savages and backward adults in that piecemeal fashion; when one has once solved the problem of making a beginning with an animal of highly developed intelligence one has no need for those halting methods. Tobermory can speak our language with perfect correctness."

This time Clovis very distinctly said, "Beyond-rats!" Sir Wilfrid was more polite, but equally sceptical.

"Hadn't we better have the cat in and judge for ourselves?" suggested Lady Blemley.

Sir Wilfrid went in search of the animal, and the company settled themselves down to the languid expectation of witnessing some more or less adroit drawing-room ventriloquism.

In a minute Sir Wilfrid was back in the room, his face white beneath its tan and his eyes dilated with excitement.

"By Gad, it's true!"

His agitation was unmistakably genuine, and his hearers started forward in a thrill of awakened interest.

Collapsing into an armchair he continued breathlessly: "I found him dozing in the smoking-room and called out to him to come for his tea. He blinked at me in his usual way, and I said, 'Come on, Toby; don't keep us waiting'; and, by Gad! he drawled out in a most horribly natural voice that he'd come when he dashed well pleased! I nearly jumped out of my skin!"

Appin had preached to absolutely incredulous hearers; Sir Wilfrid's statement carried instant conviction. A Babel-like chorus of startled exclamation arose, amid which the scientist sat mutely enjoying the first fruit of his stupendous discovery.

In the midst of the clamour Tobermory entered the room and made his way with velvet tread and studied unconcern across to the group seated round the tea-table.

A sudden hush of awkwardness and constraint fell on the company. Somehow there seemed an element of embarrassment in addressing on equal terms a domestic cat of acknowledged dental ability.

"Will you have some milk, Tobermory?" asked Lady Blemley in a rather strained voice.

"I don't mind if I do," was the response, couched in a tone of even indifference. A shiver of suppressed excitement went through the listeners, and Lady Blemley might be excused for pouring out the saucerful of milk rather unsteadily.

"I'm afraid I've spilt a good deal of it," she said apologetically.

"After all, it's not my Axminster," was Tobermory's rejoinder.

Another silence fell on the group, and then Miss Resker, in her best district-visitor manner, asked if the human language had been difficult to learn. Tobermory looked squarely at her for a moment and then fixed his gaze serenely on the middle distance. It was obvious that boring questions lay outside his scheme of life.

"What do you think of human intelligence?" asked Mavis Pellington lamely.

"Of whose intelligence in particular?" asked Tobermory coldly.

"Oh, well, mine for instance," said Mavis, with a feeble laugh.

"You put me in an embarrassing position," said Tobermory, whose tone and attitude certainly did not suggest a shred of embarrassment. "When your inclusion in this house-party was suggested Sir Wilfrid protested that you were the most brainless woman of his acquaintance, and that there was a wide distinction between hospitality and the care of the feeble-minded. Lady Blemley replied that your lack of brain-power was the precise quality which had earned you your invitation, as you were the only person she could think of who might be idiotic enough to buy their old car. You know, the one they call 'The Envy of Sisyphus,' because it goes quite nicely up-hill if you push it."

Lady Blemley's protestations would have had greater effect if she had not casually suggested to Mavis only that morning that the car in question would be just the thing for her down at her Devonshire home.

Major Barfield plunged in heavily to effect a diversion.

"How about your carryings-on with the tortoise-shell puss up at the stables, eh?"

The moment he had said it every one realized the blunder.

"One does not usually discuss these matters in public," said Tobermory frigidly. "From a slight observation of your ways since you've been in this house I should imagine you'd find it inconvenient if I were to shift the conversation on to your own little affairs."

The panic which ensued was not confined to the Major.

"Would you like to go and see if cook has got your dinner ready?" suggested Lady Blemley hurriedly, affecting to ignore the fact that it wanted at least two hours to Tobermory's dinner-time.

"Thanks," said Tobermory, "not quite so soon after my tea. I don't want to die of indigestion."

"Cats have nine lives, you know," said Sir Wilfrid heartily.

"Possibly," answered Tobermory; "but only one liver."

"Adelaide!" said Mrs. Cornett, "do you mean to encourage that cat to go out and gossip about us in the servants' hall?"

The panic had indeed become general. A narrow ornamental balustrade ran in front of most of the bedroom windows at the Towers, and it was recalled with dismay that this had formed a favourite promenade for Tobermory at all hours, whence he could watch the pigeons—and heaven knew what else besides. If he intended to become reminiscent in his present outspoken strain the effect would be something more than disconcerting. Mrs. Cornett, who spent much time at her toilet table, and whose complexion was reputed to be of a nomadic though punctual disposition, looked as ill at ease as the Major. Miss Scrawen, who wrote fiercely sensuous poetry and led a blameless life, merely displayed irritation; if you are methodical and virtuous in private you don't necessarily want every one to know it. Bertie van Tahn, who was so depraved at seventeen that he had long ago given up trying to be any worse, turned a dull shade of gardenia white, but he did not commit the error of dashing out of the room like Odo Finsberry, a young gentleman who was understood to be reading for the Church and who was possibly disturbed at the thought of scandals he might hear concerning other people. Clovis had the presence of mind to maintain a composed exterior; privately he was calculating how long it would take to procure a box of fancy mice through the agency of the *Exchange and Mart* as a species of hushmoney.

Even in a delicate situation like the present, Agnes Resker could not endure to remain too long in the background.

"Why did I ever come down here?" she asked dramatically.

Tobermory immediately accepted the opening.

"Judging by what you said to Mrs. Cornett on the croquet-lawn yesterday, you were out for food. You described the Blemleys as the dullest people to stay with that you knew, but said they were clever enough to employ a first-rate cook; otherwise they'd find it difficult to get any one to come down a second time."

"There's not a word of truth in it! I appeal to Mrs. Cornett—" exclaimed the discomfited Agnes.

"Mrs. Cornett repeated your remark afterwards to Bertie van Tahn," continued Tobermory, "and said, 'That woman is a regular Hunger Marcher; she'd go anywhere for four square meals a day,' and Bertie van Tahn said—"

At this point the chronicle mercifully ceased. Tobermory had caught a glimpse of the big yellow Tom from the Rectory working his way through the shrubbery towards the stable wing. In a flash he had vanished through the open French window.

With the disappearance of his too brilliant pupil Cornelius Appin found himself beset by a hurricane of bitter upbraiding, anxious inquiry, and frightened entreaty. The responsibility for the situation lay with him, and he must prevent matters from becoming worse. Could Tobermory impart his dangerous gift to other cats? was the first question he had to answer. It was possible, he replied, that he might have initiated his intimate friend the stable puss into his new accomplishment, but it was unlikely that his teaching could have taken a wider range as yet.

"Then," said Mrs. Cornett, "Tobermory may be a valuable cat and a great pet; but I'm sure you'll agree, Adelaide, that both he and the stable cat must be done away with without delay."

"You don't suppose I've enjoyed the last quarter of an hour, do you?" said Lady Blemley bitterly. "My husband and I are very fond of Tobermory—at least, we were before this horrible accomplishment was infused into him; but now, of course, the only thing is to have him destroyed as soon as possible."

"We can put some strychnine in the scraps he always gets at dinnertime," said Sir Wilfrid, "and I will go and drown the stable cat myself. The coachman will be very sore at losing his pet, but I'll say a very catching form of mange has broken out in both cats and we're afraid of its spreading to the kennels."

"But my great discovery!" expostulated Mr. Appin; "after all my years of research and experiment—"

"You can go and experiment on the short-horns at the farm, who are under proper control," said Mrs. Cornett, "or the elephants at the Zoological Gardens. They're said to be highly intelligent, and they have this recommendation, that they don't come creeping about our bedrooms and under chairs, and so forth."

An archangel ecstatically proclaiming the Millennium, and then finding that it clashed unpardonably with Henley and would have to be indefinitely postponed, could hardly have felt more crestfallen than Cornelius Appin at the reception of his wonderful achievement. Public opinion, however, was against him—in fact, had the general voice been consulted on the subject it is probable that a strong minority vote would have been in favour of including him in the strychnine diet.

Defective train arrangements and a nervous desire to see matters brought to a finish prevented an immediate dispersal of the party, but dinner that evening was not a social success. Sir Wilfrid had had rather a trying time with the stable cat and subsequently with the coachman. Agnes Resker ostentatiously limited her repast to a morsel of dry toast, which she bit as though it were a personal enemy; while Mavis Pellington maintained a vindictive silence throughout the meal. Lady Blemley kept up a flow of what she hoped was conversation, but her attention was fixed on the doorway. A plateful of carefully dosed fish scraps was in readiness on the sideboard, but sweets and savoury and dessert went their way, and no Tobermory appeared either in the dining-room or kitchen.

The sepulchral dinner was cheerful compared with the subsequent vigil in the smoking-room. Eating and drinking had at least supplied a distraction and cloak to the prevailing embarrassment. Bridge was out of the question in the general tension of nerves and tempers, and after Odo Finsberry had given a lugubrious rendering of "Mélisande in the Wood" to a frigid audience, music was tacitly avoided. At eleven the servants went to bed, announcing that the small window in the pantry had been left open as usual for Tobermory's private use. The guests read steadily through the current batch of magazines, and fell back gradually on the "Badminton Library" and bound volumes of *Punch*. Lady Blemley made periodic visits to the pantry, returning each time with an expression of listless depression which forestalled questioning.

At two o'clock Clovis broke the dominating silence.

"He won't turn up tonight. He's probably in the local newspaper office at the present moment, dictating the first instalment of his reminiscences. Lady What's-her-name's book won't be in it. It will be the event of the day."

Having made this contribution to the general cheerfulness, Clovis went to bed. At long intervals the various members of the house-party followed his example.

The servants taking round the early tea made a uniform announcement in reply to a uniform question. Tobermory had not returned.

Breakfast was, if anything, a more unpleasant function than dinner had been, but before its conclusion the situation was relieved. Tobermory's corpse was brought in from the shrubbery, where a gardener had just discovered it. From the bites on his throat and the yellow fur which coated his claws it was evident that he had fallen in unequal combat with the big Tom from the Rectory.

By midday most of the guests had quitted the Towers, and after lunch Lady Blemley had sufficiently recovered her spirits to write an extremely nasty letter to the Rectory about the loss of her valuable pet.

Tobermory had been Appin's one successful pupil, and he was destined to have no successor. A few weeks later an elephant in the Dresden Zoological Garden, which had shown no previous signs of irritability, broke loose and killed an Englishman who had apparently been teasing it. The victim's name was variously reported in the papers as Oppin and Eppelin, but his front name was faithfully rendered Cornelius.

"If he was trying German irregular verbs on the poor beast," said Clovis, "he deserved all he got."

The Creatures

❦

WALTER DE LA MARE
(English, 1873–1956)

It was the ebbing light of evening that recalled me out of my story to a consciousness of my whereabouts. I dropped the squat little red book to my knee and glanced out of the narrow and begrimed oblong window. We were skirting the eastern coast of cliffs, to the very edge of which a ploughman, stumbling along behind his two great horses, was driving the last of his dark furrows. In a cleft far down between the rocks a cold and idle sea was soundlessly laying its frigid garlands of foam. I stared over the flat stretch of waters, then turned my head, and looked with a kind of suddenness into the face of my one fellow-traveller.

He had entered the carriage, all but unheeded, yet not altogether un-resented, at the last country station. His features were a little obscure in the fading daylight that hung between our four narrow walls, but appar-ently his eyes had been fixed on my face for some little time.

He narrowed his lids at this unexpected confrontation, jerked back his head, and cast a glance out of his mirky glass at the bit of greenish-bright moon that was struggling into its full brilliance above the dun, swelling uplands.

"It's a queer experience, railway-travelling," he began abruptly, in a low, almost deprecating voice, drawing his hand across his eyes. "One is cast into a passing privacy with a fellow-stranger and then is gone." It was as if he had been patiently awaiting the attention of a chosen listener.

I nodded, looking at him. *"That* privacy, too," he ejaculated, "all that!" My eyes turned towards the window again: bare, thorned, black January hedge, inhospitable salt coast, flat waste of northern water. Our engine-driver promptly shut off his steam, and we slid almost noiselessly out of sight of sky and sea into a cutting.

"It's a desolate country," I ventured to remark.

"Oh, yes, 'desolate'!" he echoed a little wearily. "But what always frets me is the way we have of arrogating to ourselves the offices of judge, jury, and counsel all in one. For my part, I never forget it—the futility, the presumption. It *leads* nowhere. We drive in—into all this silence, this—this 'forsakenness,' this dream of a world between her lights of day and night time. Consciousness! . . . What restless monkeys men are!" He recovered himself, swallowed his indignation with an obvious gulp. "As if," he continued, in more chastened tones—"as if that other gate were not for ever ajar, into God knows what of peace and mystery." He stooped forward, lean, darkened, objurgatory. "Don't we *make* our world? Isn't *that* our blessed, our betrayed responsibility?"

I nodded, and ensconced myself, like a dog in straw, in the basest of all responses to a rare, even if eccentric, candour—caution.

"Well," he continued, a little weariedly, "that's the indictment. Small wonder if it will need a trumpet to blare us into that last 'Family Prayers.' Then perhaps a few solitaries—just a few—will creep out of their holes and fastnesses, and draw mercy from the merciful on the cities of the plain. The buried talent will shine none the worse for the long, long looming of its napery spun from dream and desire.

"Years ago—ten, fifteen, perhaps—I chanced on the queerest specimen of this order of the 'talented.' Much the same country, too. This"—he swept his glance out towards the now invisible sea—"this is a kind of dwarf replica of it. More naked, smoother, more sudden and precipitous, more 'forsaken,' moody. Alone! The trees are shorn there, as if with monstrous shears, by the winter gales. The air's salt. It is a country of stones and emerald meadows, of green, meandering, aimless lanes, of farms set in their clifts and valleys like rough time-bedimmed jewels, as if by some angel of humanity, wandering between dark and daybreak.

"I was younger then—in body: the youth of the mind is for men of an age—yours, maybe, and mine. Even then, even at that, I was sickened of crowds, of that unimaginable London—swarming wilderness of mankind in which a poor lost thirsty dog from Otherwhere tastes first the full meaning of that idle word 'forsaken.' 'Forsaken by whom?' is the question I ask myself now. Visitors to my particular paradise were few then— as if, my dear sir, we are not all of us visitors, visitants, revenants, on earth, panting for time in which to tell and share our secrets, roving in search of the marks that shall prove our quest not vain, not unprecedented, not a treachery. But let that be.

"I would start off morning after morning, bread and cheese in pocket, from the bare old house I lodged in, bound for that unforeseen nowhere for which the heart, the fantasy aches. Lingering hot noondays would find me stretched in a state half-comatose, yet vigilant, on the close-flowered turf of the fields or cliffs, on the sun-baked sands and rocks, soaking in the scene and life around me like some pilgrim chameleon. It was in hope to lose my way that I would set out. How shall a man find his way unless he lose it? Now and then I succeeded. That country is large, and its land and sea marks easily cheat the stranger. I was still of an age, you see, when my 'small door' was ajar, and I planted a solid foot to keep it from shutting. But how could I know what I was after? One just shakes the tree of life, and the rare fruits come tumbling down, to rot for the most part in the lush grasses.

"What was most haunting and provocative in that far-away country was its fleeting resemblance to the country of dream. You stand, you sit, or lie prone on its bud-starred heights, and look down; the green, dispersed, treeless landscape spreads beneath you, with its hollows and mounded slopes, clustering farmstead, and scatter of village, all motionless under the vast wash of sun and blue, like the drop-scene of some enchanted playhouse centuries old. So, too, the visionary bird-haunted

headlands, veiled faintly in a mist of unreality above their broken stones
and the enormous saucer of the sea.

"You cannot guess there what you may not chance upon, or whom.
Bells clash, boom, and quarrel hollowly on the edge of darkness in those
breakers. Voices waver across the fainter winds. The birds cry in a tongue
unknown yet not unfamiliar. The sky is the hawks' and the stars'. *There*
one is on the edge of life, of the unforeseen, whereas our cities—are not
our desiccated jaded minds ever continually pressing and edging further
and further away from freedom, the vast unknown, the infinite presence,
picking a fool's journey from sensual fact to fact at the tail of that he-ass
called Reason? I suggest that in that solitude the spirit within us realises
that it treads the outskirts of a region long since called the Imagination. I
assert we have strayed, and in our blindness abandoned——"

My stranger paused in his frenzy, glanced out at me from his obscure
corner as if he had intended to stun, to astonish me with some violent
heresy. We puffed out slowly, laboriously, from a "Halt" at which in the
gathering dark and moonshine we had for some while been at a standstill.
Never was wedding-guest more desperately at the mercy of ancient mari-
ner.

"Well, one day," he went on, lifting his voice a little to master the
resounding heart-beats of our steam-engine—"one late afternoon, in my
goal-less wanderings, I had climbed to the summit of a steep grass-grown
cart-track, winding up dustily between dense, untended hedges. Even
then I might have missed the house to which it led, for, hair-pin fashion,
the track here abruptly turned back on itself, and only a far fainter foot-
path led on over the hill-crest. I might, I say, have missed the house and
—and its inmates, if I had not heard the musical sound of what seemed
like the twangling of a harp. This thin-drawn, sweet, tuneless warbling
welled over the close green grass of the height as if out of space. Truth
cannot say whether it was of that air or of my own fantasy. Nor did I
ever discover what instrument, whether of man or Ariel, had released a
strain so pure and yet so bodiless.

"I pushed on and found myself in command of a gorse-strewn height, a
stretch of country that lay a few hundred paces across the steep and
sudden valley in between. In a V-shaped entry to the left, and sunwards,
lay an azure and lazy tongue of the sea. And as my eye slid softly thence
and upwards and along the sharp, green horizon line against the glass-

clear turquoise of space, it caught the flinty glitter of a square chimney. I pushed on, and presently found myself at the gate of a farmyard.

"There was but one straw-mow upon its staddles. A few fowls were sunning themselves in their dust-baths. White and pied doves preened and cooed on the roof of an outbuilding as golden with its lichens as if the western sun had scattered its dust for centuries upon the large slate slabs. Just that life and the whispering of the wind, nothing more. Yet even at one swift glimpse I seemed to have trespassed upon a peace that had endured for ages; to have crossed the viewless border that divides time from eternity. I leaned, resting, over the gate, and could have remained there for hours, lapsing ever more profoundly into the blessed quietude that had stolen over my thoughts.

"A bent-up woman appeared at the dark entry of a stone shed opposite to me, and, shading her eyes, paused in prolonged scrutiny of the stranger. At that I entered the gate and, explaining that I had lost my way and was tired and thirsty, asked for some milk. She made no reply, but after peering up at me, with something between suspicion and apprehension on her weather-beaten old face, led me towards the house which lay to the left on the slope of the valley, hidden from me till then by plumy bushes of tamarisk.

"It was a low grave house, grey-chimneyed, its stone walls traversed by a deep shadow cast by the declining sun, its dark windows rounded and uncurtained, its door wide open to the porch. She entered the house, and I paused upon the threshold. A deep unmoving quiet lay within, like that of water in a cave renewed by the tide. Above a table hung a wreath of wild flowers. To the right was a heavy oak settle upon the flags. A beam of sunlight pierced the air of the staircase from an upper window.

"Presently a dark long-faced gaunt man appeared from within, contemplating me, as he advanced, out of eyes that seemed not so much to fix the intruder as to encircle his image, as the sea contains the distant speck of a ship on its wide blue bosom of water. They might have been the eyes of the blind; the windows of a house in dream to which the inmate must make something of a pilgrimage to look out upon actuality. Then he smiled, and the long, dark features, melancholy yet serene, took light upon them, as might a bluff of rock beneath a thin passing wash of sunshine. With a gesture he welcomed me into the large dark-flagged kitchen, cool as a cellar, airy as a belfry, its sweet air traversed by a long oblong of light out of the west.

"The wide shelves of the painted dresser were laden with crockery. A wreath of freshly-gathered flowers hung over the chimney-piece. As we entered, a twittering cloud of small birds, robins, hedge-sparrows, chaffinches fluttered up a few inches from floor and sill and window-seat, and once more, with tiny starry-dark eyes observing me, soundlessly alighted.

"I could hear the infinitesimal *tic-tac* of their tiny claws upon the slate. My gaze drifted out of the window into the garden beyond, a cavern of clearer crystal and colour than that which astounded the eyes of young Aladdin. Apart from the twisted garland of wild flowers, the shining metal of range and copper candlestick, and the bright-scoured crockery, there was no adornment in the room except a rough frame, hanging from a nail in the wall, and enclosing what appeared to be a faint patterned fragment of blue silk or fine linen. The chairs and table were old and heavy. A low light warbling, an occasional *skirr* of wing, a haze-like drone of bee and fly—these were the only sounds that edged a quiet intensified in its profundity by the remote stirrings of the sea.

"The house was stilled as by a charm, yet thought within me asked no questions; speculation was asleep in its kennel. I sat down to the milk and bread, the honey and fruit which the old woman laid out upon the table, and her master seated himself opposite to me, now in a low sibilant whisper—a tongue which they seemed to understand—addressing himself to the birds, and now, as if with an effort, raising those strange greygreen eyes of his to bestow a quiet remark upon me. He asked, rather in courtesy than with any active interest, a few questions, referring to the world, its business and transports—*our* beautiful world—as an astronomer in the small hours might murmur a few words to the chance-sent guest of his solitude concerning the secrets of Uranus or Saturn. There is another, an inexplorable side to the moon. Yet he said enough for me to gather that he, too, was of that small tribe of the aloof and wild to which our cracked old word 'forsaken' might be applied, hermits, clay-matted fakirs, and such-like, the snowy birds that play and cry amid mid-oceanic surges, the living of an oasis of the wilderness, which share a reality only distantly dreamed of by the time-driven thought-corroded congregations of man.

"Yet so narrow and hazardous I somehow realised was the brink of fellow-being (shall I call it?) which we shared, he and I, that again and again fantasy within me seemed to hover over that precipice Night knows as fear. It was he, it seemed, with that still embracive contemplation of his, with that far-away yet reassuring smile, that kept my poise, my balance. 'No,' some voice within him seemed to utter, 'you are safe; the bounds are fixed; though hallucination chaunt its decoy, you shall not irretrievably pass over. Eat and drink, and presently return to "life." ' And I listened, and, like that of a drowsy child in its cradle, my consciousness sank deeper and deeper, stilled, pacified, into the dream amid which, as it seemed, this soundless house of stone now reared its walls.

"I had all but finished my meal when I heard footsteps approaching on the flags without. The murmur of other voices, distinguishably shrill yet guttural, even at a distance, and in spite of the dense stones and beams of the house which had blunted their timbre, had already reached me. Now the feet halted. I turned my head—cautiously, even perhaps apprehensively—and confronted two figures in the doorway.

"I cannot now guess the age of my entertainer. These children—for children they were in face and gesture and effect, though as to form and stature apparently in their last teens—these children were far more problematical. I say 'form and stature,' yet obviously they were dwarfish. Their heads were sunken between their shoulders, their hair thick, their eyes disconcertingly deep-set. They were ungainly, their features peculiarly irregular, as if two races from the ends of the earth had in them intermingled their blood and strangeness; as if, rather, animal and angel had connived in their creation.

"But if some inward light lay on the still eyes, on the gaunt, sorrowful, quixotic countenance that now was fully and intensely bent on mine, emphatically that light was theirs also. He spoke to them; they answered —in English, my own language, without a doubt: but an English slurred, broken, and unintelligible to me, yet clear as bell, haunting, penetrating, pining as voice of nix or siren. My ears drank in the sound as an Arab parched with desert sand falls on his dried belly and gulps in mouthfuls of crystal water. The birds hopped nearer, as if beneath the rod of an enchanter. A sweet continuous clamour arose from their small throats. The exquisite colours of plume and bosom burned, greened, melted in the level sun-ray, in the darker air beyond.

"A kind of mournful gaiety, a lamentable felicity, such as rings in the cadences of an old folk-song, welled into my heart. I was come back to the borders of Eden, bowed and outwearied, gazing from out of dream into dream, homesick, 'forsaken.'

"Well, years have gone by," muttered my fellow-traveller deprecatingly, "but I have not forgotten that Eden's primeval trees and shade.

"They led me out, these bizarre companions, a he and a she, if I may put it as crudely as my apprehension of them put it to me then. Through a broad door they conducted me—if one who leads may be said to be conducted—into their garden. Garden! A full mile long, between undiscerned walls, it sloped and narrowed towards a sea at whose dark unfoamed blue, even at this distance, my eyes dazzled. Yet how can one call that a garden which reveals no ghost of a sign of human arrangement, of human slavery, of spade or hoe?

"Great boulders shouldered up, tessellated, embossed, powdered with a thousand various mosses and lichens, between a flowering greenery of weeds. Wind-stunted, clear-emerald, lichen-tufted trees smoothed and crisped the inflowing airs of the ocean with their leaves and spines, sibilating a thin scarce-audible music. Scanty, rank, and uncultivated fruits hung close their vivid-coloured cheeks to the gnarled branches. It was the harbourage of birds, the small embowering parlour of their house of life, under an evening sky, pure and lustrous as a waterdrop. It cried 'Hospital' to the wanderers of the universe.

"As I look back in ever-thinning nebulous remembrance on my two companions, hear their voices gutturally sweet and shrill, catch again their being, so to speak, I realise that there was a kind of Orientalism in their effect. Their instant courtesy was not Western, the smiles that greeted me, whenever I turned my head to look back at them, were infinitely friendly, yet infinitely remote. So ungainly, so far from our notions of beauty and symmetry were their bodies and faces, those heads thrust heavily between their shoulders, their disproportioned yet graceful arms and hands, that the children in some of our English villages might be moved to stone them, while their elders looked on and laughed.

"Dusk was drawing near; soon night would come. The colours of the sunset, sucking its extremest dye from every leaf and blade and petal, touched my consciousness even then with a vague fleeting alarm.

"I remember I asked these strange and happy beings, repeating my question twice or thrice, as we neared the surfy entry of the valley upon whose sands a tiny stream emptied its fresh waters—I asked them if it was they who had planted this multitude of flowers, many of a kind utterly unknown to me and alien to a country inexhaustibly rich. 'We wait; we wait!' I think they cried. And it was as if their cry woke echo from the green-walled valleys of the mind into which I had strayed. Shall I confess that tears came into my eyes as I gazed hungrily around me on the harvest of their patience?

"Never was actuality so close to dream. It was not only an unknown country, slipped in between these placid hills, on which I had chanced in my ramblings. I had entered for a few brief moments a strange region of consciousness. I was treading, thus accompanied, amid a world of welcoming and fearless life—oh, friendly to me!—the paths of man's imagination, the kingdom from which thought and curiosity, vexed scrutiny and lust—a lust it may be for nothing more impious than the actual—had prehistorically proved the insensate means of his banishment. 'Reality,' 'Consciousness': had he for 'the time being' unwittingly, unhappily missed his way? Would he be led back at length to that garden wherein cockatrice and basilisk bask, harmlessly, at peace?

"I speculate now. In that queer, yes, and possibly sinister, company, sinister only because it was alien to me, I did not speculate. In their garden, the familiar was become the strange—'the strange' that lurks in the inmost heart, unburdens its riches in trance, flings its light and gilding upon love, gives heavenly savour to the intemperate bowl of passion, and is the secret of our incommunicable pity. What is yet queerer, these beings were evidently glad of my company. They stumped after me (as might yellow men after some Occidental quadruped never before seen) in merry collusion of nods and wreathed smiles at this perhaps unprecedented intrusion.

"I stood for a moment looking out over the placid surface of the sea. A ship in sail hung phantom-like on the horizon. I pined to call my discovery to its seamen. The tide gushed, broke, spent itself on the bare boulders, I was suddenly cold and alone, and gladly turned back into the garden, my companions instinctively separating to let me pass between them. I breathed in the rare, almost exotic heat, the tenuous, honeyed, almond-laden air of its flowers and birds—gull, sheldrake, plover, wagtail, finch, robin, which as I half-angrily, half-sadly realised fluttered up in momentary dismay only at *my* presence—the embodied spectre of their enemy, man. Man? Then who were these? . . .

"I lost again a way lost early that morning, as I trudged inland at night. The dark came, warm and starry. I was tired, dejected, exhausted beyond words. That night I slept in a barn and was awakened soon after daybreak by the crowing of cocks. I went out, dazed and blinking into the sunlight, bathed face and hands in a brook near by, and came to a village before a soul was stirring. So I sat under a thrift-cushioned, thorn-crowned wall in a meadow, and once more drowsed off and fell asleep. When again I awoke, it was ten o'clock. The church clock in its tower knelled out the strokes, and I went into an inn for food.

"A corpulent, blonde woman, kindly and hospitable, with a face comfortably resembling her own sow's, that yuffed and nosed in at the open door as I sat on my stool, served me with what I called for. I described—not without some vanishing shame, as if it were a treachery—my farm, its whereabouts.

"Her small blue eyes 'pigged' at me with a fleeting expression which I failed to translate. The name of the farm, it appeared, was Trevarras. 'And did you see any of the Creatures?' she asked me in a voice not entirely her own. 'The Creatures'! I sat back for an instant and stared at her; then realised that Creature was the name of my host, and Maria and Christus (though here her dialect may have deceived me) the names of my two gardeners. She spun an absurd story, so far as I could tack it together and make it coherent. Superstitious stuff about this man who had wandered in upon the shocked and curious inhabitants of the district and made his home at Trevarras—a stranger and pilgrim, a 'foreigner,' it seemed, of few words, dubious manners, and both uninformative.

"Then there was something (she placed her two fat hands, one of them wedding-ringed, on the zinc of the bar-counter, and peered over at me, as if I were a delectable 'wash'), then there was something about a woman 'from the sea.' In a 'blue gown,' and either dumb, inarticulate, or mistress of only a foreign tongue. She must have lived in sin, moreover, those pig's eyes seemed to yearn, since the children were 'simple,' 'naturals'—as God intends in such matters. It was useless. One's stomach may sometimes reject the cold sanative aerated water of 'the next morning,' and my ridiculous intoxication had left me dry but not yet quite sober.

"Anyhow, this she told me, that my blue woman, as fair as flax, had died and was buried in the neighbouring churchyard (the nearest to, though miles distant from, Trevarras). She repeatedly assured me, as if I might otherwise doubt so sophisticated a fact, that I should find her grave there, her 'stone.'

"So indeed I did—far away from the elect, and in a shade-ridden north-west corner of the sleepy, cropless acre: a slab, scarcely rounded, of granite, with but a name bitten out of the dark rough surface, *'Femina Creature.'* "

The Colonel's Lady

W. SOMERSET MAUGHAM
(English, 1874–1965)

All this happened two or three years before the outbreak of the war.

The Peregrines were having breakfast. Though they were alone and the table was long they sat at opposite ends of it. From the walls George Peregrine's ancestors, painted by the fashionable painters of the day, looked down upon them. The butler brought in the morning post. There were several letters for the colonel, business letters, *The Times* and a small parcel for his wife Evie. He looked at his letters and then, opening *The Times,* began to read it. They finished breakfast and rose from the table. He noticed that his wife hadn't opened the parcel.

"What's that?" he asked.

"Only some books."

"Shall I open it for you?"

"If you like."

He hated to cut string and so with some difficulty untied the knots.

"But they're all the same," he said when he had unwrapped the parcel. "What on earth d'you want six copies of the same book for?" He opened one of them. "Poetry." Then he looked at the title page. *When Pyramids Decay,* he read, by E. K. Hamilton. Eva Katherine Hamilton: that was his wife's maiden name. He looked at her with smiling surprise. "Have you written a book, Evie? You are a slyboots."

"I didn't think it would interest you very much. Would you like a copy?"

"Well, you know poetry isn't much in my line, but—yes, I'd like a copy; I'll read it. I'll take it along to my study. I've got a lot to do this morning."

He gathered up *The Times,* his letters and the book, and went out. His study was a large and comfortable room, with a big desk, leather armchairs and what he called "trophies of the chase" on the walls. On the bookshelves were works of reference, books on farming, gardening, fishing and shooting, and books on the last war, in which he had won an M.C. and a D.S.O. For before his marriage he had been in the Welsh Guards. At the end of the war he retired and settled down to the life of a country gentleman in the spacious house, some twenty miles from Sheffield, which one of his forebears had built in the reign of George III. George Peregrine had an estate of some fifteen hundred acres which he managed with ability; he was a Justice of the Peace and performed his duties conscientiously. During the season he rode to hounds two days a week. He was a good shot, a golfer and though now a little over fifty could still play a hard game of tennis. He could describe himself with propriety as an all-round sportsman.

He had been putting on weight lately, but was still a fine figure of a man; tall, with grey curly hair, only just beginning to grow thin on the crown, frank blue eyes, good features and a high colour. He was a public-spirited man, chairman of any number of local organisations and, as became his class and station, a loyal member of the Conservative Party. He looked upon it as his duty to see to the welfare of the people on his estate and it was a satisfaction to him to know that Evie could be trusted to tend the sick and succour the poor. He had built a cottage hospital on the outskirts of the village and paid the wages of a nurse out of his own pocket. All he asked of the recipients of his bounty was that at elections, county or general, they should vote for his candidate. He was a friendly man, affable to his inferiors, considerate with his tenants and popular with the neighbouring gentry. He would have been pleased and at the same time slightly embarrassed if someone had told him he was a jolly good fellow. That was what he wanted to be. He desired no higher praise.

It was hard luck that he had no children. He would have been an excellent father, kindly but strict, and would have brought up his sons as gentlemen's sons should be brought up, sent them to Eton, you know, taught them to fish, shoot and ride. As it was, his heir was a nephew, son of his brother killed in a motor accident, not a bad boy, but not a chip off the old block, no, sir, far from it; and would you believe it, his fool of a mother was sending him to a co-educational school. Evie had been a sad disappointment to him. Of course she was a lady, and she had a bit of money of her own; she managed the house uncommonly well and she was a good hostess. The village people adored her. She had been a pretty little thing when he married her, with a creamy skin, light brown hair and a trim figure, healthy too and not a bad tennis player; he couldn't understand why she'd had no children; of course she was faded now, she must be getting on for five and forty; her skin was drab, her hair had lost its sheen and she was as thin as a rail. She was always neat and suitably dressed, but she didn't seem to bother how she looked, she wore no make-up and didn't even use lipstick; sometimes at night when she dolled herself up for a party you could tell that once she'd been quite attractive, but ordinarily she was—well, the sort of woman you simply didn't notice. A nice woman, of course, a good wife, and it wasn't her fault if she was barren, but it was tough on a fellow who wanted an heir of his own loins; she hadn't any vitality, that's what was the matter with her. He supposed he'd been in love with her when he asked her to marry him, as least sufficiently in love for a man who wanted to marry and settle down, but with time he discovered that they had nothing much in common. She didn't care about hunting, and fishing bored her. Naturally they'd drifted apart. He had to do her the justice to admit that she'd never bothered him. There'd been no scenes. They had no quarrels. She seemed to take it for granted that he should go his own way. When he went up to London now and then she never wanted to come with him. He had a girl there, well, she wasn't exactly a girl, she was thirty-five if she was a day, but she was blonde and luscious and he only had to wire ahead of time and they'd dine, do a show and spend the night together. Well, a man, a healthy normal man had to have some fun in his life. The thought crossed his mind that if Evie hadn't been such a good woman she'd have been a better wife; but it was not the sort of thought that he welcomed and he put it away from him.

George Peregrine finished his *Times* and being a considerate fellow rang the bell and told the butler to take it to Evie. Then he looked at his watch. It was half-past ten and at eleven he had an appointment with one of his tenants. He had half an hour to spare.

"I'd better have a look at Evie's book," he said to himself.

He took it up with a smile. Evie had a lot of highbrow books in her sitting-room, not the sort of books that interested him, but if they amused her he had no objection to her reading them. He noticed that the volume he now held in his hand contained no more than ninety pages. That was all to the good. He shared Edgar Allan Poe's opinion that poems should be short. But as he turned the pages he noticed that several of Evie's had long lines of irregular length and didn't rhyme. He didn't like that. At his first school, when he was a little boy, he remembered learning a poem that began: *The boy stood on the burning deck,* and later, at Eton, one that started: *Ruin seize thee, ruthless king;* and then there was Henry V; they'd had to take that, one half. He stared at Evie's pages with consternation.

"That's not what I call poetry," he said.

Fortunately it wasn't all like that. Interspersed with the pieces that looked so odd, lines of three or four words and then a line of ten or fifteen, there were little poems, quite short, that rhymed, thank God, with the lines all the same length. Several of the pages were just headed with the word *Sonnet,* and out of curiosity he counted the lines; there were fourteen of them. He read them. They seemed all right, but he didn't quite know what they were all about. He repeated to himself: *Ruin seize thee, ruthless king.*

"Poor Evie," he sighed.

At that moment the farmer he was expecting was ushered into the study, and putting the book down he made him welcome. They embarked on their business.

"I read your book, Evie," he said as they sat down to lunch. "Jolly good. Did it cost you a packet to have it printed?"

"No, I was lucky. I sent it to a publisher and he took it."

"Not much money in poetry, my dear," he said in his good-natured, hearty way.

"No, I don't suppose there is. What did Bannock want to see you about this morning?"

Bannock was the tenant who had interrupted his reading of Evie's poems.

"He's asked me to advance the money for a pedigree bull he wants to buy. He's a good man and I've half a mind to do it."

George Peregrine saw that Evie didn't want to talk about her book and he was not sorry to change the subject. He was glad she had used her maiden name on the title page; he didn't suppose anyone would ever hear about the book, but he was proud of his own unusual name and he wouldn't have liked it if some damned penny-a-liner had made fun of Evie's effort in one of the papers.

During the few weeks that followed he thought it tactful not to ask Evie any questions about her venture into verse, and she never referred to it. It might have been a discreditable incident that they had silently agreed not to mention. But then a strange thing happened. He had to go to London on business and he took Daphne out to dinner. That was the name of the girl with whom he was in the habit of passing a few agreeable hours whenever he went to town.

"Oh, George," she said, "is that your wife who's written a book they're all talking about?"

"What on earth d'you mean?"

"Well, there's a fellow I know who's a critic. He took me out to dinner the other night and he had a book with him. 'Got anything for me to read?' I said. 'What's that?' 'Oh, I don't think that's your cup of tea,' he said. 'It's poetry. I've just been reviewing it.' 'No poetry for me,' I said. 'It's about the hottest stuff I ever read,' he said. 'Selling like hot cakes. And it's damned good.' "

"Who's the book by?" asked George.

"A woman called Hamilton. My friend told me that wasn't her real name. He said her real name was Peregrine. 'Funny,' I said, 'I know a fellow called Peregrine.' 'Colonel in the army,' he said. 'Lives near Sheffield.' "

"I'd just as soon you didn't talk about me to your friends," said George with a frown of vexation.

"Keep your shirt on, dearie. Who d'you take me for? I just said: 'It's not the same one.' " Daphne giggled. "My friend said: 'They say he's a regular Colonel Blimp.' "

George had a keen sense of humour.

"You could tell them better than that," he laughed. "If my wife had written a book I'd be the first to know about it, wouldn't I?"

"I suppose you would."

Anyhow the matter didn't interest her and when the colonel began to talk of other things she forgot about it. He put it out of his mind too. There was nothing to it, he decided, and that silly fool of a critic had just been pulling Daphne's leg. He was amused at the thought of her tackling that book because she had been told it was hot stuff and then finding it just a lot of bosh cut up into unequal lines.

He was a member of several clubs and next day he thought he'd lunch at one in St. James's Street. He was catching a train back to Sheffield early in the afternoon. He was sitting in a comfortable arm-chair having a glass of sherry before going into the dining-room when an old friend came up to him.

"Well, old boy, how's life?" he said. "How d'you like being the husband of a celebrity?"

George Peregrine looked at his friend. He thought he saw an amused twinkle in his eyes.

"I don't know what you're talking about," he answered.

"Come off it, George. Everyone knows E. K. Hamilton is your wife. Not often a book of verse has a success like that. Look here, Henry Dashwood is lunching with me. He'd like to meet you."

"Who the devil is Henry Dashwood and why should he want to meet me?"

"Oh, my dear fellow, what do you do with yourself all the time in the country? Henry's about the best critic we've got. He wrote a wonderful review of Evie's book. D'you mean to say she didn't show it you?"

Before George could answer his friend had called a man over. A tall, thin man, with a high forehead, a beard, a long nose and a stoop, just the sort of man whom George was prepared to dislike at first sight. Introductions were effected. Henry Dashwood sat down.

"Is Mrs. Peregrine in London by any chance? I should very much like to meet her," he said.

"No, my wife doesn't like London. She prefers the country," said George stiffly.

"She wrote me a very nice letter about my review. I was pleased. You know, we critics get more kicks than halfpence. I was simply bowled over by her book. It's so fresh and original, very modern without being obscure. She seems to be as much at her ease in free verse as in the classical metres." Then because he was a critic he thought he should criticise. "Sometimes her ear is a trifle at fault, but you can say the same of Emily Dickinson. There are several of those short lyrics of hers that might have been written by Landor."

All this was gibberish to George Peregrine. The man was nothing but a disgusting highbrow. But the colonel had good manners and he answered with proper civility: Henry Dashwood went on as though he hadn't spoken.

"But what makes the book so outstanding is the passion that throbs in every line. So many of these young poets are so anaemic, cold, bloodless, dully intellectual, but here you have real naked, earthy passion; of course deep, sincere emotion like that is tragic—ah, my dear Colonel, how right Heine was when he said that the poet makes little songs out of his great sorrows. You know, now and then, as I read and re-read those heart-rending pages I thought of Sappho."

This was too much for George Peregrine and he got up.

"Well, it's jolly nice of you to say such nice things about my wife's little book. I'm sure she'll be delighted. But I must bolt, I've got to catch a train and I want to get a bite of lunch."

"Damned fool," he said irritably to himself as he walked upstairs to the dining-room.

He got home in time for dinner and after Evie had gone to bed he went into his study and looked for her book. He thought he'd just glance through it again to see for himself what they were making such a fuss about, but he couldn't find it. Evie must have taken it away.

"Silly," he muttered.

He'd told her he thought it jolly good. What more could a fellow be expected to say? Well, it didn't matter. He lit his pipe and read the *Field* till he felt sleepy. But a week or so later it happened that he had to go into Sheffield for the day. He lunched there at his club. He had nearly finished when the Duke of Haverel came in. This was the great local magnate and of course the colonel knew him, but only to say how d'you do to; and he was surprised when the Duke stopped at his table.

"We're so sorry your wife couldn't come to us for the week-end," he said, with a sort of shy cordiality. "We're expecting rather a nice lot of people."

George was taken aback. He guessed that the Haverels had asked him and Evie over for the week-end and Evie, without saying a word to him about it, had refused. He had the presence of mind to say he was sorry too.

"Better luck next time," said the Duke pleasantly and moved on.

Colonel Peregrine was very angry and when he got home he said to his wife:

"Look here, what's this about our being asked over to Haverel? Why on earth did you say we couldn't go? We've never been asked before and it's the best shooting in the county."

"I didn't think of that. I thought it would only bore you."

"Damn it all, you might at least have asked me if I wanted to go."

"I'm sorry."

He looked at her closely. There was something in her expression that he didn't quite understand. He frowned.

"I suppose *I* was asked?" he barked.

Evie flushed a little.

"Well, in point of fact you weren't."

"I call it damned rude of them to ask you without asking me."

"I suppose they thought it wasn't your sort of party. The Duchess is rather fond of writers and people like that, you know. She's having Henry Dashwood, the critic, and for some reason he wants to meet me."

"It was damned nice of you to refuse, Evie."

"It's the least I could do," she smiled. She hesitated a moment. "George, my publishers want to give a little dinner party for me one day towards the end of the month and of course they want you to come too."

"Oh, I don't think that's quite my mark. I'll come up to London with you if you like. I'll find someone to dine with."

Daphne.

"I expect it'll be very dull, but they're making rather a point of it. And the day after, the American publisher who's taken my book is giving a cocktail party at Claridge's. I'd like you to come to that if you wouldn't mind."

"Sounds like a crashing bore, but if you really want me to come I'll come."

"It would be sweet of you."

George Peregrine was dazed by the cocktail party. There were a lot of people. Some of them didn't look so bad, a few of the women were decently turned out, but the men seemed to him pretty awful. He was introduced to everyone as Colonel Peregrine, E. K. Hamilton's husband, you know. The men didn't seem to have anything to say to him, but the women gushed.

"You *must* be proud of your wife. Isn't it *wonderful?* You know, I read it right through at a sitting, I simply couldn't put it down, and when I'd finished I started again at the beginning and read it right through a second time. I was simply *thrilled.*"

The English publisher said to him:

"We've not had a success like this with a book of verse for twenty years. I've never seen such reviews."

The American publisher said to him:

"It's swell. It'll be a smash hit in America. You wait and see."

The American publisher had sent Evie a great spray of orchids. Damned ridiculous, thought George. As they came in, people were taken up to Evie, and it was evident that they said flattering things to her, which she took with a pleasant smile and a word or two of thanks. She was a trifle flushed with the excitement, but seemed quite at her ease. Though he thought the whole thing a lot of stuff and nonsense George noted with approval that his wife was carrying it off in just the right way.

"Well, there's one thing," he said to himself, "you can see she's a lady and that's a damned sight more than you can say of anyone else here."

He drank a good many cocktails. But there was one thing that bothered him. He had a notion that some of the people he was introduced to looked at him in rather a funny sort of way, he couldn't quite make out what it meant, and once when he strolled by two women who were sitting together on a sofa he had the impression that they were talking about him and after he passed he was almost certain they tittered. He was very glad when the party came to an end.

In the taxi on their way back to their hotel Evie said to him:

"You were wonderful, dear. You made quite a hit. The girls simply raved about you: they thought you so handsome."

"Girls," he said bitterly. "Old hags."

"Were you bored, dear?"

"Stiff."

She pressed his hand in a gesture of sympathy.

"I hope you won't mind if we wait and go down by the afternoon train. I've got some things to do in the morning."

"No, that's all right. Shopping?"

"I do want to buy one or two things, but I've got to go and be photographed. I hate the idea, but they think I ought to be. For America, you know."

He said nothing. But he thought. He thought it would be a shock to the American public when they saw the portrait of the homely, desiccated little woman who was his wife. He'd always been under the impression that they liked glamour in America.

He went on thinking, and next morning when Evie had gone out he went to his club and up to the library. There he looked up recent numbers of *The Times Literary Supplement, The New Statesman* and *The Spectator.* Presently he found reviews of Evie's book. He didn't read them very carefully, but enough to see that they were extremely favourable. Then he went to the bookseller's in Piccadilly where he occasionally bought books. He'd made up his mind that he had to read this damned thing of Evie's properly, but he didn't want to ask her what she'd done with the copy she'd given him. He'd buy one for himself. Before going in he looked in the window and the first thing he saw was a display of *When Pyramids Decay.* Damned silly title! He went in. A young man came forward and asked if he could help him.

"No, I'm just having a look round." It embarrassed him to ask for Evie's book and he thought he'd find it for himself and then take it to the salesman. But he couldn't see it anywhere and at last, finding the young man near him, he said in a carefully casual tone: "By the way, have you got a book called *When Pyramids Decay?*"

"The new edition came in this morning. I'll get a copy."

In a moment the young man returned with it. He was a short, rather stout young man, with a shock of untidy carroty hair and spectacles. George Peregrine, tall, upstanding, very military, towered over him.

"Is this a new edition then?" he asked.

"Yes, sir. The fifth. It might be a novel the way it's selling."

George Peregrine hesitated a moment.

"Why d'you suppose it's such a success? I've always been told no one reads poetry."

"Well, it's good, you know. I've read it meself." The young man, though obviously cultured, had a slight Cockney accent, and George quite instinctively adopted a patronising attitude. "It's the story they like. Sexy, you know, but tragic."

George frowned a little. He was coming to the conclusion that the young man was rather impertinent. No one had told him anything about there being a story in the damned book and he had not gathered that from reading the reviews. The young man went on:

"Of course it's only a flash in the pan, if you know what I mean. The way I look at it, she was sort of inspired like by a personal experience, like Housman was with *The Shropshire Lad.* She'll never write anything else."

"How much is the book?" said George coldly to stop his chatter. "You needn't wrap it up, I'll just slip it into my pocket."

The November morning was raw and he was wearing a greatcoat.

At the station he bought the evening papers and magazines and he and Evie settled themselves comfortably in opposite corners of a first-class carriage and read. At five o'clock they went along to the restaurant car to have tea and chatted a little. They arrived. They drove home in the car which was waiting for them. They bathed, dressed for dinner, and after dinner Evie, saying she was tired out, went to bed. She kissed him, as was her habit, on the forehead. Then he went into the hall, took Evie's book out of his greatcoat pocket and going into the study began to read it. He didn't read verse very easily and though he read with attention, every word of it, the impression he received was far from clear. Then he began at the beginning again and read it a second time. He read with increasing malaise, but he was not a stupid man and when he had finished he had a distinct understanding of what it was all about. Part of the book was in free verse, part in conventional metres, but the story it related was coherent and plain to the meanest intelligence. It was the story of a passionate love affair between an older woman, married, and a young man. George Peregrine made out the steps of it as easily as if he had been doing a sum in simple addition.

Written in the first person, it began with the tremulous surprise of the woman, past her youth, when it dawned upon her that the young man was in love with her. She hesitated to believe it. She thought she must be deceiving herself. And she was terrified when on a sudden she discovered that she was passionately in love with him. She told herself it was absurd; with the disparity of age between them nothing but unhappiness could come to her if she yielded to her emotion. She tried to prevent him from speaking but the day came when he told her that he loved her and forced her to tell him that she loved him too. He begged her to run away with him. She couldn't leave her husband, her home; and what life could they look forward to, she an ageing woman, he so young? How could she expect his love to last? She begged him to have mercy on her. But his love was impetuous. He wanted her, he wanted her with all his heart, and at last trembling, afraid, desirous, she yielded to him. Then there was a period of ecstatic happiness. The world, the dull, humdrum world of every day, blazed with glory. Love songs flowed from her pen. The woman worshipped the young, virile body of her lover. George flushed darkly when she praised his broad chest and slim flanks, the beauty of his legs and the flatness of his belly.

Hot stuff, Daphne's friend had said. It was that all right. Disgusting.

There were sad little pieces in which she lamented the emptiness of her life when as must happen he left her, but they ended with a cry that all she had to suffer would be worth it for the bliss that for a while had been hers. She wrote of the long, tremulous nights they passed together and the languor that lulled them to sleep in one another's arms. She wrote of the rapture of brief stolen moments when, braving all danger, their passion overwhelmed them and they surrendered to its call.

She thought it would be an affair of a few weeks, but miraculously it lasted. One of the poems referred to three years having gone by without lessening the love that filled their hearts. It looked as though he continued to press her to go away with him, far away, to a hill town in Italy, a Greek island, a walled city in Tunisia, so that they could be together always, for in another of the poems she besought him to let things be as they were. Their happiness was precarious. Perhaps it was owing to the difficulties they had to encounter and the rarity of their meetings that their love had retained for so long its first enchanting ardour. Then on a sudden the young man died. How, when or where George could not discover. There followed a long, heart-broken cry of bitter grief, grief she could not indulge in, grief that had to be hidden. She had to be cheerful, give dinner-parties and go out to dinner, behave as she had always behaved, though the light had gone out of her life and she was bowed down with anguish. The last poem of all was a set of four short stanzas in which the writer, sadly resigned to her loss, thanked the dark powers that rule man's destiny that she had been privileged at least for a while to enjoy the greatest happiness that we poor human beings can ever hope to know.

It was three o'clock in the morning when George Peregrine finally put the book down. It had seemed to him that he heard Evie's voice in every line, over and over again he came upon turns of phrase he had heard her use, there were details that were as familiar to him as to her: there was no doubt about it; it was her own story she had told, and it was as plain as anything could be that she had had a lover and her lover had died. It was not anger so much that he felt, nor horror or dismay, though he was dismayed and he was horrified, but amazement. It was as inconceivable that Evie should have had a love affair, and a wildly passionate one at that, as that the trout in a glass case over the chimney piece in his study, the finest he had ever caught, should suddenly wag its tail. He understood now the meaning of the amused look he had seen in the eyes of that man he had spoken to at the club, he understood why Daphne when she was talking about the book had seemed to be enjoying a private joke, and why those two women at the cocktail party had tittered when he strolled past them.

He broke out into a sweat. Then on a sudden he was seized with fury and he jumped up to go and awake Evie and ask her sternly for an explanation. But he stopped at the door. After all, what proof had he? A book. He remembered that he'd told Evie he thought it jolly good. True, he hadn't read it, but he'd pretended he had. He would look a perfect fool if he had to admit that.

"I must watch my step," he muttered.

He made up his mind to wait for two or three days and think it all over. Then he'd decide what to do. He went to bed, but he couldn't sleep for a long time.

"Evie," he kept on saying to himself. "Evie, of all people."

They met at breakfast next morning as usual. Evie was as she always was, quiet, demure and self-possessed, a middle-aged woman who made no effort to look younger than she was, a woman who had nothing of what he still called It. He looked at her as he hadn't looked at her for years. She had her usual placid serenity. Her pale blue eyes were untroubled. There was no sign of guilt on her candid brow. She made the same little casual remarks she always made.

"It's nice to get back to the country again after those two hectic days in London. What are you going to do this morning?"

It was incomprehensible.

Three days later he went to see his solicitor. Henry Blane was an old friend of George's as well as his lawyer. He had a place not far from Peregrine's and for years they had shot over one another's preserves. For two days a week he was a country gentleman and for the other five a busy lawyer in Sheffield. He was a tall, robust fellow, with a boisterous manner and a jovial laugh, which suggested that he liked to be looked upon essentially as a sportsman and a good fellow and only incidentally as a lawyer. But he was shrewd and worldly-wise.

"Well, George, what's brought you here today?" he boomed as the colonel was shown into his office. "Have a good time in London? I'm taking my missus up for a few days next week. How's Evie?"

"It's about Evie I've come to see you," said Peregrine, giving him a suspicious look. "Have you read her book?"

His sensitivity had been sharpened during those last days of troubled thought and he was conscious of a faint change in the lawyer's expression. It was as though he were suddenly on his guard.

"Yes, I've read it. Great success, isn't it? Fancy Evie breaking out into poetry. Wonders will never cease."

George Peregrine was inclined to lose his temper.

"It's made me look a perfect damned fool."

"Oh, what nonsense, George! There's no harm in Evie's writing a book. You ought to be jolly proud of her."

"Don't talk such rot. It's her own story. You know it and everyone else knows it. I suppose I'm the only one who doesn't know who her lover was."

"There is such a thing as imagination, old boy. There's no reason to suppose the whole thing isn't made up."

"Look here, Henry, we've known one another all our lives. We've had all sorts of good times together. Be honest with me. Can you look me in the face and tell me you believe it's a made-up story?"

Harry Blane moved uneasily in his chair. He was disturbed by the distress in old George's voice.

"You've got no right to ask me a question like that. Ask Evie."

"I daren't," George answered after an anguished pause. "I'm afraid she'd tell me the truth."

There was an uncomfortable silence.

"Who was the chap?"

Harry Blane looked at him straight in the eye.

"I don't know, and if I did I wouldn't tell you."

"You swine. Don't you see what a position I'm in? Do you think it's very pleasant to be made absolutely ridiculous?"

The lawyer lit a cigarette and for some moments silently puffed it.

"I don't see what I can do for you," he said at last.

"You've got private detectives you employ, I suppose. I want you to put them on the job and let them find everything out."

"It's not very pretty to put detectives on one's wife, old boy; and besides, taking for granted for a moment that Evie had an affair, it was a good many years ago and I don't suppose it would be possible to find out a thing. They seem to have covered their tracks pretty carefully."

"I don't care. You put the detectives on. I want to know the truth."

"I won't, George. If you're determined to do that you'd better consult someone else. And look here, even if you got evidence that Evie had been unfaithful to you what would you do with it? You'd look rather silly divorcing your wife because she'd committed adultery ten years ago."

"At all events I could have it out with her."

"You can do that now, but you know just as well as I do that if you do she'll leave you. D'you want her to do that?"

George gave him an unhappy look.

"I don't know. I always thought she'd been a damned good wife to me. She runs the house perfectly, we never have any servant trouble; she's done wonders with the garden and she's splendid with all the village people. But damn it, I have my self-respect to think of. How can I go on living with her when I know that she was grossly unfaithful to me?"

"Have you always been faithful to her?"

"More or less, you know. After all, we've been married for nearly twenty-four years and Evie was never much for bed."

The solicitor slightly raised his eyebrows, but George was too intent on what he was saying to notice.

"I don't deny that I've had a bit of fun now and then. A man wants it. Women are different."

"We only have men's word for that," said Harry Blane, with a faint smile.

"Evie's absolutely the last woman I'd have suspected of kicking over the traces. I mean, she's a very fastidious, reticent woman. What on earth made her write the damned book?"

"I suppose it was a very poignant experience and perhaps it was a relief to her to get it off her chest like that."

"Well, if she had to write it why the devil didn't she write it under an assumed name?"

"She used her maiden name. I suppose she thought that was enough, and it would have been if the book hadn't had this amazing boom."

George Peregrine and the lawyer were sitting opposite one another with a desk between them. George, his elbow on the desk, his cheek on his hand, frowned at his thought.

"It's so rotten not to know what sort of a chap he was. One can't even tell if he was by way of being a gentleman. I mean, for all I know he may have been a farm-hand or a clerk in a lawyer's office."

Harry Blane did not permit himself to smile and when he answered there was in his eyes a kindly, tolerant look.

"Knowing Evie so well I think the probabilities are that he was all right. Anyhow I'm sure he wasn't a clerk in my office."

"It's been a shock to me," the colonel sighed. "I thought she was fond of me. She couldn't have written that book unless she hated me."

"Oh, I don't believe that. I don't think she's capable of hatred."

"You're not going to pretend that she loves me."

"No."

"Well, what does she feel for me?"

Harry Blane leaned back in his swivel chair and looked at George reflectively.

"Indifference, I should say."

The colonel gave a little shudder and reddened.

"After all, you're not in love with her, are you?"

George Peregrine did not answer directly.

"It's been a great blow to me not to have any children, but I've never let her see that I think she's let me down. I've always been kind to her. Within reasonable limits I've tried to do my duty by her."

The lawyer passed a large hand over his mouth to conceal the smile that trembled on his lips.

"It's been such an awful shock to me," Peregrine went on. "Damn it all, even ten years ago Evie was no chicken and God knows, she wasn't much to look at. It's so ugly." He sighed deeply. "What would *you* do in my place?"

"Nothing."

George Peregrine drew himself bolt upright in his chair and he looked at Harry with the stern set face that he must have worn when he inspected his regiment.

"I can't overlook a thing like this. I've been made a laughingstock. I can never hold up my head again."

"Nonsense," said the lawyer sharply, and then in a pleasant, kindly manner, "Listen, old boy: the man's dead; it all happened a long while back. Forget it. Talk to people about Evie's book, rave about it, tell 'em how proud you are of her. Behave as though you had so much confidence in her, you *knew* she could never have been unfaithful to you. The world moves so quickly and people's memories are so short. They'll forget."

"I shan't forget."

"You're both middle-aged people. She probably does a great deal more for you than you think and you'd be awfully lonely without her. I don't think it matters if you don't forget. It'll be all to the good if you can get it into that thick head of yours that there's a lot more in Evie than you ever had the gumption to see."

"Damn it all, you talk as if *I* was to blame."

"No, I don't think you were to blame, but I'm not so sure that Evie was either. I don't suppose she wanted to fall in love with this boy. D'you remember those verses right at the end? The impression they gave me was that though she was shattered by his death, in a strange sort of way she welcomed it. All through she'd been aware of the fragility of the tie that bound them. He died in the full flush of his first love and had never known that love so seldom endures; he'd only known its bliss and beauty. In her own bitter grief she found solace in the thought that he'd been spared all sorrow."

"All that's a bit above my head, old boy. I see more or less what you mean."

George Peregrine stared unhappily at the inkstand on the desk. He was silent and the lawyer looked at him with curious, yet sympathetic, eyes.

"Do you realise what courage she must have had never by a sign to show how dreadfully unhappy she was?" he said gently.

Colonel Peregrine sighed.

"I'm broken. I suppose you're right; it's no good crying over spilt milk and it would only make things worse if I made a fuss."

"Well?"

George Peregrine gave a pitiful little smile.

"I'll take your advice. I'll do nothing. Let them think me a damned fool and to hell with them. The truth is, I don't know what I'd do without Evie. But I'll tell you what, there's one thing I shall never understand till my dying day: What in the name of heaven did the fellow ever see in her?"

Arabesque—The Mouse

A. E. COPPARD
(English, 1878–1957)

In the main street amongst tall establishments of mart and worship was a high narrow house pressed between a coffee factory and a bootmaker's. It had four flights of long dim echoing stairs, and at the top, in a room that was full of the smell of dried apples and mice, a man in the middle age of life had sat reading Russian novels until he thought he was mad. Late was the hour, the night outside black and freezing, the pavements below empty and undistinguishable when he closed his book and sat motionless in front of the glowing but flameless fire. He felt he was very tired, yet he could not rest. He stared at a picture on the wall until he wanted to cry; it was a colour print by Utamaro of a suckling child caressing its mother's breast as she sits in front of a black-bound mirror. Very chaste and decorative it was, in spite of its curious anatomy. The man gazed, empty of sight though not of mind, until the sighing of the gas jet maddened him. He got up, put out the light, and sat down again in the darkness trying to compose his mind before the comfort of the fire. And he was just about to begin a conversation with himself when a mouse crept from a hole in the skirting near the fireplace and scurried into the fender. The man had the crude dislike for such sly nocturnal things, but this mouse was so small and bright, its antics so pretty, that he drew his feet carefully from the fender and sat watching it almost with amusement. The mouse moved along the shadows of the fender, out upon the hearth, and sat before the glow, rubbing its head, ears, and tiny belly with its paws as if it were bathing itself with the warmth, until, sharp and sudden, the fire sank, an ember fell, and the mouse flashed into its hole.

The man reached forward to the mantelpiece and put his hand upon a pocket lamp. Turning on the beam, he opened the door of a cupboard beside the fireplace. Upon one of the shelves there was a small trap baited with cheese, a trap made with a wire spring, one of those that smashed down to break the back of ingenuous and unwary mice.

"Mean—so mean," he mused, "to appeal to the hunger of any living thing just in order to destroy it."

He picked up the empty trap as if to throw it in the fire.

"I suppose I had better leave it though—the place swarms with them." He still hesitated. "I hope that little beastie won't go and do anything foolish." He put the trap back quite carefully, closed the door of the cupboard, sat down again, and extinguished the lamp.

Was there anyone else in the world so squeamish and foolish about such things! Even his mother, mother so bright and beautiful, even she had laughed at his childish horrors. He recalled how once in his childhood, not long after his sister Yosine was born, a friendly neighbour had sent him home with a bundle of dead larks tied by the feet "for supper." The pitiful inanimity of the birds had brought a gush of tears; he had run weeping home and into the kitchen, and there he had found the strange thing doing. It was dusk; mother was kneeling before the fire. He dropped the larks.

"Mother!" he exclaimed softly. She looked at his tearful face.

"What's the matter, Filip?" she asked, smiling too at his astonishment.

"Mother! What are you doing?"

Her bodice was open and she was squeezing her breasts; long thin streams of milk spurted into the fire with a little plunging noise.

"Weaning your little sister," laughed mother. She took his little inquisitive face and pressed it against the delicate warmth of her bosom, and he forgot the dead birds behind him.

"Let me do it, mother," he cried, and doing so he discovered the throb of the heart in his mother's breast. Wonderful it was for him to experience it, although she could not explain it to him.

"Why does it do that?"

"If it did not beat, little son, I should die and the Holy Father would take me from you."

"God?"

She nodded. He put his hand upon his own breast. "Oh, feel it, Mother!" he cried. Mother unbuttoned his little coat and felt the gentle *tick tick* with her warm palm.

"Beautiful!" she said.

"Is it a good one?"

She kissed his upsmiling lips. "It is good if it beats truly. Let it always beat truly, Filip, let it always beat truly."

There was the echo of a sigh in her voice, and he had divined some grief, for he was very wise. He kissed her bosom in his ecstasy and whispered soothingly: "Little mother! little mother!" In such joys he forgot his horror of the dead larks; indeed, he helped mother to pluck them and spit them for supper.

It was a black day that succeeded, and full of tragedy for the child. A great bay horse with a tawny mane had knocked down his mother in the lane, and a heavy cart had passed over her, crushing both her hands. She was borne away moaning with anguish to the surgeon, who cut off the two hands. She died in the night. For years the child's dreams were filled with the horror of the stumps of arms, bleeding unendingly. Yet he had never seen them, for he was sleeping when she died.

While this old woe was come vividly before him he again became aware of the mouse. His nerves stretched upon him in repulsion, but he soon relaxed to a tolerant interest, for it was really a most engaging little mouse. It moved with curious staccato scurries, stopping to rub its head or flicker with its ears; they seemed almost transparent ears. It spied a red cinder and skipped innocently up to it . . . sniffing . . . sniffing . . . until it jumped back scorched. It would crouch as a cat does, blinking in the warmth, or scamper madly as if dancing, and then roll upon its side rubbing its head with those pliant paws. The melancholy man watched it until it came at last to rest and squatted meditatively upon its haunches, hunched up, looking curiously wise, a pennyworth of philosophy; then once more the coals sank with a rattle and again the mouse was gone.

The man sat on before the fire and his mind filled again with unaccountable sadness. He had grown into manhood with a burning generosity of spirit and rifts of rebellion in him that proved too exacting for his fellows and seemed mere wantonness to men of casual rectitudes. "Justice and Sin," he would cry, "Property and Virtue—incompatibilities! There can be no sin in a world of justice, no property in a world of virtue!" With an engaging extravagance and a certain clear-eyed honesty of mind he had put his two and two together and seemed then to rejoice, as in some topsy-turvy dream, in having rendered unto Caesar, as you might say, the things that were due to Napoleon! But this kind of thing could not pass unexpiated in a world of men having an infinite regard for Property and a pride in their traditions of Virtue and Justice. They could indeed forgive him his sins but they could not forgive him his compassions; so he had to go seek for more melodious-minded men and fair unambiguous women. But rebuffs can deal more deadly blows than daggers; he became timid—a timidity not of fear but of pride—and grew with the years into misanthropy, susceptible to trivial griefs and despairs, a vessel of emotion that emptied as easily as it filled, until he came at last to know that his griefs were half deliberate, his despairs half unreal, and to live but for beauty—which is tranquillity—to put her wooing hand upon him.

Now, while the mouse hunts in the cupboard, one fair recollection stirs in the man's mind—of Cassia and the harmony of their only meeting, Cassia, who had such rich red hair, and eyes, yes, her eyes were full of starry inquiry like the eyes of mice. It was so long ago that he had forgotten how he came to be in it, that unaccustomed orbit of vain vivid things—a village festival, all oranges and houp-la. He could not remember how he came to be there, but at night, in the court hall, he had danced with Cassia—fair and unambiguous indeed!—who had come like the wind from among the roses and swept into his heart.

"It is easy to guess," he had said to her, "what you like most in the world."

She laughed. "To dance? Yes, and you—?"

"To find a friend."

"I know, I know," she cried, caressing him with recognitions. "Ah, at times I quite love my friends—until I begin to wonder how much they hate me!"

He had loved at once that cool pale face, the abundance of her strange hair as light as the autumn's clustered bronze, her lilac dress and all the sweetness about her like a bush of lilies. How they had laughed at the two old peasants whom they had overheard gabbling of trifles like sickness and appetite!

"There's a lot of nature in a parsnip," said one, a fat person of the kind that swells grossly when stung by a bee, "a lot of nature when it's young, but when it's old it's like everything else."

"True it is."

"And I'm very fond of vegetables, yes, and I'm very fond of bread."

"Come out with me," whispered Cassia to Filip, and they walked out in the blackness of midnight into what must have been a garden.

"Cool it is here," she said, "and quiet, but too dark even to see your face—can you see mine?"

"The moon will not rise until after dawn," said he, "it will be white in the sky when the starlings whistle in your chimney."

They walked silently and warily about until they felt the chill of the air. A dull echo of the music came to them through the walls, then stopped, and they heard the bark of a fox away in the woods.

"You are cold," he whispered, touching her bare neck with timid fingers. "Quite, quite cold," drawing his hand tenderly over the curves of her chin and face. "Let us go in," he said moving with discretion from the rapture he desired. "We will come out again," said Cassia.

But within the room the ball was just at an end, the musicians were packing up their instruments and the dancers were flocking out and homewards, or to the buffet, which was on a platform at one end of the room. The two old peasants were there, munching hugely.

"I tell you," said one of them, "there's nothing in the world for it but the grease of an owl's liver. That's it, that's it! Take something on your stomach now? Just to offset the chill of the dawn?"

Filip and Cassia were beside them, but there were so many people crowding the platform that Filip had to jump down. He stood then looking up adoringly at Cassia, who had pulled a purple cloak around her.

"For Filip, Filip, Filip," she said, pushing the last bite of her sandwich into his mouth, and pressing upon him her glass of Loupiac. Quickly he drank it with a great gesture, and flinging the glass to the wall, took Cassia into his arms, shouting: "I'll carry you home, the whole way home, yes, I'll carry you!"

"Put me down!" she cried, beating his head and pulling his ears, as they passed among the departing dancers. "Put me down, you wild thing!"

Dark, dark was the lane outside, and the night an obsidian net, into which he walked carrying the girl. But her arms were looped around him, she discovered paths for him, clinging more tightly as he staggered against a wall, stumbled upon a gulley, or when her sweet hair was caught in the boughs of a little lime tree.

"Do not loose me, Filip, will you, do not loose me," Cassia said, putting her lips against his temple.

His brain seemed bursting, his heart rocked within him, but he adored the rich grace of her limbs against his breast. "Here it is," she murmured, as he carried her into a path that led to her home in a little lawned garden where the smell of ripe apples upon the branches and the heavy lustre of roses stole upon the air. Roses and apples! Roses and apples! He carried her right into the porch before she slid down and stood close to him with her hands still upon his shoulders. He could breathe happily at the release, standing silent and looking round at the sky sprayed with wondrous stars but without a moon.

"You are stronger than I thought you, stronger than you look, you are really very strong," she whispered, nodding her head to him. Opening the buttons of his coat she put her palm against his breast.

"Oh, how your heart does beat! Does it beat truly—and for whom?"

He had seized her wrists in a little fury of love, crying: "Little mother, little mother!"

"What are you saying?" asked the girl, but before he could continue there came a footstep sounding behind the door, and the clack of a bolt. . . .

What was that? Was that really a bolt or was it . . . was it . . . the snap of the trap. The man sat up in his room intently listening, with nerves quivering again, waiting for the trap to kill the little philosopher. When he felt it was all over he reached guardedly in the darkness for the lantern, turned on the beam, and opened the door of the cupboard. Focusing the light upon the trap, he was amazed to see the mouse sitting on its haunches before it, uncaught. Its head was bowed, but its beadlike eyes were full of brightness, and it sat blinking, it did not flee.

"Shoosh!" said the man, but the mouse did not move. "Why doesn't it go? Shoosh!" he said again, and suddenly the reason of the mouse's strange behaviour was made clear. The trap had not caught it completely, but it had broken off both its forefeet, and the thing crouched there holding out its two bleeding stumps humanly, too stricken to stir.

Horror flooded the man, and conquering his repugnance he plucked the mouse up quickly by the neck. Immediately the little thing fastened its teeth in his finger; the touch was no more than the slight prick of a pin. The man's impulse then exhausted itself. What should he do with it? He put his hand behind him, he dared not look, but there was nothing to be done except kill it at once, quickly, quickly. Oh, how should he do it? He bent towards the fire as if to drop the mouse into its quenching glow; but he paused and shuddered, he would hear its cries, he would have to listen. Should he crush it with finger and thumb? A glance towards the window decided him. He opened the sash with one hand and flung the wounded mouse far into the dark street. Closing the window with a crash, he sank into a chair, limp with pity too deep for tears.

So he sat for two minutes, five minutes, ten minutes. Anxiety and shame filled him with heat. He opened the window again, and the freezing air poured in and cooled him. Seizing his lantern he ran down the echoing stairs, into the empty street, searching long and vainly for the little philosopher until he had to desist and return to his room, shivering, frozen to his very bones.

When he had recovered some warmth he took the trap from its shelf. The two feet dropped into his hand; he cast them into the fire. Then he once more set the trap and put it back carefully into the cupboard.

The Boarding House

❧❀❧

JAMES JOYCE
(Irish, 1882–1941)

Mrs. Mooney was a butcher's daughter. She was a woman who was quite able to keep things to herself: a determined woman. She had married her father's foreman and opened a butcher's shop near Spring Gardens. But as soon as his father-in-law was dead Mr. Mooney began to go to the devil. He drank, plundered the till, ran headlong into debt. It was no use making him take the pledge: he was sure to break out again a few days after. By fighting his wife in the presence of customers and by buying bad meat he ruined his business. One night he went for his wife with the cleaver and she had to sleep in a neighbour's house.

After that they lived apart. She went to the priest and got a separation from him with care of the children. She would give him neither money nor food nor house-room; and so he was obliged to enlist himself as a sheriff's man. He was a shabby stooped little drunkard with a white face and a white moustache and white eyebrows, pencilled above his little eyes, which were pink-veined and raw; and all day long he sat in the bailiff's room, waiting to be put on a job. Mrs. Mooney, who had taken what remained of her money out of the butcher business and set up a boarding house in Hardwicke Street, was a big imposing woman. Her house had a floating population made up of tourists from Liverpool and the Isle of Man and, occasionally, *artistes* from the music halls. Its resident population was made up of clerks from the city. She governed the house cunningly and firmly, knew when to give credit, when to be stern and when to let things pass. All the resident young men spoke of her as *The Madam*.

Mrs. Mooney's young men paid fifteen shillings a week for board and lodgings (beer or stout at dinner excluded). They shared in common tastes and occupations and for this reason they were very chummy with one another. They discussed with one another the chances of favourites and outsiders. Jack Mooney, the Madam's son, who was clerk to a commission agent in Fleet Street, had the reputation of being a hard case. He was fond of using soldiers' obscenities; usually he came home in the small hours. When he met his friends he had always a good one to tell them and he was always sure to be on to a good thing—that is to say, a likely horse or a likely *artiste*. He was also handy with the mits and sang comic songs. On Sunday nights there would often be a reunion in Mrs. Mooney's front drawing-room. The music-hall *artistes* would oblige; and Sheridan played waltzes and polkas and vamped accompaniments. Polly Mooney, the Madam's daughter, would also sing. She sang:

> *"I'm a . . . naughty girl.*
> *You needn't sham:*
> *You know I am."*

Polly was a slim girl of nineteen; she had light soft hair and a small full mouth. Her eyes, which were grey with a shade of green through them, had a habit of glancing upwards when she spoke with anyone, which made her look like a little perverse madonna. Mrs. Mooney had first sent her daughter to be a typist in a corn-factor's office but, as a disreputable sheriff's man used to come every other day to the office, asking to be allowed to say a word to his daughter, she had taken her daughter home again and set her to do housework. As Polly was very lively the intention was to give her the run of the young men. Besides, young men like to feel that there is a young woman not very far away. Polly, of course, flirted with the young men but Mrs. Mooney, who was a shrewd judge, knew that the young men were only passing the time away: none of them meant business. Things went on so for a long time and Mrs. Mooney began to think of sending Polly back to typewriting when she noticed that something was going on between Polly and one of the young men. She watched the pair and kept her own counsel.

Polly knew that she was being watched, but still her mother's persistent silence could not be misunderstood. There had been no open complicity between mother and daughter, no open understanding but, though people in the house began to talk of the affair, still Mrs. Mooney did not intervene. Polly began to grow a little strange in her manner and the young man was evidently perturbed. At last, when she judged it to be the right moment, Mrs. Mooney intervened. She dealt with moral problems as a cleaver deals with meat: and in this case she had made up her mind.

It was a bright Sunday morning of early summer, promising heat, but with a fresh breeze blowing. All the windows of the boarding house were open and the lace curtains ballooned gently towards the street beneath the raised sashes. The belfry of George's Church sent out constant peals and worshippers, singly or in groups, traversed the little circus before the church, revealing their purpose by their self-contained demeanour no less than by the little volumes in their gloved hands. Breakfast was over in the boarding house and the table of the breakfast-room was covered with plates on which lay yellow streaks of eggs with morsels of bacon-fat and bacon-rind. Mrs. Mooney sat in the straw arm-chair and watched the servant Mary remove the breakfast things. She made Mary collect the crusts and pieces of broken bread to help to make Tuesday's bread-pudding. When the table was cleared, the broken bread collected, the sugar and butter safe under lock and key, she began to reconstruct the interview which she had had the night before with Polly. Things were as she had suspected: she had been frank in her questions and Polly had been frank in her answers. Both had been somewhat awkward, of course. She had been made awkward by her not wishing to receive the news in too cavalier a fashion or to seem to have connived and Polly had been made awkward not merely because allusions of that kind always made her awkward but also because she did not wish it to be thought that in her wise innocence she had divined the intention behind her mother's tolerance.

Mrs. Mooney glanced instinctively at the little gilt clock on the mantelpiece as soon as she had become aware through her revery that the bells of George's Church had stopped ringing. It was seventeen minutes past eleven: she would have lots of time to have the matter out with Mr. Doran and then catch short twelve at Marlborough Street. She was sure she would win. To begin with she had all the weight of social opinion on her side: she was an outraged mother. She had allowed him to live beneath her roof, assuming that he was a man of honour, and he had simply abused her hospitality. He was thirty-four or thirty-five years of age, so that youth could not be pleaded as his excuse; nor could ignorance be his excuse since he was a man who had seen something of the world. He had simply taken advantage of Polly's youth and inexperience: that was evident. The question was: What reparation would he make?

There must be reparation made in such case. It is all very well for the man: he can go his ways as if nothing had happened, having had his moment of pleasure, but the girl has to bear the brunt. Some mothers would be content to patch up such an affair for a sum of money; she had known cases of it. But she would not do so. For her only one reparation could make up for the loss of her daughter's honour: marriage.

She counted all her cards again before sending Mary up to Mr. Doran's room to say that she wished to speak with him. She felt sure she would win. He was a serious young man, not rakish or loud-voiced like the others. If it had been Mr. Sheridan or Mr. Meade or Bantam Lyons her task would have been much harder. She did not think he would face publicity. All the lodgers in the house knew something of the affair; details had been invented by some. Besides, he had been employed for thirteen years in a great Catholic wine-merchant's office and publicity would mean for him, perhaps, the loss of his job. Whereas if he agreed all might be well. She knew he had a good screw for one thing and she suspected he had a bit of stuff put by.

Nearly the half-hour! She stood up and surveyed herself in the pier-glass. The decisive expression of her great florid face satisfied her and she thought of some mothers she knew who could not get their daughters off their hands.

Mr. Doran was very anxious indeed this Sunday morning. He had made two attempts to shave but his hand had been so unsteady that he had been obliged to desist. Three days' reddish beard fringed his jaws and every two or three minutes a mist gathered on his glasses so that he had to take them off and polish them with his pocket-handkerchief. The recollection of his confession of the night before was a cause of acute pain to him; the priest had drawn out every ridiculous detail of the affair and in the end had so magnified his sin that he was almost thankful at being afforded a loophole of reparation. The harm was done. What could he do now but marry her or run away? He could not brazen it out. The affair would be sure to be talked of and his employer would be certain to hear of it. Dublin is such a small city: everyone knows everyone else's business. He felt his heart leap warmly in his throat as he heard in his excited imagination old Mr. Leonard calling out in his rasping voice: "Send Mr. Doran here, please."

All his long years of service gone for nothing! All his industry and diligence thrown away! As a young man he had sown his wild oats, of course; he had boasted of his free-thinking and denied the existence of God to his companions in public-houses. But that was all passed and done with . . . nearly. He still bought a copy of *Reynolds's Newspaper* every week but he attended to his religious duties and for nine-tenths of the year lived a regular life. He had money enough to settle down on; it was not that. But the family would look down on her. First of all there was her disreputable father and then her mother's boarding house was beginning to get a certain fame. He had a notion that he was being had. He could imagine his friends talking of the affair and laughing. She *was* a little vulgar; some times she said "I seen" and "If I had've known." But what would grammar matter if he really loved her? He could not make up his mind whether to like her or despise her for what she had done. Of course he had done it too. His instinct urged him to remain free, not to marry. Once you are married you are done for, it said.

While he was sitting helplessly on the side of the bed in shirt and trousers she tapped lightly at his door and entered. She told him all, that she had made a clean breast of it to her mother and that her mother would speak with him that morning. She cried and threw her arms round his neck, saying:

"O Bob! Bob! What am I to do? What am I to do at all?"

She would put an end to herself, she said.

He comforted her feebly, telling her not to cry, that it would be all right, never fear. He felt against his shirt the agitation of her bosom.

It was not altogether his fault that it had happened. He remembered well, with the curious patient memory of the celibate, the first casual caresses her dress, her breath, her fingers had given him. Then late one night as he was undressing for bed she had tapped at his door, timidly. She wanted to relight her candle at his for hers had been blown out by a gust. It was her bath night. She wore a loose open combing jacket of printed flannel. Her white instep shone in the opening of her furry slippers and the blood glowed warmly behind her perfumed skin. From her hands and wrists too as she lit and steadied her candle a faint perfume arose.

On nights when he came in very late it was she who warmed up his dinner. He scarcely knew what he was eating feeling her beside him alone, at night, in the sleeping house. And her thoughtfulness! If the night was anyway cold or wet or windy there was sure to be a little tumbler of punch ready for him. Perhaps they could be happy together. . . .

They used to go upstairs together on tiptoe, each with a candle, and on the third landing exchange reluctant good-nights. They used to kiss. He remembered well her eyes, the touch of her hand and his delirium. . . .

But delirium passes. He echoed her phrase, applying it to himself: *"What am I to do?"* The instinct of the celibate warned him to hold back. But the sin was there; even his sense of honour told him that reparation must be made for such a sin.

While he was sitting with her on the side of the bed Mary came to the door and said that the missus wanted to see him in the parlour. He stood up to put on his coat and waistcoat, more helpless than ever. When he was dressed he went over to her to comfort her. It would be all right, never fear. He left her crying on the bed and moaning softly: *"O my God!"*

Going down the stairs his glasses became so dimmed with moisture that he had to take them off and polish them. He longed to ascend through the roof and fly away to another country where he would never hear again of his trouble and yet a force pushed him downstairs step by step. The implacable faces of his employer and of the Madam stared upon his discomfiture. On the last flight of stairs he passed Jack Mooney who was coming up from the pantry nursing two bottles of *Bass.* They saluted coldly; and the lover's eyes rested for a second or two on a thick bulldog face and a pair of thick short arms. When he reached the foot of the staircase he glanced up and saw Jack regarding him from the door of the return-room.

Suddenly he remembered the night when one of the music-hall *artistes,* a little blond Londoner, had made a rather free allusion to Polly. The reunion had been almost broken up on account of Jack's violence. Everyone tried to quiet him. The music-hall *artiste,* a little paler than usual, kept smiling and saying that there was no harm meant: but Jack kept shouting at him that if any fellow tried that sort of a game on with his sister he'd bloody well put his teeth down his throat, so he would.

Polly sat for a little time on the side of the bed, crying. Then she dried her eyes and went over to the looking-glass. She dipped the end of the towel in the water-jug and refreshed her eyes with the cool water. She looked at herself in profile and readjusted a hairpin above her ear. Then she went back to the bed again and sat at the foot. She regarded the pillows for a long time and the sight of them awakened in her mind secret, amiable memories. She rested the nape of her neck against the cool iron bed-rail and fell into a revery. There was no longer any perturbation visible on her face.

She waited on patiently, almost cheerfully, without alarm, her memories gradually giving place to hopes and visions of the future. Her hopes and visions were so intricate that she no longer saw the white pillows on which her gaze was fixed or remembered that she was waiting for anything.

At last she heard her mother calling. She started to her feet and ran to the banisters.

"Polly! Polly!"

"Yes, mamma?"

"Come down, dear. Mr. Doran wants to speak to you."

Then she remembered what she had been waiting for.

The Duchess and the Jeweller

 ~~~

VIRGINIA WOOLF
(English, 1882–1941)

Oliver Bacon lived at the top of a house overlooking the Green Park. He had a flat; chairs jutted out at the right angles—chairs covered in hide. Sofas filled the bays of the windows—sofas covered in tapestry. The windows, the three long windows, had the proper allowance of discreet net and figured satin. The mahogany sideboard bulged discreetly with the right brandies, whiskeys and liqueurs. And from the middle window he looked down upon the glossy roofs of fashionable cars packed in the narrow straits of Piccadilly. A more central position could not be imagined. And at eight in the morning he would have his breakfast brought in on a tray by a man-servant: the man-servant would unfold his crimson dressing-gown; he would rip his letters open with his long pointed nails and would extract thick white cards of invitation upon which the engraving stood up roughly from duchesses, countesses, viscountesses and Honourable Ladies. Then he would wash; then he would eat his toast; then he would read his paper by the bright burning fire of electric coals.

"Behold Oliver," he would say, addressing himself. "You who began life in a filthy little alley, you who . . ." and he would look down at his legs, so shapely in their perfect trousers; at his boots; at his spats. They were all shapely, shining; cut from the best cloth by the best scissors in Savile Row. But he dismantled himself often and became again a little boy in a dark alley. He had once thought that the height of his ambition —selling stolen dogs to fashionable women in Whitechapel. And once he had been done. "Oh, Oliver," his mother had wailed. "Oh, Oliver! When will you have sense, my son?" . . . Then he had gone behind a counter; had sold cheap watches; then he had taken a wallet to Amsterdam. . . . At that memory he would chuckle—the old Oliver remembering the young. Yes, he had done well with the three diamonds; also there was the commission on the emerald. After that he went into the private room behind the shop in Hatton Garden; the room with the scales, the safe, the thick magnifying glasses. And then . . . and then . . . He chuckled. When he passed through the knots of jewellers in the hot evening who were discussing prices, gold mines, diamonds, reports from South Africa, one of them would lay a finger to the side of his nose and murmur, "Hum —m—m," as he passed. It was no more than a murmur; no more than a nudge on the shoulder, a finger on the nose, a buzz that ran through the cluster of jewellers in Hatton Garden on a hot afternoon—oh, many years ago now! But still Oliver felt it purring down his spine, the nudge, the murmur that meant, "Look at him—young Oliver, the young jeweller —there he goes." Young he was then. And he dressed better and better; and had, first a hansom cab; then a car; and first he went up to the dress circle, then down into the stalls. And he had a villa at Richmond, overlooking the river, with trellises of red roses; and Mademoiselle used to pick one every morning and stick it in his buttonhole.

"So," said Oliver Bacon, rising and stretching his legs. "So . . ."

And he stood beneath the picture of an old lady on the mantelpiece and raised his hands. "I have kept my word," he said, laying his hands together, palm to palm, as if he were doing homage to her. "I have won my bet." That was so; he was the richest jeweller in England; but his nose, which was long and flexible, like an elephant's trunk, seemed to say by its curious quiver at the nostrils (but it seemed as if the whole nose quivered, not only the nostrils) that he was not satisfied yet; still smelt something under the ground a little further off. Imagine a giant hog in a pasture rich with truffles; after unearthing this truffle and that, still it smells a bigger, a blacker truffle under the ground further off. So Oliver snuffed always in the rich earth of Mayfair another truffle, a blacker, a bigger further off.

Now then he straightened the pearl in his tie, cased himself in his smart blue overcoat; took his yellow gloves and his cane; and swayed as he descended the stairs and half snuffed, half sighed through his long sharp nose as he passed out into Piccadilly. For was he not still a sad man, a dissatisfied man, a man who seeks something that is hidden, though he had won his bet?

He swayed slightly as he walked, as the camel at the zoo sways from side to side when it walks along the asphalt paths laden with grocers and their wives eating from paper bags and throwing little bits of silver paper crumpled up on to the path. The camel despises the grocers; the camel is dissatisfied with its lot; the camel sees the blue lake and the fringe of palm trees in front of it. So the great jeweller, the greatest jeweller in the whole world, swung down Piccadilly, perfectly dressed, with his gloves, with his cane; but dissatisfied still, till he reached the dark little shop, that was famous in France, in Germany, in Austria, in Italy, and all over America—the dark little shop in the street off Bond Street.

As usual, he strode through the shop without speaking, though the four men, the two old men, Marshall and Spencer, and the two young men, Hammond and Wicks, stood straight and looked at him, envying him. It was only with one finger of the amber-coloured glove, waggling, that he acknowledged their presence. And he went in and shut the door of his private room behind him.

Then he unlocked the grating that barred the window. The cries of Bond Street came in; the purr of the distant traffic. The light from reflectors at the back of the shop struck upwards. One tree waved six green leaves, for it was June. But Mademoiselle had married Mr. Pedder of the local brewery—no one stuck roses in his buttonhole now.

"So," he half sighed, half snorted, "so——"

Then he touched a spring in the wall and slowly the panelling slid open, and behind it were the steel safes, five, no, six of them, all of burnished steel. He twisted a key; unlocked one; then another. Each was lined with a pad of deep crimson velvet; in each lay jewels—bracelets, necklaces, rings, tiaras, ducal coronets; loose stones in glass shells; rubies, emeralds, pearls, diamonds. All safe, shining, cool, yet burning, eternally, with their own compressed light.

"Tears!" said Oliver, looking at the pearls.

"Heart's blood!" he said, looking at the rubies.

"Gunpowder!" he continued, rattling the diamonds so that they flashed and blazed.

"Gunpowder enough to blow Mayfair—sky high, high, high!" He threw his head back and made a sound like a horse neighing as he said it.

The telephone buzzed obsequiously in a low muted voice on his table. He shut the safe.

"In ten minutes," he said. "Not before." And he sat down at his desk and looked at the heads of the Roman emperors that were graved on his sleeve links. And again he dismantled himself and became once more the little boy playing marbles in the alley where they sell stolen dogs on Sunday. He became that wily astute little boy, with lips like wet cherries. He dabbled his fingers in ropes of tripe; he dipped them in pans of frying fish; he dodged in and out among the crowds. He was slim, lissome, with eyes like licked stones. And now—now—the hands of the clock ticked on, one two, three, four. . . . The Duchess of Lambourne waited his pleasure; the Duchess of Lambourne, daughter of a hundred Earls. She would wait for ten minutes on a chair at the counter. She would wait his pleasure. She would wait till he was ready to see her. He watched the clock in its shagreen case. The hand moved on. With each tick the clock handed him—so it seemed—pâté de foie gras, a glass of champagne, another of fine brandy, a cigar costing one guinea. The clock laid them on the table beside him as the ten minutes passed. Then he heard soft slow footsteps approaching; a rustle in the corridor. The door opened. Mr. Hammond flattened himself against the wall.

"Her Grace!" he announced.

And he waited there, flattened against the wall.

And Oliver, rising, could hear the rustle of the dress of the Duchess as she came down the passage. Then she loomed up, filling the door, filling the room with the aroma, the prestige, the arrogance, the pomp, the pride of all the Dukes and Duchesses swollen in one wave. And as a wave breaks, she broke, as she sat down, spreading and splashing and falling over Oliver Bacon, the great jeweller, covering him with sparkling bright colours, green, rose, violet; and odours; and iridescences; and rays shooting from fingers, nodding from plumes, flashing from silk; for she was very large, very fat, tightly girt in pink taffeta, and past her prime. As a parasol with many flounces, as a peacock with many feathers, shuts its flounces, folds its feathers, so she subsided and shut herself as she sank down in the leather armchair.

"Good morning, Mr. Bacon," said the Duchess. And she held out her hand which came through the slit of her white glove. And Oliver bent low as he shook it. And as their hands touched the link was forged between them once more. They were friends, yet enemies; he was master, she was mistress; each cheated the other, each needed the other, each feared the other, each felt this and knew this every time they touched hands thus in the little back room with the white light outside, and the tree with its six leaves, and the sound of the street in the distance and behind them the safes.

"And to-day, Duchess—what can I do for you to-day?" said Oliver, very softly.

The Duchess opened her heart, her private heart, gaped wide. And with a sigh but no words she took from her bag a long washleather pouch —it looked like a lean yellow ferret. And from a slit in the ferret's belly she dropped pearls—ten pearls. They rolled from the slit in the ferret's belly—one, two, three, four—like the eggs of some heavenly bird.

"All's that's left me, dear Mr. Bacon," she moaned. Five, six, seven— down they rolled, down the slopes of the vast mountain sides that fell between her knees into one narrow valley—the eighth, the ninth, and the tenth. There they lay in the glow of the peach-blossom taffeta. Ten pearls.

"From the Appleby cincture," she mourned. "The last . . . the last of them all."

Oliver stretched out and took one of the pearls between finger and thumb. It was round, it was lustrous. But real was it, or false? Was she lying again? Did she dare?

She laid her plump padded finger across her lips. "If the Duke knew . . ." she whispered. "Dear Mr. Bacon, a bit of bad luck . . ."

Been gambling again, had she?

"That villain! That sharper!" she hissed.

The man with the chipped cheek bone? A bad 'un. And the Duke was straight as a poker; with side whiskers; would cut her off, shut her up down there if he knew—what I know, thought Oliver, and glanced at the safe.

"Araminta, Daphne, Diana," she moaned. "It's for *them.*"

The ladies Araminta, Daphne, Diana—her daughters. He knew them; adored them. But it was Diana he loved.

"You have all my secrets," she leered. Tears slid; tears fell; tears, like diamonds, collecting powder in the ruts of her cherry blossom cheeks.

"Old friend," she murmured, "old friend."

"Old friend," he repeated, "old friend," as if he licked the words.

"How much?" he queried.

She covered the pearls with her hand.

"Twenty thousand," she whispered.

But was it real or false, the one he held in his hand? The Appleby cincture—hadn't she sold it already? He would ring for Spencer or Hammond. "Take it and test it," he would say. He stretched to the bell.

"You will come down to-morrow?" she urged, she interrupted. "The Prime Minister—His Royal Highness . . ." She stopped. "And Diana . . ." she added.

Oliver took his hand off the bell.

He looked past her, at the backs of the houses in Bond Street. But he saw, not the houses in Bond Street, but a dimpling river; and trout rising and salmon; and the Prime Minister; and himself too, in white waistcoat; and then, Diana. He looked down at the pearl in his hand. But how could he test it, in the light of the river, in the light of the eyes of Diana? But the eyes of the Duchess were on him.

"Twenty thousand," she moaned. "My honour!"

The honour of the mother of Diana! He drew his cheque book towards him; he took out his pen.

"Twenty——" he wrote. Then he stopped writing. The eyes of the old woman in the picture were on him—of the old woman his mother.

"Oliver!" she warned him. "Have sense! Don't be a fool!"

"Oliver!" the Duchess entreated—it was "Oliver" now, not "Mr. Bacon." "You'll come for a long weekend?"

Alone in the woods with Diana! Riding alone in the woods with Diana!

"Thousand," he wrote, and signed it.

"Here you are," he said.

And there opened all the flounces of the parasol, all the plumes of the peacock, the radiance of the wave, the swords and spears of Agincourt, as she rose from her chair. And the two old men and the two young men, Spencer and Marshall, Wicks and Hammond, flattened themselves behind the counter envying him as he led her through the shop to the door. And he waggled his yellow glove in their faces, and she held her honour —a cheque for twenty thousand pounds with his signature—quite firmly in her hands.

"Are they false or are they real?" asked Oliver, shutting his private door. There they were, ten pearls on the blotting-paper on the table. He took them to the window. He held them under his lens to the light. . . .

This, then, was the truffle he had routed out of the earth! Rotten at the centre—rotten at the core!

"Forgive me, oh, my mother!" he sighed, raising his hand as if he asked pardon of the old woman in the picture. And again he was a little boy in the alley where they sold dogs on Sunday.

"For," he murmured, laying the palms of his hands together, "it is to be a long week-end."

Bachelors

HUGH WALPOLE
(English, 1884–1941)

I

In any cathedral town there must of necessity be certain characters who are bound and tied to the cobble-stones of the place from whose heart they have sprung. One can picture them in no other town or country— they are that place's property as surely as are the Town Hall, the Baths, the Market Place, and the Cathedral. Their very peculiarities, their little idiosyncrasies, are proudly suggested in that column of the local newspaper headed, "Are You Aware That——?" and, always, their names are to be found after "Amongst those present were——" when any kind of festivity, civic or personal, has occurred.

The cathedral town of S—— in Glebeshire boasted Henry and Robert Chandler, Esqs., amongst their most distinguished "features." "Features" they were, and no visitor could spend a week in that pleasant city without having them pointed out to him, just as he had already been directed towards the great west-end window of the cathedral or the magnificent golden tomb of the Dryden St. Pomfrets.

Harry and Robin Chandler had spent all their days enclosed by the pleasant shelter of S——. They had indeed gone first to Rugby and afterwards to Trinity, Cambridge, but from these places they had always returned to S—— with such precipitation and eagerness that it was evident that when whilst their bodies were being harassed and driven in wilder places their souls were resting in S——.

Robin Chandler was, at the time of this crisis in his history, fifty-five years of age, Harry ten years younger, and they lived at the corner of the Close in a house shaped like a teapot, and had a motherly and rotund widow as their housekeeper. Of the two, Robin was most certainly the "character." He *looked* a "character." He was precisely the kind of old gentleman whom you would expect to find in the close of an English cathedral. You would say, on seeing Robin Chandler, "Ah! *there* he is!" and you would connect him with the other old gentlemen and the other old maids whom you had, in your time, met in cathedral cities. Robin looked more than his age because his hair was white and his figure rotund. His face was round and amiable and a little foolish, and this foolishness was to be attributed to the fact that he was never sure what he would do with his mouth. He would be amused and would laugh heartily, but even in the climax of the laugh his mouth would wander a little and tremble uncertainly at the corners. He had a dimple in each cheek, and a fine high forehead from which his hair was brushed straight back into a kind of white waterfall that tumbled down the back of his head. He was short and fat and very neat, being dressed generally in pepper-and-salt trousers, a brown velvet waistcoat with brass buttons, a black coat and a black tie. When out of doors he wore a soft black hat cocked jauntily over one ear, and he always trotted along, moving his feet very slightly one in front of the other. He stopped a thousand times during his walk down the High Street, greeting his friends (he had no enemies in the world), and he always had a number of gentle queer things to say—things that no one else would have thought of saying. His interests were natural history, stamps, bowls, and, of course, his brother—and this last swallowed up the others even as the serpent in the Bible swallowed up all the other serpents.

Harry Chandler was of quite another kind: of middle height, red-faced, short brown moustache, brown hair cut close to his head, his eyes confident and unintelligent, his attitude that of a man who knows his world, takes many baths, and has no doubts about anything. He stood at the head of the sporting interests of S——, being president of the golf club and the cricket club; his interests were also apparently political, for he was a most important member of the Conservative Club that had its palatial apartments half-way down the High Street. He might be seen any morning of the week striding along in a tweed jacket and large and balloon-like knickerbockers, his face very red, his eyes very wide and staring, his air that of a man who knows his power and values it. "Ha, Benson!" he would say, or, "Ha, Rawlings!" or even, "Good-day to you, Bumpus!" and sometimes, when a local infant threatened his progress, "Out of the way, little one, out of the way!"

People said, with considerable truth, that it was strange that two brothers, who were so continually together, should be so different, but when one knew Robin Chandler intimately one discovered that he had been endeavouring, all his days, to acquire some of his brother's habits and characteristics. He would try at times to be domineering, hearty, and monosyllabic, and of course he always failed. He had the pleasantest of voices, but it was the voice of an amiable canary, and he never could express himself without using a great number of words. That Robin worshipped his brother was one of the items of natural history treasured by the city of S——.

He had worshipped from that day, so many years ago, when a lonely little boy of ten, he had been informed that he was henceforth to have a companion in life.

He had been, always, from the first a submissive character who depended very much on other people's affection for happiness. It had been, the ladies of S—— always said, a shamefully one-sided affair.

Harry Chandler's attitude to his brother was one of indulgent tolerance. "Dear old fellow," he would call him. "He's an odd kind of chap, my brother," he would confide to a listening friend. "You'd never think we were brothers, now, would you? You should just see him try to play golf. Stands there with his legs apart, his body stiff as a rod, biting his lips, don't you know—serious as anything—and then he clean misses it, you know. He's a dear old fellow, but, between you and me, a bit of an old woman."

Robin was quite aware of his brother's attitude, but, indeed, no other seemed possible. He had watched, with wide-eyed wonder, his brother's growth. The things Harry could do! Was there anyone who played games with such confidence, anyone who could hold his own in a gathering of men with such assurance and success, anyone so fascinating in a drawing-room, anyone in the world with such captivating *savoir-faire?* Robin, himself, was afraid of women, except very old and lonely ones. He had, long ago, been "horribly" in love, and she might, one imagines, have loved him in return had he pursued the matter; but—what *would* Harry do without him? No, until Harry himself married, Robin must send the other sex to limbo. And through all these years what agitations there had been! For a long time it had seemed as certain that Harry would marry as that night must follow the day. That his brother was fascinating to women Robin held as surely as that he himself had no attraction for them whatever! Terrible hours! Terrible apparitions of beautiful young women to whom Harry would give their first golfing lesson! Terrible "alarums and excursions"! "Oh! I hear, Mr. Chandler, that we are to congratulate your brother . . . !" Is not S—— a cathedral city?

And yet, always, Robin was delivered. Through all these years Harry had not been even engaged. Robin wondered at the women, but, from his heart, was grateful to them, and, with every year, the assurance of safety grew. Now, always, he put the terrible thought from him. Sometimes in the night it would leap out from the dark, with mouth a-grin and widespread claws. "What'll you do, my friend, if it *does* happen? It may, you know. Plenty of time yet. . . . A nice kind of time you'll have alone——" Well, that was a bad half-hour, but at the end of it the grinning beast was beaten back to its lair.

There was nothing that Harry could do that did not interest Robin, and this, men at the club said, was bad for Harry.

"Really, Chandler's getting a bit of a bore. Thinks the least little thing he's done ought to be sent up to the *Times.* All that silly old brother of his."

But they liked "the silly old brother"—liked him, were the truth known, better than Harry. Robin would have been immensely surprised at his popularity had he ever known it.

There came an afternoon. It was half-past four on a day of late October, and the cathedral bells were drowsily ringing for evensong. Robin was standing at the window of the little smoking-room, where they always had tea, waiting his brother's return from golf. It was dusk, and at the farther end of the Close, above an ivy-covered wall, low between two old Georgian houses, the blue evening sky, fading into palest saffron, showed. The cobbles had caught the evening light, and figures—two old ladies, a canon, an old gentleman in a bath-chair—were moving, like notes in a piece of music, across the grass square to the cathedral doors. It was a sight that Robin had seen year after year from that same window, and it had always for him drama as intense as anything that Napoleon or Wellington can have felt from the top of some smoke-clad hill. "There's Miss Barton. I thought she was in London. I wonder whether her brother's left her anything in his will. There's Prendergast. It's his month, I suppose. How cross it will make him, having to come in from his golf!"

He was conscious, as he heard the bells, of the quiet, cosy little room behind him filled with dusty old things that belonged to every period of his experiences—old college photographs, old books, old caps that his brother had worn in different teams which his presence had honoured. There, too, the kettle was humming, the tea-cake was hot, the clock—the same old gold clock—ticked the minutes away. He ruffled his hair with his hand, until he looked more than ever like an amiable, well-fed bird. The bells had fallen to a slow monotone—"Hurry up—hurry up—hurry up." . . . There were steps on the cobbles, a key in the door, a pause in the hall, then his brother had come in.

"Fancy, Harry," said Robin, moving towards the tea-things, "Miss Brandon's back. I wonder whether——"

"I say, old man"—Harry's voice was, for perhaps the first time in his life, nervous and hesitating—"Robin, old boy—hem! You must congratulate me—hem—yes—ha!—I'm engaged to Miss Pinsent. She—hum—accepted me on the—hum—golf-course this afternoon."

II

There followed then for Robin Chandler the most terrible weeks, weeks far more terrible than anything that he had ever imagined possible for human courage to support.

It was demanded of him, on every side, that he should be false. He must be false to his brother; he must pretend to him that he was glad and happy that this had occurred; he must be false to all the old women of S——, who crowded about him, eagerly watching for any sign of that wound which, they were assured amongst themselves, his brother's engagement must have dealt him; above all, he must be false to the girl, Iris Pinsent, who instantly demanded his affection and (such was always her attitude to the other sex) protection from the roughness of the world.

Iris Pinsent—golden, fragile, and appealing—was straight from the schoolroom. Her father had, six months before, arrived at S—— as governor of its prison, and, during those six months, Iris had put up her hair and "come out." She had seemed to Robin so entirely of the schoolroom that he had never, for the wildest instant, considered her as a possible wife for anybody. Now every day she appeared, ran over their old teapot house as though it were her own, won the instant and undying hatred of Mrs. Rumbold, the housekeeper, sat upon Harry's knee, pulled Harry's hair, untied his tie and tied it up again, laughed and sang and danced about the two elderly men as though they were puppies quite new to a brilliant world.

No one—not Robin himself—had any conception of the depths of Robin's suffering. "Mr. Robert Chandler *must* be feeling his brother's engagement," said one old lady to another old lady, and *another* old lady to *another* old lady. "But really you wouldn't think so, to look at him. He'll feel it after the marriage though, when he's all alone"—and the old ladies either licked their lips or wiped their eyes, according to their characters.

To Robin it was exactly as though he were standing on the very edge of a slimy and bottomless pit. Towards this pit his feet were slipping, and soon, very soon, the inevitable moment of descent would come; but meanwhile, gripping with his feet, digging his hands into the slime, he would hold on as long as he could . . . the world should not know until it must.

He trotted about the town, went to tea parties, played bowls, was as neat and as careful, as interested in his neighbours' affairs, as kind and thoughtful as ever he had been. Harry Chandler, who was, of course, not a discerning man, was hurt at this indifference.

"Really, Robin," he said one evening, when they were alone, "I don't believe you'll mind it a bit when I'm gone."

Robin paused, then said—"Of course, Harry, I shall miss you—terribly," and that was all.

Robin, in fact, ran from his despair. There were horrible moments when it caught him up, and then there was a grinding cold at his heart;

but these moments with all the force of his character he beat down. But what was he to do? What should he, could he, do? He had devoted his life, every moment and thought of it, to his brother's interests. He could not now, at his age, build up other gods, worship at other shrines. His bowls, his stamps, he laughed aloud when he thought of them. His life had been simply that he should watch his brother's triumphs, soften his brother's defeats, listen to his brother's ideas, anticipate his brother's wants. This may seem to many a humiliating rôle for a man: Robin Chandler did not feel it so; he was simply grateful that he had so splendid a person as his brother to play shadow to. He fancied that many people in the town thought him a lucky fellow.

No longer, even now, was there any need of him as audience, no longer was his opinion invited, no longer his praise demanded—and yet, even in these early weeks of the engagement, Robin fancied that Miss Pinsent was not proving quite so good a listener as she might. Indeed he began to wonder whether Miss Pinsent liked being a listener at all. She had so much to say, so many of her own achievements and triumphs to recount. Robin, as he watched the two of them together, wondered at first how any one *could* treat his brother with such casual equality; then, as the days passed and this became a common sight, he wondered whether there had not been something a little absurd about his own attitude.

Very reluctantly and only after a very considerable time Robin was compelled to confess to himself that Harry was not quite at his best as a lover. Harry, whilst Miss Pinsent sprang around him, laughed at him, mocked him, imitated him, burlesqued him, was often at a loss. He had found at once that his heavy, authoritative manner had no effect upon Miss Pinsent.

"Ha!—hum——" she would imitate him. "How d'y do, Rawlings."

Robin, listening in amazement, wondered whether there could be any love in Miss Pinsent's heart, but apparently love there really was, of a kittenish, puppyish kind. Another astonishing thing was that Miss Pinsent was, it seemed, more afraid of Robin than of Harry. She was only, on the rarest occasions, "kittenish" with Robin, but would stand in front of him and ask him quite serious questions about Life and bowls and bird's eggs, and Robin would ruffle his hair and answer her to the best of his ability. Really, Robin was forced to confess to himself, poor Harry looked quite foolish and even silly on many occasions. "Why does he let her behave like that?" he thought. "I do hope that other people don't notice it."

He was pleasantly aware—if anything could be pleasant at this terrible time—that he was acquiring now an independent existence in people's eyes. This had begun, of course, with people being sorry for him, but that the proud little man would not allow for a moment. He had been, for many, many years, overshadowed by his brother; but now that his brother was allotted and disposed of, Robin Chandler stood out all by himself. "Poor little Mr. Chandler!" the ladies said. "We must show him a little kindness just now." And Robin was obliged to confess that he liked it. Nevertheless, it must not be supposed that, during all this time, he was not an utterly miserable man.

Then, as the weeks passed, his discomfort grew. He wished, how fervently, that his brother would deal with the girl in some more dignified and satisfactory fashion. "Why, even I," Robin thought to himself, "have more influence over her than he has. She never plays about with me like that. Really, Harry——"

But the tragic side of it all was that Harry was not a happy lover. Why was he a lover at all, if not a happy one? All Harry's fine spirit had departed. His honest brow wore a puzzled look that never in all its five-and-forty years it had worn before. He began sentences, "I wonder whether——" "Do you think, Robin——" and then never finished them. He abandoned the Conservative Club, and although he played golf with Miss Pinsent on most afternoons of the week, that beloved game seemed to have lost most of its charm.

He no longer on his return would proclaim to his brother that he had done a bogey five in three, or beaten old Major Waggett (his special foe) by two up and three to play. No, he returned and drank his tea in silence. Robin's heart ached for him.

Once the two of them had, in Robin's presence, a most horrible quarrel. They were all having tea together in the little dusty smoking-room, and Miss Pinsent, striking unexpectedly her lover in the chest (one of her loving, playful tricks), upset his tea. He swore then with a frank volubility that spoke of many weeks' difficult restraint. She cried, rushed from the room and the house, vowing that she would never return. . . .

But, of course, she did return, and that very shortly afterwards. There was a reconciliation—but Robin found, to his own exceeding surprise, that he was rather ashamed of both of them. "I wish—I wish," he thought, "that I didn't see Harry like this. Love affects people very strangely."

Then, on an afternoon of pouring rain, Robin Chandler was beating his way up the High Street, hastening home to warmth and tea. He was sheltered by an enormous umbrella, and this gave him precisely the appearance of a walking mushroom. His arm was touched, and, turning round, he saw Miss Pinsent, who was looking bedraggled and unhappy, without any umbrella at all.

"I didn't know it was going to rain. It looked so fine . . ." Her voice trembled and she betrayed the imminence of tears—she took his arm and they walked along together. Then, suddenly, he was aware that she was talking about Harry, and speaking as though she needed Robin's advice about him. Robin's heart began to beat fast. "Did he really think that Harry loved her? . . . Would Harry really be kind to her? . . . Of course she was very fond of him, but . . . Did he think that differences in ages *really* made much trouble afterwards? . . . Of course she was very fond . . ."

This may be definitely put down as the most critical moment in all Mr. Robin Chandler's long life. The Tempter, with that bewildering precipitance and complete disregard for the justice of a forewarning prelude that he invariably betrays, sprang, there and then, in the dripping High Street of S——, upon the poor little man.

Robin saw, with a horrible distinctness, that the power was given him to sway Miss Pinsent. A little hesitation on his part, an unexpressed but nevertheless definite agreement with her as to the danger of unequal ages in marriage, a hint or two as to possible harshnesses and brutalities in Harry's character—he saw with amazing and horrible clearness that these things would be quite enough. By to-morrow afternoon Mr. Henry Chandler would no longer be engaged to Miss Iris Pinsent. . . .

They halted for an instant at the top of the High Street. The wind was rushing round the corner and the rain lashed the umbrella. Robin could see the wall of the cathedral, very grey and grim, and one corner of the Close with the rain running in little driven lines across the cobbles.

"You'll have your brother back again. . . . You won't be a lonely, lonely old man. . . ."

Then with a shake of his shoulders the thing was gone and, as they drove their way into the Close, he began eagerly, exhaustively, almost breathlessly, to prove to her that his brother was indeed a god among men.

III

It was arranged that Harry should go and stay with the Pinsents for a week in a house that they had in the country some miles from S——, and that during that time the date of the wedding should be settled. Robin saw with confused feelings his brother's departure; it was the first time for many years that they had been separated—this was melancholy enough—but also he was compelled to admit that it was a relief to him that, for a week at any rate, he would not be forced to watch his brother under such conditions. He found, indeed, that in a resigned, rather dejected kind of fashion, he was quite happy. Mrs. Rumbold, the housekeeper, could not make enough fuss of him. Harry had always been so emphatically the master in the house that she had never considered Mr. Robert. It had always been Harry who had arranged the hours of meals, and did he in the summer come in very late, well, then, Mr. Robert waited.

But now——! No, Mr. Harry had acted as a selfish and inconsiderate man, leaving poor Mr. Robert all alone "without a thought." What did an old thing of his age want to do with marriage—choosing so young a girl, too—almost indecent! Had Miss Pinsent treated Mrs. Rumbold with care and deference, then there might have been another opinion altogether. As it was—"She's a regular young Slap-in-the-face, if you ask me," said Mrs. Rumbold to her chosen friends. "Slap and come again, that's what *she* is. You mark my words."

Therefore Robin received an attention, a deference, that had never been his before. And not only from Mrs. Rumbold! The whole town offered it him. The town had always been fond of him, but so modest, and retiring had he been that the comment always was—"Mr. Robert Chandler? . . . Oh yes! . . . Such a nice little man. No one sees very much of him. No one *knows* him, you might say, but you couldn't help liking him!"

But, during this week, in what an amazing way did he expand, flourish, blossom! It was at first incredible to him that people should be interested in him for himself, and fifty-five years' convictions about life are difficult things to shake. But behold! Whereas before it had been, "Oh, Mr. Chandler, your brother has so kindly promised to dine with us on Thursday night, I wonder whether you could come too?" Now it was, "Do come and dine, Mr. Chandler, *any* night as long as you give us a day or two's notice." People found him indeed a great deal more amusing by himself than he had been before in his brother's company. Always there had been that anxious glance in his brother's direction to see whether everything were well, always that modest hesitation about giving any opinion at all whilst his brother was present. Now he would sit perched on the edge of a sofa, his hands on his fat little knees, the dimples dancing in his cheeks, his hair on end, his chuckle (a chuckle entirely his own) over some joke that he saw ahead of him and would very shortly deliver to his audience. By the end of the week he had decided that:

(1) He liked women after all.

(2) He would be perfectly wretched alone, but that he would bear up as well as he could.

(3) He'd really no idea that he'd got so much to say.

(4) He felt younger than he had ever done before.

"Still," he said to himself, "dear old Harry's marriage will be too dreadful. I simply don't know what I shall do with myself."

The afternoon of Harry's return arrived. Robin stood at the window as he had done on that other horrible day when he had first heard of the engagement.

He was inevitably reminded of that day, for now again there, above the low wall, pale blue was fading into saffron, across the grass figures were stealing; already the bell was dropping into its "Hurry up—hurry up—hurry up."

Robin watched, and then suddenly, like a flame, like a fire, came the truth. He knew, yes, he knew, let him deny it as he might, that never in all his five-and-fifty years had he enjoyed a week as he had enjoyed this last one. He had tasted delights, known extravagances and excitements that had never before been his. He had been free!

He stared round bewildered. What treachery to Harry! What irony that so soon he should have changed from despair to what was not far from triumph! He remembered the bitter dismay that so short a time ago had, in this very room, wrapped him round.

But now he was a man of freedom! No one's shadow, depending upon no one in the world for his independent happiness! His eyes fell upon a picture above the fireplace, a water-colour painting of a grey fell and a blue lake at evening. It was a picture that he loved, but Harry had declared it "A dreary thing"—and it was only this week that it had been raised to that place of honour. After all, Harry would not care now, now when so soon he was to have a house of his own.

The door was flung open, and Harry was there, there with him in the room.

"I say!" he closed the door behind him and came forward. "Robin, she's chucked me!"

"Oh!"

"Yes—jolly well chucked me—last night when we were alone she told me. Been mistaken . . . misjudged her feelings—was too young . . . all the rest of it."

"Oh! Harry. . . . Oh, I'm sorry!"

Harry strode twice or thrice up and down the room. "Yes, chucked, by Jove! At first, you know, you could have knocked me down with a feather. But now—damn it—I don't know, Robin, that I'm not glad. She said it was largely some talk she'd had with you about me—how you'd praised me no end, and then she'd seen that she didn't feel about me quite like that, and that she couldn't marry me unless she did. The contrast struck her, don't you know. . . ."

He paused, then went on: "But I'm glad, dashed if I'm not. It's awful being engaged. . . . I felt it all the time, really. She never said things about me as you've always done—never knew me a bit as you do. It's a relief to be free—it *is* really. I missed you like anything. You were always so sympathetic and understanding. It'll be jolly to have you to tell things to again. . . . Yes—dash it—hum—ha——Won't the fellows at the club laugh? . . . Well, I must go and clean. Tell old Ma Rumbold to hurry with the tea."

He went out.

Robin waited a little, then, with the very shadow of a sigh, walked to the window. He looked out for a moment at the gathering dusk, then got a chair, climbed on to it and carefully took down the water-colour from the wall.

The Prussian Officer

D. H. LAWRENCE
(English, 1885–1930)

I

They had marched more than thirty kilometres since dawn, along the white, hot road where occasional thickets of trees threw a moment of shade, then out into the glare again. On either hand, the valley, wide and shallow, glittered with heat; dark-green patches of rye, pale young corn, fallow and meadow and black pine woods spread in a dull, hot diagram under a glistening sky. But right in front the mountains ranged across, pale blue and very still, snow gleaming gently out of the deep atmosphere. And towards the mountains, on and on, the regiment marched between the rye-fields and the meadows, between the scraggy fruit trees set regularly on either side the high road. The burnished, dark-green rye threw off a suffocating heat, the mountains drew gradually nearer and more distinct. While the feet of the soldiers grew hotter, sweat ran through their hair under their helmets, and their knapsacks could burn no more in contact with their shoulders, but seemed instead to give off a cold, prickly sensation.

He walked on and on in silence, staring at the mountains ahead, that rose sheer out of the land, and stood fold behind fold, half earth, half heaven, the heaven, the barrier with slits of soft snow, in the pale, bluish peaks.

He could now walk almost without pain. At the start, he had determined not to limp. It had made him sick to take the first steps, and during the first mile or so, he had compressed his breath, and the cold drops of sweat had stood on his forehead. But he had walked it off. What were they after all but bruises! He had looked at them, as he was getting up: deep bruises on the backs of his thighs. And since he had made his first step in the morning, he had been conscious of them, till now he had a tight, hot place in his chest, with suppressing the pain, and holding himself in. There seemed no air when he breathed. But he walked almost lightly.

The Captain's hand had trembled at taking his coffee at dawn: his orderly saw it again. And he saw the fine figure of the Captain wheeling on horseback at the farmhouse ahead, a handsome figure in pale-blue uniform with facings of scarlet, and the metal gleaming on the black helmet and the sword-scabbard, and dark streaks of sweat coming on the silky bay horse. The orderly felt he was connected with that figure moving so suddenly on horseback: he followed it like a shadow, mute and inevitable and damned by it. And the officer was always aware of the tramp of the company behind, the march of his orderly among the men.

The Captain was a tall man of about forty, grey at the temples. He had a handsome, finely-knit figure, and was one of the best horsemen in the West. His orderly, having to rub him down, admired the amazing riding-muscles of his loins.

For the rest, the orderly scarcely noticed the officer any more than he noticed himself. It was rarely he saw his master's face: he did not look at it. The Captain had reddish-brown, stiff hair, that he wore short upon his skull. His moustache was also cut short and bristly over a full, brutal mouth. His face was rather rugged, the cheeks thin. Perhaps the man was the more handsome for the deep lines in his face, the irritable tension of his brow, which gave him the look of a man who fights with life. His fair eyebrows stood bushy over light-blue eyes that were always flashing with cold fire.

He was a Prussian aristocrat, haughty and overbearing. But his mother had been a Polish countess. Having made too many gambling debts when he was young, he had ruined his prospects in the Army, and remained an infantry captain. He had never married: his position did not allow of it, and no woman had ever moved him to it. His time he spent riding— occasionally he rode one of his own horses at the races—and at the officers' club. Now and then he took himself a mistress. But after such an event, he returned to duty with his brow still more tense, his eyes still more hostile and irritable. With the men, however, he was merely impersonal, though a devil when roused; so that, on the whole, they feared him, but had no great aversion from him. They accepted him as the inevitable.

To his orderly he was at first cold and just and indifferent: he did not fuss over trifles. So that his servant knew practically nothing about him, except just what orders he would give, and how he wanted them obeyed. That was quite simple. Then the change gradually came.

The orderly was a youth of about twenty-two, of medium height, and well built. He had strong, heavy limbs, was swarthy, with a soft, black, young moustache. There was something altogether warm and young about him. He had firmly marked eyebrows over dark, expressionless eyes, that seemed never to have thought, only to have received life direct through his senses, and acted straight from instinct.

Gradually the officer had become aware of his servant's young vigorous, unconscious presence about him. He could not get away from the sense of the youth's person, while he was in attendance. It was like a warm flame upon the older man's tense, rigid body, that had become almost unliving, fixed. There was something so free and self-contained about him, and something in the young fellow's movement, that made the officer aware of him. And this irritated the Prussian. He did not choose to be touched into life by his servant. He might easily have changed his man, but he did not. He now very rarely looked direct at his orderly, but kept his face averted, as if to avoid seeing him. And yet as the young soldier moved unthinking about the apartment, the elder watched him, and would notice the movement of his strong young shoulders under the blue cloth, the bend of his neck. And it irritated him. To see the soldier's young, brown, shapely peasant's hand grasp the loaf or the wine-bottle sent a flash of hate or of anger through the elder man's blood. It was not that the youth was clumsy: it was rather the blind, instinctive sureness of movement of an unhampered young animal that irritated the officer to such a degree.

Once, when a bottle of wine had gone over, and the red gushed out on to the tablecloth, the officer had started up with an oath, and his eyes, bluey like fire, had held those of the confused youth for a moment. It was a shock for the young soldier. He felt something sink deeper, deeper into his soul, where nothing had ever gone before. It left him rather blank and wondering. Some of his natural completeness in himself was gone, a little uneasiness took its place. And from that time an undiscovered feeling had held between the two men.

Henceforward the orderly was afraid of really meeting his master. His subconsciousness remembered those steely blue eyes and the harsh brows, and did not intend to meet them again. So he always stared past his master, and avoided him. Also, in a little anxiety, he waited for the three months to have gone, when his time would be up. He began to feel a constraint in the Captain's presence, and the soldier even more than the officer wanted to be left alone, in his neutrality as servant.

He had served the Captain for more than a year, and knew his duty. This he performed easily, as if it were natural to him. The officer and his commands he took for granted, as he took the sun and the rain, and he served as a matter of course. It did not implicate him personally.

But now if he were going to be forced into a personal interchange with his master he would be like a wild thing caught, he felt he must get away.

But the influence of the young soldier's being had penetrated through the officer's stiffened discipline, and perturbed the man in him. He, however, was a gentleman, with long, fine hands and cultivated movements, and was not going to allow such a thing as the stirring of his innate self. He was a man of passionate temper, who had always kept himself suppressed. Occasionally there had been a duel, an outburst before the soldiers. He knew himself to be always on the point of breaking out. But he kept himself hard to the idea of the Service. Whereas the young soldier seemed to live out his warm, full nature, to give it off in his very movements, which had a certain zest, such as wild animals have in free movement. And this irritated the officer more and more.

In spite of himself, the Captain could not regain his neutrality of feeling towards his orderly. Nor could he leave the man alone. In spite of himself, he watched him, gave him sharp orders, tried to take up as much of his time as possible. Sometimes he flew into a rage with the young soldier, and bullied him. Then the orderly shut himself off, as it were out of earshot, and waited, with sullen, flushed face, for the end of the noise. The words never pierced to his intelligence, he made himself, protectively, impervious to the feelings of his master.

He had a scar on his left thumb, a deep seam going across the knuckle. The officer had long suffered from it, and wanted to do something to it. Still it was there, ugly and brutal on the young, brown hand. At last the

Captain's reserve gave way. One day, as the orderly was smoothing out the tablecloth, the officer pinned down his thumb with a pencil, asking: "How did you come by that?"

The young man winced and drew back at attention.

"A wood axe, Herr Hauptmann," he answered.

The officer waited for further explanation. None came. The orderly went about his duties. The elder man was sullenly angry. His servant avoided him. And the next day he had to use all his will-power to avoid seeing the scarred thumb. He wanted to get hold of it and——A hot flame ran in his blood.

He knew his servant would soon be free, and would be glad. As yet, the soldier had held himself off from the elder man. The Captain grew madly irritable. He could not rest when the soldier was away, and when he was present, he glared at him with tormented eyes. He hated those fine, black brows over the unmeaning, dark eyes, he was infuriated by the free movement of the handsome limbs, which no military discipline could make stiff. And he became harsh and cruelly bullying, using contempt and satire. The young soldier only grew more mute and expressionless.

"What cattle were you bred by, that you can't keep straight eyes? Look me in the eyes when I speak to you."

And the soldier turned his dark eyes to the other's face, but there was no sight in them: he stared with the slightest possible cast, holding back his sight, perceiving the blue of his master's eyes, but receiving no look from them. And the elder man went pale, and his reddish eyebrows twitched. He gave his order, barrenly.

Once he flung a heavy military glove into the young soldier's face. Then he had the satisfaction of seeing the black eyes flare up into his own, like a blaze when straw is thrown on a fire. And he had laughed with a little tremor and a sneer.

But there were only two months more. The youth instinctively tried to keep himself intact: he tried to serve the officer as if the latter were an abstract authority and not a man. All his instinct was to avoid personal contact, even definite hate. But in spite of himself the hate grew, responsive to the officer's passion. However, he put it in the background. When he had left the Army he could dare acknowledge it. By nature he was active, and had many friends. He thought what amazing good fellows they were. But, without knowing it, he was alone. Now this solitariness was intensified. It would carry him through his term. But the officer seemed to be going irritably insane, and the youth was deeply frightened.

The soldier had a sweetheart, a girl from the mountains, independent and primitive. The two walked together, rather silently. He went with her, not to talk, but to have his arm round her, and for the physical contact. This eased him, made it easier for him to ignore the Captain; for he could rest with her held fast against his chest. And she, in some unspoken fashion, was there for him. They loved each other.

The Captain perceived it, and was mad with irritation. He kept the young man engaged all the evenings long, and took pleasure in the dark look that came on his face. Occasionally, the eyes of the two men met, those of the younger sullen and dark, doggedly unalterable, those of the elder sneering with restless contempt.

The officer tried hard not to admit the passion that had got hold of him. He would not know that his feeling for his orderly was anything but that of a man incensed by his stupid, perverse servant. So, keeping quite justified and conventional in his consciousness, he let the other thing run on. His nerves, however, were suffering. At last he slung the end of a belt in his servant's face. When he saw the youth start back, the pain-tears in his eyes and the blood on his mouth, he had felt at once a thrill of deep pleasure and of shame.

But this, he acknowledged to himself, was a thing he had never done before. The fellow was too exasperating. His own nerves must be going to pieces. He went away for some days with a woman.

It was a mockery of pleasure. He simply did not want the woman. But he stayed on for his time. At the end of it, he came back in an agony of irritation, torment, and misery. He rode all the evening, then came straight in to supper. His orderly was out. The officer sat with his long, fine hands lying on the table, perfectly still, and all his blood seemed to be corroding.

At last his servant entered. He watched the strong, easy young figure, the fine eyebrows, the thick black hair. In a week's time the youth had got back his old well-being. The hands of the officer twitched and seemed to be full of mad flame. The young man stood at attention, unmoving, shut off.

The meal went in silence. But the orderly seemed eager. He made a clatter with the dishes.

"Are you in a hurry?" asked the officer, watching the intent, warm face of his servant. The other did not reply.

"Will you answer my question?" said the Captain.

"Yes, sir," replied the orderly, standing with his pile of deep Army plates. The Captain waited, looked at him, then asked again:

"Are you in a hurry?"

"Yes, sir," came the answer, that sent a flash through the listener.

"For what?"

"I was going out, sir."

"I want you this evening."

There was a moment's hesitation. The officer had a curious stiffness of countenance.

"Yes, sir," replied the servant, in his throat.

"I want you to-morrow evening also—in fact you may consider your evenings occupied, unless I give you leave."

The mouth with the young moustache set close.

"Yes, sir," answered the orderly, loosening his lips for a moment.

He again turned to the door.

"And why have you a piece of pencil in your ear?"

The orderly hesitated, then continued on his way without answering. He set the plates in a pile outside the door, took the stump of pencil from his ear, and put it in his pocket. He had been copying a verse for his sweetheart's birthday card. He returned to finish clearing the table. The officer's eyes were dancing, he had a little, eager smile.

"Why have you a piece of pencil in your ear?" he asked.

The orderly took his hands full of dishes. His master was standing near the great green stove, a little smile on his face, his chin thrust forward. When the young soldier saw him his heart suddenly ran hot. He felt blind. Instead of answering, he turned dazedly to the door. As he was crouching to set down the dishes, he was pitched forward by a kick from behind. The pots went in a stream down the stairs, he clung to the pillar of the banisters. And as he was rising he was kicked heavily again and again, so that he clung sickly to the post for some moments. His master had gone swiftly into the room and closed the door. The maid-servant downstairs looked up the staircase and made a mocking face at the crockery disaster.

The officer's heart was plunging. He poured himself a glass of wine, part of which he spilled on the floor, and gulped the remainder, leaning against the cool, green stove. He heard his man collecting the dishes from the stairs. Pale, as if intoxicated, he waited. The servant entered again. The Captain's heart gave a pang, as of pleasure, seeing the young fellow bewildered and uncertain on his feet with pain.

"Schöner!" he said.

The soldier was a little slower in coming to attention.

"Yes, sir!"

The youth stood before him, with pathetic young moustache, and fine eyebrows very distinct on his forehead of dark marble.

"I asked you a question."

"Yes, sir."

The officer's tone bit like acid.

"Why had you a pencil in your ear?"

Again the servant's heart ran hot, and he could not breathe. With dark, strained eyes, he looked at the officer, as if fascinated. And he stood there sturdily planted, unconscious. The withering smile came into the Captain's eyes, and he lifted his foot.

"I forgot it—sir," panted the soldier, his dark eyes fixed on the other man's dancing blue ones.

"What was it doing there?"

He saw the young man's breast heaving as he made an effort for words.

"I had been writing."

"Writing what?"

Again the soldier looked him up and down. The officer could hear him panting. The smile came into the blue eyes. The soldier worked his dry throat, but could not speak. Suddenly the smile lit like a flame on the officer's face, and a kick came heavily against the orderly's thigh. The youth moved sideways. His face went dead, with two black, staring eyes.

"Well?" said the officer.

The orderly's mouth had gone dry, and his tongue rubbed in it as on dry brown-paper. He worked his throat. The officer raised his foot. The servant went stiff.

"Some poetry, sir," came the crackling, unrecognisable sound of his voice.

"Poetry, what poetry?" asked the Captain, with a sickly smile.

Again there was the working in the throat. The Captain's heart had suddenly gone down heavily, and he stood sick and tired.

"For my girl, sir," he heard the dry, inhuman sound.

"Oh!" he said, turning away. "Clear the table."

"Click!" went the soldier's throat; then again, "click!" and then the half-articulate:

"Yes, sir."

The young soldier was gone, looking old, and walking heavily.

The officer, left alone, held himself rigid, to prevent himself from thinking. His instinct warned him that he must not think. Deep inside him was the intense gratification of his passion, still working powerfully. Then there was a counteraction, a horrible breaking down of something inside him, a whole agony of reaction. He stood there for an hour motionless, a chaos of sensations, but rigid with a will to keep blank his consciousness, to prevent his mind grasping. And he held himself so until the worst of the stress had passed, when he began to drink, drank himself to an intoxication, till he slept obliterated. When he woke in the morning he was shaken to the base of his nature. But he had fought off the realisation of what he had done. He had prevented his mind from taking it in, had suppressed it along with his instincts, and the conscious man had nothing to do with it. He felt only as after a bout of intoxication, weak, but the affair itself all dim and not to be recovered. Of the drunkenness of his passion he successfully refused remembrance. And when his orderly appeared with coffee, the officer assumed the same self he had had the morning before. He refused the event of the past night—denied it had ever been—and was successful in his denial. He had not done any such thing—not he himself. Whatever there might be lay at the door of a stupid insubordinate servant.

The orderly had gone about in a stupor all the evening. He drank some beer because he was parched, but not much, the alcohol made his feeling come back, and he could not bear it. He was dulled, as if nine-tenths of the ordinary man in him were inert. He crawled about disfigured. Still, when he thought of the kicks, he went sick, and when he thought of the threat of more kicking, in the room afterwards, his heart went hot and faint, and he panted, remembering the one that had come. He had been forced to say: "For my girl." He was much too done even to want to cry. His mouth hung slightly open, like an idiot's. He felt vacant, and wasted. So, he wandered at his work, painfully, and very slowly and clumsily, fumbling blindly with the brushes, and finding it difficult, when he sat down, to summon the energy to move again. His limbs, his jaw, were slack and nerveless. But he was very tired. He got to bed at last, and slept inert, relaxed, in a sleep that was rather stupor than slumber, a dead night of stupefaction shot through with gleams of anguish.

In the morning were the manoeuvres. But he woke even before the bugle sounded. The painful ache in his chest, the dryness of his throat, the awful steady feeling of misery made his eyes come awake and dreary at once. He knew, without thinking, what had happened. And he knew that the day had come again, when he must go on with his round. The last bit of darkness was being pushed out of the room. He would have to move his inert body and go on. He was so young, and had known so little trouble, that he was bewildered. He only wished it would stay night, so that he could lie still, covered up by the darkness. And yet nothing would prevent the day from coming, nothing would save him from having to get up and saddle the Captain's horse, and make the Captain's coffee. It was there, inevitable. And then, he thought, it was impossible. Yet they would not leave him free. He must go and take the coffee to the Captain. He was too stunned to understand it. He only knew it was inevitable—inevitable, however long he lay inert.

At last, after heaving at himself, for he seemed to be a mass of inertia, he got up. But he had to force every one of his movements from behind, with his will. He felt lost, and dazed, and helpless. Then he clutched hold of the bed, the pain was so keen. And looking at his thighs he saw the darker bruises on his swarthy flesh, and he knew that if he pressed one of his fingers on one of the bruises, he should faint. But he did not want to faint—he did not want anybody to know. No one should ever know. It was between him and the Captain. There were only the two people in the world now—himself and the Captain.

Slowly, economically, he got dressed and forced himself to walk. Everything was obscure, except just what he had his hands on. But he managed to get through his work. The very pain revived his dull senses. The worst remained yet. He took the tray and went up to the Captain's room. The officer, pale and heavy, sat at the table. The orderly, as he saluted, felt himself put out of existence. He stood still for a moment submitting to his own nullification—then he gathered himself, seemed to regain himself, and then the Captain began to grow vague, unreal, and the younger soldier's heart beat up. He clung to this situation—that the Captain did not exist—so that he himself might live. But when he saw his officer's hand tremble as he took the coffee, he felt everything falling shattered. And he went away, feeling as if he himself were coming to pieces, disintegrated. And when the Captain was there on horseback, giving orders, while he himself stood, with rifle and knapsack, sick with pain, he felt as if he must shut his eyes—as if he must shut his eyes on everything. It was only the long agony of marching with a parched throat that filled him with one single, sleep-heavy intention: to save himself.

II

He was getting used even to his parched throat. That the snowy peaks were radiant among the sky, that the whity-green glacier-river twisted through its pale shoals, in the valley below, seemed almost supernatural. But he was going mad with fever and thirst. He plodded on uncomplaining. He did not want to speak, not to anybody. There were two gulls, like flakes of water and snow, over the river. The scent of green rye soaked in sunshine came like a sickness. And the march continued, monotonously, almost like a bad sleep.

At the next farmhouse, which stood low and broad near the high road, tubs of water had been put out. The soldiers clustered round to drink. They took off their helmets, and the steam mounted from their wet hair. The Captain sat on horseback, watching. He needed to see his orderly. His helmet threw a dark shadow over his light, fierce eyes, but his moustache and mouth and chin were distinct in the sunshine. The orderly must move under the presence of the figure of the horseman. It was not that he was afraid, or cowed. It was as if he was disembowelled, made empty, like an empty shell. He felt himself as nothing, a shadow creeping under the sunshine. And, thirsty as he was, he could scarcely drink, feeling the Captain near him. He would not take off his helmet to wipe his wet hair. He wanted to stay in shadow, not to be forced into consciousness. Starting, he saw the light heel of the officer prick the belly of the horse; the Captain cantered away, and he himself could relapse into vacancy.

Nothing, however, could give him back his living place in the hot, bright morning. He felt like a gap among it all. Whereas the Captain was prouder, overriding. A hot flash went through the young servant's body. The Captain was firmer and prouder with life, he himself was empty as a shadow. Again the flash went through him, dazing him out. But his heart ran a little firmer.

The company turned up the hill, to make a loop for the return. Below, from among the trees, the farm-bell clanged. He saw the labourers, mowing bare-foot at the thick grass, leave off their work and go downhill, their scythes hanging over their shoulders, like long, bright claws curving down behind them. They seemed like dream-people, as if they had no relation to himself. He felt as in a blackish dream: as if all the other things were there and had form, but he himself was only a consciousness, a gap that could think and perceive.

The soldiers were tramping silently up the glaring hill-side. Gradually his head began to revolve, slowly, rhythmically. Sometimes it was dark before his eyes, as if he saw this world through a smoked glass, frail shadows and unreal. It gave him a pain in his head to walk.

The air was too scented, it gave no breath. All the lush green-stuff seemed to be issuing its sap, till the air was deathly, sickly with the smell of greenness. There was the perfume of clover, like pure honey and bees. Then there grew a faint acrid tang—they were near the beeches; and then a queer clattering noise, and a suffocating, hideous smell; they were passing a flock of sheep, a shepherd in a black smock, holding his crook. Why should the sheep huddle together under this fierce sun? He felt that the shepherd would not see him, though he could see the shepherd.

At last there was the halt. They stacked rifles in a conical stack, put down their kit in a scattered circle around it, and dispersed a little, sitting on a small knoll high on the hill-side. The chatter began. The soldiers were steaming with heat, but were lively. He sat still, seeing the blue mountains rising upon the land, twenty kilometres away. There was a blue fold in the ranges, then out of that, at the foot, the broad, pale bed of the river, stretches of whity-green water between pinkish-grey shoals among the dark pine woods. There it was, spread out a long way off. And it seemed to come downhill, the river. There was a raft being steered, a mile away. It was a strange country. Nearer, a red-roofed, broad farm with white base and square dots of windows crouched beside the wall of beech foliage on the wood's edge. There were long strips of rye and clover and pale green corn. And just at his feet, below the knoll, was a darkish bog, where globe flowers stood breathless still on their slim stalks. And some of the pale gold bubbles were burst, and a broken fragment hung in the air. He thought he was going to sleep.

Suddenly something moved into this coloured mirage before his eyes. The Captain, a small, light-blue and scarlet figure, was trotting evenly between the strips of corn, along the level brow of the hill. And the man making flag-signals was coming on. Proud and sure moved the horseman's figure, the quick, bright thing, in which was concentrated all the light of this morning, which for the rest lay fragile, shining shadow. Submissive, apathetic, the young soldier sat and stared. But as the horse slowed to a walk, coming up the last steep path, the great flash flared over the body and soul of the orderly. He sat waiting. The back of his head felt as if it were weighted with a heavy piece of fire. He did not want to eat. His hands trembled slightly as he moved them. Meanwhile the officer on horseback was approaching slowly and proudly. The tension grew in the orderly's soul. Then again, seeing the Captain ease himself on the saddle, the flash blazed through him.

The Captain looked at the patch of light blue and scarlet, and dark head, scattered closely on the hill-side. It pleased him. The command pleased him. And he was feeling proud. His orderly was among them in common subjection. The officer rose a little on his stirrups to look. The young soldier sat with averted, dumb face. The Captain relaxed on his seat. His slim-legged, beautiful horse, brown as a beech nut, walked proudly uphill. The Captain passed into the zone of the company's atmosphere: a hot smell of men, of sweat, of leather. He knew it very well. After a word with the lieutenant, he went a few paces higher, and sat there, a dominant figure, his sweat-marked horse swishing its tail, while he looked down on his men, on his orderly, a nonentity among the crowd.

The young soldier's heart was like fire in his chest, and he breathed with difficulty. The officer, looking downhill, saw three of the young soldiers, two pails of water between them, staggering across a sunny green field. A table had been set up under a tree, and there the slim lieutenant stood, importantly busy. Then the Captain summoned himself to an act of courage. He called his orderly.

The flame leapt into the young soldier's throat as he heard the command, and he rose blindly, stifled. He saluted, standing below the officer. He did not look up. But there was the flicker in the Captain's voice.

"Go to the inn and fetch me . . ." the officer gave his commands. "Quick!" he added.

At the last word, the heart of the servant leapt with a flash, and he felt the strength come over his body. But he turned in mechanical obedience, and set off at a heavy run downhill, looking almost like a bear, his trousers bagging over his military boots. And the officer watched this blind, plunging run all the way.

But it was only the outside of the orderly's body that was obeying so humbly and mechanically. Inside had gradually accumulated a core into which all the energy of that young life was compact and concentrated. He executed his commission, and plodded quickly back uphill. There was a pain in his head as he walked that made him twist his features unknowingly. But hard there in the centre of his chest was himself, himself, firm, and not to be plucked to pieces.

The Captain had gone up into the wood. The orderly plodded through the hot, powerfully smelling zone of the company's atmosphere. He had a curious mass of energy inside him now. The Captain was less real than himself. He approached the green entrance to the wood. There, in the half-shade, he saw the horse standing, the sunshine and the flickering shadow of leaves dancing over his brown body. There was a clearing where timber had lately been felled. Here, in the gold-green shade beside the brilliant cup of sunshine, stood two figures, blue and pink, the bits of pink showing out plainly. The Captain was talking to his lieutenant.

The orderly stood on the edge of the bright clearing, where great trunks of trees, stripped and glistening, lay stretched like naked, brown-skinned bodies. Chips of wood littered the trampled floor, like splashed light, and the bases of the felled trees stood here and there, with their raw, level tops. Beyond was the brilliant, sunlit green of a beech.

"Then I will ride forward," the orderly heard his Captain say. The lieutenant saluted and strode away. He himself went forward. A hot flash passed through his belly, as he tramped towards his officer.

The Captain watched the rather heavy figure of the young soldier stumble forward, and his veins, too, ran hot. This was to be man to man between them. He yielded before the solid, stumbling figure with bent head. The orderly stooped and put the food on a level-sawn tree-base. The Captain watched the glistening, sun-inflamed, naked hands. He wanted to speak to the young soldier, but could not. The servant propped a bottle against his thigh, pressed open the cork, and poured out the beer into the mug. He kept his head bent. The Captain accepted the mug.

"Hot!" he said, as if amiably.

The flame sprang out of the orderly's heart, nearly suffocating him.

"Yes, sir," he replied, between shut teeth.

And he heard the sound of the Captain's drinking, and he clenched his fists, such a strong torment came into his wrists. Then came the faint clang of the closing of the pot-lid. He looked up. The Captain was watching him. He glanced swiftly away. Then he saw the officer stoop and take a piece of bread from the tree-base. Again the flash of flame went through the young soldier, seeing the stiff body stoop beneath him, and his hands jerked. He looked away. He could feel the officer was nervous. The bread fell as it was being broken. The officer ate the other piece. The two men stood tense and still, the master laboriously chewing his bread, the servant staring with averted face, his fist clenched.

Then the young soldier started. The officer had pressed open the lid of the mug again. The orderly watched the lip of the mug, and the white hand that clenched the handle, as if he were fascinated. It was raised. The youth followed it with his eyes. And then he saw the thin, strong throat of the elder man moving up and down as he drank, the strong jaw working. And the instinct which had been jerking at the young man's wrists suddenly jerked free. He jumped, feeling as if it were rent in two by a strong flame.

The spur of the officer caught in a tree root, he went down backwards with a crash, the middle of his back thudding sickeningly against a sharp-edged tree-base, the pot flying away. And in a second the orderly, with serious, earnest young face, and underlip between his teeth, had got his knee in the officer's chest and was pressing the chin backward over the farther edge of the tree-stump, pressing, with all his heart behind in a passion of relief, the tension of his wrists exquisite with relief. And with the base of his palms he shoved at the chin, with all his might. And it was pleasant, too, to have that chin that hard jaw already slightly rough with beard, in his hands. He did not relax one hair's breadth, but, all the force of all his blood exulting in his thrust, he shoved back the head of the other man, till there was a little "cluck" and a crunching sensation. Then he felt as if his head went to vapour. Heavy convulsions shook the body of the officer, frightening and horrifying the young soldier. Yet it pleased him, too, to repress them. It pleased him to keep his hands pressing back the chin, to feel the chest of the other man yield in expiration to the weight of his strong, young knees, to feel the hard twitchings of the prostrate body jerking his own whole frame, which was pressed down on it.

But it went still. He could look into the nostrils of the other man, the eyes he could scarcely see. How curiously the mouth was pushed out, exaggerating the full lips, and the moustache bristling up from them. Then, with a start, he noticed the nostrils gradually filled with blood. The red brimmed, hesitated, ran over, and went in a thin trickle down the face to the eyes.

It shocked and distressed him. Slowly, he got up. The body twitched and sprawled there, inert. He stood and looked at it in silence. It was a pity *it* was broken. It represented more than the thing which had kicked and bullied him. He was afraid to look at the eyes. They were hideous now, only the whites showing, and the blood running to them. The face of the orderly was drawn with horror at the sight. Well, it was so. In his heart he was satisfied. He had hated the face of the Captain. It was extinguished now. There was a heavy relief in the orderly's soul. That was as it should be. But he could not bear to see the long, military body lying broken over the tree-base, the fine fingers crisped. He wanted to hide it away.

Quickly, busily, he gathered it up and pushed it under the felled tree trunks, which rested their beautiful, smooth length either end on the logs. The face was horrible with blood. He covered it with the helmet. Then he pushed the limbs straight and decent, and brushed the dead leaves off the fine cloth of the uniform. So, it lay quite still in the shadow under there. A little strip of sunshine ran along the breast, from a chink between the logs. The orderly sat by it for a few moments. Here his own life also ended.

Then, through his daze, he heard the lieutenant, in a loud voice, explaining to the men outside the wood, that they were to suppose the bridge on the river below was held by the enemy. Now they were to march to the attack in such and such a manner. The lieutenant had no gift of expression. The orderly, listening from habit, got muddled. And when the lieutenant began it all again he ceased to hear.

He knew he must go. He stood up. It surprised him that the leaves were glittering in the sun, and the chips of wood reflecting white from the ground. For him a change had come over the world. But for the rest it had not—all seemed the same. Only he had left it. And he could not go back. It was his duty to return with the beer-pot and the bottle. He could not. He had left all that. The lieutenant was still hoarsely explaining. He must go, or they would overtake him. And he could not bear contact with anyone now.

He drew his fingers over his eyes, trying to find out where he was.

Then he turned away. He saw the horse standing in the path. He went up to it and mounted. It hurt him to sit in the saddle. The pain of keeping his seat occupied him as they cantered through the wood. He would not have minded anything, but he could not get away from the sense of being divided from the others. The path led out of the trees. On the edge of the wood he pulled up and stood watching. There in the spacious sunshine of the valley soldiers were moving in a little swarm. Every now and then, a man harrowing on a strip of fallow shouted to his oxen, at the turn. The village and the white-towered church was small in the sunshine. And he no longer belonged to it—he sat there, beyond, like a man outside in the dark. He had gone out from everyday life into the unknown and he could not, he even did not want to go back.

Turning from the sun-blazing valley, he rode deep into the wood. Tree trunks, like people standing grey and still, took no notice as he went. A doe, herself a moving bit of sunshine and shadow, went running through the flecked shade. There were bright green rents in the foliage. Then it was all pine wood, dark and cool. And he was sick with pain, and had an intolerable great pulse in his head, and he was sick. He had never been ill in his life. He felt lost, quite dazed with all this.

Trying to get down from the horse, he fell, astonished at the pain and his lack of balance. The horse shifted uneasily. He jerked its bridle and sent it cantering jerkily away. It was his last connection with the rest of things.

But he only wanted to lie down and not be disturbed. Stumbling through the trees, he came on a quiet place where beeches and pine trees grew on a slope. Immediately he had lain down and closed his eyes, his consciousness went racing on without him. A big pulse of sickness beat in him as if it throbbed through the whole earth. He was burning with dry heat. But he was too busy, too tearingly active in the incoherent race of delirium to observe.

III

He came to with a start. His mouth was dry and hard, his heart beat heavily, but he had not the energy to get up. His heart beat heavily. Where was he?—the barracks—at home? There was something knocking. And, making an effort, he looked round—trees, and litter of greenery, and reddish, bright, still pieces of sunshine on the floor. He did not believe he was himself, he did not believe what he saw. Something was knocking. He made a struggle towards consciousness, but relapsed. Then he struggled again. And gradually his surroundings fell into relationship with himself. He knew, and a great pang of fear went through his heart. Somebody was knocking. He could see the heavy, black rags of a fir tree overhead. Then everything went black. Yet he did not believe he had closed his eyes. He had not. Out of the blackness sight slowly emerged again. And someone was knocking. Quickly, he saw the blood-disfigured face of his Captain, which he hated. And he held himself still with horror. Yet, deep inside him, he knew that it was so, the Captain should be dead. But the physical delirium got hold of him. Someone was knocking. He lay perfectly still, as if dead, with fear. And he went unconscious.

When he opened his eyes again he started, seeing something creeping swiftly up a tree trunk. It was a little bird. And the bird was whistling overhead. Tap-tap-tap—it was the small, quick bird rapping the tree trunk with its beak, as if its head were a little round hammer. He watched it curiously. It shifted sharply, in its creeping fashion. Then, like a mouse, it slid down the bare trunk. Its swift creeping sent a flash of revulsion through him. He raised his head. It felt a great weight. Then, the little bird ran out of the shadow across a still patch of sunshine, its little head bobbing swiftly, its white legs twinkling brightly for a moment. How neat it was in its build, so compact, with piece of white on its wings. There were several of them. They were so pretty—but they crept like swift, erratic mice, running here and there among the beech-mast.

He lay down again exhausted, and his consciousness lapsed. He had a horror of the little creeping birds. All his blood seemed to be darting and creeping in his head. And yet he could not move.

He came to with a further ache of exhaustion. There was the pain in his head, and the horrible sickness, and his inability to move. He had never been ill in his life. He did not know where he was or what he was. Probably he had got sunstroke. Or what else?—he had silenced the Captain for ever—some time ago—oh, a long time ago. There had been blood on his face, and his eyes had turned upwards. It was all right, somehow. It was peace. But now he had got beyond himself. He had never been here before. Was it life, or not life? He was by himself. They were in a big, bright place, those others, and he was outside. The town, all the country, a big bright place of light: and he was outside, here, in the darkened open beyond, where each thing existed alone. But they would all have to come out there sometime, those others. Little, and left behind him, they all were. There had been father and mother and sweetheart. What did they all matter? This was the open land.

He sat up. Something scuffled. It was a little brown squirrel running in lovely undulating bounds over the floor, its red tail completing the undulation of its body—and then, as it sat up, furling and unfurling. He watched it, pleased. It ran on again, friskily, enjoying itself. It flew wildly at another squirrel, and they were chasing each other, and making little scolding, chattering noises. The soldier wanted to speak to them. But only a hoarse sound came out of his throat. The squirrels burst away— they flew up the trees. And then he saw the one peeping round at him, half-way up a tree trunk. A start of fear went through him, though in so far as he was conscious, he was amused. It still stayed, its little keen face staring at him half-way up the tree trunk, its little ears pricked up, its clawey little hands clinging to the bark, its white breast reared. He started from it in panic.

Struggling to his feet, he lurched away. He went on walking, walking, looking for something—for a drink. His brain felt hot and inflamed for want of water. He stumbled on: Then he did not know anything. He went unconscious as he walked. Yet he stumbled on, his mouth open.

When, to his dumb wonder, he opened his eyes on the world again, he no longer tried to remember what it was. There was thick, golden light behind golden-green glitterings, and tall, grey-purple shafts, and darknesses farther off, surrounding him, growing deeper. He was conscious of a sense of arrival. He was amid the reality, on the real, dark bottom. But there was the thirst burning in his brain. He felt lighter, not so heavy. He supposed it was newness. The air was muttering with thunder. He thought he was walking wonderfully swiftly and was coming straight to relief—or was it to water?

Suddenly he stood still with fear. There was a tremendous flare of gold, immense—just a few dark trunks like bars between him and it. All the young level wheat was burnished gold glaring on its silky green. A woman, full-skirted, a black cloth on her head for head-dress, was passing like a block of shadow through the glistening, green corn, into the full glare. There was a farm, too, pale blue in shadow, and the timber black. And there was a church spire, nearly fused away in the gold. The woman moved on, away from him. He had no language with which to speak to her. She was the bright, solid unreality. She would make a noise of words that would confuse him, and her eyes would look at him without seeing him. She was crossing there to the other side. He stood against a tree.

When at last he turned, looking down the long, bare grove whose flat bed was already filling dark, he saw the mountains in a wonder-light, not far away, and radiant. Behind the soft, grey ridge of the nearest range the farther mountains stood golden and pale grey, the snow all radiant like pure, soft gold. So still, gleaming in the sky, fashioned pure out of the ore of the sky, they shone in their silence. He stood and looked at them, his face illuminated. And like the golden, lustrous gleaming of the snow he felt his own thirst bright in him. He stood and gazed, leaning against a tree. And then everything slid away into space.

During the night the lightning fluttered perpetually, making the whole sky white. He must have walked again. The world hung livid round him for moments, fields a level sheen of grey-green light, trees in dark bulk, and the range of clouds black across a white sky. Then the darkness fell like a shutter, and the night was whole. A faint flutter of a half-revealed world, that could not quite leap out of the darkness!—Then there again stood a sweep of pallor for the land, dark shapes looming, a range of clouds hanging overhead. The world was a ghostly shadow, thrown for a moment upon the pure darkness, which returned ever whole and complete.

And the mere delirium of sickness and fever went on inside him—his brain opening and shutting like the night—then sometimes convulsions of terror from something with great eyes that stared round a tree—then the long agony of the march, and the sun decomposing his blood—then the pang of hate for the Captain, followed by a pang of tenderness and ease. But everything was distorted, born of an ache and resolving into an ache.

In the morning he came definitely awake. Then his brain flamed with the sole horror of thirstiness! The sun was on his face, the dew was steaming from his wet clothes. Like one possessed, he got up. There, straight in front of him, blue and cool and tender, the mountains ranged across the pale edge of the morning sky. He wanted them—he wanted them alone—he wanted to leave himself and be identified with them. They did not move, they were still and soft, with white, gentle markings of snow. He stood still, mad with suffering, his hands crisping and clutching. Then he was twisting in a paroxysm on the grass.

He lay still, in a kind of dream of anguish. His thirst seemed to have separated itself from him, and to stand apart, a single demand. Then the pain he felt was another single self. Then there was the clog of his body, another separate thing. He was divided among all kinds of separate things. There was some strange, agonised connection between them, but they were drawing farther apart. Then they would all split. The sun, drilling down on him, was drilling through the bond. Then they would all fall, fall through the everlasting lapse of space. Then again, his consciousness reasserted itself. He roused on to his elbow and stared at the gleaming mountains. There they ranked, all still and wonderful between earth and heaven. He stared till his eyes went black, and the mountains, as they stood in their beauty, so clean and cool, seemed to have it, that which was lost in him.

IV

When the soldiers found him, three hours later, he was lying with his face over his arm, his black hair giving off heat under the sun. But he was still alive. Seeing the open, black mouth the young soldiers dropped him in horror.

He died in the hospital at night, without having seen again.

The doctors saw the bruises on his legs, behind, and were silent.

The bodies of the two men lay together, side by side, in the mortuary, the one white and slender, but laid rigidly at rest, the other looking as if every moment it must rouse into life again, so young and unused, from a slumber.

New Women

JOYCE CARY
(Anglo-Irish, 1888–1957)

Samuel Thompson, civil servant, was the only child of Athenia Battersby, the famous feminist leader. She is said to have been the original
inventor of the plan for burning letter-boxes. She designed the suffrage
hat, and wrote a book proving that Shakespeare was Queen Elizabeth.
But it is a shame for the modern generation of women to laugh at
Athenia. They owe her a big debt. She had courage and character, she
really did a great deal to get them votes and sacrificed much of herself in
the process—her sense of humour, for instance.

She forbade marriage to her followers, as a degradation, but after
women's votes were granted, she married Sandy Thompson, a feminist as
enthusiastic as herself, and taught him to cook; in fact, made him a
modern husband thirty years before his time. He would do the washing-
up while she dashed out to meetings.

Not that Sandy was put upon. He himself proposed to do the washing-
up and learned how to sew. He was a man of pugnacious temperament
who loved any excuse for a fight. If he had not been brought up a Christian pacifist, he would have made a first-class thug. As an organiser of
suffrage demonstrations, he loved to bash policemen, and he hemmed
dusters to show how much he considered women a superior sex.

Their marriage was very happy in its own way. But dedicated parents
are bad for children, whose imaginations, like their bodies, cannot bear to
remain fixed in any one position. Samuel had an austere upbringing—
both parents taught him from his earliest years that boys were little better

than brutes. But, as friends later pointed out to him, he had no right to complain of anything, he was lucky to exist at all, and had almost certainly been an accident. Athenia was even more against motherhood, at least for feminist pioneers, than marriage. She held that responsible educated women should devote themselves to the professions, in order to take a commanding place in the life of the country.

Samuel took the point and was humbly grateful for life, such as it was. He grew up a modest and retiring character. Even in his office in the Ministry of Energy, he was hardly known, except as a signature, by anyone outside his own staff. He belonged to no clubs and played no games except Patience. His hobby was collecting stamps, but he also took an absorbed interest in the latest scientific developments, as recorded in his morning paper, an old Liberal daily which, by tradition, gave at least half a column a week to general culture. The theory of the expanding universe occupied him for months and drove his acquaintances distracted. He was also extremely concerned in nuclear physics and the possibility of the disappearance of the world one morning owing to an accident at Harwell.

He especially avoided the company of women; he appeared a confirmed old bachelor. But at forty-six, to everyone's astonishment, he fell in love with one of the secretaries at the office and married her. Aminta was a very smart young woman direct from college and right up to date. She condescended to Picasso and was completely bored with the subject of homosexuality. She wore a Victorian cameo in her hat and had two fine drawings by Millais in her flat.

The wedding was in church. Aminta was a keen churchwoman. This was slightly embarrassing to Samuel, who had never even been baptised. Athenia Battersby had strong views about religion. As a scientist, she called it nonsense; as a feminist, a man-made device for the subjection of women. But Aminta pushed him through the service and he did not disgrace himself.

They settled in a charming little villa at Kew, Ruskin Gothic, and furnished it with some good mid-Victorian mahogany. Aminta was lucky enough to find a Clarkson Stansfield sea picture in a junk shop and to get it for ten pounds. This fine work gave great distinction to their sitting-room. Aminta's treasure was a gilt clock under an original glass dome, which required and received a draped mantelpiece.

Aminta now proposes to entertain Samuel's friends and is surprised to find he hasn't any. She has dozens of both sexes and all ages, especially friends from college. All these young women are in jobs or just married or both. They arrive every day to see Aminta, bringing small babies or bottles of claret. All of them want to see Samuel, and gaze curiously at him, tell him that Aminta will make a very good wife in spite of her intelligence, and, when they go away, say to each other, like all friends of a new-married person, 'But how extraordinary—how on earth did it happen—can it last?'

They suspect that their dear but reckless Aminta has acquired Samuel as a collector's piece.

Samuel is embarrassed by all these young people, especially the girls. They shock him by their conversation about the most intimate details of their love affairs and the complexes of their lovers; they startle him by their strong views on the subject of marriage, and especially the duties of a wife and mother. They have no patience with a girl who can't cook, clean, wash, drive any make of car, mend linen, put in a fuse, do running repairs on household gadgets, choose, store and decant a respectable wine, and pick a smokable cigar at a smokable price.

As for children, they all want six apiece and take the view that if any child does not turn out a perfectly integrated and responsible member of society, the mother will be entirely to blame.

When Samuel dares to murmur that there can be bad fathers, they gaze at him for a moment and then say that no doubt mothers sometimes make that excuse, but it's not really an excuse. They obviously think that any woman ought to be able to cope with any kind of man, including the worst of fathers. Cope is their great word. Though polite to Samuel, they don't take him very seriously. When he raises the question of the expanding universe one evening, he is assured by two girls at once, of whom one has taken a first-class in mathematics and is a Fellow of her college, that it is a stunt for the tabloids. The universe, they say, can be made to dance the polka with a suitable equation; it depends only on which system you use. The mathematician, who is in the eighth month of her second child, then returns to the subject of lyings-in. Is it better to have a monthly nurse at home or go to hospital? Either way things can go wrong, and then the party discusses some cases that have gone wrong, with the technical elaboration of experts. It is, for instance, quite wrong to suppose that the widest hips are a guarantee of safety. Samuel listens with horror, and breaks into cold sweats. Aminta is small, with an eighteen-inch waist and hips of that rare type that look slim even in jeans.

Aminta, after two months of marriage, is already expecting. She has been decided on six children from the age of ten. She, too, has had a feminist mother.

Samuel mutters in his sleep and wakes up with a moan. Next day he begins to flutter about Aminta like a nervous hen. She must not lift that chair, she must not use her arms, she must not run on the stairs, she must not go out this morning, it is too hot or too cold. Aminta laughs at him and obeys till he has gone to the office. Luckily, at this time his newspaper brings out some articles on painless childbirth, and Samuel rushes out at once to buy all the books. Aminta is commanded to do exercises, to learn how to relax. And she obeys. For Aminta herself has been a little apprehensive, even if she says nothing about it. What girl doesn't have some anxiety in her first pregnancy?

Aminta has lost her parents young, and her family was small and scattered—Service people. A naval cousin dropped in from Hong Kong one day with a real Chinese jar of the genuine ginger. An elder sister, an Anglican nun, brought her an original Negro carving from Central Africa. A great-aunt from the Midlands, who had sent her, for wedding present, a plated muffineer dating from her own wedding, asked herself for a week because she could stand anything except modern hotels.

She was a little thin woman of seventy-six with the complexion of a sea captain. Her nose was Atlantic blue, a dark fierce blue like the middle of a storm cloud. Her mahogany cheeks were as dark as a cabin door. Her forehead, a sharp line above her eyebrows, was dead white, like that of an old sailor. But she had not the suave and ingratiating manner of the liner captain; she was bluff and gruff. She had got her complexion from sixty years in the hunting field where she had made a distinguished career as the first woman M.F.H., at least of a smart pack.

Even in town she wore the mannish dress affected by pioneer women of the late 'eighties; a Tyrol felt, a double-breasted reefer, a man's hard collar and four-in-hand tie.

She was amazed and disgusted by the furniture, especially the gilt clock and the draped chimney board. 'Good God,' she said. 'Just like my granny's, and *she* was a stuffy old relic even for Dawlish. All that dusty rubbish went out with moustache cups.'

She thought the Stansfield equally out of date. She herself possessed a seascape, a Boudin: 'But of course, I know this modern French stuff doesn't appeal to everyone.'

She brought a brace of pheasants and two bottles of port, Croft '26. She instructed Aminta to cook the pheasants, an anxious job for so particular a gourmet, but she allowed no one but herself to decant the port.

And over a second glass that evening, she unbent so far as to say she could forgive Samuel everything but his mother.

'My God,' she said, 'what a disaster—that vote. When I was young, women ran the civilised world, let's say, France down to Longchamp and England up to Newmarket, but they don't run anything now, except those ridiculous nylons. My generation were people; we made ourselves respected, but you girls are just a sex. Look at the advertisements.'

When she heard of Aminta's relaxing exercises, she snorted, 'There you are—just what I said—as if women were all the same size and shape, just lumps of sex stamped out from the same batch of cake mixture and served up in the same frills.'

She poured and savoured her third glass, accepted a cigar, glanced at the name on the box, said, 'How do you afford Havanas? You young ones today spoil yourselves.'

'They were for you,' said Aminta.

'I thought so,' said she with the grim smile of an M.F.H. 'Getting round the old fool on her weak side.'

Suddenly she became extraordinarily genial, in the way of so many gruff old people who seemed astonished and overwhelmed at the least mark of affection. Probably the old woman paid for her local glory in loneliness. All at once she couldn't do too much for her dear Aminta and Sammy. She would send them game every week and her own recipe for bread sauce. She would order a dozen of burgundy at once—that was the stuff for breeding gals, nothing like it to make blood. As for the lying-in, there was only one man in England—one that a woman could trust—her own man, Dr McMurdo.

'He's delivered all the Hunt children for forty years, and he's set my collar-bone five times. He's been retired since the war, but he'd do anything for me. I'll bring him up at once to look over the ground.'

And she wired the next morning. She belonged to the generation before phones.

Samuel swore that no Blankshire bone-setter should come near his Aminta. But Dr McMurdo came the next day. It was apparently true that he would do anything for a lady so distinguished in history as Aminta's aunt. He was also in his seventies, an enormous man with a huge, round purple face and a great swag belly. He was dressed in a shaggy yellow tweed with four-inch blue check and a duster-pattern white flannel waistcoat. He ate and drank with all the gusto of a Falstaff. To see him at table would have been an inspiration to Stratford. He, too, was an expert on port. His manner with the patient was less fatherly than familiar. He did not exactly slap her on the behind after his examination, but it was more than a pat.

When she talked about her relaxing exercises and painless childbirth, he grinned like a satyr and answered with more affectionate pats, 'Leave it to me, dear. That's what I'm here for. Just you relax.'

And he winked at Thompson—a wink combining all the genial villainy of a Falstaff with all the cynicism, as Thompson put it, of an abortionist. And, as soon as Aminta had her first real pain, out came the chloroform mask. She knew nothing more till she waked up feeling beautifully flat and heard, as in the far distance, a baby crying somewhere, and gradually realised that this was her baby.

After that, it somehow came about that McMurdo attended also for the other two children. They are brought up in the new style, to mind their manners, and to get up when their papa comes to table—just as Aminta promised to obey, so she says a house must have its head and supports the authority of the father. The result is that when she threatens them, 'I'll tell Papa,' they become instantly as good as gold and amenable as lambs. They are happy, lively, and reasonable; they have no moral problems and always know the right thing to do even when they don't mean to do it.

The Thompson family, in short, is a very happy one—Aminta's friends, who assured Samuel that her intelligence would not prevent her from making a success of marriage, were right. Samuel adores her. Their only subject of occasional difference is the vote. As a son of his mother he thinks Aminta takes the vote too lightly.

Not that she despises it. 'Of course, it's a thing one has to have,' she says, 'like mumps. But why do they always have elections on wet days and put the polling booths in back-yards among municipal dustbins? What do votes *do* after all?'

Though Aminta makes a great deal of Samuel's authority as master of the house, it is noticed that she runs everything; looks after all the money, pays all the bills, even at Samuel's new croquet club, drives the car and chooses the family holiday. What's more, when in that frantic fortnight before Budget Day, Samuel, like all senior Government clerks, brings back memos in the evenings and even for the Sunday, she will sit down and knock up a quite masterly report on the Calorific Value of Brick Dust, or the Profitable Utilisation of Factory Smoke.

In this happiness, Samuel has bloomed in a late florescence. He has given up stamps and collects glass paperweights. He wears a bowler and fancy waistcoats. His trousers grow narrower and narrower. He says that nowadays there is so little difference between political parties that old Liberals like himself might as well vote blindfold. And last election he very nearly did vote Conservative. The only reason why he refrained at the last moment was because he discovered that the Liberal candidate was a strong supporter of Sunday observance, and he has become a devoted churchman with a leaning to evangelism. In short, he is nearly a new man.

Bliss

KATHERINE MANSFIELD
(New Zealander, 1888–1923)

Although Bertha Young was thirty she still had moments like this when she wanted to run instead of walk, to take dancing steps on and off the pavement, to bowl a hoop, to throw something up in the air and catch it again, or to stand still and laugh at—nothing—at nothing, simply.

What can you do if you are thirty and, turning the corner of your own street, you are overcome, suddenly, by a feeling of bliss—absolute bliss!—as though you'd suddenly swallowed a bright piece of that late afternoon sun and it burned in your bosom, sending out a little shower of sparks into every particle, into every finger and toe? . . .

Oh, is there no way you can express it without being "drunk and disorderly"? How idiotic civilization is! Why be given a body if you have to keep it shut up in a case like a rare, rare fiddle?

"No, that about the fiddle is not quite what I mean," she thought, running up the steps and feeling in her bag for the key—she'd forgotten it, as usual—and rattling the letter-box. "It's not what I mean, be-cause——Thank you, Mary"—she went into the hall. "Is nurse back?"

"Yes, M'm."

"And has the fruit come?"

"Yes, M'm. Everything's come."

"Bring the fruit up to the dining-room, will you? I'll arrange it before I go upstairs."

It was dusky in the dining-room and quite chilly. But all the same

Bertha threw off her coat; she could not bear the tight clasp of it another moment, and the cold air fell on her arms.

But in her bosom there was still that bright glowing place—that shower of little sparks coming from it. It was almost unbearable. She hardly dared to breathe for fear of fanning it higher, and yet she breathed deeply, deeply. She hardly dared to look into the cold mirror—but she did look, and it gave her back a woman, radiant, with smiling, trembling lips, with big, dark eyes and an air of listening, waiting for something . . . divine to happen . . . that she knew must happen . . . infallibly.

Mary brought in the fruit on a tray and with it a glass bowl, and a blue dish, very lovely, with a strange sheen on it as though it had been dipped in milk.

"Shall I turn on the light, M'm?"

"No, thank you. I can see quite well."

There were tangerines and apples stained with strawberry pink. Some yellow pears, smooth as silk, some white grapes covered with a silver bloom and a big cluster of purple ones. These last she had bought to tone in with the new dining-room carpet. Yes, that did sound rather far-fetched and absurd, but it was really why she had bought them. She had thought in the shop: "I must have some purple ones to bring the carpet up to the table." And it had seemed quite sense at the time.

When she had finished with them and had made two pyramids of these bright round shapes, she stood away from the table to get the effect—and it really was most curious. For the dark table seemed to melt into the dusky light and the glass dish and the blue bowl to float in the air. This, of course in her present mood, was so incredibly beautiful. . . . She began to laugh.

"No, no. I'm getting hysterical." And she seized her bag and coat and ran upstairs to the nursery.

Nurse sat at a low table giving Little B her supper after her bath. The baby had on a white flannel gown and a blue woollen jacket, and her dark, fine hair was brushed up into a funny little peak. She looked up when she saw her mother and began to jump.

"Now, my lovey, eat it up like a good girl," said Nurse, setting her lips in a way that Bertha knew, and that meant she had come into the nursery at another wrong moment.

"Has she been good, Nanny?"

"She's been a little sweet all the afternoon," whispered Nanny. "We went to the park and I sat down on a chair and took her out of the pram and a big dog came along and put its head on my knee and she clutched its ear, tugged it. Oh, you should have seen her."

Bertha wanted to ask if it wasn't rather dangerous to let her clutch at a strange dog's ear. But she did not dare to. She stood watching them, her hands by her side, like the poor little girl in front of the rich little girl with the doll.

The baby looked up at her again, stared, and then smiled so charmingly that Bertha couldn't help crying:

"Oh, Nanny, do let me finish giving her her supper while you put the bath things away."

"Well, M'm, she oughtn't to be changed hands while she's eating," said Nanny, still whispering. "It unsettles her; it's very likely to upset her."

How absurd it was. Why have a baby if it has to be kept—not in a case like a rare, rare fiddle—but in another woman's arms?

"Oh, I must!" said she.

Very offended, Nanny handed her over.

"Now, don't excite her after her supper. You know you do, M'm. And I have such a time with her after!"

Thank heaven! Nanny went out of the room with the bath towels.

"Now I've got you to myself, my little precious," said Bertha, as the baby leaned against her.

She ate delightfully, holding up her lips for the spoon and then waving her hands. Sometimes she wouldn't let the spoon go; and sometimes, just as Bertha had filled it, she waved it away to the four winds.

When the soup was finished Bertha turned round to the fire.

"You're nice—you're very nice!" said she, kissing her warm baby. "I'm fond of you. I like you."

And, indeed, she loved Little B so much—her neck as she bent forward, her exquisite toes as they shone transparent in the firelight—that all her feeling of bliss came back again, and again she didn't know how to express it—what to do with it.

"You're wanted on the telephone," said Nanny, coming back in triumph and seizing *her* Little B.

Down she flew. It was Harry.

"Oh, is that you, Ber? Look here. I'll be late. I'll take a taxi and come

along as quickly as I can, but get dinner put back ten minutes—will you?
All right?"

"Yes, perfectly. Oh, Harry!"

"Yes?"

What had she to say? She'd nothing to say. She only wanted to get in
touch with him for a moment. She couldn't absurdly cry: "Hasn't it been
a divine day!"

"What is it?" rapped out the little voice.

"Nothing. *Entendu,*" said Bertha, and hung up the receiver, thinking
how more than idiotic civilization was.

They had people coming to dinner. The Norman Knights—a very
sound couple—he was about to start a theatre, and she was awfully keen
on interior decoration, a young man, Eddie Warren, who had just published a little book of poems and whom everybody was asking to dine,
and a "find" of Bertha's called Pearl Fulton. What Miss Fulton did,
Bertha didn't know. They had met at the club and Bertha had fallen in
love with her, as she always did fall in love with beautiful women who
had something strange about them.

The provoking thing was that, though they had been about together
and met a number of times and really talked, Bertha couldn't yet make
her out. Up to a certain point Miss Fulton was rarely, wonderfully frank,
but the certain point was there, and beyond that she would not go.

Was there anything beyond it? Harry said "No." Voted her dullish,
and "cold like all blond women, with a touch, perhaps, of anaemia of the
brain." But Bertha wouldn't agree with him; not yet, at any rate.

"No, the way she has of sitting with her head a little on one side, and
smiling, has something behind it, Harry, and I must find out what that
something is."

"Most likely it's a good stomach," answered Harry.

He made a point of catching Bertha's heels with replies of that kind
. . . "liver frozen, my dear girl," or "pure flatulence," or "kidney disease," . . . and so on. For some strange reason Bertha liked this, and
almost admired it in him very much.

She went into the drawing-room and lighted the fire; then, picking up
the cushions, one by one, that Mary had disposed so carefully, she threw
them back on to the chairs and the couches. That made all the difference;
the room came alive at once. As she was about to throw the last one she

surprised herself by suddenly hugging it to her, passionately, passionately. But it did not put out the fire in her bosom. Oh, on the contrary! The windows of the drawing-room opened on to a balcony overlooking the garden. At the far end, against the wall, there was a tall, slender pear tree in fullest, richest bloom; it stood perfect, as though becalmed against the jade-green sky. Bertha couldn't help feeling, even from this distance, that it had not a single bud or a faded petal. Down below, in the garden beds, the red and yellow tulips, heavy with flowers, seemed to lean upon the dusk. A grey cat, dragging its belly, crept across the lawn, and a black one, its shadow, trailed after. The sight of them, so intent and so quick, gave Bertha a curious shiver.

"What creepy things cats are!" she stammered, and she turned away from the window and began walking up and down. . . .

How strong the jonquils smelled in the warm room. Too strong? Oh, no. And yet, as though overcome, she flung down on a couch and pressed her hands to her eyes.

"I'm too happy—too happy!" she murmured.

And she seemed to see on her eyelids the lovely pear tree with its wide open blossoms as a symbol of her own life.

Really—really—she had everything. She was young. Harry and she were as much in love as ever, and they got on together splendidly and were really good pals. She had an adorable baby. They didn't have to worry about money. They had this absolutely satisfactory house and garden. And friends—modern, thrilling friends, writers and painters and poets or people keen on social questions—just the kind of friends they wanted. And then there were books, and there was music, and she had found a wonderful little dressmaker, and they were going abroad in the summer, and their new cook made the most superb omelettes. . . .

"I'm absurd. Absurd!" She sat up; but she felt quite dizzy, quite drunk. It must have been the spring.

Yes, it was the spring. Now she was so tired she could not drag herself upstairs to dress.

A white dress, a string of jade beads, green shoes and stockings. It wasn't intentional. She had thought of this scheme hours before she stood at the drawing-room window.

Her petals rustled softly into the hall, and she kissed Mrs. Norman Knight, who was taking off the most amusing orange coat with a procession of black monkeys round the hem and up the fronts.

". . . Why! Why! Why is the middle-class so stodgy—so utterly without a sense of humour! My dear, it's only by a fluke that I am here at all —Norman being the protective fluke. For my darling monkeys so upset the train that it rose to a man and simply ate me with its eyes. Didn't laugh—wasn't amused—that I should have loved. No, just stared—and bored me through and through."

"But the cream of it was," said Norman, pressing a large tortoiseshell-rimmed monocle into his eye, "you don't mind me telling this, Face, do you?" (In their home and among their friends they called each other Face and Mug.) "The cream of it was when she, being full fed, turned to the woman beside her and said: 'Haven't you ever seen a monkey before?' "

"Oh, yes!" Mrs. Norman Knight joined in the laughter. "Wasn't that too absolutely creamy?"

And a funnier thing still was that now her coat was off she did look like a very intelligent monkey—who had even made that yellow silk dress out of scraped banana skins. And her amber ear-rings; they were like little dangling nuts.

"This is a sad, sad fall!" said Mug, pausing in front of Little B's perambulator. "When the perambulator comes into the hall——" and he waved the rest of the quotation away.

The bell rang. It was lean, pale Eddie Warren (as usual) in a state of acute distress.

"It *is* the right house, *isn't* it?" he pleaded.

"Oh, I think so—I hope so," said Bertha brightly.

"I have had such a *dreadful* experience with a taxi-man; he was *most* sinister. I couldn't get him to *stop*. The *more* I knocked and called the *faster* he went. And *in* the moonlight this *bizarre* figure with the *flattened* head *crouching* over the *lit-tle* wheel. . . ."

He shuddered, taking off an immense white silk scarf. Bertha noticed that his socks were white, too—most charming.

"But how dreadful!" she cried.

"Yes, it really was," said Eddie, following her into the drawing-room. "I saw myself *driving* through Eternity in a *timeless* taxi."

He knew the Norman Knights. In fact, he was going to write a play for N. K. when the theatre scheme came off.

"Well, Warren, how's the play?" said Norman Knight, dropping his monocle and giving his eye a moment in which to rise to the surface before it was screwed down again.

And Mrs. Norman Knight: "Oh, Mr. Warren, what happy socks?"

"I *am* so glad you like them," said he, staring at his feet. "They seem to have got so *much* whiter since the moon rose." And he turned his lean sorrowful young face to Bertha. "There *is* a moon, you know."

She wanted to cry: "I am sure there is—often—often!"

He really was a most attractive person. But so was Face, crouched before the fire in her banana skins, and so was Mug, smoking a cigarette and saying as he flicked the ash: "Why doth the bridegroom tarry?"

"There he is, now."

Bang went the front door open and shut. Harry shouted: "Hullo, you people. Down in five minutes." And they heard him swarm up the stairs. Bertha couldn't help smiling; she knew how he loved doing things at high pressure. What, after all, did an extra five minutes matter? But he would pretend to himself that they mattered beyond measure. And then he would make a great point of coming into the drawing-room, extravagantly cool and collected.

Harry had such a zest for life. Oh, how she appreciated it in him. And his passion for fighting—for seeking in everything that came up against him another test of his power and of his courage—that, too, she understood. Even when it made him just occasionally, to other people, who didn't know him well, a little ridiculous perhaps. . . . For there were moments when he rushed into battle where no battle was. . . . She talked and laughed and positively forgot until he had come in (just as she had imagined) that Pearl Fulton had not turned up.

"I wonder if Miss Fulton has forgotten?"

"I expect so," said Harry. "Is she on the 'phone?"

"Ah! There's a taxi, now." And Bertha smiled with that little air of proprietorship that she always assumed while her women finds were new and mysterious. "She lives in taxis."

"She'll run to fat if she does," said Harry coolly, ringing the bell for dinner. "Frightful danger for blond women."

"Harry—don't," warned Bertha, laughing up at him.

Came another tiny moment, while they waited, laughing and talking, just a trifle too much at their ease, a trifle too unaware. And then Miss Fulton, all in silver, with a silver fillet binding her pale blond hair, came in smiling, her head a little on one side.

"Am I late?"

"No, not at all," said Bertha. "Come along." And she took her arm and they moved into the dining-room.

What was there in the touch of that cool arm that could fan—fan—start blazing—blazing—the fire of bliss that Bertha did not know what to do with?

Miss Fulton did not look at her; but then she seldom did look at people directly. Her heavy eyelids lay upon her eyes and the strange half smile came and went upon her lips as though she lived by listening rather than seeing. But Bertha knew, suddenly, as if the longest, most intimate look had passed between them—as if they had said to each other: "You, too?" —that Pearl Fulton, stirring the beautiful red soup in the grey plate, was feeling just what she was feeling.

And the others? Face and Mug, Eddie and Harry, their spoons rising and falling—dabbing their lips with their napkins, crumbling bread, fiddling with the forks and glasses and talking.

"I met her at the Alpha show—the weirdest little person. She'd not only cut off her hair, but she seemed to have taken a dreadfully good snip off her legs and arms and her neck and her poor little nose as well."

"Isn't she very *liée* with Michael Oat?"

"The man who wrote *Love in False Teeth?*"

"He wants to write a play for me. One act. One man. Decides to commit suicide. Gives all the reasons why he should and why he shouldn't. And just as he has made up his mind either to do it or not to do it—curtain. Not half a bad idea."

"What's he going to call it—'Stomach Trouble'?"

"I *think* I've come across the *same* idea in a lit-tle French review, *quite* unknown in England."

No, they didn't share it. They were dears—dears—and she loved having them there, at her table, and giving them delicious food and wine. In fact, she longed to tell them how delightful they were, and what a decorative group they made, how they seemed to set one another off and how they reminded her of a play by Tchekhov!

Harry was enjoying his dinner. It was part of his—well, not his nature, exactly, and certainly not his pose—his—something or other—to talk about food and to glory in his "shameless passion for the white flesh of the lobster" and "the green of pistachio ices—green and cold like the eyelids of Egyptian dancers."

When he looked up at her and said: "Bertha, this is a very admirable *soufflée!*" she almost could have wept with child-like pleasure.

Oh, why did she feel so tender towards the whole world to-night? Everything was good—was right. All that happened seemed to fill again her brimming cup of bliss.

And still, in the back of her mind, there was the pear tree. It would be silver now, in the light of poor dear Eddie's moon, silver as Miss Fulton, who sat there turning a tangerine in her slender fingers that were so pale a light seemed to come from them.

What she simply couldn't make out—what was miraculous—was how she should have guessed Miss Fulton's mood so exactly and so instantly. For she never doubted for a moment that she was right, and yet what had she to go on? Less than nothing.

"I believe this does happen very, very rarely between women. Never between men," thought Bertha. "But while I am making the coffee in the drawing-room perhaps she will 'give a sign.' "

What she meant by that she did not know, and what would happen after that she could not imagine.

While she thought like this she saw herself talking and laughing. She had to talk because of her desire to laugh.

"I must laugh or die."

But when she noticed Face's funny little habit of tucking something down the front of her bodice—as if she kept a tiny, secret hoard of nuts there, too—Bertha had to dig her nails into her hands—so as not to laugh too much.

It was over at last. And: "Come and see my new coffee machine," said Bertha.

"We only have a new coffee machine once a fortnight," said Harry. Face took her arm this time; Miss Fulton bent her head and followed after.

The fire had died down in the drawing-room to a red, flickering "nest of baby phoenixes," said Face.

"Don't turn up the light for a moment. It is so lovely." And down she crouched by the fire again. She was always cold . . . "without her little red flannel jacket, of course," thought Bertha.

At that moment Miss Fulton "gave the sign."

"Have you a garden?" said the cool, sleepy voice.

This was so exquisite on her part that all Bertha could do was to obey. She crossed the room, pulled the curtains apart, and opened those long windows.

"There!" she breathed.

And the two women stood side by side looking at the slender, flowering tree. Although it was so still it seemed, like the flame of a candle, to stretch up, to point, to quiver in the bright air, to grow taller and taller as they gazed—almost to touch the rim of the round, silver moon.

How long did they stand there? Both, as it were, caught in that circle of unearthly light, understanding each other perfectly, creatures of another world, and wondering what they were to do in this one with all this blissful treasure that burned in their bosoms and dropped, in silver flowers, from their hair and hands?

For ever—for a moment? And did Miss Fulton murmur: "Yes. Just *that.*" Or did Bertha dream it?

Then the light was snapped on and Face made the coffee and Harry said: "My dear Mrs. Knight, don't ask me about my baby. I never see her. I shan't feel the slightest interest in her until she has a lover," and Mug took his eye out of the conservatory for a moment and then put it under glass again and Eddie Warren drank his coffee and set down the cup with a face of anguish as though he had drunk and seen the spider.

"What I want to do is to give the young men a show. I believe London is simply teeming with first-chop, unwritten plays. What I want to say to 'em is: 'Here's the theatre. Fire ahead.' "

"You know, my dear, I am going to decorate a room for the Jacob Nathans. Oh, I am so tempted to do a fried-fish scheme, with the backs of the chairs shaped like frying pans and lovely chip potatoes embroidered all over the curtains."

"The trouble with our young writing men is that they are still too romantic. You can't put out to sea without being seasick and wanting a basin. Well, why won't they have the courage of those basins?"

"A *dreadful* poem about a *girl* who was *violated* by a beggar *without* a nose in a lit-tle wood. . . ."

Miss Fulton sank into the lowest, deepest chair and Harry handed round the cigarettes.

From the way he stood in front of her shaking the silver box and saying abruptly: "Egyptian? Turkish? Virginian? They're all mixed up," Bertha realized that she not only bored him; he really disliked her. And she decided from the way Miss Fulton said: "No, thank you, I won't smoke," that she felt it, too, and was hurt.

"Oh, Harry, don't dislike her. You are quite wrong about her. She's wonderful, wonderful. And, besides, how can you feel so differently about someone who means so much to me. I shall try to tell you when we are in bed to-night what has been happening. What she and I have shared."

At those last words something strange and almost terrifying darted into Bertha's mind. And this something blind and smiling whispered to her: "Soon these people will go. The house will be quiet—quiet. The lights will be out. And you and he will be alone together in the dark room —the warm bed. . . ."

She jumped up from her chair and ran over to the piano.

"What a pity someone does not play!" she cried. "What a pity somebody does not play."

For the first time in her life Bertha Young desired her husband.

Oh, she'd loved him—she'd been in love with him, of course, in every other way, but just not in that way. And, equally, of course, she'd understood that he was different. They'd discussed it so often. It had worried her dreadfully at first to find that she was so cold, but after a time it had not seemed to matter. They were so frank with each other—such good pals. That was the best of being modern.

But now—ardently! ardently! The word ached in her ardent body! Was this what that feeling of bliss had been leading up to? But then then——

"My dear," said Mrs. Norman Knight, "you know our shame. We are the victims of time and train. We live in Hampstead. It's been so nice."

"I'll come with you into the hall," said Bertha. "I loved having you. But you must not miss the last train. That's so awful, isn't it?"

"Have a whisky, Knight, before you go?" called Harry.

"No, thanks, old chap."

Bertha squeezed his hand for that as she shook it.

"Good night, good-bye," she cried from the top step, feeling that this self of hers was taking leave of them for ever.

When she got back into the drawing-room the others were on the move.

". . . Then you can come part of the way in my taxi."

"I shall be *so* thankful *not* to have to face *another* drive *alone* after my *dreadful* experience."

"You can get a taxi at the rank just at the end of the street. You won't have to walk more than a few yards."

"That's a comfort. I'll go and put on my coat."

Miss Fulton moved towards the hall and Bertha was following when Harry almost pushed past.

"Let me help you."

Bertha knew that he was repenting his rudeness—she let him go. What a boy he was in some ways—so impulsive—so—simple.

And Eddie and she were left by the fire.

"I *wonder* if you have seen Bilks' *new* poem called *Table d'Hôte,*" said Eddie softly. "It's *so* wonderful. In the last Anthology. Have you got a copy? I'd *so* like to *show* it to you. It begins with an *incredibly* beautiful line: 'Why Must it Always be Tomato Soup?' "

"Yes," said Bertha. And she moved noiselessly to a table opposite the drawing-room door and Eddie glided noiselessly after her. She picked up the little book and gave it to him; they had not made a sound.

While he looked it up she turned her head towards the hall. And she saw . . . Harry with Miss Fulton's coat in his arms and Miss Fulton with her back turned to him and her head bent. He tossed the coat away, put his hands on her shoulders and turned her violently to him. His lips said: "I adore you," and Miss Fulton laid her moonbeam fingers on his cheeks and smiled her sleepy smile. Harry's nostrils quivered; his lips curled back in a hideous grin while he whispered: "To-morrow," and with her eyelids Miss Fulton said: "Yes."

"Here it is," said Eddie. " 'Why Must it Always be Tomato Soup?' It's so *deeply* true, don't you feel? Tomato soup is so *dreadfully* eternal."

"If you prefer," said Harry's voice, very loud, from the hall, "I can phone you a cab to come to the door."

"Oh, no. It's not necessary," said Miss Fulton, and she came up to Bertha and gave her the slender fingers to hold.

"Good-bye. Thank you so much."

"Good-bye," said Bertha.

Miss Fulton held her hand a moment longer.

"Your lovely pear tree!" she murmured.

And then she was gone, with Eddie following, like the black cat following the grey cat.

"I'll shut up shop," said Harry, extravagantly cool and collected.
"Your lovely pear tree—pear tree—pear tree!"
Bertha simply ran over to the long windows.
"Oh, what is going to happen now?" she cried.
But the pear tree was as lovely as ever and as full of flower and as still.

Idenborough

~~~~~~

SYLVIA TOWNSEND WARNER
(English, 1893–1978)

The car was a Rover, a 1939 model. In the December of that year
Amabel's husband, Thomas Serpell, had bought it to put by, saying that
at the end of a war there is no decent metal or decent leather left. It was
still on blocks when, three years later, he died.

When wealthy men die, there is always a sensation of poverty, and
under the stress of death-duties the executors had spoken of selling the
car; but Thomas, Amabel's stepson, had cabled from Canada, where he
was training pilots, that it must be kept, so it remained in the garage,
draped in dust sheets and looking like a funeral trophy. Amabel also
remained, living on with her mother-in-law for company, a dull, kind,
preservative life, so preservative that when Thomas finally came home he
exclaimed, 'Good God, Amabel, is this really you? You look like my
niece!' Her smooth skin and her flowering full lips were the more remarkable for being encountered among Serpell aunts and cousins, fine large
specimens of a North Country stock, brief in bloom and durable as pigskin. Amabel, an alien, had reversed this. She looked young and she felt
elderly.

Her answer was defensive: 'Rather fat for a niece, Thomas.'

'Well, that will soon come off,' he said. 'You should do exercises, and swim, and play tennis.' Sojourning for so long in a new world. Thomas had brought back an embarrassing insistence on youthfulness, and smartness and spryness.

'Now we must get out the Rover,' said his grandmother, speaking as though it were a ceremonial teapot.

Thomas replied that it was scarcely worth the trouble, since in Cambridge he would use a bicycle. Thomas had also brought back a craving for culture and scholasticism and was going to Cambridge to read history.

When Thomas came north for Christmas, he brought his friend, Winter Gregory. Winter Gregory was a don, a kind of being Amabel had never set eyes on. She wished she had the sangfroid of her mother-in-law, who had never seen a don either but supposed he would eat and drink like any other mortal. After a couple of days, it was evident that he could fall in love like any other mortal, too. Amabel ceased to feel elderly, and refused his first proposal of marriage with such headlong vigour that the most cloistered and artless don might have taken hope from it. Winter was not notably cloistered. He had viewed with horror the bald solitaire diamond with which the deceased Mr Serpell had expressed his intentions of matrimony. The ring that he took with him on his second visit spelled out *Regard* with a ruby, an emerald, a garnet, an amethyst, another ruby and a quite moderate diamond. It looked very pretty on Amabel's old-fashioned small hand. There seemed no reason why the hand should not immediately become his, but she evaded marriage for over a year, and was finally routed into it by her mother-in-law's scorn for a woman of forty who hadn't the spunk to take a second husband. Her rough tongue succeeded where Thomas's encouragement had failed. Amabel had been abashed by the encouragements. It seemed to her like robbing a blind beggar to accept so much kind approval from her stepson when for the second time in her life she was violently in love, and on this occasion, too, not with his father.

The Rover preceded her to Cambridge. Thomas had given it to Winter as a wedding-present. This was so much what Thomas's father would have done that Amabel had a polyandrous impression that Thomas's father had almost done so.

Now, in the second year of their happy marriage, the car was swivelling along lanes and byroads whose banks were brooched with primroses and veined with the heavy blue of wild hyacinths still in bud. Winter had wanted to visit Amabel's birthplace in Somerset. She had not seen it since her fifth year, when her father went to a London parish, and there was very little she recognized except an archway under which he had driven her hoop. She felt a complete stranger and sightseer. It was the Cockney Winter who knew Priddy in the Mendips and the sudden violent view of the Bristol Channel from the road above Clapton-in-Gordano, and who, saying calmly, 'We shall find it down here,' turned the car down a one-in-five rabbit-run. But it was Wiltshire, he said, as they crossed the county boundary—especially the unattended-to, undramatic country north of Salisbury Plain—that he was more at home in.

'Stonehenge,' said Amabel, catching at something she could be sure of. 'I should like to see Stonehenge.'

Without comment on her geography, he began to drive south-eastward toward the smooth rampart of the chalk. On the timelessness of Salisbury Plain, Amabel suddenly became aware that the Rover looked somewhat out of date.

'You know, Winter, it's only just struck me that this car does look rather odd—spinsterish, and as if we ought to be wearing toques trimmed with autumn leaves.'

'If I had to choose between a spinster and a chromium-plated strumpet —' He broke off, and pointed ahead. 'Look!'

'Oh!' Her exclamation sounded like a cry of pity. 'Oh, Winter, is that Stonehenge?'

'Are you disappointed?'

'No! But somehow I feel so sorry for it. It is so small, so very small, and so neat.'

'Amabel, you don't know how I love you for things like that. You are the only perfectly sincere person I have ever known.'

He halted the car. Presently, he turned it and they drove away. She felt vaguely surprised. Winter's spendthrift treatment of historical monuments was something she could not get accustomed to. Thomas her husband never quitted a castle or a waterfall (he had been equally prone to both) without having, as he said 'thoroughly taken it in.' Thomas her stepson, though immune to nature and the Middle Ages, could take quite as long to absorb a portico, and talked much more. At times, she felt a certain nostalgia for the Serpell method of sightseeing. Though tiring to the legs, it was restful to the mind; there was none of this hit-or-miss, sharpshooting responsibility for saying the right thing. Having been so lucky with Stonehenge, she was the more anxiously aware of her inadequacies during the rest of the day's journey, for when they turned aside for a manor house, she could think of nothing but living in it, and when Winter stopped the car with a shout of laughter before a Baptist chapel, she asked him what he was laughing at. Above all, she was estranged by the duplicity of the landscape, so intricate and so indeterminate. After the large, hymn-tune solemnity of the North of England, it was perplexing as a fugue.

She's tired, Winter thought, and in his concern for her he lost his sense of direction, and took a wrong turning. He began to hurry, and so overshot a signpost, and had to back. It stood where the road branched left and right, and the left-hand pointer read, 'Great Wimble 9, Oxford 31.'

Sighing with relief, he said, 'There! Oxford. We shan't be long now. After Wimble, we shall strike a main road.' Even as he spoke, he noticed the right-hand pointer 'Idenborough! I had no idea we were so near it.'

'Ten miles,' Amabel said. 'And a dreadful road.'

'Yes, but Idenborough at the end of it. It's almost the loveliest small town in England, and there's quite a good inn. Why don't we spend the night there, instead of in Oxford?'

Amabel had read the name before he spoke it, and had been nerving herself to hear it spoken. It was at Idenborough, twenty years before, that she and Harry had spent a day, and two long autumn nights lying in a lumpy bed—so short a time, and yet outweighing all the rest of her life. She had gone there by train, abandoning her Thomases on the pretext of an old school friend just leaving for India. Blinded by excitement and sick headache, she had got out at a station on a branch line, where Harry was waiting on the platform, his face so stern with love that for a moment she had not recognized him, while he, glaring at the other end of the train, was so sunk in his conviction that she had changed her mind that she was compelled to take him by the sleeve and shake him before he noticed her. All rapture, all romance, and all leave-taking were sealed up under that word, *Idenborough,* and now it was a name on a signpost, and a place where she and Winter might spend the night.

'Oxford's only thirty miles on, and you wanted to show me Oxford.' Her voice shook as if she had been running.

Glancing round, he saw that she looked pale. Oxford be damned, with its bells and its buses, and its admirers settling with veneration on all the fakes! 'Oxford can wait,' he said, and turned off for Idenborough.

If only I could sometimes tell the truth, if only I could learn to speak out, she thought—and remembered how, earlier in the day, Winter had praised her for her sincerity. But now it was too late. Deceit must accumulate on deceit, and with her second husband she would visit Idenborough, where she had cuckolded her first one. Winter was assuring her how much she would like Idenborough, and comparing its grape-coloured roof-tiles with roofs in Burgundy, while, faithless once again, she sat staring ahead, licking her lips with excitement as she waited for the first recognition. The lane ran into a main road. Ahead was a wide, placid street, and the silhouette of a church tower, old and owlish. She did not particularly recognize anything, but no doubt that was because they were entering from another direction. The tower had been there, of course, for she remembered the bells chiming the hours and the quarters, and Harry saying that he had an uncle whose conversation was precisely similar. And, in fact, what did she remember of Idenborough? So little— only everything. But when Winter stopped in front of a porch surmounted by a mild bear painted plum colour, she nearly said, 'This isn't the right hotel.'

While he was garaging the car, she followed the servant to the room allotted to them, her legs moving under her like the legs of some other person, legs imperfectly attached and rather too short for her. Strewing her coat and gloves and bag on twin beds of blameless springs, she went to the window. Roofs of weathered tiles, fig trees and lilacs emerging from walled gardens, the leaden haunches of a church, and beyond, a row of tall poplars. . . . She knew those trees. They signalled everything into place. The hotel where she had stayed with Harry must be at the farther end of the town. There was the true Idenborough. The poplars grew close to that hotel, aligned along a bridle-path that led to a cemetery and the gasworks. There they had walked up and down, in a gentle drizzling rain, saying that it was really too wet to stay out any longer and yet continuing to walk up and down. And there she had known the inexhaustible melancholy of youth, extending below her like an ocean and endlessly surrounding her while she floated onward, immortally buoyant and serene.

When Winter came in, she turned from the window, saying, 'I am so glad we came here instead of Oxford. Shall we go out for a little walk?'

'Not till you've had a drink. I only hope I haven't gone and overtired you, jaunting about all day. Besides, it's nearly dinner-time.'

'Well, after dinner, then?'

The drink mounted lightly to her head. All through dinner, she felt a detached, competent animation, as though she were behaving to music. Exactly on the beat, she said, 'What horrible coffee! Don't let's waste time on it. I'd rather walk round Idenborough.'

The direction of the poplar trees was so perfectly established in her mind that she felt no impatience when Winter set off in the opposite direction, talking of a town hall. A lion and a unicorn decorated the town hall, plump and suave as though they were in sugar on a biscuit. They were just what Harry would have liked, and she almost wished that they had come this way instead of going by bus to that rather tiresome village with a wishing-well. Winter liked the lion and the unicorn, too, and agreed about the biscuit. They walked down several streets, pausing to admire doorways and converse with evening cats, and finding a chemist's shop still open and lit up like an Elizabethan jewel with its coloured flasks and rosy patent tonics, they went in for the pleasure of buying something in Idenborough. The purchase of a small hot-water bottle led to a long conversation between Winter and the chemist that wound its way to leeches and local survivals of traditional remedies, such as stolen potatoes and fried mice.

When they left the shop, the twilight had changed to a blue dusk, and Amabel could hear doors being shut and bolted. But still she was not impatient, though it was apparent that Winter had something more up his sleeve, some special beauty that he was saving for the last. While she was waiting in the chemist's shop, it occurred to her that if this evening were frittered away, there would still be to-morrow morning. It would be easy to make an excuse of wanting to shop by herself in order to buy him a surprise present, and then all she need do would be to find the railway station and from there retrace her way to the hotel and the poplar trees, and on the way back she could buy a mug. Idenborough was full of shops where mugs could be bought, and when you have taken the first step of deceiving a husband, nothing is easier than to go on.

Reposing on this, she accompanied Winter down a street so narrow that there was no inducement to stop and admire anything. At the foot of the hill, the street turned sharply. She received a sudden impression of light and space, and felt the air freshened, and heard the slap of water against stone. They were on a quay, and before them extended a narrow bridge of many arches. Half-way across it, he stopped.

'Look, Amabel. That's why I wanted to bring you here.'

Behind them the town, catching the revenant light of the eastern sky, was a muddle of brown and mulberry-coloured velvets. The tower and the high nave of the church rose above it, and the sky showed through the clerestory windows. But she only looked at it long enough to steady herself, and then returned her gaze to the wide, pale river, whose waters swirled with a kind of sleepwalking impetus from between the piers of the bridge. So wide a river. . . . How could they not have known there was this river? She looked along its course and saw on the far bank a row of poplar trees, rising lugubriously tall from an unlit, unbroken flatness of water-meadows.

Laying her hand on the parapet and finding it quite real, she asked, 'What river is this?'

'The Thames.'

Another strong swirl of water emerged from under the bridge and spread itself onward, as though in calm assent and confirmation.

'What did you say this place was called?'

'Idenborough.'

A small black dazzle flashed in front of her and disappeared under the bridge.

'A bat,' she said, fastening on a certainty.

Not hearing her, he went on, 'Idenborough Regis, to give it its full name. There's another Idenborough, in Bedfordshire. A dull place— though now I suppose it glitters with cinemas and garages, for there's an aerodrome near by.'

After a while, still looking down on the river, Amabel said, 'Is there anywhere you haven't been?'

There was such rancour in her voice that he was nearly stampeded into asking her if she felt tired. Taking his cue from an oncoming yawn, he replied, 'Bed, perhaps. Judging from my present sensations, I have never been to bed.'

The yawn achieved itself, and on its close he took her by the arm and began walking back to the hotel.

'I expect it's driving that old-fashioned car that tires you,' she said.

His car, his dearest possession (since one does not number a wife among possessions), which throughout their holiday of by-roads and hysterical contours had behaved like a duchess—not satisfied with attacking him, Amabel must needs turn against the Rover, too. This time, he asserted himself. 'With a good car, it's mileage that counts, Amabel, not years. The same with wives.'

'Yes, but it *is* an old car, Winter. One's only got to look at it to see that. And though it's very chivalrous of you to feel affection for your old dowdy. . . .'

All the way back to the hotel she talked in this strain, flagellating herself under the guise of depreciating the car, condoling with him on his faithfulness to an old car and an ageing wife. It rent his heart to hear her. It appalled his heart to admit an identity between his gentle, modest, complying Amabel and this provincial harridan at his side.

She saw his grief and his dismay, but she dared not weaken to them. If she were to change her harsh tune, if for one moment between now and when she heard him grunt and fall from her into the solitude of sleep she were to let him be kind to her, she would be done for; she would give way and tell him about Harry and the other Idenborough, and how, merely by her own despicable shilly-shallying and playing for safety, there had been no more to tell. To Winter, unjudging, unblaming, possibly even approving, it would seem next to nothing, and by length of time diminished to nothing at all. Indeed, there was not much of it: two nights and a day, a rapture so inattentively, unbelievingly entertained that she did not even know what county Idenborough was in. Unbelievingly entertained, weakly lost, negligently remembered (for months at a time she did not give it a thought), yet it was all she had. Thinking this, she reversed the thought. She was all it had. It existed by her secrecy; to speak of it would be to dismiss it, like the small crystal world of a bubble, into common air. Any infidelity but that.

Fard

ALDOUS HUXLEY
(English, 1894–1963)

They had been quarrelling now for nearly three-quarters of an hour. Muted and inarticulate, the voices floated down the corridor, from the other end of the flat. Stooping over her sewing, Sophie wondered, without much curiosity, what it was all about this time. It was Madame's voice that she heard most often. Shrill with anger and indignant with tears, it burst out in gusts, in gushes. Monsieur was more self-controlled, and his deeper voice was too softly pitched to penetrate easily the closed doors and to carry along the passage. To Sophie, in her cold little room, the quarrel sounded, most of the time, like a series of monologues by Madame, interrupted by strange and ominous silences. But every now and then Monsieur seemed to lose his temper outright, and then there was no silence between the gusts, but a harsh, deep, angry shout. Madame kept up her loud shrillness continuously and without flagging; her voice had, even in anger, a curious, level monotony. But Monsieur spoke now loudly, now softly, with emphases and modulations and sudden outbursts, so that his contributions to the squabble, when they were audible, sounded like a series of separate explosions. Bow, wow, wow-wow-wow, wow—a dog barking rather slowly.

After a time Sophie paid no more heed to the noise of quarrelling. She was mending one of Madame's camisoles, and the work required all her attention. She felt very tired; her body ached all over. It had been a hard day; so had yesterday, so had the day before. Every day was a hard day, and she wasn't so young as she had been. Two years more and she'd be fifty. Every day had been a hard day ever since she could remember. She thought of the sacks of potatoes she used to carry when she was a little girl in the country. Slowly, slowly she was walking along the dusty road with the sack over her shoulder. Ten steps more; she could manage that. Only it never was the end; one always had to begin again.

She looked up from her sewing, moved her head from side to side, blinked. She had begun to see lights and spots of colour dancing before her eyes; it often happened to her now. A sort of yellowish bright worm was wriggling up towards the right-hand corner of her field of vision; and though it was always moving upwards, upwards, it was always there in the same place. And there were stars of red and green that snapped and brightened and faded all around the worm. They moved between her and her sewing; they were there when she shut her eyes. After a moment she went on with her work; Madame wanted her camisole most particularly to-morrow morning. But it was difficult to see round the worm.

There was suddenly a great increase of noise from the other end of the corridor. A door had opened; words articulated themselves.

'. . . bien tort, mon ami, si tu crois que je suis ton esclave. Je ferai ce que je voudrai.'

'Moi aussi.' Monsieur uttered a harsh, dangerous laugh. There was the sound of heavy footsteps in the passage, a rattling in the umbrella stand; then the front door banged.

Sophie looked down again at her work. Oh, the worm, the coloured stars, the aching fatigue in all her limbs! If one could only spend a whole day in bed—in a huge bed, feathery, warm, and soft, all the day long . . .

The ringing of the bell startled her. It always made her jump, that furious wasp-like buzzer. She got up, put her work down on the table, smoothed her apron, set straight her cap, and stepped out into the corridor. Once more the bell buzzed furiously. Madame was impatient.

'At last, Sophie. I thought you were never coming.'

Sophie said nothing; there was nothing to say. Madame was standing in front of the open wardrobe. A bundle of dresses hung over her arm, and there were more of them lying in a heap on the bed.

'Une beauté à la Rubens,' her husband used to call her when he was in an amorous mood. He liked these massive, splendid, great women. None of your flexible drain-pipes for him. 'Hélène Fourmont' was his pet name for her.

'Some day,' Madame used to tell her friends, 'some day I really must go to the Louvre and see my portrait. By Rubens, you know. It's extraordinary that one should have lived all one's life in Paris and never have seen the Louvre. Don't you think so?'

She was superb to-night. Her cheeks were flushed; her blue eyes shone with an unusual brilliance between their long lashes; her short, red-brown hair had broken wildly loose.

'To-morrow, Sophie,' she said dramatically, 'we start for Rome. To-morrow morning.' She unhooked another dress from the wardrobe as she spoke, and threw it on to the bed. With the movement her dressing-gown flew open, and there was a vision of ornate underclothing and white exuberant flesh. 'We must pack at once.'

'For how long, Madame?'

'A fortnight, three months—how should I know?'

'It makes a difference, Madame.'

'The important thing is to get away. I shall not return to this house, after what has been said to me to-night, till I am humbly asked to.'

'We had better take the large trunk, then, Madame; I will go and fetch it.'

The air in the box-room was sickly with the smell of dust and leather. The big trunk was jammed in a far corner. She had to bend and strain at it in order to pull it out. The worm and the coloured stars flickered before her eyes; she felt dizzy when she straightened herself up. 'I'll help you to pack, Sophie,' said Madame, when the servant returned, dragging the heavy trunk after her. What a death's-head the old woman looked nowadays! She hated having old, ugly people near her. But Sophie was so efficient; it would be madness to get rid of her.

'Madame need not trouble.' There would be no end to it, Sophie knew, if Madame started opening drawers and throwing things about. 'Madame had much better go to bed. It's late.'

No, no. She wouldn't be able to sleep. She was to such a degree enervated. These men . . . What an embeastment! One was not their slave. One would not be treated in this way.

Sophie was packing. A whole day in bed, in a huge, soft bed, like Madame's. One would doze, one would wake up for a moment, one would doze again.

'His latest game,' Madame was saying indignantly, 'is to tell me he hasn't got any money. I'm not to buy any clothes, he says. Too grotesque.

I can't go about naked, can I?' She threw out her hands. 'And as for
saying he can't afford, that's simply nonsense. He can, perfectly well.
Only he's mean, mean, horribly mean. And if he'd only do a little honest
work, for a change, instead of writing silly verses and publishing them at
his own expense, he'd have plenty and to spare.' She walked up and down
the room. 'Besides,' she went on, 'there's his old father. What's he for, I
should like to know? "You must be proud of having a poet for a husband," he says.' She made her voice quaver like an old man's. 'It's all I
can do not to laugh in his face. "And what beautiful verses Hégésippe
writes about you! What passion, what fire!" ' Thinking of the old man,
she grimaced, wobbled her head, shook her finger, doddered on her legs.
'And when one reflects that poor Hégésippe is bald, and dyes the few
hairs he has left.' She laughed. 'As for the passion he talks so much about
in his beastly verses,' she laughed—'that's all pure invention. But, my
good Sophie, what are you thinking of? Why are you packing that hideous old green dress?'

Sophie pulled out the dress without saying anything. Why did the
woman choose this night to look so terribly ill? She had a yellow face and
blue teeth. Madame shuddered; it was too horrible. She ought to send her
to bed. But, after all, the work had to be done. What could one do about
it? She felt more than ever aggrieved.

'Life is terrible.' Sighing, she sat down heavily on the edge of the bed.
The buoyant springs rocked her gently once or twice before they settled
to rest. 'To be married to a man like this. I shall soon be getting old and
fat. And never once unfaithful. But look how he treats me.' She got up
again and began to wander aimlessly about the room. 'I won't stand it,
though,' she burst out. She had halted in front of the long mirror, and
was admiring her own splendid tragic figure. No one would believe, to
look at her, that she was over thirty. Behind the beautiful tragedian she
could see in the glass a thin, miserable, old creature, with a yellow face
and blue teeth, crouching over the trunk. Really, it was too disagreeable.
Sophie looked like one of those beggar women one sees on a cold morning, standing in the gutter. Does one hurry past, trying not to look at
them? Or does one stop, open one's purse, and give them one's copper
and nickel—even as much as a two-franc note, if one has no change? But
whatever one did, one always felt uncomfortable, one always felt apolo-
getic for one's furs. That was what came of walking. If one had a car—
but that was another of Hégésippe's meannesses—one wouldn't, rolling

along behind closed windows, have to be conscious of them at all. She turned away from the glass.

'I won't stand it,' she said, trying not to think of the beggar women, of blue teeth in a yellow face; 'I won't stand it.' She dropped into a chair. But think of a lover with a yellow face and blue, uneven teeth! She closed her eyes, shuddered at the thought. It would be enough to make one sick. She felt impelled to take another look: Sophie's eyes were the colour of greenish lead, quite without life. What was one to do about it? The woman's face was a reproach, an accusation. And besides, the sight of it was making her feel positively ill. She had never been so profoundly enervated.

Sophie rose slowly and with difficulty from her knees; an expression of pain crossed her face. Slowly she walked to the chest of drawers, slowly counted out six pairs of silk stockings. She turned back towards the trunk. The woman was a walking corpse!

'Life is terrible,' Madame repeated with conviction, 'terrible, terrible, terrible.'

She ought to send the woman to bed. But she would never be able to get her packing done by herself. And it was so important to get off tomorrow morning. She had told Hégésippe she would go, and he had simply laughed; he hadn't believed it. She must give him a lesson this time. In Rome she would see Luigino. Such a charming boy, and a marquis, too. Perhaps . . . But she could think of nothing but Sophie's face; the leaden eyes, the bluish teeth, the yellow, wrinkled skin.

'Sophie,' she said suddenly; it was with difficulty that she prevented herself screaming, 'look on my dressing-table. You'll see a box of rouge, the Dorin number twenty-four. Put a little on your cheeks. And there's a stick of lip salve in the right-hand drawer.'

She kept her eyes resolutely shut while Sophie got up—with what a horrible creaking of the joints!—walked over to the dressing-table, and stood there, rustling faintly, through what seemed an eternity. What a life, my God, what a life! Slow footsteps trailed back again. She opened her eyes. Oh, that was far better, far better.

'Thank you, Sophie. You look much less tired now.' She got up briskly. 'And now we must hurry.' Full of energy, she ran to the wardrobe. 'Goodness me,' she exclaimed, throwing up her hands, 'you've forgotten to put in my blue evening dress. How could you be so stupid, Sophie?'

Spring Sowing

LIAM O'FLAHERTY
(Irish, 1896–1984)

It was still dark when Martin Delaney and his wife Mary got up. Martin stood in his shirt by the window a long time looking out, rubbing his eyes and yawning, while Mary raked out the live coals that had lain hidden in the ashes on the hearth all night. Outside, cocks were crowing and a white streak was rising from the ground, as it were, and beginning to scatter the darkness. It was a February morning, dry, cold and starry.

The couple sat down to their breakfast of tea, bread and butter, in silence. They had only been married the previous autumn and it was hateful leaving a warm bed at such an early hour. They both felt in a bad humour and ate, wrapped in their thoughts. Martin, with his brown hair and eyes, his freckled face and his little fair moustache, looked too young to be married, and his wife looked hardly more than a girl, red-cheeked and blue-eyed, her black hair piled at the rear of her head with a large comb gleaming in the middle of the pile, Spanish fashion. They were both dressed in rough homespuns, and both wore the loose white frieze shirt that Inverara peasants use for work in the fields.

They ate in silence, sleepy and bad-humoured and yet on fire with excitement, for it was the first day of their first spring sowing as man and wife. And each felt the glamour of that day on which they were to open up the earth together and plant seeds in it. So they sat in silence and bad humour, for somehow the imminence of an event that had been long expected, loved, feared and prepared for made them dejected. Mary, with her shrewd woman's mind, munched her bread and butter and thought of

. . . Oh, what didn't she think of? Of as many things as there are in life does a woman think in the first joy and anxiety of her mating. But Martin's mind was fixed on one thought. Would he be able to prove himself a man worthy of being the head of a family by doing his spring sowing well?

In the barn after breakfast, when they were getting the potato seeds and the line for measuring the ground and the spade, a cross word or two passed between them, and when Martin fell over a basket in the half-darkness of the barn, he swore and said that a man would be better off dead than . . . But before he could finish whatever he was going to say, Mary had her arms around his waist and her face to his. "Martin," she said, "let us not begin this day cross with one another." And there was a tremor in her voice. And somehow, as they embraced and Martin kept mumbling in his awkward peasant's voice, "pulse of my heart, treasure of my life," and such traditional phrases, all their irritation and sleepiness left them. And they stood there embracing until at last Martin pushed her from him with pretended roughness and said: "Come, come, girl, it will be sunset before we begin at this rate."

Still, as they walked silently in their rawhide shoes through the little hamlet, there was not a soul about. Lights were glimmering in the windows of a few cabins. The sky had a big grey crack in it in the east, as if it were going to burst in order to give birth to the sun. Birds were singing somewhere at a distance. Martin and Mary rested their baskets of seeds on a fence outside the village and Martin whispered to Mary proudly: "We are first, Mary." And they both looked back at the little cluster of cabins that was the centre of their world, with throbbing hearts. For the joy of spring had now taken complete hold of them.

They reached the little field where they were to sow. It was a little triangular patch of ground under an ivy-covered limestone hill. The little field had been manured with seaweed some weeks before, and the weeds had rotted and whitened on the grass. And there was a big red heap of fresh seaweed lying in a corner by the fence to be spread under the seeds as they were laid. Martin, in spite of the cold, threw off everything above his waist except his striped woollen shirt. Then he spat on his hands, seized his spade and cried: "Now you are going to see what kind of a man you have, Mary."

"There, now," said Mary, tying a little shawl closer under her chin.

"Aren't we boastful this early hour of the morning? Maybe I'll wait till sunset to see what kind of a man I have got."

The work began. Martin measured the ground by the southern fence for the first ridge, a strip of ground four feet wide, and he placed the line along the edge and pegged it at each end. Then he spread fresh seaweed over the strip. Mary filled her apron with seeds and began to lay them in rows, four, three, four. When she was a little distance down the ridge, Martin advanced with his spade to the head, eager to commence.

"Now in the name of God," he cried, spitting on his palms, "let us raise the first sod!"

"Oh, Martin, wait till I'm with you!" cried Mary, dropping her seeds on the ridge and running up to him. Her fingers outside her woollen mittens were numb with the cold, and she couldn't wipe them in her apron. Her cheeks seemed to be on fire. She put an arm round Martin's waist and stood looking at the green sod his spade was going to cut, with the excitement of a little child.

"Now for God's sake, girl, keep back!" said Martin gruffly. "Suppose anybody saw us trapesing about like this in the field of our spring sowing, what would they take us for but a pair of useless, soft, empty-headed people that would be sure to die of the hunger. Huh!" He spoke very rapidly, and his eyes were fixed on the ground before him. His eyes had a wild, eager light in them as if some primeval impulse were burning within his brain and driving out every other desire but that of asserting his manhood and of subjugating the earth.

"Oh, what do we care who is looking?" said Mary; but she drew back at the same time and gazed distantly at the ground. Then Martin cut the sod, and pressing the spade deep into the earth with his foot, he turned up the first sod with a crunching sound as the grass roots were dragged out of the earth. Mary sighed and walked back hurriedly to her seeds with furrowed brows. She picked up her seeds and began to spread them rapidly to drive out the sudden terror that had seized her at that moment when the first sod was turned up and she saw the fierce, hard look in her husband's eyes, that were unconscious of her presence. She became suddenly afraid of that pitiless, cruel earth, the peasant's slave master, that would keep her chained to hard work and poverty all her life until she would sink again into its bosom. Her short-lived love was gone. Henceforth she was only her husband's helper to till the earth. And Martin, absolutely without thought, worked furiously, covering the ridge with black earth, his sharp spade gleaming white as he whirled it sideways to beat the sods.

Then, as the sun rose, the little valley beneath the ivy-covered hills became dotted with white frieze shirts, and everywhere men worked madly, without speaking, and women spread seeds. There was no heat in the light of the sun, and there was a sharpness in the still thin air that made the men jump on their spade halts ferociously and beat the sods as if they were living enemies. Birds hopped silently before the spades, with their heads cocked sideways, watching for worms. Made brave by hunger, they often dashed under the spades to secure their food.

Then, when the sun reached a certain point, all the women went back to the village to get dinner for their men, and the men worked on without stopping. Then the women returned, almost running, each carrying a tin can with a flannel tied around it and a little bundle tied with a white cloth. Martin threw down his spade when Mary arrived back in the field. Smiling at one another they sat under the hill for their meal. It was the same as their breakfast, tea and bread and butter.

"Ah," said Martin, when he had taken a long draught of tea from his mug, "is there anything in this world as fine as eating dinner out in the open like this after doing a good morning's work? There, I have done two ridges and a half. That's more than any man in the village could do. Ha!" And he looked at his wife proudly.

"Yes, isn't it lovely," said Mary, looking at the black ridges wistfully. She was just munching her bread and butter. The hurried trip to the village and the trouble of getting the tea ready had robbed her of her appetite. She had to keep blowing at the turf fire with the rim of her skirt, and the smoke nearly blinded her. But now, sitting on that grassy knoll, with the valley all round glistening with fresh seaweed and a light smoke rising from the freshly turned earth, a strange joy swept over her. It overpowered that other feeling of dread that had been with her during the morning.

Martin ate heartily, revelling in his great thirst and his great hunger, with every pore of his body open to the pure air. And he looked around at his neighbours' fields boastfully, comparing them with his own. Then he looked at his wife's little round black head and felt very proud of having her as his own. He leaned back on his elbow and took her hand in his. Shyly and in silence, not knowing what to say and ashamed of their gentle feelings, for peasants are always ashamed of feeling refined, they finished eating and still sat hand in hand looking away into the distance. Everywhere the sowers were resting on little knolls, men, women and children sitting in silence. And the great calm of nature in spring filled the atmosphere around them. Everything seemed to sit still and wait until midday had passed. Only the gleaming sun chased westwards at a mighty pace, in and out through white clouds.

Then in a distant field an old man got up, took his spade and began to clean the earth from it with a piece of stone. The rasping noise carried a long way in the silence. That was the signal for a general rising all along the little valley. Young men stretched themselves and yawned. They walked slowly back to their ridges.

Martin's back and his wrists were getting a little sore, and Mary felt that if she stooped again over her seeds her neck would break, but neither said anything and soon they had forgotten their tiredness in the mechanical movement of their bodies. The strong smell of the upturned earth acted like a drug on their nerves.

In the afternoon, when the sun was strongest, the old men of the village came out to look at their people sowing. Martin's grandfather, almost bent double over his thick stick, stopped in the land outside the field and, groaning loudly, he leaned over the fence.

"God bless the work," he called wheezily.

"And you, grandfather," replied the couple together, but they did not stop working.

"Ha!" muttered the old man to himself. "Ha! He sows well and that woman is good, too. They are beginning well."

It was fifty years since he had begun with his Mary, full of hope and pride, and the merciless soil had hugged them to its bosom ever since, each spring without rest. But he did not think of that. The soil gives forgetfulness. Only the present is remembered in the spring, even by the aged who have spent their lives tilling the earth; so the old man, with his huge red nose and the spotted handkerchief tied around his skull under his black soft felt hat, watched his grandson work and gave him advice.

"Don't cut your sods so long," he would wheeze, "you are putting too much soil on your ridge."

"Ah, woman! Don't plant a seed so near the edge. The stalk will come out sideways."

And they paid no heed to him.

"Ah," grumbled the old man, "in my young days, when men worked from morning till night without tasting food, better work was done. But of course it can't be expected to be the same as it was. The breed is getting weaker. So it is."

Then he began to cough in his chest and hobbled away to another field where his son Michael was working.

By sundown Martin had five ridges finished. He threw down his spade and stretched himself. All his bones ached and he wanted to lie down and rest. "It's time to be going home, Mary," he said.

Mary straightened herself, but she was too tired to reply. She looked at Martin wearily and it seemed to her that it was a great many years since they had set out that morning. Then she thought of the journey home and the trouble of feeding the pigs, putting the fowls into their coops and getting the supper ready, and a momentary flash of rebellion against the slavery of being a peasant's wife crossed her mind. It passed in a moment. Martin was saying, as he dressed himself:

"Ha! My soul from the devil, it has been a good day's work. Five ridges done, and each one of them as straight as a steel rod. Begob, Mary, it's no boasting to say that ye might well be proud of being the wife of Martin Delaney. And that's not saying the whole of it, my girl. You did your share better than any woman in Inverara could do it this blessed day."

They stood for a few moments in silence, looking at the work they had done. All her dissatisfaction and weariness vanished from Mary's mind with the delicious feeling of comfort that overcame her at having done this work with her husband. They had done it together. They had planted seeds in the earth. The next day and the next and all their lives, when spring came they would have to bend their backs and do it until their hands and bones got twisted with rheumatism. But night would always bring sleep and forgetfulness.

As they walked home slowly, Martin walked in front with another peasant talking about the sowing, and Mary walked behind, with her eyes on the ground, thinking.

Cows were lowing at a distance.

Hand in Glove

❦

ELIZABETH BOWEN
(Anglo-Irish, 1899–1973)

Jasmine Lodge was favourably set on a residential, prettily-wooded hill-side in the south of Ireland, overlooking a river and, still better, the roofs of a lively garrison town. Around 1904, which was the flowering period of the Miss Trevors, girls could not have had a more auspicious home—the neighbourhood spun merrily round the military. Ethel and Elsie, a spirited pair, garnered the full advantage—no ball, hop, picnic, lawn tennis, croquet or boating party was complete without them; in winter, though they could not afford to hunt, they trimly bicycled to all meets, and on frosty evenings, with their guitars, set off to *soirées,* snug inside their cab in their fur-tipped capes.

They possessed an aunt, a Mrs Varley de Grey, *née* Elysia Trevor, a formerly notable local belle, who, drawn back again in her widowhood to what had been the scene of her early triumphs, occupied a back bedroom in Jasmine Lodge. Mrs Varley de Grey had had no luck: her splashing match, in its time the talk of two kingdoms, had ended up in disaster—the well-born captain in a cavalry regiment having gone so far as to blow out his brains in India, leaving behind him nothing but her and debts. Mrs Varley de Grey had returned from India with nothing but seven large trunks crammed with recent finery; and she also had been impaired by shock. This had taken place while Ethel and Elsie, whose father had married late, were still unborn—so it was that, for as long as the girls recalled, their aunt had been the sole drawback to Jasmine Lodge. Their parents had orphaned them, somewhat thoughtlessly, by simultaneously dying of scarlet fever when Ethel was just out and Elsie soon to be—they were therefore left lacking a chaperone and, with their gift for putting everything to some use, propped the aunt up in order that she might play that role. Only when her peculiarities became too marked did they feel it necessary to withdraw her: by that time, however, all the surrounding ladies could be said to compete for the honour of taking into society the sought-after Miss Trevors. From then on, no more was seen or heard of Mrs Varley de Grey. ('Oh, just a trifle unwell, but nothing much!') She remained upstairs, at the back: when the girls were giving one of their little parties, or a couple of officers came to call, the key of her room would be turned in the outer lock.

The girls hung Chinese lanterns from the creepered veranda, and would sit lightly strumming on their guitars. Not less fascinating was their badinage, accompanied by a daring flash of the eyes. They were known as the clever Miss Trevors, not because of any taint of dogmatism or book-learning—no, when a gentleman cried, 'Those girls have brains!' he meant it wholly in admiration—but because of their accomplishments, ingenuity and agility. They took leading parts in theatricals, lent spirit to numbers of drawing-room games, were naughty mimics, and sang duets. Nor did their fingers lag behind their wits—they constructed lampshades, crêpe paper flowers and picturesque hats; and, above all, varied their dresses marvellously—no one could beat them for ideas, nipping, slashing or fitting. Once more allowing nothing to go to waste, they had remodelled the trousseau out of their aunt's trunks, causing sad old tulles and tarlatans, satins and *moiré* taffetas, to appear to have come from Paris only today. They re-stitched spangles, pressed ruffles crisp, and revived many a corsage of squashed silk roses. They went somewhat softly about that task, for the trunks were all stored in the attic immediately over the back room.

They wore their clothes well. 'A pin on either of those two would look smart!' declared other girls. All that they were short of was evening gloves—they had two pairs each, which they had been compelled to buy. *What* could have become of Mrs Varley de Grey's presumably sumptuous numbers of this item, they were unable to fathom, and it was too bad. Had gloves been overlooked in her rush from India?—or, were they here, in that *one* trunk the Trevors could not get at? All other locks had yielded to pulls or pickings, or the sisters found keys to fit them, or they had used the tool-box; but this last stronghold defied them. In that sad little soiled silk sack, always on her person, Mrs Varley de Grey, they became convinced, hoarded the operative keys, along with some frippery rings and brooches—all true emeralds, pearls and diamonds having been long ago, as they knew, sold. Such contrariety on their aunt's part irked them—meanwhile, gaieties bore hard on their existing gloves. Last thing at nights when they came in, last thing in the evenings before they went out, they would manfully dab away at the fingertips. So, it must be admitted that a long whiff of benzine pursued them as they whirled round the ballroom floor.

They were tall and handsome—nothing so soft as pretty, but in those days it was a vocation to be a handsome girl; many of the best marriages had been made by such. They carried themselves imposingly, had good busts and shoulders, waists firm under the whalebone, and straight backs. Their features were striking, their colouring high; low on their foreheads bounced dark mops of curls. Ethel was, perhaps, the dominant one, but both girls were pronounced to be full of character.

Whom, and still more when, did they mean to marry? They had already seen regiments out and in; for quite a number of years, it began to seem, bets in the neighbourhood had been running high. Sympathetic spy-glasses were trained on the conspicuous gateway to Jasmine Lodge; each new cavalier was noted. The only trouble might be, their promoters claimed, that the clever Trevors were always so surrounded that they had not a moment in which to turn or choose. Or otherwise, could it possibly be that the admiration aroused by Ethel and Elsie, and their now institutional place in the local scene, scared out more tender feeling from the masculine breast? It came to be felt, and perhaps by the girls themselves, that, having lingered so long and so puzzlingly, it was up to them to bring off (like their aunt) a *coup*. Society around this garrison town had long plumed itself upon its romantic record; summer and winter, Cupid shot his darts. Lush scenery, the oblivion of all things else bred by the steamy climate, and perpetual gallivanting—all were conducive. Ethel's and Elsie's names, it could be presumed, were by now murmured wherever the Union Jack flew. Nevertheless, it was time they should decide.

Ethel's decision took place late one evening. She set her cap at the second son of an English marquess. Lord Fred had come on a visit, for the fishing, to a mansion some miles down the river from Jasmine Lodge. He first made his appearance, with the rest of the house party, at one of the more resplendent military balls, and was understood to be a man-about-town. The civilian glint of his pince-nez, at once serene and superb, instantaneously wrought, with his great name, on Ethel's heart. She beheld him, and the assembled audience, with approbation, looked on at the moment so big with fate. The truth, it appeared in a flash, was that Ethel, though so condescending with her charms, had not from the first been destined to love a soldier; and that here, after long attrition, her answer was. Lord Fred was, by all, at once signed over to her. For his part, he responded to her attentions quite gladly, though in a somewhat dazed way. If he did not so often dance with her—indeed, how could he, for she was much besought?—he could at least be perceived to gaze. At a swiftly organized river picnic, the next evening, he by consent fell to Ethel's lot—she had spent the foregoing morning snipping and tacking at a remaining muslin of Mrs Varley de Grey's, a very fresh forget-me-not-dotted pattern. The muslin did not survive the evening out, for when the moon should have risen, rain poured into the boats. Ethel's good-humoured drollery carried all before it, and Lord Fred wrapped his blazer around her form.

Next day, more rain; and all felt flat. At Jasmine Lodge, the expectant deck chairs had to be hurried in from the garden, and the small close rooms, with their greeneried windows and plentiful bric-à-brac, gave out a stuffy, resentful, indoor smell. The maid was out; Elsie was lying down with a migraine; so it devolved on Ethel to carry up Mrs Varley de Grey's tea—the invalid set very great store by tea, and her manifestations by door rattlings, sobs and mutters were apt to become disturbing if it did not appear. Ethel, with the not particularly dainty tray, accordingly entered the back room, this afternoon rendered dark by its outlook into a dripping uphill wood. The aunt, her visage draped in a cobweb shawl, was as usual sitting up in bed. '*Aha,*' she at once cried, screwing one eye up and glittering round at Ethel with the other, 'so what's all this in the wind today?'

Ethel, as she lodged the meal on the bed, shrugged her shoulders, saying: 'I'm in a hurry.'

'No doubt you are. The question is, will you get him?'

'Oh, drink your tea!' snapped Ethel, her colour rising.

The old wretch responded by popping a lump of sugar into her cheek, and sucking at it while she fixed her wink on her niece. She then observed: '*I* could tell you a thing or two!'

'We've had enough of *your* fabrications, Auntie!'

'Fabrications!' croaked Mrs Varley de Grey. 'And who's been the fabricator, I'd like to ask? Who's so nifty with the scissors and needle? Who's been going a-hunting in my clothes?'

'Oh, what a fib!' exclaimed Ethel, turning her eyes up. 'Those old musty miserable bundles of things of yours—would Elsie or I consider laying a finger on them?'

Mrs Varley de Grey replied, as she sometimes did, by heaving up and throwing the tray at Ethel. Nought, therefore, but cast-off kitchen china nowadays was ever exposed to risk; and the young woman, not trying to gather the debris up, statuesquely, thoughtfully stood with her arms folded, watching tea steam rise from the carpet. Today, the effort required seemed to have been too much for Aunt Elysia, who collapsed on her pillows, faintly blue in the face. 'Rats in the attic,' she muttered. *I've* heard them, rats in the attic! Now where's my tea?'

'You've had it,' said Ethel, turning to leave the room. However, she paused to study a photograph in a tarnished, elaborate silver frame. 'Really quite an Adonis, poor Uncle Harry.—From the first glance, you say, he never looked back?'

'My lovely tea,' said her aunt, beginning to sob.

As Ethel slowly put down the photograph, her eyes could be seen to calculate, her mouth hardened and a reflective cast came over her brow. Step by step, once more she approached the bed, and, as she did so, altered her tune. She suggested, in a beguiling tone: 'You said you could tell me a thing or two . . . ?'

Time went on; Lord Fred, though forever promising, still failed to come quite within Ethel's grasp. Ground gained one hour seemed to be lost the next—it seemed, for example, that things went better for Ethel in the afternoons, in the open air, than at the dressier evening functions. It was when she swept down on him in full plumage that Lord Fred seemed to contract. Could it be that he feared his passions?—she hardly thought so. Or, did her complexion not light up well? When there was a question of dancing, he came so late that her programme already was black with other names, whereupon he would heave a gallant sigh. When they did take the floor together, he held her so far at arm's length, and with his face turned so far away, that when she wished to address him she had to shout—she told herself this must be the London style, but it piqued her, naturally. Next morning, all would be as it was before, with nobody so completely assiduous as Lord Fred—but, through it all, he still never came to the point. And worse, the days of his visit were running out; he would soon be back in the heart of the London Season. 'Will you ever get him, Ethel, now, do you think?' Elsie asked, with trying solicitude, and no doubt the neighbourhood wondered also.

She conjured up all her fascinations. But was something further needed, to do the trick?

It was now that she began to frequent her aunt.

In that dank little back room looking into the hill, proud Ethel humbled herself, to prise out the secret. Sessions were close and long. Elsie, in mystification outside the door, heard the dotty voice of their relative rising, falling, with, now and then, bloodcurdling little knowing laughs. Mrs Varley de Grey was back in the golden days. Always, though, of a sudden it would break off, drop back into pleas, whimpers and jagged breathing. No doctor, though she constantly asked for one, had for years been allowed to visit Mrs Varley de Grey—the girls saw no reason for that expense, or for the interference which might follow. Aunt's affliction, they swore, was confined to the head; all she required was quiet, and that she got. Knowing, however, how gossip spreads, they would let no servant near her for more than a minute or two, and then with one of themselves on watch at the door. They had much to bear from the foetid state of her room.

'You don't think you'll kill her, Ethel?' the out-of-it Elsie asked. 'Forever sitting on top of her, as you now do. Can it be healthy, egging her on to talk? What's this attraction, all of a sudden?—whatever's this which has sprung up between you two? She and you are becoming quite hand-in-glove.'

Elsie merely remarked this, and soon forgot: she had her own fish to fry. It was Ethel who had cause to recall the words—for, the afternoon of the very day they were spoken, Aunt Elysia whizzed off on another track, screamed for what was impossible and, upon being thwarted, went into a seizure unknown before. The worst of it was, at the outset her mind cleared—she pushed her shawl back, reared up her unkempt grey head and looked at Ethel, unblinkingly studied Ethel, with a lucid accumulation of years of hate. 'You fool of a gawk,' she said, and with such contempt! 'Coming running to me to know how to trap a man. Could *you* learn, if it was from Venus herself? Wait till I show you beauty.—Bring down those trunks!'

'Oh, Auntie.'

'Bring them down, I say. I'm about to dress myself up.'

'Oh, but I cannot; they're heavy; I'm single-handed.'

'Heavy?—they came here heavy. But there've been rats in the attic.—*I* saw you, swishing downstairs in my *eau-de-nil!*'

'Oh, you dreamed that!'

'Through the crack of the door.—Let me up, then. Let us go where they are, and look—we shall soon see!' Aunt Elysia threw back the bedclothes and began to get up. 'Let's take a look,' she said, 'at the rats' work.' She set out to totter towards the door.

'Oh, but you're not fit!' Ethel protested.

'And when did a doctor say so?' There was a swaying: Ethel caught her in time and, not gently, lugged her back to the bed—and Ethel's mind the whole of this time was whirling, for tonight was the night upon which all hung. Lord Fred's last local appearance was to be, like his first, at a ball: tomorrow he left for London. So it must be tonight, at this ball, or never! How was it that Ethel felt so strangely, wildly confident of the outcome? It was time to begin on her coiffure, lay out her dress. Oh, tonight she would shine as never before! She flung back the bedclothes over the helpless form, heard a clock strike, and hastily turned to go.

'I will be quits with you,' said the voice behind her.

Ethel, in a kimono, hair half done, was in her own room, in front of the open glove drawer, when Elsie came in—home from a tennis party. Elsie acted oddly; she went at once to the drawer and buried her nose in it. 'Oh, my goodness,' she cried, 'it's all too true, and it's awful!'

'What is?' Ethel carelessly asked.

'Ethel dear, would you ever face it out if I were to tell you a certain rumour I heard today at the party as to Lord Fred?'

Ethel turned from her sister, took up the heated tongs and applied more crimps to her natural curliness. She said: 'Certainly; spit it out.'

'Since childhood, he's recoiled from the breath of benzine. He wilts away when it enters the very room!'

'Who says that's so?'

'He confided it to his hostess, who is now spitefully putting it around the country.'

Ethel bit her lip and put down the tongs, while Elsie sorrowfully concluded: 'And your gloves stink, Ethel, as I'm sure do mine.' Elsie then thought it wiser to slip away.

In a minute more, however, she was back, and this time with a still more peculiar air. She demanded: 'In what state did you leave Auntie? She was sounding so very quiet that I peeped in, and *I* don't care for the looks of her now at all!' Ethel swore, but consented to take a look. She stayed in there in the back room, with Elsie biting her thumb-nail outside the door, for what seemed an ominous length of time—when she did emerge, she looked greenish, but held her head high. The sisters' eyes met. Ethel said, stonily: 'Dozing.'

'You're certain she's *not* . . . ? She *couldn't* ever be—you know?'

'Dozing, I tell you,' Ethel stared Elsie out.

'If she *was* gone,' quavered the frailer sister, 'just think of it—why, we'd never get to the ball!—And a ball that everything hangs on,' she ended up, with a sacred but conspiratorial glance at Ethel.

'Reassure yourself. Didn't you hear me say?'

As she spoke Ethel, chiefly from habit, locked her late aunt's door on the outside. The act caused a sort of secret jingle to be heard from inside her fist, and Elsie asked: 'What's that you've got hold of, now?' 'Just a few little keys and trinkets she made me keep,' replied Ethel, disclosing the small bag she had found where she'd looked for it, under the dead one's pillow. 'Scurry on now, Elsie, or you'll never be dressed. Care to make use of my tongs, while they're so splendidly hot?'

Alone at last, Ethel drew in a breath, and, with a gesture of resolution, retied her kimono sash tightly over her corset. She shook the key from the bag and regarded it, murmuring, 'Providential!', then gave a glance upward, towards where the attics were. The late spring sun had set, but an apricot afterglow, not unlike the light cast by a Chinese lantern, crept through the upper storey of Jasmine Lodge. The cessation of all those rustlings, tappings, whimpers and moans from inside Mrs Varley de Grey's room had set up an unfamiliar, somewhat unnerving hush. Not till a whiff of singeing hair announced that Elsie was well employed did Ethel set out on the quest which held all her hopes. Success was imperative—she *must* have gloves. Gloves, gloves . . .

Soundlessly, she set foot on the attic stairs.

Under the skylight, she had to suppress a shriek, for a rat—yes, of all things!—leaped at her out of an empty hatbox; and the rodent gave her a wink before it darted away. Now Ethel and Elsie knew for a certain fact that there never *had* been rats in Jasmine Lodge. However, she continued to steel her nerves, and to push her way to the one inviolate trunk.

All Mrs Varley de Grey's other Indian luggage gaped and yawned at Ethel, void, showing its linings, on end or toppling, forming a barricade around the object of her search—she pushed, pitched and pulled, scowling as the dust flew into her hair. But the last trunk, when it came into view and reach, still had something select and bridal about it: on top, the initials E. V. de G. stared out, quite luminous in a frightening way—for indeed how dusky the attic was! Shadows not only multiplied in the corners but seemed to finger their way up the sloping roof. Silence pierced up through the floor from that room below—and, worst, Ethel had the sensation of being watched by that pair of fixed eyes she had not stayed to close. She glanced this way, that way, backward over her shoulder. But, Lord Fred was at stake!—she knelt down and got to work with the key.

This trunk had two neat brass locks, one left, one right, along the front of the lid. Ethel, after fumbling, opened the first—then, so great was her hurry to know what might be within that she could not wait but slipped her hand in under the lifted corner. She pulled out one pricelessly lacy top of what must be a bride-veil, and gave a quick laugh—must not this be an omen? She pulled again, but the stuff resisted, almost as though it were being grasped from inside the trunk—she let go, and either her eyes deceived her or the lace began to be drawn back slowly, in again, inch by inch. What was odder was, that the spotless finger-tip of a white kid glove appeared for a moment, as though exploring its way out, then withdrew.

Ethel's heart stood still—but she turned to the other lock. Was a giddy attack overcoming her?—for, as she gazed, the entire lid of the trunk seemed to bulge upward, heave and strain, so that the E. V. de G. upon it rippled.

Untouched by the key in her trembling hand, the second lock tore itself open.

She recoiled, while the lid slowly rose—of its own accord.

She should have fled. But oh, how she craved what lay there exposed! —layer upon layer, wrapped in transparent paper, of elbow-length, magnolia-pure white gloves, bedded on the inert folds of the veil. 'Lord Fred,' thought Ethel, 'now you're within my grasp!'

That was her last thought, nor was the grasp to be hers. Down on her knees again, breathless with lust and joy, Ethel flung herself forward on to that sea of kid, scrabbling and seizing. The glove she had seen before was now, however, readier for its purpose. At first it merely pounced after Ethel's fingers, as though making mock of their greedy course; but the hand within it was all the time filling out . . . With one snowy flash through the dusk, the glove clutched Ethel's front hair, tangled itself in her black curls and dragged her head down. She began to choke among the sachets and tissue—then the glove let go, hurled her back, and made its leap at her throat.

It was a marvel that anything so dainty should be so strong. So great, so convulsive was the swell of the force that, during the strangling of Ethel, the seams of the glove split.

In any case, the glove would have been too small for her.

The shrieks of Elsie, upon the attic threshold, began only when all other sounds had died down . . . The ultimate spark of the once-famous cleverness of the Miss Trevors appeared in Elsie's extrication of herself from this awkward mess—for, who was to credit how Ethel came by her end? The sisters' reputation for warmth of heart was to stand the survivor in good stead—for, could those affections nursed in Jasmine Lodge, extending so freely even to the unwell aunt, have culminated in Elsie's setting on Ethel? No. In the end, the matter was hushed up—which is to say, is still talked about even now. Ethel Trevor and Mrs Varley de Grey were interred in the same grave, as everyone understood that they would have wished. What conversation took place under the earth, one does not know.

Sinners

❧ ⁂ ❧

SEAN O'FAOLAIN
(Irish, 1900–   )

The canon, barely glancing at his two waiting penitents, entered the
confessional. From inside he looked wearily across at the rows of
penitents on each side of Father Deeley's box, all still as statues where
they sat against the wall, or leaned forward to let the light of the single
electric bulb, high up in the windy roof, fall on their prayer books. Deeley would give each about ten minutes, and that meant he would not
absolve the last until near midnight. "More trouble with the sacristan,"
sighed the canon, and closed the curtains and lifted his hand towards the
slide of the grille.

He paused. To banish a sudden restiveness he said a prayer. He often
said that prayer—an Aspiration Against Anger. He had remembered that
on the other side of the grille was a little serving-girl he had sent out of
the box last Saturday night because she had been five years away from
confession and did not seem to be a bit sorry for it. He lifted his hand, but
paused again. To add to his difficulty—for it was no help to know what,
under the sigillum, he must pretend not to know—he had just been told
in the sacristy by her employer that a pair of her best boots was missing.
Why on earth, he sighed, did people reveal such things to him? Did he
want to know the sins of his penitents? Was the confession being made to
him, or to God? Was it . . . He lowered his hand, ashamed of his irritation, and repeated the prayer. Then he drew the slide, cupped his ear in
his palm to listen, and saw her hands clasping and unclasping, as if her
courage was a little bird between her palms trying to escape.

"My poor child," he said, ever so gently, dutifully pretending to know nothing about her, "tell me how long it is since your last confession."

"It's a long time, Father," she whispered.

"How long?" To encourage her he added, "Over a year?"

"Yes, Father."

"How much? Tell me, my poor child, tell me. Two years?"

"More, Father."

"Three years?"

"More, Father."

"Well, well, you must tell me, you know."

In spite of himself his voice was a little pettish. The title "Father" instead of "Canon" was annoying him, too. She noted the change of voice, for she said, hurriedly:

" 'Tis that, Father."

" 'Tis what?" asked the canon a shade too loudly.

"Over three years, Father," she prevaricated.

He wondered if he could dare let the prevarication go; but his conscience would not let him.

"My dear child, how much over three years is it?"

" 'Tis, 'tis, Father, 'tis . . ."

The canon forestalled the lie.

"My dear child, how much over three years is it? Is it four years? And would you mind calling me *Canon?*"

The breathing became faster.

" 'Tis, Father, I mean, 'tis more, *Canon,* Father."

"Well, how much? I can't make your confession for you, you know."

" 'Tis a bit more, Father."

"But how much?" broke from the canon.

"Two months," lied the maid, and her hands made a flutter of whiteness in the dark.

The canon almost wished he could break the seal of the confessional and reveal to her that he knew exactly who she was, and how long she had been away; all he dared say was:

"I suspect you're telling me a lie."

"Oh, God, Father, it's gospel truth."

"But"—the canon tapped the cushion—"there's no use in telling me if it's not the truth. For God's sake, my poor child"—he controlled himself —"maybe it's five years?"

" 'Tis five years," admitted the maid in so low a voice that he barely heard it.

He sighed with satisfaction. He straightened his hair on his forehead. Then he leaned nearer to hear her sins, nearer and nearer until his ear was pressed against the lattice.

"Now," he warned, "that is a long time, my child. But, thank God, you have come back at last. You must try hard to remember all—all— your sins. Let me help you. My poor little child! Take the first commandment."

But when he heard the shudder of her breath he knew he had made a bad mistake; she would be seeing a long list of broken commandments before her and she would slur over many of her sins in order to shorten the ordeal.

"I mean to say," went on the canon, annoyed with his own stupidity, "that is one way of doing it. Do you wish to make your confession that way?"

"Yes, Father."

"Very well."

"The first commandment . . ." She stopped in confusion and he realized that she did not even know what the commandment was.

"Did you ever miss Mass on Sundays?" he helped her out, although his knees were beginning to dance with impatience.

"Oh, never, never in my whole life."

"Good. Did you ever swear? Take the Lord's name in vain?"

"Tututut!" said the girl in horror at the very idea.

"Did you ever disobey your parents, cause them pain in any way, give back-answers?"

"I have no parents, Father. Mrs. Higg— my mistress got me from the orphanage."

"Ah! Well . . . er . . . lies? Anger? Have you told lies, or given way to anger?"

"Wisha, I suppose I did, Father. I suppose I told a little lie now and again."

"How often in those five years? On an average? I mean, is it a weakness you have? A habit?"

"God help us, Father, I don't tell many. I only tell 'em when I do be afraid."

"Well, we will say you told lies occasionally. Now the sixth commandment. Have you ever sinned in thought, word, or deed against Holy Purity? The opposite sex, for example. Have you ever misbehaved in any way with men?"

"Oh!" gasped the maid, and her voice thickened.

"Stealing?" prompted the canon, and he waited for her to say that she had stolen Mrs. Higgins's boots.

"I never in my life, Father, stole as much as the head off of a pin. Except when I was small I once stole an apple in the nuns' orchard. And then they caught me and gave me a flaking. And they took the last bite out of my mouth."

"You never stole articles of dress?" threatened the canon, and he suddenly realized that there were only three very unlikely commandments left. "Clothes? Hats? Gloves? Shoes?"

"Never, Father."

There was a long pause.

"Boots?" he whispered.

Suddenly the girl was sobbing violently.

"Father," she wept, "Mrs. Higgins is telling you lies about me. I hate that wan. I . . . I . . . I hate her. I do. She's always prying and poking and prodding at me. She took me from the nuns five years ago and she never gave me a minute's rest. She calls me low names. She tells me I can't be good or wholesome to come out of an orphanage. She is picking at me from dawn to dusk. She's an old bitch . . ."

"My child! My child!"

"I did take the boots. I took them. But I didn't steal them. Sure I haven't a boot on my foot and she has lashings and leavings of 'em. I was going to put them back."

"My child, to take them is the same as to steal them."

"What does she want them for? But she's that mean. Her own daughter ran away from her two years ago and married an Englishman who's half a Freemason. The poor girl told me with her own mouth, only last week, how she's half starved by that husband of hers and they have no money to have a family. But do you think her mother would give her a penny?"

The girl sobbed on. The canon groaned and drew himself up to ease his chest. He could hear the wind whistling up in the roof and he could see the long queue on each side of Father Deeley's box, all still as statues in the dusk of the aisle. Seeing them he groaned again as much as to say,

"What's the use? They all deceive themselves. They all think everyone is sinful but themselves only. Or if they say they are sinners, and feel it—it only lasts while they are in the church. Then they go out and are filled with envy and pride and they have no charity." He leaned back.

"My child, my child, my child! For five years you have stayed away from God. If you had died you would have died with that mortal sin on your soul and gone to hell for all eternity. It's the law of the Church, and the law of God, that you *must*, you *must* go to confession at least once a year. Why did you stay away? Look at the way your mind is deformed so that you can't even recognize a sin when you commit it. Is there some sin you haven't told me that you were ashamed to tell?"

"No, Father."

"Didn't your good mistress send you to confession at least every month during those five years?"

"She sent me every week. But it was always of a Saturday night. And one Saturday night I didn't go because I wanted to buy a blouse before the shops shut. Then it was six months before I knew it and I was afraid to go. And, anyway, sure what had I to tell?"

The canon waved his hands weakly and with great sarcasm he said:

"Did you *never* commit a sin?"

"I suppose I told a lie, Father. And there was the apple in the nuns' orchard."

Furiously the priest turned to her, determined to wring the truth from her. In her compartment he heard Lady Nolan-White, his second penitent, coughing impatiently.

"My dear child, you simply must have committed sins during those five years. Be honest with yourself. Come now! Look! Take the most common sin of all. Have you, ever, had what we, vulgarly, call a . . . er . . . call a—boy?"

"I had—once—Father."

"Well, now!" He rubbed his forehead like a man in a great heat and he strained towards her as if he were struggling with her demon. "You were, what do we say . . . er . . . walking out with him?"

"Yes," panted the girl. "In the back lane."

"Well, what shall we say? Did, what do you say, did, er, did any intimacy take place with him?"

"I don't know, Father."

"You know what it is to be immodest, don't you?" cried the canon.

Her breath was panting in and out. She said nothing. She stared at him.

"My poor, poor child, you seem to have small experience of the world. But we must get at the truth. Did he—did you—did either of you ever go beyond the bounds of propriety?"

"I dunno, Father."

Loudly the canon expelled his breath. He was becoming exhausted, but he would not give in. He rubbed his hair all the wrong way, which gave him a wild look. He took off his pince-nez and wiped them.

"You understand plain English, don't you? Now, tell me, tell Almighty God the truth of the thing. Did you ever allow him to take liberties with you?"

"Yes, Father. I mean, no, Father. We were in the lane. No, Father. We didn't do nothing. Nothing much, I mean."

"Five years," moaned the canon, and he hammered his thigh with his fist. "And nothing to tell. What kind of Christians . . ." He determined to make one last effort—just one more effort. "Did he ever touch your body?" he asked bluntly.

"No, Father. Well, I mean—no, Father."

Seeing that she was beginning to whimper again he threw up his hands.

"All right, child," he said gently. "Say your Act of Contrition and I'll give you Absolution."

"Father," she whispered, her eyes black through the grille, "I was in bed with him once."

The canon looked at her. She drew back. He leaned away and looked from a distance at the crisscrossed face behind the grille. The he began to smile, slowly expanding his mouth into a wide beam of relief.

"My child," he whispered, "did anyone ever tell you that you were a little deficient in the head? I mean, you weren't very smart at school, were you?"

"I was always at the top of the school, Father. Mother Mary Gonzaga wanted to make a teacher of me."

"And," growled the canon, now utterly exasperated, and dancing his knees up and down on the balls of his feet like a man in the agony of toothache, "do you kneel there and tell me that you think it no sin to go to bed with a man? Who," he added casually, "isn't your husband?"

"I meant no harm, Father," she palpitated, "and it's not what is in your mind at all, for we didn't do nothing, and if it wasn't for the thunder and lightning that terrified me, I wouldn't do it at all. Mrs. Higgins was down in Crosshaven with Mrs. Kinwall, that's her daughter, and I was all alone in the house, and I was afraid of the dark and the thunder, so Mikey said he'd stay with me, so he stayed, and then it was late and I was 'fraid to be by myself in the bed, so he said, 'I'll mind you,' so I said, 'All right, Mikey, but none of that,' and he said, 'All right, Madgie, none of that,' and there wasn't any of that, Father."

She stared at the canon, who was blowing and puffing and shaking his head as if the whole world were suddenly gone mad.

"It was no harm, Father," she wailed, seeing he did not believe her.

"Once?" asked the canon shortly. "You did this once?"

"Yes, Father."

"Are you sorry for it?" he demanded briefly.

"If it was a sin. Was it, Father?"

"It was," he roared. "People can't be allowed to do this kind of thing. It was a serious occasion of sin. Anything might have happened. Are you sorry?"—and he wondered if he should throw her out of the box again.

"I'm sorry, Father."

"Tell me a sin of your past life."

"The apple in the orchard, Father."

"Say an Act of Contrition."

She ran through it swiftly, staring at him all the while. There were beads of perspiration on her upper lip.

"Say three Rosaries for your penance."

He shot the slide to and sank back, worn out. From force of habit he drew the opposite slide and at once he got the sweet scent of jasmine, but when Lady Nolan-White was in the middle of her confiteor he waved his two hands madly in the air and said, hastily:

"Excuse me, one moment . . . I can't . . . it's all absurd . . . it's impossible . . ."

And he drew the slide on her astonished, beautiful, rouged face. He put on his biretta, low down on his nose, and stalked out into the aisle. He parted the curtains on Lady Nolan-White and said:

"It's quite impossible. . . . You don't understand it. . . . Good night!"

He stalked up the dim aisle, and when he met two urchins gossiping in a corner he banged their little skulls together, and at once he became disgusted with himself to see them cowering from him in fright. He passed on, his hand under the tail of his surplice, dancing it up and down. When he saw two old women by the great Calvary, rubbing spittle into the Magdalen's foot and then rubbing the spittle to their eyes or throat, he groaned out, "Oh, dear, oh, dear," and strode on towards Father Deeley's box. There he counted heads—fourteen penitents on one side and twelve on the other—looked at his gold watch and saw it was a quarter past eight.

He strode back to the center compartment and flung aside the curtains. Out of the dimness the warm, cherubic face of the young curate looked at him—a pink Italian saint. Slowly the glow of spiritual elevation died from his face as the canon's insistent whisper hissed down at him:

"Father Deeley, it won't do. I assure you it's absolutely impossible. Half past eight and twenty-six people yet to hear confession. They're just deceiving you. They want to gabble. I am an old man and I understand them. Think of the sacristan. Electric light, too! And gas going until midnight. The organization of the Church . . ."

And so on. All the time he kept stretching and relaxing the mechanical bow of his genteel smile, and he spoke in the most polite voice. But Deeley's face grew troubled, and pained, and seeing it the canon groaned inwardly. He remembered a curate he had once who played the organ every day for hours on end, until the parishioners complained that they couldn't pray with the noise he made; the canon recalled how he had gone up into the loft to ask him to stop, and the curate had lifted to him a face like an angel, and how within one half minute it had become the face of a cruel, bitter old man.

"All right, Father Deeley," he said hastily, forestalling protests. "You are young. I know. Still, you are young . . ."

"I am not young," hissed Deeley furiously. "I know my duty. It's a matter of conscience. I can sit in the dark if you are so mean that you . . ."

"All right, all right, all right," waved the canon, smiling furiously. "We are all old nowadays. Experience counts for nothing . . ."

"Canon," said Deeley, intensely, putting his two fists on his chest, "when I was in the seminary, I used to say to myself, 'Deeley,' I used to say, 'when you are a priest . . .' "

"Oh," begged the canon, cracking his face in a smile, "don't, I beg you, please don't tell me your life story!"

Whereupon he whirled away, his head in the air, switching on and off the electric light of his smile to penitents he did not know and had never seen in his life before. He found himself before the high altar. He saw the sacristan standing on a stepladder before it arranging the flowers for the morning, and he thought it would be well to apologize to him for Deeley's late hours. But the sacristan kept turning a vase round and round and round, and at last he realized that the little man was cross with him already, was deliberately delaying up there, and would not come down until he was gone.

Sighing, he went away, and after writing some letters he realized that his stomach had ceased to belong to him and would be out on its own devices until morning, like a hound that escapes from its kennel. Wearily he took his hat and cane and decided to take a long walk to calm his nerves.

It was a tender night of floating moonlight, cozily damp, and it soothed him to look down on the city and see the roofs as white as if there were frost on them. More calm, he returned home. The river was like milk. The streets were asleep. He hummed quietly to himself and felt at peace with all men. The clocks of the city chimed at one another in a good-humored mood, slow and with silvery, singing echoes. Then he heard a woman's voice talking from the high window of a cement-faced house, and he saw that it was Mrs. Higgins's house. She was in a white nightdress.

"That's a fine story!" she cried down to the pavement. "Ha! A cockalorum of a story! Wait until I see the canon. At confession, indeed! Wait until I see the nuns! Oh, you jade! You unfortunate poor sinner!"

He saw the little girlish figure cowering down in the doorway.

"Mrs. Higgins," she wailed, "it's gospel truth. The canon threw me out again. I told him all sorts of lies. I had to go to Father Deeley. He kept me half an hour. Oh, Mrs. Higgins," wailed the child, "it's gospel truth."

"Aha!" prated the nightdress. "But you're a nice thing. Wait until I tell . . ."

The canon felt the hound of his stomach jump from the kennel again. His entrails came bodily up to his neck. He marched by, blowing and puffing.

"Oh, my God!" he whined. "Have pity on me. Oh, my God! Have pity on me!"

He turned towards the dark presbytery deep among the darkest lanes.

The Spree

V. S. PRITCHETT
(English, 1900–   )

The old man—but when does old age begin?—the old man turned over in bed and putting out his hand to the crest of his wife's beautiful white rising hip and comforting bottom, hit the wall with his knuckles and woke up. More than once during the two years since she had died he had done this and knew that if old age vanished in the morning it came on at night, filling the bedroom with people until, switching on the light, he saw it staring at him; then it shuffled off and left him looking at the face of the clock. Three hours until breakfast: the hunger of loss yawned under his ribs. Trying to make out the figures on the clock, he dropped off to sleep again and was walking up Regent Street seeing, on the other side of it, a very high-bred white dog, long in the legs and distinguished in its step, hurrying up to Oxford Circus, pausing at each street corner in doubt, looking up at each person as he passed and whimpering politely to them: "Me? Me? Me?" and going on when they did not answer. A valuable dog like that, lost! Someone will pick it up, lead it off, sell it to the hospital, and doctors will cut it up! The old man woke up with a shout to stop the crime and then he saw daylight in the room and heard bare feet running past his room and the shouts of his three grandchildren and his daughter-in-law calling "Ssh! Don't wake Grandpa."

The old man got out of bed and stood looking indignantly at the mirror over the washbasin and at his empty gums. It was awful to think, as he put his teeth in to cover the horror of his mouth, that twelve or fourteen hours of London daylight were stacked up meaninglessly wait-

ing for him. He pulled himself together. As he washed, listening to the
noises of the house, he made up a speech to say to his son, who must be
downstairs by now.

"I am not saying I am ungrateful. But old and young are not meant to
be together. You've got your life. I've got mine. The children are sweet—
you're too sharp with them—but I can't stand the noise. I don't want to
live at your expense. I want a place of my own. Where I can breathe.
Like Frenchy." And as he said this, speaking into the towel and listening
to the tap running, he could see and hear Frenchy, who was his dentist
but who looked like a rascally prophet in his white coat and was seventy
if he was a day, saying to him as he looked down into his mouth and as if
he was really tinkering with a property there, "You ought to do what I've
done. Get a house by the sea. It keeps you young."

Frenchy vanished, leaving him ten years younger. The old man got
into his shirt and trousers and was carefully spreading and puffing up his
sparse black-and-grey hair across his head when in came his daughter-in-
law, accusing him—why did she accuse? "Grandpa! You're up!"

She was like a soft Jersey cow with eyes too big and reproachful. She
was bringing him tea, the dear sweet tiresome woman.

"Of course I'm up," he said.

One glance at the tea showed him it was not like the tea he used to
make for his wife when she was alive, but had too much milk in it, always
tepid, left standing somewhere. He held his hairbrush up and he suddenly
said, asserting his right to live, to get out of the house, in air he could
breathe, "I'm going into London to get my hair cut."

"Are you sure you'll be all right?"

"Why do you say that?" he said severely. "I've got several things I
want to do."

And when she had gone, he heard her say on the stairs, "He's going to
get his hair cut!"

And his son saying, "Not again!"

This business, this defiance of the haircut! For the old man it was not a
mere scissoring and clipping of the hair. It was a ceremonial of freedom;
it had the whiff of orgy, the incitement of a ritual. As the years went by,
leaving him in such a financial mess that he was now down to not much
more than a pension, it signified desire—but what desire? To be memorable in some streets of London, or at least as evocative as an incense. The

desire would come to him, on summer days like this, when he walked in
his son's suburban garden, to sniff and to pick a rose for his buttonhole;
and then, already intoxicated, he marched out of the garden gate onto the
street and to the bus stop, upright and vigorous, carrying his weight well
and pink in the face. The scents of the barber's had been creeping into his
nostrils, his chest, even went down to his legs. To be clipped, oiled, and
perfumed was to be free.

So on this decent July morning in the sun-shot and acid suburban mist,
he stood in a queue for the bus, and if anyone had spoken to him he
would have gladly said, to put them in their place, "Times have changed.
Before I retired, when Kate was alive—though I must honestly say we
often had words about it—I always took a cab."

The bus came and whooshed him down to Knightsbridge, to his temple—the most expensive of the big shops. There, reborn on miles of
carpet, he paused and sauntered, sauntered and paused. He was inflamed
by hall after hall of women's dresses and hats, by cosmetics and jewellery. Scores of women were there. Glad to be cooled off, he passed into
the echoing hall of provisions. He saw the game, the salmon, and the
cheese. He ate them and moved on to lose twenty years in the men's
clothing department, where, among ties and brilliant shirts and jackets,
his stern yet bashful pink face woke up to the loot and his ears heard the
voices of the rich, the grave chorus of male self-approval. He went to the
end where the oak stairs led down to the barber's; there, cool as clergy,
they stood gossiping in their white coats. One came forward, seated him,
and dressed him up like a baby. And then—nothing happened. He was
the only customer, and the barber took a few steps back towards the
group, saying, "He wasn't at the staff meeting."

The old man tapped his finger irritably under his sheet. Barbers did not
cut hair, it seemed. They went to staff meetings. One called back, "Mr.
Holderness seconded it."

Who was Holderness?

"Where is Charles?" said the old man to call the barbers to order.
Obsequiously the man began that pretty music with his scissors.

"Charles?" said the barber.

"Yes. Charles. He shaved me for twenty years."

"He retired."

Another emptiness, another cavern, opened inside the old man.

"Retired? He was a child."

"All the old ones have retired."

The barber had lost his priestly look. He looked sinful, even criminal, certainly hypocritical.

And although the old man's head was being washed by lotions and oils and there was a tickling freshness about the ears and his nostrils quickened, there was something uneasy about the experience. In days gone by, the place had been baronial; now it seemed not quite to gleam. One could not be a sultan among a miserable remnant of men who held staff meetings. When the old man left, the woman at the desk went on talking as she took his money and did not know his name. When he went upstairs, he paused to look back—no, the place was a palace of pleasure no longer. It was the place where—except for the staff—no one was known.

And that was what struck him as he stepped out of the glancing swing-doors of the shop, glad to be out in the July sun: that he was a sultan, cool, scented, and light-headed, extraordinary in a way, sacred almost, ready for anything—but cut off from expectancy, unknown nowadays to anybody, free for nothing, liberty evaporating out of the tips of his shoes. He stepped out on the pavement dissembling leisure. His walk became slower and gliding. For an hour, shop windows distracted him; new shops where old had been shocked him. But, he said, pulling himself together, I must not fall into *that* trap: old people live in the past. And I am not old! Old I am not! So he stopped gliding and stepped out wilfully, looking so stern and with mouth turned down, so corrupt and purposeful with success, that he was unnoticeable. Who notices success?

It was always—he didn't like to admit it—like this on these days when he made the great stand for his haircut and the exquisite smell. He would set out with a vision, it crumbled into a rambling dream. He fell back, like a country hare, on his habitual run, to the shops which had bought his goods years ago, to see what they were selling and where he knew no one now; to a café which had changed its décor, where he ate a sandwich and drank a cup of coffee; but as the dream consoled, it dissolved into final melancholy. He with his appetite for everything, who could not pass a shop window, or an estate agent's, or a fine house, without greed watering in his mouth, could buy nothing. He hadn't the cash.

There was always this moment when the bottom began to fall out of his haircut days. He denied that his legs were tired, but he did slow down. It would occur to him suddenly in Piccadilly that he knew no one now in the city. He had been a buyer and seller, not a man for friends: he knew buildings, lifts, offices, but not people. There would be nothing for it but to return home. He would drag his way to the inevitable bus stop of defeat, and stand, as so many Londoners did, with surrender on their faces. He delayed it as long as he could, stopping at a street corner or gazing at a passing girl and looking round with that dishonest look a dog has when it is pretending not to hear its master's whistle. There was only one straw to clutch at. There was nothing wrong with his teeth, but he could ring up his dentist. He could ring up Frenchy. He could ring him and say, "Frenchy? How's tricks?" sportily, and (a man for smells) he could almost smell the starch in Frenchy's white coat, the keen, chemical hygienic smell of his room. The old gentleman considered this and then went down a couple of disheartened side streets. In a short cul-de-sac, standing outside a urinal and a few doors from a dead-looking pub, there was a telephone box. An oldish brown motor-coach was parked empty at the kerb by it, its doors closed, a small crowd waiting beside it. There was a man in the telephone box, but he came out in a temper, shouting something to the crowd. The old man went into the box. He had thought of something to say: "Hullo, Frenchy! Where is that house you were going to find me, you old rascal?"

For Frenchy came up from the sea every day. It was true that Frenchy was a rascal, especially with the women, one after the other, but looking down into the old man's mouth and chipping at a tooth, he seemed to be looking into your soul.

The old man got out his coins. He was tired but eagerness revived him as he dialled.

"Hullo, Frenchy," he said. But the voice that replied was not Frenchy's. It was a child's. The child was calling out, "Mum. Mum." The old man banged down the telephone and stared at the dial. His heart thumped. He had, he realized, not dialled Frenchy's number but the number of his old house, the one he had sold after Kate had died.

The old gentleman backed out of the box and stared, tottering with horror, at it. His legs went weak, his breath had gone, and sweat bubbled on his face. He steadied himself by the brick wall. He edged away from the bus and the crowd so as not to be seen. He thought he was going to faint. He moved to a doorway. There was a loud laugh from the crowd as a young man with long black hair gave the back of the bus a kick. And then suddenly he and a few others rushed towards the old man, shouting and laughing.

"Excuse us," someone said and pushed him aside. He saw he was standing in the doorway of the pub.

"That's true," the old man murmured to himself. "Brandy is what I need." And at that, the rest of the little crowd pushed into him or past him. One of them was a young girl with fair hair who paused as her young man pulled her by the hand and said kindly to the old man, "After you."

There he was, being elbowed, travelling backwards into the little bar. It was the small private bar of the pub and the old man found himself against the counter. The young people were stretching their arms across him and calling out orders for drinks and shouting. He was wedged among them. The wild young man with the piratical look was on one side of him, the girl and her young man on the other. The wild young man called to the others, "Wait a minute. What's yours, dad?"

The old man was bewildered. "Brandy."

"Brandy," shouted the young man across the bar.

"That's right," said the girl to the old man, studying his face. "You have one. You ought to have got on the first coach."

"You'd have been halfway to bloody Brighton by now," said the wild young man. "The first bloody outing this firm's had in its whole bloody history and they bloody forgot the driver. Are you the driver?"

Someone called out, "No, he's not the driver."

"I had a shock," the old man began, but crowded against the bar no one heard him.

"Drink it up, then," the girl said to him, and startled by her kindness, he drank. The brandy burned and in a minute fire went up into his head, and his face lost its hard bewildered look and it loosened into a smile. He heard their young voices flying about him. They were going to Brighton. No, the other side of Brighton. No, this side—well, to bloody Hampton's mansion, estate, something. The new chairman—he'd thrown the place open. Bloody thrown it, laughed the wild man, to the works and the office and, as usual, "the works get the first coach." The young girl leaned down to smell the rose in the old man's buttonhole and said to her young man, "It's lovely. Smell it." His arm was round her waist and there were the two of them bowing to the rose.

"From your garden?" said the girl.

The old man heard himself, to his astonishment, tell a lie.

"I grew it," he said.

"We shan't bloody start for hours," someone said. "Drink up."

The old man looked at his watch: a tragic look. Soon they'd be gone. Someone said, "Which department are you in?" "He's in the works," someone said. "No, I've retired," said the old man, not to cause a fuss. "Have another, dad," said the young man. "My turn."

Three of them bent their heads to hear him say again, "I have retired," and one of them said, "It was passed at the meeting. Anyone retired entitled to come."

"You've made a mistake," the old man began to explain to them. "I was just telephoning to my dentist . . ."

"No," said one of the bending young men, turning to someone in the crowd. "That bastard Fowkes talked a lot of bull but it passed."

"You're all right," the girl said to the old man.

"He's all right," said another and handed the old man another drink. If only they would stop shouting, the old man thought, I could explain.

"A mistake . . ." he began again.

"It won't do you any harm," someone said. "Drink up."

Then someone shouted from the door. "He's here. The driver."

The girl pulled the old man by the arm and he found himself being hustled to the door.

"My glass," he said.

He was pushed, holding his half-empty glass, into the street. They rushed past him and he stood there, glass in hand, trying to say good-bye and then he followed them, still holding his glass, to explain. They shouted to him, "Come on," and he politely followed to the door of the bus where they were pushing to get in.

But at the door of the bus everything changed. A woman wearing a flowered dress with a red belt, a woman as stout as himself, had a foot on the step of the bus and was trying to heave herself up while people ahead of her blocked the door. She nearly fell.

The old man, all smiles and sadness, put on a dignified anger. He pushed his way towards her. He turned forbiddingly on the youngsters.

"Allow me, madam," he said and took the woman's cool fat elbow and helped her up the step, putting his own foot on the lower one. Fatal. He was shoved up and himself pushed inside, the brandy spilling down his suit. He could not turn round. He was in, driven in deeply, to wait till the procession stopped. "I'm getting out," he said.

He flopped into the seat behind the woman.

"Young people are always in a rush," she turned to say to him.

The last to get in were the young couple.

"Break it up," said the driver. They were slow, for they were enlaced and wanted to squeeze in united.

The old man waited for them to be seated and then stood up, glass in hand, as if offering a toast, as he moved forward to get out.

"Would you mind sitting down," said the driver. He was counting the passengers, and one, seeing the old man with the glass in his hand, said, "Cheers."

For the first time in his adult life, the old man indignantly obeyed an order. He sat down, was about to explain his glass, heard himself counted, got up. He was too late. The driver pulled a bar, slammed the door, spread his arms over the wheel and off they went, to a noise that bashed people's eyeballs.

At every change of the gears, as the coach gulped out of the narrow streets, a change took place in the old man. Shaken in the kidneys, he looked around in protest, put his glass out of sight on the floor, and blushed. He was glad no one was sitting beside him, for his first idea was to scramble to the window and jump through it at the first traffic lights. The girl who had her arm round her young man looked round and smiled. Then he too looked round at all these unknown people, belonging to a firm he had never heard of, going to a destination unknown to him, and he had the inflated sensations of an enormous illegality. He had been kidnapped. He tipped back his hat and looked bounderish. The bus was hot and seemed to be frying in the packed traffic when it stopped at the lights. People had to shout to be heard. Under cover of the general shouting, he too shouted to a couple of women across the gangway, "Do we pass the Oval?"

The woman asked her friend, who asked the man in front, who asked the young couple. Blocks of offices went by in lumps. No one knew except someone who said, "Must do." The old man nodded. The moment the Oval cricket ground came into sight, he planned to go to the driver and tell him to let him off. So he kept his eyes open, thinking, What a lark. What a thing to tell them at home. Guess what? Had a free ride. "Cheek, my boy" (he'd say to his son), "that's what you need. Let me give you a bit of advice. You'll get nowhere without cheek."

His pink face beamed with shrewd frivolity as the coach groaned over the Thames that had never looked so wide and sly. Distantly a power station swerved to the west, then to the east, then rocked like a cradle as the young girl—restless like Kate she was—got out of her young man's arms and got him back into hers, in a tighter embrace. Three containers passed, the coach slackened, then choked forward so suddenly that the old man's head nearly hit the back of the head of the fat lady in front. He studied it and noticed the way the woman's thick hair, gold with grey in it, was darker as it came out of her neck like a growing plant and he thought, as he had often done, how much better a woman's head looks from behind—the face interferes with it in front. And then his own chin went slack and he began a voluptuous journey down corridors. One more look at the power station, which had become several jumping power stations, giving higher and higher leaps in the air, and he was asleep.

A snore came from him. The talking woman across the gangway was annoyed by this soliloquizing noise which seemed to offer a rival narrative; but others admired it for its steadiness, which peacefully mocked the unsteady recovery and spitting and fading energy of the coach and the desperation of the driver. Between their shouts at the driver, many glanced admiringly at the sleeper. He was swinging in some private barber's shop that swerved through space, sometimes in some airy corridor, at other times circling beneficently round a cricket match in which Frenchy, the umpire, in his white linen coat, was offering him a plate of cold salmon which his daughter-in-law was trying to stop him from eating; he was off the coach, striking his way home on foot at the tail of the longest funeral procession he had ever seen, going uphill for miles into fields that were getting greener and colder and emptier as snow came on and he sat down, plonk, out of breath, waking to hear the weeping of the crowds, all weeping for him, and then, still waking, he saw himself outside the tall glass walls of a hospital. It must be a hospital, for inside two men in white could be clearly seen in a glass-enclosed room, one of them the driver, getting ready to carry him in on a stretcher. He gasped, now fully awake. There was absolute silence. The coach had stopped; it was empty—he was alone in it, except for the woman, who, thank God, was still sitting in front of him, the hair still growing from the back of her neck.

"Where . . ." he began. Then he saw the hospital was in fact a garage. The passengers had got out, garagemen were looking under the hood of the bus. The woman turned round. He saw a mild face, without makeup.

"We've broken down," she said.

How grateful he was for her mild face. He had thought he was dead. "I've been asleep," he said. "Where are we?"

He nearly said, "Have we passed the Oval?" but swallowed that silly question.

"Quarter past three," he said. Meaning thirty miles out, stuck fast in derelict country at a crossroads, with a few villas sticking out in fields, eating into the grass among a few trees, with a billboard on the far side of the highway saying blatantly, MORTGAGES, and the cars dashing by in flights like birds, twenty at a time, still sweeping away westward into space.

The woman had turned to study him, and when he got up, flustered, she said in a strict but lofty voice, "Sit down."

He sat down.

"Don't you move," she said. "I'm not going to move. They've made a mess of it. Let them put it right."

She had twisted round and he saw her face, wide and full now, as meaty as an obstinate country girl's, and with a smile that made her look as though she were evaporating.

"This is Hampton's doing," she said. "Anything to save money. I am going to tell him what I think of him when I see him. No one in charge. Not even the driver—listen to him. Treat staff like cattle. They've got to send another coach. Don't you move until it comes."

Having said this, she was happy.

"When my husband was on the board nothing like this happened. Do you know anyone here? I don't. Everything's changed."

She studied his grey hair.

The old man clung for the moment to the fact that he and she were united in not knowing anybody. His secretiveness was coming back.

"I've retired," he said.

The woman leaned further over the back of the seat and looked around the empty bus and then back at him as if she had captured him. Her full lips were the resting lips of a stout woman between meals.

"I must have seen you at the works with John," she said. "It was always a family in those days. Or were you in the office?"

I must get out of this, the old man was thinking, and he sat forward nearer to her, getting ready to get out once more. I must find out the name of this place, get a train or a bus or something, get back home. The place looked nameless.

But since his wife had died he had never been as near to a strange woman's face. It was a wide, ordinary, baby-like face damp in the skin, with big blue eyes under fair, skimpy eyebrows, and she studied him as a soft, plump child would—for no reason beyond an assumption that he and she were together in this: they weren't such fools; at their ages, to get off the coach. It was less the nearness of the face than her voice that kept him there.

It was a soft, high voice that seemed to blow away like a child's and was far too young for her, even sounded so purely truthful as to be false. It came out in deep breaths drawn up from soft but heavy breasts that could, he imagined, kick up a hullabaloo, a voice which suggested that by some silly inconsequent right she would say whatever came into her head. It was the kind of voice that made the old man swell with a polite, immensely intimate desire to knock the nonsense out of her.

"I can smell your rose from here," she said. "There are not many left who knew the firm in John's time. It was John's lifework."

He smiled complacently. He had his secret.

She paused and then the childish voice went suddenly higher. She was not simply addressing him. She was addressing a meeting.

"I told him that when he let Hampton flatter him he'd be out in a year. I said to John, 'He's jealous. He's been jealous all the time."

The woman paused. Then her chin and her lips stuck out, and her eyes that had looked so vague began to bulge and her voice went suddenly deep, rumbling with prophecy.

" 'He wants to kill you,' I said. You," said the woman to the old man, "must have seen it. And he did kill him. We went on a trip round the world: America, Japan, India"—her voice sailed across countries— "that's where he died. If Hampton thinks he can wipe it out by throwing his place open to the staff and getting me down there on show, he's wrong."

My God, she's as dotty as Kate's sister used to get after her husband died, thought the old man. I'm sitting behind a madwoman.

"Dawson," she said and abruptly stood up as the old man rose too. "Oh," she said in her high regal style, gazing away out of the window of the bus. "I remember your name now. You had that row, that terrible row—oh, yes," she said eagerly, the conspirator. *"You* ring up Hampton. He's afraid of you. He'll listen. I've got the number here. You tell him there are twenty-seven of his employees stranded on the Brighton road."

The old man sighed. He gave up all idea of slipping out. When a woman orders you about, what do you do? He thought she looked rather fine standing there prophetically. The one thing to do in such cases was to be memorable. When is a man most memorable? When he says no.

"No, I wouldn't think of it," he said curtly. "Mr. Hampton and I are not on speaking terms."

"Why?" said the woman, distracted by curiosity.

"Mr. Hampton and I," he began, and he looked very gravely at her for a long time. "I have never heard of him. Who is he? I'm not on the staff. I've never heard of the firm." And then like a conjurer waving a handkerchief, he spread his face into a smile that had often got him an order in the old days.

"I just got on the coach for the ride. Someone said, 'Brighton.' 'Day at the sea,' I said. 'Suits me.' "

The woman's face went the colour of liver with rage and disbelief. One for the law, all the rage she had just been feeling about Hampton now switched to the old man. She was unbelieving.

"No one checked?" she said, her voice throbbing. She was boiling up like the police.

The old gentleman just shook his head gently. "No one checked"—it was a definition of paradise. If he had wings he would have spread them, taken to the air, and flown round her three times, saying, "Not a soul! Not a soul!"

She was looking him up and down. He stood with a plump man's dignity, but what saved him in her eyes were his smart, well-cut clothes, his trim hair, and the jaunty rose: he looked like an old rip, a racing man, probably a crook—at any rate, a bit of a rogue on the spree, yet innocent too. She studied his shoes and he moved a foot and kicked the brandy glass. It rolled into the gangway and he smiled slightly.

"You've got a nerve," she said, her smile spreading.

"Sick of sitting at home," he said. Weighing her up—not so much her character but her body—he said, "I've been living with my daughter-in-law since my wife died."

He burst out with confidence, for he saw he had almost conquered her. "Young and old don't mix. Brighton would suit me. I thought I would have a look around for a house."

Her eyes were still busily going over him.

"You're a spark," she said, still staring. Then she saw the glass and bent down to pick it up. As she straightened she leaned on the back of the seat and laughed out loud.

"You just got on. Oh, dear." She laughed loudly, helplessly. "Serves Hampton right.

"Sit down," she said. He sat down. She sat down on the seat opposite. He was astonished and even shy to see his peculiar case appreciated, and his peculiarity grew in his mind from a joke to a poem, from a poem to a dogma.

"I meant to get off at the Oval, but I dropped off to sleep." He laughed.

"Going to see the cricket?" she said.

"No," he said. "Home—I mean my son's place."

The whole thing began to appear lovely to him. He felt as she laughed at him, as she still held the glass, twiddling it by the stem, that he was remarkable.

"Years ago I did it once before," he said, multiplying his marvels. "When my wife was alive. I got a late train from London, went to sleep, and woke up in Bath. I did. I really did. Stayed at the Royal. Saw a customer next day. He was so surprised to see me he gave me an order worth three hundred pounds. My wife didn't believe me."

"Well, can you blame her?" the woman said.

The driver walked from the office of the garage and put his head into the coach and called out, "They're sending a new bus. Be here four o'clock."

The old man turned. "By the way, I'm getting off," he shouted to the driver.

"Aren't you going on?" said the woman. "I thought you said you were having a trip to the sea."

She wanted him to stay.

"To be frank," said the old man. "These youngsters—we'd been having a drink—they meant no harm—pushed me on when I was giving you a hand. I was in the pub. I had had a bit of a shock. I did something foolish. Painful really."

"What was that?" she said.

"Well," said the old man, swanking in his embarrassment and going very red, "I went to this telephone box, you know, where the coach started from, to ring up my dentist—Frenchy. I sometimes ring him up, but I got through to the wrong number. You know what I did? I rang the number of my old house, when Kate—when my wife—was alive. Some girl answered—maybe a boy—I don't know. It gave me a turn, doing a thing like that. I thought my mind had gone."

"Well, the number would have changed."

"I thought, I really did think, for a second, it was my wife."

The traffic on the main road sobbed or whistled as they talked. Containers, private cars, police cars, breakdown vans, cars with boats on their roofs—all sobbing their hearts out in a panic to get somewhere else.

"When did your wife die?" said the woman. "Just recently?"

"Two years ago," he said.

"It was grief. That is what it was—grief," she said gravely and looked away from him into the sky outside and to the derelict bit of country.

That voice of hers, by turns childish, silly, passing to the higher notes of the exalted and belligerent widow—all that talk of partners killing each other!—had become, as his wife's used to do after some tantrum, simply plain.

Grief. Yes, it was. He blinked away the threat of tears before her understanding. In these two years he seemed, because of his loneliness, to be dragging an increasing load of unsaid things behind him, things he had no one to tell. With his son and his daughter-in-law and their young friends he sat with his mouth open ready to speak, but he could never get a word out. The words simply fell back down his throat. He had a load of what people called boring things which he could not say: he had loved his wife; she had bored him; it had become a bond. What he needed was not friends, for since so many friends had died he had become a stranger; he needed another stranger. Perhaps like this woman whose face was as blank as his was, time having worn all expression from it. Because of that, you could see she looked now, if not as old as he was, full of life; but she had joined his lonely race and had the lost look of going nowhere. He lowered his eyes and became shy. Grief—what was it? A craving. Yet not for a face or even a voice or even for love, but for a body. But dressed. Say, in a flowered dress.

To get his mind off a thought so bold he uttered one of his boring things, a sort of sample of what he would have said to his wife. "Last night I had a dream about a dog," he began, to test her out as a stranger to whom you could say any damn silly thing. A friend would never listen to damn silly things.

The woman repeated, going back to what she had already said, as women do, "Remembering the telephone number—it was grief."

And then went off at a tangent, roughly. "Don't mention dreams to me. Last week at the bungalow I saw my husband walk across the sitting-room clean through the electric fire and the mirror over the mantelpiece and stand on the other side of it, not looking at me, but saying something to me that I couldn't hear—asking for a box of matches, I expect."

"Imagination," said the old man, sternly correcting her. He had no desire to hear of her dead husband's antics, but he did feel that warm, already possessive desire, to knock sense into her. It was a pleasant feeling.

"It wasn't imagination," she said, squaring up to him. "I packed my things and went to London at once. I couldn't stand it. I drove in to Brighton, left the car at the station, and came up to London for a few days. That is why when I heard about Hampton's party at the office I took this coach.

"Saved the train fare. Why shouldn't Hampton pay?" She grinned. "I told him I'd come to the party, but I'm not going. I'm picking up the car at Brighton and going home to the bungalow. It's only seven miles away."

She waited to see if he would laugh at their being so cunningly in the same boat. He did not laugh and that impressed her, but she frowned. Her husband would not have laughed either.

"I dread going back," she said sulkily.

"I sold my place," he said. "I know the feeling."

"You were right," said the woman. "That's what I ought to do. Sell the place. I'd get a good price for it, too. I'm not exactly looking forward to going back there this evening. It's very isolated—but the cat's there."

He said nothing. Earnestly she said, "You've got your son and daughter-in-law waiting for you," giving him a pat on the knee. "Someone to talk to. You're lucky."

The driver put his head into the door and said, "All out. The other coach is here."

"That's us," said the woman.

The crowd outside were indeed getting into the new coach. The old man followed her out and looked back at the empty seats with regret. At the door he stepped past her and handed her out. She was stout but landed light as a feather. The wild young man and his friends were shouting, full of new beer, bottles in their pockets. The others trooped in.

"Good-bye," said the old man, doing his memorable turn.

"You're not coming with us?" said the woman. And then she said quietly, looking round secretively, "I won't say anything. You can't give up now. You're worried about your daughter-in-law I know," she said.

The old man resented that.

"That doesn't worry me," he said.

"You ought to think of them," she said. "You ought to."

There was a shout of vulgar laughter from the wild young man and his friends. They had seen the two young lovers a long way off walking slowly, with all the time in the world, towards the coach. They had been off on their own.

"Worn yourselves out up in the fields?" bawled the wild young man, and he got the driver to sound the horn on the wheel insistently at them.

"You can ring from my place," said the woman.

The old man put on his air of being offended.

"You might buy my house," she tempted.

The two lovers arrived and everyone laughed. The girl—so like his wife when she was young—smiled at him.

"No. I can get the train back from Brighton," the old man said.

"Get in," called the driver.

The old man assembled seventy years of dignity. He did this because dignity seemed to make him invisible. He gave a lift to the woman's elbow, he followed her, he looked for a seat, and when she made room for him beside her, invisibly he sat there. She laughed hungrily, showing all her teeth. He gave a very wide sudden smile. The coach load chattered and some began to sing and shout and the young couple, getting into the clinch again, slept. The coach started and shook off the last of the towny places, whipped through short villages, passed pubs with animal names, The Fox, The Red Lion, The Dog and Duck, The Greyhound, and one with a new sign, The Dragon. It tunnelled under miles of trees, breathed afresh in scampering fields and thirty miles of greenery, public and private, until slowly, in an hour or so, the bald hills near the sea came up and, under them, distant slabs of chalk. Further and further the coach went and the bald hills grew taller and nearer.

The woman gazed disapprovingly at the young couple and was about to say something to the old man when suddenly, at the sight of his spry profile, she began to think—in freezing panic—of criminals. A man like this was just the kind—outwardly respectable—who would go down to Hampton's garden party to case the place, as she had read, pass as a member of the staff, steal jewellery, or plan a huge burglary. Or come to her house and bash her. The people who lived only a mile and a half from where she lived had had burglars when they were away: someone had been watching the house. They believed it was someone who had heard the house was for sale. Beside her own front door, behind a bush, she kept an iron bar. She always picked it up before she got her key out—in case. She saw herself now suddenly hitting out with it passionately, so that her heart raced; then having bashed the old man, she calmed down, or rather, she sailed into one of her exalted moods. She was wearing a heavy silver ring with a large brown stone in it, a stone which looked violet in some lights, and she said in her most genteel, faraway voice, "When I was in India, an Indian prince gave this ring to me when my husband died. It is very rare. It is one of those rings they wear for protection. He loved my husband. He gave it to me. They believe in magic."

She took it off and gave it to the old man.

"I always wear it. The people down the road were burgled."

The old man looked at the ring. It was very ugly and he gave it back to her.

What fools women are, he thought, and felt a huge access of strength. But aloud he said, "Very nice." And not to be outdone, he said, "My wife died in the Azores."

She took a deep breath. The coach had broken through the hills, and now cliffs of red houses had built up on either side and the city trees and gardens grew thicker and richer. The sunlight seemed to splash down in waves between them and over them. She grasped his arm.

"I can smell the sea already!" she said. "What are you going to tell your daughter-in-law when you ring up? I told the driver to stop at the station."

"Tell them?" said the old man. A brilliant idea occurred to him.

"I'll tell them I just dropped in on the Canary Islands," he said.

The woman let go of his arm, and after one glance, choked with laughter.

"Why not?" he said, grinning. "They ask too many questions. Where have you been? What are you doing? Or I might say Boulogne. Why not?"

"Well, it's nearer," she said. "But you must explain."

The wild young man suddenly shouted, "Where's he taking us now?" as the coach turned off the main road.

"He's dropping us at the station," the woman called out boldly. And indeed, speeding no more, grunting down side streets, the coach made for the station and stopped at the entrance to the station yard.

"Here we are," she said. "I'll get my car."

She pulled him by the sleeve to the door and he helped her out.

They stood on the pavement, surprised to see the houses and shops of the city stand still, every window looking at them. Brusquely cutting them off, the coach drove away at once downhill and left them to watch it pass out of sight. The old man blinked, staring at the last of the coach, and the woman's face aged.

It was the moment to be memorable, but he was so taken aback by her heavy look that he said, "You ought to have stayed on, gone to the party."

"No," she said, shaking brightness onto the face. "I'll get my car. It was just seeing your life drive off—don't you feel that sometimes?"

"No," he said. "Not mine. Theirs." And he straightened up, looked at his watch and then down the long hill. He put out his hand.

"I'm going to have a look at the sea."

And indeed, in a pale-blue wall on this July day, the sea showed between the houses. Or perhaps it was the sky. Hard to tell which.

She said, "Wait for me. I'll drive you down. I tell you what—I'll get my car. We'll drive to my house and have a cup of tea or a drink, and then you can telephone from there and I'll bring you back in for your train."

He still hesitated.

"I dreaded that journey. You made me laugh," she said.

And that is what they did. He admired her managing arms and knees as she drove out of the city into the confusing lanes.

"It's nice of you to come. I get nervous going back," she said as they turned into the drive of one of the ugliest bungalows he had ever seen, on top of the Downs, close to a couple of ragged firs torn and bent by the wind. A cat raced them to the door. She showed him the iron bar she kept close to it, behind the bush. A few miles away between a dip in the Downs was the pale-blue sea again, shaped like her lower lip.

There were her brass Indian objects on the wall of the sitting-room; on the mantelpiece and leaning against the mirror he had walked through was the photograph of her husband. Pull down a few walls, reface the front, move out the furniture, he thought, that's what you'd have to do, when she went off to another room, and wearing a white dress with red poppies on it came back with the tea tray.

"Now telephone," she said. "I'll get the number." But she did not give him the instrument until she heard a child answer it. That killed her last suspicion. She heard him speak to his daughter-in-law, and when he put the telephone down she said grandly, "I want thirty-one thousand pounds for the house."

The sum was so preposterous that it seemed to explode in his head and made him spill his tea in his saucer.

"If I decide to sell," she said, noticing his shock.

"If anyone offers you that," he said dryly, "I advise you to jump at it." They regarded each other with disappointment.

"I'll show you the garden. My husband worked hard in it," she said. "Are you a gardener?"

"Not any longer," he said as he followed her sulking across the lawn. She was sulking too. A thin film of cloud came over the late afternoon sky.

"Well, if you're ever interested let me know," she said. "I'll drive you to the station."

And she did, taking him the long way round the coast road, and there indeed was the sea, the real sea, all of it, spread out like the skirt of some lazy old landlady with children playing all along the fringes on the beaches. He liked being with the woman in the car, but he was sad his day was ending.

"I feel better," she said. "I think I'll go to Hampton's after all," she said, watching him. "I feel like a spree."

But he did not rise. Thirty-one thousand! The ideas women have! At the station he shook hands and she said, "Next time you come to Brighton . . ." and she touched his rose with her finger. The rose was drooping. He got on the train.

"Who is this lady friend who keeps ringing you up from Brighton?" his daughter-in-law asked in her lowing voice several times in the following weeks. Always questions.

"A couple I met at Frenchy's," he said on the spur of the moment.

"You didn't say you'd seen Frenchy. How is he?" his son said.

"Didn't I?" said the old man. "I might go down to see them next week. But I don't know. Frenchy's heard of a house."

But the old man knew that what he needed was not a house.

A Wedding-Dress

MORLEY CALLAGHAN
(Canadian, 1903–   )

For fifteen years Miss Lena Schwartz had waited for Sam Hilton to get a good job so they could get married. She lived in a quiet boarding-house on Wellesley Street, the only woman among seven men boarders. The landlady, Mrs. Mary McNab, did not want woman boarders; the house might get a bad reputation in the neighbourhood, but Miss Schwartz had been with her a long time. Miss Schwartz was thirty-two, her hair was straight, her nose turned up a little, and she was thin.

Sam got a good job in Windsor and she was going there to marry him. She was glad to think that Sam still wanted to marry her, because he was a Catholic and went to church every Sunday. Sam liked her so much he wrote a cramped homely letter four times a week.

When Miss Schwartz knew definitely that she was going to Windsor, she read part of a letter to Mrs. McNab, who was a plump, tidy woman. The men heard about the letter at the table and talked as if Lena were an old maid. 'I guess it will really happen to her all right,' they said, nudging one another.

The salesgirl mechanically lifted a brown dress from the rack. 'This is the right shade for you,' she said. 'Will you try it on?'

Miss Schwartz was disappointed. She had no idea such a plain dress would cost twenty-five dollars. She wanted something to keep alive the tempestuous feeling in her body, something to startle Sam. She had never paid so much for a dress, but Sam liked something fancy. 'I don't think I like these,' she said. 'I wanted something special.'

The salesgirl said sarcastically, 'Maybe you were thinking of a French dress. Some on the rack in the French room are marked down.'

Miss Schwartz moved away automatically. The salesgirl did not bother following her. 'Let the old maid look around,' she said to herself, following with her eyes the tall commonplace woman in the dark coat and the oddly shaped purple hat as she went into the gray French room. Miss Schwartz stood on a blue pattern on the gray carpet and guardedly fingered a dress on the rack, a black canton crepe dress with a high collar that folded back, forming petals of burnt orange. From the hem to the collar was a row of buttons, the sleeves were long with a narrow orange trimming at the cuff, and there was a wide corded silk girdle. It was marked seventy-five dollars. She liked the feeling it left in the tips of her fingers. She stood alone at the rack, toying with the material, her mind playing with thoughts she guiltily enjoyed. She imagined herself wantonly attractive in the dress, slyly watched by men with bold thoughts as she walked down the street with Sam, who would be nervously excited when he drew her into some corner and put his hands on her shoulders. Her heart began to beat heavily. She wanted to walk out of the room and over to the escalator but could not think clearly. Her fingers were carelessly drawing the dress into her wide coat sleeve, the dress disappearing steadily and finally slipping easily from the hanger, drawn into her wide sleeve.

She left the French room with a guilty feeling of satisfied exhaustion. The escalator carried her down slowly to the main floor. She hugged the parcels and the sleeve containing the dress tight to her breast. On the street-car she started to cry because Sam seemed to have become something remote, drifting away from her. She would have gone back with the dress but did not know how to go about it.

When she got to the boarding-house she went straight upstairs and put on the dress as fast as she could, to feel that it belonged to her. The black dress with the burnt orange petals on the high collar was short and loose on her thin figure.

And then the landlady knocked at the door and said that a tall man downstairs wanted to see her about something important. Mrs. McNab waited for Miss Schwartz to come out of her room.

Miss Schwartz sat on the bed. She felt that if she did not move at once she would not be able to walk downstairs. She walked downstairs in the French dress, Mrs. McNab watching her closely. Miss Schwartz saw a man with a wide heavy face and his coat collar buttoned high on his neck complacently watching her. She felt that she might just as well be walking downstairs in her underclothes; the dress was like something wicked clinging to her legs and her body. 'How do you do,' she said.

'Put on your hat and coat,' he said steadily.

Miss Schwartz, slightly bewildered, turned stupidly and went upstairs. She came down a minute later in her coat and hat and went out with the tall man. Mrs. McNab got red in the face when Miss Schwartz offered no word of explanation.

On the street he took her arm and said, 'You got the dress on and it won't do any good to talk about it. We'll go over to the station.'

'But I have to go to Windsor,' she said, 'I really have to. It will be all right. You see, I am to be married tomorrow. It's important to Sam.'

He would not take her seriously. The street lights made the slippery sidewalks glassy. It was hard to walk evenly.

At the station the sergeant said to the detective, 'She might be a bad egg. She's an old maid and they get very foxy.'

She tried to explain it clearly and was almost garrulous. The sergeant shrugged his shoulders and said the cells would not hurt her for a night. She started to cry. A policeman led her to a small cell with a plain bed.

Miss Schwartz could not think about being in the cell. Her head, heavy at first, got light and she could not consider the matter. The detective who had arrested her gruffly offered to send a wire to Sam.

The policeman on duty during the night thought she was a stupid silly woman because she kept saying over and over, 'We were going to be married. Sam liked a body to look real nice. He always said so.' The unsatisfied expression in her eyes puzzled the policeman, who said to the sergeant, 'She's a bit of a fool, but I guess she was going to get married all right.'

At half past nine in the morning they took her from the cell to the police car along with a small wiry man who had been quite drunk the night before, a coloured woman who had been keeping a bawdy-house, a dispirited fat man arrested for bigamy, and a Chinaman who had been keeping a betting-house. She sat stiffly, primly, in a corner of the car and could not cry. Snow was falling heavily when the car turned into the city hall courtyard.

Miss Schwartz appeared in the Women's Court before a little Jewish magistrate. Her legs seemed to stiffen and fall away when she saw Sam's closely cropped head and his big lazy body at a long table before the magistrate. A young man was talking rapidly and confidently to him. The magistrate and the Crown attorney were trying to make a joke at each other's expense. The magistrate found the attorney amusing. A court clerk yelled a name, the policeman at the door repeated it and then loudly yelled the name along the hall. The coloured woman who had been keeping the bawdy-house appeared with her lawyer.

Sam moved over to Miss Schwartz. He found it hard not to cry. She knew that a Salvation Army man was talking to a slightly hard-looking woman about her, and she felt strong and resentful. Sam held her hand but said nothing.

The coloured woman went to jail for two months rather than pay a fine of $200.

'Lena Schwartz,' said the clerk. The policeman at the door shouted the name along the hall. The young lawyer who had been talking to Sam told her to stand up while the clerk read the charge. She was scared and her knees were stiff.

'Where is the dress?' asked the magistrate.

A store detective with a heavy moustache explained that she had it on and told how she had been followed and later on arrested. Everybody looked at her, the dress too short and hanging loosely on her thin body, the burnt orange petals creased and twisted. The magistrate said to himself: 'She's an old maid and it doesn't even look nice on her.'

'She was to be married today,' began the young lawyer affably. 'She was to be married in this dress,' he said and good-humouredly explained that yesterday when she stole it she had become temporarily a kleptomaniac. Mr. Hilton had come up from Windsor and was willing to pay for the dress. It was a case for clemency. 'She waited a long time to be married and was not quite sure of herself,' he said seriously.

He told Sam to stand up. Sam haltingly explained that she was a good woman, a very good woman. The Crown attorney seemed to find Miss Schwartz amusing.

The magistrate scratched away with his pen and then said he would remand Miss Schwartz for sentence if Sam still wanted to marry her and would pay for the dress. Sam could hardly say anything. 'She will leave the city with you,' said the magistrate, 'and keep out of the department stores for a year.' He saw Miss Schwartz wrinkling her nose and blinking her eyes and added, 'Now go out and have a quiet wedding.' The magistrate was quite satisfied with himself.

Miss Schwartz, looking a little older than Sam, stood up in her dress that was to make men slyly watch her and straightened the corded silk girdle. It was to be her wedding-dress, all right. Sam gravely took her arm and they went out to be quietly married.

Judas

FRANK O'CONNOR
(Irish, 1903–1966)

"Sure you won't be late, Jerry?" said the mother and I going out.

"Am I ever late?" said I, and I laughed.

That was all we said, Michael John, but it stuck in my mind. As I was going down the road I was thinking it was months since I'd taken her to the pictures. Of course, you might think that funny, but after the father's death we were thrown together a lot. And I knew she hated being alone in the house after dark.

At the same time I had my own troubles. You see, Michael John, being an only child I never knocked round the way other fellows did. All the fellows in the office went out with girls, or at any rate they let on they did. They said "Who was the old doll I saw you with last night, Jerry? You'd better mind yourself, or you'll be getting into trouble." To hear them you'd imagine there was no sport in the world, only girls, and that they'd always be getting you into trouble. Paddy Kinnane, for instance, talked like that, and he never saw the way it upset me. I think he thought it was a great compliment. It wasn't until years after that I began to suspect that Paddy's acquaintance with girls was about of one kind with my own.

Then I met Kitty Doherty. Kitty was a hospital nurse, and all the chaps in the office said a fellow should never go with hospital nurses. Ordinary girls were bad enough, but nurses were a fright—they knew too much. I knew when I met Kitty that that was a lie. She was a well-educated superior girl; she lived up the river in a posh locality, and her mother was on all sorts of councils and committees. Kitty was small and wiry; a good-looking girl, always in good humour, and when she talked, she hopped from one thing to another like a robin on a frosty morning.

I used to meet her in the evening up the river road, as if I was walking there by accident and very surprised to see her. "Fancy meeting you!" I'd say or "Well, well, isn't this a great surprise!" Mind you, it usually was, for, no matter how much I was expecting her, I was never prepared for the shock of her presence. Then we'd stand talking for half an hour and I'd see her home. Several times she asked me in, but I was too nervous. I knew I'd lose my head, break the china, use some dirty word, and then go home and cut my throat. Of course, I never asked her to come to the pictures or anything of the sort. She was above that. My only hope was that if I waited long enough I might be able to save her from drowning or the white slavers or something else dramatic, which would show in a modest and dignified way how I felt about her. At the same time I had a bad conscience because I knew I should stay at home more with the mother, but the very thought that I might be missing an opportunity of fishing Kitty out of the river would spoil a whole evening on me.

That night in particular I was nearly distracted. It was three weeks since I'd seen Kitty. I was sure that, at the very least, she was dying and asking for me, and that no one knew my address. A week before, I had felt I simply couldn't bear it any longer, so I had made an excuse and gone down to the post office. I rang up the hospital and asked for Kitty. I fully expected them to say in gloomy tones that Kitty had died half an hour before, and got the shock of my life when the girl at the other end asked my name. I lost my head. "I'm afraid I'm a stranger to Miss Doherty," I said with an embarrassed laugh, "but I have a message for her from a friend."

Then I grew completely panic-stricken. What could a girl like Kitty make of a damned, deliberate lie like that? What else was it but a trap laid by an old and cunning hand? I held the receiver out and looked at it as if it was someone whose neck I was going to wring. "Moynihan," I said to it, "you're mad. An asylum, Moynihan, is the only place for you."

I heard Kitty's voice, not in my ear at all, but in the telephone booth as though she were standing before me, and nearly dropped the receiver in terror. Then I raised it and asked in what I thought of as a French accent: "Who is dat speaking, please?" "This is Kitty Doherty," she replied impatiently. "Who are you?"

That was exactly what I was wondering myself. "I am Monsieur Bertrand," I went on cautiously. "I am afraid I have the wrong number. I am so sorry." Then I put down the receiver carefully and thought how nice it would be if only I had a penknife handy to cut my throat with. It's funny, but from the moment I met Kitty I was always coveting sharp things like razors and penknives.

After that an awful idea dawned on me. Of course, I should have thought of it before, but, as you can see, I wasn't exactly knowledgeable where girls were concerned. I began to see that I wasn't meeting Kitty for the very good reason that Kitty didn't want to meet me. What her reason was, I could only imagine, but imagination was my strong point. I examined my conscience to see what I might have said to her. I remembered every remark I had made. The reason was only too clear. Every single remark I had made was either brutal, indecent or disgusting. I had talked of Paddy Kinnane as a fellow who "went with dolls." What could a pure-minded girl think of a chap who naturally used such a phrase except—what unfortunately was quite true—that he had a mind like a cesspit.

But this evening I felt more confident. It was a lovely summer evening with views of hillsides and fields between the gaps in the houses, and it raised my spirits. Perhaps I was wrong; perhaps she hadn't noticed or understood my filthy conversation, perhaps we might meet and walk home together. I walked the full length of the river road and back, and then started to walk it again. The crowds were thinning out as fellows and girls slipped off up the lanes or down to the river-bank, courting. As the streets went out like lamps about me, my hopes sank lower and lower. I saw clearly that she was avoiding me; that she knew I was not the quiet, good-natured fellow I let on to be but a volcano of brutality and lust.

"Lust, lust, lust!" I hissed to myself, clenching my fists. I could have forgiven myself anything but the lust.

Then I glanced up and saw her on a tram. I instantly forgot about the lust and smiled and waved my cap to her, but she was looking ahead and didn't see me. I raced after the car, intending to jump onto it, to sit in one of the back seats on top where she would not see me, and then say in astonishment as she got off "Fancy meeting you here!" But as if the driver knew what was in my mind, he put on speed, and the old tram went tossing and screeching down the one straight bit of road in the town, and I stood panting in the roadway, smiling as though missing a tram were the best joke in the world, and wishing all the time that I had a penknife and the courage to use it. My position was hopeless!

Then I must have gone a bit mad—really mad, I mean—for I started to race the tram. There were still lots of people out walking, and they stared after me in an incredulous way, so I lifted my fists to my chest in the attitude of a professional runner and dropped into what I fondly hoped would look like a comfortable stride and delude them into the belief that I was in training for a big race. By the time I was finished, I *was* a runner, and full of indignation against the people who still continued to stare at me.

Between my running and the tram's halts I just managed to keep it in view as far as the other side of town. When I saw Kitty get off and go up a hilly street, I collapsed and was only just able to drag myself after her. When she went into a house on a terrace, I sat on the high curb with my head between my knees until the panting stopped. At any rate I felt safe. I could afford to rest, could walk up and down before the house until she came out, and accost her with an innocent smile and say "Fancy meeting you!"

But my luck was dead out that night. As I was walking up and down, close enough to the house to keep it in view but not close enough to be observed from the windows, I saw a tall man strolling up at the opposite side of the road and my heart sank. It was Paddy Kinnane.

"Hallo, Jerry," he chuckled with that knowing grin he put on whenever he wanted to compliment you on being discovered in a compromising situation. "What are you doing here?"

"Just waiting for a chap I had a date with, Paddy," I said, trying to sound casual.

"Looks more as if you were waiting for an old doll, to me," Paddy said flatteringly. "Still waters run deep. When are you supposed to be meeting him?"

Cripes, I didn't even know what the time was!

"Half eight," I said at random.

"Half eight?" said Paddy. " 'Tis nearly nine now."

"Ah, he's a most unpunctual fellow," I said. "He's always the same. He'll turn up all right."

"I may as well wait with you," said Paddy, leaning against the wall and taking out a packet of cigarettes. "You might find yourself stuck by the end of the evening. There's people in this town that have no consideration for anyone."

That was Paddy all out: a heart of gold; no trouble too much for him if he could do you a good turn—I'd have loved to strangle him.

"Ah, to hell with him!" I said impatiently. "I won't bother waiting. It only struck me this minute that I have another appointment up the Western Road. You'll excuse me now, Paddy. I'll tell you all about it another time."

And away I went hell-for-leather to the tram. I mounted it and went on to the other terminus, near Kitty's house. There, at least, Paddy Kinnane could not get at me. I sat on the river wall in the dusk. The moon was rising, and every quarter of an hour a tram came grunting and squeaking over the old bridge and went black-out while the conductor switched his trolley. Each time I got off the wall and stood on the curb in the moonlight, searching for Kitty among the passengers. Then a policeman came along, and, as he seemed to be watching me, I slunk slowly off up the hill and stood against a wall in shadow. There was a high wall at the other side of the road as well, and behind it the roof of a house was cut out of the sky in moonlight. Every now and then a tram came in and people passed, and the snatches of conversation I caught were like the warmth from an open door to the heart of a homeless man. It was quite clear now that my position was hopeless. If Kitty had walked or been driven she could have reached home from the opposite direction. She could be at home in bed by now. The last tram came and went, and still there was no Kitty, and still I hung on despairingly. While one glimmer of a chance remained I could not go home.

Then I heard a woman's step. I couldn't even pretend to myself that it might be Kitty until she suddenly shuffled past me with that hasty little walk of hers. I started and called her name. She glanced quickly over her shoulder and, seeing a man emerge from the shadow, took fright and ran. I ran too, but she put on speed and began to outdistance me. At that I despaired. I stood on the pavement and shouted after her at the top of my voice.

"Kitty! Kitty, for God's sake, wait!"

She ran a few steps farther and then halted incredulously. She looked back, and then turned and slowly retraced her steps.

"Jerry Moynihan!" she whispered in astonishment. "What are you doing here?"

I was summoning strength to tell her that I had happened to be taking a stroll in that direction and was astonished to see her when I realized the improbability of it and began to cry instead. Then I laughed. It was hysteria, I suppose. But Kitty had had a bad fright and, now she was getting over it, she was as cross as two sticks.

"What's wrong with you, I say?" she snapped. "Are you out of your mind or what?"

"But I didn't see you for weeks," I burst out.

"I know," she replied. "I wasn't out. What about it?"

"I thought it might be something I said to you," I said desperately.

"What did you say?" she asked in bewilderment, but I couldn't repeat the hideous things I had already said. Perhaps, after all, she hadn't noticed them!

"How do I know?"

"Oh, it's not that," she said impatiently. "It's just Mother."

"Why?" I asked almost joyously. "Is there something wrong with her?"

"Ah, no, but she made such a fuss about it. I felt it wasn't worth it."

"A fuss? What did she make a fuss about?"

"About you, of course," Kitty said in exasperation.

"But what did I do?" I asked, clutching my head. This was worse than anything I had ever imagined. This was terrible!

"You didn't do anything, but people were talking about us. And you wouldn't come in and be introduced like anyone else. I know she's a bit of a fool, and her head is stuffed with old nonsense about her family. I could never see that they were different to anyone else, and anyway she married a commercial traveller herself, so she has nothing to talk about. Still, you needn't be so superior."

I felt cold shivers run through me. I had thought of Kitty as a secret between God, herself, and me and assumed that she only knew the half of it. Now it seemed I didn't even know the half. People were talking about us! I was superior! What next?

"But what has she against me?" I asked despairingly.

"She thinks we're doing a tangle, of course," snapped Kitty as if she was astonished at my stupidity, "and I suppose she imagines you're not grand enough for a great-great-grandniece of Daniel O'Connell. I told her you were above that sort of thing, but she wouldn't believe me. She said I was a deep, callous, crafty little intriguer and I hadn't a drop of Daniel O'Connell's blood in my veins." Kitty giggled at the thought of herself as an intriguer, and no wonder.

"That's all she knows," I said despairingly.

"I know," Kitty agreed. "She has no sense. And anyway she has no reason to think I'm telling lies. Cissy and I always had fellows, and we spooned with them all over the shop under her very nose, so I don't see why she thinks I'm trying to conceal anything."

At this I began to laugh like an idiot. This was worse than appalling. This was a nightmare. Kitty, whom I had thought so angelic, talking in cold blood about "spooning" with fellows all over the house. Even the bad women in the books I had read didn't talk about love-making in that cold-blooded way. Madame Bovary herself had at least the decency to pretend that she didn't like it. It was another door opening on the outside world, but Kitty thought I was laughing at her and started to apologize.

"Of course, I had no sense at the time," she said. "You were the first fellow I met that treated me properly. The others only wanted to fool around, and now, because I don't like it, Mother thinks I'm into something ghastly. I told her I liked you better than any fellow I knew, but that I'd grown out of all that sort of thing."

"And what did she say to that?" I asked fiercely. I was beginning to see that imagination wasn't enough; that all around me there was an objective reality that was a thousand times more nightmarish than any fantasy of my own. I couldn't hear enough about it, though at the same time it turned my stomach.

"Ah, I told you she was silly," Kitty said in embarrassment.

"Go on!" I shouted. "I want to know."

"Well," said Kitty with a demure grin, "she said you were a deep, designing guttersnipe who knew exactly how to get round featherpated little idiots like me. . . . You see, it's quite hopeless. The woman is common. She doesn't understand."

"Oh, God!" I said almost in tears. "I only wish she was right."

"Why do you wish she was right?" Kitty asked with real curiosity.

"Because then I'd have some chance of you," I said.

"Oh!" said Kitty, as if this was news to her. "To tell you the truth," she added after a moment, "I thought you were a bit keen at first, but then I wasn't sure. When you didn't kiss me or anything, I mean."

"God," I said bitterly, "when I think what I've been through in the past few weeks!"

"I know," said Kitty, biting her lip. "I was a bit fed up too."

Then we said nothing for a few moments.

"You're sure you mean it?" she asked suspiciously.

"But I tell you I was on the point of committing suicide," I said angrily.

"What good would that be?" she asked with another shrug, and this time she looked at me and laughed outright—the little jade!

I insisted on telling her about my prospects. She didn't want to hear about my prospects; she wanted me to kiss her, but that seemed to me a very sissy sort of occupation, so I told her just the same, in the intervals. It was as if a stone had been lifted off my heart, and I went home in the moonlight, singing. Then I heard the clock strike, and the singing stopped. I remembered the mother's "Sure you won't be late?" and my own "Am I ever late?" This was desperation too, but of a different sort.

The door was ajar and the kitchen in darkness. I saw her sitting before the fire by herself, and just as I was about to throw my arms round her, I smelt Kitty's perfume and was afraid to go near her. God help us, as though that would have told her anything!

"Hullo, Mum," I said with a nervous laugh, rubbing my hands. "You're all in darkness."

"You'll have a cup of tea?" she said.

"I might as well."

"What time is it?" she said, lighting the gas. "You're very late."

"I met a fellow from the office," I said, but at the same time I was stung by the complaint in her tone.

"You frightened me," she said with a little whimper. "I didn't know what happened to you. What kept you at all?"

"Oh, what do you think?" I said, goaded by my own sense of guilt. "Drinking and blackguarding as usual."

I could have bitten my tongue off as I said it; it sounded so cruel, as if some stranger had said it instead of me. She turned to me with a frightened stare as if she were seeing the stranger too, and somehow I couldn't bear it.

"God Almighty!" I said. "A fellow can have no life in his own house."

I went hastily upstairs, lit the candle, undressed, and got into bed. A chap could be a drunkard and blackguard and not be made to suffer what I was being made to suffer for being out late one single night. This, I felt, was what you got for being a good son.

"Jerry," she called from the foot of the stairs, "will I bring you up your cup?"

"I don't want it now, thanks," I said.

I heard her sigh and turn away. Then she locked the doors, front and back. She didn't wash up, and I knew that my cup of tea was standing on the table with a saucer on top in case I changed my mind. She came slowly upstairs and her walk was that of an old woman. I blew out the candle before she reached the landing, in case she came in to ask if I wanted anything else, and the moonlight came in the attic window and brought me memories of Kitty. But every time I tried to imagine her face as she grinned up at me, waiting for me to kiss her, it was the mother's face that came up instead, with that look like a child's when you strike him for the first time—as if he suddenly saw the stranger in you. I remembered all our life together from the night my father died; our early Mass on Sunday; our visits to the pictures, and our plans for the future, and Christ! Michael John, it was as if I was inside her mind while she sat by the fire waiting for the blow to fall. And now it had fallen, and I was a stranger to her, and nothing I could ever do would make us the same to one another again. There was something like a cannon-ball stuck in my chest, and I lay awake till the cocks started crowing. Then I could bear it no longer. I went out on the landing and listened.

"Are you awake, Mother?" I asked in a whisper.

"What is it, Jerry?" she replied in alarm, and I knew that she hadn't slept any more than I had.

"I only came to say I was sorry," I said, opening the door of her room, and then as I saw her sitting up in bed under the Sacred Heart lamp, the cannon-ball burst inside me and I began to cry like a kid.

"Oh, child, child, child!" she exclaimed, "what are you crying for at all, my little boy?" She spread out her arms to me. I went to her and she hugged me and rocked me as she did when I was only a nipper. "Oh, oh, oh," she was saying to herself in a whisper, "my storeen bawn, my little man!"—all the names she hadn't called me in years. That was all we said. I couldn't bring myself to tell her what I had done, nor could she confess to me that she was jealous: all she could do was to try and comfort me for the way I'd hurt her, to make up to me for the nature she had given me. "My storeen bawn!" she said. "My little man!"

A Drink in the Passage

❧❧❧

ALAN PATON
(South African, 1903–   )

In the year 1960 the Union of South Africa celebrated its Golden Jubilee, and there was a nationwide sensation when the one-thousand-pound prize for the finest piece of sculpture was won by a black man, Edward Simelane. His work, *African Mother and Child*, not only excited the admiration, but touched the conscience or heart or whatever it was that responded, of white South Africa, and seemed likely to make him famous in other countries.

It was by an oversight that his work was accepted, for it was the policy of the government that all the celebrations and competitions should be strictly segregated. The committee of the sculpture section received a private reprimand for having been so careless as to omit the words "for whites only" from the conditions, but was told, by a very high personage it is said, that if Simelane's work "was indisputably the best", it should receive the award. The committee then decided that this prize must be given along with the others, at the public ceremony which would bring this particular part of the celebrations to a close.

For this decision it received a surprising amount of support from the white public; but in certain powerful quarters, there was an outcry against any departure from the "traditional policies" of the country, and a threat that many white prize-winners would renounce their prizes. However a crisis was averted, because the sculptor was "unfortunately unable to attend the ceremony".

"I wasn't feeling up to it," Simelane said mischievously to me. "My parents, and my wife's parents, and our priest, decided that I wasn't feeling up to it. And finally I decided so too. Of course Majosi and Sola and the others wanted me to go and get my prize personally, but I said, 'boys, I'm a sculptor, not a demonstrator'."

"This cognac is wonderful," he said, "especially in these big glasses. It's the first time I've had such a glass. It's also the first time I've drunk a brandy so slowly. In Orlando you develop a throat of iron, and you just put back your head and pour it down, in case the police should arrive."

He said to me, "This is the second cognac I've had in my life. Would you like to hear the story of how I had my first?"

You know the Alabaster Bookshop in von Brandis Street? Well, after the competition they asked me if they could exhibit my *African Mother and Child*. They gave a whole window to it, with a white velvet backdrop, if there is anything called white velvet, and some complimentary words.

Well somehow I could never go and look in that window. On my way from the station to the *Herald* office, I sometimes went past there, and I felt good when I saw all the people standing there; but I would only squint at it out of the corner of my eye.

Then one night I was working late at the *Herald,* and when I came out there was hardly anyone in the streets, so I thought I'd go and see the window, and indulge certain pleasurable human feelings. I must have got a little lost in the contemplation of my own genius, because suddenly there was a young white man standing next to me.

He said to me, "What do you think of that, mate?" And you know, one doesn't get called "mate" every day.

"I'm looking at it," I said.

"I live near here," he said, "and I come and look at it nearly every night. You know it's by one of your own boys, don't you? See, Edward Simelane."

"Yes, I know."

"It's beautiful," he said. "Look at that mother's head. She's loving that child, but she's somehow watching too. Do you see that? Like someone guarding. She knows it won't be an easy life."

He cocked his head on one side, to see the thing better.

"He got a thousand pounds for it," he said. "That's a lot of money for one of your boys. But good luck to him. You don't get much luck, do you?"

Then he said confidentially, "Mate, would you like a drink?"

Well honestly I didn't feel like a drink at that time of night, with a white stranger and all, and a train still to catch to Orlando.

"You know we black people must be out of the city by eleven," I said.

"It won't take long. My flat's just round the corner. Do you speak Afrikaans?"

"Since I was a child," I said in Afrikaans.

"We'll speak Afrikaans then. My English isn't too wonderful. I'm van Rensburg. And you?"

I couldn't have told him my name. I said I was Vakalisa, living in Orlando.

"Vakalisa, eh? I haven't heard that name before."

By this time he had started off, and I was following, but not willingly. That's my trouble, as you'll soon see. I can't break off an encounter. We didn't exactly walk abreast, but he didn't exactly walk in front of me. He didn't look constrained. He wasn't looking round to see if anyone might be watching.

He said to me, "Do you know what I wanted to do?"

"No," I said.

"I wanted a bookshop, like that one there. I always wanted that, ever since I can remember. When I was small, I had a little shop of my own." He laughed at himself. "Some were real books, of course, but some of them I wrote myself. But I had bad luck. My parents died before I could finish school."

Then he said to me, "Are you educated?"

I said unwillingly, "Yes." Then I thought to myself, how stupid, for leaving the question open.

And sure enough he asked, "Far?"

And again unwillingly, I said, "Far."

He took a big leap. "Degree?"

"Yes."

"Literature?"

"Yes."

He expelled his breath, and gave a long "ah". We had reached his building, Majorca Mansions, not one of those luxurious places. I was glad to see that the entrance lobby was deserted. I wasn't at my ease. I don't feel at my ease in such places, not unless I am protected by friends, and this man was a stranger. The lift was at ground level, marked *Whites Only. Slegs vir Blankes.* Van Rensburg opened the door and waved me in. Was he constrained? To this day I don't know. While I was waiting for him to press the button, so that we could get moving and away from that ground floor, he stood with his finger suspended over it, and looked at me with a kind of honest, unselfish envy.

"You were lucky," he said. "Literature, that's what I wanted to do."

He shook his head and pressed the button, and he didn't speak again until we stopped high up. But before we got out he said suddenly, "If I had had a bookshop, I'd have given that boy a window too."

We got out and walked along one of those polished concrete passage-ways, I suppose you could call it a stoep if it weren't so high up, let's call it a passage. On the one side was a wall, and plenty of fresh air, and far down below von Brandis Street. On the other side were the doors, impersonal doors; you could hear radios and people talking, but there wasn't a soul in sight. I wouldn't like living so high; we Africans like being close to the earth. Van Rensburg stopped at one of the doors, and said to me, "I won't be a minute." Then he went in, leaving the door open, and inside I could hear voices. I thought to myself, he's telling them who's here. Then after a minute or so, he came back to the door, holding two glasses of red wine. He was warm and smiling.

"Sorry there's no brandy," he said. "Only wine. Here's happiness."

Now I certainly had not expected that I would have my drink in the passage. I wasn't only feeling what you may be thinking, I was thinking that one of the impersonal doors might open at any moment, and someone might see me in a "white" building, and see me and van Rensburg breaking the liquor laws of the country. Anger could have saved me from the whole embarrassing situation, but you know I can't easily be angry. Even if I could have been, I might have found it hard to be angry with this particular man. But I wanted to get away from there, and I couldn't. My mother used to say to me, when I had said something anti-white, "Son, don't talk like that, talk as you are." She would have understood at once why I took a drink from a man who gave it to me in the passage.

Van Rensburg said to me, "Don't you know this fellow Simelane?"

"I've heard of him," I said.

"I'd like to meet him," he said. "I'd like to talk to him." He added in explanation, "You know, talk out my heart to him."

A woman of about fifty years of age came from the room beyond, bringing a plate of biscuits. She smiled and bowed to me. I took one of the biscuits, but not for all the money in the world could I have said to her *dankie, my nooi,* or that disgusting *dankie, missus,* nor did I want to speak to her in English because her language was Afrikaans, so I took the risk of it and used the word *mevrou,* for the politeness of which some Afrikaners would knock a black man down, and I said, in high Afrikaans, with a smile and a bow too, *"Ek is u dankbaar, Mevrou."*

But nobody knocked me down. The woman smiled and bowed, and van Rensburg, in a strained voice that suddenly came out of nowhere, said, "Our land is beautiful. But it breaks my heart."

The woman put her hand on his arm, and said, "Jannie, Jannie."

Then another woman and a man, all about the same age, came up and stood behind van Rensburg.

"He's a B.A.," van Rensburg told them. "What do you think of that?"

The first woman smiled and bowed to me again, and van Rensburg said, as though it were a matter for grief, "I wanted to give him brandy, but there's only wine."

The second woman said, "I remember, Jannie. Come with me."

She went back into the room, and he followed her. The first woman said to me, "Jannie's a good man. Strange, but good."

And I thought the whole thing was mad, and getting beyond me, with me a black stranger being shown a testimonial for the son of the house, with these white strangers standing and looking at me in the passage, as though they wanted for God's sake to touch me somewhere and didn't know how, but I saw the earnestness of the woman who had smiled and bowed to me, and I said to her, "I can see that, *Mevrou."*

"He goes down every night to look at the statue," she said. "He says only God could make something so beautiful, therefore God must be in the man who made it, and he wants to meet him and talk out his heart to him."

She looked back at the room, and then she dropped her voice a little, and said to me, "Can't you see, it's somehow because it's a black woman and a black child?"

And I said to her, "I can see that, *Mevrou.*"

She turned to the man and said of me, "He's a good boy."

Then the other woman returned with van Rensburg, and van Rensburg had a bottle of brandy. He was smiling and pleased, and he said to me, "This isn't ordinary brandy, it's French."

He showed me the bottle, and I, wanting to get the hell out of that place, looked at it and saw it was cognac. He turned to the man and said, "Uncle, you remember? When you were ill? The doctor said you must have good brandy. And the man at the bottle-store said this was the best brandy in the world."

"I must go," I said. "I must catch that train."

"I'll take you to the station," he said. "Don't you worry about that."

He poured me a drink and one for himself.

"Uncle," he said, "what about one for yourself?"

The older man said, "I don't mind if I do," and he went inside to get himself a glass.

Van Rensburg said, "Happiness," and lifted his glass to me. It was a good brandy, the best I've ever tasted. But I wanted to get the hell out of there. I stood in the passage and drank van Rensburg's brandy. Then Uncle came back with his glass, and van Rensburg poured him a brandy, and Uncle raised his glass to me too. All of us were full of goodwill, but I was waiting for the opening of one of those impersonal doors. Perhaps they were too, I don't know. Perhaps when you want so badly to touch someone, you don't care. I was drinking my brandy almost as fast as I would have drunk it in Orlando.

"I must go," I said.

Van Rensburg said, "I'll take you to the station." He finished his brandy, and I finished mine too. We handed the glasses to Uncle, who said to me, "Good night my boy." The first woman said, "May God bless you," and the other woman bowed and smiled. Then van Rensburg and I went down in the lift to the basement, and got into his car.

"I told you I'd take you to the station," he said. "I'd take you home, but I'm frightened of Orlando at night."

We drove up Eloff Street, and he said, "Did you know what I meant?" I knew that he wanted an answer to something, and I wanted to answer him, but I couldn't, because I didn't know what that something was. He couldn't be talking about being frightened of Orlando at night, because what more could one mean than just that?

"By what?" I asked.

"You know," he said, "about our land being beautiful?"

Yes, I knew what he meant, and I knew that for God's sake he wanted to touch me too and he couldn't; for his eyes had been blinded by years in the dark. And I thought it was a pity, for if men never touch each other, they'll hurt each other one day. And it was a pity he was blind, and couldn't touch me, for black men don't touch white men any more; only by accident, when they make something like *Mother and Child*.

He said to me, "What are you thinking?"

I said, "Many things," and my inarticulateness distressed me, for I knew he wanted something from me. I felt him fall back, angry, hurt, despairing, I didn't know. He stopped at the main entrance to the station, but I didn't tell him I couldn't go in there. I got out and said to him, "Thank you for the sociable evening."

"They liked having you," he said. "Did you see that?"

I said, "Yes, I saw that."

He sat slumped in his seat, like a man with a burden of incomprehensible, insoluble grief. I wanted to touch him, but I was thinking about the train. He said Good night and I said it too. We each saluted the other. What he was thinking, God knows, but I was thinking he was like a man trying to run a race in iron shoes, and not understanding why he cannot move.

When I got back to Orlando, I told my wife the story, and she wept.

Mortmain

GRAHAM GREENE
(English, 1904–   )

How wonderfully secure and peaceful a genuine marriage seemed to
Carter, when he attained it at the age of forty-two. He even enjoyed every
moment of the church service, except when he saw Josephine wiping
away a tear as he conducted Julia down the aisle. It was typical of this
new frank relationship that Josephine was there at all. He had no secrets
from Julia; they had often talked together of his ten tormented years with
Josephine, of her extravagant jealousy, of her well-timed hysterics. 'It
was her insecurity,' Julia argued with understanding, and she was quite
convinced that in a little while it would be possible to form a friendship
with Josephine.

'I doubt it, darling.'

'Why? I can't help being fond of anyone who loved you.'

'It was a rather cruel love.'

'Perhaps at the end when she knew she was losing you, but darling,
there *were* happy years.'

'Yes.' But he wanted to forget that he had ever loved anyone before
Julia.

Her generosity sometimes staggered him. On the seventh day of their
honeymoon, when they were drinking retsina in a little restaurant on the
beach by Sunium, he accidentally took a letter from Josephine out of his
pocket. It had arrived the day before and he had concealed it, for fear of
hurting Julia. It was typical of Josephine that she could not leave him
alone for the brief period of the honeymoon. Even her handwriting was

now abhorrent to him—very neat, very small, in black ink the colour of her hair. Julia was platinum-fair. How had he ever thought that black hair was beautiful? Or been impatient to read letters in black ink?

'What's the letter, darling? I didn't know there had been a post.'

'It's from Josephine. It came yesterday.'

'But you haven't even opened it!' she exclaimed without a word of reproach.

'I don't want to think about her.'

'But, darling, she may be ill.'

'Not she.'

'Or in distress.'

'She earns more with her fashion-designs than I do with my stories.'

'Darling, let's be kind. We can afford to be. We are so happy.'

So he opened the letter. It was affectionate and uncomplaining and he read it with distaste.

Dear Philip, I didn't want to be a death's head at the reception, so I had no chance to say goodbye and wish you both the greatest possible happiness. I thought Julia looked terribly beautiful and so very, very young. You must look after her carefully. I know how well you can do that, Philip dear. When I saw her, I couldn't help wondering why you took such a long time to make up your mind to leave me. Silly Philip. It's much less painful to act quickly.

I don't suppose you are interested to hear about my activities now, but just in case you are worrying a little about me—you know what an old worrier you are—I want you to know that I'm working very hard at a whole series for—guess, the French Vogue. *They are paying me a fortune in francs, and I simply have no time for unhappy thoughts. I've been back once—I hope you don't mind—to our apartment (slip of the tongue) because I'd lost a key sketch. I found it at the back of our communal drawer —the ideas-bank, do you remember? I thought I'd taken all my stuff away, but there it was between the leaves of the story you started that heavenly summer, and never finished, at Napoule. Now I'm rambling on when all I really wanted to say was: Be happy both of you. Love, Josephine.*

Carter handed the letter to Julia and said, 'It could have been worse.'

'But would she like me to read it?'

'Oh, it's meant for both of us.' Again he thought how wonderful it was to have no secrets. There had been so many secrets during the last ten years, even innocent secrets, for fear of misunderstanding, of Josephine's rage or silence. Now he had no fear of anything at all: he could have trusted even a guilty secret to Julia's sympathy and comprehension. He said, 'I was a fool not to show you the letter yesterday. I'll never do anything like that again.' He tried to recall Spenser's line—'. . . port after stormie seas'.

When Julia had finished reading the letter she said, 'I think she's a wonderful woman. How very, very sweet of her to write like that. You know I was—only now and then of course—just a little worried about her. After all *I* wouldn't like to lose you after ten years.'

When they were in the taxi going back to Athens she said, 'Were you very happy at Napoule?'

'Yes, I suppose so. I don't remember, it wasn't like this.'

With the antennae of a lover he could feel her moving away from him, though their shoulders still touched. The sun was bright on the road from Sunium, the warm sleepy loving siesta lay ahead, and yet . . . 'Is anything the matter, darling?' he asked.

'Not really. . . . It's only . . . do you think one day you'll say the same about Athens as about Napoule? "I don't remember, it wasn't like this." '

'What a dear fool you are,' he said and kissed her. After that they played a little in the taxi going back to Athens, and when the streets began to unroll she sat up and combed her hair. 'You aren't really a cold man, are you?' she asked and he knew that all was right again. It was Josephine's fault that—momentarily—there had been a small division.

When they got out of bed to have dinner, she said, 'We must write to Josephine.'

'Oh no!'

'Darling, I know how you feel, but really it was a wonderful letter.'

'A picture-postcard then.'

So they agreed on that.

Suddenly it was autumn when they arrived back in London—if not winter already, for there was ice in the rain falling on the tarmac, and they had quite forgotten how early the lights came on at home—passing Gillette and Lucozade and Smith's Crisps, and no view of the Parthenon anywhere. The BOAC posters seemed more than usually sad—'BOAC takes you there and brings you back'.

'We'll put on all the electric fires as soon as we get in,' Carter said, 'and it will be warm in no time at all.' But when they opened the door of the apartment they found the fires were already alight. Little glows greeted them in the twilight from the depths of the living-room and the bedroom.

'Some fairy has done this,' Julia said.

'Not a fairy of any kind,' Carter said. He had already seen the envelope on the mantelpiece addressed in black ink to 'Mrs Carter'.

Dear Julia, you won't mind my calling you Julia, will you? I feel we have so much in common, having loved the same man. Today was so icy that I could not help thinking of how you two were returning from the sun and the warmth to a cold flat. (I know how cold the flat can be. I used to catch a chill every year when we came back from the south of France.) So I've done a very presumptuous thing. I've slipped in and put on the fires, but to show you that I'll never do such a thing again, I've hidden my key under the mat outside the front door. That's just in case your plane is held up in Rome or somewhere. I'll telephone the airport and if by some unlikely chance you haven't arrived, I'll come back and turn out the fires for safety (and economy! the rates are awful). Wishing you a very warm evening in your new home, love from Josephine.

P.S. I did notice that the coffee jar was empty, so I've left a packet of Blue Mountain in the kitchen. It's the only coffee Philip really cares for.

'Well,' Julia said laughing, 'she does think of everything.'

'I wish she'd just leave us alone,' Carter said.

'We wouldn't be warm like this, and we wouldn't have any coffee for breakfast.'

'I feel that she's lurking about the place and she'll walk in at any moment. Just when I'm kissing you.' He kissed Julia with one careful eye on the door.

'You *are* a bit unfair, darling. After all, she's left her key under the mat.'

'She might have had a duplicate made.'

She closed his mouth with another kiss.

'Have you noticed how erotic an aeroplane makes you after a few hours?' Carter asked.

'Yes.'

'I suppose it's the vibration.'

'Let's do something about it, darling.'

'I'll just look under the mat first. To make sure she wasn't lying.'

He enjoyed marriage—so much that he blamed himself for not having married before, forgetting that in that case he would have been married to Josephine. He found Julia, who had no work of her own, almost miraculously available. There was no maid to mar their relationship with habits. As they were always together, at cocktail parties, in restaurants, at small dinner parties, they had only to meet each other's eyes . . . Julia soon earned the reputation of being delicate and easily tired, it occurred so often that they left a cocktail party after a quarter of an hour or abandoned a dinner after the coffee—'Oh dear, I'm so sorry, such a vile headache, so stupid of me. Philip, *you* must stay . . .'

'Of course I'm not going to stay.'

Once they had a narrow escape from discovery on the stairs while they were laughing uncontrollably. Their host had followed them out to ask them to post a letter. Julia in the nick of time changed her laughter into what seemed to be a fit of hysterics. . . . Several weeks went by. It was a really successful marriage. . . . They liked—between whiles—to discuss its success, each attributing the main merit to the other. 'When I think you might have married Josephine,' Julia said. 'Why didn't you marry Josephine?'

'I suppose at the back of our minds we knew it wasn't going to be permanent.'

'Are we going to be permanent?'

'If we aren't, nothing will ever be.'

It was early in November that the time-bombs began to go off. No doubt they had been planned to explode earlier, but Josephine had not taken into account the temporary change in his habits. Some weeks passed before he had occasion to open what they used to call the ideas-bank in the days of their closest companionship—the drawer in which he used to leave notes for stories, scraps of overheard dialogue and the like, and she would leave roughly sketched ideas for fashion advertisements.

Directly he opened the drawer he saw her letter. It was labelled heavily 'Top Secret' in black ink with a whimsically drawn exclamation mark in the form of a girl with big eyes (Josephine suffered in an elegant way from exophthalmic goitre) rising genie-like out of a bottle. He read the letter with extreme distaste:

Dear, you didn't expect to find me here, did you? But after ten years I can't not now and then say, Good-night or good-morning, how are you? Bless you. Lots of love (really and truly), Your Josephine.

The threat of 'now and then' was unmistakable. He slammed the drawer shut and said 'Damn' so loudly that Julia looked in. 'Whatever is it, darling?'

'Josephine again.'

She read the letter and said, 'You know, I can understand the way she feels. Poor Josephine. Are you tearing it up, darling?'

'What else do you expect me to do with it? Keep it for a collected edition of her letters?'

'It just seems a bit unkind.'

'Me unkind to *her?* Julia, you've no idea of the sort of life that we led those last years. I can show you scars: when she was in a rage she would stub her cigarettes *anywhere.'*

'She felt she was losing you, darling, and she got desperate. They are my fault really, those scars, every one of them.' He could see growing in her eyes that soft amused speculative look which always led to the same thing.

Only two days passed before the next time-bomb went off. When they got up Julia said, 'We really ought to change the mattress. We both fall into a kind of hole in the middle.'

'I hadn't noticed.'

'Lots of people change the mattress every week.'

'Yes. Josephine always did.'

They stripped the bed and began to roll the mattress. Lying on the springs was a letter addressed to Julia. Carter saw it first and tried to push it out of sight, but Julia saw him.

'What's that?'

'Josephine, of course. There'll soon be too many letters for one volume. We shall have to get them properly edited at Yale like George Eliot's.'

'Darling, this is addressed to me. What were you planning to do with it?'

'Destroy it in secret.'

'I thought we were going to have no secrets.'

'I had counted without Josephine.'

For the first time she hesitated before opening the letter. 'It's certainly a bit bizarre to put a letter here. Do you think it got there accidentally?' 'Rather difficult, I should think.'

She read the letter and then gave it to him. She said with relief, 'Oh, she explains why. It's quite natural really.' He read:

Dear Julia, how I hope you are basking in a really Greek sun. Don't tell Philip (Oh, but of course you wouldn't have secrets yet) but I never really cared for the south of France. Always that mistral, drying the skin. I'm glad to think you are not suffering there. We always planned to go to Greece when we could afford it, so I know Philip will be happy. I came in today to find a sketch and then remembered that the mattress hadn't been turned for at least a fortnight. We were rather distracted, you know, the last weeks we were together. Anyway I couldn't bear the thought of your coming back from the lotus islands and finding bumps in your bed the first night, so I've turned it for you. I'd advise you to turn it every week: otherwise a hole always develops in the middle. By the way I've put up the winter curtains and sent the summer ones to the cleaners at 153 Brompton Road. Love, Josephine.

'If you remember, she wrote to me that Napoule had been heavenly,' he said. 'The Yale editor will have to put in a cross-reference.'

'You *are* a bit cold-blooded,' Julia said. 'Darling, she's only trying to be helpful. After all I never knew about the curtains or the mattress.'

'I suppose you are going to write a long cosy letter in reply, full of household chat.'

'She's been waiting weeks for an answer. This is an *ancient* letter.'

'And I wonder how many more ancient letters there are waiting to pop out. By God, I'm going to search the flat through and through. From attic to basement.'

'We don't have either.'

'You know very well what I mean.'

'I only know you are getting fussed in an exaggerated way. You really behave as though you are frightened of Josephine.'

'Oh hell!'

Julia left the room abruptly and he tried to work. Later that day a squib went off—nothing serious, but it didn't help his mood. He wanted to find the dialling number for overseas telegrams and he discovered inserted in volume one of the directory a complete list in alphabetical order, typed on Josephine's machine on which O was always blurred, a complete list of the numbers he most often required. John Hughes, his oldest friend, came after Harrods; and there were the nearest taxi-rank, the chemist's, the butcher's, the bank, the dry-cleaner's, the greengrocer's, the fishmonger's, his publisher and agent, Elizabeth Arden's and local hairdressers'—marked in brackets ('For J. please note, quite reliable and very inexpensive')—it was the first time he noticed they had the same initials.

Julia, who saw him discover the list, said, 'The angel-woman. We'll pin it up over the telephone. It's really terribly complete.'

'After the crack in her last letter I'd have expected her to include Cartier's.'

'Darling, it wasn't a crack. It was a bare statement of fact. If I hadn't a little money, we would have gone to the south of France too.'

'I suppose you think I married you to get to Greece.'

'Don't be an owl. You don't see Josephine clearly, that's all. You twist every kindness she does.'

'Kindness?'

'I expect it's the sense of guilt.'

After that he really began a search. He looked in cigarette-boxes, drawers, filing-cabinets, he went through all the pockets of the suits he had left behind, he opened the back of the television-cabinet, he lifted the lid of the lavatory-cistern, and even changed the roll of toilet-paper (it was quicker than unwinding the whole thing). Julia came to look at him, as he worked in the lavatory, without her usual sympathy. He tried the pelmets (who knew what they mightn't discover when next the curtains were sent for cleaning?), he took their dirty clothes out of the basket in case something had been overlooked at the bottom. He went on hands-and-knees through the kitchen to look under the gas-stove, and once, when he found a piece of paper wrapped around a pipe, he exclaimed in a kind of triumph, but it was nothing at all—a plumber's relic. The afternoon post rattled through the letter-box and Julia called to him from the hall—'Oh, good, you never told me you took in the French *Vogue*.'

'I don't.'

'Sorry, there's a kind of Christmas card in another envelope. A subscription's been taken out for us by Miss Josephine Heckstall-Jones. I do call that sweet of her.'

'She's sold a series of drawings to them. I won't look at it.'

'Darling, you are being childish. Do you expect her to stop reading your books?'

'I only want to be left alone with you. Just for a few weeks. It's not so much to ask.'

'You're a bit of an egoist, darling.'

He felt quiet and tired that evening, but a little relieved in mind. His search had been very thorough. In the middle of dinner he had remembered the wedding-presents, still crated for lack of room, and insisted on making sure between the courses that they were still nailed down—he knew Josephine would never have used a screwdriver for fear of injuring her fingers, and she was terrified of hammers. The peace of a solitary evening at last descended on them: the delicious calm which they knew either of them could alter at any moment with a touch of the hand. Lovers cannot postpone as married people can. 'I am grown peaceful as old age tonight,' he quoted to her.

'Who wrote that?'

'Browning.'

'I don't know Browning. Read me some.'

He loved to read Browning aloud—he had a good voice for poetry, it was his small harmless Narcissism. 'Would you really like it?'

'Yes.'

'I used to read to Josephine,' he warned her.

'What do I care? We can't help doing *some* of the same things, can we, darling?'

'There is something I never read to Josephine. Even though I was in love with her, it wasn't suitable. We weren't—permanent.' He began:

> How well I know what I mean to do
> When the long dark autumn-evenings come . . .

He was deeply moved by his own reading. He had never loved Julia so much as at this moment. Here was home—nothing else had been other than a caravan.

> . . . I will speak now,
> No longer watch you as you sit
> Reading by firelight, that great brow

And the spirit-small hand propping it,
Mutely, my heart knows how.

He rather wished that Julia had really been reading, but then of course
she wouldn't have been listening to him with such adorable attention.

. . . If two lives join, there is oft a scar.
They are one and one, with a shadowy third;
One near one is too far.

He turned the page and there lay a sheet of paper (he would have discovered it at once, before reading, if she had put it in an envelope) with the
black neat handwriting.

*Dearest Philip, only to say goodnight to you between the pages of your
favourite book—and mine. We are so lucky to have ended in the way we
have. With memories in common we shall for ever be a little in touch.
Love, Josephine.*

He flung the book and the paper on the floor. He said, 'The bitch. The
bloody bitch.'

'I won't have you talk of her like that,' Julia said with surprising
strength. She picked up the paper and read it.

'What's wrong with that?' she demanded. 'Do you hate memories?
What's going to happen to our memories?'

'But don't you see the trick she's playing? Don't you understand? Are
you an idiot, Julia?'

That night they lay in bed on opposite sides, not even touching with
their feet. It was the first night since they had come home that they had
not made love. Neither slept much. In the morning Carter found a letter
in the most obvious place of all, which he had somehow neglected: between the leaves of the unused single-lined foolscap on which he always
wrote his stories. It began, 'Darling, I'm sure you won't mind my using
the old term . . .'

The Spring Hat

❦

H. E. BATES
(English, 1905–1974)

Miss Manktelow, who in desperation had begun to tint her hair a shade of unobtrusive brown, never openly expressed her opinion that the profession of millinery was better than any other. But in her heart she had always known it was.

From her small back sitting-room, where chairs and tables and even the mantelpiece were hung about with grey skulls of buckram and rolls of coloured ribbon and frayed strips of trimming, she looked out on an asphalt yard in which two cut-down beer-barrels supported the dead frames of a pair of rhododendrons. She did not quite remember when the rhododendrons had been planted; she knew only that they had never flowered and then had died. But one day, when she had time, she was going to take the brown skeletons of them out and in their places she was going to plant something brighter. Perhaps nasturtiums or geraniums or even tobacco plants—they would smell beautifully when the yard was dark and hot on summer evenings. She was very fond of flowers, but the constant trouble with flowers was cats. You planted something and immediately, next day, cats scratched it up again and killed it. That was the worst, she thought, of living in a neighbourhood like East Street. All its earth was asphalt. All its back-yards were alive with cats and there were never any flowers.

Mrs Daley, a customer who had a large crusty head with a depressed forehead and pale ears that were something like pieces of uncooked pastry pricked at the bottom with skewers, looked uneasily at a hat Miss Manktelow was finishing on a wooden block.

She was not quite sure what to think of this hat. It did not seem, she thought, to suit her character. It appeared to be rather loud for her and she said:

'I had in mind something rather in the way of a plain velour.'

'Velour?' Miss Manktelow said. 'I wouldn't think velour was you.'

'What Joe said was——'

'Joe?' Miss Manktelow said. She pricked her bottom lip as she took out of it, too hastily, one of the pins she was using for the hat. 'How is Joe?'

The flower she was pinning on Mrs Daley's hat was something like a cross between a trampled peony and an overblown crimson poppy. It was a little dusty in the heart but that would brush off and in the completed hat it would never be seen.

'You know Joe,' Mrs Daley said. 'You know what Joe is. Joe's always the same.'

Her voice was flat with indifference about Joe. She reached out and touched the hat. Her feeling that it was not right for her made her mouth drop loosely. A narrow gap appeared above the upper set of her false teeth and gave her a look of disjointed vacancy.

'I've had the velour in my mind all winter,' she said.

'Winter—yes, that's all right,' Miss Manktelow said. 'In winter I grant you. But you want a bit more colour now spring is here.'

In the yard and beyond it, in East Street, there was no sign of spring. On the tarred fence a brown cat was crouching and the wind of February prickled its fur. A fog of black smoke hung about the bakery. The bakery was also an outdoor beer-house and there were all sorts of sounds that came from it that Miss Manktelow knew well. Beer barrels rolling in the side jetty. Men's voices. Shovels scraping on the bakehouse floor.

She was familiar also with the sound of Joe Daley, laughing with the baker.

'The thing to do is to try it,' she said. She took the last of the pins from her mouth. Under the flabby flower of crimson and dusty black the entire hat on its wooden skull was submerged. 'That's the only way.'

Joe Daley was a large man with fierce pink flesh and light dancing blue eyes that because of their vivacity seemed to stick out, like a shrimp's, from the front of his head. In summer the beer-house was cool. In winter the bakehouse was always fiery and snug and nearly always Joe was there. People were not permitted drink in the beer-house because it had an off-licence only, but there was nothing to prevent the baker and Joe Daley having bottles of beer in the bakehouse at the back. They had many bottles of beer there and sometimes Joe stayed for the night-baking. He and the baker laughed over the beer while the bread was cooking and Miss Manktelow, waking, could hear them from her room.

'This is temporary,' she said, 'nothing is fixed.'

When she put the hat on Mrs. Daley's head the large dough-like ears supported it uncertainly. In a strange fashion the flower made Mrs Daley look heavier, older, more misshapen than before.

'I fancy the flower wants to be further up,' Miss Manktelow said. 'That will give you a bit of height. That's what you need.'

Mrs Daley was small in all ways except for her head and ears. Miss Manktelow did not understand how a large healthy boisterous man like Joe Daley came to fall for a woman so undersized. She did not know how people fell for each other anyway. It was a mystery how one person got into the way of being entranced or familiar with another.

'Let's try it there.' The flower, fixed high on the crown of the hat, seemed as big as a train signal. 'I'll just pin it and you can see what you feel.'

Joe was extraordinary, always laughing. Miss Manktelow was fond of having new bread and cocoa at night. And sometimes, about ten o'clock, when she went into the bakehouse to fetch bread fresh and hot from the oven, Joe would be there. That would be the first baking. The air would be strong with the heat of the bakehouse, the smell of bread and the laughter of Joe. There would be a yeasty smell of baking and beer, the loud boisterous blowing laugh of Joe as he sprawled in a floury chair.

'I feel as if I'm going to over-balance,' Mrs Daley said, 'with the flower all that much on one side——'

'I don't think so,' Miss Manktelow said. 'Don't let that worry you——'

When Mrs Daley peered into the mirror above the mantelpiece she saw the critical face of Miss Manktelow rise above her shoulder.

'Now forget that it's you,' Miss Manktelow said. 'Try to imagine it's someone else. Detach yourself and look at the hat.'

Mrs Daley looked at the top-heavy familiar reflection of herself with an expression of troubled uncertainty. She could not imagine she was anyone else and her mouth fell open again. She felt insecure and touched the side of the flower, pushing it up a little, and Miss Manktelow said: 'No, no. Not too much. I think it's right as it is.'

'I fancy it ought to go more in the middle——'

'Well, let's try in the middle then. We can but try.'

The flower, set in the middle of the hat, seemed to pull down the entire front of Mrs Daley's face into a puzzled scowl. Mrs Daley's hair was spidery and grey. Pieces of it stuck out from under the hat like straying sheep's wool, making her look as if she wore a wig that did not sit correctly.

Miss Manktelow said she thought the flower in the middle of the hat looked marvellous. She felt it was just the thing. 'It gives balance,' she said. 'And yet there's just that touch.'

Mrs Daley fingered the hat, the flower and bits of her hair uncertainly, as if wondering exactly what that touch could be. Miss Manktelow thought of Joe.

There had once been an evening when Joe had been extra boisterous in the bakehouse, full of extraordinary larks.

She often thought of that evening. Joe was sitting on the dough-board in his shirt sleeves. You never knew what Joe was going to say to you next and that evening he had kept on calling her Miss Mangeltoe. It was the way he said it that was so funny and every few moments he roared with laughter. For a time she did her best not to laugh. Her name after all was rather an exceptional one; she was in a profession; she did not want to lower herself at all. She had once heard someone say too that her name was French and that it was possibly a corruption of something like Manque de l'eau, whatever that meant.

But after Joe had called her Miss Mangeltoe several times she could not help herself and began laughing. At first she tittered and then Joe gave a shriek of laughter, the beginning of which she saw plainly, a series of stirring tremulous flutters, in the great strong belly above the tops of his trousers.

After that she could not keep her face straight. Joe roared and kept slapping his fat tight thighs with both hands. There were beads of yeasty beer on his mouth, a tipsy flare in his blue eyes and a smell of fire and baking in the air. She felt the laughter, the warmth and the way Joe called her Miss Mangeltoe having a strange effect on her. It fired her, although she laughed so much, into a curious sadness that became an ache above her heart.

Then another disturbing and in fact almost terrifying thing had happened. All at once Joe, swinging his legs excitedly under the dough-table, said he would take her home.

'Could we try it plain?' Mrs Daley said, 'without the flower?'

Miss Manktelow stuck pins into her mouth and again she felt one of them sharply prick her lips.

'It's nothing without the flower,' she said. 'The flower is *it*. It's the whole point of the hat. You can see for yourself if we put it on the block.'

On the block, that was so like a bony and skinless skull, the hat did not look more ugly than when it sat on Mrs Daley's flabby, paste-like ears. Mrs Daley stared at it with open mouth, in dismay, her false teeth dropping weakly. She said that Joe had all the time fancied her in a velour, that all the time that had been Joe's idea.

'Men never know about hats,' Miss Manktelow said.

Mrs Daley had cut her hair in an old-fashioned bob that had the effect of shortening her stature still further now that she had taken off the hat. Looking at it, Miss Manktelow wondered again how on earth a man like Joe could fall for a person who looked so dwarf and crushed and then she said:

'I think I've got it. I think I've got the answer. We'll put the flower at the back.'

She had thought again and again of that evening when Joe had said he would take her home. She wondered what might have happened if she had taken him into the house. She had never been able to make up her mind whether he meant it or not. Joe was always larking of course. Perhaps he was drunk? You never quite knew with Joe. But he had in fact actually jumped off the dough-board; he had actually taken her by the arm and pretended he was ready.

'At the back,' she said to Mrs Daley. 'I'm perfectly sure that that's the answer.'

She remembered Joe roaring with laughter and winking at the baker and saying: 'We're ready. Eh, Fred? We're ready. Only got to get Miss Mangeltoe ready now, Fred, and then we're all set. That right, Fred? Always got to get the lady ready.'

She did not think it could have been a joke; but then again, she often told herself, it could have been and perhaps it was. All the same she wondered what might have happened. Joe in the dark house, Joe having another glass of beer and a plate of bread and cheese, Joe talking and laughing among the trimmings and hats and skulls. Joe alone with her. Joe saying he was ready and pulling her leg and calling her Miss Mangeltoe. She could never be quite certain that what she imagined might not have been real. There was no way of saying it might not have happened.

The hat, without the flower at the front, sat on Mrs Daley more hideously than ever; but when Mrs Daley looked into the mirror again she was aware only of a sense of relief because she could not see the flower.

'I think that's better,' she said. 'Heaps. I like it better like that.'

'It's always a question of trying things one way and the other until you get the thing that fits the personality,' Miss Manktelow said.

She had learnt all that during her years with Curtis and Co. You had to make the personality fit the hat. Naturally customers resisted and had their own ideas but they never really knew what was best for them. That was why they were always rushing back and changing hats because they did not fit their change of mood. Women were stupid about hats. They simply never knew.

She had learned all those things at Curtis and Co. She had been a very promising girl there. She had wanted to get on. But somehow things had not turned out very brightly. One way or another they had never quite clicked. She had started up on her own in the back room and somehow had never got out of it. The truth was you needed capital and influence to get on.

'Now we've got it right,' she said, 'I'll sew it on.'

Mrs Daley, wearing the hat at last, gave off a terribly troubled impression of two-fold misfortune. There was something naked and unfinished about the hat as seen from the front. Her ears protruded grossly, like two pale gargoyles deformed and wrinkled. From the back the flower seemed as if hooked to the wrong hat and then forgotten.

'I don't think it will need altering,' Miss Manktelow said. 'I don't think it will need a touch.'

'I hope to goodness Joe won't hate it,' Mrs Daley said.

From the street-side window Miss Manktelow watched Mrs Daley blown beyond the bakehouse, across East Street, by the February wind. There was no sign of spring in East Street. The hat was altogether too large for Mrs Daley and seemed to rock on her ears. In the wind Mrs

Daley looked ugly and comfortless and held the hat with one hand as if feeling it was top-heavy and did not belong to her and would blow away.

Through the back window Miss Manktelow stared at the yard. The rhododendrons were stark and hideous and would have to come out this spring. She removed the naked wooden skull from the table and thought of the bakehouse at night, of Joe laughing and of the smell of bread and fire.

She turned and looked at her face in the mirror. It really wasn't a bad face, she thought. She really couldn't understand how a man like Joe could fall for a face so crushed and out of proportion as Mrs Daley's, with those enormous ears and the scraggle of bleached grey hair.

She lifted the front of her own hair with her fingers. The new streak of grey growing out from the roots was something she would have to tint in when she went to bed. How did people fall for each other? How did it come about that a man preferred one face to another?

In the yard the brown cat leapt from the fence, driven by a black tom-cat that slid like a panther behind the rhododendrons. In rage Miss Manktelow saw the flash of its reflection in the mirror and rushed to the window, beating on it angrily.

'Psst!' she shouted. 'Psst! You big black brute!—go home! Psst! Psst! Get out!—go home!'

That was what killed things, she thought. That's what made it impossible to have any flowers.

'Psst!' she said. She spat with angry breath against the glass. 'Psst! Go home, you brute!' It was no wonder you could never have anything. 'Psst! Psst!—go home where you belong. Psst!—you great ugly thing!'

In hatred Miss Manktelow glared at the cat; and the cat, with green-proud eyes, glared back at Miss Manktelow.

Under the Banyan Tree

R. K. NARAYAN
(Indian, 1906–   )

The village Somal, nestling away in the forest tracts of Mempi, had a population of less than three hundred. It was in every way a village to make the heart of a rural reformer sink. Its tank, a small expanse of water, right in the middle of the village, served for drinking, bathing, and washing the cattle, and it bred malaria, typhoid, and heaven knew what else. The cottages sprawled anyhow and the lanes twisted and wriggled up and down and strangled each other. The population used the highway as the refuse ground and in the backyard of every house drain water stagnated in green puddles.

Such was the village. It is likely that the people of the village were insensitive: but it is more than likely that they never noticed their surroundings because they lived in a kind of perpetual enchantment. The enchanter was Nambi, the story-teller. He was a man of about sixty or seventy. Or was he eighty or one hundred and eighty? Who could say? In a place so much cut off as Somal (the nearest bus-stop was ten miles away) reckoning could hardly be in the familiar measures of time. If anyone asked Nambi what his age was he referred to an ancient famine or an invasion or the building of a bridge and indicated how high he had stood from the ground at the time.

He was illiterate, in the sense that the written word was a mystery to him; but he could make up a story, in his head, at the rate of one a month; each story took nearly ten days to narrate.

His home was the little temple which was at the very end of the village.

No one could say how he had come to regard himself as the owner of the temple. The temple was a very small structure with red-striped walls, with a stone image of the Goddess, *Shakti,* in the sanctum. The front portion of the temple was Nambi's home. For aught it mattered any place might be his home; for he was without possessions. All that he possessed was a broom with which he swept the temple; and he had also a couple of *dhoties* and upper cloth. He spent most part of the day in the shade of the banyan which spread out its branches in front of the temple. When he felt hungry he walked into any house that caught his fancy and joined the family at dinner. When he needed new clothes they were brought to him by the villagers. He hardly ever had to go out in search of company; for the banyan shade served as a club house for the village folk. All through the day people came seeking Nambi's company and squatted under the tree. If he was in a mood for it he listened to their talk and entertained them with his own observations and anecdotes. When he was in no mood he looked at the visitors sourly and asked, "What do you think I am? Don't blame me if you get no story at the next moon. Unless I meditate how can the Goddess give me a story? Do you think stories float in the air?"; and moved out to the edge of the forest and squatted there contemplating the trees.

On Friday evenings the village turned up at the temple for worship, when Nambi lit a score of mud lamps and arranged them around the threshold of the sanctuary. He decorated the image with flowers, which grew wildly in the backyard of the temple. He acted as the priest and offered to the Goddess fruits and flowers brought in by the villagers.

On the nights he had a story to tell he lit a small lamp and placed it in a niche in the trunk of the banyan tree. Villagers as they returned home in the evenings saw this, went home, and said to their wives, "Now, now, hurry up with the dinner, the story-teller is calling us." As the moon crept up behind the hillock, men, women and children, gathered under the banyan tree. The story-teller would not appear yet. He would be sitting in the sanctum, before the Goddess, with his eyes shut, in deep meditation. He sat thus as long as he liked and when he came out, with his forehead ablaze with ash and vermilion, he took his seat on a stone platform in front of the temple. He opened the story with a question. Jerking his finger towards a vague, far-away destination, he asked, "A thousand years ago, a stone's throw in that direction, what do you think there was? It was not the weed-covered waste it is now, for donkeys to roll in. It was not the ash-pit it is now. It was the capital of the king. . . ." The king would be Dasaratha, Vikramaditya, Asoka, or anyone that came into the old man's head; the capital was called Kapila, Kridapura, or anything. Opening thus the old man went on without a pause for three hours. By then brick by brick the palace of the king was raised. The old man described the dazzling *durbar* hall where sat a hundred vassal kings, ministers, and subjects; in another part of the palace all the musicians in the world assembled and sang; and most of the songs were sung over again by Nambi to his audience; and he described in detail the pictures and trophies that hung on the walls of the palace. . . .

It was story-building on an epic scale. The first day barely conveyed the setting of the tale, and Nambi's audience as yet had no idea who were all coming into the story. As the moon slipped behind the trees of Mempi Forest Nambi said, "Now friends, Mother says this will do for the day." He abruptly rose, went in, lay down, and fell asleep long before the babble of the crowd ceased.

The light in the niche would again be seen two or three days later, and again and again throughout the bright half of the month. Kings and heroes, villains and fairy-like women, gods in human form, saints and assassins, jostled each other in that world which was created under the banyan tree. Nambi's voice rose and fell in an exquisite rhythm, and the moonlight and the hour completed the magic. The villagers laughed with Nambi, they wept with him, they adored the heroes, cursed the villains, groaned when the conspirator had his initial success, and they sent up to the gods a heartfelt prayer for a happy ending. . . .

On the last day when the story ended, the whole gathering went into the sanctum and prostrated before the Goddess. . . .

By the time the next moon peeped over the hillock Nambi was ready with another story. He never repeated the same kind of story or brought in the same set of persons, and the village folk considered Nambi a sort of miracle, quoted his words of wisdom, and lived on the whole in an exalted plane of their own, though their life in all other respects was hard and drab.

And yet it had gone on for years and years. And one moon he lit the lamp in the tree. The audience came. The old man took his seat and began the story. ". . . When King Vikramaditya lived, his minister was . . ." He paused. He could not get beyond it. He made a fresh beginning. "There was the king . . ." he said, repeated it, and then his words trailed off into a vague mumbling. "What has come over me?" he asked pathetically. "Oh, Mother, great Mother, why do I stumble and falter? I know the story. I had the whole of it a moment ago. What was it about? I can't understand what has happened?" He faltered and looked so miserable that his audience said, "Take your own time. You are perhaps tired."

"Shut up!" he cried. "Am I tired? Wait a moment; I will tell you the story presently." Following this there was utter silence. Eager faces looked up at him. "Don't look at me!" he flared up. Somebody gave him a tumbler of milk. The audience waited patiently. This was a new experience. Some persons expressed their sympathy aloud. Some persons began to talk among themselves. Those who sat in the outer edge of the crowd silently slipped away. Gradually, as it neared midnight, others followed this example. Nambi sat staring at the ground, his head bowed in thought. For the first time he realized that he was old. He felt he would never more be able to control his thought or express them cogently. He looked up. Everyone had gone except his friend Mari the blacksmith. "Mari, why aren't you also gone?"

Mari apologized for the rest: "They didn't want to tire you; so they have gone away."

Nambi got up. "You are right. Tomorrow I will make it up. Age, age. What is my age? It has come on suddenly." He pointed at his head and said, "This says 'Old fool, don't think I shall be your servant any more. You will be my servant hereafter.' It is disobedient and treacherous."

He lit the lamp in the niche next day. The crowd assembled under the banyan faithfully. Nambi had spent the whole day in meditation. He had been fervently praying to the Goddess not to desert him. He began the story. He went on for an hour without a stop. He felt greatly relieved, so much so that he interrupted his narration to remark, "Oh, friends. The Mother is always kind. I was seized with a foolish fear . . ." and continued the story. In a few minutes he felt dried up. He struggled hard: "And then . . . and then . . . what happened?" He stammered. There followed a pause lasting an hour. The audience rose without a word and went home. The old man sat on the stone brooding till the cock crew. "I can't blame them for it," he muttered to himself. "Can they sit down here and mope all night?" Two days later he gave another instalment of the story, and that, too, lasted only a few minutes. The gathering dwindled. Fewer persons began to take notice of the lamp in the niche. Even these came only out of a sense of duty. Nambi realized that there was no use in prolonging the struggle. He brought the story to a speedy and premature end.

He realized what was happening. He was harrowed by the thoughts of his failure. "I should have been happier if I had dropped dead years ago," he said to himself. "Mother, why have you struck me dumb. . . ?" He shut himself up in the sanctum, hardly ate any food, and spent the greater part of the day sitting motionless in meditation.

The next moon peeped over the hillock, Nambi lit the lamp in the niche. The villagers as they returned home saw the lamp, but only a handful turned up at night. "Where are the others?" the old man asked. "Let us wait." He waited. The moon came up. His handful of audience waited patiently. And then the old man said, "I won't tell the story today, nor tomorrow unless the whole village comes here. I insist upon it. It is a mighty story. Everyone must hear it." Next day he went up and down the village street shouting, "I have a most wonderful tale to tell tonight. Come one and all; don't miss it. . . ." This personal appeal had a great effect. At night a large crowd gathered under the banyan. They were happy that the story-teller had regained his powers. Nambi came out of the temple when everyone had settled and said: "It is the Mother who gives the gifts; and it is She who takes away the gifts. Nambi is a dotard. He speaks when the Mother has anything to say. He is struck dumb when She has nothing to say. But what is the use of the jasmine when it has lost its scent? What is the lamp for when all the oil is gone? Goddess be thanked. . . . These are my last words on this earth; and this is my greatest story." He rose and went into the sanctum. His audience hardly understood what he meant. They sat there till they became weary. And then some of them got up and stepped into the sanctum. There the story-teller sat with his eyes shut. "Aren't you going to tell us a story?" they asked. He opened his eyes, looked at them, and shook his head. He indicated by gesture that he had spoken his last words.

When he felt hungry he walked into any cottage and silently sat down for food, and walked away the moment he had eaten. Beyond this he had hardly anything to demand of his fellow-beings. The rest of his life (he lived for a few more years) was one great consummate silence.

The Old Man

DAPHNE DU MAURIER
(English, 1907–)

Did I hear you asking about the Old Man? I thought so. You're a new-comer to the district, here on holiday. We get plenty these days, during the summer months. Somehow they always find their way eventually over the cliffs down to this beach, and then they pause and look from the sea back to the lake. Just as you did.

It's a lovely spot, isn't it? Quiet and remote. You can't wonder at the old man choosing to live here.

I don't remember when he first came. Nobody can. Many years ago, it must have been. He was here when I arrived, long before the war. Per-haps he came to escape from civilisation, much as I did myself. Or maybe, where he lived before, the folks around made things too hot for him. It's hard to say. I had the feeling, from the very first, that he had done something, or something had been done to him, that gave him a grudge against the world. I remember the first time I set eyes on him I said to myself, "I bet that old fellow is one hell of a character."

Yes, he was living here beside the lake, along of his missus. Funny sort of lash-up they had, exposed to all the weather, but they didn't seem to mind.

I had been warned about him by one of the fellows from the farm, who advised me, with a grin, to give the old man who lived down by the lake a wide berth—he didn't care for strangers. So I went warily, and I didn't stay to pass the time of day. Nor would it have been any use if I had, not knowing a word of his lingo. The first time I saw him he was standing by the edge of the lake, looking out to sea, and from tact I avoided the piece of planking over the stream, which meant passing close to him, and crossed to the other side of the lake by the beach instead. Then, with an awkward feeling that I was trespassing and had no business to be there, I bobbed down behind a clump of gorse, took out my spy-glass, and had a peep at him.

He was a big fellow, broad and strong—he's aged, of course, lately; I'm speaking of several years back—but even now you can see what he must have been once. Such power and drive behind him, and that fine head, which he carried like a king. There's an idea in that, too. No, I'm not joking. Who knows what royal blood he carries inside him, harking back to some remote ancestor? And now and again, surging in him—not through his own fault—it gets the better of him and drives him fighting mad. I didn't think about that at the time. I just looked at him, and ducked behind the gorse when I saw him turn, and I wondered to myself what went on in his mind, whether he knew I was there, watching him.

If he should decide to come up the lake after me I should look pretty foolish. He must have thought better of it, though, or perhaps he did not care. He went on staring out to sea, watching the gulls and the incoming tide, and presently he ambled off his side of the lake, heading for the missus and home and maybe supper.

I didn't catch a glimpse of her that first day. She just wasn't around. Living as they do, close in by the left bank of the lake, with no proper track to the place, I hardly had the nerve to venture close and come upon her face to face. When I did see her, though, I was disappointed. She wasn't much to look at after all. What I mean is, she hadn't got anything like his character. A placid, mild-tempered creature, I judged her.

They had both come back from fishing when I saw them, and were making their way up from the beach to the lake. He was in front, of course. She tagged along behind. Neither of them took the slightest notice of me, and I was glad, because the old man might have paused, and waited, and told her to get on back home, and then come down towards the rocks where I was sitting. You ask what I would have said, had he done so? I'm damned if I know. Maybe I would have got up, whistling and seeming unconcerned, and then, with a nod and a smile—useless, really, but instinctive, if you know what I mean—said good day and pottered off. I don't think he would have done anything. He'd just have stared after me, with those strange narrow eyes of his, and let me go.

After that, winter and summer, I was always down on the beach or the rocks, and they went on living their curious, remote existence, sometimes fishing in the lake, sometimes at sea. Occasionally I'd come across them in the harbour on the estuary, taking a look at the yachts anchored there, and the shipping. I used to wonder which of them made the suggestion. Perhaps suddenly he would be lured by the thought of the bustle and life of the harbour, and all the things he had either wantonly given up or never known, and he would say to her, "Today we are going into town." And she, happy to do whatever pleased him best, followed along.

You see, one thing that stood out—and you couldn't help noticing it— was that the pair of them were devoted to one another. I've seen her greet him when he came back from a day's fishing and had left her back home, and towards evening she'd come down the lake and on to the beach and down to the sea to wait for him. She'd see him coming from a long way off, and I would see him too, rounding the corner of the bay. He'd come straight in to the beach, and she would go to meet him, and they would embrace each other, not caring a damn who saw them. It was touching, if you know what I mean. You felt there was something lovable about the old man, if that's how things were between them. He might be a devil to outsiders, but he was all the world to her. It gave me a warm feeling for him, when I saw them together like that.

You asked if they had any family. I was coming to that. It's about the family I really wanted to tell you. Because there was a tragedy, you see. And nobody knows anything about it except me. I suppose I could have told someone, but if I had, I don't know . . . They might have taken the old man away, and she'd have broken her heart without him, and anyway, when all's said and done, it wasn't my business. I know the evidence against the old man was strong, but I hadn't positive proof, it might have been some sort of accident, and anyway, nobody made any enquiries at the time the boy disappeared, so who was I to turn busybody and informer?

I'll try and explain what happened. But you must understand that all this took place over quite a time, and sometimes I was away from home or busy, and didn't go near the lake. Nobody seemed to take any interest in the couple living there but myself, so that it was only what I observed with my own eyes that makes this story, nothing that I heard from anybody else, no scraps of gossip, or tales told about them behind their backs.

Yes, they weren't always alone, as they are now. They had four kids. Three girls and a boy. They brought up the four of them in that ramshackle old place by the lake, and it was always a wonder to me how they did it. God, I've known days when the rain lashed the lake into little waves that burst and broke on the muddy shore near by their place, and turned the marsh into a swamp, and the wind driving straight in. You'd have thought anyone with a grain of sense would have taken his missus and his kids out of it and gone off somewhere where they could get some creature comforts at least. Not the old man. If he could stick it, I guess he decided she could too, and the kids as well. Maybe he wanted to bring them up the hard way.

Mark you, they were attractive youngsters. Especially the youngest girl. I never knew her name, but I called her Tiny, she had so much go to her. Chip off the old block, in spite of her size. I can see her now, as a little thing, the first to venture paddling in the lake, on a fine morning, way ahead of her sisters and the brother.

The brother I nicknamed Boy. He was the eldest, and between you and me a bit of a fool. He hadn't the looks of his sisters and was a clumsy sort of fellow. The girls would play around on their own, and go fishing, and he'd hang about in the background, not knowing what to do with himself. If he possibly could he'd stay around home, near his mother. Proper mother's boy. That's why I gave him the name. Not that she seemed to fuss over him any more than she did the others. She treated the four alike, as far as I could tell. Her thoughts were always for the old man rather than for them. But Boy was just a great baby, and I have an idea he was simple.

Like their parents, the youngsters kept themselves to themselves. Been dinned into them, I dare say, by the old man. They never came down to the beach on their own and played; and it must have been a temptation, I thought, in full summer, when people came walking over the cliffs down to the beach to bathe and picnic. I suppose, for those strange reasons best known to himself, the old man had warned them to have no truck with strangers.

They were used to me pottering, day in, day out, fetching driftwood and that. And often I would pause and watch the kids playing by the lake. I didn't talk to them, though. They might have gone back and told the old man. They used to look up when I passed by, then glance away

again, sort of shy. All but Tiny. Tiny would toss her head and do a
somersault, just to show off.

I sometimes watched them go off, the six of them—the old man, the
missus, Boy, and the three girls, for a day's fishing out to sea. The old
man, of course, in charge; Tiny eager to help, close to her dad; the missus
looking about her to see if the weather was going to keep fine; the two
other girls alongside; and Boy, poor simple Boy, always the last to leave
home. I never knew what sport they had. They used to stay out late, and
I'd have left the beach by the time they came back again. But I guess they
did well. They must have lived almost entirely on what they caught. Well,
fish is said to be full of vitamins, isn't it? Perhaps the old man was a food
faddist in his way.

Time passed, and the youngsters began to grow up. Tiny lost something of her individuality then, it seemed to me. She grew more like her
sisters. They were a nice-looking trio, all the same. Quiet, you know,
well-behaved.

As for Boy, he was enormous. Almost as big as the old man, but with
what a difference! He had none of his father's looks, or strength, or
personality; he was nothing but a great clumsy lout. And the trouble was,
I believe the old man was ashamed of him. He didn't pull his weight in
the home, I'm certain of that. And out fishing he was perfectly useless.
The girls would work away like beetles, with Boy, always in the background, making a mess of things. If his mother was there he just stayed
by her side.

I could see it rattled the old man to have such an oaf of a son. Irritated
him, too, because Boy was so big. It probably didn't make sense to his
intolerant mind. Strength and stupidity didn't go together. In any normal
family, of course, Boy would have left home by now and gone out to
work. I used to wonder if they argued about it back in the evenings, the
missus and the old man, or if it was something never admitted between
them but tacitly understood—Boy was no good.

Well, they did leave home at last. At least, the girls did.

I'll tell you how it happened.

It was a day in late autumn, and I happened to be over doing some
shopping in the little town overlooking the harbour, three miles from this
place, and suddenly I saw the old man, the missus, the three girls and
Boy all making their way up to Pont—that's at the head of a creek going
eastward from the harbour. There are a few cottages at Pont, and a farm

and a church up behind. The family looked washed and spruced up, and so did the old man and the missus, and I wondered if they were going visiting. If they were, it was an unusual thing for them to do. But it's possible they had friends or acquaintances up there, of whom I knew nothing. Anyway, that was the last I saw of them, on the fine Saturday afternoon, making for Pont.

It blew hard over the weekend, a proper easterly gale. I kept indoors and didn't go out at all. I knew the seas would be breaking good and hard on the beach. I wondered if the old man and the family had been able to get back. They would have been wise to stay with their friends up Pont, if they had friends there.

It was Tuesday before the wind dropped and I went down to the beach again. Seaweed, driftwood, tar and oil all over the place. It's always the same after an easterly blow. I looked up the lake, towards the old man's shack, and I saw him there, with the missus, just by the edge of the lake. But there was no sign of the youngsters.

I thought it a bit funny, and waited around in case they should appear. They never did. I walked right round the lake, and from the opposite bank I had a good view of their place, and even took out my old spy-glass to have a closer look. They just weren't there. The old man was pottering about as he often did when he wasn't fishing, and the missus had settled herself down to bask in the sun. There was only one explanation. They had left the family with friends in Pont. They had sent the family for a holiday.

I can't help admitting I was relieved, because for one frightful moment I thought maybe they had started off back home on the Saturday night and got struck by the gale; and, well—that the old man and his missus had got back safely, but not the kids. It couldn't be that, though. I should have heard. Someone would have said something. The old man wouldn't be pottering there in his usual unconcerned fashion and the missus basking in the sun. No, that must have been it. They had left the family with friends. Or maybe the girls and Boy had gone up country, gone to find themselves jobs at last.

Somehow it left a gap. I felt sad. So long now I had been used to seeing them all around, Tiny and the others. I had a strange sort of feeling that they had gone for good. Silly, wasn't it? To mind, I mean. There was the old man, and his missus, and the four youngsters, and I'd more or less watched them grow up, and now for no reason they had gone.

I wished then I knew even a word or two of his language, so that I could have called out to him, neighbour-like, and said, "I see you and the missus are on your own. Nothing wrong, I hope?"

But there, it wasn't any use. He'd have looked at me with his strange eyes and told me to go to hell.

I never saw the girls again. No, never. They just didn't come back. Once I thought I saw Tiny, somewhere up the estuary, with a group of friends, but I couldn't be sure. If it was, she'd grown, she looked different. I tell you what I think. I think the old man and the missus took them with a definite end in view, that last weekend, and either settled them with friends they knew or told them to shift for themselves.

I know it sounds hard, not what you'd do for your own son and daughters, but you have to remember the old man was a tough customer, a law unto himself. No doubt he thought it would be for the best, and so it probably was, and if only I could know for certain what happened to the girls, especially Tiny, I wouldn't worry.

But I do worry sometimes, because of what happened to Boy.

You see, Boy was fool enough to come back. He came back about three weeks after that final weekend. I had walked down through the woods— not my usual way, but down to the lake by the stream that feeds it from a higher level. I rounded the lake by the marshes to the north, some distance from the old man's place, and the first thing I saw was Boy.

He wasn't doing anything. He was just standing by the marsh. He looked dazed. He was too far off for me to hail him; besides, I didn't have the nerve. But I watched him, as he stood there in his clumsy loutish way, and I saw him staring at the far end of the lake. He was staring in the direction of the old man.

The old man, and the missus with him, took not the slightest notice of Boy. They were close to the beach, by the plank bridge, and were either just going out to fish or coming back. And here was Boy, with his dazed stupid face, but not only stupid—frightened.

I wanted to say, "Is anything the matter?" but I didn't know how to say it. I stood there, like Boy, staring at the old man.

Then what we both must have feared would happen, happened.

The old man lifted his head, and saw Boy.

He must have said a word to his missus, because she didn't move, she stayed where she was, by the bridge, but the old man turned like a flash of lightning and came down the other side of the lake towards the marshes, towards Boy. He looked terrible. I shall never forget his appearance. That magnificent head I had always admired now angry, evil; and he was cursing Boy as he came. I tell you, I heard him.

Boy, bewildered, scared, looked hopelessly about him for cover. There was none. Only the thin reeds that grew beside the marsh. But the poor fellow was so dumb he went in there, and crouched, and believed himself safe—it was a horrible sight.

I was just getting my own courage up to interfere when the old man stopped suddenly in his tracks, pulled up short as it were, and then, still cursing, muttering, turned back again and returned to the bridge. Boy watched him, from his cover of reeds, then, poor clot that he was, came out on to the marsh again, with some idea, I suppose, of striking for home.

I looked about me. There was no one to call. No one to give any help. And if I went and tried to get someone from the farm they would tell me not to interfere, that the old man was best left alone when he got in one of his rages, and anyway that Boy was old enough to take care of himself. He was as big as the old man. He could give as good as he got. I knew different. Boy was no fighter. He didn't know how.

I waited quite a time beside the lake but nothing happened. It began to grow dark. It was no use my waiting there. The old man and the missus left the bridge and went on home. Boy was still standing there on the marsh, by the lake's edge.

I called to him, softly. "It's no use. He won't let you in. Go back to Pont, or wherever it is you've been. Go to some place, anywhere, but get out of here."

He looked up, that same queer dazed expression on his face, and I could tell he hadn't understood a word I said.

I felt powerless to do any more. I went home myself. But I thought about Boy all evening, and in the morning I went down to the lake again, and I took a great stick with me to give me courage. Not that it would have been much good. Not against the old man.

Well . . . I suppose they had come to some sort of agreement, during the night. There was Boy, by his mother's side, and the old man was pottering on his own.

I must say, it was a great relief. Because, after all, what could I have said or done? If the old man didn't want Boy home, it was really his affair. And if Boy was too stupid to go, that was Boy's affair.

But I blamed the mother a good deal. After all, it was up to her to tell Boy he was in the way, and the old man was in one of his moods, and Boy had best get out while the going was good. But I never did think she had great intelligence. She did not seem to show much spirit at any time.

However, what arrangement they had come to worked for a time. Boy stuck close to his mother—I suppose he helped her at home, I don't know—and the old man left them alone and was more and more by himself.

He took to sitting down by the bridge, humped, staring out to sea, with a queer brooding look on him. He seemed strange, and lonely. I didn't like it. I don't know what his thoughts were, but I'm sure they were evil. It suddenly seemed a very long time since he and the missus and the whole family had gone fishing, a happy, contented party. Now everything had changed for him. He was thrust out in the cold, and the missus and Boy stayed together.

I felt sorry for him, but I felt frightened too. Because I felt it could not go on like this indefinitely; something would happen.

One day I went down to the beach for driftwood—it had been blowing in the night—and when I glanced towards the lake I saw that Boy wasn't with his mother. He was back where I had seen him that first day, on the edge of the marsh. He was as big as his father. If he'd known how to use his strength he'd have been a match for him any day, but he hadn't the brains. There he was, back on the marsh, a great big frightened foolish fellow, and there was the old man, outside his home, staring down towards his son with murder in his eyes.

I said to myself, "He's going to kill him." But I didn't know how or when or where, whether by night, when they were sleeping, or by day, when they were fishing. The mother was useless, she would not prevent it. It was no use appealing to the mother. If only Boy would use one little grain of sense, and go . . .

I watched and waited until nightfall. Nothing happened.

It rained in the night. It was grey, and cold, and dim. December was everywhere, trees all bare and bleak. I couldn't get down to the lake until late afternoon, and then the skies had cleared and the sun was shining in that watery way it does in winter, a burst of it, just before setting below the sea.

I saw the old man, and the missus too. They were close together, by the old shack, and they saw me coming for they looked towards me. Boy wasn't there. He wasn't on the marsh, either. Nor by the side of the lake.

I crossed the bridge and went along the right bank of the lake, and I had my spy-glass with me, but I couldn't see Boy. Yet all the time I was aware of the old man watching me.

Then I saw him. I scrambled down the bank, and crossed the marsh, and went to the thing I saw lying there, behind the reeds.

He was dead. There was a great gash on his body. Dried blood on his back. But he had lain there all night. His body was sodden with the rain.

Maybe you'll think I'm a fool, but I began to cry, like an idiot, and I shouted across to the old man, "You murderer, you bloody God-damned murderer." He did not answer. He did not move. He stood there, outside his shack with the missus, watching me.

You'll want to know what I did. I went back and got a spade, and I dug a grave for Boy, in the reeds behind the marsh, and I said one of my own prayers for him, being uncertain of his religion. When I had finished I looked across the lake to the old man.

And do you know what I saw?

I saw him lower his great head, and bend towards her and embrace her. And she lifted her head to him and embraced him too. It was both a requiem and a benediction. An atonement, and a giving of praise. In their strange way they knew they had done evil, but now it was over, because I had buried Boy and he was gone. They were free to be together again, and there was no longer a third to divide them.

They came out into the middle of the lake, and suddenly I saw the old man stretch his neck and beat his wings, and he took off from the water, full of power, and she followed him. I watched the two swans fly out to sea right into the face of the setting sun, and I tell you it was one of the most beautiful sights I ever saw in my life: the two swans flying there, alone, in winter.

Eterna

MARY LAVIN
(Irish, 1912–   )

Out in the street at last, the doctor stopped running and looked back at the steps of the gallery. The woman was not following him. All the same, he went across to where the car was parked. But as there was still no sign of her he didn't drive away. His wife would be along shortly—she was only picking up odds and ends for the kids at some shop around the corner where there was a closing-down sale. What a fool he was to have gone into that cursed gallery. Just because he had found a parking place opposite it! If he'd bought an evening paper and waited for Annie in the car, he'd have saved himself a nasty fright, because now he felt certain that the crazy woman could not possibly have been Eterna. Not in those outlandish clothes! Not with that daft look in her eyes as she strayed from painting to painting, causing everyone to stare.

If it was Eterna, wouldn't he have noticed her the minute he went into the place, instead of merely turning to see why other people were staring? Even then, he wouldn't have given the poor soul a second glance if he hadn't fancied a resemblance. But when he found her eyes fixed on him he lost his head and ran, although he was vaguely aware, even then, that her daft gaze had already wandered away from him. That was another thing. If it was Eterna, wouldn't she have recognized him?

It was mortifying to think that he had lost control to such an extent that he *ran*. Supposing one of his patients had been there and seen him. It was unlikely, though, that anyone up from the country for a precious half day in Dublin would waste time in the National Gallery. He relaxed. He lit a cigarette and settled down to wait for Annie.

Why had he gone into the gallery at all? He had probably fallen into a nostalgic mood, thinking of all the exhibitions he'd attended there before he was qualified and when he still entertained notions of a practice in Dublin. In those days, going to art exhibitions, symphony concerts, operas, and that sort of thing seemed as important for his advancement as going to his lectures. Ah, well, he'd better not tell Annie about his little adventure. Not that she'd give a damn whether it was Eterna or not—she'd be concerned only at his having gone into the gallery at all, at his backsliding into intellectual snobbery, or what she called professional posturing. 'Tommyrot' was the word she had actually used the first time he met her, or, rather the first time they had had what could be considered a real conversation.

'It's not as if you were a specialist,' she had said bluntly. 'A district doctor doesn't have to put on airs like the bigwigs up in Dublin. That kind of thing might impress Dublin people, but it won't go down in a country town, it will only do you harm. The people in this town are simple, but they are not fools. They see through you, Doctor, the way they see through a pane of glass.' She had looked at him so contemptuously that he winced. But she kept on. 'You know damn well, Doctor, that you wouldn't have deigned to talk to me tonight if you weren't in such a state over that silly nun.'

That had cut through to the bone. It was so true. He had never taken the slightest notice of her before that night, had hardly looked in her direction. In the four months he'd been in the Central Hotel, where she was receptionist, he had hardly spoken a word to her beyond the meagre civilities of good night and good morning. Anyway, she was seldom to be seen except behind the brass grille of her dark little office at the back of the entrance hall. To him, she was just another dreary feature of the broken-down, third-rate hotel.

He himself only spent weekdays in the place. Saturday always saw him hitting out for Dublin. He never bothered to hunt for decent accommodation in the town, being certain that such was not to be found. The whole town was a cultural desert—although, mind you, he knew he was lucky to get his appointment, considering his marks in the Finals. All the same, if he had been lucky he might have got a town with more to offer than the Central Hotel.

It was a dump. The lounge was small and dark, with frosted glass in the windows, and the fire in the shallow grate was kept so tightly banked down with clinkers that once when he threw an orange peel on top of the coals it was still unconsumed when he came back from his rounds at the end of the day. As for the company! It seldom varied—a few commercial travellers, a bank clerk or two, and an elderly, unmarried schoolteacher. If an occasional tourist appeared, he or she very shortly became aware of being misplaced, and accordingly sat all evening in disgruntled silence. He himself had no alternative but to engage in the inanities that passed for conversation and then retire to his dismal bedroom and lie on his bed.

When the call first came to go up to the convent, he was at his lowest. It was a cold night in February, a dreadful night of wind and rain, yet he was glad to get away from the hotel for an hour or so. Admittedly, too, the week that followed gave a bit of spice to his life, but the good was taken out of that by the hideous embarrassment he brought upon himself on his last visit up there.

Back at the Central after that last visit, scarcely tasting the miserable evening meal, he had left the dining room with a vague intention of stepping out in the fresh air. He saw it was raining. And it was as he turned back that he saw the receptionist—Annie—coming out of her box at the back of the hall and taking her coat from the rack.

'It's raining. Did you know that?' he asked. She answered by merely indicating that the coat was a mackintosh, and this made him feel so foolish that he had to detain her to correct the bad impression he'd made. From the few curt words he drew out of her, he gathered that she went for a walk at that hour every evening regularly, wet or fine.

'There's not much else to do, I grant you that,' he said bitterly.

'Oh, I enjoy my walks,' she protested, and then, to his astonishment, she came out with a vehement attack on him. 'Of course, I don't claim to have your sophisticated tastes!' she said, and when he asked what she meant by that remark she shrugged her shoulders. That really provoked him. He hurried after her to the door.

'Do you ever take anyone with you?' he asked. And when, again, she gave no answer he took it she had no objection. Grabbing his own coat from the rack, he stepped out after her into the dark street. The rain had eased off. She had a strong stride and she held up her face as if she liked the slap of the wet, cold air.

The town was badly lit, but when they got out of it, and the stars began to pierce the sky, he found that he enjoyed striding along beside her. They didn't talk much and soon he forgot about the nuns—until they came to a point where the road forked, and Annie, who was slightly ahead, took the one that went past the convent. He stopped.

'Let's not go that way,' he said abruptly.

'Why not? It's the way I always go.' She stopped, too, and he thought she was deferring to him, but he was wrong.

'What's the matter with going this way?' she demanded. Then and there, he blurted out what had happened at the convent that afternoon.

He could not have told a better person. To begin with, Annie had at once dismissed Eterna as silly, and not worth consideration. Then she turned on him. 'If you ask me, you got what you deserved—a good come-down,' she said. And she proceeded from that to give him the worst bawling out he'd had in his life. 'You may be a good doctor, but you won't cut much ice in this town unless you change your tune,' she said, and although the mixed metaphor made him wince, she was obviously so sincere that he listened to her with respect. When she put it to him flatly that he would not have stopped to speak to her if he hadn't been upset, he made no attempt at denial.

'I did not deserve that you should be so kind to me,' he said quietly. He was glad to see, however, that this disconcerted her.

'Well . . . if you're enjoying the walk . . .' she murmured, and moved on again. But he noticed that when they were passing the convent gates she began to talk more animatedly, and he felt she was hoping to distract him. She didn't altogether succeed, but he was grateful to her, and by the time they got back to the Central he certainly felt better than when he had set out. He asked if he might perhaps accompany her the following night. She gave her consent, and after that they went walking every evening.

It wasn't long until he gave up going to Dublin at the week-ends. And before the end of the year they were married. Naturally, after their first conversation, he felt no further need to mention Eterna, and Annie didn't bring her name up, either, except once, when they were on their honey-moon. She told him she had heard that Eterna had left the convent.

'But don't let it bother you!' she added, seeing that he was a bit upset at the news. 'You flatter yourself if you think her decision had anything to do with you. You'll never see her again. She's left the town.'

He put the whole incident out of his mind. Indeed, he tried to forget everything about those awful months before he met Annie. It was the most miserable time in his entire existence. The incident with Eterna was a fitting climax to it.

The night he first saw her, the night he was called to the convent, was wet and miserable. It was freezing cold, and the rain was as fierce as hail. It lashed at the windows of the car, and his flesh anticipated the cascade of icy raindrops that would be dashed over his hands when he dragged at the massive gates to gain admission to the long, dark avenue.

He'd been up there twice before—once to inoculate a group of nuns leaving for the missions, and once to sign the death certificate of an old lay sister. On both of those occasions, though, it had been daytime. Now, in the darkness, the twisting drive seemed endless. Several times he swerved when he ought to have gone straight. From time to time wet laurels slapped against the sides of his car, and a hazy light over the far-off convent door seemed to shift position, because when the wind swayed the branches it seemed it was not them but the light that moved. The gleam of that light was eerie, and he was reminded of how he used to quake as a child, listening to tales of a light that flickered over the bogs and lured the unwary to extinction in bottomless holes full of black water. By the time he reached the convent door, he was completely unnerved. To make matters worse, before he had a chance to ring the bell the door was opened by a small bundle in black who was obviously on the wait for him. It was a lay sister so doubled up by age and rheumatism that she was almost on all fours. She had to crane her neck upwards to bid him enter. What a cross old face! Yet at the time he took no exception to her. As far as he was concerned, that was the look of true sanctity. He'd seen it often on the faces of lay sisters in hospital wards and in homes for old people, where it was the lay sisters, and not the haughty choir nuns, who did all the hard work. He'd often said that if he were God he would not trade a single one of those cranky creatures for a whole conventful of the other sort.

'It's a bad night, Sister,' he said, more amicably than he felt, as he went to help her close the heavy door. But without his help she slammed it shut, and he began to feel that his amiability was superfluous. Ostentatiously, the old woman wiped her bone-dry slippers on a fibre mat inside the door, and bobbing her head for him to follow, she set off with a remarkable gait, for one so old and deformed, across floorboards that were dangerously overwaxed.

Assuming that his patient would be confined to her cell, he looked uneasily at the steep staircase that rose up as bare and ominous as a glass hill, when, to his relief, the old nun came to a stop before reaching it and threw open the door of a parlour to the left. Even then, he thought he was being shown in there to wait for his patient to be brought to him. But she was already there. Sitting stiffly on a straight-backed chair, with her hands primly folded on her lap and her eyes downcast, was how he first saw Eterna.

Eterna? Why was it that from the start his mind discarded the prefix that connoted her dedicated state? She was still only a novice. She was wearing a white veil, but that, of course, did not exonerate him. The truth was that the moment he first laid eyes on her he experienced a most unprofessional desire to humiliate her. Perhaps it was because in spite of her outward appearance of meekness she had instantly conveyed—to him, at least—an impression of unspeakable arrogance. 'All I ask is martyrdom,' she seemed to say, and left it to the old lay sister to explain why a doctor had been called. She had apparently cut her arm.

'Roll up your sleeve and show the cut to the doctor. Hurry up, Sister,' said the old nun, and when Eterna's white fingers fumbled ineffectually with the masculine-looking studs on her wristband the old nun reached out impatiently and rolled up the sleeve with her own crabbed, red hands. When, however, the tender white skin of her arm was bared, Eterna blushed. Good, he thought, as he bent to examine the cut. This might teach her that high aspirations do not turn human beings into angels overnight.

The cut was not deep, but the skin around it was inflamed and angry-looking. There being no antibiotics in those days, he honestly thought at first that it might be necessary to get his patient into a hospital, but, suspecting that this would cause consternation in the community, he decided to dress the cut and see how it would be after a couple of hours.

'Can we get some hot water, Sister, please?' he asked, and when the old nun went over and tugged at a leather bellpull beside the door he understood that the water would be brought. While waiting for it, he told the pair that he would like to call back in three hours. 'At eleven,' he added, to clarify matters. The nuns looked at each other in some confusion.

'The rule of silence is enjoined on us at nine o'clock, Doctor,' the old nun said with severity.

If he had been strictly honest, he would have admitted to himself that, providing the arm was kept motionless, another examination could wait until morning. But a curious obstinancy had taken possession of him. With a stony look, he conceded an hour. 'Ten at the earliest,' he said.

The two veils, the white and the black, veered together like sails in a storm, and the nuns whispered urgently. From a word caught here and there, he gathered that the Reverend Mother had retired to her cell. To whom would they look for guidance and direction? To comply with his wishes, it might be necessary to get the assent of the chaplain, who occupied a cottage in the grounds. But would the Reverend Father be available at that hour? A second session of whispering took place. Perhaps the matter was not grave enough to justify disturbing the priest? More whispering. Finally, the old nun, whose name was Sister Bernadine, fixed him with steely eyes and said that in the extreme emergency she was herself prepared to give the permission necessary for the late call although she was clearly in a state of perturbation.

Putting away his thermometer and closing his bag, the doctor looked disapprovingly at the novice. 'How did you get this cut anyway?' he asked curtly. It was a measure of the effect she'd had on him that he had omitted to ask this routine question at the proper time. And since neither nun had volunteered the information, he began to suspect that the accident was not sympathetically viewed by the rest of the community.

'Tell the doctor what happened, Sister,' said old Bernadine. He thought he detected a note of malice in her voice.

'I fell off a step-ladder, Doctor,' Eterna said, her voice painfully low.

He raised his eyebrows. 'Oh? Are you a carpenter?' he asked, with mock surprise, it being his experience that nuns were forever scrambling up step-ladders and climbing on to tables and chairs to disfigure their convents with shrines and grottoes. 'How did it get infected? And why didn't you bandage it—or don't you believe in remedying bodily ailments?'

'I think perhaps I may have let some turpentine soak through the bandage,' Eterna whispered, her voice now almost impossible to hear.

'Turpentine? Step-ladders? So you really are a sort of handyman hereabouts?' he said, with a cynical smile he could not control.

He turned back to the old nun. 'What exactly happened?' he asked.

She gave him a surly look. 'Sister is an artist, Doctor. She was painting a replica of Our Lady of Good Counsel on the wall of the chapel.' Clearly, such goings on were not her notion of proper behaviour for nuns. 'Our present Superior believes talent may be put to use—but only in the service of God, of course!'

He was taken aback. An artist? He stared at Eterna. To think that this was the first person of talent he had encountered since he came to the district—and she had to be a nun! He felt cheated.

'I should have been told of this earlier,' he said disagreeably. 'I would have kept a closer watch on my words. Artists are such sensitive souls.'

Then, as if Eterna were incapable of understanding, much less executing, his orders, he wrote out a prescription and handed it to the old sister. 'Have that filled in the morning, and meanwhile see that the cut is kept open. Put hot poultices on it, and change them frequently. I'll be back in two hours.' He went towards the door. There, however, he turned and, staring at the novice, added a rider to his orders. 'Water as hot as the patient can stand,' he said. 'How about martyrdom now,' his eyes seemed to ask her as he allowed himself to be let out into the dark by Sister Bernadine.

He had by then only one thought in his head, and that was to be finished with the case. The next two hours dragged, and he thought the time would never come to be back and be done with the tiresome business. Nevertheless, when he did get back, and asked Bernadine for more hot water, it crossed his mind that at that hour everyone else might be asleep, and she might have to amble off and fetch it herself. He felt a strange elation at the thought of being alone with Eterna. But little he knew of convent life! Never in a million years would he be left alone with a novice. The old nun reached for the bellpull, as before, and the hot water was brought immediately. He gave his attention to the cut.

He was glad he had insisted on seeing it again. The swelling had not gone down. He pressed out some pus, put on a dressing, reminded them to get the prescription filled first thing next morning, and said he would call again the following afternoon.

That afternoon of his third call, old Bernadine, as before, was close on the heels of her charge, and kept so close to her throughout the visit that she considerably hampered his movements. He repeatedly had to ask her to get out of his way. 'Excuse me, Sister. . . . If you please, Sister. . . .

Pardon me, please.' To his further annoyance, when he did manage to attend to the cut, and was about to leave, the old nun stopped him.

'Will this be your last visit, Doctor?' she asked.

The danger of septicaemia was by then almost negligible, but he decided to be on the safe side. 'I'm afraid not, Sister. One can never be too careful in some matters.' He said it ironically, because the old woman had conveyed the impression that they were all three engaged in an operation highly dangerous to faith and morals! 'I'll be back in two days,' he said.

He intended that fourth visit to be his last. He could have devised no further pretext for calling—the healing process had definitely started. When he arrived at the convent, however, a small change occurred in the order of events, and the door was opened not by Bernadine but by a nun so old that, by comparison, Bernadine could be considered sprightly. This old crone was so doddering that she misapprehended the nature of his visit, and taking him to be the chaplain bearing the Host, blessed herself at sight of him and genuflected.

'This way, Father,' she said reverentially, and he had to manoeuvre her towards the parlour, where Eterna sat sedately. The saintly old soul settled herself down in an armchair that almost swallowed her alive, and took up her beads. In a second, she was lost to this world. Passing the big wooden beads between forefinger and thumb as if she were fashioning pellets of bread, or rolling pills, her whispered Paters and Aves soon had the parlour as sibilant as an aviary.

Taking advantage of the lack of vigilance on the part of the old saint, the doctor ventured a joke with Eterna. 'I see we have a new chaperon,' he said. He was surprised and delighted to see a glint come into the novice's eye—until, to his chagrin, he realized that it was a glint of anger. What matter! It showed that she was at least in part human. But why did that gratify him? Quite aside from professional ethics, this disdainful creature did not in any way attract him. On the contrary! Perhaps he wanted to penetrate her unnatural indifference and send a shaft of some kind into her cold heart?

Whatever it was, after having assured himself there was no further festering in the cut, he pronounced it to be no longer dangerous, and went over to the window to make a comment on the view from it—this being his standard practice when terminating a case.

There wasn't much of a view, though. The window opened on to a small court, where at that moment the entire community of nuns was taking recreation, walking up and down the narrow asphalt paths that separated stiffly planted flower beds. 'I see the chestnuts are in bud,' he said. There wasn't much else to comment on, and he'd been surprised to see them in bud so early. But to his own ears the words didn't seem to have the proper valedictory undertones, and as he stared out at those big buds, ready to burst into leaf, he felt his heart lift at the thought that winter was over and spring well on its way. To his surprise, Eterna came and stood beside him. She looked out, too, but she still didn't smile.

'They're sticky,' she said. But although her remark may have been as inconsequential as his own, he couldn't help feeling dejected—for her—because when those sticky buds broke open and the sprawling leaves unfurled, that garden would be positively claustrophobic. The slatted seats set at regular intervals along the paths were so near to each other that there would be no more privacy out there than in the parlour.

'In the name of God, how can you be content to spend the sum of all your mortal days in this place?' he asked impulsively. Then he gave a nervous glance in the direction of the old nun in the armchair. 'Is she really deaf?' he asked.

'Stone deaf. When there is thunder and lightning, she cannot even hear the lightning,' Eterna said, almost vindictively. Then she noticed her mistake, and was overcome by the absurdity of it. 'Thunder, I mean,' she added and, yes—he could scarcely believe it—she giggled.

He laughed, too—and loudly at that. Neither of them thought of the old soul in the corner. And there was a sudden sense of freedom between them such as there might have been with any other young couple.

'Seriously,' he said, 'human relations are complicated enough at the best of times and under the best of conditions, without people locking themselves up together under the same roof for the whole of their lives. How do you stand it? Even the good Lord Himself, if we are to believe His own words, does not propose to house us all up together in His heavenly mansion!'

As he hoped she might, Eterna laughed again. 'It may be impertinent of me to say it,' he went on, 'but don't you think it is a poor thanks to your Creator to turn your back on His creation?'

'A fat lot I'd have seen of God's creation,' she said, and the unexpected colloquialism surprised him. 'I was born in this town. The oldest of ten!

But for the nuns, I'd never have got anything more than elementary schooling. They educated me for nothing! And it was they who taught me to draw and to paint. There was a nun who had done her novitiate in Louvain, and she taught me all I know.' She paused, and her voice went lower. 'When I entered, I had no dowry. They took me without one because of my'—she hesitated, obviously from modesty—'because of my gifts,' she finished, evidently unable to find another word. She blushed. The impetuosity of her outburst would have embarrassed him, too, if it were not for how amazingly that blush transformed her.

'Surely you could have got a scholarship to the College of Art, or a grant of some kind?' he said. Then he realized that he had seen nothing of her work. 'The standard is fairly high, of course,' he said hastily.

'And I am not very good, either,' she said, with a humility he would not have credited her with a few days earlier. 'My only regret is that I never saw any of the great masterpieces before I left the world—especially the moderns. You may not believe it, but I was never in the National Gallery in Dublin, much less . . .' Her voice trailed off on a note of regret.

'Oh, there's nothing much of importance in Dublin,' he lied. He didn't like the turn the conversation was taking, and he was disturbed by the sad look that had come over her face. 'Anyway, you can always get reproductions. The experts claim that detail can best be studied in photographs.'

Eterna gave a barely perceptible shrug to her shoulders. 'By students, perhaps,' she said politely, 'but I don't think anything could compensate for not being able to stand in front of the original.' The wistful expression on her face made her really beautiful. He felt it was high time for him to take his departure.

'Let's hope there will be art galleries in heaven,' he said as he took up his bag to depart. Eterna was not listening, though. Glancing back at the old soul behind them, who by her incantations had induced in herself such a state of paradisical bliss that her eyes had rolled back in her head, leaving only the whites showing, the novice detained him with a gesture.

'I'd like to show you something. Can you stay another second?' she asked breathlessly. And throwing her veil over her shoulder she seemed to send a flicker of light over his face in the way a sheet flapping on a clothes-line can seem to flash light into a sunless room. She ran out of the parlour. It entered his head fleetingly that he should leave while she was gone. But before there was time for that she was back, her face radiant.

'I found this in a wastepaper basket in one of the dormitories after the boarders went home last summer,' she said. From the thick black folds of her habit she produced a booklet. He recognized it as an ordinary catalogue from the National Gallery, but she was clasping it to her bosom with all the ardour of a saint at the stake clasping a crucifix. 'It's from the National Gallery,' she said as she placed it on a table and began to leaf through it. 'Did you know there is a Monet there? And a Sisley?' she cried. 'Have you seen them?'

Giving him no time to answer, she was feverishly searching through the illustrations. 'Ah, here it is! My favourite!' she cried, flattening out the catalogue at a colour reproduction of Monet's *River Scene*. He did not know that there was a Monet in Dublin and this one was not, as far as he knew, an important painting, but the reproduction was good, and Eterna was certainly deeply affected by it.

'How I'd love to see it,' she said. Her eyes were shining, and her parted lips showed her pearly little teeth.

He was completely swept off his feet. 'How I'd love to show it to you, Eterna,' he whispered back.

But oh, the look of shock that came on her face!

As a doctor, he could not miss it, nor mistake its implications. Neither could he fail to feel an appalling guilt at his breach of ethics. For a second that seemed as if it would last forever, they stared at each other, and from her stare he knew that to her he was some slimy, toadlike thing that had crawled out of a painting of Bosch's *Temptation of St Anthony*. Letting her treasure fall to the floor, she ran across to the armchair and, assisting the old crone to her feet, she half led, half carried her from the room like a doll.

He waited only to make sure they had vanished before he fled the place, not waiting for anyone to show him out.

It was early afternoon, but cancelling his other calls for the day, he went back to the hotel and lay on his bed in a state of shock. He thought the hour for the evening meal would never come. Although he had no appetite, he would have welcomed any gabble that would take his mind off what had occurred. Yet when the meal-time arrived, for once there was not a soul in the dining room. After barely touching his food, he went into the lounge. Two travellers were there, but they were obviously talking about something confidential, their heads close together, and he felt he could not intrude on them. Finally, he went to the hall door, thinking he might walk up the street. He saw that it was raining and he turned back into the hotel. It was then that he saw Annie taking down her coat. Cold fish that she had seemed to him at the time, he was so desperate for company that he spoke to her. What luck for him that she had been sensible, so practical!

And now, sitting waiting for her in the car, he was filled with impatience to see her. They were intending to go home after the shops shut, but the traffic was always bad at that hour, and it occurred to him that it might be a good idea to stay and have a meal in town first. They could phone home. Ah, there she was, coming up the street towards the car with her arms full of parcels as usual. He sprang out of the car to go to meet her, when suddenly panic engulfed him again and he looked across at the gallery. But there was no sign of the crazy woman, and bolstered up by the sight of Annie advancing stoutly towards him, he relaxed again. Why should he care even if it was Eterna? If she'd gone a bit cracked, what about it? As Annie would say, she was probably headed that way from the start. People had to learn to clip their wings if they wanted to survive in this world. They had to keep their feet on the ground. That was what Annie had taught him to do—God bless her.

Willy-Wagtails by Moonlight

❧❀❧

PATRICK WHITE
(Australian, 1912–   )

The Wheelers drove up to the Mackenzies' punctually at six-thirty. It was the hour for which they had been asked. My God, thought Jum Wheeler. It had been raining a little, and the tyres sounded blander on the wet gravel.

In front of the Mackenzies', which was what is known as a Lovely Old Home—colonial style—amongst some carefully natural-looking gums, there stood a taxi.

'Never knew Arch and Nora ask us with anyone else,' Eileen Wheeler said.

'Maybe they didn't. Even now. Maybe it's someone they couldn't get rid of.'

'Or an urgent prescription from the chemist's.'

Eileen Wheeler yawned. She must remember to show sympathy, because Nora Mackenzie was going through a particularly difficult one.

Anyway, they were there, and the door stood open on the lights inside. Even the lives of the people you know, even the lives of Nora and Arch look interesting for a split second, when you drive up and glimpse them through a lit doorway.

'It's that Miss Cullen,' Eileen said.

For there was Miss Cullen, doing something with a brief-case in the hall.

'Ugly bitch,' Jum said.

'Plain is the word,' corrected Eileen.

'Arch couldn't do without her. Practically runs the business.'

Certainly that Miss Cullen looked most methodical, shuffling the immaculate papers, and slipping them into a new pigskin brief-case in Arch and Nora's hall.

'Got a figure,' Eileen conceded.

'But not a chin.'

'Oh, hello, Miss Cullen. It's stopped raining.'

It was too bright stepping suddenly into the hall. The Wheelers brightly blinked. They looked newly made.

'Keeping well, Miss Cullen, I hope?'

'I have nothing to complain about, Mr Wheeler,' Miss Cullen replied. She snapped the catch. Small, rather pointed breasts under the raincoat. But, definitely, no chin.

Eileen Wheeler was fixing her hair in the reproduction Sheraton mirror.

She had been to the hairdresser's recently, and the do was still set too tight.

'Well, good-bye now,' Miss Cullen said.

When she smiled there was a hint of gold, but discreet, no more than a bridge. Then she would draw her lips together, and lick them ever so slightly, as if she had been sucking a not unpleasantly acid sweetie.

Miss Cullen went out the door, closing it firmly but quietly behind her.

'That was Miss Cullen,' said Nora Mackenzie coming down. 'She's Arch's secretary.'

'He couldn't do without her,' she added, as though they did not know.

Nora was like that. Eileen wondered how she and Nora had tagged along together, ever since Goulburn, all those years.

'God, she's plain!' Jum said.

Nora did not exactly frown, but pleated her forehead the way she did when other people's virtues were assailed. Such attacks seemed to affect her personally, causing her almost physical pain.

'But Mildred is so kind,' she insisted.

Nora Mackenzie made a point of calling her husband's employees by first names, trying to make them part of a family which she alone, perhaps, would have liked to exist.

'She brought me some giblet soup, all the way from Balgowlah, that time I had virus 'flu.'

'Was it good, darling?' Eileen asked.

She was going through the routine, rubbing Nora's cheek with her own. Nora was pale. She must remember to be kind.

Nora did not answer, but led the way into the lounge-room.

Nora said:

'I don't think I'll turn on the lights for the present. They hurt my eyes, and it's so restful sitting in the dusk.'

Nora *was* pale. She had, in fact, just taken a couple of Disprin.

'Out of sorts, dear?' Eileen asked.

Nora did not answer, but offered some dry martinis.

Very watery, Jum knew from experience, but drink of a kind.

'Arch will be down presently,' Nora said. 'He had to attend to some business, some letters Miss Cullen brought. Then he went in to have a shower.'

Nora's hands were trembling as she offered the dry martinis, but Eileen remembered they always had.

The Wheelers sat down. It was all so familiar, they did not have to be asked, which was fortunate, as Nora Mackenzie always experienced difficulty in settling guests into chairs. Now she sat down herself, far more diffidently than her friends. The cushions were standing on their points.

Eileen sighed. Old friendships and the first scent of gin always made her nostalgic.

'It's stopped raining,' she said, and sighed.

'Arch well?' Jum asked.

As if he cared. She had let the ice get into the cocktail, turning it almost to pure water.

'He has his trouble,' Nora said. 'You know, his back.'

Daring them to have forgotten.

Nora loved Arch. It made Eileen feel ashamed.

So fortunate for them to have discovered each other. Nora Leadbeatter and Arch Mackenzie. Two such bores. And with bird-watching in common. Though Eileen Wheeler had never believed Nora did not make herself learn to like watching birds.

At Goulburn, in the early days, Nora would come out to Glen Davie sometimes to be with Eileen at week-ends. Mr Leadbeatter had been manager at the Wales for a while. He always saw that his daughter had the cleanest notes. Nora was shy, but better than nothing, and the two girls would sit about on the veranda those summer evenings, buffing their nails, and listening to the sheep cough in the home paddock. Eileen gave Nora lessons in making-up. Nora had protested, but was pleased.

'Mother well, darling?' Eileen asked, sipping that sad, watery gin.

'Not exactly *well,*' Nora replied, painfully.

Because she had been to Orange, to visit her widowed mother, who suffered from Parkinson's disease.

'You know what I mean, dear,' said Eileen.

Jum was dropping his ash on the carpet. It might be better when poor bloody Arch came down.

'I have an idea that woman, that Mrs Galloway, is unkind to her,' Nora said.

'Get another,' Eileen advised. 'It isn't like after the War.'

'One can never be sure,' Nora debated. 'One would hate to hurt the woman's feelings.'

Seated in the dusk Nora Mackenzie was of a moth colour. Her face looked as though she had been rubbing it with chalk. Might have, too, in spite of those lessons in make-up. She sat and twisted her hands together.

How very red Nora's hands had been, at Goulburn, at the convent, to which the two girls had gone. Not that they belonged to *those.* It was only convenient. Nora's hands had been red and trembly after practising a tarantella, early, in the frost. So very early all of that. Eileen had learnt about life shortly after puberty. She had tried to tell Nora one or two things, but Nora did not want to hear. Oh, no, no, *please,* Eileen, Nora cried. As though a boy had been twisting her arm. She had those long, entreating, sensitive hands.

And there they were still. Twisting together, making their excuses. For what they had never done.

Arch came in then. He turned on the lights, which made Nora wince, even those lights which barely existed in all the neutrality of Nora's room. Nora did not comment, but smiled, because it was Arch who had committed the crime.

Arch said:

'You two toping hard as usual.'

He poured himself the rest of the cocktail.

Eileen laughed her laugh which people found amusing at parties.

Jum said, and bent his leg, if it hadn't been for Arch and the shower, they wouldn't have had the one too many.

'A little alcohol releases the vitality,' Nora remarked ever so gently.

She always grew anxious at the point where jokes became personal.

Arch composed his mouth under the handle-bars moustache, and Jum knew what they were in for.

'Miss Cullen came out with one or two letters,' Arch was taking pains to explain. 'Something she thought should go off tonight. I take a shower most evenings. Summer, at least.'

'Such humidity,' Nora helped.

Arch looked down into his glass. He might have been composing further remarks, but did not come out with them.

That silly, bloody English-air-force-officer's moustache. It was the only thing Arch had ever dared. War had given him the courage to pinch a detail which did not belong to him.

'That Miss Cullen, useful girl,' Jum suggested.

'Runs the office.'

'Forty, if a day,' Eileen said, whose figure was beginning to slacken off.

Arch said he would not know, and Jum made a joke about Miss Cullen's *cul-de-sac*.

The little pleats had appeared again in Nora Mackenzie's chalky brow. 'Well,' she cried, jumping up, quite girlish, 'I do hope the dinner will be a success.'

And laughed.

Nora was half-way through her second course with that woman at the Chanticleer. Eileen suspected there would be avocadoes stuffed with prawns, chicken *Mornay*, and *crêpes Suzette*.

Eileen was right.

Arch seemed to gain in authority sitting at the head of his table.

'I'd like you to taste this wine,' he said. 'It's very light.'

'Oh, yes?' said Jum.

The wine was corked, but nobody remarked. The second bottle, later on, was somewhat better. The Mackenzies were spreading themselves tonight.

Arch flipped his napkin once or twice, emphasizing a point. He smoothed the handle-bars moustache, which should have concealed a harelip, only there wasn't one. Jum dated from before the moustache, long, long, very long.

Arch said:

'There was a story Armitage told me at lunch. There was a man who bought a mower. Who suffered from indigestion. Now, how, exactly, did it . . . go?'

Jum had begun to make those little pellets out of bread. It always fascinated him how grubby the little pellets turned out. And himself not by any means dirty.

Arch failed to remember the point of the story Armitage had told.

It was difficult to understand how Arch had made a success of his business. Perhaps it was that Miss Cullen, breasts and all, under the rain-coat. For a long time Arch had messed around. Travelled in something. Separator parts. Got the agency for some sort of phoney machine for supplying *ozone* to public buildings. The Mackenzies lived at Burwood then. Arch continued to mess around. The War was quite a godsend. Arch was the real adje type. Did a conscientious job. Careful with his allowances, too.

Then, suddenly, after the War, Arch Mackenzie had launched out, started the import-export business. Funny the way a man will suddenly hit on the idea to which his particular brand of stupidity can respond.

The Mackenzies had moved to the North Shore, to the house which still occasionally embarrassed Nora. She felt as though she ought to apol-ogize for success. But there was the bird-watching. Most week-ends they went off to the bush, to the Mountains or somewhere. She felt happier in humbler circumstances. In time she got used to the tape recorder which they took along. She made herself look upon it as a necessity rather than ostentation.

Eileen was dying for a cigarette.

'May I smoke, Arch?'

'We're amongst friends, aren't we?'

Eileen did not answer that. And Arch fetched the ash-tray they kept handy for those who needed it.

Nora in the kitchen dropped the beans. Everybody heard, but Arch asked Jum for a few tips on investments, as he always did when Nora happened to be out of the room. Nora had some idea that the Stock Exchange was immoral.

Then Nora brought the dish of little, pale tinned peas.

'Ah! *Pet—ty pwah!*' said Jum.

He formed his full, and rather greasy lips into a funnel through which the little rounded syllables poured most impressively.

Nora forgot her embarrassment. She envied Jum his courage in foreign languages. Although there were her lessons in Italian, she would never have dared utter in public.

'Can you bear *crêpes Suzette?*' Nora had to apologize.

'Lovely, darling.' Eileen smiled.

She would have swallowed a tiger. But was, *au fond,* at her gloomiest.

What was the betting Nora would drop the *crêpes Suzette?* It was those long, trembly hands, on which the turquoise ring looked too small and innocent. The Mackenzies were still in the semi-precious bracket in the days when they became engaged.

'How's the old bird-watching?'

Jum had to force himself, but after all he had drunk their wine.

Arch Mackenzie sat deeper in his chair, almost completely at his ease.

'Got some new tapes,' he said. 'We'll play them later. Went up to Kurrajong on Sunday, and got the bell-birds. I'll play you the lyre-bird, too. That was Mount Wilson.'

'Didn't we hear the lyre-bird last time?' Eileen asked.

Arch said:

'Yes.'

Deliberately.

'But wouldn't you like to hear it again? It's something of a collector's piece.'

Nora said they'd be more comfortable drinking their coffee in the lounge.

Then Arch fetched the tape recorder. He set it up on the Queen Anne walnut piecrust. It certainly was an impressive machine.

'I'll play you the lyre-bird.'

'The *pièce de résistance?* Don't you think we should keep it?'

'He can never wait for the lyre-bird.'

Nora had grown almost complacent. She sat holding her coffee, smiling faintly through the steam. The children she had never had with Arch were about to enter.

'Delicious coffee,' Eileen said.

She had finished her filter-tips. She had never felt drearier.

The tape machine had begun to snuffle. There was quite an unusual amount of crackle. Perhaps it was the bush. Yes, that was it. The bush!

'Well, it's really quite remarkable how you people have the patience,' Eileen Wheeler had to say.

'Ssh!'

Arch Mackenzie was frowning. He had sat forward in the period chair. 'This is where it comes in.'

His face was tragic in the shaded light.

'Get it?' he whispered.

His hand was helping. Or commanding.

'Quite remarkable,' Eileen repeated.

Jum was shocked to realize he had only two days left in which to take up the ICI rights for old Thingummy.

Nora sat looking at her empty cup. But lovingly.

Nora could have been beautiful, Eileen saw. And suddenly felt old, she who had stripped once or twice at amusing parties. Nora Mackenzie did not know about that.

Somewhere in the depths of the bush Nora was calling that it had just turned four o'clock, but she had forgotten to pack the thermos.

The machine snuffled.

Arch Mackenzie was listening. He was biting his moustache.

'There's another passage soon.' He frowned.

'Darling,' Nora whispered, 'after the lyre-bird you might slip into the kitchen and change the bulb. It went while I was making the coffee.'

Arch Mackenzie's frown deepened. Even Nora was letting him down. But she did not see. She was so in love.

It might have been funny if it was not also pathetic. People were horribly pathetic, Eileen Wheeler decided, who had her intellectual moments. She was also feeling sick. It was Nora's *crêpes Suzette,* lying like blankets.

'You'll realize there are one or two rough passages,' Arch said, coming forward when the tape had ended. 'I might cut it.'

'It could do with a little trimming,' Eileen agreed. 'But perhaps it's more natural without.'

'Am I a what's-this, a masochist,' she asked.

'Don't forget the kitchen bulb,' Nora prompted.

Very gently. Very dreamy.

Her hair had strayed, in full dowdiness, down along her white cheek. 'I'll give you the bell-birds for while I'm gone.'

Jum's throat had begun to rattle. He sat up in time, though, and saved his cup in the same movement.

'I remember the bell-birds,' he said.

'Not these ones, you don't. These are new. These are the very latest. The best bell-birds.'

Arch had started the tape, and stalked out of the room, as if to let the bell-birds themselves prove his point.

'It is one of our loveliest recordings,' Nora promised.

They all listened or appeared to.

When Nora said:

'Oh, dear'—getting up—'I do believe'—panting almost—'the bell-bird tape'—trembling—'is damaged.'

Certainly the crackle was more intense.

'Arch will be so terribly upset.'

She had switched off the horrifying machine. With surprising skill for one so helpless. For a moment it seemed to Eileen Wheeler that Nora Mackenzie was going to hide the offending tape somewhere in her bosom. But she thought better of it, and put it aside on one of those little superfluous tables.

'Perhaps it's the machine that's broken,' suggested Jum.

'Oh, no,' said Nora, 'it's the tape. I know. We'll have to give you something else.'

'I can't understand,'—Eileen grinned—'how you ever got around, Nora, to being mechanical.'

'If you're determined,' Nora said.

Her head was lowered in concentration.

'If you want a thing enough.'

She was fixing a fresh tape.

'And we do love our birds. Our Sundays together in the bush.'

The machine had begun its snuffling and shuffling again. Nora Mackenzie raised her head, as if launched on an invocation.

Two or three notes of bird-song fell surprisingly pure and clear, out of the crackle, into the beige and string-coloured room.

'This is one,' Nora said, 'I don't think I've ever heard before.'

She smiled, however, and listened to identify.

'Willy-Wagtails,' Nora said.

Willy-Wagtails were suited to tape. The song tumbled and exulted.

'It must be something,' Nora said, 'that Arch made while I was with Mother. There were a couple of Sundays when he did a little field-work on his own.'

Nora might have given way to a gentle melancholy for all she had foregone if circumstances had not heightened the pitch. There was Arch standing in the doorway. Blood streaming.

'Blasted bulb collapsed in my hand!'

'Oh, darling! Oh *dear!*' Nora cried.

The Wheelers were both fascinated. There was the blood dripping on the beige wall-to-wall.

How the willy-wagtails chortled.

Nora Mackenzie literally staggered at her husband, to take upon herself, if possible, the whole ghastly business.

'Come along, Arch,' she moaned. 'We'll fix. In just a minute,' Nora panted.

And simply by closing the door, she succeeded in blotting the situation, all but the drops of blood that were left behind on the carpet.

'Poor old Arch! Bleeding like a pig!' Jum Wheeler said, and laughed.

Eileen added:

'We shall suffer the willy-wags alone.'

Perhaps it was better like that. You could relax. Eileen began to pull. Her step-ins had eaten into her.

The willy-wagtails were at it again.

'Am I going crackers?' asked Jum. 'Listening to those bloody birds!'

When somebody laughed. Out of the tape. The Wheelers sat. Still.

Three-quarters of the bottle! Snuffle crackle. *Arch Mackenzie, you're a fair trimmer!* Again that rather brassy laughter.

'Well, I'll be blowed!' said Jum Wheeler.

'But it's that Miss Cullen,' Eileen said.

The Wheeler spirits soared as surely as plummets dragged the notes of the wagtail down.

But it's far too rocky, and far too late. Besides, it's willy-wagtails we're after. How Miss Cullen laughed. *Willy-wagtails by moonlight!* Arch was less intelligible, as if he had listened to too many birds, and caught the habit. Snuffle crackle went the machine . . . *the buttons are not made to undo . . .* Miss Cullen informed. *Oh, stop it. Arch!* ARCH! *You're* TEARING *me!*

So that the merciless machine took possession of the room. There in the crackle of twigs, the stench of ants, the two Wheelers sat. There was that long, thin Harry Edwards, Eileen remembered, with bony wrists, had got her down behind the barn. She had hated it at first. All mirth had been exorcized from Miss Cullen's recorded laughter. Grinding out.

Grinding out. So much of life was recorded by now. Returning late from a country dance, the Wheelers had fallen down amongst the sticks and stones, and made what is called love, and risen in the grey hours, to find themselves numb and bulging.

If only the tape, if you knew the trick with the wretched switch.

Jum Wheeler decided not to look at his wife: Little guilty, pockets were turning themselves out in his mind. That woman at the Locomotive Hotel. Pockets and pockets of putrefying trash. Down along the creek, amongst the tussocks and the sheep pellets, the sun burning his boy's skin, he played his overture to sex. Alone.

This sort of thing's all very well, Miss Cullen decided. *It's time we turned practical. Are you sure we can find our way back to the car?*

Always trundling. Crackling. But there were the blessed wagtails again.

'Wonder if they forgot the machine?'

'Oh, God! Hasn't the tape bobbed up in Pymble?'

A single willy-wagtail sprinkled its grace-notes through the stuffy room.

'Everything's all right,' Nora announced. 'He's calmer now. I persuaded him to take a drop of brandy.'

'That should fix him,' Jum said.

But Nora was listening to the lone wagtail. She was standing in the bush. Listening. The notes of bird-song falling like mountain water, when they were not chiselled in moonlight.

'There is nothing purer,' Nora said, 'than the song of the wagtail. Excepting Schubert,' she added, 'some of Schubert.'

She was so shyly glad it had occurred to her.

But the Wheelers just sat.

And again Nora Mackenzie was standing alone amongst the inexorable moonlit gums. She thought perhaps she had always felt alone, even with Arch, while grateful even for her loneliness.

'Ah, there you are!' Nora said.

It was Arch. He stood holding out his bandaged wound. Rather rigid. He could have been up for court martial.

'I've missed the willy-wagtails,' Nora said, raising her face to him, exposing her distress, like a girl. 'Some day you'll have to play it to me. When you've the time. And we can concentrate.'

The Wheelers might not have existed.

As for the tape it had discovered silence.
Arch mumbled they'd all better have something to drink.
Jum agreed it was a good idea.
'Positively brilliant,' Eileen said.

The True Story

❦

DYLAN THOMAS
(Welsh, 1914–1953)

The old woman upstairs had been dying since Helen could remember. She had lain like a wax woman in her sheets since Helen was a child coming with her mother to bring fresh fruit and vegetables to the dying. And now Helen was a woman under her apron and print frock and her pale hair was bound in a bunch behind her head. Each morning she got up with the sun, lit the fire, let in the red-eyed cat. She made a pot of tea and, going up to the bedroom at the back of the cottage, bent over the old woman whose unseeing eyes were never closed. Each morning she looked into the hollows of the eyes and passed her hands over them. But the lids did not move, and she could not tell if the old woman breathed. "Eight o'clock, eight o'clock now," she said. And at once the eyes smiled. A ragged hand came out from the sheets and stayed there until Helen took it in her padded hand and closed it round the cup. When the cup was empty Helen filled it, and when the pot was dry she pulled back the white sheets from the bed. There the old woman was, stretched out in her nightdress, and the colour of her flesh was grey as her hair. Helen tidied the sheets and attended to the old woman's wants. Then she took the pot away.

Each morning she made breakfast for the boy who worked in the garden. She went to the back door, opened it, and saw him in the distance with his spade. "Half past eight now," she said. He was an ugly boy and his eyes were redder than the cat's, two crafty cuts in his head forever spying on the first shadows of her breast. She put his food in front of him. When he stood up he always said, "Is there anything you want me to do?" She had never said, "Yes." The boy went back to dig potatoes out of the patch or to count the hens' eggs, and if there were berries to be picked off the garden bushes she joined him before noon. Seeing the red currants pile up in the palm of her hand, she would think of the stain of the money under the old woman's mattress. If there were hens to be killed she could cut their throats far more cleanly than the boy who let his knife stay in the wound and wiped the blood on the knife along his sleeves. She caught a hen and killed it, felt its warm blood, and saw it run headless up the path. Then she went in to wash her hands.

It was in the first weeks of spring that she made up her mind to kill the old woman upstairs. She was twenty years old. There was so much that she wanted. She wanted a man of her own and a black dress for Sundays and a hat with a flower. She had no money at all. On the days that the boy took the eggs and the vegetables to market she gave him sixpence that the old woman gave her, and the money the boy brought back in his handkerchief she put into the old woman's hand. She worked for her food and shelter as the boy worked for his, though she slept in a room upstairs and he slept in a straw bed over the empty sheds.

On a market morning she walked into the garden so that the plan might be cooled in her head. It was a fine May day with no more than two clouds in the sky, two unshapely hands closing round the head of the sun. "If I could fly," she thought, "I could fly in at the open window and fix my teeth in her throat." But the cool wind blew the thought away. She knew that she was no common girl, for she had read books in the winter evenings when the boy was dreaming in the straw and the old woman was alone in the dark. She had read of a god who came down like money, of snakes with the voices of men, and of a man who stood on the top of a hill talking with a piece of fire.

At the end of the garden where the fence kept out the wild, green fields she came to a mound of earth. There she had buried the dog she had killed for catching and killing the hens. On a rough cross the date of the death was written backwards so that the dog had not died yet. "I could bury her here," said Helen to herself, "by the side of the grave, so that nobody could find her." And she patted her hands and reached the back door of the cottage before the two clouds got round the sun.

Inside there was a meal to be prepared for the old woman, potatoes to be mashed up in the tea. With the knife in her hand and the skins in her lap, she thought of the murder she was about to do. The knife made the only sound, the wind had dropped down, her heart was as quiet as though she had wrapped it up. Nothing moved in the cottage; her hand was dead on her lap; she could not think that smoke went up the chimney and out into the still sky. Her mind, alone in the world, was ticking away. Then, when all things were dead, a cock crew, and she remembered the boy who would soon be back from market. She had made up her mind to kill before he returned, but the grave must be dug and the hole filled up. Helen felt her hand die again in her lap. And in the middle of death she heard the boy's hand lift the latch. He came into the kitchen, saw that she was cleaning potatoes, and dropped his handkerchief on the table. Hearing the rattle of money, she looked up at him and smiled. He had never seen her smile before.

Soon she put his meal in front of him, and sat sideways by the fire. As he raised the knife to his mouth, he felt the full glance of her eyes on the sides of his eyes. "Have you taken up her dinner?" he asked. She did not answer. When he had finished he stood up from the table and asked, "Is there anything you want me to do?" as he had asked a thousand times. "Yes," said Helen.

She had never said "Yes" to him before. He had never heard a woman speak as she did then. The first shadow of her breast had never been so dark. He stumbled across the kitchen to her and she lifted her hands to her shoulders. "What will you do for me?" she said, and loosened the straps of her frock so that it fell about her and left her breast bare. She took his hand and placed it on her flesh. He stared at her nakedness, then said her name and caught hold of her. She held him close. "What will you do for me?" She let her frock fall on the floor and tore the rest of her clothes away. "You will do what I want," she said as his hands dropped on her.

After a minute she struggled out of his arms and ran softly across the room. With her naked back to the door that led upstairs, she beckoned him and told him what he was to do. "You help me, we shall be rich," she said. He smiled and nodded. He tried to finger her again but she caught his fingers and opened the door and led him upstairs. "You stay here quiet," she said. In the old woman's room she looked around her as if for the last time, at the cracked jug, the half-open window, the bed and the text on the wall. "One o'clock now," she said into the old woman's ear, and the blind eyes smiled. Helen put her fingers round the old woman's throat. "One o'clock now," she said, and with a sudden movement knocked the old woman's head against the wall. It needed but three little knocks, and the head burst like an egg.

"What have you done?" cried the boy. Helen called for him to come in. He stared at the naked woman who cleaned her hands on the bed and at the blood that made a round, red stain on the wall, and screamed out in horror. "Be quiet," said Helen, but he screamed again at her quiet voice and scurried downstairs.

"So Helen must fly," she said to herself, "fly out of the old woman's room." She opened the window wider and stepped out. "I am flying," she said.

But she was not flying.

Royal Jelly

❦⟊⟊❦

ROALD DAHL
(English, 1916–   )

"It worries me to death, Albert, it really does," Mrs. Taylor said.

She kept her eyes fixed on the baby who was now lying absolutely motionless in the crook of her left arm.

"I just know there's something wrong."

The skin on the baby's face had a pearly translucent quality, and was stretched very tightly over the bones.

"Try again," Albert Taylor said.

"It won't do any good."

"You have to keep trying, Mabel," he said.

She lifted the bottle out of the saucepan of hot water and shook a few drops of milk onto the inside of her wrist, testing for temperature.

"Come on," she whispered. "Come on, my baby. Wake up and take a bit more of this."

There was a small lamp on the table close by that made a soft yellow glow all around her.

"Please," she said. "Take just a weeny bit more."

The husband watched her over the top of his magazine. She was half dead with exhaustion, he could see that and the pale oval face, usually so grave and serene, had taken on a kind of pinched and desperate look. But even so, the drop of her head as she gazed down at the child was curiously beautiful.

"You see," she murmured. "It's no good. She won't have it."

She held the bottle up to the light, squinting at the calibrations.

"One ounce again. That's all she's taken. No—it isn't even that. It's only three quarters. It's not enough to keep body and soul together, Albert, it really isn't. It worries me to death."

"I know," he said.

"If only they could *find out* what was wrong."

"There's nothing wrong, Mabel. It's just a matter of time."

"Of course there's something wrong."

"Dr. Robinson says no."

"Look," she said, standing up. "You can't tell me it's natural for a six-weeks-old child to weigh less, less by more than *two whole pounds* than she did when she was born! Just look at those legs! They're nothing but skin and bone!"

The tiny baby lay limply on her arm, not moving.

"Dr. Robinson said you was to stop worrying, Mabel. So did that other one."

"Ha!" she said. "Isn't that wonderful! I'm to stop worrying!"

"Now, Mabel."

"What does he want me to do? Treat it as some sort of a joke?"

"He didn't say that."

"I hate doctors! I hate them all!" she cried, and she swung away from him and walked quickly out of the room toward the stairs, carrying the baby with her.

Albert Taylor stayed where he was and let her go.

In a little while he heard her moving about in the bedroom directly over his head, quick nervous footsteps going tap tap tap on the linoleum above. Soon the footsteps would stop, and then he would have to get up and follow her, and when he went into the bedroom he would find her sitting beside the cot as usual, staring at the child and crying softly to herself and refusing to move.

"She's starving, Albert," she would say.

"Of course she's not starving."

"She *is* starving. I know she is. And Albert?"

"Yes?"

"I believe you know it too, but you won't admit it. Isn't that right?"

Every night now it was like this.

Last week they had taken the child back to the hospital, and the doctor had examined it carefully and told them that there was nothing the matter.

"It took us nine years to get this baby, Doctor," Mabel had said. "I think it would kill me if anything should happen to her."

That was six days ago and since then it had lost another five ounces.

But worrying about it wasn't going to help anybody, Albert Taylor told himself. One simply had to trust the doctor on a thing like this. He picked up the magazine that was still lying on his lap and glanced idly down the list of contents to see what it had to offer this week:

AMONG THE BEES IN MAY
HONEY COOKERY
THE BEE FARMER AND THE B. PHARM.
EXPERIENCES IN THE CONTROL OF NOSEMA
THE LATEST ON ROYAL JELLY
THIS WEEK IN THE APIARY
THE HEALING POWER OF PROPOLIS
REGURGITATIONS
BRITISH BEEKEEPERS ANNUAL DINNER
ASSOCIATION NEWS

All his life Albert Taylor had been fascinated by anything that had to do with bees. As a small boy he used often to catch them in his bare hands and go running with them into the house to show to his mother, and sometimes he would put them on his face and let them crawl about over his cheeks and neck, and the astonishing thing about it all was that he never got stung. On the contrary, the bees seemed to enjoy being with him. They never tried to fly away, and to get rid of them he would have to brush them off gently with his fingers. Even then they would frequently return and settle again on his arm or hand or knee, any place where the skin was bare.

His father, who was a bricklayer, said there must be some witch's stench about the boy, something noxious that came oozing out through the pores of the skin, and that no good would ever come of it, hypnotizing insects like that. But the mother said it was a gift given him by God, and even went so far as to compare him with St. Francis and the birds.

As he grew older, Albert Taylor's fascination with bees developed into an obsession, and by the time he was twelve he had built his first hive. The following summer he had captured his first swarm. Two years later, at the age of fourteen, he had no less than five hives standing neatly in a row against the fence in his father's small back yard, and already—apart from the normal task of producing honey—he was practising the delicate and complicated business of rearing his own queens, grafting larvae into artificial cell cups, and all the rest of it.

He never had to use smoke when there was work to do inside a hive, and he never wore gloves on his hands or a net over his head. Clearly there was some strange sympathy between this boy and the bees, and down in the village, in the shops and pubs, they began to speak about him with a certain kind of respect, and people started coming up to the house to buy his honey.

When he was eighteen, he had rented one acre of rough pasture alongside a cherry orchard down the valley about a mile from the village, and there he had set out to establish his own business. Now, eleven years later, he was still in the same spot, but he had six acres of ground instead of one, two hundred and forty well-stocked hives, and a small house that he'd built mainly with his own hands. He had married at the age of twenty and that, apart from the fact that it had taken them over nine years to get a child, had also been a success. In fact, everything had gone pretty well for Albert until this strange little baby girl came along and started frightening them out of their wits by refusing to eat properly and losing weight every day.

He looked up from the magazine and began thinking about his daughter.

This evening, for instance, when she had opened her eyes at the beginning of the feed, he had gazed into them and seen something that frightened him to death—a kind of misty vacant stare, as though the eyes themselves were not connected to the brain at all but were just lying loose in their sockets like a couple of small grey marbles.

Did those doctors really know what they were talking about?

He reached for an ashtray and started slowly picking the ashes out from the bowl of his pipe with a matchstick.

One could always take her along to another hospital, somewhere in Oxford perhaps. He might suggest that to Mabel when he went upstairs.

He could still hear her moving around in the bedroom, but she must have taken off her shoes now and put on slippers because the noise was very faint.

He switched his attention back to the magazine and went on with his reading. He finished an article called "Experiences in the Control of

Nosema," then turned over the page and began reading the next one, "The Latest on Royal Jelly." He doubted very much whether there would be anything in this that he didn't know already:

What is this wonderful substance called royal jelly?

He reached for the tin of tobacco on the table beside him and began filling his pipe, still reading.

Royal jelly is a glandular secretion produced by the nurse bees to feed the larvae immediately they have hatched from the egg. The pharingeal glands of bees produce this substance in much the same way as the mammary glands of vertebrates produce milk. The fact is of great biological interest because no other insects in the world are known to have evolved such a process.

All old stuff, he told himself, but for want of anything better to do, he continued to read.

Royal jelly is fed in concentrated form to all bee larvae for the first three days after hatching from the egg; but beyond that point, for all those who are destined to become drones or workers, this precious food is greatly diluted with honey and pollen. On the other hand, the larvae which are destined to become queens are fed throughout the whole of their larval period on a concentrated diet of pure royal jelly. Hence the name.

Above him, up in the bedroom, the noise of the footsteps had stopped altogether. The house was quiet. He struck a match and put it to his pipe.

Royal jelly must be a substance of tremendous nourishing power, for on this diet alone, the honey-bee larva increases in weight fifteen hundred times in five days.

That was probably about right, he thought, although for some reason it had never occurred to him to consider larval growth in terms of weight before.

This is as if a seven-and-a-half-pound baby should increase in that time to five tons.

Albert Taylor stopped and read that sentence again.

He read it a third time.

This is as if a seven-and-a-half-pound baby . . .

"Mabel!" he cried, jumping up from his chair. "Mabel! Come here!"

He went out into the hall and stood at the foot of the stairs calling for her to come down.

There was no answer.

He ran up the stairs and switched on the light on the landing. The bedroom door was closed. He crossed the landing and opened it and stood in the doorway looking into the dark room. "Mabel," he said. "Come downstairs a moment, will you please? I've just had a bit of an idea. It's about the baby."

The light from the landing behind him cast a faint glow over the bed and he could see her dimly now, lying on her stomach with her face buried in the pillow and her arms up over her head. She was crying again.

"Mabel," he said, going over to her, touching her shoulder. "Please come down a moment. This may be important."

"Go away," she said. "Leave me alone."

"Don't you want to hear about my idea?"

"Oh, Albert, I'm *tired,*" she sobbed. "I'm so tired I don't know what I'm doing any more. I don't think I can go on. I don't think I can stand it."

There was a pause. Albert Taylor turned away from her and walked slowly over to the cradle where the baby was lying, and peered in. It was too dark for him to see the child's face, but when he bent down close he could hear the sound of breathing, very faint and quick. "What time is the next feed?" he asked.

"Two o'clock, I suppose."

"And the one after that?"

"Six in the morning."

"I'll do them both," he said. "You go to sleep."

She didn't answer.

"You get properly into bed, Mabel, and go straight to sleep, you understand? And stop worrying. I'm taking over completely for the next twelve hours. You'll give yourself a nervous breakdown going on like this."

"Yes," she said. "I know."

"I'm taking the nipper and myself *and* the alarm clock into the spare room this very moment, so you just lie down and relax and forget all about us. Right?" Already he was pushing the cradle out through the door.

"Oh, Albert," she sobbed.

"Don't you worry about a thing. Leave it to me."

"Albert . . ."

"Yes?"

"I love you, Albert."

"I love you too, Mabel. Now go to sleep."

Albert Taylor didn't see his wife again until nearly eleven o'clock the next morning.

"Good *gracious* me!" she cried, rushing down the stairs in dressing-gown and slippers. "Albert! Just look at the time! I must have slept twelve hours at least! Is everything all right? What happened?"

He was sitting quietly in his armchair, smoking a pipe and reading the morning paper. The baby was in a sort of carrier cot on the floor at his feet, sleeping.

"Hullo, dear," he said, smiling.

She ran over to the cot and looked in. "Did she take anything, Albert? How many times have you fed her? She was due for another one at ten o'clock, did you know that?"

Albert Taylor folded the newspaper neatly into a square and put it away on the side table. "I fed her at two in the morning," he said, "and she took about half an ounce, no more. I fed her again at six and she did a bit better that time, two ounces . . ."

"*Two ounces!* Oh, Albert, that's marvellous!"

"And we just finished the last feed ten minutes ago. There's the bottle on the mantelpiece. Only one ounce left. She drank three. How's that?" He was grinning proudly, delighted with his achievement.

The woman quickly got down on her knees and peered at the baby.

"Don't she look better?" he asked eagerly. "Don't she look fatter in the face?"

"It may sound silly," the wife said, "but I actually think she does. Oh, Albert, you're a marvell! How did you do it?"

"She's turning the corner," he said. "That's all it is. Just like the doctor prophesied, she's turning the corner."

"I pray to God you're right, Albert."

"Of course I'm right. From now on, you watch her go."

The woman was gazing lovingly at the baby.

"You look a lot better yourself too, Mabel."

"I feel wonderful. I'm sorry about last night."

"Let's keep it this way," he said. "I'll do all the night feeds in future. You do the day ones."

She looked up at him across the cot, frowning. "No," she said. "Oh no, I wouldn't allow you to do that."

"I don't want you to have a breakdown, Mabel."

"I won't, not now I've had some sleep."

"Much better we share it."

"No, Albert. This is my job and I intend to do it. Last night won't happen again."

There was a pause. Albert Taylor took the pipe out of his mouth and examined the grain on the bowl. "All right," he said. "In that case I'll just relieve you of the donkey work, I'll do all the sterilizing and the mixing of the food and getting everything ready. That'll help you a bit, anyway."

She looked at him carefully, wondering what could have come over him all of a sudden.

"You see, Mabel, I've been thinking . . ."

"Yes, dear."

"I've been thinking that up until last night I've never even raised a finger to help you with this baby."

"That isn't true."

"Oh yes it is. So I've decided that from now on I'm going to do *my* share of the work. I'm going to be the feed-mixer and the bottle-sterilizer. Right?"

"It's very sweet of you, dear, but I really don't think it's necessary. . . ."

"Come on!" he cried. "Don't change the luck! I done it the last three times and just *look* what happened! When's the next one? Two o'clock, isn't it?"

"Yes."

"It's all mixed," he said. "Everything's all mixed and ready and all you've got to do when the time comes is to go out there to the larder and take it off the shelf and warm it up. That's *some* help, isn't it?"

The woman got up off her knees and went over to him and kissed him on the cheek. "You're such a nice man," she said. "I love you more and more every day I know you."

Later, in the middle of the afternoon, when Albert was outside in the sunshine working among the hives, he heard her calling to him from the house.

"Albert!" she shouted. "Albert, come here!" She was running through the buttercups toward him.

He started forward to meet her, wondering what was wrong.

"Oh, Albert! Guess what!"

"What?"

"I've just finished giving her the two-o'clock feed and she's taken the whole lot!"

"No!"

"Every drop of it! Oh, Albert, I'm so happy! She's going to be all right! She's turned the corner just like you said!" She came up to him and threw her arms around his neck and hugged him, and he clapped her on the back and laughed and said what a marvellous little mother she was.

"Will you come in and watch the next one and see if she does it again, Albert?"

He told her he wouldn't miss it for anything, and she hugged him again, then turned and ran back to the house, skipping over the grass and singing all the way.

Naturally, there was a certain amount of suspense in the air as the time approached for the six-o'clock feed. By five thirty both parents were already seated in the living-room waiting for the moment to arrive. The bottle with the milk formula in it was standing in a suacepan of warm water on the mantelpiece. The baby was asleep in its carrier cot on the sofa.

At twenty minutes to six it woke up and started screaming its head off.

"There you are!" Mrs. Taylor cried. "She's asking for the bottle. Pick her up quick, Albert, and hand her to me here. Give me the bottle first."

He gave her the bottle, then placed the baby on the woman's lap. Cautiously, she touched the baby's lips with the end of the nipple. The baby seized the nipple between its gums and began to suck ravenously with a rapid powerful action.

"Oh, Albert, isn't it wonderful?" she said, laughing.

"It's terrific, Mabel."

In seven or eight minutes, the entire contents of the bottle had disappeared down the baby's throat.

"You clever girl," Mrs. Taylor said. "Four ounces again."

Albert Taylor was leaning forward in his chair, peering intently into the baby's face. "You know what?" he said. "She even seems as though she's put on a touch of weight already. What do you think?"

The mother looked down at the child.

"Don't she seem bigger and fatter to you, Mabel, than she was yesterday?"

"Maybe she does, Albert. I'm not sure. Although actually there couldn't be any *real* gain in such a short time as this. The important thing is that she's eating normally."

"She's turned the corner," Albert said. "I don't think you need worry about her any more."

"I certainly won't."

"You want me to go up and fetch the cradle back into our own bedroom, Mabel?"

"Yes, please," she said.

Albert went upstairs and moved the cradle. The woman followed with the baby, and after changing its nappy, she laid it gently down on its bed. Then she covered it with sheet and blanket.

"Doesn't she look lovely, Albert?" she whispered. "Isn't that the most beautiful baby you've ever seen in your *entire* life?"

"Leave her be now, Mabel," he said. "Come on downstairs and cook us a bit of supper. We both deserve it."

After they had finished eating, the parents settled themselves in armchairs in the living-room, Albert with his magazine and his pipe, Mrs. Taylor with her knitting. But this was a very different scene from the one of the night before. Suddenly, all tensions had vanished. Mrs. Taylor's handsome oval face was glowing with pleasure, her cheeks were pink, her eyes were sparkling bright, and her mouth was fixed in a little dreamy smile of pure content. Every now and again she would glance up from her knitting and gaze affectionately at her husband. Occasionally, she would stop the clicking of her needles altogether for a few seconds and sit quite still, looking at the ceiling, listening for a cry or a whimper from upstairs. But all was quiet.

"Albert," she said after a while.

"Yes, dear?"

"What was it you were going to tell me last night when you came rushing up to the bedroom? You said you had an idea for the baby."

Albert Taylor lowered the magazine onto his lap and gave her a long sly look.

"Did I?" he said.

"Yes." She waited for him to go on, but he didn't.

"What's the big joke?" she asked. "Why are you grinning like that?"

"It's a joke all right," he said.

"Tell it to me, dear."

"I'm not sure I ought to," he said. "You might call me a liar."

She had seldom seen him looking so pleased with hmself as he was now, and she smiled back at him, egging him on.

"I'd just like to see your face when you hear it, Mabel, that's all."

"Albert, what *is* all this?"

He paused, refusing to be hurried.

"You do think the baby's better, don't you?" he asked.

"Of course I do."

"You agree with me that all of a sudden she's feeding marvellously and looking one-hundred-per-cent different?"

"I do, Albert, yes."

"That's good," he said, the grin widening. "You see, it's me that did it."

"Did what?"

"I cured the baby."

"Yes, dear, I'm sure you did." Mrs. Taylor went right on with her knitting.

"You don't believe me, do you?"

"Of course I believe you, Albert. I give you all the credit, every bit of it."

"Then how did I do it?"

"Well," she said, pausing a moment to think. "I suppose it's simply that you're a brilliant feed-mixer. Ever since you started mixing the feeds she's got better and better."

"You mean there's some sort of an art in mixing the feeds?"

"Apparently there is." She was knitting away and smiling quietly to herself, thinking how funny men were.

"I'll tell you a secret," he said. "You're absolutely right. Although, mind you, it isn't so much *how* you mix it that counts. It's what you put in. You realize that, don't you, Mabel?"

Mrs. Taylor stopped knitting and looked up sharply at her husband. "Albert," she said, "don't tell me you've been putting things into that child's milk?"

He sat there grinning.

"Well, have you or haven't you?"

"It's possible," he said.

"I don't believe it."

He had a strange fierce way of grinning that showed his teeth.

"Albert," she said. "Stop playing with me like this."

"Yes, dear, all right."

"You haven't *really* put anything into her milk, have you? Answer me properly, Albert. This could be serious with such a tiny baby."

"The answer is yes, Mabel."

"Albert Taylor! How could you?"

"Now don't get excited," he said. "I'll tell you all about it if you really want me to, but for heaven's sake keep your hair on."

"It was beer!" she cried. "I just know it was beer!"

"Don't be so daft, Mabel, please."

"Then what was it?"

Albert laid his pipe down carefully on the table beside him and leaned back in his chair. "Tell me," he said, "did you ever by any chance happen to hear me mentioning something called royal jelly?"

"I did not."

"It's magic," he said. "Pure magic. And last night I suddenly got the idea that if I was to put some of this into the baby's milk . . ."

"How *dare* you!"

"Now, Mabel, you don't even know what it is yet."

"I don't care what it is," she said. "You can't go putting foreign bodies like that into a tiny baby's milk. You must be mad."

"It's perfectly harmless, Mabel, otherwise I wouldn't have done it. It comes from bees."

"I might have guessed that."

"And it's so precious that practically no one can afford to take it. When they do, it's only one little drop at a time."

"And how much did you give to our baby, might I ask?"

"Ah," he said, "that's the whole point. That's where the difference lies. I reckon that our baby, just in the last four feeds, has already swallowed about fifty times as much royal jelly as anyone else in the world has ever swallowed before. How about that?"

"Albert, stop pulling my leg."

"I swear it," he said proudly.

She sat there staring at him, her brow wrinkled, her mouth slightly open.

"You know what this stuff actually costs, Mabel, if you want to buy it? There's a place in America advertising it for sale this very moment for something like five hundred dollars a pound jar! *Five hundred dollars!* That's more than gold, you know!"

She hadn't the faintest idea what he was talking about.

"I'll prove it," he said, and he jumped up and went across to the large bookcase where he kept all his literature about bees. On the top shelf, the back numbers of *The American Bee Journal* were neatly stacked alongside those of *The British Bee Journal, Beecraft,* and other magazines. He took down the last issue of *The American Bee Journal* and turned to a page of small classified advertisements at the back.

"Here you are," he said. "Exactly as I told you. 'We sell royal jelly— $480 per lb. jar wholesale.' "

He handed her the magazine so she could read it herself.

"Now do you believe me? This is an actual shop in New York, Mabel. It says so."

"It doesn't say you can go stirring it into the milk of a practically newborn baby," she said. "I don't know what's come over you, Albert, I really don't."

"It's curing her, isn't it?"

"I'm not so sure about that, now."

"Don't be so damn silly, Mabel. You know it is."

"Then why haven't other people done it with *their* babies?"

"I keep telling you," he said. "It's too expensive. Practically nobody in the world can afford to buy royal jelly just for *eating* except maybe one or two multimillionaires. The people who buy it are the big companies that make women's face creams and things like that. They're using it as a stunt. They mix a tiny pinch of it into a big jar of face cream and it's selling like hot cakes for absolutely enormous prices. They claim it takes out the wrinkles."

"And does it?"

"Now how on earth would I know that, Mabel? Anyway," he said, returning to his chair, "that's not the point. The point is this. It's done so much good to our little baby just in the last few hours that I think we ought to go right on giving it to her. Now don't interrupt, Mabel. Let me finish. I've got two hundred and forty hives out there and if I turn over maybe a hundred of them to making royal jelly, we ought to be able to supply her with all she wants."

"Albert Taylor," the woman said, stretching her eyes wide and staring at him. "Have you gone out of your mind?"

"Just hear me through, will you please?"

"I forbid it," she said, "absolutely. You're not to give my baby another drop of that horrid jelly, you understand?"

"Now, Mabel . . ."

"And quite apart from that, we had a shocking honey crop last year, and if you go fooling around with those hives now, there's no telling what might not happen."

"There's nothing wrong with my hives, Mabel."

"You know very well we had only half the normal crop last year."

"Do me a favour, will you?" he said. "Let me explain some of the marvellous things this stuff does."

"You haven't even told me what it is yet."

"All right, Mabel. I'll do that too. Will you listen? Will you give me a chance to explain it?"

She sighed and picked up her knitting once more. "I suppose you might as well get it off your chest, Albert. Go on and tell me."

He paused, a bit uncertain now how to begin. It wasn't going to be easy to explain something like this to a person with no detailed knowledge of apiculture at all.

"You know, don't you," he said, "that each colony has only one queen?"

"Yes."

"And that this queen lays all the eggs?"

"Yes, dear. That much I know."

"All right. Now the queen can actually lay two different kinds of eggs. You didn't know that, but she can. It's what we call one of the miracles of the hive. She can lay eggs that produce drones, and she can lay eggs that produce workers. Now if that isn't a miracle, Mabel, I don't know what is."

"Yes, Albert, all right."

"The drones are the males. We don't have to worry about them. The workers are all females. So is the queen, of course. But the workers are unsexed females, if you see what I mean. Their organs are completely undeveloped, whereas the queen is tremendously sexy. She can actually lay her own weight in eggs in a single day."

He hesitated, marshalling his thoughts.

"Now what happens is this. The queen crawls around on the comb and lays her eggs in what we call cells. You know all those hundreds of little holes you see in a honeycomb? Well, a brood comb is just about the same except the cells don't have honey in them, they have eggs. She lays one egg to each cell, and in three days each of these eggs hatches out into a tiny grub. We call it a larva.

"Now, as soon as this larva appears, the nurse bees—they're young workers—all crowd round and start feeding it like mad. And you know what they feed it on?"

"Royal jelly," Mabel answered patiently.

"Right!" he cried. "That's exactly what they do feed it on. They get this stuff out of a gland in their heads and they start pumping it into the cell to feed the larva. And what happens then?"

He paused dramatically, blinking at her with his small watery-grey eyes. Then he turned slowly in his chair and reached for the magazine that he had been reading the night before.

"You want to know what happens then?" he asked, wetting his lips.

"I can hardly wait."

" 'Royal jelly,' " he read aloud, " 'must be a substance of tremendous nourishing power, for on this diet alone, the honey-bee larva increases in weight *fifteen hundred times* in five days!' "

"How much?"

"Fifteen hundred times, Mabel. And you know what that means if you put it in terms of a human being? It means," he said, lowering his voice, leaning forward, fixing her with those small pale eyes, "it means that in five days a baby weighing seven and a half pounds to start off with would increase in weight to *five tons!"*

For the second time, Mrs. Taylor stopped knitting.

"Now you mustn't take that too literally, Mabel."

"Who says I mustn't?"

"It's just a scientific way of putting it, that's all."

"Very well, Albert. Go on."

"But that's only half the story," he said. "There's more to come. The really amazing thing about royal jelly, I haven't told you yet. I'm going to show you now how it can transform a plain dull-looking little worker bee with practically no sex organs at all into a great big beautiful fertile queen."

"Are you saying our baby is dull-looking and plain?" she asked sharply.

"Now don't go putting words into my mouth, Mabel, please. Just listen to this. Did you know that the queen bee and the worker bee, although they are completely different when they grow up, are both hatched out of exactly the same kind of egg?"

"I don't believe that," she said.

"It's true as I'm sitting here, Mabel, honest it is. Any time the bees want a queen to hatch out of the egg instead of a worker, they can do it."

"How?"

"Ah," he said, shaking a thick forefinger in her direction. "That's just what I'm coming to. That's the secret of the whole thing. Now—what do *you* think it is, Mabel, that makes this miracle happen?"

"Royal jelly," she answered. "You already told me."

"Royal jelly it is!" he cried, clapping his hands and bouncing up on his seat. His big round face was glowing with excitement now, and two vivid patches of scarlet had appeared high up on each cheek.

"Here's how it works. I'll put it very simply for you. The bees want a new queen. So they build an extra-large cell, a queen cell we call it, and they get the old queen to lay one of her eggs in there. The other one thousand nine hundred and ninety-nine eggs she lays in ordinary worker cells. Now. As soon as these eggs hatch out into larvae, the nurse bees rally round and start pumping in the royal jelly. All of them get it, workers as well as queen. But here's the vital thing, Mabel, so listen carefully. Here's where the difference comes. The worker larvae only receive this special marvelous food for the *first three days* of their larval life. After that they have a complete change of diet. What really happens is they get weaned, except that it's not like an ordinary weaning because it's so sudden. After the third day they're put straight away onto more or less routine bees' food—a mixture of honey and pollen—and then about two weeks later they emerge from the cells as workers.

"But not so the larva in the queen cell! This one gets royal jelly *all the way through its larval life.* The nurse bees simply pour it into the cell, so much so in fact that the little larva is literally floating in it. And that's what makes it into a queen!"

"You can't prove it," she said.

"Don't talk so damn silly, Mabel, please. Thousands of people have proved it time and time again, famous scientists in every country in the world. All you have to do is take a larva out of a worker cell and put it in a queen cell—that's what we call grafting—and just so long as the nurse bees keep it well supplied with royal jelly, then presto!—it'll grow up into a queen! And what makes it more marvellous still is the absolutely enormous difference between a queen and a worker when they grow up. The abdomen is a different shape. The sting is different. The legs are different. The . . ."

"In what way are the legs different?" she asked, testing him.

"The legs? Well, the workers have little pollen baskets on their legs for carrying the pollen. The queen has none. Now here's another thing. The queen has fully developed sex organs. The workers don't. And most amazing of all, Mabel, the queen lives for an average of four to six years. The worker hardly lives that many months. And all this difference simply because one of them got royal jelly and the other didn't!"

"It's pretty hard to believe," she said, "that a food can do all that."

"Of course it's hard to believe. It's another of the miracles of the hive. In fact it's the biggest ruddy miracle of them all. It's such a hell of a big miracle that it's baffled the greatest men of science for hundreds of years. Wait a moment. Stay there. Don't move."

Again he jumped up and went over to the bookcase and started rummaging among the books and magazines.

"I'm going to find you a few of the reports. Here we are. Here's one of them. Listen to this." He started reading aloud from a copy of *The American Bee Journal:*

" 'Living in Toronto at the head of a fine research laboratory given to him by the people of Canada in recognition of his truly great contribution to humanity in the discovery of insulin, Dr. Frederick A. Banting became curious about royal jelly. He requested his staff to do a basic fractional analysis. . . .' "

He paused.

"Well, there's no need to read it all, but here's what happened. Dr. Banting and his people took some royal jelly from queen cells that contained two-day-old larvae, and then they started analyzing it. And what d'you think they found?

"They found," he said, "that royal jelly contained phenols, sterols, glycerils, dextrose, *and*—now here it comes—and eighty to eighty-five per cent *unidentified* acids!"

He stood beside the bookcase with the magazine in his hand, smiling a funny little furtive smile of triumph, and his wife watched him, bewildered.

He was not a tall man; he had a thick plump pulpy-looking body that was built close to the ground on abbreviated legs. The legs were slightly bowed. The head was huge and round, covered with bristly short-cut hair, and the greater part of the face—now that he had given up shaving altogether—was hidden by a brownish yellow fuzz about an inch long. In one way and another, he was rather grotesque to look at, there was no denying that.

"Eighty to eighty-five per cent," he said, "unidentified acids. Isn't that fantastic?" He turned back to the bookshelf and began hunting through the other magazines.

"What does it mean, unidentified acids?"

"That's the whole point! No one knows! Not even Banting could find out. You've heard of Banting?"

"No."

"He just happens to be about the most famous living doctor in the world today, that's all."

Looking at him now as he buzzed around in front of the bookcase with his bristly head and his hairy face and his plump pulpy body, she couldn't help thinking that somehow, in some curious way, there was a touch of the bee about this man. She had often seen women grow to look like the horses that they rode, and she had noticed that people who bred birds or bull terriers or pomeranians frequently resembled in some small but startling manner the creature of their choice. But up until now it had never occurred to her that her husband might look like a bee. It shocked her a bit.

"And did Banting ever try to eat it," she asked, "this royal jelly?"

"Of course he didn't eat it, Mabel. He didn't have enough for that. It's too precious."

"You know something?" she said, staring at him but smiling a little all the same. "You're getting to look just a teeny bit like a bee yourself, did you know that?"

He turned and looked at her.

"I suppose it's the beard mostly," she said. "I do wish you'd stop wearing it. Even the colour is sort of bee-ish, don't you think?"

"What the hell are you talking about, Mabel?"

"Albert," she said. "Your language."

"Do you want to hear any more of this or don't you?"

"Yes, dear, I'm sorry. I was only joking. Do go on."

He turned away again and pulled another magazine out of the bookcase and began leafing through the pages. "Now just listen to this, Mabel.

'In 1939, Heyl experimented with twenty-one-day-old rats, injecting them with royal jelly in varying amounts. As a result, he found a precocious follicular development of the ovaries directly in proportion to the quantity of royal jelly injected.' "

"There!" she cried. "I knew it!"

"Knew what?"

"I knew something terrible would happen."

"Nonsense. There's nothing wrong with that. Now here's another, Mabel. 'Still and Burdett found that a male rat which hitherto had been unable to breed, upon receiving a minute daily dose of royal jelly, became a father many times over.' "

"Albert," she cried, "this stuff is *much* too strong to give to a baby! I don't like it at all."

"Nonsense, Mabel."

"Then why do they only try it out on rats, tell me that? Why don't some of these famous scientists take it themselves? They're too clever, that's why. Do you think Dr. Banting is going to risk finishing up with precious ovaries? Not him."

"But they *have* given it to people, Mabel. Here's a whole article about it. Listen." He turned the page and again began reading from the magazine. " 'In Mexico, in 1953, a group of enlightened physicians began prescribing minute doses of royal jelly for such things as cerebral neuritis, arthritis, diabetes, autointoxication from tobacco, impotence in men, asthma, croup, and gout. . . . There are stacks of signed testimonials. . . . A celebrated stock-broker in Mexico City contracted a particularly stubborn case of psoriasis. He became physically unattractive. His clients began to forsake him. His business began to suffer. In desperation he turned to royal jelly—one drop with every meal—and presto!—he was cured in a fortnight. A waiter in the Café Jena, also in Mexico City, reported that his father, after taking minute doses of this wonder substance in capsule form, sired a healthy boy child at the age of ninety. A bullfight promoter in Acapulco, finding himself landed with a rather lethargic-looking bull, injected it with one gram of royal jelly (an excessive dose) just before it entered the arena. Thereupon, the beast became so swift and savage that it promptly dispatched two picadors, three horses, and a matador, and finally . . .' "

"Listen!" Mrs. Taylor said, interrupting him. "I think the baby's crying."

Albert glanced up from his reading. Sure enough, a lusty yelling noise was coming from the bedroom above.

"She must be hungry," he said.

His wife looked at the clock. "Good gracious me!" she cried, jumping up. "It's past her time again already! You mix the feed, Albert, quickly, while I bring her down! But hurry! I don't want to keep her waiting."

In half a minute, Mrs. Taylor was back, carrying the screaming infant in her arms. She was flustered now, still quite unaccustomed to the ghastly nonstop racket that a healthy baby makes when it wants its food. "Do be quick, Albert!" she called, settling herself in the armchair and arranging the child on her lap. "Please hurry!"

Albert entered from the kitchen and handed her the bottle of warm milk. "It's just right," he said. "You don't have to test it."

She hitched the baby's head a little higher in the crook of her arm, then pushed the rubber teat straight into the wide-open yelling mouth. The baby grabbed the teat and began to suck. The yelling stopped. Mrs. Taylor relaxed.

"Oh, Albert, isn't she lovely?"

"She's terrific, Mabel—thanks to royal jelly."

"Now, dear, I don't want to hear another word about that nasty stuff. It frightens me to death."

"You're making a big mistake," he said.

"We'll see about that."

The baby went on sucking the bottle.

"I do believe she's going to finish the whole lot again, Albert."

"I'm sure she is," he said.

And a few minutes later, the milk was all gone.

"Oh, what a good girl you are!" Mrs. Taylor cried, as very gently she started to withdraw the nipple. The baby sensed what she was doing and sucked harder, trying to hold on. The woman gave a quick little tug, and *plop,* out it came.

"Waa! Waa! Waa! Waa! Waa!" the baby yelled.

"Nasty old wind," Mrs. Taylor said, hoisting the child onto her shoulder and patting its back.

It belched twice in quick succession.

"There you are, my darling, you'll be all right now."

For a few seconds, the yelling stopped. Then it started again.

"Keep belching her," Albert said. "She's drunk it too quick."

His wife lifted the baby back onto her shoulder. She rubbed its spine. She changed it from one shoulder to the other. She lay it on its stomach on her lap. She sat it up on her knee. But it didn't belch again, and the yelling became louder and more insistent every minute.

"Good for the lungs," Albert Taylor said, grinning. "That's the way they exercise their lungs, Mabel, did you know that?"

"There, there, there," the wife said, kissing it all over the face. "There, there, there."

They waited another five minutes, but not for one moment did the screaming stop.

"Change the nappy," Albert said. "It's got a wet nappy, that's all it is." He fetched a clean one from the kitchen, and Mrs. Taylor took the old one off and put the new one on.

This made no difference at all.

"Waa! Waa! Waa! Waa! Waa!" the baby yelled.

"You didn't stick the safety pin through the skin, did you, Mabel?"

"Of course I didn't," she said, feeling under the nappy with her fingers to make sure.

The parents sat opposite one another in their armchairs, smiling nervously, watching the baby on the mother's lap, waiting for it to tire and stop screaming.

"You know what?" Albert Taylor said at last.

"What?"

"I'll bet she's still hungry. I'll bet all she wants is another swig at that bottle. How about me fetching her an extra lot?"

"I don't think we ought to do that, Albert."

"It'll do her good," he said, getting up from his chair. "I'm going to warm her up a second helping."

He went into the kitchen, and was away several minutes. When he returned he was holding a bottle brimful of milk.

"I made her a double," he announced. "Eight ounces. Just in case."

"Albert! Are you mad! Don't you know it's just as bad to overfeed as it is to underfeed?"

"You don't have to give her the lot, Mabel. You can stop any time you like. Go on," he said, standing over her. "Give her a drink."

Mrs. Taylor began to tease the baby's upper lip with the end of the nipple. The tiny mouth closed like a trap over the rubber teat and suddenly there was silence in the room. The baby's whole body relaxed and a look of absolute bliss came over its face as it started to drink.

"There you are, Mabel! What did I tell you?"

The woman didn't answer.

"She's ravenous, that's what she is. Just look at her suck."

Mrs. Taylor was watching the level of the milk in the bottle. It was dropping fast, and before long three or four ounces out of the eight had disappeared.

"There," she said. "That'll do."

"You can't pull it away now, Mabel."

"Yes, dear. I must."

"Go on, woman. Give her the rest and stop fussing."

"But *Albert* . . ."

"She's famished, can't you see that? Go on, my beauty," he said. "You finish that bottle."

"I don't like it, Albert," the wife said, but she didn't pull the bottle away.

"She's making up for lost time, Mabel, that's all she's doing."

Five minutes later the bottle was empty. Slowly, Mrs. Taylor withdrew the nipple, and this time there was no protest from the baby, no sound at all. It lay peacefully on the mother's lap, the eyes glazed with contentment, the mouth half open, the lips smeared with milk.

"Twelve whole ounces, Mabel!" Albert Taylor said. "Three times the normal amount! Isn't that amazing!"

The woman was staring down at the baby. And now the old anxious tight-lipped look of the frightened mother was slowly returning to her face.

"What's the matter with *you?*" Albert asked. "You're not worried by that, are you? You can't expect her to get back to normal on a lousy four ounces, don't be ridiculous."

"Come here, Albert," she said.

"What?"

"I said come here."

He went over and stood beside her.

"Take a good look and tell me if you see anything different."

He peered closely at the baby. "She seems bigger, Mabel, if that's what you mean. Bigger and fatter."

"Hold her," she ordered. "Go on, pick her up."

He reached out and lifted the baby up off the mother's lap. "Good God!" he cried. "She weighs a ton!"

"Exactly."

"Now isn't that marvellous!" he cried, beaming. "I'll bet she must almost be back to normal already!"

"It frightens me, Albert. It's too quick."

"Nonsense, woman."

"It's that disgusting jelly that's done it," she said. "I hate the stuff."

"There's nothing disgusting about royal jelly," he answered, indignant.

"Don't be a fool, Albert! You think it's *normal* for a child to start putting on weight at this speed?"

"You're never satisfied!" he cried. "You're scared stiff when she's losing and now you're absolutely terrified because she's gaining! What's the matter with you, Mabel?"

The woman got up from her chair with the baby in her arms and started toward the door. "All I can say is," she said, "it's lucky I'm here to see you don't give her any more of it, that's all I can say." She went out, and Albert watched her through the open door as she crossed the hall to the foot of the stairs and started to ascend, and when she reached the third or fourth step she suddenly stopped and stood quite still for several seconds as though remembering something. Then she turned and came down again rather quickly and re-entered the room.

"Albert," she said.

"Yes?"

"I assume there wasn't any royal jelly in this last feed we've just given her?"

"I don't see why you should assume that, Mabel."

"Albert!"

"What's wrong?" he asked, soft and innocent.

"How *dare* you!" she cried.

Albert Taylor's great bearded face took on a pained and puzzled look. "I think you ought to be very glad she's got another big dose of it inside her," he said. "Honest I do. And this *is* a big dose, Mabel, believe you me."

The woman was standing just inside the doorway clasping the sleeping baby in her arms and staring at her husband with huge eyes. She stood very erect, her body absolutely stiff with fury, her face paler, more tight-lipped than ever.

"You mark my words," Albert was saying, "you're going to have a nipper there soon that'll win first prize in any baby show in the *entire* country. Hey, why don't you weigh her now and see what she is? You want me to get the scales, Mabel, so you can weigh her?"

The woman walked straight over to the large table in the centre of the room and laid the baby down and quickly started taking off its clothes. "Yes!" she snapped. "Get the scales!" Off came the little nightgown, then the undervest.

Then she unpinned the nappy and she drew it away and the baby lay naked on the table.

"But Mabel!" Albert cried. "It's a miracle! She's fat as a puppy!"

Indeed, the amount of flesh the child had put on since the day before was astounding. The small sunken chest with the rib-bones showing all over it was now plump and round as a barrel, and the belly was bulging high in the air. Curiously, though, the arms and legs did not seem to have grown in proportion. Still short and skinny, they looked like little sticks protruding from a ball of fat.

"Look!" Albert said. "She's even beginning to get a bit of fuzz on the tummy to keep her warm!" He put out a hand and was about to run the tips of his fingers over the powdering of silky yellowy-brown hairs that had suddenly appeared on the baby's stomach.

"Don't you touch her!" the woman cried. She turned and faced him, her eyes blazing, and she looked suddenly like some kind of a little fighting bird with her neck arched over toward him as though she were about to fly at his face and peck his eyes out.

"Now wait a minute," he said, retreating.

"You must be mad!" she cried.

"Now wait just one minute, Mabel, will you please, because if you're still thinking this stuff is dangerous . . . That *is* what you're thinking, isn't it? All right, then. Listen carefully. I shall now proceed to *prove* to you once and for all, Mabel, that royal jelly is absolutely harmless to human beings, even in enormous doses. For example—why do you think we had only half the usual honey crop last summer? Tell me that."

His retreat, walking backwards, had taken him three or four yards away from her, where he seemed to feel more comfortable.

"The reason we had only half the usual crop last summer," he said slowly, lowering his voice, "was because I turned one hundred of my hives over to the production of royal jelly."

"You *what?*"

"Ah," he whispered. "I thought that might surprise you a bit. And I've been making it ever since right under your very nose." His small eyes were glinting at her, and a slow sly smile was creeping around the corners of his mouth.

"You'll never guess the reason, either," he said. "I've been afraid to mention it up to now because I thought it might . . . well . . . sort of embarrass you."

There was a slight pause. He had his hands clasped high in front of him, level with his chest, and he was rubbing one palm against the other, making a soft scraping noise.

"You remember that bit I read you out of the magazine? That bit about the rat? Let me see now, how does it go? 'Still and Burdett found that a male rat which hitherto had been unable to breed . . .' " He hesitated, the grin widening, showing his teeth.

"You get the message, Mabel?"

She stood quite still, facing him.

"The very first time I ever read that sentence, Mabel, I jumped straight out of my chair and I said to myself if it'll work with a lousy rat, I said, then there's no reason on earth why it shouldn't work with Albert Taylor."

He paused again, craning his head forward and turning one ear slightly in his wife's direction, waiting for her to say something. But she didn't.

"And here's another thing," he went on. "It made me feel so absolutely marvellous, Mabel, and so sort of completely different to what I was before that I went right on taking it even after you'd announced the joyful tidings. *Buckets* of it I must have swallowed during the last twelve months."

The big heavy haunted-looking eyes of the woman were moving intently over the man's face and neck. There was no skin showing at all on the neck, not even at the sides below the ears. The whole of it, to a point where it disappeared into the collar of the shirt, was covered all the way around with those shortish silky hairs, yellowy black.

"Mind you," he said, turning away from her, gazing lovingly now at the baby, "it's going to work far better on a tiny infant than on a fully developed man like me. You've only got to look at her to see that, don't you agree?"

The woman's eyes travelled slowly downward and settled on the baby.

The baby was lying naked on the table, fat and white and comatose, like some gigantic grub that was approaching the end of its larval life and would soon emerge into the world complete with mandibles and wings.

"Why don't you cover her up, Mabel?" he said. "We don't want our little queen to catch a cold."

The Fathers' Daughters

MURIEL SPARK
(Scottish, 1918–   )

She left the old man in his deck-chair on the front, having first adjusted the umbrella awning with her own hand, and with her own hand, put his panama hat at a comfortable angle. The beach attendant had been sulky, but she didn't see why one should lay out tips only for adjusting an umbrella and a panama hat. Since the introduction of the new franc it was impossible to tip less than a franc. There seemed to be a conspiracy all along the coast to hide the lesser coins from the visitors, and one could only find franc pieces in one's purse, and one had to be careful not to embarrass Father, and one . . .

She hurried along the Rue Paradis, keeping in the hot shade, among all the old, old smells of Nice, not only garlic wafting from the cafés, and of the hot invisible air itself, but the smells from her memory, from thirty-five summers at Nice in apartments of long-ago, Father's summer salon, Father's friends' children, Father's friends, writers, young artists dating back five years at Nice, six, nine years; and then, before the war, twenty years ago—when we were at Nice, do you remember, Father? Do you remember the pension on the Boulevard Victor Hugo when we were rather poor? Do you remember the Americans at the Negresco in 1937—

how changed, how demure they are now! Do you remember, Father, how in the old days we disliked the thick carpets—at least, you disliked them, and what you dislike, I dislike, isn't it so, Father?

Yes, Dora, we don't care for luxury. Comfort, yes, but luxury, no.

I doubt if we can afford to stay at an hotel on the front this year, Father.

What's that? What's that you say?

I said I doubt if we ought to stay on the front this year, Father; the Promenade des Anglais is becoming very trippery. Remember you disliked the thick carpets. . . .

Yes, yes, of course.

Of course, and so we'll go, I suggest, to a little place I've found on the Boulevard Gambetta, and if we don't like that there's a very good place on the Boulevard Victor Hugo. Within our means, Father, modest and . . .

What's that you say?

I said it wasn't a vulgar place, Father.

Ah. No.

And so I'll just drop them a note and book a couple of bedrooms. They may be small, but the food . . .

Facing the sea, Dora.

They are all very vulgar places facing the sea, Father. Very distracting. No peace at all. Times have changed, you know.

Ah. Well, I leave it to you, dear. Tell them I desire a large room, suitable for entertaining. Spare no expense, Dora.

Oh, of course not, Father.

And I hope to God we've won the lottery, she thought, as she hurried up the little street to the lottery kiosk. Someone's got to win it out of the whole of France. The dark-skinned blonde at the lottery kiosk took an interest in Dora who came so regularly each morning rather than buy a newspaper to see the results. She leaned over the ticket, holding her card of numbers, comparing it with Dora's ticket, with an expression of earnest sympathy.

'No luck,' Dora said.

'Try again tomorrow,' said the woman. 'One never knows. Life is a lottery . . .'

Dora smiled as one who must either smile or weep. On her way back to the sea-front she thought, tomorrow I will buy five hundred francs' worth. Then she thought, no, no, I'd better not, I may run short of francs and have to take Father home before time. Dora, the food here is inferior. —I know, Father, but it's the same everywhere in France now, times have changed.—I think we should move to another hotel, Dora.—The others are all very expensive, Father.—What's that? What's that you say? —There are no other rooms available, Father, because of the tourists, these days.

The brown legs of lovely young men and girls passed her as she approached the sea. I ought to appreciate every minute of this, she thought, it may be the last time. This thoroughly blue sea, these brown limbs, these white teeth and innocent inane tongues, these palm trees—all this is what we are paying for.

'Everything all right, Father?'

'Where have you been, dear?'

'Only for a walk round the back streets to smell the savours.'

'Dora, you are a chip off the old block. What did you see?'

'Brown limbs, white teeth, men in shirt sleeves behind café windows, playing cards with green bottles in front of them.'

'Good—you see everything with my eyes, Dora.'

'Heat, smell, brown legs—it's what we are paying for, Father.'

'Dora, you are becoming vulgar, if you don't mind my saying so. The eye of the true artist doesn't see life in the way of goods paid for. The world is ours. It is our birthright. We take it without payment.'

'I'm not an artist like you, Father. Let me move the umbrella—you mustn't get too much sun.'

'Times have changed,' he said, glancing along the pebble beach, 'the young men today have no interest in life.'

She knew what her father meant. All along the beach, the young men playing with the air, girls, the sun; they were coming in from the sea, shaking the water from their heads; they were walking over the pebbles, then splashing into the water; they were taking an interest in their environment with every pore of their skin, as Father would have said in younger days when he was writing his books. What he meant, now, when he said, 'the young men today have no interest in life' was that his young disciples, his admirers, had all gone, they were grown old and preoccupied, and had not been replaced. The last young man to seek out Father had been a bloodless-looking youth—not that one judged by appearances —who had called about seven years ago at their house in Essex. Father had made the most of him, giving up many of his mornings to sitting in the library talking about books with the young man, about life and the old days. But this, the last of Father's disciples, had left after two weeks with a promise to send them the article he was going to write about Father and his works. Indeed he had sent a letter: 'Dear Henry Castlemaine,—Words cannot express my admiration . . .' After that they had heard no more. Dora was not really sorry. He was a poor specimen compared with the men who, in earlier days, used to visit Father. Dora in her late teens could have married one of three or four vigorous members of the Henry Castlemaine set, but she had not done so because of her widowed father and his needs as a public figure; and now she sometimes felt it would have served Father better if she had married, because of Father—one could have contributed from a husband's income, perhaps, to his declining years.

Dora said, 'We must be going back to the hotel for lunch.'

'Let us lunch somewhere else. The food there is . . .'

She helped her father from the deck chair and, turning to the sea, took a grateful breath of the warm blue breeze. A young man, coming up from the sea, shook his head blindly and splashed her with water; then noticing what he had done he said—turning and catching her by the arm— 'Oh, I'm so sorry.' He spoke in English, was an Englishman, and she knew already how unmistakably she was an Englishwoman. 'All right,' she said, with a quick little laugh. The father was fumbling with his stick, the incident had passed, was immediately forgotten by Dora as she took his arm and propelled him across the wide hot boulevard where the white-suited policemen held up the impetuous traffic. 'How would you like to be arrested by one of those, Dora?' He gave his deep short laugh and looked down at her. 'I'd love it, Father.' Perhaps he wouldn't insist on lunching elsewhere. If only they could reach the hotel, it would be all right; Father would be too exhausted to insist. But already he was saying, 'Let's find somewhere for lunch.'

'Well, we've paid for it at the hotel, Father.'

'Don't be vulgar, my love.'

In the following March, when Dora met Ben Donadieu for the first time, she had the feeling she had seen him somewhere before, she knew not where. Later, she told him of this, but he could not recall having seen her. But this sense of having seen him somewhere remained with Dora all her life. She came to believe she had met him in a former existence. In fact, it was on the beach at Nice that she had seen him, when he came up among the pebbles from the sea, and shook his hair, wetting her, and took her arm, apologising.

'Don't be vulgar, my love. The hotel food is appalling. Not French at all.'

'It's the same all over France, Father, these days.'

'There used to be a restaurant—what was its name?—in one of those little streets behind the Casino. Let's go there. All the writers go there.'

'Not any more, Father.'

'Well, so much the better. Let's go there in any case. What's the name of the place?—Anyway, come on, I could go there blindfold. All the writers used to go . . .'

She laughed, because, after all, he was sweet. As she walked with him towards the Casino she did not say—Not any more, Father, do the writers go there. The writers don't come to Nice, not those of moderate means. But there's one writer here this year, Father, called Kenneth Hope, whom you haven't heard about. He uses our beach, and I've seen him once—a shy, thin, middle-aged man. But he won't speak to anyone. He writes wonderfully, Father. I've read his novels, they open windows in the mind that have been bricked-up for a hundred years. I have read *The Inventors,* which made great fame and fortune for him. It is about the inventors of patent gadgets, what lives they lead, how their minds apply themselves to invention and to love, and you would think, while you were reading *The Inventors,* that the place they live in was dominated by inventors. He has that magic, Father—he can make you believe anything. Dora did not say this, for her father had done great work too, and deserved a revival. His name was revered, his books were not greatly spoken of, they were not read. He would not understand the fame of Kenneth Hope. Father's novels were about the individual consciences of men and women, no one could do the individual conscience like Father.

'Here we are, Father—this is the place, isn't it?'

'No, Dora, it's further along.'

'Oh, but that's the Tumbril; it's wildly expensive.'

'Really, darling!'

She decided to plead the heat, and to order only a slice of melon for lunch with a glass of her father's wine. Both tall and slim, they entered the restaurant. Her hair was drawn back, the bones of her face were good, her eyes were small and fixed ready for humour, for she had decided to be a spinster and do it properly; she looked forty-six and she did not look forty-six; her skin was dry; her mouth was thin, and was growing thinner with the worry about money. The father looked eighty years old, as he was. Thirty years ago people used to turn round and say, as he passed, 'That's Henry Castlemaine'.

Ben lay on his stomach on his mattress on the beach enclosure. Carmelita Hope lay on her mattress, next to him. They were eating rolls and cheese and drinking white wine which the beach attendant had brought to them from the café. Carmelita's tan was like a perfect garment, drawn skin-tight over her body. Since leaving school she had been in numerous jobs behind the scenes of film and television studios. Now she was out of a job again. She thought of marrying Ben, he was so entirely different from all the other men of her acquaintance, he was joyful and he was serious. He was also good-looking: he was half French, brought up in England. And an interesting age, thirty-one. He was a school teacher, but Father could probably get him a job in advertising or publishing. Father could do a lot of things for them both if only he would exert himself. Perhaps if she got married he would exert himself.

'Did you see your father at all yesterday, Carmelita?'

'No; as a matter of fact he's driven up the coast. I think he's gone to stay at some villa on the Italian border.'

'I should like to see more of him,' said Ben. 'And have a talk with him. I've never really had a chance to have a talk with him.'

'He's awfully shy,' said Carmelita, 'with my friends.'

Sometimes she felt a stab of dissatisfaction when Ben talked about her father. Ben had read all his books through and through—that seemed rather obsessive to Carmelita, reading books a second time and a third, as if one's memory was defective. It seemed to her that Ben loved her only because she was Kenneth Hope's daughter, and then, again, it seemed to her that this couldn't be so, for Ben wasn't attracted by money and success. Carmelita knew lots of daughters of famous men, and they were beset by suitors who were keen on their fathers' money and success. But it was the books that Ben liked about her father.

'He never interferes with me,' she said. 'He's rather good that way.'

'I would like to have a long talk with him,' Ben said.

'What about?—He doesn't like talking about his work.'

'No, but a man like that. I would like to know his mind.'

'What about my mind?'

'You've got a lovely mind. Full of pleasant laziness. No guile.' He drew his forefinger from her knee to her ankle. She was wearing a pink bikini. She was very pretty and had hoped to become a starlet before her eighteenth birthday. Now she was very close to twenty-one and was thinking of marrying Ben instead, and was relieved that she no longer wanted to be an actress. He had lasted longer than any other boy friend. She had often found a boy exciting at first but usually went off him quite soon. Ben was an intellectual, and intellectuals, say what you like, seemed to last longer than anyone else. There was more in them to find out about. One was always discovering new things—she supposed it was Father's blood in her that drew her towards the cultivated type, like Ben.

He was staying at a tiny hotel in a back street near the old quay. The entrance was dark, but the room itself was right at the top of the house, with a little balcony. Carmelita was staying with friends at a villa. She spent a lot of time in Ben's room, and sometimes slept there. It was turning out to be a remarkably happy summer.

'You won't see much of Father,' she said, 'if we get married. He works and sees nobody. When he doesn't write he goes away. Perhaps he'll get married again and——'

'That's all right,' he said, 'I don't want to marry your father.'

Dora Castlemaine had several diplomas for elocution which she had never put to use. She got a part-time job, after the Christmas holidays that year, in Basil Street Grammar School in London, and her job was to try to reform the more pronounced Cockney accents of the more promising boys into a near-standard English. Her father was amazed.

'Money, money, you are always talking about money. Let us run up debts. One is nobody without debts.'

'One's credit is limited, Father. Don't be an old goose.'

'Have you consulted Waite?' Waite was the publisher's young man who looked after the Castlemaine royalties, diminishing year by year.

'We've drawn more than our due for the present.'

'Well, it's a bore, you going out to teach.'

'It may be a bore for you,' she said at last, 'but it isn't for me.'

'Dora, do you really mean you want to go to this job in London?'

'Yes, I want to. I'm looking forward to it.'

He didn't believe her. But he said, 'I suppose I'm a bit of a burden on you, Dora, these days. Perhaps I ought to go off and die.'

'Like Oates at the South Pole,' Dora commented.

He looked at her and she looked at him. They were shrewd in their love for each other.

She was the only woman teacher in the school, with hardly the status of a teacher. She had her own corner of the common room and, anxious to reassure the men that she had no intention of intruding upon them, would, during free periods, spread out on the table one of the weekly journals and study it intently, only looking up to say good morning or good afternoon to the masters who came in with piles of exercise books under their arms. Dora had no exercise books to correct, she was something apart, a reformer of vowel sounds. One of the masters, and then another, made conversation with her during morning break, when she passed round the sugar for the coffee. Some were in their early thirties. The ginger-moustached science master was not long graduated from Cambridge. Nobody said to her, as intelligent men had done as late as fifteen years ago, 'Are you any relation, Miss Castlemaine, to Henry Castlemaine the writer?'

Ben walked with Carmelita under the trees of Lincoln's Inn Fields in the spring of the year, after school, and watched the children at their games. They were a beautiful couple. Carmelita was doing secretarial work in the City. Her father was in Morocco, having first taken them out to dinner to celebrate their engagement. Ben said, 'There's a woman at the school, teaching elocution.'

'Oh?' said Carmelita. She was jumpy, because since her father's departure for Morocco Ben had given a new turn to their relationship. He would not let her stay overnight in his flat in Bayswater, not even at the week-ends. He said it would be nice, perhaps, to practise restraint until they were married in the summer, and that would give them something to look forward to. 'And I'm interested to see,' said Ben, 'what we mean to each other without sex.'

This made her understand how greatly she had become obsessed with him. She thought perhaps he was practising a form of cruelty to intensify her obsession. In fact, he did want to see what they meant to each other without sex.

She called at his flat unexpectedly and found him reading, with piles of other books set out on the table as if waiting to be read.

She accused him: You only want to get rid of me so that you can read your books.

'The fourth form is reading Trollope,' he explained, pointing to a novel of Trollope's among the pile.

'But you aren't studying Trollope just now.'

He had been reading a life of James Joyce. He banged it down and said. 'I've been reading all my life, and you won't stop me, Carmelita.'

She sat down. 'I don't want to stop you,' she said.

'I know,' he said.

'We aren't getting on at all well without sex,' she said, and on that occasion stayed the night.

He was writing an essay on her father. She wished that her father had taken more interest in it. Father had taken them out to dinner with his party face, smiling and boyish. Carmelita had seen him otherwise—in his acute dejection, when he seemed hardly able to endure the light of day.

'What's the matter, Father?'

'There's a comedy of errors going on inside me, Carmelita.' He sat at his desk most of the day while he was in these moods, doing nothing. Then, during the night, he would perhaps start writing, and sleep all the next morning, and gradually in the following days the weight would pass.

'There's a man on the phone wants you, Father—an interview.'

'Tell him I'm in the Middle East.'

'What did you think of Ben, Father?'

'A terribly nice man, Carmelita. You've made the right choice, I think.'

'An intellectual—I do like them best, you know.'

'I'd say he was the student type. Always will be.'

'He wants to write an essay about you, Father. He's absolutely mad about your books.'

'Yes.'

'I mean, couldn't you help him, Father? Couldn't you talk to him about your work, you know?'

'Oh, God, Carmelita. It would be easier to write the bloody essay myself.'

'All right, all right. I was only asking.'

'I don't want any disciples, Carmelita. They give me the creeps.'

'Yes, yes, all right. I know you're an artist, Father, there's no need to show off your temperament. I only wanted you to help Ben. I only . . .'

I only, she thought as she walked in Lincoln's Inn Fields with Ben, wanted him to help me. I should have said, 'I want you to talk more to Ben, to help me.' And Father would have said, 'How do you mean?' And I would have said, 'I don't know, quite.' And he would have said, 'Well, if you don't know what you mean, how the hell do I?'

Ben was saying, 'There's a woman at the school, teaching elocution.'

'Oh?' said Carmelita jumpily.

'A Miss Castlemaine. She's been there four months, and I only found out today that she's the daughter of Henry Castlemaine.'

'But he's dead!' said Carmelita.

'Well, I thought so, too. But apparently he isn't dead, he's very much alive in a house in Essex.'

'How old is Miss Castlemaine?' said Carmelita.

'Middle-aged. Middle forties. Perhaps late forties. She's a nice woman, a classic English spinster. She teaches the boys to say "How now brown cow". You could imagine her doing wood engravings in the Cotswolds. I only found out today——'

'You might manage to get invited to meet him, with any luck,' Carmelita said.

'Yes, she said I must come and see him, perhaps for a weekend. Miss Castlemaine is going to arrange it. She was awfully friendly when she found I was a Castlemaine admirer. A lot of people must think he's dead. Of course, his work belongs to a past world, but it's wonderful. Do you know *The Pebbled Shore?*—that's an early one.'

'No, but I've read *Sin of Substance,* I think. It——'

'You mean *The Sinner and the Substance.* Oh, it has fine things in it. Castlemaine's due for a revival.'

Carmelita felt a sharp stab of anger with her father, and then a kind of despair which was not as yet entirely familiar to her, although already she wondered if this was how Father felt in his great depressions when he sat all day, staring and enduring, and all night miraculously wrote the ache out of his system in prose of harsh merriment.

Helplessly, she said, 'Castlemaine's novels aren't as good as Father's, are they?'

'Oh, there's no comparison. Castlemaine is quite different. You can't say one type is *better* than another—goodness me!' He was looking aca-

demically towards the chimney stacks of Lincoln's Inn. This was the look
in which she loved him most. After all, she thought, the Castlemaines
might make everything easier for both of us.

'Father, it's really rather absurd. A difference of sixteen years. . . .
People will say——'

'Don't be vulgar, Dora dear. What does it matter what people say?
Mere age makes no difference when there's a true affinity, a marriage of
true minds.'

'Ben and I have a lot in common.'

'I know it,' he said, and sat a little higher in his chair.

'I shall be able to give up my job, Father, and spend my time here with
you again. I never really wanted that job. And you are so much in better
health now . . .'

'I know.'

'And Ben will be here in the evenings and the weekends. You get on
well with Ben, don't you?'

'A remarkably fine man, Dora. He'll go far. He's perceptive.'

'He's keen to revive your work.'

'I know. He should give up that job, as I told him, and devote himself
entirely to literary studies. A born essayist.'

'Oh, Father, he'll have to keep his job for the meantime, anyhow. We'll
need the money. It will help us all; we——'

'What's that? What's that you say?'

'I said he finds work in the grammar school stimulating, Father.'

'Do you love the man?'

'It's a little difficult to say, at my age, Father.'

'To me, you both seem children. Do you love him?'

'I feel,' she said, 'that I have known him much longer than I have.
Sometimes I think I've known him all my life. I'm sure we have met
before, perhaps even in a former existence. That's the decisive factor.
There's something of *destiny* about my marrying Ben; do you know what
I mean?'

'Yes, I think I do.'

'He was engaged, last year for a short time, to marry quite a young
girl,' she said. 'The daughter of a novelist called Kenneth Hope. Have
you heard of him, Father?'

'Vaguely,' he said. 'Ben,' he said, 'is a born disciple.'

She looked at him and he looked at her, shrewd in their love for each other.

Two Potters

❦

DORIS LESSING
(English, 1919–   )

I have only known one potter in this country, Mary Tawnish, and she lives out of London in a village where her husband is a school-teacher. She seldom comes to town, and I seldom leave it, so we write.

The making of pots is not a thing I often think of, so when I dreamed about the old potter it was natural to think of Mary. But it was difficult to tell her; there are two kinds of humanity, those who dream and those who don't, and both tend to despise, or to tolerate, the other. Mary Tawnish says, when others relate their dreams: "I've never had a dream in my life." And adds, to soften or placate: "At least, I don't remember. They say it's a question of remembering?"

I would have guessed her to be a person who would dream a good deal, I don't know why.

A tall woman, and rather large, she has bright brown clustering hair, and brown eyes that give the impression of light, though not from their surface: it is not a "bright" or "brilliant" glance. She looks at you, smiling or not, but always calm, and there is an impression of light, which seems caught in the structure of colour in the iris, so sometimes her eyes look yellow; set off by smooth brown eyebrows.

A large, slow-moving woman, with large white slow hands. And a silent one—she is a listener.

Her life has been a series of dramas: a childhood on the move with erratic parents, a bad first marriage, a child that died, lovers, but none lasting; then a second marriage to William Tawnish who teaches physics and biology. He is a quick, biting, bitter little man with whom she has three half-grown children.

More than once I have told her story, without comment, in order to observe the silent judgement: Another misfit, another unhappy soul, only to see the judger confounded on meeting her, for there was never a woman less fitted by nature for discord or miseries. Or so it would seem. So it seems she feels herself, for she disapproves of other people's collisions with themselves, just as if her own life had nothing to do with her.

The first dream about the potter was simple and short. Once upon a time . . . there was a village or a settlement, not in England, that was certain, for the scene was of a baked red-dust bareness. Low rectangular structures, of simple baked mud, also reddish-brown, were set evenly on the baked soil, yet because some were roofless and others in the process of crumbling, and others half-built, there was nothing finished or formed about this place. And for leagues and leagues, in all directions, the great plain, of reddish earth, and in the middle of the plain the settlement that looked as if it were hastily moulded by a great hand out of wet clay, allowed to dry, and left there. It seemed uninhabited, but in an empty space among the huts, all by himself, working away on a primitive potter's wheel turned by foot, was an old man. He wore a garment of coarse sacking over yellowish and dusty limbs. One bare foot was set in the dust near me, the cracked toes spread and curled. He had a bit of yellow straw stuck in close grizzling hair.

When I woke from this dream I was rested and excited, in spite of the great dried-up plain and the empty settlement one precarious stage from the dust. In the end I sat down and wrote to Mary Tawnish, although I could hear her flat comment very clearly: Well, that's interesting. Our letters are usually of the kind known as "keeping in touch." First I enquired about her children, and about William, and then I told the dream: "For some reason I thought of you. I did know a man who made pots in Africa. The farmer he worked for discovered he had a talent for potmaking (it seemed his tribe were potters by tradition), because when they made bricks for the farm, this man, Elija, slipped little dishes and bowls into the kiln to bake with the bricks. The farmer used to pay him a couple of shillings a week extra, and sold the dishes to a dealer in the city. He made simple things, not like yours. He had no wheel, of course. He didn't use colour. His things were a darkish yellow, because of the kind of soil on that farm. A bit monotonous after a bit. And they broke easily. If you come up to London give me a ring. . . ."

She didn't come, but soon I had a letter with a postscript: "What an interesting dream, thanks so much for telling me."

I dreamed about the old potter again. There was the great, flat, dust-beaten reddish plain, ringed by very distant blue-hazed mountains, so far away they were like mirages, or clouds, or low-lying smoke. There was the settlement. And there the old potter, sitting on one of his own up-turned pots, one foot set firmly in the dust, and the other moving the wheel; one palm shaping the clay, the other shedding water which glittered in the low sullen glare in flashes of moving light on its way to the turning wet clay. He was extremely old, his eyes faded and of the same deceiving blue as the mountains. All around him, drying in rows on a thin scattering of yellow straw, were pots of different sizes. They were all round. The huts were rectangular, the pots round. I looked at these two different manifestations of the earth, separated by shape; and then through a gap in the huts to the plain. No one in sight. It seemed no one lived there. Yet there sat the old man, with the hundreds of pots and dishes drying in rows on the straw, dipping his hand into an enormous jar of water and scattering drops that smelled sweet as they hit the dust and pitted it.

Again I thought of Mary. But they had nothing in common, that poor old potter who had no one to buy his work, and Mary who sold her strange coloured bowls and jugs to the big shops in London. I wondered what the old potter would think of Mary's work—particularly what he'd think of a square flat dish I'd bought from her, coloured a greenish-yellow. The square had, as it were, slipped out of whack, and the surface is rough, with finger marks left showing. I serve cheese on it. The old man's jars were for millet, I knew that, or for soured milk.

I wrote and told Mary the second dream, thinking: Well, if it bores or irritates her, it's too bad. This time she rang me up. She wanted me to go down to one of the shops which had been slow in making a new order. Weren't her things selling? she wanted to know. She added she was getting a fellow feeling for the old potter; he didn't have any customers either, from the size of his stock. But it turned out that the shop had sold all Mary's things, and had simply forgotten to order more.

I waited, with patient excitement, for the next instalment, or unfolding, of the dream.

The settlement was now populated, indeed, teeming, and it was much bigger. The low flat rooms of dull earth had spread over an area of some miles. They were not separated now, but linked. I walked through a system of these rooms. They were roughly the same size, but set at all angles to each other so that, standing in one, it might have one, two, three doors, leading to a corresponding number of mud rooms. I walked for something like half a mile through low dark rooms without once needing to cross a roofless space, and when I emerged in the daylight, there was the potter, and beyond him a marketplace. But a poor one. From out of his great jars, women, wearing the same sort of yellowish sacking as he, sold grain and milk to dusty, smallish, rather listless people. The potter worked on, under heavy sunlight, with his rows and rows of clay vessels drying on the glinting yellow straw. A very small boy crouched by him, watching every movement he made. I saw how the water shaken from the old fingers on the whirling pot flew past it and spattered the small intent poverty-shaped face with its narrowed watching eyes. But the face received the water unflinching, probably unnoticed.

Beyond the settlement stretched the plain. Beyond that, the thin, illusory mountains. Over the red flat plain drifted small shadows: they were from great birds wheeling and banking and turning.

I wrote to Mary and she wrote back that she was glad the old man had some customers at last, she had been worried about him. As for her, she thought it was time he used some colour, all that red dust was depressing. She said she could see the settlement was short of water, since I hadn't mentioned a well, let alone a river, only the potter's great brimming jar which reflected the blue sky, the sun, the great birds. Wasn't a diet of milk and millet bad for people? Here she broke off to say she supposed I couldn't help all this, it was my nature, and "Apropos, isn't it time your poor village had a storyteller at least? How bored the poor things must be!"

I wrote back to say I was not responsible for this settlement, and whereas if I had my way, it would be set in groves of fruit trees and surrounded by whitening cornfields, with a river full of splashing brown children. I couldn't help it, that's how things were in this place, wherever it was.

One day in a shop I saw a shelf of her work and noticed that some of them were of smooth, dully shining brown, like polished skin—jars, and flat round plates. Our village potter would have known these, nothing to surprise him here. All the same, there was a difference between Mary's consciously simple vessels and the simplicity of the old potter. I looked at them and thought: Well, my dear, that's not going to get you very far. . . . But I would have found it hard to say exactly what I meant, and in fact I bought a plate and a jar, and they gave me great pleasure, thinking of Mary and the old potter linked in them, between my hands.

Quite a long time passed. When I dreamed again, all the plain was populated. The mountains had come closer in, reaching up tall and blue into blue sky, circumscribing the plain. The settlements, looked at from the height of the mountain tops, seemed like patches of slightly raised surface on the plain. I understood their nature and substance: a slight raising of the dust here and there, like the frail patterning of raindrops hitting dry dust, pitting it, then the sun coming out swiftly to dry the dust. The resulting tiny fragile patterned crust of dried dust—that gives, as near as I can, the feeling the settlements gave me, viewed from the mountains. Except that the raised dried crusts were patterned in rectangles. I could see the tiny patternings all over the plain. I let myself down from the mountains, through the great birds that wheeled and floated, and descended to the settlement I knew. There sat the potter, the clay curving under his left hand as he flicked water over it from his right. It was all going on as usual—I was reassured by his being there, creating his pots. Nothing much had changed, though so much time had passed. The low flat monotonous dwellings were the same, though they had crumbled to dust and raised themselves from it a hundred times since I had been here last. No green yet, no river. A scum-covered creek had goats grazing beside it, and the millet grew in straggly patches, flattened and brown from drought. In the marketplace were pinkish fruits, lying in heaps by the soft piles of millet, on woven straw mats. I didn't know the fruit: it was small, about plum-size, smooth-skinned, and I felt it had a sharp pulpy taste. Pinky-yellow skins lay scattered in the dust. A man passed me, with a low slinking movement of the hips, holding his sacklike garment in position at his side with the pressure of an elbow, staring in front of him over the pink fruit which he pressed against sharp yellow teeth.

I wrote and told Mary the plain was more populated, but that things hadn't improved much, except for the fruit. But it was astringent, I wouldn't care for it myself.

She wrote back to say she was glad she slept so soundly, she would find such dreams depressing.

I said there was nothing depressing about it. I entered the dream with pleasure, as if listening to a storyteller say: Once upon a time . . .

But the next was discouraging, I woke depressed. I stood by the old potter in the marketplace, and for once his hands were still, the wheel at rest. His eyes followed the movements of the people buying and selling, and his mouth was bitter. Beside him, his vessels stood in rows on the warm glinting straw. From time to time a woman came picking her way along the rows, bending to narrow her eyes at the pots. Then she chose one, dropped a coin in the potter's hand, and bore it off over her shoulder.

I was inside the potter's mind and I knew what he was thinking. He said: "Just once, Lord, just once, just once!" He put his hand down into a patch of hot shade under the wheel and lifted on his palm a small clay rabbit which he held out to the ground. He sat motionless, looking at the sky, then at the rabbit, praying: "Please, Lord, just once." But nothing happened.

I wrote Mary that the old man was tired with long centuries of making pots whose life was so short: the litter of broken pots under the settlement had raised its level twenty feet by now, and every pot had come off his wheel. He wanted God to breathe life into his clay rabbit. He had hoped to see it lift up its long red-veined ears, to feel its furry feet on his palm, and watch it hop down and off among the great earthenware pots, sniffing at them and twitching its ears—a live thing among the forms of clay.

Mary said the old man was getting above himself. She said further: "Why a *rabbit?* I simply don't *see* a rabbit. What use would a rabbit be? Do you realise that apart from goats (you say they have milk), and those vultures overhead, they have no animals at all? Wouldn't a cow be better than a rabbit?"

I wrote: "I can't do anything about that place when I'm dreaming it, but when I'm awake, why not? Right then, the rabbit hopped off the old man's hand into the dust. It sat twitching its nose and throbbing all over, the way rabbits do. Then it sprang slowly off and began nibbling at the straw, while the old man wept with happiness. Now what have you to say? If I say there was a rabbit, a rabbit there was. Besides, that poor old man deserves one, after so long. God could have done so much, it wouldn't have cost Him anything."

I had no reply to that letter, and I stopped dreaming about the settlement. I knew it was because of my effrontery in creating that rabbit, inserting myself into the story. Very well, then . . . I wrote to Mary: "I've been thinking: suppose it had been you who'd dreamed about the potter—all right, all right, just suppose it. Now. Next morning you sat at the breakfast table, your William at one end, and the children between eating cornflakes and drinking milk. You were rather silent. (Of course you usually are.) You looked at your husband and you thought: What on earth would he say if I told him what I'm going to do? You said nothing, presiding at the table; then you sent the children off to school, and your husband to his classes. Then you were alone and when you'd washed the dishes and put them away, you went secretly into the stone-floored room where your wheel and the kiln are, and you took some clay and you made a small rabbit and you set it on a high shelf behind some finished vases to dry. You didn't want anyone to see that rabbit. One day, a week later, when it was dry, you waited until your family was out of the house, then you put your rabbit on your palm, and you went into a field, and you knelt down and held the rabbit out to the grass, and you waited. You didn't pray, because you don't believe in God, but you wouldn't have been in the least surprised if that rabbit's nose had started to twitch and its long soft ears stood up. . . ."

Mary wrote: "There aren't any rabbits any more, had you forgotten myxomatosis? Actually I did make some small rabbits recently, for the children, in blue and green glaze, because it occurred to me the two youngest haven't seen a rabbit out of a picture book. Still, they're coming back in some parts, I hear. The farmers will be angry."

I wrote: "Yes, I had forgotten. Well then . . . sometimes at evening, when you walk in the fields, you think: How nice to see a rabbit lift his paws and look at us. You remember the rotting little corpses of a few years back. You think: *I'll try again.* Meantime, you're nervous of what William will say, he's such a rationalist. Well of course, so are we, but he wouldn't even play a little. I may be wrong, but I think you're afraid of William catching you out, and you are careful not to be caught. One sunny morning you take it out onto the field and . . . all right, all right then, it *doesn't* hop away. You can't decide whether to lay your clay rabbit down among the warm grasses (it's a sunny day) and let it crumble back into the earth, or whether to bake it in your kiln. You haven't baked it, it's even rather damp still: the old potter's rabbit was wet, just before he held it out into the sun he sprinkled water on it, I saw him.

"Later you decide to tell your husband. Out of curiosity? The children are in the garden, you can hear their voices, and William sits opposite you reading the newspaper. You have a crazy impulse to say: I'm going to take my rabbit into the field tonight and pray for God to breathe life into it, a field without rabbits is empty. Instead you say: 'William, I had a dream last night. . . .' First he frowns, a quick frown, then he turns those small quick sandy-lashed intelligent eyes on you, taking it all in. To your surprise, instead of saying: 'I don't remember your ever dreaming,' he says: 'Mary, I didn't know you disapproved of the farmers killing off their rabbits.' You say: 'I didn't disapprove. I'd have done the same, I suppose.' The fact that he's not reacted with sarcasm or impatience, as he might very well, makes you feel guilty when you lift the clay rabbit down, take it out to a field and set it in a hedge, its nose pointing out towards some fresh grass. That night William says, casual: 'You'll be glad to hear the rabbits are back. Basil Smith shot one in his field—the first for eight years, he says. Well, I'm glad myself, I've missed the little beggars.' You are delighted. You slip secretly into a cold misty moonlight and you run to the hedge and of course the rabbit is gone. You stand, clutching your thick green stole around you, because it's cold, shivering, but delighted, delighted! Though you know quite well one of your children, or someone else's child, has slipped along this hedge, seen the rabbit, and taken it off to play with."

Mary wrote: "Oh all right, if you say so, so it is. But I must tell you, if you are interested in *facts,* that the only thing that has happened is that Dennis (the middle one) put his blue rabbit out in a hedge for a joke near the Smiths' gate, and Basil Smith shot it to smithereens one dusk thinking it was real. He used to lose a small fortune every year to rabbits, he didn't think it was a funny joke at all. Anyway, why don't you come down for a weekend?"

The Tawnishes live in an old farmhouse on the edge of the village. There is a great garden, with fruit trees, roses—everything. The big house and the three boys mean a lot of work, but Mary spends all the time she can in the shed that used to be a dairy where she pots. I arrived to find them in the kitchen, having lunch. Mary nodded to me to sit down. William was in conflict with the middle boy, Dennis, who was, as the

other two boys kept saying, "showing off." Or, rather, he was in that
torment of writhing self-consciousness that afflicts small boys sometimes,
rolling his eyes while he stuttered and wriggled, his whole sandy freckled
person scarlet and miserable.

"Well I did I did I did I did I did. . . ." He paused for breath, his eyes
popping, and his older brother chanted: "No you didn't, you didn't, you
didn't."

"Yes I did I did I did I did. . . ."

And the father said, brisk but irritated: "Now then, Dennis, use your
loaf, you couldn't have, because it is obvious you have *not.*"

"But I did I did I did I did. . . ."

"Well, then, you had better go out of the room until you come to your
senses and are fit company for rational people," said his father, trium-
phantly in the right.

The child choked on his battling breath, and ran howling out into the
garden. Where, after a minute, the older boy followed, ostensibly to control him.

"He did what?" I asked.

"Who knows?" said Mary. There she sat, at the head of the table,
bright-eyed and smiling, serving apple pie and custard, a dark changeling
in the middle of her gingery, freckled family.

Her husband said, brisk: "What do you mean, who knows? You know
quite well."

"It's his battle with Basil Smith," said Mary to me. "Ever since Basil
Smith shot at his blue rabbit and broke it, there's been evil feeling on
both sides. Dennis claims that he set fire to the Smith farmhouse last
night."

"*What?*"

Mary pointed through a low window, where the Smiths' house
showed, two fields away, like a picture in a frame.

William said: "He's hysterical and he's got to stop it."

"Well," said Mary, "if Basil shot my blue rabbit I'd want to burn his
house down too. It seems quite reasonable to me."

William let out an exclamation of rage, checked himself because of my
presence, shot fiery glances all round, and went out, taking the youngest
boy with him.

"Well," said Mary. "Well . . ." She smiled. "Come into the pottery,
I've got something to show you." She went ahead along a stone passage,

a tall, lazy-moving woman, her bright brown hair catching the light. As we passed an open window, there was a fearful row of shrieks, yells, blows; and we saw the three boys rolling and tussling in the grass, while William danced futilely around them shouting: "Stop it, stop it at once!" Their mother proceeded, apparently uninterested, into the potting room.

This held the potting apparatus, and a great many jars, plates, and jugs of all colours and kinds, ranged on shelves. She lifted down a creature from a high shelf, and set it before me. Then she left it with me, while she bent to attend to the kiln.

It was yellowish-brown, a sort of rabbit or hare, but with ears like neither—narrower, sharp, short, like the pointed unfolding shoots of a plant. It had a muzzle more like a dog's than a rabbit's; it looked as if it did not eat grass—perhaps insects and beetles? Yellowish eyes were set on the front of its head. Its hind legs were less powerful than a rabbit's, or hare's; and I saw its talents were for concealment, not for escaping enemies in great pistoning leaps. It rested on short, stubby hind legs, with front paws held up in a queer, twisted, almost affected posture, head turned to one side, and ears furled around each other. It looked as if it had been wound up like a spring, and had half-unwound. It looked like a strangely shaped rock, or like the harsh twisted plants that sometimes grow on rocks.

Mary came back and stood by me, her head slightly on one side, with her characteristic small patient smile that nevertheless held a sweet concealed exasperation.

"Well," she said, "there it is."

I hesitated, because it was not the creature I had seen on the old potter's palm.

"What was an English rabbit doing there at all?" she asked.

"I didn't say it was an English rabbit."

But of course, she was right: this animal was far more in keeping with the dried mud houses, the dusty plain, than the pretty furry rabbit I had dreamed.

I smiled at Mary, because she was humouring me, as she humoured her husband and her children. For some reason I thought of her first husband and her lovers, two of whom I had known. At moments of painful crisis, or at parting, had she stood thus—a calm, pretty woman, smiling her sweetly satirical smile, as if to say: "Well, make a fuss if you like, it's got nothing at all to do with me"? If so, I'm surprised that one of them didn't murder her.

"Well," I said at last, "thanks. Can I take this thing, whatever it is?"

"Of course. I made it for you. You must admit, it may not be pretty, but it's more likely to be *true.*"

I accepted this, as I had to; and I said: "Well, thanks for coming down to our level long enough to play games with us."

At which there was a flash of yellow light from her luminous eyes, while her face remained grave, as if amusement, or acknowledgement of the *truth,* could only be focussed in her thus, through a change of light in her irises.

A few minutes later, the three boys and the father came round this part of the house in a whirlwind of quarrelling energy. The aggrieved Dennis was in tears, and the father almost beside himself. Mary, who until now had remained apart from it all, gave an exclamation, slipped on a coat, and said: "I can't stand this. I'm going to talk to Basil Smith."

She went out, and I watched her cross the fields to the other house.

Meanwhile Dennis, scarlet and suffering, came into the pottery in search of his mother. He whirled about, looking for her, then grabbed my creature, said: "Is that for me?", snatched it possessively to him when I said: "No, it's for me," set it down when I told him to, and stood breathing like a furnace, his freckles like tea leaves against his skin.

"Your mother's gone to see Mr. Smith," I said.

"He shot my rabbit," he said.

"It wasn't a real rabbit."

"But he thought it was a real rabbit."

"Yes, but you knew he would think so, and that he'd shoot at it."

"He killed it!"

"You wanted him to!"

At which he let out a scream and danced up and down like a mad boy, shouting: "I didn't I didn't I didn't I didn't. . . ."

His father, entering on this scene, grabbed him by his flailing arms, fought the child into a position of tensed stillness, and held him there, saying, in a frenzy of incredulous common-sense: "I've never—in—my—life—heard—such—lunacy!"

Now Mary came in, accompanied by Mr. Smith, a large, fair, youngish man, with a sweet open face, which was uncomfortable now, because of what he had agreed to do.

"Let that child go," said Mary to her husband. Dennis dropped to the floor, rolled over, and lay face down, heaving with sobs.

"Call the others!"

Resignation itself, William went to the window, and shouted: "Harry, John, Harry, John, come here at once, your mother wants you!" He then stood, with folded arms, a defeated philosopher, grinning angrily while the two other children came in and stood waiting by the door.

"Now," said Mary. "Get up, Dennis."

Dennis got up, his face battered with suffering, and looked with hope towards his mother.

Mary looked at Basil Smith.

Who said, careful to get the words right: "I am very sorry that I killed your rabbit."

The father let out a sharp outraged breath, but kept quiet at a glance from his wife.

The chest of Dennis swelled and sank—in one moment there would be a storm of tears.

"Dennis," said Mary, "say after me: 'Mr. Smith, I'm very sorry I set fire to your house.' "

Dennis said in a rush, to get it out in time: "Mr. Smith I'm very sorry I set fire to your . . . to your . . . to your . . ." He sniffed and heaved, and Mary said firmly: *"House,* Dennis."

"House," said Dennis, in a wail. He then rushed at his mother, buried his head in her waist, and stood howling and wrestling, while she laid large hands on his ginger head and smiled over it at Mr. Basil Smith.

"Dear God," said her husband, letting his folded arms drop dramatically, now the ridiculous play was over. "Come and have a drink, Basil."

The men went off. The two other children stood silent and abashed, because of the force of Dennis's emotion, for which they clearly felt partly responsible. Then they slipped out to play. The house was tranquil again, save for Dennis's quietening sobs. Soon Mary took the boy up to his room to sleep it off. I stayed in the great, stone-floored pottery, looking at my strange twisted animal, and at the blues and greens of Mary's work all around the walls.

Supper was early and soon over. The boys were silent, Dennis too limp to eat. Bed was prescribed for everyone. William kept looking at his wife, his mouth set under his ginger moustache, and he could positively be heard thinking: Filling them full of this nonsense while I try to bring

them up reasonable human beings! But she avoided his eyes, and sat calm
and remote, serving mashed potatoes and brown stew. It was only when
we had finished the washing-up that she smiled at him—her sweet,
amused smile. It was clear they needed to be alone. I said I wanted an
early night and left them: he had gone to touch her before I was out of
the room.

Next day, a warm summer Sunday, everyone was relaxed, the old
house peaceful. I left that evening, with my clay creature, and Mary said
smiling, humouring me: "Let me know how things go on with your place,
wherever it is." But I had her beautiful animal in my suitcase, so I did
not mind being humoured.

That night, at home, I went into the marketplace, and up to the old
potter, who stilled his wheel when he saw me coming. The small boy
lifted his frowning attentive eyes from the potter's hands and smiled at
me. I held out Mary's creature. The old man took it, screwed up his eyes
to examine it, nodded. He held it in his left hand, scattered water on it
with his right, held his palm down towards the littered dust, and the
creature jumped off it and away, with quick, jerky movements, not stopping until it was through the huts, clear of the settlement, and against a
small outcrop of jagged brown rocks where it raised its front paws and
froze in the posture Mary had created for it. Overhead an eagle or a
hawk floated by, looked down, but failed to see Mary's creature, and
floated on, up and away into the great blue spaces over the flat dry plain
to the mountains. I heard the wheel creak; the old man was back at work.
The small boy crouched, watching, and the water flung by the potter's
right hand sprayed the bowl he was making and the child's face, in a
beautiful curving spray of glittering light.

The Confirmation Suit

❦

BRENDAN BEHAN
(Irish, 1923–1964)

For weeks it was nothing but simony and sacrilege, and the sins crying to heaven for vengeance, the big green Catechism in our hands, walking home along the North Circular Road. And after tea, at the back of the brewery wall, with a butt too, to help our wits, what is a pure spirit, and don't kill that, Billser has to get a drag out of it yet, what do I mean by apostate, and hell and heaven and despair and presumption and hope. The big fellows, who were now thirteen and the veterans of last year's Confirmation, frightened us, and said the Bishop would fire us out of the Chapel if we didn't answer his questions, and we'd be left wandering around the streets, in a new suit and top-coat with nothing to show for it, all dressed up and nowhere to go. The big people said not to mind them; they were only getting it up for us, jealous because they were over their Confirmation, and could never make it again. At school we were in a special room to ourselves, for the last few days, and went round, a special class of people. There were worrying times too, that the Bishop would light on you, and you wouldn't be able to answer his questions. Or you might hear the women complaining about the price of boys' clothes.

'Twenty-two and sixpence for tweed, I'd expect a share in the shop for that. I've a good mind to let him go in jersey and pants for that.'

'Quite right, ma'am,' says one to another, backing one another up, 'I always say what matter if they are good and pure.' What had that got to do with it, if you had to go into the Chapel in a jersey and pants, and every other kid in a new suit, kid gloves and tan shoes and a school cap.

The Cowan brothers were terrified. They were twins, and twelve years old, and every old one in the street seemed to be wishing a jersey and pants on them, and saying their poor mother couldn't be expected to do for two in the one year, and she ought to go down to Sister Monica and tell her to put one back. If it came to that, the Cowans agreed to fight it out, at the back of the brewery wall, whoever got best, the other would be put back.

I wasn't so worried about this. My old fellow was a tradesman, and made money most of the time. Besides, my grandmother, who lived at the top of the next house, was a lady of capernosity and function. She had money and lay in bed all day, drinking porter or malt, and taking pinches of snuff, and talking to the neighbours that would call up to tell her the news of the day. She only left her bed to go down one flight of stairs and visit the lady in the back drawing room, Miss McCann.

Miss McCann worked a sewing machine, making habits for the dead. Sometimes girls from our quarter got her to make dresses and costumes, but mostly she stuck to the habits. They were a steady line, she said, and you didn't have to be always buying patterns, for the fashions didn't change, not even from summer to winter. They were like a long brown shirt, and a hood attached, that was closed over the person's face before the coffin lid was screwn down. A sort of little banner hung out of one arm, made of the same material, and four silk rosettes in each corner, and in the middle, the letters I.H.S., which mean, Miss McCann said: 'I Have Suffered'.

My grandmother and Miss McCann liked me more than any other kid they knew. I like being liked, and could only admire their taste.

My Aunt Jack, who was my father's aunt as well as mine, sometimes came down from where she lived, up near the Basin, where the water came from before they started getting it from Wicklow. My Aunt Jack said it was much better water, at that. Miss McCann said she ought to be a good judge. For Aunt Jack was funny. She didn't drink porter or malt, or take snuff, and my father said she never thought much about men, either. She was also very strict about washing yourself very often. My grandmother took a bath every year, whether she was dirty or not, but she was in no way bigoted in the washing line in between times.

Aunt Jack made terrible raids on us now and again, to stop snuff and drink, and made my grandmother get up in the morning, and wash herself, and cook meals and take food with them. My grandmother was a gilder by trade, and served her time in one of the best shops in the city, and was getting a man's wages at sixteen. She liked stuff out of the pork butchers, and out of cans, but didn't like boiling potatoes, for she said she was no skivvy, and the chip man was better at it. When she was left alone it was a pleasure to eat with her. She always had cans of lovely things and spicy meat and brawn, and plenty of seasoning, fresh out of the German man's shop up the road. But after a visit from Aunt Jack, she would have to get up and wash for a week, and she would have to go and make stews and boil cabbage and pig's cheeks. Aunt Jack was very much up for sheep's heads too. They were so cheap and nourishing.

But my grandmother only tried it once. She had been a first-class gilder in Eustace Street, but never had anything to do with sheep's heads before. When she took it out of the pot, and laid it on the plate, she and I sat looking at it, in fear and trembling. It was bad enough going into the pot, but with the soup streaming from its eyes, and its big teeth clenched in a very bad temper, it would put the heart crossways in you. My grandmother asked me, in a whisper, if I ever thought sheep could look so vindictive, but that it was more like the head of an old man, and would I for God's sake take it up and throw it out of the window. The sheep kept glaring at us, but I came the far side of it, and rushed over to the window and threw it out in a flash. My grandmother had to drink a Baby Power whiskey, for she wasn't the better of herself.

Afterwards she kept what she called her stock-pot on the gas. A heap of bones, and as she said herself, any old muck that would come in handy, to have boiling there, night and day, on a glimmer. She and I ate happily of cooked ham and California pineapple and sock-eye salmon, and the pot of good nourishing soup was always on the gas even if Aunt Jack came down the chimney, like the Holy Souls at midnight. My grandmother said she didn't begrudge the money for the gas. Not when she remembered the looks that sheep's head was giving her. And all that she had to do with the stock-pot was to throw in another sup of water, now and again, and a handful of old rubbish the pork butcher would send over, in the way of lights or bones. My Aunt Jack thought a lot about barley, too, so we had a package of that lying beside the gas, and threw a sprinkle in any time her foot was heard on the stairs. The stock-pot bubbled away on the gas for years after, and only when my grandmother was dead did someone notice it. They tasted it, and spat it out just as quick, and wondered what it was. Some said it was paste, and more that it was gold size, and there were other people and they maintained it was glue. They all agreed on one thing, that it was dangerous tack to leave lying around, where there might be young children, and in the heel of the reel, it went out the same window as the sheep's head.

Miss McCann told my grandmother not to mind Aunt Jack but to sleep as long as she liked in the morning. They came to an arrangement that Miss McCann would cover the landing and keep an eye out. She would call Aunt Jack in for a minute, and give the signal by banging the grate, letting on to poke the fire, and have a bit of a conversation with Aunt Jack about dresses and costumes, and hats and habits. One of these mornings, and Miss McCann delaying a fighting action, to give my grandmother time to hurl herself out of bed and into her clothes and give her face the rub of a towel, the chat between Miss McCann and Aunt Jack came to my Confirmation suit.

When I made my first Communion, my grandmother dug deep under the mattress, and myself and Aunt Jack were sent round expensive shops, and I came back with a rig that would take the sight of your eye. This time, however, Miss McCann said there wasn't much stirring in the habit line, on account of the mild winter, and she would be delighted to make the suit, if Aunt Jack would get the material. I nearly wept, for terror of what these old women would have me got up in, but I had to let on to be delighted, Miss McCann was so set on it. She asked Aunt Jack did she remember my father's Confirmation suit. He did. He said he would never forget it. They sent him out in a velvet suit, of plum colour, with a lace collar. My blood ran cold when he told me.

The stuff they got for my suit was blue serge, and that was not so bad. They got as far as the pants, and that passed off very civil. You can't do much to a boy's pants, one pair is like the next, though I had to ask them not to trouble themselves putting three little buttons on either side of the legs. The waistcoat was all right, and anyway the coat would cover it. But the coat itself, that was where Aughrim was lost.

The lapels were little wee things, like what you'd see in pictures like *Ring* magazine of John L. Sullivan, or Gentleman Jim, and the buttons were the size of saucers, or within the bawl of an ass of it, and I nearly cried when I saw them being put on, and ran down to my mother, and begged her to get me any sort of a suit, even a jersey and pants, than have me set up before the people in this get-up. My mother said it was very kind of Aunt Jack and Miss McCann to go to all this trouble and expense, and I was very ungrateful not to appreciate it. My father said that Miss McCann was such a good tailor that people were dying to get into her creations, and her handiwork was to be found in all the best cemeteries. He laughed himself sick at this, and said if it was good enough for him to be sent down to North William Street in plum-coloured velvet and lace, I needn't be getting the needle over a couple of big buttons and little lapels. He asked me not to forget to get up early the morning of my Confirmation, and let him see me, before he went to work: a bit of a laugh started the day well. My mother told him to give over and let me alone, and said she was sure it would be a lovely suit, and that Aunt Jack would never buy poor material, but stuff that would last forever. That nearly finished me altogether, and I ran through the hall up to the corner, fit to cry my eyes out, only I wasn't much of a hand at crying. I went more for cursing, and I cursed all belonging to me, and I was hard at it on my father, and wondering why his lace collar hadn't choked him, when I remembered that it was a sin to go on like that, and I going up for Confirmation, and I had to simmer down, and live in fear of the day I'd put on that jacket.

The days passed, and I was fitted and refitted, and every old one in the house came up to look at the suit, and took a pinch of snuff, and a sup out of the jug, and wished me long life and the health to wear and tear it, and they spent that much time viewing it round, back, belly and sides, that Miss McCann hadn't time to make the overcoat, and like an answer to a prayer, I was brought down to Talbot Street, and dressed out in a dinging overcoat, belted, like a grown-up man's. And my shoes and gloves were dear and dandy, and I said to myself that there was no need to let anyone see the suit with its little lapels and big buttons. I could keep the topcoat on all day, in the chapel, and going round afterwards.

The night before Confirmation day, Miss McCann handed over the suit to my mother, and kissed me, and said not to bother thanking her. She would do more than that for me, and she and my grandmother cried and had a drink on the strength of my having grown to be a big fellow, in the space of twelve years, which they didn't seem to consider a great deal of time. My father said to my mother, and I getting bathed before the fire, that since I was born Miss McCann thought the world of me. When my mother was in hospital, she took me into her place till my mother came out, and it near broke her heart to give me back.

In the morning I got up, and Mrs. Rooney in the next room shouted in to my mother that her Liam was still stalling, and not making any move to get out of it, and she thought she was cursed; Christmas or Easter, Communion or Confirmation, it would drive a body into Riddleys, which is the mad part of Grangegorman, and she wondered she wasn't driven out of her mind, and above in the puzzle factory years ago. So she shouted again at Liam to get up, and washed and dressed. And my mother shouted at me, though I was already knotting my tie, but you might as well be out of the world, as out of fashion, and they kept it up like a pair of mad women, until at last Liam and I were ready and he came in to show my mother his clothes. She hanselled him a tanner, which he put in his pocket and Mrs. Rooney called me in to show her my clothes. I just stood at her door and didn't open my coat, but just grabbed the sixpence out of her hand, and ran up the stairs like the hammers of hell. She shouted at me to hold on a minute, she hadn't seen my suit, but I muttered something about it not being lucky to keep a Bishop waiting, and ran on.

The Church was crowded, boys on one side and the girls on the other, and the altar ablaze with lights and flowers, and a throne for the Bishop to sit on when he wasn't confirming. There was a cheering crowd outside, drums rolled, trumpeters from Jim Larkin's band sounded the Salute. The Bishop came in and the doors were shut. In short order I joined the queue to the rails, knelt and was whispered over, and touched on the cheek. I had my overcoat on the whole time, though it was warm, and I was in a lather of sweat waiting for the hymns and the sermon.

The lights grew brighter and I got warmer, was carried out fainting. But though I didn't mind them loosening my tie, I clenched firmly my overcoat, and nobody saw the jacket with the big buttons and the little lapels. When I went home, I got into bed, and my father said I went into a sickness just as the Bishop was giving us the pledge. He said this was a master stroke, and showed real presence of mind.

Sunday after Sunday, my mother fought over the suit. She said I was a liar and a hypocrite, putting it on for a few minutes every week, and running into Miss McCann's and out again, letting her think I wore it every week-end. In a passionate temper my mother said she would show me up, and tell Miss McCann, and up like a shot with her, for my mother was always slim, and light on her feet as a feather, and in next door. When she came back she said nothing, but sat at the fire looking into it. I didn't really believe she would tell Miss McCann. And I put on the suit and thought I would go in and tell her I was wearing it this week-night, because I was going to the Queen's with my brothers. I ran next door and upstairs, and every step was more certain and easy that my mother hadn't told her. I ran, shoved in the door, saying: 'Miss Mc., Miss Mc., Rory and Sean and I are going to the Queen's. . . .' She was bent over the sewing-machine and all I could see was the top of her old grey head, and the rest of her shaking with crying, and her arms folded under her head, on a bit of habit where she had been finishing the I.H.S. I ran down the stairs and back into our place, and my mother was sitting at the fire, sad and sorry, but saying nothing.

I needn't have worried about the suit lasting forever. Miss McCann didn't. The next winter was not so mild, and she was whipped before the year was out. At her wake people said how she was in a habit of her own making, and my father said she would look queer in anything else, seeing as she supplied the dead of the whole quarter for forty years, without one complaint from a customer.

At the funeral, I left my topcoat in the carriage and got out and walked in the spills of rain after her coffin. People said I would get my end, but I went on till we reached the graveside, and I stood in my Confirmation suit drenched to the skin. I thought this was the least I could do.

Native Country

NADINE GORDIMER
(South African, 1923–   )

Among the things in Anita's bedroom there was a clock as well as a
Renaissance chair with a bit of string tied between its arms so that no one
could sit in it. It was a mantel clock with only one hand and until she
grew old enough to be taught at school to tell the time she had always
thought that other people's clocks were strange. "I didn't know there was
something wrong with ours," she told her father. "There is nothing
'wrong' with ours," he said in the tone of distant disgust with which he
approached the subject of the people among whom they lived. He was a
very pale man with eyes as pale, though blue, as his fine skin and thick
silky white hair that waved back high all round from temples and brow.
"It is a seventeenth-century clock and at that time they were made with
only one hand, to mark the hours, only of course these people know
nothing about such things. They know the tin alarm clock that wakes
them up in the morning."

Other children's parents were young and red-armed; they played golf
and tennis and dug in the garden. In their houses they had only furniture
whose purpose was obvious, beds to sleep in and chairs to sit in, and
everything was new. They had smart standing ashtrays that swallowed
cigarette stubs down into a chromium column when you pressed a button.

Anita had never known the Europe which, as she knew from her parents' own house and the friends who came in and out of it, was an
interior peopled and furnished quite differently. The sun was kept out

from objects like faces. The chairs, tables, bureaux, and commodes had each their inlay, carving, or encrustation of coloured lacquer just as Dr. Manides, Mr. Gruntz, the Terbegens, and the Crespignys had their different accents. The lisps and intonations in their English kept present other tongues, ancient civilizations, philosophies growing into political systems, and political systems growing one out of the other; the objects kept present concepts of beauty laid one upon the other, the skill of guilds that had evolved and disappeared, and the proportions of other rooms. So Anita knew from an early age that the strange faded beast in which her father sat with his hands resting on its two snarling heads, belonged somewhere. When a child she had brought home with her from the neighbouring streets was struck dumb before the presence of her father and Mr. Gruntz sitting in silence over the chess table, and gazed round in a growing oppression that almost entirely inhibited breathing as the gaze reached the harpsichord, Anita would whisper, "A kind of piano."

The street outside into which she and the friend then burst was white with blazing afternoon sunlight. Black nannies yelled gossip where they congregated restlessly with their white charges. Barefoot boys cycled to buy milk or bread from the Greek shop on the corner. Sometimes the older children played cricket with an upended fruit box for wicket, or *bok-bok,* a wild game rougher than leapfrog, from which Anita would emerge with her fringe drenched in sweat. Every Saturday afternoon she went with her school friends to the cinema down the road, where they traded American comics with each other, blew bubble gum, and stopped their ears when the schoolboys whistled between their teeth at the love scenes. After rain, she and the other children in their street paddled in the swirling gutters of warm brown water and teased black delivery men by throwing bunches of wet leaves at them as they rode by. Now and then there were fights; a party of jeering boys would provoke the girls. Anita always came back into the house with an exhilarated face that slowly took on the indoor calm of heavy curtains and the smell of coffee brewing.

"Anita has been enjoying herself." Her father would push his chair away from the table, as if inviting the guests to contemplate her. "And where she has been?" Frau Gruntz gave singing lessons (ex-Vienna opera) and at sixty, in a smart linen costume, she offered the white bosom and wide painted smile of the moment when the first note of an aria is about to be sounded. Dr. Manides, who regarded it as an affront to his esteemed friend Gruntz that she should be married to him, said, "Is Anita's business."

Her mother said, "Your hair . . ." with resigned acceptance and a certain timidity towards this apparition from activities not so much unthinkable as discounted.

"Oh Mommy, man!" Anita spoke as the other children did.

But these were elderly city people who had spent a large part of their lives talking in cafés and the interruption of Anita was hardly more than a pause; quickly and absently passed over.

The family was living in a working-class suburb of bungalows out towards the mine dumps on the south side of Johannesburg. After the war they moved to the crush of flat buildings squeezing out older houses of the town's beginnings on the ridge of the north side. There were many more people like themselves, now; Italians, Hollanders, half the Polish aristocracy. Later came Germans; and after 1956, the Hungarians were to follow. There were delicatessen shops, an audience for chamber music, *espresso,* and even one or two cafés where the newspapers hung from wooden spines. Anita's father's bookkeeping job (he had been in the family bank, at home) gave way to something better, though he did not rise to a new prosperity, as some of the others did—the German Jews in the clothing industry, the Italians in engineering and building. Into the shabby double-story house he brought the things he began to pick up; Persian rugs, a *guéridon,* gilt clocks, *gesso* frames, a single English lead wineglass that one of the local "antique" dealers had known no better than to include in a job lot of modern Czechoslovakian rubbish. The new waves of refugees and immigrants had brought, like the sand that is found among clothes when one unpacks after a holiday at the sea, some residue of Europe. Professor Terbegen went to auctions too, and there was an endless rivalry pursued in the discussion of chipped and gilded objects, now doubly removed, in latitude as well as time, from their inspiration.

Once, while they were still living in the humble suburb, Anita's father had shown another round his treasures—but not an immigrant, not a refugee with the dust of interrupted conversation in a long-bombed café hanging in his mind. He was a man with the self-assured handsomeness that good looks take on at the end of the thirties, and at that time he was in the uniform of a colonel of one of the "free" forces of an occupied country, attached to British Intelligence. A staff car waited outside; he talked to Anita's mother and father in their own tongue and brought alive animation and laughter, a draught of their world in common. In him it was not a memory; he was Europe, living and present, the special dry humour of the capital, the logical mind of a particular university, the eyes and hands sensually accustomed to marble and chestnut trees in bloom. Anita, fifteen years old, knew only the South African privates with baggy khaki trousers strapped down over their clumsy boots, who came home to the neighbourhood houses on weekend leave. She followed her father and this visitor round, keeping out of the way and studying him in secrecy and amazement.

Axelrod was in South Africa for over a year and he came to the house often. He was the son of friends in the old Europe, whom Anita had never met, but who belonged to the best period of her parents' lives. He was an expert on German porcelain and French furniture, English silver and Italian glass—in fact all the furnishings and ornaments of that interior which Anita had never inhabited. Although he became an intimate, his visits (sometimes he spent the weekend) were always an event. Anita knew every seam and braid of his uniform. She knew his phrasing in French; his play on words in German. He got her a special seat at a military tattoo and he paid her mock grown-up compliments like giving her French perfume on her birthday—a celebration at which he held all the attention and provided all the fun. While he was in the house he made it his own, but he would leave at a time confirmed by a quick glance at his watch, so that the high note of his presence was maintained by the sudden sense of the width of his life, opening out here and there and everywhere, beyond them, and yet at the same time taking them up into it. He would come back with the same smile of lively participation with which he had gone out; he had been to a party, or with a woman. In the meantime, Anita was asked by one of the young South African soldiers to go to a dance in the Scout Hall, but she was too afraid to ask permission from her parents. The boy said, "But why can't you even try, man?" His lips came together humbly as waiting hands.

After the war Axelrod came out from Europe on a visit because he had the idea that he might acquire some African pieces—there was a small band of collectors who were interested in Benin bronzes and old wooden sculpture from West Africa. He and Anita's father stood looking at two crouching figures unwrapped upon the plush cloth on her mother's table. The heavy black wood was covered with a clinging spiderweb of the spores of dried mould. The protuding navel stood out like a Cyclopean eye. The gash of the female sex, the third limb of the male were statements beyond the age of chivalry or the prurience of a Marquis de Sade. One had, tied on its belly, a small cloth bundle stiff with a dried, still reddish stain. A piece of tarnished mirror set into its chest showed your face rotting and falling away like something dug up from a grave.

Axelrod smiled with the corners of his mouth dipped comically; her father looked at the things with his head instinctively drawn back, sourly sideways out of his pale eyes. They appraised each other in the way of people who knew each other's thoughts, and in a moment, began to laugh. "Don't try to make a fool of me, Axelrod."

"No, Felix, these are good pieces. At least a hundred and fifty years old. Mrs. van Rose will go mad about them."

They laughed delightedly at each other's disgust, Axelrod shaking his head and holding the older man's shoulder.

It was extraordinary to have Axelrod in the house again. Now it was the house in Hillbrow, of course. His voice downstairs when he talked on the telephone. The smell of his cigarettes. His expensive English suits being carried upstairs after Beauty, the servant girl, had pressed them. Anita was nearly eighteen and she emerged from the chrysalis of her room, awkward, hot-faced under her wild-falling short hair. She was present as she had been, following them round as a child; but now she accompanied them to restaurants and shared the wine at dinner, silently listening and following with her eyes not only the guest's face, but the invisible contours of his conversation. There was always something out-of-breath about her; now and then they would turn to her with a parenthetic smile or remark, as to a child who has just run in.

When she was back in her room she would stand at the window like a person who has lost his memory. The scene that she knew intimately, down there in the yard between the flat buildings, was unrecognizable to her, as if she had never been there before. And yet how much of her time did she spend, watching the life that moved in and out the slanting bifurcation of shade that, cast by high buildings, travelled like the arm of a compass round the well of bright sunlight. Black men and women who were cleaners and maids in the flats lived there; they slept in dormitories on the roofs, and their life zigzagged up and down the iron fire escapes, and rebounded in shouts of anger and laughter from wall to wall. The men gambled on their haunches at lunchtime. At night they drank the brew that, she knew so well, was kept hidden in the electrical-installation kiosk. They argued, barbered each other's hair, put their hands on the lovely backsides of the girls, and, on their respective days off, went up to the roof in the kitchen-boy garb and came down again as bold, well-dressed men with brushed hats and polished shoes. Down there, the servant, Beauty, had another being than that of Anita's parents' house.

But with Axelrod's presence in the rooms behind her, Anita heard and saw nothing that was before her eyes. She was alive in the streets whose names he let fall in his anecdotes ("near the rue de Courcelles," "in the Quaistrasse") and in the houses, hidden in winter rain, among the elaborate objects he and her father admired and understood.

One of the pleasantries with which Axelrod took his leave at the airport was "And Anita? You must send her when she finishes school. Elisabeth will look after her." There had been a wife at some time, but they were parted; Elisabeth was an old family retainer he had taken with him when he set up house in London.

Like all such pleasantries, it was smiled at and meant nothing, yet when Anita was taken by her mother to Europe for the first time, just after her eighteenth birthday, it was Axelrod who showed them the Wallace Collection ("my favourite place in London") and, in the British Museum, swept them past rooms they mustn't waste their time with, to stand in homage before certain selected objects. Anita was left by her mother to spend a year with relatives in Lausanne and to attend some secretarial school there. But when Axelrod, passing through on business, took her out to lunch like an uncle giving a niece a treat and found her mutely miserable, he disposed of her homesickness in a sentence—"I'll take you to London." He added, "That's the place for you. You can learn your typewriting with some nice young ladies from Kensington."

"I want to go home."

Axelrod smiled with absent adult indulgence, and said, "Oh there. I shouldn't think Felix and your mother would stick it out much longer. They'll be here soon, too, I'm sure."

He wrote to Felix and without even waiting for an answer, packed the girl into his car and drove her round Switzerland for a week before taking her to London. Installed in his house, with Elisabeth to keep her company when she came home from her secretarial college, she saw little of Axelrod. She soon discovered that he was having an affair with a pianist; that had been his reason for being in Switzerland: so long as the affair lasted, he combined business with his preoccupation and followed his mistress round Europe while she fulfilled concert engagements. Later he was in love with the beautiful wife of Lord T———(Anita got to know the lovely croaky voice over the telephone), and there were others. He began to look older but never less attractive, with deep lines accentuating the strength of his mouth and his youthful slenderness turned to lean- ness. When Anita finished her secretarial course, he took her to her first night club. She was telling him her experiences as applicant for several jobs. They laughed about them and he said, "What about applying to me?" She made some joking remark; but his careless, impulsive sugges- tions were part of his acquisitive flair, and as he spoke the joke became perfectly sensible: "I need a secretary at home as well as at the rooms. Someone to pick up the bits of paper I scrawl important things on, eh? Someone to write down what I think before I forget it. Someone to follow me round . . ." While he was talking she was following him in a differ- ent way, on the dim concourse of the dance floor. Her legs and body moved with his, in all its assurance of the love of women.

Her mother and father came over on a visit that year and stayed in the house in London. There were important sales of seventeenth-century fur- niture and rare glass and above various objects the eyes of the old man and Axelrod met in the passion of assessment and appreciation. At din- ner, at the theatre, over morning coffee, the talk was of nothing but rarities. Anita knew the difference between a *tazza* and *caqueteuse*, now —she had been working with Axelrod among such things for some months, and she could place them, like the strange faces of foreigners once one has seen their counterparts in their home countries. Her father looked at her with pride, as he would at some *objet d'art* that had emerged well from its saleroom obscurity. "There is nothing there for anybody. A lot of blacks and the white people are worse—agh!"

Axelrod, on his travels about the collections and salerooms of the world, continued to send her the kind of grown-up presents that flatter a child. From Japan came an absurd tinned oyster, guaranteed to contain a cultured pearl. He himself always carried in his pocket, the rosary of his religion of beautiful objects, an oblong alexandrite to fondle while he thought or talked. His letters were as amusing as his gifts: *My little amanuensis, Meet me in Paris, Thursday—M. Jarnoux has some bargains to show me and I need someone to conspire with against him. You will be wanting to replenish your wardrobe anyway; the spring showings are on.*

. . . It was a joke with him to pretend that she was not a shy girl who wore nothing but skirts and jerseys. In the open-air cafés of Rome and Paris they looked like a handsome youngish father and his suddenly shot-up daughter, who find they get on tremendously well together. She had a few young friends, a boy or two, but Axelrod—a job like hers, that was, took up one's life completely: how could a young man with a couple of tickets for the cinema compete with a sudden summons to meet Axelrod in Paris?

In Vienna he made love to her for the first time, in a hotel that delighted him in its perfect restoration to the rococo splendour that he remembered from before the war. They had had a most successful few days, there; a treasure of wonderful porcelain that had emerged from some hiding place, one of the most important collections he had acquired in years—and it was in the sweet buoyancy of success that he gave in to her: for, of course, it was plain as the nose on her face that she was in love with him. "It's incest, eh?" he said tenderly, honestly. "But I know you are a big girl. Yes? You have been a big girl with me for a long time, now."

But she misunderstood the extent of the indulgence.

When they got back to London, he said, "Write to them and tell them the news about their bachelor friend. We are going to be married. You can't compromise me in this way, my darling Anita. What about my reputation?" Coming from Axelrod, it was a declaration beyond her wildest fantasies: the single fantasy that had been begun out of the seams of his uniform, the smell of his cigarettes when she was fifteen years old. Her parents had no qualms; Axelrod was the son they might have had if they had not had Anita, child of their exile and old age, born, like the people around them who were strangers to them, in a strange land. In a way, he would always be more a son of theirs than Anita would ever be a daughter. Yet by the fact of Axelrod's marrying her, she became more of a daughter than she had been.

Married to Axelrod, she changed remarkably little. She was there at the head of the table at his brilliant dinner parties, of course, and on her hand were his rings—for one crazy moment she had thought he would give her his alexandrite as her engagement ring, but no, it was still in his pocket, and she was thankful she had said nothing. She bore three children, and gained confidence among his friends and in her indispensability to him in his work—as time went by she was able to take all practical matters, including complicated financial transactions from country to country, off his hands. Yet her appearance, even in her thirties, continued to have something about it of the awkward schoolgirl: this, after all, was what Axelrod had married. He took her to Italy to buy her clothes (Paris, he said, was not her style); her suède skirts and raw silk blouses were really only more expensive versions of the old jerseys and skirts.

As she grew towards maturity, and he towards age (there were twenty-five years between them) their relationship evened out somewhat. She accepted without her former humbleness his affairs with women. Her gauche appearance became her style; and rather stylish. She was no longer conscious of a certain helplessness before other women's beauti-fully manicured hands, skilfully raised breasts, and those deliberately fake faces that Axelrod enjoyed as much as he did the enamelled ones on his favourite French miniatures. He had still, unchanged, what people thought of as his charm—for her, the old affectionate amusement with which he had treated her all her life. He was a better lover than ever, and they had the one ground on which, at least, they had been equals from the start: their interest and pleasure in their children. If she had never had from him the one proof—and that she had never had it was con-firmed by the fact that she did not know what form it would take—if she had never had the one proof that he loved her, then at least she had made her life with him just as if that proof had been in the house all the time, along with all the other treasures that belonged there.

In the spring of his fifty-eighth year Axelrod went away for a few days on one of his usual quick trips. He telephoned from Rome to the country house in Berkshire they had had for some years, to say that he would be back on Monday at lunchtime; the sun was shining and the leaves were out, already, in the Pincio Gardens—he wished they were all there with him. Anita and her eldest child, Daniel, spent the weekend beside the fire, in a furious chess battle. On Monday morning she drove the children back to town in time for school and as she opened the front door she saw Axelrod's partner and the secretary from the offices standing up to con-front her. Axelrod had collapsed and died of a heart attack in a terrace café.

There was a seat booked for her on a plane and she went without telling anyone, not even their closest friends. She sat alone in the plane looking at the condensed moisture vibrating on the window as she had done all the other times she had gone to join Axelrod. She went to him at the mortuary and saw that he had not known he would die; his death had taken him on impulse while the pleasure of some new acquisition was still on his face. She walked about the streets of Rome and past the café where they had told her he had died and the absurd expression that one's heart could be "sore" became true for her, she felt a rough soreness inside her as if some organ were being manhandled. Then she followed the way, by fountain, by marble triton and square, along the chestnuts coming into new leaf, back to his hotel, and packed his things. And as she put her hand blindly, for comfort, into the pocket of his trousers in the gesture with which he always felt for the jewel that he fingered there, she touched a small hard box. She took out a jeweller's case. In it was Axelrod's oblong alexandrite, made up into a ring.

The air blotched before her eyes and her ears began to sing; she sat on the bed and thrust her head down over her knees, her hands raked up into her hair.

The blood flowed back to her brain and she was able to get up again. She took the ring out of its slot in the velvet pad and put it on her third finger; it was just a little tight; unless a jeweller had the actual finger from which to take his measurements, it was difficult to be accurate to a millimetre. This very week, on the Thursday, they would have been married fourteen years. Every year on the anniversary Axelrod brought her a present, one of the objects she had learned from him were beautiful and precious, but the truth was that of all the lovely things with which their house was filled she had coveted only one—the jewel that Axelrod played with in his pocket. And she could never ask him for it; had long ago accepted that although he knew she wanted it, he delicately saved her the humiliation of his admitting this since he knew he could never give it to her.

She hid her face in her hands with a panting gasp. Joy buffeted her body unfamiliarly, she turned her head this way and that; a blazing pride of fulfilment shocked and delighted her. Sorrow came back; but it was not the sediment of old sorrow, that had been dissolved in her veins.

With the summer, some months later, she began to feel that the ring really was too tight. She took it to a jeweller. While he was taking the correct measurement of her finger on a bunch of metal rings, she thought suddenly as if someone spoke out loud: Was the ring meant for her?

Why had she never thought of this before?

What reason was there to have assumed that Axelrod had had the alexandrite made up for her? The coming anniversary had not been a special landmark. He had never been ill before that first and fatal blood clot and he was the last sort of person to have any romantic premonition of death.

What on earth had made her so sure? After fourteen years, might the ring not just as well have been made for some other woman? All his life Axelrod had had his love affairs just as he had his childhood memories of the Guignol in Paris parks, and his passionate familiarity with the objects that had piled up through the centuries as if in some junk room of the trappings of empires and principalities, before the Wall, waiting for the Bomb—that life of Europe to which he belonged and which it had never been expected, either by her parents or by him, she would ever really understand as one born to it. She found herself thinking of the crude afternoon sun in the street where she had played *bok-bok.* The soldier with his sunburnt, razor-nicked face and issue boots, who had wanted to take her to a dance. The black men in the ridiculous shorts and tunics who gambled and talked and drank and made love with their women in the bare well between the buildings, where there was nothing but strong sun, and strong shade marking the passage of the sun like the hand of a clock: she thought of the single hand of the clock that had stood in her room in Africa. Oh why had she come in from the street? Why had she not gone to the dance with the clumsy young soldier? Why had she not gone down there among the black men and women and learned what they were laughing at and tasted what they tasted when they tipped the jam tin and the beer went down their throats?

Long ago, that time, Axelrod and her father had looked with ridicule on the heavy black wooden figures with bellies and breasts and sex plainly stated. She tried to remember the figures but it was too far away, and she could not. And yet she had cared for nothing of the things *they* had valued. Nothing.

Only the alexandrite.

Prizes

JANET FRAME
(New Zealander, 1924–   )

Life is hell, but at least there are prizes. Or so one thought. One knew of the pit ahead, of the grownups lying there rewarded, arranged, and faded, who were so long ago bright as poppies. One learned to take one's own deserved place on the edge, ready to leap, not to hang back in a status-free huddle where bodies were warm together and the future darkness seemed less frightening. Therefore, one learned to win prizes, to be surrounded in sleep by a dream of ordinal numbers, to stand in best clothes upon platforms in order to receive medals threaded upon black-and-gold ribbons, books "bound in calf," scrolled certificates. One's face became, from habit, incandescent with achievement.

I had my share of prizes, and of resentment when nobody recognized my efforts; for instance, year after year, when the New Zealand Agricultural and Pastoral Society held its show in the Onui Drill Hall, I made a buttonhole of a rose and a sprig of maidenhair fern tied together with raffia, which I entered for the Flower Display, Gentleman's Buttonhole. It was never displayed, and it never won a prize. One morning, a militant woman in a white coat made a speech to the whole school from the front steps, before Bertie Dowling played the kettledrum for us to march inside, and in her speech the woman accused too many people of entering for the Buttonhole Section, and advised us not to try to make buttonholes, as they were an art beyond our years that even grownups found difficult to master. "It has never been explained," the woman said, "why so many children enter buttonholes in the Flower Show." (Bertie Dowling had the sticks raised, ready to play the drum. He was very clever at it; he was a small, sunburned, wiry boy with long feet like a rabbit.)

I felt antagonistic toward the woman visitor. Who was she to order me not to make buttonholes for the Flower Show? I persisted, as I say, year after year, yet always, once I had surrendered my exhibit, neat in its little box cadged from the jeweler's, I never heard of it again. I had so much determination and so little wisdom that I never grasped the futility of my struggle, although I realized that when talents were being devised and distributed my name was not included in the short list of those blessed with the power to make gentlemen's buttonholes that would reach the display table at the Flower Show in the Drill Hall and win First, Second, or Third Prize.

I won six and fourpence for handwriting. At that time, I was in love with my parents; therefore, I decided to buy my mother a best-china cup, saucer, and plate with the entire six and fourpence, even though at that time I also had a fondness for Sante Chocolate Bars, jelly beans, and chocolate fish whose insides were a splurge of pink rubbery substance with tiny air holes in it. When I gave my mother the best-china cup, saucer, and plate she said, "You shouldn't have," and, wrapping the set carefully in tissue paper, she placed it in the sideboard cupboard with the other dishes that we never used—not even for the banquet to see the New Year in—like the gravy boat, the tiny cream jug with the picture of a Dutch girl, the vegetable dishes with the picture of a rooster crowing on each one. Then my mother locked the door. I never saw her using the cup, saucer, and plate. It was best china, too, the man in Peak's told me. My mother always said she was keeping the set for when she could *really* use it, drinking out of the cup, resting a silver spoon in the saucer, tasting (with a cake fork) a slice of marble cake upon the plate. Although I could not then discern the difference between using something and *really* using it, there was evidently a distinction so important that when my mother died she had still not been able to use, really to use, my six-and-fourpenny gift to her.

My next prize was for a poem that revealed both my lack of scientific knowledge and my touching disbelief in change by concluding with the lines

And till the sky falls from above,
These things of nature I shall love.

Uncle Ted, of my favorite wireless station in Christchurch, read my poem
over the air, between a recording of "The Nutcracker, Waltz of the Flowers," and the fifth episode of *David and Dawn in Fairyland,* and two days
later I received through the post an order for ten shillings, with part of
which I bought for myself an unsatisfactory diary and a John Bull Printing Set, which I used, printing my name, and rude rhymes, and insults to
the rest of the family, until the ink dried on the navy-blue pad; the
remainder of the ten shillings I saved in a Post Office Bank, which could
not be opened unless it was taken to the Post Office. I broke into it with a
kitchen knife when my bathing cap perished and the weather was warm
enough for swimming.

Prizes. They arrived unexpectedly, or I waited greedily for them at the
end of every school year, when I received one or two, sometimes three,
books with the school motto, "Pleasure from Work," inscribed on the
flyleaf beneath the cramped, detailed writing of the form mistress setting
out the reasons for my prize. Reasons were necessary, for no school had
yet learned to distribute prizes at random, first come, first served, in the
manner that my mother had adopted, in exasperation, when she was
pestered for raisins, dates, or the last of the chocolate biscuits. I collected
so many books: *Treasure Island; Silas Marner; Emma; Poems of Longfel-
low,* with a heart-throbbing picture of Hiawatha bearing Minnehaha
across the river:

Over wide and rushing rivers
In his arms he bore the maiden;

India, with illustrations colored as if with cochineal; *Boys and Girls Who
Became Famous;* and—during the war, when books were scarce—a
musty old rained-on and stained volume of poems about blossoms, barns,
and wine presses, printed in tall, dark type, where snakes lurked in every
capital letter.
  Prizes. Some did not get prizes. Dotty Baker with the greasy hair never
got a prize. Maud Gray, who found it hard to read even simple sentences
aloud, never got a prize. Maud Gray! She was the stodgiest girl in the

class; all the teachers made fun of her, and most of the pupils, including myself, followed their example. Her eyes were brittle and brown, like cracked acorn shells; her face was pale and blotched, like milk on the turn.

Years later, I was visiting Onui. I was walking desolately in the rain along the main street, wearing my dirty old gabardine and my dowdy clothes and feeling fifteen instead of twenty-five, when, just beyond the bed of poppies in the center of the street, I saw two beautiful women wheeling prams, and their proud gait was so noticeable I tried to recall when and where I had seen before that superior parading of the victorious. And then I realized that I had walked onto the platform in the same way, year after year, to receive my prizes. Dotty Baker, Maud Gray! As they passed with their cocooned, quilted, embroidered treasure, I could not even assert my superiority by whispering, "You cheated in history, you couldn't learn poetry by heart, you never had your name in the paper. . . . First in geometry, French, English, history. . . ."

They smiled at me and I smiled at them. We shared the pit, each in her place. The rain poured upon the bed of crushed poppies between us. Yet the delicacy and distance of the two women were unmistakable; I grudged their proud cloaks as they trooped, clients of love, on their specially reserved side of the world. But—prizes. They never won prizes. My only retaliation was prizes—listing them, remembering.

I wrote to a children's newspaper, sending poems that were awarded ten or five or three marks. When I had earned one hundred marks, I received the usual prize of two guineas. For one guinea my father bought me a tennis racket, as he said, "on the cheap," but when he showed it to me I was alarmed to discover that the strings were black instead of white, and the name was unfamiliar—Double Duke. I was the loneliest person in the world with my black-stringed Double Duke. Why had my father not realized that every other girl at school possessed a white-stringed Vantage? Ah, it was sad enough to have an old wireless at home with a name no one had heard of and with tubes so few in number compared with the tubes in other sets. The conversations in class went: "Have you got a wireless at home? How many tubes?" The prestige of owning things mattered so much, and to have a tennis racket with a strange name and grotesque strings was punishment indeed. I was so ashamed of my tennis racket that I seldom used it.

With my other guinea from the newspaper I had the unexpected fortune to be chosen by Hessie Sutton, a woman up the road, as her pupil for music lessons—the piano—at a reduced rate, and every Tuesday and Friday after school I claimed an hour of Hessie Sutton's time in the front room of the house where she lived with her mother and a white parrot whose perpetual screaming inspired complaining letters to the evening paper.

The front room was large and carpeted, with sparkling, bubble-shaped windows. The piano made wonderfully clean sounds as the keys sank into and sprang from their green bedding; the sounds filled me with a polished sense of opulence and cleanliness, and each note emerged bravely and milkily alone and poured into me, up to my neck. I swallowed. I liked Hessie Sutton's piano. We had none at home. At my aunt's house, where I went to practice once a week, there was an old piano with soapy yellow keys that stuck halfway, and the lower or upper half of each sound had been weathered down so that each note came forth deprived, diseased, with an invalid petulance and stricture.

"But you must not bite your nails," Hessie Sutton warned me. "You will never be able to play the piano if you bite your nails!" That was my first intimation that Hessie Sutton was a spy. I clenched my fists, hiding my fingernails.

At school, I said, "I learn music, do you?" Dotty Baker, Maud Gray, and others learned music, but mostly they were like uncooked pastry at it; they suffered a dearth of warmth, expansion, gold finish. On the cold June days, when the Music Festival was held, we sat miserably in the hall, our coats over our knees, listening to a "Marche Militaire" being played by schoolgirl dentists and carpenters.

My first piece was named "Puck." I went down to the stationer's to buy it on tick, and the ginger-haired boy served me, and his face had a rust-colored blush, like a dock leaf in autumn, because he had to go to the small room at the back of the shop and ask his parents if it would be all right to serve me, as our bill had not been paid. On my way home with "Puck," I met Hessie Sutton and smiled at her, shyly and excitedly, but when she glanced at the parcel under my arm and the music half wrapped, and gave an understanding smile, my face clouded in a fierce frown. How dare she see me and divine my excitement! How dare she! How I hated her!

That afternoon, when I went for my lesson, she heightened my sense of shame. "I saw you." She pounced as soon as I entered the room. "I saw you," she said, like a detective giving evidence, "coming home with your new piece of music. I guessed how excited you were!"

"I wasn't caring at all," I said sullenly.

"Yes, you were," Hessie Sutton insisted. "I saw it in your face! I *knew!*"

I did not understand why she should appear so triumphant, as if by seizing on a momentary aspect of my behavior she had uncovered a life of deceit in me. Why, she honked with triumph like the soldier who brought back the golden horn from the underworld as proof of the secret activities of the twelve dancing princesses! I did not realize that people's actions are mysteries that are so seldom solved.

"I knew, I knew!" Hessie Sutton kept saying as I sat down to try out "Puck."

From that day, I no longer enjoyed my music lessons. I was weary of being spied upon. People were saying, observing me closely, "She's filling out, she's growing tall, look at her hair, isn't that Grace's chin she's got, and there's no doubting where her smile comes from!"

You see how derivative I was made out to be? Nothing belonged to me, not even my body, and now with Hessie Sutton and her spying ways I could not call my feelings my own. Why did people have so much need to stake their claim in other people? Were they scared of the bailiffs' arriving in their own house? I stopped learning music. I was in despair. I could no longer use prizes as a fortress. In spite of my books bound in calf, my scrolled certificates, the prize essay on the Visit to the Flour Mill, and my marks of merit in the children's newspaper, I was being invaded by people who wanted *their* prizes from *me*.

And now I lie in the pit, finally arranged, faded, robbed of all prizes, while still under every human sky the crows wheel and swoop, dividing, dividing the spoils of the dead.

Timoshenko

IAIN CRICHTON SMITH
(Scottish, 1928–   )

When I went into the thatched house as I always did at nine o'clock at night, he was lying on the floor stabbed with a bread knife, his usually brick-red face pale and his ginger moustache a dark wedge under his nose. His eyes were wide open like blue marbles. I wondered where she was. The radio was still on and I went over and switched it off. At the moment she came down from the other room and sat on the bench. There was no point in going for a doctor; he was obviously dead: even I could tell that. She sat like a child, her knees close together, her hands folded in her lap.

I had regarded the two of them as children. He had a very bad limp and sat day after day at the earthen wall which bordered the road, his glassy hands resting on his stick, talking to the passers-by. Sometimes he would blow on his fingers, his cheeks red and globular. She on the other hand sat in the house most of the time, perhaps cooking a meal or washing clothes. Of the two I considered her the simpler, though she had been away from the island a few times, in her youth, at the fishing, but had to be looked after by the other girls in case she did something silly.

'Did you do that?' I said, pointing to the body which seemed more eloquent than either of us. She nodded wordlessly. As a matter of fact I hadn't liked him very much. He was always asking me riddles to which I did not know the answer, and when I was bewildered he would nod his head and say, 'I don't understand what they are teaching at these schools nowadays.' He had an absolutely bald head which shone in the light and

a sarcastic way of speaking. He would call his sister Timoshenko or
Voroshilov, because the Russians at that time were driving the Germans
out of their country and these generals were always in the news.
'Timoshenko will know about it,' he would say and she would stand there
smiling, a teapot in her hands.

But of course I never thought what it was like for the two of them
when I wasn't there. Perhaps he persecuted her. Perhaps his sarcasm was
a perpetual wound. Perhaps, lame as he was, sitting at the wall all day, he
was petrified by boredom and his tiny mind squirmed like the snail-like
meat inside a whelk. He had never left the island in his whole life and I
didn't know what had caused his limp which was so serious that he had
to drag himself along by means of two sticks.

The blood had stopped flowing and the body lay on the floor like a log.
The fire was out and the dishes on the dresser were clean and colourful
rising in tier after tier. The floor which was made of clay seemed to
undulate slightly. I felt unreal as if at any moment the body would rise
from the floor like a question mark and ask me another riddle, the moustache twitching like an antenna. But this didn't happen. It stayed there
solid and heavy, the knife sticking from its breast.

I knew that soon I would have to get someone, perhaps the policeman
or a doctor or perhaps a neighbour. But I was so fascinated by the
woman that I stayed, wondering why she had done it. Girlishly she sat
on the bench, her hands in her lap, not even twisting them nervously.

Suddenly she said, 'I don't know why but I took the knife and I . . . I
don't know why.'

She looked past me, then added, 'I can't remember why I did it. I don't
understand.'

I waited for her to talk and after a while she went on.

'Many years ago,' she said, 'I was going to be married. He made fun of
me when Norman came into the house. He said I couldn't cook and I
couldn't wash, and that was wrong. That must have been twenty years
ago. He was limping then too. He told Norman I was a bit daft. That was
many years ago. But that wasn't it. Anyway, he told Norman I was silly.
Norman had put on his best suit when he came to the house. He wasn't
rich or anything like that. You don't know him. Anyway he's dead now.
He died last week in the next village. He was on his own and they found
him in the house dead. He had been dead for a week; of course he was
quite old. He was older than me then. Anyway he came into the house

and he was wearing his best suit and he had polished his shoes and I
thought that he looked very handsome. Well, Donald said that I wasn't
any good at cooking and that I was silly. He made fun of me and all the
time he made fun of me Norman looked at me, as if he wanted me to say
something. I remember he had a white handkerchief in his pocket and it
looked very clean. Norman didn't have much to say for himself. In those
days he worked a croft and he was building a house. I was thirty years
old then and he was forty-two. I was wearing a long brown skirt which I
had got at the fishing and I was sitting as I am sitting now with my hands
in my lap as my mother taught me. Donald said that I smoked when I
was away from home. That was wicked of him. Of course to him it was a
joke but it wasn't true. I think Norman believed him and he didn't like
women smoking. My brother, you see, would make jokes all the time,
they were like knives in my body, and my mind wasn't quick enough to
say something back to him. Norman maybe didn't love me but we would
have been happy together. Donald believed that his jokes were very
funny, that people looked up to him, and that he was a clever man. But of
course he . . . Maybe if it hadn't been for his limp he might have carried on in school, so he said anyway. I left school at twelve. I had to look
after him even when my parents were alive.

'It didn't matter what I did, it was wrong. The tea was too hot or too
cold. The potatoes weren't cooked right or the herring wasn't salt
enough. "Who would marry you?" he would say to me. But I think
Norman would have married me. Norman was a big man but he was
slow and honest. He wasn't sarcastic at all and he couldn't think like my
brother. "She was in Yarmouth," Donald told him, "but they won't have
her back, she's too stupid. Aren't you, Mary?" he asked me. That wasn't
true. The reason I couldn't go to Yarmouth was because I had to stay at
home and look after him. I was going to go but he made me stop. He got
very ill the night before I was due to leave and I had to stay behind.
Anyway Norman went away that night and he never came back. I can
still see him going out the door in his new suit back to the new house he
was building. I found out afterwards that my brother had seen him and
told him that I used to have fits at the time of the new moon, and that
wasn't true.

'So I never married, and Donald would say to me, if I did something
that he didn't like, "That's why Norman never married you, you're too

stupid. And you shouldn't be going about with your stockings hanging down to your ankles. It doesn't look ladylike." '

I remembered how I used to come and listen to the News in this very house and it would tell of the German armies being inexorably strangled by the Russians. I would have visions of myself like Timoshenko standing up in my tank with dark goggles over my eyes as the Germans cowered in the snow and the rope of cold was drawn tighter and tighter. And he would say to me, 'Now then, tell me how many mackerel there are in a barrel. Go on now, tell me that.' And he would put his bald head on one side and look at me, his ginger moustache bristling. Or he would say, 'Tell me, then, what is the Gaelic for a compass. Eh? The proper Gaelic, I mean. Timoshenko will tell you that. Won't you, Timoshenko? She was at the fishing, weren't you, Timoshenko?'

And he would shift his aching legs, sighing heavily, his face becoming redder and redder.

'He thought I knew nothing,' she said. 'Other times he would threaten to put me out of the house because it belongs to him, you see.' She looked down at the body as if he were still alive and he were liable to stand up and throw her out of the house, crowing like a cockerel, his red cheeks inflated, and his red wings beating.

'He would say, "I'll get a housekeeper in. There's plenty who would make a good housekeeper. You're so stupid you don't know anything. And you leave everything so dirty. Look at this shirt you're supposed to have washed!" '

Was all this really true, I wondered. Had this woman lived in this village for so many years without anyone knowing anything about her suffering? It seemed so strange and unreal. All the time we had thought of the two as likeable comedians and one was cruel and vicious and the other was tormented and resentful. We had thought of them as nice, pleasant people, characters in the village. We didn't think of them as people at all, human beings who were locked in a death struggle. When people talked about her she became a sunny figure out of a comic, blundering about in a strange English world when she left the island, but happy all the same. We hadn't imagined that she was suffering like this in her dim world. And when we saw him sitting by the wall we thought of him as a fixture and we would shout greetings to him and he would shout back some quaint witticism. How odd it all was.

'But I knew what was going on all the time,' she continued. 'I could follow the news too. I knew what the Germans were doing, and the Russians. But he made me out to be a fool. And the thing was even after I heard of Norman's death I didn't say anything, though he said a few things himself. He told me one day, "You should have been his house-keeper and he wouldn't have been found dead like that on his own. But you weren't good enough for him. Poor man." And he would look at me with those small eyes of his. They had found Norman, you see, by the fire. He had fallen into it, he was ill and old. He hadn't been well for years. I often thought of taking him food but Donald wouldn't let me. After all we're all human and a little food wouldn't have been missed. I used to think of when we were young so many years ago. And when I was young I wasn't ugly. I wasn't beautiful but I wasn't ugly. I used to go to the dances when I was young, like the others. And of course I was at Yarmouth. He had never been out of the island though he was a man and I was only a woman and we used to bring presents home at the end of the season. I bought him a pipe once and another time I got him a melodeon but he wouldn't play it. So you see, there was that.'

There was another longish silence. Outside, it was pitch black and there was ice on the roads. In fact coming over from my own house I nearly slipped and fell but I had a torch so that was all right.

I wasn't at all afraid of her. I was in a strange way enjoying our conversation or rather her monologue. It was as if I was listening to an important story about life, a warning and a disaster. I remembered how as children we would be frightened by her brother waving his sticks from the wall where he was sitting. And we would run away full tilt as if we were running away from a monster. Our parents would say, 'It's only his joking,' and think how kind he was to go out of his way to entertain the children, but I wondered now whether in fact it might not be that he hated children and it wasn't acting at all, that cockerel clapping his sticks at us as we scattered across the moor.

Maybe too he had been more in pain than we had thought.

The trouble was that we didn't visit the two of them much at all. I did so, but only because I wished to listen to their radio to hear the news. Also, I was a quiet, reserved person who was happier in the company of people older than myself. But I hadn't actually looked at either of them with a clear hard look. To me she was a simple creature who smiled when her brother made some joke about Timoshenko, for his jokes tended to be remorselessly repetitive. It didn't occur to me that she was perhaps being pierced to the core by his primitive witticisms and it didn't occur to me either that they were meant to be cruel and were in fact outcrops from a perpetual war.

Suddenly she said to me, 'Would you like a cup of tea?' Without thinking I said 'Yes,' as if it was the most natural remark in the world while the body lay on the floor between us. I was amazed at how calmly I had accepted the presence of the body, though I had always thought of myself as sensitive and delicate. But on the other hand it was as if the body was not real, as if, as I have said, it would get to its feet, place its sticks under its arms, and walk towards me asking me riddles. Naturally however this didn't happen. And so we drank the tea out of neat cups with thin blue stripes at the rim.

'I had to give him all my saccharins,' she said, 'because he liked sweet things. It's a long time since I've had such a sweet cup of tea.' I noticed then that she had put saccharins in my tea and I realised that this was the first time that I had had tea in her house. She was in a strange way savouring her transient freedom.

'I remember now,' she said. 'It was the Germans and Timoshenko. The Germans had been trying to destroy Russia. I knew that, I'm not daft. And now the Russians were killing them. I heard that on the six o'clock news. And Timoshenko, he was doing that, he was winning. It was then that I . . .' She stopped then, the cup at her lips. 'I remember now. It was when it said about Timoshenko and he said the tea wasn't sweet enough. That was when I . . . I must have been cutting bread. I must . . .'

She looked at me in amazement as if it was just at that moment that she realised she had killed him. As she began to tremble I took the cup from her hands—it was spilling over—and put my arm around her and comforted her while she cried.

The Ballroom of Romance

ᑫᒍᒎᒪᒍᒎᒪᒍ

WILLIAM TREVOR
(Irish, 1928–   )

On Sundays, or on Mondays if he couldn't make it and often he couldn't, Sunday being his busy day, Canon O'Connell arrived at the farm in order to hold a private service with Bridie's father, who couldn't get about any more, having had a leg amputated after gangrene had set in. They'd had a pony and cart then and Bridie's mother had been alive: it hadn't been difficult for the two of them to help her father on to the cart in order to make the journey to Mass. But two years later the pony had gone lame and eventually had to be destroyed; not long after that her mother had died. 'Don't worry about it at all,' Canon O'Connell had said, referring to the difficulty of transporting her father to Mass. 'I'll slip up by the week, Bridie.'

The milk lorry called daily for the single churn of milk, Mr Driscoll delivered groceries and meal in his van, and took away the eggs that Bridie had collected during the week. Since Canon O'Connell had made his offer, in 1953, Bridie's father hadn't left the farm.

As well as Mass on Sundays and her weekly visits to a wayside dance-hall Bridie went shopping once every month, cycling to the town early on a Friday afternoon. She bought things for herself, material for a dress, knitting wool, stockings, a newspaper, and paper-backed Wild West novels for her father. She talked in the shops to some of the girls she'd been at school with, girls who had married shop-assistants or shop-keep-ers, or had become assistants themselves. Most of them had families of their own by now. 'You're lucky to be peaceful in the hills,' they said to

Bridie, 'instead of stuck in a hole like this.' They had a tired look, most of them, from pregnancies and their efforts to organize and control their large families.

As she cycled back to the hills on a Friday Bridie often felt that they truly envied her her life, and she found it surprising that they should do so. If it hadn't been for her father she'd have wanted to work in the town also, in the tinned meat factory maybe, or in a shop. The town had a cinema called the Electric, and a fish-and-chip shop where people met at night, eating chips out of newspaper on the pavement outside. In the evenings, sitting in the farmhouse with her father, she often thought about the town, imagining the shop-windows lit up to display their goods and the sweetshops still open so that people could purchase chocolates or fruit to take with them to the Electric cinema. But the town was eleven miles away, which was too far to cycle, there and back, for an evening's entertainment.

'It's a terrible thing for you, girl,' her father used to say, genuinely troubled, 'tied up to a one-legged man.' He would sigh heavily, hobbling back from the fields, where he managed as best he could. 'If your mother hadn't died,' he'd say, not finishing the sentence.

If her mother hadn't died her mother could have looked after him and the scant acres he owned, her mother could somehow have lifted the milk-churn on to the collection platform and attended to the few hens and the cows. 'I'd be dead without the girl to assist me,' she'd heard her father saying to Canon O'Connell, and Canon O'Connell replied that he was certainly lucky to have her.

'Amn't I as happy here as anywhere?' she'd say herself, but her father knew she was pretending and was saddened because the weight of circumstances had so harshly interfered with her life.

Although her father still called her a girl, Bridie was thirty-six. She was tall and strong: the skin of her fingers and her palms were stained, and harsh to touch. The labour they'd experienced had found its way into them, as though juices had come out of vegetation and pigment out of soil: since childhood she'd torn away the rough scotch grass that grew each spring among her father's mangolds and sugar beet; since childhood she'd harvested potatoes in August, her hands daily rooting in the ground she loosened and turned. Wind had toughened the flesh of her face, sun had browned it; her neck and nose were lean, her lips touched with early wrinkles.

But on Saturday nights Bridie forgot the scotch grass and the soil. In different dresses she cycled to the dance-hall, encouraged to make the journey by her father. 'Doesn't it do you good, girl?' he'd say, as though he imagined she begrudged herself the pleasure. 'Why wouldn't you enjoy yourself?' She'd cook him his tea and then he'd settle down with the wireless, or maybe a Wild West novel. In time, while still she danced, he'd stoke the fire up and hobble his way upstairs to bed.

The dance-hall, owned by Mr Justin Dwyer, was miles from anywhere, a lone building by the roadside with treeless boglands all around and a gravel expanse in front of it. On pink pebbled cement its title was painted in an azure blue that matched the depth of the background shade yet stood out well, unfussily proclaiming *The Ballroom of Romance*. Above these letters four coloured bulbs—in red, green, orange and mauve—were lit at appropriate times, an indication that the evening rendezvous was open for business. Only the façade of the building was pink, the other walls being a more ordinary grey. And inside, except for pink swing-doors, everything was blue.

On Saturday nights Mr Justin Dwyer, a small, thin man, unlocked the metal grid that protected his property and drew it back, creating an open mouth from which music would later pour. He helped his wife to carry crates of lemonade and packets of biscuits from their car, and then took up a position in the tiny vestibule between the drawn-back grid and the pink swing-doors. He sat at a card-table, with money and tickets spread out before him. He'd made a fortune, people said: he owned other ballrooms also.

People came on bicycles or in old motor-cars, country people like Bridie from remote hill farms and villages. People who did not often see other people met there, girls and boys, men and women. They paid Mr Dwyer and passed into his dance-hall, where shadows were cast on pale-blue walls and light from a crystal bowl was dim. The band, known as the Romantic Jazz Band, was composed of clarinet, drums and piano. The drummer sometimes sang.

Bridie had been going to the dance-hall since first she left the Presentation Nuns, before her mother's death. She didn't mind the journey, which was seven miles there and seven miles back: she'd travelled as far every day to the Presentation Nuns on the same bicycle, which had once been the property of her mother, an old Rudge purchased originally in 1936.

On Sundays she cycled six miles to Mass, but she never minded either: she'd grown quite used to all that.

'How're you, Bridie?' inquired Mr Justin Dwyer when she arrived in a new scarlet dress one autumn evening in 1971. She said she was all right and in reply to Mr Dwyer's second query she said that her father was all right also. 'I'll go up one of these days,' promised Mr Dwyer, which was a promise he'd been making for twenty years.

She paid the entrance fee and passed through the pink swing-doors. The Romantic Jazz Band was playing a familiar melody of the past, 'The Destiny Waltz'. In spite of the band's title, jazz was not ever played in the ballroom: Mr Dwyer did not personally care for that kind of music, nor had he cared for various dance movements that had come and gone over the years. Jiving, rock and roll, twisting, and other such variations had all been resisted by Mr Dwyer, who believed that a ballroom should be, as much as possible, a dignified place. The Romantic Jazz Band consisted of Mr Maloney, Mr Swanton, and Dano Ryan on drums. They were three middle-aged men who drove out from the town in Mr Maloney's car, amateur performers who were employed otherwise by the tinned-meat factory, the Electricity Supply Board, and the County Council.

'How're you, Bridie?' inquired Dano Ryan as she passed him on her way to the cloakroom. He was idle for a moment with his drums, 'The Destiny Waltz' not calling for much attention from him.

'I'm all right, Dano,' she said. 'Are you fit yourself? Are the eyes better?' The week before he'd told her that he'd developed a watering of the eyes that must have been some kind of cold or other. He'd woken up with it in the morning and it had persisted until the afternoon: it was a new experience, he'd told her, adding that he'd never had a day's illness or discomfort in his life.

'I think I need glasses,' he said now, and as she passed into the cloak-room she imagined him in glasses, repairing the roads, as he was em-ployed to do by the County Council. You hardly ever saw a road-mender with glasses, she reflected, and she wondered if all the dust that was inherent in his work had perhaps affected his eyes.

'How're you, Bridie?' a girl called Eenie Mackie said in the cloakroom, a girl who'd left the Presentation Nuns only a year ago.

'That's a lovely dress, Eenie,' Bridie said. 'Is it nylon, that?'

'Tricel actually. Drip-dry.'

Bridie took off her coat and hung it on a hook. There was a small wash-basin in the cloakroom above which hung a discoloured oval mirror. Used tissues and pieces of cotton-wool, cigarette-butts and matches covered the concrete floor. Lengths of green-painted timber partitioned off a lavatory in a corner.

'Jeez, you're looking great, Bridie,' Madge Dowding remarked, waiting for her turn at the mirror. She moved towards it as she spoke, taking off a pair of spectacles before endeavouring to apply make-up to the lashes of her eye. She stared myopically into the oval mirror, humming while the other girls became restive.

'Will you hurry up, for God's sake!' shouted Eenie Mackie. 'We're standing here all night, Madge.'

Madge Dowding was the only one who was older than Bridie. She was thirty-nine, although often she said she was younger. The girls sniggered about that, saying that Madge Dowding should accept her condition— her age and her squint and her poor complexion—and not make herself ridiculous going out after men. What man would be bothered with the like of her anyway? Madge Dowding would do better to give herself over to do Saturday-night work for the Legion of Mary: wasn't Canon O'Connell always looking for aid?

'Is that fellow there?' she asked now, moving away from the mirror. 'The guy with the long arms. Did anyone see him outside?'

'He's dancing with Cat Bolger,' one of the girls replied. 'She has herself glued to him.'

'Lover boy,' remarked Patty Byrne, and everyone laughed because the person referred to was hardly a boy any more, being over fifty it was said, a bachelor who came only occasionally to the dance-hall.

Madge Dowding left the cloakroom rapidly, not bothering to pretend she wasn't anxious about the conjunction of Cat Bolger and the man with the long arms. Two sharp spots of red had come into her cheeks, and when she stumbled in her haste the girls in the cloakroom laughed. A younger girl would have pretended to be casual.

Bridie chatted, waiting for the mirror. Some girls, not wishing to be delayed, used the mirrors of their compacts. Then in twos and threes, occasionally singly, they left the cloakroom and took their places on upright wooden chairs at one end of the dance-hall, waiting to be asked to dance. Mr Maloney, Mr Swanton and Dano Ryan played 'Harvest Moon' and 'I Wonder Who's Kissing Her Now' and 'I'll Be Around'.

Bridie danced. Her father would be falling asleep by the fire; the wireless, tuned in to Radio Eireann, would be murmuring in the background. Already he'd have listened to *Faith and Order* and *Spot the Talent.* His Wild West novel, *Three Rode Fast* by Jake Matall, would have dropped from his single knee on to the flagged floor. He would wake with a jerk as he did every night and, forgetting what night it was, might be surprised not to see her, for usually she was sitting there at the table, mending clothes or washing eggs. 'Is it time for the News?' he'd automatically say.

Dust and cigarette smoke formed a haze beneath the crystal bowl, feet thudded, girls shrieked and laughed, some of them dancing together for want of a male partner. The music was loud, the musicians had taken off their jackets. Vigorously they played a number of tunes from *State Fair* and then, more romantically, 'Just One of Those Things'. The tempo increased for a Paul Jones, after which Bridie found herself with a youth who told her he was saving up to emigrate, the nation in his opinion being finished. 'I'm up in the hills with the uncle,' he said, 'labouring fourteen hours a day. Is it any life for a young fellow?' She knew his uncle, a hill farmer whose stony acres were separated from her father's by one other farm only. 'He has me gutted with work,' the youth told her. 'Is there sense in it at all, Bridie?'

At ten o'clock there was a stir, occasioned by the arrival of three middle-aged bachelors who'd cycled over from Carey's public house. They shouted and whistled, greeting other people across the dancing area. They smelt of stout and sweat and whiskey.

Every Saturday at just this time they arrived, and, having sold them their tickets, Mr Dwyer folded up his card-table and locked the tin box that held the evening's takings: his ballroom was complete.

'How're you, Bridie?' one of the bachelors, known as Bowser Egan, inquired. Another one, Tim Daly, asked Patty Byrne how she was. 'Will we take the floor?' Eyes Horgan suggested to Madge Dowding, already pressing the front of his navy-blue suit against the net of her dress. Bridie danced with Bowser Egan, who said she was looking great.

The bachelors would never marry, the girls of the dance-hall considered: they were wedded already, to stout and whiskey and laziness, to three old mothers somewhere up in the hills. The man with the long arms didn't drink but he was the same in all other ways: he had the same look of a bachelor, a quality in his face.

'Great,' Bowser Egan said, feather-stepping in an inaccurate and inebriated manner. 'You're a great little dancer, Bridie.'

'Will you lay off that!' cried Madge Dowding, her voice shrill above the sound of the music. Eyes Horgan had slipped two fingers into the back of her dress and was now pretending they'd got there by accident. He smiled blearily, his huge red face streaming with perspiration, the eyes which gave him his nickname protuberant and bloodshot.

'Watch your step with that one,' Bowser Egan called out, laughing so that spittle sprayed on to Bridie's face. Eenie Mackie, who was also dancing near the incident, laughed also and winked at Bridie. Dano Ryan left his drums and sang. 'Oh, how I miss your gentle kiss,' he crooned, 'and long to hold you tight.'

Nobody knew the name of the man with the long arms. The only words he'd ever been known to speak in the Ballroom of Romance were the words that formed his invitation to dance. He was a shy man who stood alone when he wasn't performing on the dance-floor. He rode away on his bicycle afterwards, not saying good night to anyone.

'Cat has your man leppin' tonight,' Tim Daly remarked to Patty Byrne, for the liveliness that Cat Bolger had introduced into foxtrot and waltz was noticeable.

'I think of you only,' sang Dano Ryan. 'Only wishing, wishing you were by my side.'

Dano Ryan would have done, Bridie often thought, because he was a different kind of bachelor: he had a lonely look about him, as if he'd become tired of being on his own. Every week she thought he would have done, and during the week her mind regularly returned to that thought. Dano Ryan would have done because she felt he wouldn't mind coming to live in the farmhouse while her one-legged father was still about the place. Three could live as cheaply as two where Dano Ryan was concerned because giving up the wages he earned as a road-worker would be balanced by the saving made on what he paid for lodgings. Once, at the end of an evening, she'd pretended that there was a puncture in the back wheel of her bicycle and he'd concerned himself with it while Mr Maloney and Mr Swanton waited for him in Mr Maloney's car. He'd blown the tyre up with the car pump and had said he thought it would hold.

It was well known in the dance-hall that she fancied her chances with Dano Ryan. But it was well known also that Dano Ryan had got into a set way of life and had remained in it for quite some years. He lodged with a widow called Mrs Griffin and Mrs Griffin's mentally affected son, in a cottage on the outskirts of the town. He was said to be good to the affected child, buying him sweets and taking him out for rides on the cross-bar of his bicycle. He gave an hour or two of his time every week to the Church of Our Lady Queen of Heaven, and he was loyal to Mr Dwyer. He performed in the two other rural dance-halls that Mr Dwyer owned, rejecting advances from the town's more sophisticated dance-hall, even though it was more conveniently situated for him and the fee was more substantial than that paid by Mr Dwyer. But Mr Dwyer had discovered Dano Ryan and Dano had not forgotten it, just as Mr Maloney and Mr Swanton had not forgotten their discovery by Mr Dwyer either.

'Would we take a lemonade?' Bowser Egan suggested. 'And a packet of biscuits, Bridie?'

No alcoholic liquor was ever served in the Ballroom of Romance, the premises not being licensed for this added stimulant. Mr Dwyer in fact had never sought a licence for any of his premises, knowing that romance and alcohol were difficult commodities to mix, especially in a dignified ballroom. Behind where the girls sat on the wooden chairs Mr Dwyer's wife, a small stout woman, served the bottles of lemonade, with straws, and the biscuits and the crisps. She talked busily while doing so, mainly about the turkeys she kept. She'd once told Bridie that she thought of them as children.

'Thanks,' Bridie said, and Bowser Egan led her to the trestle table. Soon it would be the intermission: soon the three members of the band would cross the floor also for refreshment. She thought up questions to ask Dano Ryan.

When first she'd danced in the Ballroom of Romance, when she was just sixteen, Dano Ryan had been there also, four years older than she was, playing the drums for Mr Maloney as he played them now. She'd hardly noticed him then because of his not being one of the dancers: he was part of the ballroom's scenery, like the trestle table and the lemonade bottles, and Mrs Dwyer and Mr Dwyer. The youths who'd danced with her then in their Saturday-night blue suits had later disappeared into the town, or to Dublin or Britain, leaving behind them those who became the middle-aged bachelors of the hills. There'd been a boy called Patrick Grady whom she had loved in those days. Week after week she'd ridden away from the Ballroom of Romance with the image of his face in her mind, a thin face, pale beneath black hair. It had been different, dancing with Patrick Grady, and she'd felt that he found it different dancing with her, although he'd never said so. At night she'd dreamed of him and in the daytime too, while she helped her mother in the kitchen or her father with the cows. Week by week she'd returned to the ballroom, smiling on its pink façade and dancing then in the arms of Patrick Grady. Often they'd stood together drinking lemonade, not saying anything, not knowing what to say. She knew he loved her, and she believed then that he would lead her one day from the dim, romantic ballroom, from its blueness and its pinkness and its crystal bowl of light and its music. She believed he would lead her into sunshine, to the town and the Church of Our Lady Queen of Heaven, to marriage and smiling faces. But someone else had got Patrick Grady, a girl from the town who'd never danced in the wayside ballroom. She'd scooped up Patrick Grady when he didn't have a chance.

Bridie had wept, hearing that. By night she'd lain in her bed in the farmhouse, quietly crying, the tears rolling into her hair and making the pillow damp. When she woke in the early morning the thought was still naggingly with her and it remained with her by day, replacing her daytime dreams of happiness. Someone told her later on that he'd crossed to Britain, to Wolverhampton, with the girl he'd married, and she imagined him there, in a place she wasn't able properly to visualize, labouring in a factory, his children being born and acquiring the accent of the area. The Ballroom of Romance wasn't the same without him, and when no one else stood out for her particularly over the years and when no one offered her marriage, she found herself wondering about Dano Ryan. If you couldn't have love, the next best thing was surely a decent man.

Bowser Egan hardly fell into that category, nor did Tim Daly. And it was plain to everyone that Cat Bolger and Madge Dowding were wasting their time over the man with the long arms. Madge Dowding was already a figure of fun in the ballroom, the way she ran after the bachelors; Cat Bolger would end up the same if she wasn't careful. One way or another it wasn't difficult to be a figure of fun in the ballroom, and you didn't have to be as old as Madge Dowding: a girl who'd just left the Presentation Nuns had once asked Eyes Horgan what he had in his trouser pocket and he told her it was a penknife. She'd repeated this afterwards in the cloakroom, how she'd requested Eyes Horgan not to dance so close to her because his penknife was sticking into her. 'Jeez, aren't you the right baby!' Patty Byrne had shouted delightedly: everyone had laughed, knowing that Eyes Horgan only came to the ballroom for stuff like that. He was no use to any girl.

'Two lemonades, Mrs Dwyer,' Bowser Egan said, 'and two packets of Kerry Creams. Is Kerry Creams all right, Bridie?'

She nodded, smiling. Kerry Creams would be fine, she said.

'Well, Bridie, isn't that the great outfit you have!' Mrs Dwyer remarked. 'Doesn't the red suit her, Bowser?'

By the swing-doors stood Mr Dwyer, smoking a cigarette that he held cupped in his left hand. His small eyes noted all developments. He had been aware of Madge Dowding's anxiety when Eyes Horgan had inserted two fingers into the back opening of her dress. He had looked away, not caring for the incident, but had it developed further he would have spoken to Eyes Horgan, as he had on other occasions. Some of the younger lads didn't know any better and would dance very close to their partners, who generally were too embarrassed to do anything about it, being young themselves. But that, in Mr Dwyer's opinion, was a different kettle of fish altogether because they were decent young lads who'd in no time at all be doing a steady line with a girl and would end up as he had himself with Mrs Dwyer, in the same house with her, sleeping in a bed with her, firmly married. It was the middle-aged bachelors who required the watching: they came down from the hills like mountain goats, released from their mammies and from the smell of animals and soil. Mr Dwyer continued to watch Eyes Horgan, wondering how drunk he was.

Dano Ryan's song came to an end, Mr Swanton laid down his clarinet, Mr Maloney rose from the piano. Dano Ryan wiped sweat from his face and the three men slowly moved towards Mrs Dwyer's trestle table.

'Jeez, you have powerful legs,' Eyes Horgan whispered to Madge Dowding, but Madge Dowding's attention was on the man with the long arms, who had left Cat Bolger's side and was proceeding in the direction of the men's lavatory. He never took refreshments. She moved, herself, towards the men's lavatory, to take up a position outside it, but Eyes Horgan followed her. 'Would you take a lemonade, Madge?' he asked. He had a small bottle of whiskey on him: if they went into a corner they could add a drop of it to the lemonade. She didn't drink spirits, she reminded him, and he went away.

'Excuse me a minute,' Bowser Egan said, putting down his bottle of lemonade. He crossed the floor to the lavatory. He too, Bridie knew, would have a small bottle of whiskey on him. She watched while Dano

Ryan, listening to a story Mr Maloney was telling, paused in the centre of the ballroom, his head bent to hear what was being said. He was a big man, heavily made, with black hair that was slightly touched with grey, and big hands. He laughed when Mr Maloney came to the end of his story and then bent his head again, in order to listen to a story told by Mr Swanton.

'Are you on your own, Bridie?' Cat Bolger asked, and Bridie said she was waiting for Bowser Egan. 'I think I'll have a lemonade,' Cat Bolger said.

Younger boys and girls stood with their arms still around one another, queueing up for refreshments. Boys who hadn't danced at all, being nervous because they didn't know any steps, stood in groups, smoking and making jokes. Girls who hadn't been danced with yet talked to one another, their eyes wandering. Some of them sucked at straws in lemonade bottles.

Bridie, still watching Dano Ryan, imagined him wearing the glasses he'd referred to, sitting in the farmhouse kitchen, reading one of her father's Wild West novels. She imagined the three of them eating a meal she'd prepared, fried eggs and rashers and fried potato-cakes and tea and bread and butter and jam, brown bread and soda and shop bread. She imagined Dano Ryan leaving the kitchen in the morning to go out to the fields in order to weed the mangolds, and her father hobbling off behind him, and the two men working together. She saw hay being cut, Dano Ryan with the scythe that she'd learned to use herself, her father using a rake as best he could. She saw herself, because of the extra help, being able to attend to things in the farmhouse, things she'd never had time for because of the cows and the hens and the fields. There were bedroom curtains that needed repairing where the net had ripped, and wallpaper that had become loose and needed to be stuck up with flour paste. The scullery required whitewashing.

The night he'd blown up the tyre of her bicycle she'd thought he was going to kiss her. He'd crouched on the ground in the darkness with his ear to the tyre, listening for escaping air. When he could hear none he'd straightened up and said he thought she'd be all right on the bicycle. His face had been quite close to hers and she'd smiled at him. At that moment, unfortunately, Mr Maloney had blown an impatient blast on the horn of his motor-car.

Often she'd been kissed by Bowser Egan, on the nights when he insisted on riding part of the way home with her. They had to dismount in order to push their bicycles up a hill and the first time he'd accompanied her he'd contrived to fall against her, steadying himself by putting a hand on her shoulder. The next thing she was aware of was the moist quality of his lips and the sound of his bicycle as it clattered noisily on the road. He'd suggested then, regaining his breath, that they should go into a field.

That was nine years ago. In the intervening passage of time she'd been kissed as well, in similar circumstances, by Eyes Horgan and Tim Daly. She'd gone into fields with them and permitted them to put their arms about her while heavily they breathed. At one time or another she had imagined marriage with one or other of them, seeing them in the farmhouse with her father, even though the fantasies were unlikely.

Bridie stood with Cat Bolger, knowing that it would be some time before Bowser Egan came out of the lavatory. Mr Maloney, Mr Swanton and Dano Ryan approached, Mr Maloney insisting that he would fetch three bottles of lemonade from the trestle table.

'You sang the last one beautifully,' Bridie said to Dano Ryan. 'Isn't it a beautiful song?'

Mr Swanton said it was the finest song ever written, and Cat Bolger said she preferred 'Danny Boy', which in her opinion was the finest song ever written.

'Take a suck of that,' said Mr Maloney, handing Dano Ryan and Mr Swanton bottles of lemonade. 'How's Bridie tonight? Is your father well, Bridie?'

Her father was all right, she said.

'I hear they're starting a cement factory,' said Mr Maloney. 'Did anyone hear talk of that? They're after striking some commodity in the earth that makes good cement. Ten feet down, over at Kilmalough.'

'It'll bring employment,' said Mr Swanton. 'It's employment that's necessary in this area.'

'Canon O'Connell was on about it,' Mr Maloney said. 'There's Yankee money involved.'

'Will the Yanks come over?' inquired Cat Bolger. 'Will they run it themselves, Mr Maloney?'

Mr Maloney, intent on his lemonade, didn't hear the questions and Cat Bolger didn't repeat them.

'There's stuff called Optrex,' Bridie said quietly to Dano Ryan, 'that

my father took the time he had a cold in his eyes. Maybe Optrex would
settle the watering, Dano.'

'Ah sure, it doesn't worry me that much—'

'It's terrible, anything wrong with the eyes. You wouldn't want to take
a chance. You'd get Optrex in a chemist, Dano, and a little bowl with it
so that you can bathe the eyes.'

Her father's eyes had become red-rimmed and unsightly to look at.
She'd gone into Riordan's Medical Hall in the town and had explained
what the trouble was, and Mr Riordan had recommended Optrex. She
told this to Dano Ryan, adding that her father had had no trouble with
his eyes since. Dano Ryan nodded.

'Did you hear that, Mrs Dwyer?' Mr Maloney called out. 'A cement
factory for Kilmalough.'

Mrs Dwyer wagged her head, placing empty bottles in a crate. She'd
heard references to the cement factory, she said: it was the best news for a
long time.

'Kilmalough'll never know itself,' her husband commented, joining her
in her task with the empty lemonade bottles.

' 'Twill bring prosperity certainly,' said Mr Swanton. 'I was saying just
there, Justin, that employment's what's necessary.'

'Sure, won't the Yanks—' began Cat Bolger, but Mr Maloney interrupted her.

'The Yanks'll be in at the top, Cat, or maybe not here at all—maybe
only inserting money into it. It'll be local labour entirely.'

'You'll not marry a Yank, Cat,' said Mr Swanton, loudly laughing.
'You can't catch those fellows.'

'Haven't you plenty of homemade bachelors?' suggested Mr Maloney.
He laughed also, throwing away the straw he was sucking through and
tipping the bottle into his mouth. Cat Bolger told him to get on with
himself. She moved towards the men's lavatory and took up a position
outside it, not speaking to Madge Dowding, who was still standing there.

'Keep a watch on Eyes Horgan,' Mrs Dwyer warned her husband,
which was advice she gave him at this time every Saturday night, knowing that Eyes Horgan was drinking in the lavatory. When he was drunk
Eyes Horgan was the most difficult of the bachelors.

'I have a drop of it left, Dano,' Bridie said quietly. 'I could bring it
over on Saturday. The eye stuff.'

'Ah, don't worry yourself, Bridie—'

'No trouble at all. Honestly now—'

'Mrs Griffin has me fixed up for a test with Dr Cready. The old eyes are no worry, only when I'm reading the paper or at the pictures. Mrs Griffin says I'm only straining them due to lack of glasses.'

He looked away while he said that, and she knew at once that Mrs Griffin was arranging to marry him. She felt it instinctively: Mrs Griffin was going to marry him because she was afraid that if he moved away from her cottage, to get married to someone else, she'd find it hard to replace him with another lodger who'd be good to her affected son. He'd become a father to Mrs Griffin's affected son, to whom already he was kind. It was a natural outcome, for Mrs Griffin had all the chances, seeing him every night and morning and not having to make do with weekly encounters in a ballroom.

She thought of Patrick Grady, seeing in her mind his pale, thin face. She might be the mother of four of his children now, or seven or eight maybe. She might be living in Wolverhampton, going out to the pictures in the evenings, instead of looking after a one-legged man. If the weight of circumstances hadn't intervened she wouldn't be standing in a wayside ballroom, mourning the marriage of a road-mender she didn't love. For a moment she thought she might cry, standing there thinking of Patrick Grady in Wolverhampton. In her life, on the farm and in the house, there was no place for tears. Tears were a luxury, like flowers would be in the fields where the mangolds grew, or fresh whitewash in the scullery. It wouldn't have been fair ever to have wept in the kitchen while her father sat listening to *Spot the Talent:* her father had more right to weep, having lost a leg. He suffered in a greater way, yet he remained kind and concerned for her.

In the Ballroom of Romance she felt behind her eyes the tears that it would have been improper to release in the presence of her father. She wanted to let them go, to feel them streaming on her cheeks, to receive the sympathy of Dano Ryan and of everyone else. She wanted them all to listen to her while she told them about Patrick Grady who was now in Wolverhampton and about the death of her mother and her own life since. She wanted Dano Ryan to put his arm around her so that she could lean her head against it. She wanted him to look at her in his decent way and to stroke with his road-mender's fingers the backs of her hands. She might wake in a bed with him and imagine for a moment that he was Patrick Grady. She might bathe his eyes and pretend.

'Back to business,' said Mr Maloney, leading his band across the floor to their instruments.

'Tell your father I was asking for him,' Dano Ryan said. She smiled and she promised, as though nothing had happened, that she would tell her father that.

She danced with Tim Daly and then again with the youth who'd said he intended to emigrate. She saw Madge Dowding moving swiftly towards the man with the long arms as he came out of the lavatory, moving faster than Cat Bolger. Eyes Horgan approached Cat Bolger. Dancing with her, he spoke earnestly, attempting to persuade her to permit him to ride part of the way home with her. He was unaware of the jealousy that was coming from her as she watched Madge Dowding holding close to her the man with the long arms while they performed a quickstep. Cat Bolger was in her thirties too.

'Get away out of that,' said Bowser Egan, cutting in on the youth who was dancing with Bridie. 'Go home to your mammy, boy.' He took her into his arms, saying again that she was looking great tonight. 'Did you hear about the cement factory?' he said. 'Isn't it great for Kilmalough?'

She agreed. She said what Mr Swanton and Mr Maloney had said: that the cement factory would bring employment to the neighbourhood.

'Will I ride home with you a bit, Bridie?' Bowser Egan suggested, and she pretended not to hear him. 'Aren't you my girl, Bridie, and always have been?' he said, a statement that made no sense at all.

His voice went on whispering at her, saying he would marry her tomorrow only his mother wouldn't permit another woman in the house. She knew what it was like herself, he reminded her, having a parent to look after: you couldn't leave them to rot, you had to honour your father and your mother.

She danced to 'The Bells Are Ringing', moving her legs in time with Bowser Egan's while over his shoulder she watched Dano Ryan softly striking one of his smaller drums. Mrs Griffin had got him even though she was nearly fifty, with no looks at all, a lumpish woman with lumpish legs and arms. Mrs Griffin had got him just as the girl had got Patrick Grady.

The music ceased, Bowser Egan held her hard against him, trying to touch her face with his. Around them, people whistled and clapped: the evening had come to an end. She walked away from Bowser Egan, knowing that not ever again would she dance in the Ballroom of Romance.

She'd been a figure of fun, trying to promote a relationship with a middle-aged County Council labourer, as ridiculous as Madge Dowding dancing on beyond her time.

'I'm waiting outside for you, Cat,' Eyes Horgan called out, lighting a cigarette as he made for the swing-doors.

Already the man with the long arms—made long, so they said, from carrying rocks off his land—had left the ballroom. Others were moving briskly. Mr Dwyer was tidying the chairs.

In the cloakroom the girls put on their coats and said they'd see one another at Mass the next day. Madge Dowding hurried. 'Are you O.K., Bridie?' Patty Byrne asked and Bridie said she was. She smiled at little Patty Byrne, wondering if a day would come for the younger girl also, if one day she'd decide that she was a figure of fun in a wayside ballroom.

'Good night so,' Bridie said, leaving the cloakroom, and the girls who were still chatting there wished her good night. Outside the cloakroom she paused for a moment. Mr Dwyer was still tidying the chairs, picking up empty lemonade bottles from the floor, setting the chairs in a neat row. His wife was sweeping the floor. 'Good night, Bridie,' Mr Dwyer said. 'Good night, Bridie,' his wife said.

Extra lights had been switched on so that the Dwyers could see what they were doing. In the glare the blue walls of the ballroom seemed tatty, marked with hair-oil where men had leaned against them, inscribed with names and initials and hearts with arrows through them. The crystal bowl gave out a light that was ineffective in the glare; the bowl was broken here and there, which wasn't noticeable when the other lights weren't on.

'Good night so,' Bridie said to the Dwyers. She passed through the swing-doors and descended the three concrete steps on the gravel expanse in front of the ballroom. People were gathered on the gravel, talking in groups, standing with their bicycles. She saw Madge Dowding going off with Tim Daly. A youth rode away with a girl on the cross-bar of his bicycle. The engines of motor-cars started.

'Good night, Bridie,' Dano Ryan said.

'Good night, Dano,' she said.

She walked across the gravel towards her bicycle, hearing Mr Maloney, somewhere behind her, repeating that no matter how you looked at it the cement factory would be a great thing for Kilmalough. She heard the bang of a car-door and knew it was Mr Swanton banging the door of

Mr Maloney's car because he always gave it the same loud bang. Two other doors banged as she reached her bicycle and then the engine started up and the headlights went on. She touched the two tyres of the bicycle to make certain she hadn't a puncture. The wheels of Mr Maloney's car traversed the gravel and were silent when they reached the road.

'Good night, Bridie,' someone called, and she replied, pushing her bicycle towards the road.

'Will I ride a little way with you?' Bowser Egan asked.

They rode together and when they arrived at the hill for which it was necessary to dismount she looked back and saw in the distance the four coloured bulbs that decorated the façade of the Ballroom of Romance. As she watched the lights went out, and she imagined Mr Dwyer pulling the metal grid across the front of his property and locking the two padlocks that secured it. His wife would be waiting with the evening's takings, sitting in the front of their car.

'D'you know what it is, Bridie,' said Bowser Egan, 'you were never looking better than tonight.' He took from a pocket of his suit the small bottle of whiskey he had. He uncorked it and drank some and then handed it to her. She took it and drank. 'Sure, why wouldn't you?' he said, surprised to see her drinking because she never had in his company before. It was an unpleasant taste, she considered, a taste she'd experienced only twice before, when she'd taken whiskey as a remedy for toothache. 'What harm would it do you?' Bowser Egan said as she raised the bottle again to her lips. He reached out a hand for it, though, suddenly concerned lest she should consume a greater share than he wished her to.

She watched him drinking more expertly than she had. He would always be drinking, she thought. He'd be lazy and useless, sitting in the kitchen with the *Irish Press*. He'd waste money buying a second-hand motor-car in order to drive into the town to go to the public houses on fair-days.

'She's shook these days,' he said, referring to his mother. 'She'll hardly last two years, I'm thinking.' He threw the empty whiskey bottle into the ditch and lit a cigarette. They pushed their bicycles. He said:

'When she goes, Bridie, I'll sell the bloody place up. I'll sell the pigs and the whole damn one and twopence worth.' He paused in order to raise the cigarette to his lips. He drew in smoke and exhaled it. 'With the cash that I'll get I could improve some place else, Bridie.'

They reached a gate on the left-hand side of the road and automatically they pushed their bicycles towards it and leaned them against it. He climbed over the gate into the field and she climbed after him. 'Will we sit down here, Bridie?' he said, offering the suggestion as one that had just occurred to him, as though they'd entered the field for some other purpose.

'We could improve a place like your own one,' he said, putting his right arm around her shoulders. 'Have you a kiss in you, Bridie?' He kissed her, exerting pressure with his teeth. When his mother died he would sell his farm and spend the money in the town. After that he would think of getting married because he'd have nowhere to go, because he'd want a fire to sit at and a woman to cook food for him. He kissed her again, his lips hot, the sweat on his cheeks sticking to her. 'God, you're great at kissing,' he said.

She rose, saying it was time to go, and they climbed over the gate again. 'There's nothing like a Saturday,' he said. 'Good night to you so, Bridie.'

He mounted his bicycle and rode down the hill, and she pushed hers to the top and then mounted it also. She rode through the night as on Saturday nights for years she had ridden and never would ride again because she'd reached a certain age. She would wait now and in time Bowser Egan would seek her out because his mother would have died. Her father would probably have died also by then. She would marry Bowser Egan because it would be lonesome being by herself in the farmhouse.

A Day in the Country

DAN JACOBSON
(South African, 1929–   )

We had spent the day on the farm, as we usually did every Sunday. Rather a dull day it had been, I remember, in April, too cold to go swimming in the river, and there had been nothing much else to do except sit in the car and watch my father as he helped the boys round up the cattle driven down from the veld, and then walk through them, stick in hand, prodding their sides, stopping to discuss at length what to do about the heifer who was going blind in one eye, or what a pity it was that this miserable beast should be in calf again when what it needed was a long rest. My father could spend hours like that, perfectly happy among the slow red cows and oxen, with the African herd boy who knew each head of cattle as an individual and respected it as such. And my father prodded, leaned against his stick, screwed his face up against the sun, listened to the herd boy's comments, and twisted his ankle on one of the rocks that littered the piece of veld where the cattle were gathered.

When he ricked his ankle, my father had had enough. He got back into the car and we set off home, with the herd-boy's children riding with us on the back bumper, as far as the gate. At the gate they climbed off and opened it for us; we passed through, they waved, and we waved back. Now there was just the thirty-mile run home, through Rietpan, by-passing Dors River, meeting the tarred road to take us to the Boer War Memorial—and so home. My brother was driving, my father and mother sat in front with him, and my sister and I were in the back seat. The first stretch of road was really bad, not a road at all, but a cart-track across

Rietpan Commonage, a piece of veld that had been grazed to complete nudity by the donkeys of the villagers. A few donkeys, a cow or two, one or two goats: those were generally the sole possessions of the Rietpan villagers, that and a mud-walled house and five irrigated acres. But though Rietpan was poor, it had its location, even poorer, where the black-skinned inhabitants of the village lived. They were conducting some sort of religious rite as we passed the location, and a man held up a cross of plaited twigs towards us. He was wearing a blue cowl on his head. The wind blew all their clothes in bright fluttering rags as they walked behind the leader. The sun shone bare upon them through the wind.

Inside the car it was dull and dusty, with the Sunday newspapers in a mess on the floor. My sister was knitting. We passed through Rietpan quickly, in a cloud of dust, with a greeting for Major le Roy on his front stoep and a pause to give way for someone's sheep. The road between Rietpan and Dors River was better, and my brother increased his speed.

My father looked up from the comic he was reading. He read it with an air of absolute puzzlement: "Who reads these things?" he asked. Then: "Oh, oh, oh, boy, slow down." He placed a hand on my brother's arm. There was a car standing in the middle of the road, and a group of people at the side of the road, looking down at something.

We thought it was an accident. It looked like an accident. We prepared ourselves for something horrible and warily our car crept up to the other, then drove past it and stopped.

"What is it?" my sister said shrilly.

"I don't know." We couldn't see. The other car was blocking our view of what the little group was seeing. Our car went forward a few feet. Dear God, it was an accident. The group stood over a little African child, a group of white men and women. A few Africans stood a little way off, looking at what was going on, and saying nothing. The white people were talking to one another. They seemed quite unmoved, almost light-hearted, but the black child lay still on the ground. I could see its spindly legs like winter branches of a tree, lying still on the ground.

"What is it?" my father called out through the window of the car, and as he did so, one of the white men stooped and picked the child up. The black legs kicked wildly, and a shriek went up from the child. I saw one of the Africans take a pace forward, then fall back. The group turned to their car, one man still carrying the child. And then I saw a strange thing. They were laughing, all of them were laughing. The child still screamed and kicked, and then writhed over in the man's arms, away from the motor-car, butting its head into the broad grey-shirted chest, as a child turns into its mother's arms for protection. We saw white face after face, all bared in smiles, and their laughter surrounded the thin screams of the child, until one could no longer believe that what one heard was truly a scream of fear.

"What is it?" my father called again. But no one took any notice. One of the men ran forward and opened the bonnet of the car. We heard him say in Afrikaans, "Come on, put him in," and the child screamed again, awfully.

But we knew now. It wasn't an accident, it was a game. I don't know whether we felt more relief or disgust. One of the grinning men saw us watching them, and still with his grin, he waved to us that we could go on. They didn't need our help; it wasn't an accident. None of us grinned back at him. I think he saw that we weren't amused at his game for he looked away.

"For God's sake let's go."

"I've had enough of this."

My brother started the car. As we drove off I said, "What dirty swine." I looked through the back window of the car. They had put the child back on the road, one of the men was standing half-way in his car, the bonnet was down. Apparently the game was breaking up. We hoped that it was our condemnation that had broken it up. Yet there was the taste of guilt in each of our mouths that we had just looked our condemnation and not said anything to them, not made a protest in the name of humanity. But we were used to that sort of scene and that sort of guilt. Together they almost make up a way of life.

We had driven on only a short distance when with a roar of wind and a cloud of dust the car passed us. As it whipped past, one of the men in it leaned his head, half his body, out of the window, and shouted something at us. None of us heard what he was shouting, it was lost in the wind and the dust. All we saw was a white shirt and a white face and a pair of bright red lips opening and closing grotesquely.

Now you don't shout insults at my father. My brother and I swore ineffectually at the billows of dust which followed their car, but my father, in a moment, was trembling with rage.

"Chase them," he shouted.

"Don't be mad," my brother said.

"Then stop the car."

"Why? What for."

"I'll show you why. Stop the car." My brother didn't, so my father leaned over and switched off the ignition key.

My brother lost his temper as the car slowed down and stopped. "All right, take your bloody car," he said and got out and came in the back, slamming the door behind him.

"Michael, what are you going to do?" my mother asked.

My brother and I were both yelling at my father to leave it, cut it out, forget the whole business and he was saying, "No one shouts at me like that. No one shouts at me like that," as we tore along the road. We could see the other car ahead of us, still raising dust. But we were catching up with it. Soon we were in the car's cloud of dust. Small stones struck against the windshield, and we could see very little through the grey murk.

"Michael, you're going to have an accident."

"I'm not going to have an accident."

"For God's sake, Dad, let's not have a scene."

"What do you mean let's not have a scene, when they shout at me like that?"

"You don't even know what he shouted."

"I know well enough what he shouted."

"What did he shout?"

"No one shouts at me like that."

We came to the crossroads of the main road to Lyndhurst and the Rietpan-Dors River road. The front car went towards Dors River, so we went that way too, still at a dangerously high speed.

"Michael, you're going to have an accident."

Dors River was about us. J. Wassenaar *Algemene Handelaar*/General Dealer. There was the station. The road passed J. Wassenaar and then turned round a corner, the hotel, the Savoy, with two petrol-pumps in front of it. Then there was a house, another, a piece of veld, two more houses, and a last shop. In front of the last shop stood the black Dodge we had been chasing. The people were climbing out of it. One of them, the man in the white shirt, the one who had shouted, saw us coming and stood looking at us with his mouth open.

Again we drew level with the car. Inside our car, everyone with the exception of my father, was dreading the scene that we knew was about to follow.

We stopped. My father said: "How dare you shout at me like that."

Now they were all out of their car. There were six of them, three men and three women. They stood at various points round their car, looking at us.

The young man in the grey shirt said, "What's the matter with you?" He was big and dirty, the one who had been carrying the child. He wore a broad-brimmed hat on the back of his head, and it made his face look round and flabby, under the circling rim of his hat. But he was big and strong, with enormous bare arms folded on his chest. I knew that if it did come to a fight he would be the one to give us the most trouble, and the one who would probably beat us at that. He walked over to our car, arms still folded, contemptuously, and said again: "What's the matter with you?"

But he was speaking English. Was that already a victory for us? He was speaking our language, we weren't speaking his. But he was big, much bigger than any of us as he stood at the driver's window of the car and said: "What's the matter with you?"

My father suddenly blazed out at him. "What sort of a person are you? First you torture a child that's done nothing to you, and then you scream at someone you're passing on the road. Well, let me tell you that I'm not a little Kaffir piccanin. You can't do what you like with me. I'll teach you manners before I'm finished with you."

The man said, "How?" He added: "You're too old." And it was true, pitifully true, my father was too old to fight him. He could have killed the old man.

This was the cue for my brother and myself. We climbed out of the car and walked round. The big man wheeled to face us. I saw his muscles tighten under the hair of his arms and I knew that if we were to win this argument it wouldn't be by force. But we stared at each other as though we weren't frightened. He probably wasn't.

My father said: "You people make me sick. You've got no idea how to behave. But if you think you can go round bullying everybody like you bully that Kaffir child you're mistaken." He opened the door of the car as though to come out, and quickly the man darted at it, to slam it on him. With me a little way behind him my brother moved towards the man. My brother said: "No you don't." He was panting as he spoke, as though he had been running in a race.

Now, if there was to be a fight, it would be now. But there was no fight, and I did not understand why, as the old man, apparently the father of the two younger ones, came up and said, "You've got no right to talk like that about my people. We weren't doing anything to the piccanin." He gestured, almost appealingly.

We stared at him. He said again, "You've got no right to talk like that about my people"—and then I realised that our fear—the fear that we would be called "Bloody Jews", the fear which perhaps had kept our mouths closed when we had seen the piccanin being tortured—was his fear too. He, the Afrikaner who spoke English to us, felt that my father was sitting in his car and despising him for the race he belonged to, and judging him and his race by what we had seen on the road; and I realised, how happily, that the father did not want to be judged by that act, and did not want his son to fight us, for even if we should fight and his son should beat us, our original and damning judgment would remain, would even be confirmed. He didn't want to beat us, he wanted us to think well of his race, and how could he do that while the piccanin screamed with terror and kicked helplessly against his son's arms? He stayed his son's arm, and said, "It was only a bit of fun and you had no right to swear at us."

"Swear at you?" my father asked.

"Yes, swear at us," the other son said, coming up. I saw then why his lips were so red. It was lipstick on his mouth. It must have come from the lips of one of the girls who were leaning against the mudguards of the other car, watching the scene. Like his father, this son did not want to fight. He said, "We heard you swearing as you drove off."

"You were the one," my father said, interrupting him. "You were the one who leaned out of the car and shouted." My father looked at him.

He wiped his mouth with his hand. There was another smear of lipstick on his cheek-bone. He said, "I shouted at you to mind your own business."

"But we said nothing to you. We didn't like what you were doing, but we didn't say anything to you."

"You said 'bloody swine'."

"That's simply not true," my father said.

I said nothing.

"I heard you," the man repeated.

"You couldn't have heard it because no one said it."

And despite this foolish wrangling, the tension remained where it had been all along, where it had been when it had looked as though there was to be a physical fight. The unspoken words lay heavily on our tongues: *Dutchmen, Jews.* But they were never used. Racial tensions usually hasten fights, but this time they didn't, for they were too widely shared. Our fear was theirs: it was almost as though we co-operated with one another to keep the significance of the argument hidden, yet never for a moment forgot it. Had we not been Jews, we might have reproved them more strongly for what they did to the piccanin—for kinship in oppression, or fear of oppression, has two sides, one less noble than the other; and had they not been Afrikaners who feared that their reputation was one of brutality, uncouthness and oppression—all of which they had confirmed, they feared—they might simply have fought us off. But we were all prevented from fighting, and prevented from peace.

I remember the father saying, "Do you think we would have done anything to that piccanin? We aren't mad people. It was just a bit of fun among ourselves."

And the younger son, who did not want to fight, spoke earnestly to me. "You see, this little native child ran right across our car, in front of our car, and I had to brake like hell not to knock him over. So we thought we'll give him a lesson he'll remember. It's for his own good too, you know. He'll be a damn sight more careful now. He'll look what's going on before he runs across the road. Perhaps he'll live longer that way." Tentatively he smiled at me.

The father was saying, "You see that boy there, he goes to university. In Pretoria. Already he's in his second-year studies. A university student. Do you think that people like that, university students, gentlemen, educated people, are going to do anything that they'll be ashamed of afterwards? . . ."

I said, "You made a mistake. No one shouted 'bloody swine'." What I said was true, but it was a lie too. In all that squalor it hardly mattered, but I had to add: "But we didn't like what you were doing."

"All right, then I shouldn't have shouted at you from my car. But it was our business what we were doing with that piccanin, especially as we weren't going to hurt him. It was only a bit of sport."

"Not a very nice sport," my mother called out. We seemed to be winning all the way down the line. The big son had moved away and was being ignored by everybody. The other two continued their laboured explanations, struggling for English words to express themselves in. Once the father veered towards an aggressive tone, and then, as though remembering the faces in the car, closed and hostile, with the struggling black body in his son's arms, as guilty as blood, he became defensive again.

So a sort of peace did come, and we got back into the car. No one shook hands with anyone, there had been no reconciliation to warrant that. But no blows had been struck, and no one had called anyone a bloody Dutchman or a bloody Jew, so everything was as well as could be expected. Better really, for us, because we still despised them. We despised that family: it is not our fault they misinterpreted it. And they should have known that we were as frightened of them as they were of us. We left them there, outside their white-washed shop with the house behind it, that looked across the sand road to the railway line and the railway paddock where one chestnut horse was growing thin in transit between two lost farms.

It was a quiet journey home. Everyone was feeling depressed and beaten, though, as I have explained, the victory was ours. But we had all lost, so much, somewhere, farther back, along that dusty road.

Weekend

SHIRLEY HAZZARD
(Australian, 1931–   )

Lilian, on waking, reached up her arm to pull back the curtain from the window above her bed. The cretonne roses, so recently hung that their folds were still awkward and raw-smelling, tinkled back on brass rings, and sunlight fell around the walls in honey-colored warpings. It was like being under water, she thought, bathed in that delicate light; she had forgotten these contradictions of spring in England—chill, dreary evenings like yesterday's, and bright mornings full of early flowers. She pushed the blankets away and knelt up on the bed to look out the small, paned window. The outer air, the garden glittered; the meadows—for they could hardly be called anything less—unfolded beyond, crowned by a glimpse of the village and the fifteenth-century church. All as suitable, as immaculate as the white window sill on which her elbows rested.

But the room was, of course, cold, and she sank back into the bedclothes. During the night, she had wakened several times to hear the wind rattling the windowpanes and had pushed herself further down the bed, trying to warm her shoulders. (The little electric radiator had been taken away during the day to dry the baby's washing and had not been returned.) Going to bed last night, she had actually consoled herself with the prospect of departure—that it would be her last night in the house. And tonight, no doubt, back in London, she would wonder about the weekend, and comfort herself by telephoning Julie and by thinking out the long, loving letter she would write when she got back to New York. The letter, in her mind, was already some paragraphs advanced.

Like some desolating childhood disappointment, she thought, this anxiety to get away when she had so longed to come here—so longed to see them, and to see Julie most of all. Because, even though Ben was her own brother, it was to Julie she felt closer; Julie she had missed more in these two years away. Given only this weekend, Lilian felt the need to precipitate confidences—"Are you happy, is this really what you want?" she had almost asked Julie last night, coming upstairs. Which was nonsense, impertinence; one couldn't ask it, and in any case Julie would have laughed and told Ben afterward ("What ever do you think Lilian said to me?"). Married couples always betrayed their friends that way—probably for something to say, being so much together. And Ben, indifferent, would say: "How perfectly extraordinary," or "I'm not in the least surprised," or "Poor old Lilian."

Lilian's room was in the old part of the house—seventeenth-century, Julie had said. Lilian allowed a century either way, for Julie's imprecision and the exaggeration of the estate agent. She lay approving the uneven walls, the heavy beams of the roof, the sturdy irregularities of the window and door. The only furniture other than her bed was a new chest of drawers, a cane chair, and a small, unsteady table. On this table stood a china lamp and *Poets of the Present*, a frayed volume in which Thomas Hardy was heavily represented. The room—in fact, the whole house—looked bare. They needed so many things, Julie had said—practically everything—but for a while nothing more could be done; buying the house had taken every penny. On Friday, when Lilian arrived, Julie had shown her around, walking through the rooms with her hand in the crook of Lilian's arm, separating apologetically at doorways. (All the rooms were at slightly different levels, and there was a step or two at each entrance—sometimes dropping, dangerously, beyond a closed door.) Julie's shy, artless face, lowered so that strands of silky hair drooped on Lilian's shoulder, had seemed tired, frail. Her sweater and skirt were aged, unheeded. Too much for her, Lilian thought, this house, and the baby, though I'm sure it's lovely. "Lovely," she had repeated later, in the nursery, over a mound of blue blanket. In the hallway, it was Lilian who linked their arms again.

She pushed the bedclothes back once more, and lowered her feet to the cold, glossy floor. And Ben, she thought, shivering and resting her elbow on her knee and her chin on her hand. She found it hard to believe in Ben as Julie's husband, Simon's father, a member (as she supposed he must be) of the community, traveling up to London every morning of the week, and at home seeming settled and domestic, reading the evening paper with the air of one who must not be disturbed. She supposed that in his way he must love Julie, but she couldn't really imagine him intimate with anyone. She thought of him as a source of knowledge rather than experience; a good, though not contemporary mind, a person rather than a man.

"I adore you," Ben said, without opening his eyes, "but why are you up so early?"

Julie, at the mirror, uttered a strangled sound. She took a bobby pin from between her teeth and fastened up the last, escaping lock of hair. "I have to take care of Simon until the girl arrives. And think about lunch. . . . And then, there's Lilian."

"What about her?" Ben stretched out into the depression left by Julie's body in the other half of the bed. His eyes, now open, were surprisingly alert. "Come and talk to me."

She came and sat beside him, reaching her arm across his body to rest her hand on the bed. "I just mean I have to think of her—make sure she's not cold or anything."

"Difficult to see how she can be anything else, when we've got both the radiators."

"Oh, Lord! I forgot. . . . *Don't*, darling, after all the trouble I took combing it."

"Why is it done differently?" He loosened another strand.

"I don't know—I suppose because Lilian eyes me as though I should Do Something with myself. She makes me feel that I look . . . *married.*"

"Scarcely astonishing, in the circumstances." He drew her elbow back so that, losing the support of her arm, she collapsed against his breast. She remained there, and he put his arm around her. " 'Old, married, and in despair'—is that the idea?"

"Something like that."

"Too soon for that," he observed, encouragingly. "But I know what you mean. Since she's been here I can hardly read the paper without feeling that I've sold my immortal soul."

Julie giggled. "Don't be awful." She drew away from him and put her hands up to her hair, assessing the damage. "Do you think she's happy? I get the feeling she doesn't *want* anything—you know, doesn't know what she should do with her life. . . ." She opened another bobby pin with her teeth and replaced it at the back of her head. "We, at least know where we are."

" 'I am between water and stone fruit in India,' " declared Ben, looking up at Lilian over the *Times*. "In eleven letters."

"Any clues?"

"None."

"Pondicherry," Lilian said, after a moment's silence.

Ben wrote. Pleased with herself, Lilian curled her legs up on the sofa and wondered if she should be in the kitchen, helping Julie. There were to be guests for lunch.

" 'A secret'—blank—'in the stream.' Tennyson. Nine letters."

"No clues?"

"Begins and ends with 's.' "

"Sweetness," said Julie unexpectedly from the dining room. She appeared for a moment in the doorway and added: *"In Memoriam,"* polishing a glass with a dish towel.

"Twenty across," Ben resumed, but Lilian got up and followed Julie.

The kitchen smelled of roasting lamb, and of floor polish and mint sauce. What an appalling stove, Lilian thought; surely they'll replace it.

"Do sit down," Julie told her, pulling out a chair by the table. "We'll be five for lunch—some neighbors called Marchant and the three of us. No, darling, thank you, there's nothing; everything's done. Unless perhaps you'd like to shell the peas." She turned her attention to the meat. "It's quite efficient, really, this kitchen—though, as you see, we had to put in a new stove."

Lilian began to break pods over a colander. "What are they like, your neighbors?"

"The Marchants? We scarcely know them. They drove over one day, in a Volkswagen, to call—we'd been introduced by the previous owners of the house. And they asked us to dinner last week, but we couldn't leave the baby. Seem all right—a bit dull." Having basted the lamb, Julie slid it back into the oven and straightened up. She plunged the basting spoon into suds in the sink. "Nothing against them, really, apart from the car."

Arriving late in their Volkswagen, the Marchants brought with them a big, restless Dalmatian called Spot. Mr. Marchant was stocky and bald, with heavy glasses and a suit of limp tweed. Mrs. Marchant was slight and ginger-haired, and wore a green pullover and a gray flannel skirt. They stood for some minutes in the hall, commenting on improvements in high, authoritative voices, before they could be induced to enter the living room. Mrs. Marchant did not sit down at once, but moved across the room to stare at a picture before veering sharply away to the window. Rather, Lilian could not help thinking, like a small colored fish in an aquarium. Spot after a brisk canter around the furniture, flopped down to pant in a corner, where Ben was preparing drinks.

Mrs. Marchant gave Lilian her divided attention. "You've just been—thank you, with a little water—to America?"

"She lives there," Ben said, stepping over the dog. "Out of the way, Fido."

"Spot," corrected Mrs. Marchant, scenting disparagement.

Mr. Marchant, who was a lawyer, produced some formidably documented views on the conduct of government in the United States. Congressional legislation appeared to him as a series of venal disasters—catalogued, Lilian felt, with a certain satisfaction.

Julie was quietly interrogating the dog, now sitting at her feet. "Are you a good doggie?" Spot smiled, but kept his counsel.

Unable to refute Mr. Marchant, and badly situated for conversation with Spot, Lilian kept silent. Perhaps it's a system, something one gets used to again, she told herself—like doing the *Times* crossword puzzle.

Mrs. Marchant was inclined to be tolerant. "The Americans who come over here seem pleasant enough, don't you think?"

"Oh, absolutely," Ben agreed. He put out his cigarette, and added: "A trifle assiduous, perhaps," before lighting another.

Mrs. Marchant persisted. "But I've always got on well with them. We had four in our house—remember, Hugh?—during the war. Well-behaved boys. They read aloud in the evenings." She nodded to reinforce this surprising memory.

"Did they really?" Julie, who had risen, paused at the door of the dining room. "What?"

Mrs. Marchant's approval diminished. "Well, I *was* hoping for Wordsworth, which Daddy would have so loved—my father was living with us then. But instead they read an interminable thing about a whale—a *whale,* I assure you. I thought we'd never see the back of that whale. But mercifully, when the good weather came, they opened the Second Front."

Lilian, glancing up in dismay, was astonished to find Julie's face disarrayed with amusement.

They sat down to lunch, and Ben carved the meat. Spot, having found his way under the table, squeezed back and forth among their legs, his firm, bristly sides heaving with cheerful interest, his tail slapping wildly. Julie looked pained, and once laid down her knife and fork as though she were about to speak—but didn't. At last Mr. Marchant got up from the table, apologizing, and called the dog to the door.

"Out, damned Spot," he said, pointing. Everyone laughed except Mrs. Marchant, who had heard the joke a hundred times. The dog pattered out as if he had intended this all along.

Julie washed the dishes, and Lilian dried them. The Marchants, waving, had disappeared with Spot in their car, shortly after lunch. Ben had gone out to work in the garden ("Before the rain comes," Julie said, although there was no sign of rain). In the sun outside the kitchen window, Simon slept in his pram.

"Is he warm enough there?" Lilian asked.

Julie looked up, her hands in the sink. "Oh, don't you think so?" she asked anxiously, alarming Lilian, who had expected a confident reassurance.

"It's beginning to get chilly," she said. Together, they looked uncertainly at the strip of sunshine on the grass. Their shoulders touched.

"Oh, God!" shouted Ben from the garden. He crossed rapidly in front of the kitchen window and came in at the back door, a bundle of drooping plants in his hands. "Julia," he said, using her full name to emphasize his displeasure. (How infantile men are, Lilian thought.) "Julia, the lupines are all dug up. Will you please tell those people for Christ's sake not to bring their filthy dog here again?"

"Yes, dear," Julie replied seriously, apparently memorizing the message in order to convey it with complete accuracy. "Can't they be replanted?"

He shook his head. "The blighter's chewed them."

Lilian wiped the draining board and hung the wet dish towel on a rod to dry. "I'll bring Simon in, shall I?" she said smoothly, and made her way past Ben into the garden.

"Leave the pram," Julie called. "Ben will bring it."

Outside the kitchen door, the grass was sparse and trampled, and flaked with wood shavings from the recent passage and unpacking of furniture. Beyond, however, it became lavishly green, in need of cutting and scattered with spring flowers. The garden, more delicate than ever in the already dying light, was surrounded by ancient trees and, on one side, by a thick, trim hedge of box. A memory even as one stands here, Lilian thought, saddened by anticipation of her own nostalgia—and yet pleased all at once to have come out at this moment, to find the scene imposing some sort of misty symmetry on the untidy events of the day. I may cry, she told herself with surprise, as she lifted the sleeping Simon.

Ben, still grasping the ravished lupines, looked at her with interest as he came out of the house.

Lilian gathered up the trailing blanket with her free hand and walked slowly away. He will say: "Poor old Lilian," after I've left, she reminded herself. In the kitchen, she handed Simon over to his mother. "Now I must really go and pack," she said.

Lilian leaned from the window of the train. "I'll telephone you from London," she told Julie.

It will come right again, on the telephone, they assured each other silently.

Julie, suddenly pale and tired, brushed away tears. "It's cold. I should have brought a coat."

"What?"

"It's cold."

"Next time I'll come in the summer."

Crying, Julie laughed. "It'll still be cold. But come back soon."

"Do you have everything you need?" Ben asked, too late for ambiguity, glancing at the magazine stall.

"Yes, thanks. Oh, goodbye." The train drew away. "Goodbye!"

"Goodbye! Lilian . . . goodbye."

They waved, close at last for a moment, before the train ran into the darkness.

The two on the platform stood still for a few seconds, convalescent, before they walked away to their little car. In the clear, black, country air outside the station, Julie shivered again. The wind had risen, as it had the night before. They got into the car without speaking. Only when the

engine started, on the third try, did Julie move up against Ben. He put his
arm briefly around her, and then withdrew it. The car moved off.

"Poor old Lilian," Julie said.

Prue

ALICE MUNRO
(Canadian, 1931–   )

Prue used to live with Gordon. This was after Gordon had left his wife
and before he went back to her—a year and four months in all. Some
time later, he and his wife were divorced. After that came a period of
indecision, of living together off and on; then the wife went away to New
Zealand, most likely for good.

Prue did not go back to Vancouver Island, where Gordon had met her
when she was working as a dining-room hostess in a resort hotel. She got
a job in Toronto, working in a plant shop. She had many friends in
Toronto by that time, most of them Gordon's friends and his wife's
friends. They liked Prue and were ready to feel sorry for her, but she
laughed them out of it. She is very likable. She has what eastern Canadi-
ans call an English accent, though she was born in Canada—in Duncan,
on Vancouver Island. This accent helps her to say the most cynical things
in a winning and lighthearted way. She presents her life in anecdotes, and
though it is the point of most of her anecdotes that hopes are dashed,
dreams ridiculed, things never turn out as expected, everything is altered
in a bizarre way and there is no explanation ever, people always feel
cheered up after listening to her; they say of her that it is a relief to meet
somebody who doesn't take herself too seriously, who is so unintense,
and civilized, and never makes any real demands or complaints.

The only thing she complains about readily is her name. Prue is a schoolgirl, she says, and Prudence is an old virgin; the parents who gave her that name must have been too shortsighted even to take account of puberty. What if she had grown a great bosom, she says, or developed a sultry look? Or was the name itself a guarantee that she wouldn't? In her late forties now, slight and fair, attending to customers with a dutiful vivacity, giving pleasure to dinner guests, she might not be far from what those parents had in mind: bright and thoughtful, a cheerful spectator. It is hard to grant her maturity, maternity, real troubles.

Her grownup children, the products of an early Vancouver Island marriage she calls a cosmic disaster, come to see her, and instead of wanting money, like other people's children, they bring presents, try to do her accounts, arrange to have her house insulated. She is delighted with their presents, listens to their advice, and, like a flighty daughter, neglects to answer their letters.

Her children hope she is not staying on in Toronto because of Gordon. Everybody hopes that. She would laugh at the idea. She gives parties and goes to parties; she goes out sometimes with other men. Her attitude toward sex is very comforting to those of her friends who get into terrible states of passion and jealousy, and feel cut loose from their moorings. She seems to regard sex as a wholesome, slightly silly indulgence, like dancing and nice dinners—something that shouldn't interfere with people's being kind and cheerful to each other.

Now that his wife is gone for good, Gordon comes to see Prue occasionally, and sometimes asks her out for dinner. They may not go to a restaurant; they may go to his house. Gordon is a good cook. When Prue or his wife lived with him he couldn't cook at all, but as soon as he put his mind to it he became—he says truthfully—better than either of them.

Recently he and Prue were having dinner at his house. He had made Chicken Kiev, and crème brûlée for dessert. Like most new, serious cooks, he talked about food.

Gordon is rich, by Prue's—and most people's—standards. He is a neurologist. His house is new, built on a hillside north of the city, where there used to be picturesque, unprofitable farms. Now there are one-of-a-kind, architect-designed, very expensive houses on half-acre lots. Prue, describing Gordon's house, will say, "Do you know there are four bathrooms? So that if four people want to have baths at the same time there's no problem. It seems a bit much, but it's very nice, really, and you'd never have to go through the hall."

Gordon's house has a raised dining area—a sort of platform, surrounded by a conversation pit, a music pit, and a bank of heavy greenery under sloping glass. You can't see the entrance area from the dining area, but there are no intervening walls, so that from one area you can hear something of what is going on in the other.

During dinner the doorbell rang. Gordon excused himself and went down the steps. Prue heard a female voice. The person it belonged to was still outside, so she could not hear the words. She heard Gordon's voice, pitched low, cautioning. The door didn't close—it seemed the person had not been invited in—but the voices went on, muted and angry. Suddenly there was a cry from Gordon, and he appeared halfway up the steps, waving his arms.

"The crème brûlée," he said. "Could you?" He ran back down as Prue got up and went into the kitchen to save the dessert. When she returned he was climbing the stairs more slowly, looking both agitated and tired.

"A friend," he said gloomily. "Was it all right?"

Prue realized he was speaking of the crème brûlée, and she said yes, it was perfect, she had got it just in time. He thanked her but did not cheer up. It seemed it was not the dessert he was troubled over but whatever had happened at the door. To take his mind off it, Prue started asking him professional questions about the plants.

"I don't know a thing about them," he said. "You know that."

"I thought you might have picked it up. Like the cooking."

"She takes care of them."

"Mrs. Carr?" said Prue, naming his housekeeper.

"Who did you think?"

Prue blushed. She hated to be thought suspicious.

"The problem is that I think I would like to marry you," said Gordon, with no noticeable lightening of his spirits. Gordon is a large man, with heavy features. He likes to wear thick clothing, bulky sweaters. His blue eyes are often bloodshot, and their expression indicates that there is a helpless, baffled soul squirming around inside this doughty fortress.

"What a problem," said Prue lightly, though she knew Gordon well enough to know that it was.

The doorbell rang again, rang twice, three times, before Gordon could get to it. This time there was a crash, as of something flung and landing hard. The door slammed and Gordon was immediately back in view. He staggered on the steps and held his hand to his head, meanwhile making a gesture with the other hand to signify that nothing serious had happened, Prue was to sit down.

"Bloody overnight bag," he said. "She threw it at me."

"Did it hit you?"

"Glancing."

"It made a hard sound for an overnight bag. Were there rocks in it?"

"Probably cans. Her deodorant and so forth."

"Oh."

Prue watched him pour himself a drink. "I'd like some coffee, if I might," she said. She went to the kitchen to put the water on, and Gordon followed her.

"I think I'm in love with this person," he said.

"Who is she?"

"You don't know her. She's quite young."

"Oh."

"But I do think I want to marry you, in a few years' time."

"After you get over being in love?"

"Yes."

"Well. I guess nobody knows what can happen in a few years' time."

When Prue tells about this, she says, "I think he was afraid I was going to laugh. He doesn't know why people laugh or throw their overnight bags at him, but he's noticed they do. He's such a proper person, really. The lovely dinner. Then she comes and throws her overnight bag. And it's quite reasonable to think of marrying me in a few years' time, when he gets over being in love. I think he first thought of telling me to sort of put my mind at rest."

She doesn't mention that the next morning she picked up one of Gordon's cufflinks from his dresser. The cufflinks are made of amber and he bought them in Russia, on the holiday he and wife took when they got back together again. They look like squares of candy, golden, translucent, and this one warms quickly in her hand. She drops it into the pocket of her jacket. Taking one is not a real theft. It could be a reminder, an intimate prank, a piece of nonsense.

She is alone in Gordon's house; he has gone off early, as he always does. The housekeeper does not come till nine. Prue doesn't have to be at the shop until ten; she could make herself breakfast, stay and have coffee with the housekeeper, who is her friend from olden times. But once she has the cufflink in her pocket she doesn't linger. The house seems too bleak a place to spend an extra moment in. It was Prue, actually, who helped choose the building lot. But she's not responsible for approving the plans—the wife was back by that time.

When she gets home she puts the cufflink in an old tobacco tin. The children bought this tobacco tin in a junk shop years ago, and gave it to her for a present. She used to smoke, in those days, and the children were worried about her, so they gave her this tin full of toffees, jelly beans, and gumdrops, with a note saying, "Please get fat instead." That was for her birthday. Now the tin has in it several things besides the cufflink—all small things, not of great value but not worthless, either. A little enamelled dish, a sterling-silver spoon for salt, a crystal fish. These are not sentimental keepsakes. She never looks at them, and often forgets what she has there. They are not booty, they don't have ritualistic significance. She does not take something every time she goes to Gordon's house, or every time she stays over, or to mark what she might call memorable visits. She doesn't do it in a daze and she doesn't seem to be under a compulsion. She just takes something, every now and then, and puts it away in the dark of the old tobacco tin, and more or less forgets about it.

Legend for a Painting

JULIA O'FAOLAIN
(Irish, 1933–   )

A knight rode to a place where a lady was living with a dragon. She was a gently bred creature with a high forehead, and her dress—allowing for her surroundings—was neat. While the dragon slept, the knight had a chance to present himself.

'I have come,' he told the lady, 'to set you free.' He pointed at a stout chain linking her to her monstrous companion. It had a greenish tinge, due the knight supposed to some canker oozing from the creature's flesh.

Green was the dragon's colour. Its tail was green; so were its wings, with the exception of the pale pink eyes which were embedded in them and which glowed like water-lilies and expanded when the dragon flew, as eyes do on the spread tails of peacocks. Greenest of all was the dragon's under-belly which swelled like sod on a fresh grave. It was heaving just now and emitting gurgles. The knight shuddered.

'What,' the lady wondered, 'do you mean by "free"?'

The knight spelled it: 'F-R-E-E', although he was unsure whether or not she might be literate. 'To go!' he gasped for he was grappling with distress.

'But where?' the lady insisted. 'I like it here, you know. Draggie and I' —the knight feared her grin might be mischievous or even mad—'have a perfect symbiotic relationship!'

The knight guessed at obscenities.

'I clean his scales,' she said, 'and he prepares my food. We have no cutlery so he chews it while it cooks in the fire from his throat: a labour-saving device. He can do rabbit stew, braised wood pigeon, even liver Venetian style when we can get a liver.'

'God's blood!' the knight managed to swear. His breath had been taken away.

'I don't know that recipe. Is it good? I can see,' the lady wisely soothed, 'you don't approve. But remember that fire scours. His mouth is germ free. Cleaner than mine or your own, which, if I may say so with respect, has been breathing too close. Have you perhaps been chewing wild garlic?'

The knight crossed himself. 'You,' he told the lady, 'must be losing your wits as a result of living with this carnal beast!' He sprinkled her with a little sacred dust from a pouch that he carried about his person. He had gathered it on the grave of Saint George the Dragon Killer and trusted in its curative properties. 'God grant,' he prayed, 'you don't lose your soul as well. Haven't you heard that if a single drop of dragon's blood falls on the mildest man or maid, they grow as carnal as the beast itself? Concupiscent!' he hissed persuasively. 'Bloody! Fierce!'

The lady sighed. 'Blood does obsess you!' she remarked. 'Draggie never bleeds. You needn't worry. His skin's prime quality. Very resistant and I care for him well. He may be "carnal" as you say. We're certainly both carnivores. I take it you're a vegetarian?'

The knight glanced at the cankered chain and groaned. 'You're mad!' he ground his teeth. 'Your sense of values has been perverted. The fact that you can't see it proves it!'

'A tautology, I think?' The lady grinned. 'Why don't you have a talk with old Draggie when he wakes up? You'll see how gentle he can be. That might dispel your prejudices.'

But the knight had heard enough. He neither liked long words nor thought them proper in a woman's mouth. *Deeds not words* was the motto emblazoned on his shield, for he liked words that condemned words and this, as the lady could have told him, revealed inner contradictions likely to lead to trouble in the long run.

'Enough!' he yelled and, lifting his lance, plunged it several times between the dragon's scales. He had no difficulty in doing this, for the dragon was a slow-witted, somnolent beast at best and just now deep in a private dragon-dream. Its eyes, when they opened, were iridescent and flamed in the sunlight, turning, when the creature wept, into great, con-

centric, rainbow wheels of fire. 'Take that!' the knight was howling glee-
fully, 'and that and that!'

Blood spurted, gushed, and spattered until his face, his polished armour and the white coat of his charger were veined and flecked like
porphyry. The dragon was soon dead but the knight's rage seemed un-
stoppable. For minutes, as though battening on its own release, it continued to discharge as he hacked at the unresisting carcass. Butchering, his
sword swirled and slammed. His teeth gnashed. Saliva flowed in stringy
beardlets from his chin and the lady stared at him with horror. She had
been pale before but now her cheeks seemed to have gathered sour,
greenish reflections into their brimming hollows.

Abruptly, she dropped the chain. Its clank, as it hit a stone, interrupted the knight's frenzy. As though just awakened, he turned dull eyes
to her. Questioning.

'Then,' slowly grasping what this meant, 'you were never his prisoner,
after all?'

The lady pointed at a gold collar encircling the dragon's neck. It had
been concealed by an overlap of scales but had slipped into view during
the fight. One end of the chain was fastened to it.

'He was mine,' she said. 'But as I told you he was gentle and more a
pet than a prisoner.'

The knight wiped his eyelids which were fringed with red. He looked
at his hands.

'Blood!' he shrieked. 'Dragon's blood!'

'Yes,' she said in a cold, taut voice, 'you're bloody. Concupiscent, no
doubt? Fierce, certainly! Carnal?' She kicked the chain, which had broken when she threw it down and, bending, picked up a link that had
become detached. 'I'll wear this,' she said bitterly, 'in token of my servi-
tude. I'm your prisoner now.' She slipped the gold, green-tinged metal
ring on to the third finger of her left hand. It too was stained with blood.

Threnody

∾

FAY WELDON
(English, 1935–   )

1976/77

I don't want to take up too much of your time and attention, Miss
Jacobs. I am sure there are many others in a far worse state than me. I
met a couple of them on the way here, in fact, in the High Street. An old
woman walked behind me shouting that Sainsbury's was the worst den of
iniquity in the world and that the police station was a brothel. And a
beautiful young woman passed me, weeping. Her face was so wet I
thought for a minute it was raining. Well, I am in neither of those sorry
states. I am prepared to take the world at its face value, and nothing
distresses me very much any more. Look at me! My skirt and blouse are
neat: my hair is combed: I am not distressed. I look what I am; a solicitor's wife, aged thirty-five, well set up for the slow run down to old age
and death.

Depressed? No. I don't think so. Realistic, perhaps. Do I look depressed?
I notice I am sitting in the bright light from the window, while you sit
almost in the dark. I find that uncomfortable. I am not used to it. Usually
the self remains obscure while others are brilliantly lit. Self-knowledge is
hard to come by. That is why I am here. I want to say the things I do not
like to say at home, for fear of making the milk curdle and the children
anxious. I have blisters on my tongue, from biting words back.

Start at the beginning? Very well.

My mother named me Threnody. No. It isn't written on my card. I am known as Anne; well, who wants a name like Threnody? My husband Eric certainly does not. The name was a mistake on my mother's part. She thought Threnody meant some kind of happy, lilting melody. In fact, it means dirge, or lament. My mother's friend Elsie, who was to bring me up, pointed this out, but only after the deed was done. I don't hold the error against my mother. It was 1940, after all. Bombs fell and food was short, and I dare say she thought that Davis was a dull and ordinary surname, and that I deserved all the help I could get, and that was why she plucked Threnody out of the air, and used it for a name, instead of fishing Jane or Mary or Helen out of the common pool. And if more excuses were needed for my mother, she was only twenty when I was born, and my father was not available for consultation. What's more, according to Elsie, she had a milk ulcer. That helps no one think straight. I had one with Robert. He's my younger. And the Registrar would have been too busy entering deaths—Elsie said the week I was born was the week of the worst of the London bombings—to have had time or energy to help my mother out.

Yes. Elsie spoke a lot to me about my early childhood: yes. Perhaps I remember with her memory. See with her eyes. The world according to Elsie. We have grown apart for various reasons but I remain fond of her. I think those war years were the best of Elsie's life. She had three children and her husband was in the navy, and she lived next door to my mum and me, when I was a baby, in Riley Street. By all accounts it was a casual, slap-dash street; a woman's world, for the husbands were away fighting Germany. Meals were seldom served on time, and came straight out of saucepans, not from serving dishes, and children shared beds with mothers and were the happier for it.

Yes, of course, Miss Jacobs. All these attitudes and assumptions of mine will be examined in the course of time. I know that and am prepared to change them. That's why I'm here. In the meantime I am just giving you the broad outline, so you know the kind of person I am. A solicitor's wife, burdened by the fact that her mother named her Threnody. A dirge or lament.

Where were we, before you interrupted? Though I must say you are very silent. It must be quite a good way to make money. Sitting there like a voyeur, saying nothing in particular, getting on with your knitting. Yes, a very good way indeed. I must try it some time. Set myself up so nice and cosy.

No. It doesn't make me feel better to have lost my temper with you. It makes me feel worse. Fourteen sessions before I was honest with you about my feelings? Is that good or bad? If it's neither good nor bad, why fucking well mention it? Can I now get on with my story, please? Christ, isn't that what I pay you for?

Riley Street in the war. Local schools had closed and such mothers as had stood out against evacuation now had the company of their children all day long. Bombs fell by night, of course, but quite a lot of the women claimed that air-raids were preferable to their husband's attentions. According to Elsie. Yes. All this is according to Elsie. I was only a child, not Einstein. I do not have total recall.

Elsie wasn't like the others. Elsie liked sex. So did my mother. I don't think they were real lesbians, not in the modern sense. No, certainly I have no sense of disgust. Why should I? I can see it all clearly. The general feeling between them of a sensuous common bond; the slap-happy life of early nights and late risings, and cheerful neighbours and cups of tea, and time passing and no one caring, and mother-skin touching child-skin in the glow of the coal fire, and no one ever bothering to sweep up, and the money from the army coming through the letter box every week, so there was no hassle getting it out of husbands—and every night the bombers going over and real physical fear and the need for relief from it—well, I can see how all these things would combine so that Jan's and Elsie's lips were all but bound to meet, if only casually, and more in the expectation of comfort than in any actual desire for sexual gratification.

What do you mean, protest too much? I see that you're wearing a nice new jumper. Is that the one you've been knitting at my expense? You are not, if you don't mind me saying so, too good a knitter. You can't mind me saying so. I pay you not to mind.

Yes, I know that children like to deny their parents' sexual experiences; I have even heard my little Rosalind say Mummy and Daddy only did it the twice; once for Robert and once for me, and it made me laugh, though the way Eric's going these days, she wouldn't be so far out. But for me, you see, it was true. I haven't mentioned my father much since I've been seeing you, for the I would have thought obvious reason that he died before I was born. He never even got to know I had been named Threnody. My mother wrote a letter to him and posted it, confessing all, but she needn't have bothered. He died before he could read it. He was on the African front. He was trapped in a blazing tank. No. Not a nice way to go. But that was the war. People got burned alive or asphyxiated or cut into bits or crushed flat or starved to death or died of disease: a nice clean bullet hole was rare. Killed in Action. If you disintegrated altogether and just weren't there any more you were posted Missing, Presumed Killed. They must have found bits of my father, I suppose. How do you mourn a father you never saw? He and my mother met, married and conceived me all in the space of two months, as was not unusual at the time. Then my father was sent back to the front, buttons shining, leaving my poor young mother to cope.

I know it wasn't his fault. What are you implying? my difficulties with Eric are because of my father? My *father?* What father? Look, I don't have difficulties with Eric; he has difficulties with himself. What are you *talking* about?

No. That my mother had this relationship with Elsie is not fantasy. One day when I'm feeling strong enough I'll tell you how I know.

Poetry? Write poetry? Me? Do solicitors' wives write poetry? I suppose I wasn't always a solicitor's wife, though it seems hard to believe.

As a baby I had a transparent look—Elsie said so. My mother didn't quite believe in my existence, according to Elsie, and that was the reason for my transparency. I think my mother was lucky: she was not quite able to believe in the desperate reality of anything. Why should she? She was Eve in the Garden of Eden, happy in Riley Street, until when I was four she bit into the apple of knowledge, and we were all cast out into outer darkness. Yesterday I sent a poem off to the Cheltenham Festival competition. I must be mad.

Talking about must be mad, I have to keep secret from everyone the fact that I come to see you. Eric says people will not just think, but know I'm mad, if they don't already. I expect he's right. He's always right. I married him because he was so right, and generally in charge. Never mind. Mustn't grumble. Elsie used to say mustn't grumble.

The apple my mother bit into was the apple of love. Had it just been sex no harm would have been done. Love doesn't just move mountains it sends them toppling down upon the innocent.

I don't want to come here any more. I can't afford it. I can't face it. It's doing more harm than good. My mother went dancing. She and Elsie had a row about it. I remember it. I was four. Elsie didn't want her to go. My mother had a pair of the new black glassy nylons and she put them on and Elsie called her names, but she went off to the dance and met a U.S. serviceman called Gus and they fell in love. Gus wanted my Mum to put her past behind her, and that included me. Threnody. Dirge or lament.

I remember him saying to my Mum when she brought him home, 'Funny names you English give your kids,' and I remember Elsie saying, 'Not as funny as Gus. What's it short for? Disgusting?'

My Mum married Gus in Seattle and Elsie got one thousand pounds from Gus' family to take me in.

Sold to the nice lady next door. For the sum of one thousand pounds.

Well, Elsie was nice. Nicer than my Mum, I dare say. My Mum was a flibbertygibbet. The lady at No. 8 said so.

God, I feel about six. No, four. Christ!

1977/8

Historically, women have always abandoned their children in favour of their husbands. All through the days of empire, middle-class mothers left their little ones with nannies and schools and followed their men and thought themselves virtuous for doing so. Working-class women, of course, behaved more naturally. Perhaps my Mum was just being up-market.

Yes, I feel myself again. Surprisingly mature. I am runner-up in the Cheltenham Poetry Prize. Eric brought half a bottle of champagne. Had I won, it would have been a whole bottle. He's like that.

I remember when the war came to an end. Bells and flags and kissing in the streets. And then all up and down Riley Street husbands returned and children were pushed out of their mother's beds and lived for ever with a sense of Paradise Lost. Meals became meat and two veg again: male voices demanded quiet and clean socks: and the pot plants began to flourish again. They do, I am quite convinced, in houses where normal sex is frequently practised. You are right: lately mine have been dying off. That's coincidence. Please let me get on, Miss Jacobs. Always butting in. If you're not too silent you're too talkative.

As for me, I belonged to nobody and had my own fate. Threnody. Dirge or lament. I had a little back bedroom at the top of Elsie's house and everyone was kind to me, and yes, I have always said I had a very happy childhood. I liked my name in those days. I was always good at turning misfortune into advantage. 'It's a Russian name,' I'd say to my friends. 'My father, who died the day I was born, was a prince. My mother was a princess. She was abducted by secret agents: she is imprisoned in a castle!' No. She never wrote to me.

I suppose in fact I was always a little ashamed of Elsie. I thought she was coarse and vulgar. I was very sensitive. I swelled up terribly if bitten by a wasp. I couldn't wear wool next to my skin. Remember the vagrant girl in the Hans Andersen story? They knew she was a princess because when she slept on a hundred mattresses she could still feel the pea underneath.

Ted? Elsie's husband? Ted my foster-father? Oh, Ted. Him. Well.

Elsie had another baby when I was eleven and Ted didn't like me very much in those days—I'm not surprised. If there were beans and chips I'd say isn't there any salad, that kind of thing—and they needed my bedroom so Elsie wrote to my Mum, but the letter was returned Gone Away. My father's family? Elsie went along to the Registrar because all she knew, all anyone knew, about my father was his name, Arthur Davis, but the Registrar was gone with all his files. V2 rocket. Direct hit. That's war. People appear, and disappear, and history with them.

If anything goes wrong at home Eric says, 'Of course, you can't be expected to concentrate. You're a poet, after all.' It's all your fault, Miss Jacobs. Encouraging me to be something I'm not. I'd have thought you weren't supposed to do things like that.

I think I was a very pretty child. Well, that's the feeling I have. I loved nice dresses and button shoes. I remember Elsie saying, when I said I wanted to go to grammar school, 'Christ, that child gives herself airs.' But Ted backed me, surprisingly enough, and paid for my uniform without even complaining. He'd quite come round to me by the time I was thirteen. Yes, I was frightened of him. I'd wedge a chair beneath my door handle at night. No. I wasn't exactly frightened of him, more of the way Elsie didn't ever let me be in the room alone with him.

Anyway, Elsie was rescued from the threat of me by the government. They brought out a scheme for the residential education of war-disadvantaged children, so I was wrenched out of the grammar school where I was doing English Lit and learning to be a journalist and put into this institution and taught shorthand typing and office management.

Institution? Well, actually, it wasn't too bad. It was a stately home, which had been requisitioned from some ducal family in the war. Gold stucco flaked on to the filing cabinets and the canteen was set up beneath faded tapestries, and stone cherubs lay on their backs in the weeds and smiled. It suited my mood.

I slept alone in the servants' attic, beneath a sloping roof, and icicles formed outside my dormer window, but I knew it was better than Riley Street.

Yes, I made lots of friends at college. I entertained them. They were mostly very plain—being disadvantaged does tend to make people plain —and I felt in some way responsible for them. I always felt I had a future: but they only seemed to have pasts. They still write to me. One of them became a countess, for all her cross eyes. You can never tell.

Of course I see good looks as the way a woman gets on. Her face is her future. Would you be sitting there knitting shrouds—I assume you're knitting shrouds—if you hadn't been born with a face like a flat iron?

Flat iron? No, I have no particular association with flat irons. It just reminds me of your fucking face. Or vice versa. Look, I'm sorry. Yes, there's something coming up.

Ted. Foster-father Ted. I learned office routine, bookkeeping, shorthand typing. I'd given up wanting to be a journalist. You could be a secretary until you got married; but if you were a journalist that was a career. If you had a career you couldn't be married, and vice versa. And I wanted to be married, oh yes. I wanted to marry out of Riley Street for ever and into stately homes, however decayed. I settled for Eric, in the end, and Georgian country. Madness!

Love? What do you mean? Of course I love my husband. You're supposed to, aren't you? That's what it's all about.

Ted. Why do you keep bringing me back to Ted? It was better when you sat silent and gently snored; did you know you snored?—now I seem to hear your gratey whiny voice in my ears all day and all night. 'Ted— whine, sniffle—what about—whine, sniffle—Ted, whine, sniffle.' It was nothing. It was the kind of thing that happens to girls all the time. Ted came to visit me at the stately home. Stump, stump, stump up the wide staircase in brown boots. He was a good looking man. Horrible, and old, and bristly, with a moustache. And angry, always. Not as if I'd done something wrong, but as if I *was* something wrong. Do you know? No, you wouldn't. You're always right.

Ted. He described himself as my uncle, and they allowed him up into my attic bedroom and he made love to me. Rape? I don't know. That's another word like love. I don't know what it means. I didn't want him to and yet I let him. I hated him and feared him and despised him and I wanted him to wrong me. He knew it was wrong, and I knew it was wrong, and he knew that I knew, and I acquiesced in this monstrous ugly act: I think perhaps it has made me passive. More passive than I need be. In order to accept that deed and incorporate it in my sweet vision of myself, I had to accept and incorporate everything else. The monstrous crime. Incest: in the spirit if not the deed.

Yes, of course I'm rationalising, Miss Jacobs, whatever that means. If you'll excuse me I'll leave this session now. I know it's early, but I'm sure your other clients are clamouring at the door. They always are. I'm surprised you can tell us apart. Perhaps you can't.

Why are you suggesting I start a business of some kind? I don't *want* to be independent. I think women should be looked after and it's the husband's place to do it. You know that.

Thank you. I had a good Christmas. I hope you did. Eric decided the turkey wasn't properly cooked, so everything had to go back into the oven, and it was all rather spoiled. Eric fears food poisoning. I don't. I hope for it. I have blisters on my tongue again. Haven't had those for ages. And I'm getting back pains.

Listen, I've got the premises for the Press, and raised the money for the lease. I'll print leaflets and wedding invitations, and circulars and handbooks and when I've managed to scrape together a little capital, even try doing volumes of poetry. I have quite a gift for handprinting, it seems.

I have been thinking about the Ted episode. He justified himself, as he adjusted his dress. Gentlemen were required to do that in public conveniences, at that time. Gentlemen will kindly adjust their dress. Meaning, don't forget your flies. He didn't. Some men make love without even taking off their trousers. Did you know? Well, you are *Miss* Jacobs. For all I know you're a virgin and have no idea what I'm talking about half the time.

Incidentally I have an Arts Council grant for the poetry editions. They needn't think they can dictate to me culturally, just because I take their money.

Ted's justification was that while he'd been away in the war Elsie had been having it off with my mother, so he owed her no fidelity. He thought a balance had been righted. And I'm sure he thought sex with me was his just reward for the money he had expended on me. Well, men do, don't they? But it was hit and run, really. He didn't write or phone and I was glad and I put it out of my mind, or thought I did. No. I felt no guilt towards Elsie. Should I have? But there has been a barrier between my life before and my life after; between my present and my past. I have become someone to whom the early life, the magic of infancy and total love, has been lost. I suppose that is how the traumatised live. Most of us are traumatised. Will knowing it make any difference?

1979

Miss Jacobs, I am in love. I shall tell you about it presently. A woman of 37 in love! Ridiculous. Heart pounding, mouth dry, loins melting. Oh! No. I shan't say any more about it. Not yet. Wonderful. I am so happy. Do you like my new jeans?

Eric. It was as much my fault as his. Now I am in love I can afford to forgive him. Look at my own part in it all. I was a tough little thing, really. After I left college I pushed my accent up a notch or so, acquired a fantasy Mummy and Daddy, and a country home and a horsy head square or two, and shared a Knightsbridge flat with a gaggle of secretaries who had all these things by natural right. Manners and attitudes brushed off. I meant to catch a man: the best man I could. I got a job with a firm of West End solicitors. I don't think anyone doubted me. I had the same clear honest eyes then as I have now. People believe what you say you are, if you say it loud and clear. So I did. Anne Threnody-Davis. Hyphenated. Madness!

Eric was the youngest partner in the law firm. Twenty-eight, unmarried, public school, private income, good background. There was, in those days, a very special kind of war between men and women. The woman's virginity was the trophy. The man's desire was to seduce the woman, prove her bad, and then abandon her as she deserved. The woman's was to snare and fascinate by sexual wiles, but exact marriage as the price of bed. Well I wasn't a virgin, was I, but I sure as shit tried.

Yes. My language has become freer. I think it's the company I'm keeping more than anything you've done for me. Freudian or sub-Freudian analysis doesn't go down too well in the circles I move in, I can tell you. But the Press is going very well. Do you think I should change its name to the Threnody Press? I'd like to do that. A kind of half-way acknowledgment. Eric won't like it, though.

I manoeuvred Eric into marrying me: sitting in his office as cool and sweet as could be, making up imaginary suitors for myself until he was so sick with anxiety and lust he proposed marriage. Once engaged, my various deceptions were quickly and horribly exposed. Served me right. I know I was a victim of a system which led women to weak survival by deceit but even so I behaved badly. I think Eric could have accepted Riley Street and Elsie and Ted with perfect equanimity if I'd been open and honest about it. But I was ashamed of it, and so he was too. He kept his word and married me but I knew he really didn't want to. He fell a third out of love with me when he discovered Threnody was my Christian name and not attached to Davis by a hyphen, and the second third when he actually made love to me on our wedding night and I confessed I wasn't a virgin, and the last third when we just somehow didn't get on in bed together, anyway. Look, I was only eighteen.

We both did our best. We lived in the country so I could put my past behind me, including the name Threnody. We had a nice house and nice children and I kept them both well. We entertained. I was a model wife. I went through all the motions; and we are always polite to each other. I felt so guilty about those initial deceptions that I thereafter behaved impeccably. But I died. I was dead. And even you couldn't revive me. Not so bad a crime? How can you say that? Think of the harm I've done! The damage. I killed my father: I drove my mother away; I stole poor Elsie's husband, I cheated my husband and my children of the life they should have had. You can say what you like to me. But that is the truth.

The truth of what I feel, not the truth of what happened, all right, but that is the greater truth and how am I to live with that? That I'm not just dirt: but poisonous dirt as well. I must be punished, obliterated. You know you have made me suicidal? Sheila says she hopes you know what you are doing. Sheila is the person I am in love with.

What's the matter? Why did you cough like that? Do you think you have failed? I *know* you have succeeded. I don't think you meant to, mind you. But I know my true nature now. I am lesbian. I am going to come out. What is coming out? Don't you *know?* Where have you been the last few years? Coming out is declaring your sexual nature to the world. The theory being that if everyone does it, then straight society will stop being so censorious, and isolated gays will stop being so miserable, and realise what an ordinary, lovely, everyday thing same-sex-sexuality is. You might even start wondering about your own nature, Miss Jacobs. What do you mean, caution? No haste? God, you are so boring. Don't you realise I am in love?

Good heavens! Yes, ages and ages ago I said that. Sex isn't as dangerous as love. Mountains move and topple on the innocent. But I'm not deserting my children. Sheila is so good with them. They'll move in with us. It may be a bit difficult with Robert—I mean, he may be my son but he's still male, and male is the enemy, when you come down to it. But of course Eric will be reasonable when I tell him. We'll be so much happier apart. I really think he's a bit gay too, you see. People like me and him do tend to drift together, Sheila says.

Sheila says a lot, as Elsie did? What are you implying? No, I don't think so. In fact, Sheila doesn't believe in small talk. She's quite tall; nearly six foot, and really striking looking. She has a sort of husky, languorous voice. It really turns me on. I was publishing the newsletter for the lesbian commune she runs—well, she doesn't run it; it's a group thing: no male hierarchical organisation.

What do you mean, the world according to Sheila? As it used to be the world according to Elsie? What are you trying to *say?* You're jealous. I think you're jealous because I'm happy and you're not. Yes, I know about my outer shell. My carapace. Sheila says all women married to men grow them, in self defence. We must use our sisters to help crack the shell, Sheila says, so the true self can emerge.

How much money have I given you, over the years? When I think how it could have helped the commune! You know the trouble I was having with the back? Sheila says its because I've been playing heterosexual. She says she dare say if she submitted to male sexual aggression nightly she'd have a bad back too. Not *nightly?* Well, all right. You have a funny air, Miss Jacobs, crouched in your dark corner, of being girded for battle. Yes, I do see all male sex as assault, frankly. No, not an expression of love. Love between men and women can't be the love between equals, because men believe women are their inferiors. They can't help it. It's in the language. He before she. *Man* kind. *His*-story, John and Mary. The love men show towards women is at its best patronising. The penis is after all a weapon of mastery. Good heavens, look at rockets. Missiles. Whee! What a humdinger of an ejaculation! Wow.

I'm afraid Eric isn't being co-operative at all. He's being vindictive. Sheila says gays are, if they're under cover.

Sex with Sheila. It's wonderful. How can I explain to you? Peaceful. There is so much time. No fear of the other's failure, which will later be revenged. No fear of your own. Everything waits. The seasons. The earth in its orbit. Everything. It's love, as I have never known it. Eric won't give me a divorce. He has thrown me out. Well, he's a solicitor. He has friends. He is claiming custody of the children. He will only let me see them in the presence of a third party. Specifically not Sheila! It's barbaric, monstrous! Male vengeance. The man whose pride has been injured. That's all it is. Not *feeling.*

But I have the Threnody Press, which is just about now breaking even, and I have Sheila. I have no savings, no house, no children, no possessions: and many of my friends don't understand the truth and have taken Eric's side: but a few understand. Especially Paula. She's very supportive. And I have my dignity, and I have love, and when I have recovered from these blows, I will be happy. I am very calm, and very confident.

They are so kind to us at the commune. My sisters. Sheila and I have our own room: We're not in the dormitories. There are a lot of things I have to get used to. It is good of you to let me see you for nothing, even though it is only once a week. I would have thought, considering—well, never mind. You live as a woman in the old male world—you have to have your props. Money, status, possessions. We're different. Even our clothing we have in common.

Sheila has moved back into the dormitory. We talked it out. She feels there is something destructive in our exclusiveness. I see what she means. I think. No, I'm not depressed. It's just I haven't had time to mend my sandal thongs.

Of course it's a feather in Sheila's cap to have seduced a married woman with children. It's happening all the time. All over the country women are realising their true natures, coming out, leaving husband and children. It's nothing to do with fashion. If we are strong, if we hold together, as sisters, all will be well—

What do you mean, I use words without meaning? Miss Jacobs, I think I am going mad. Eric owns half the Threnody Press. He says I may keep it if I buy out his share. But that's two thousand pounds. I haven't got it. It will have to be sold. I am destroyed.

Miss Jacobs, Sheila says that emotions are political. That I should hand mine over to the group for discussion and direction, and not to you. But I don't know. I do love Sheila. I'm sure I do. I must, mustn't I? I mean, that's what's supposed to happen. Now when did I say that before? Round and round: circles within circles, little wheels within big wheels. Cogs grinding. Dear God, forgive me my sins.

Miss Jacobs, I met Paula in the street. I thought she was a good friend, even though she was heterosexual, but she was getting a bit funny and I asked her straight out why, and she said it's not that she thought it was disgusting or anything like that: just that she couldn't trust me any more. She couldn't relax in my company. She said it was as if I were one of the men, weighing her up for attractiveness or otherwise, dismissing her because of her body, not her self. As if I would! But it's true that now when I look at the lips of women I wonder what kissing them would be like.

No. Pre-Sheila, I never had thoughts like that.

Do you mind if I cry? Sheila doesn't like me crying, and I have blisters on my tongue again. Why do I cry? Because of the children. Sheila says why shouldn't Eric take care of them for a change: much as she liked them they were something of a nuisance: it was difficult to be properly sexually spontaneous when kids were around. I remarked that heterosexuals waited 'til they'd gone to bed, and Sheila said yes, and look how miserable they are!

No. I don't see eye to eye with Sheila all the time, not any more. I think that's your fault. Eric has custody of the children. The case has been taken up by the Society for Lesbian Mothers. There's been a lot of press about, and even television interviews. God, I did look a mess. I'd no idea. Anyway, now everyone knows. Everyone. If I even put my head out of the door people stare.

It all reminds me of Ted, I don't know why. Stump, stump, stump, up the stairs, dreadful but inevitable. My doom.

My name is Threnody. It means dirge or lament. My mother didn't make a mistake. She had a foreknowledge, that's all.

Sheila wants Ellen to be included in our relationship. Ellen's twenty-two. Sheila says I've been a real drag lately, miserable and depressing and self-centred and unable to break out of my sexist conditioning, so that she's sometimes wondered if I weren't just a heterosexual playing sick fashionable games. I cried, which really made her angry, but the blisters on my tongue have gone. She said Rose Ellen would be good for all of us, being

cheerful and positive—twenty-two, is what I think she means—and a bit
confused politically, Sheila says, but fantastic in bed! Well, she should
know. What does that mean anyway? Good in bed! She said to me Threnody by name, and Threnody by nature. A real drag, Sheila said. The
world according to Sheila.

I accept that. Threnody. I fully accept my name. What did I do about
Rose Ellen? I packed my one suitcase, which is all I have left of my life,
and I went out into the world. Rose Ellen is *not* fantastic in bed: or at any
rate she doesn't turn me on in the least, and she is very, very stupid. I
have the suitcase in your waiting room. I shall go and stay with Paula if
she'll have me now. You wanted me punished, I seem to remember. You
didn't? It was what *I* wanted? Are you sure? I certainly feel much better.
I mean quite dreadful, as befits my circumstances, which is totally
ruined, everything lost: but nothing on either side of that, except a most
wonderful cheerfulness. I shan't see you now for some time. I can't afford
you. I mean, emotionally afford *not* paying for you, if you see what I
mean. No, frankly, I don't think I have manoeuvred this whole situation
just to get out of treatment. Goodbye, and thank you. I mean really,
thank you from the bleeding, beating heart of Threnody.

1980

I see you have some new knitting. I love the colours. Much brighter! I
hope it wasn't me who depressed you? I was going to post you the money
I owe you but Tim said why not come and visit you and do it in person. I
said you'd probably not be able to find the time to fit me in, but he said of
course you would and he was right. Tim is often right, but not always,
the way Eric was. Did I tell you about Tim? I don't know if seeing you
did me the slightest good: perhaps all that was required was for me to
meet the right person? Tim is a doctor. He was a widower when I met
him. Now he is married to me. We have five children between us. Three
of his and two of mine. Mine come at weekends. I am quite good friends
with Eric now. He married again very soon after the divorce—a local
farmer's daughter. Perhaps he was never the snob I thought he was, and
it was me all the time? But since this is a social visit and I'm not paying
you, I don't suppose you'll see the need to go into all that. In any case

Tim likes me as I am and does not see the need for alteration. Do you know what he said to me the other day? He said, 'Don't tell me your mother made a mistake when she called you Threnody. She didn't. So far as I am concerned,' said Tim, 'the word Threnody now means a happy, lilting melody, and not dirge, or lament, at all.'

So you see, Miss Jacobs, all is well. What did you say? Nothing is ever as good as one hopes, or as bad as one fears? What a very sort of *intermediate* remark.

Cords

EDNA O'BRIEN
(Irish, 1936–   )

Everything was ready, the suitcase closed, her black velvet coat-collar carefully brushed, and a list pinned to the wall reminding her husband when to feed the hens and turkeys, and what foodstuffs to give them. She was setting out on a visit to her daughter Claire in London, just like any mother, except that *her* daughter was different: she'd lost her faith, and she mixed with queer people and wrote poems. If it was stories one could detect the sin in them, but these poems made no sense at all and therefore seemed more wicked. Her daughter had sent the money for the air-ticket. She was going now, kissing her husband goodbye, tender towards him in a way that she never was, throughout each day, as he spent his time looking through the window at the wet currant bushes, grumbling about the rain, but was in fact pleased at the excuse to hatch indoors, and asked for tea all the time, which he lapped from a saucer, because it was more pleasurable.

'The turkeys are the most important,' she said, kissing him good-bye, and thinking faraway to the following Christmas, to the turkeys she would sell, and the plumper ones she would give as gifts.

'I hope you have a safe flight,' he said. She'd never flown before.

'All Irish planes are blessed, they never crash,' she said, believing totally in the God that created her, sent her this venial husband, a largish farmhouse, hens, hardship, and one daughter who'd changed, become moody, and grown away from them completely.

The journey was pleasant once she'd got over the shock of being strapped down for the take-off. As they went higher and higher she looked out at the very white, wispish cloud and thought of the wash tub and hoped her husband would remember to change his shirt while she was away. The trip would have been perfect but that there was a screaming woman who had to be calmed down by the air hostess. She looked like a woman who was being sent to a mental institution, but did not know it.

Claire met her mother at the airport and they kissed warmly, not having seen each other for over a year.

'Have you stones in it?' Claire said, taking the fibre suitcase. It was doubly secured with a new piece of binding twine. Her mother wore a black straw hat with clusters of cherries on both sides of the brim.

'You were great to meet me,' the mother said.

'Of course I'd meet you,' Claire said, easing her mother right back on the taxi seat. It was a long ride and they might as well be comfortable.

'I could have navigated,' the mother said, and Claire said nonsense a little too brusquely. Then to make amends she asked gently how the journey was.

'Oh I must tell you, there was this very peculiar woman and she was screaming.'

Claire listened and stiffened, remembering her mother's voice that became low and dramatic in a crisis, the same voice that said, 'Sweet Lord your father will kill us,' or, 'What's to become of us, the bailiff is here,' or, 'Look, look, the chimney is on fire.'

'But otherwise?' Claire said. This was a holiday, not an expedition into the past.

'We had tea and sandwiches. I couldn't eat mine, the bread was buttered.'

'Still faddy?' Claire said. Her mother got bilious if she touched butter, fish, olive oil, or eggs; although her daily diet was mutton stew, or home-cured bacon.

'Anyhow, I have nice things for you,' Claire said. She had bought in stocks of biscuits, jellies and preserves because these were the things her mother favoured, these foods that she herself found distasteful.

The first evening passed well enough. The mother unpacked the presents—a chicken, bread, eggs, a tapestry of a church spire which she'd done all winter, stitching at it until she was almost blind, a holy water font, ashtrays made from shells, lamps converted from bottles, and a picture of a matador assembled by sticking small varnished pebbles on to hardboard.

Claire laid them along the mantelshelf in the kitchen, and stood back, not so much to admire them as to see how incongruous they looked, piled together.

'Thank you,' she said to her mother, as tenderly as she might have when she was a child. These gifts touched her, especially the tapestry, although it was ugly. She thought of the winter nights and the Aladdin lamp smoking (they expected the electricity to be installed soon), and her mother hunched over her work, not even using a thimble to ease the needle through, because she believed in sacrifice, and her father turning to say, 'Could I borrow your glasses, Mam, I want to have a look at the paper?' He was too lazy to have his own eyes tested and believed that his wife's glasses were just as good. She could picture them at the fire night after night, the turf flames green and fitful, the hens locked up, foxes prowling around in the wind, outside.

'I'm glad you like it, I did it specially for you,' the mother said gravely, and they both stood with tears in their eyes, savouring those seconds of tenderness, knowing that it would be short-lived.

'You'll stay seventeen days,' Claire said, because that was the length an economy ticket allowed. She really meant, 'Are you staying seventeen days?'

'If it's all right,' her mother said over-humbly. 'I don't see you that often, and I miss you.'

Claire withdrew into the scullery to put on the kettle for her mother's hot water bottle; she did not want any disclosures now, any declaration about how hard life had been and how near they'd been to death during many of the father's drinking deliriums.

'Your father sent you his love,' her mother said, nettled because Claire had not asked how he was.

'How is he?'

'He's great now, never touches a drop.'

Claire knew that if he had, he would have descended on her, the way he used to descend on her as a child when she was in the convent, or else she would have had a telegram, of clipped urgency, 'Come home. Mother.'

'It was God did it, curing him like that,' the mother said.

Claire thought bitterly that God had taken too long to help the thin frustrated man who was emaciated, crazed and bankrupted by drink. But she said nothing, she merely filled the rubber bottle, pressed the air from it with her arm, and then conducted her mother upstairs to bed.

Next morning they went up to the centre of London and Claire presented her mother with fifty pounds. The woman got flushed and began to shake her head, the quick uncontrolled movements resembling those of a beast with the staggers.

'You always had a good heart, too good,' she said to her daughter, as her eyes beheld racks of coats, raincoats, skirts on spinning hangers, and all kinds and colours of hats.

'Try some on,' Claire said. 'I have to make a phone call.'

There were guests due to visit her that night—it had been arranged weeks before—but as they were bohemian people, she could not see her mother suffering them, or them suffering her mother. There was the added complication that they were a 'trio'—one man and two women; his wife and his mistress. At that point in their lives the wife was noticeably pregnant.

On the telephone the mistress said they were looking forward, awfully, to the night, and Claire heard herself substantiate the invitation by saying she had simply rung up to remind them. She thought of asking another man to give a complexion of decency to the evening, but the only three unattached men she could think of had been lovers of hers and she could not call on them; it seemed pathetic.

'Damn,' she said, irritated by many things, but mainly by the fact that she was going through one of those bleak, loveless patches that come in everyone's life, but, she imagined, came more frequently the older one got. She was twenty-eight. Soon she would be thirty. Withering.

'How do?' her mother said in a ridiculous voice when Claire returned.

She was holding a hand mirror up to get a back view of a ridiculous hat, which she had tried on. It resembled the shiny straw she wore for her trip, except that it was more ornamental and cost ten guineas. That was the second point about it that Claire noted. The white price tag was hanging over the mother's nose. Claire hated shopping the way other people might hate going to the dentist. For herself she never shopped. She merely saw things in windows, ascertained the size, and bought them.

'Am I too old for it?' the mother said. A loaded question in itself.

'You're not,' Claire said. 'You look well in it.'

'Of course I've always loved hats,' her mother said, as if admitting to some secret vice. Claire remembered drawers with felt hats laid into them, and bobbins on the brims of hats, and little aprons of veiling, with spots which, as a child, she thought might crawl over the wearer's face.

'Yes, I remember your hats,' Claire said, remembering too the smell of empty perfume bottles and camphor, and a saxe-blue hat that her mother once got on approbation, by post, and wore to Mass before returning it to the shop.

'If you like it, take it,' Claire said indulgently.

The mother bought it, along with a reversible raincoat and a pair of shoes. She told the assistant who measured her feet about a pair of shoes which lasted her for seventeen years, and were eventually stolen by a tinker-woman, who afterwards was sent to jail for the theft.

'Poor old creature I wouldn't have wished jail on her,' the mother said, and Claire nudged her to shut up. The mother's face flushed under the shelter of her new, wide-brimmed hat.

'Did I say something wrong?' she said as she descended uneasily on the escalator, her parcels held close to her.

'No, I just thought she was busy, it isn't like shops at home,' Claire said.

'I think she was enjoying the story,' her mother said, gathering courage before she stepped off, on to the ground floor.

At home they prepared the food and the mother tidied the front room before the visitors arrived. Without a word she carried all her own trophies—the tapestry, the pebble picture, the ashtrays, the holy water font and the other ornaments—and put them in the front room alongside the books, the pencil drawings and the poster of Bengal that was a left-over from Claire's dark-skinned lover.

'They're nicer in here,' the mother said, apologizing for doing it, and at the same time criticizing the drawing of the nude.

'I'd get rid of some of those things if I were you,' she said in a serious tone to her daughter.

Claire kept silent, and sipped the whiskey she felt she needed badly. Then to get off the subject she asked after her mother's feet. They were fixing a chiropodist appointment for the next day.

The mother had changed into a blue blouse, Claire into velvet pants, and they sat before the fire on low pouffes with a blue-shaded lamp casting a restful light on their very similar faces. At sixty, and made-up, the mother still had a poem of a face: round, pale, perfect and with soft eyes, expectant, in spite of what life had brought. On the whites there had appeared blobs of green, the sad green of old age.

'You have a tea-leaf on your eyelid,' she said to Claire, putting up her hand to brush it away. It was mascara which got so smeared that Claire had to go upstairs to repair it.

At that precise moment the visitors came.

'They're here,' the mother said when the hall bell shrieked.

'Open the door,' Claire called down.

'Won't it look odd, if you don't do it?' the mother said.

'Oh, open it,' Claire called impatiently. She was quite relieved that they would have to muddle through their own set of introductions.

The dinner went off well. They all liked the food and the mother was not as shy as Claire expected. She told about her journey, but kept the 'mad woman' episode out of it, and about a television programme she'd once seen, showing how bird's nest soup was collected. Only her voice was unnatural.

After dinner Claire gave her guests enormous brandies, because she felt relieved that nothing disastrous had been uttered. Her mother never drank spirits of course.

The fulfilled guests sat back, sniffed brandy, drank their coffee, laughed, tipped their cigarette ash on the floor, having missed the ashtray by a hair's breadth, gossiped, and re-filled their glasses. They smiled at the various new ornaments but did not comment, except to say that the tapestry was nice.

'Claire likes it,' the mother said timidly, drawing them into another silence. The evening was punctuated by brief but crushing silences.

'You like Chinese food then?' the husband said. He mentioned a restaurant which she ought to go and see. It was in the East End of London and getting there entailed having a motor-car.

'You've been there?' his wife said to the young blonde mistress who had hardly spoken.

'Yes and it was super except for the pork which was drowned in Chanel Number Five. Remember?' she said, turning to the husband, who nodded.

'We must go some time,' his wife said. 'If ever you can spare an evening.' She was staring at the big brandy snifter that she let rock back and forth in her lap. It was for rose petals but when she saw it she insisted on drinking from it. The petals were already dying on the mantelshelf.

'That was the night we found a man against a wall, beaten up,' the mistress said, shivering, recalling how she had actually shivered.

'You were so sorry for him,' the husband said, amused.

'Wouldn't anyone be?' the wife said tartly, and Claire turned to her mother and promised that they would go to that restaurant the following evening.

'We'll see,' the mother said. She knew the places she wanted to visit: Buckingham Palace, the tower of London and the waxworks museum. When she went home it was these places she would discuss with her neighbours who'd already been to London, not some seamy place where men were flung against walls.

'No, not another, it's not good for the baby,' the husband said, as his wife balanced her empty glass on the palm of her hand and looked towards the bottle.

'Who's the more important, me or the baby?'

'Don't be silly, Marigold,' the husband said.

'Excuse me,' she said in a changed voice. 'Whose welfare are you thinking about?' She was on the verge of an emotional outburst, her cheeks flushed from brandy and umbrage. By contrast Claire's mother had the appearance of a tombstone, chalk white and deadly still.

'How is the fire?' Claire said, staring at it. On that cue her mother jumped up and sailed off with the coal scuttle.

'I'll get it,' Claire said following. The mother did not even wait until they reached the kitchen.

'Tell me,' she said, her blue eyes pierced with insult, 'which of those two ladies is he married to?'

'It's not your concern,' Claire said, hastily. She had meant to smooth it over, to say that the pregnant woman had some mental disturbance, but instead she said hurtful things about her mother being narrow-minded and cruel.

'Show me your friends and I know who you are,' the mother said and went away to shovel the coal. She left the filled bucket outside the living-room door and went upstairs. Claire, who had gone back to her guests, heard the mother's footsteps climbing the stairs and going into the bedroom overhead.

'Is your mother gone to bed?' the husband asked.

'She's tired I expect,' Claire said, conveying weariness too. She wanted them to go. She could not confide in them even though they were old friends. They might sneer. They were not friends any more than the ex-lovers, they were all social appendages, extras, acquaintances cultivated in order to be able to say to other acquaintances, 'Well one night a bunch of us went mad and had a nude sit-in . . .' There was no one she trusted, no one she could produce for her mother and feel happy about it.

'Music, brandy, cigarettes . . .' They were recalling her, voicing their needs, wondering who would go to the machine for the cigarettes. Pauline did. They stayed until they'd finished the packet, which was well after midnight.

Claire hurried to her mother's room and found her awake with the light on, fingering her horn rosary beads. The same old black ones.

'I'm sorry,' Claire said.

'You turned on me like a tinker,' her mother said, in a voice cracked with emotion.

'I didn't mean to,' Claire said. She tried to sound reasonable, assured; she tried to tell her mother that the world was a big place and contained many people, all of whom held various views about various things.

'They're not sincere,' her mother said, stressing the last word.

'And who is?' Claire said, remembering the treacherous way the lovers vanished, or how former landladies rigged meters so that units of electricity cost double. Her mother had no notion of how lonely it was to read manuscripts all day, and write a poem once in a while, when one became consumed with a memory or an idea, and then to constantly go out, seeking people, hoping that one of them might fit, might know the short-hand of her, body and soul.

'I was a good mother, I did everything I could, and this is all the thanks I get.' It was spoken with such justification that Claire turned and laughed, hysterically. An incident leaped to her tongue, something she had never recalled before.

'You went to the hospital,' she said to her mother, 'to have your toe lanced, and you came home and told me, *me,* that the doctor said, "Raise your right arm until I give you an injection," but when you did, he gave you no injection, he just cut into your toe. Why did you tell it?' The words fell out of her mouth unexpectedly, and she became aware of the awfulness when she felt her knees shaking.

'What are you talking about?' her mother said numbly. The face that was round, in the evening, had become old, twisted, bitter.

'Nothing,' Claire said. Impossible to explain. She had violated all the rules: decency, kindness, caution. She would never be able to laugh it off in the morning. Muttering an apology she went to her own room and sat on her bed, trembling. Since her mother's arrival every detail of her childhood kept dogging her. Her present life, her work, the friends she had, seemed insubstantial compared with all that had happened before. She could count the various batches of white, hissing geese—it was geese in those days—that wandered over the swampy fields, one year after another, hid in memory she could locate the pot-holes on the driveway where rain lodged, and where leaking oil from a passing car made rainbows. Looking down into rainbows to escape the colour that was in her mind, or on her tongue. She'd licked four fingers once that were slit by an unexpected razor blade which was wedged upright in a shelf where she'd reached to find a sweet, or to finger the secret dust up there. The same colour had been on her mother's violated toe underneath the big, bulky bandage. In chapel too, the sanctuary light was a bowl of blood with a flame laid into it. These images did not distress her at the time. She used to love to slip into the chapel, alone, in the daytime, moving from one Station of the Cross to the next, being God's exclusive pet, praying that she would die before her mother did, in order to escape being the scapegoat of her father. How could she have known, how could any of them have known that twenty years later, zipped into a heated, plastic tent, treating herself to a steam bath she would suddenly panic and cry out convinced that her sweat became as drops of blood. She put her hands through the flaps and begged the masseuse to protect her, the way she had begged her mother, long ago. Made a fool of herself. The way she made a fool of herself with the various men. The first night she met the

Indian she was wearing a white fox collar, and its whiteness under his dark, well-chiselled chin made a stark sight as they walked through a mirrored room to a table, and saw, and were seen, in mirrors. He said something she couldn't hear.

'Tell me later,' she said, already putting her little claim on him, already saying, 'You are not going to abandon me in this room of mirrors, in my bluish-white fox that so compliments your bluish-black lips.' But after a few weeks he left, like the others. She was familiar with the various tactics of withdrawal—abrupt, honest, nice. Flowers, notes posted from the provinces, and the 'I don't want you to get hurt' refrain. They reminded her of the trails that slugs leave on a lawn in summer mornings, the sad, silver trails of departure. Their goings were far more vivid than their comings, or was she only capable of remembering the worst? Remembering everything, solving nothing. She undressed, she told herself that her four fingers had healed, that her mother's big toe was now like any other person's big toe, that her father drank tea and held his temper, and that one day she would meet a man whom she loved and did not frighten away. But it was brandy optimism. She'd gone down and carried the bottle up. The brandy gave her hope but it disturbed her heart beats and she was unable to sleep. As morning approached she rehearsed the sweet and conciliatory things she would say to her mother.

They went to Mass on Sunday, but it was obvious that Claire was not in the habit of going: they had to ask the way. Going in, her mother took a small liquer bottle from her handbag and filled it with holy water from the font.

'It's always good to have it,' she said to Claire, but in a bashful way. The outburst had severed them, and they were polite now in a way that should never have been.

After Mass they went—because the mother had stated her wishes—to the waxworks museum, saw the Tower of London and walked across the park that faced Buckingham Palace.

'Very good grazing here,' the mother said. Her new shoes were getting spotted from the damp, highish grass. It was raining. The spokes of the mother's umbrella kept tapping Claire's, and no matter how far she drew away, the mother moved accordingly, to prong her, it seemed.

'You know,' the mother said. 'I was thinking.'

Claire knew what was coming. Her mother wanted to go home; she was worried about her husband, her fowls, the washing that would have piled up, the spring wheat that would have to be sown. In reality she was miserable. She and her daughter were farther away now than when they wrote letters each week and discussed the weather, or work, or the colds they'd had.

'You're only here six days,' Claire said. 'And I want to take you to the theatre and restaurants. Don't go.'

'I'll think about it,' the mother said. But her mind was made up.

Two evenings later they waited in the airport lounge, hesitant to speak, for fear they might miss the flight number.

'The change did you good,' Claire said. Her mother was togged out in new clothes and looked smarter. She had two more new hats in her hand, carrying them in the hope they would escape the notice of the customs men.

'I'll let you know if I have to pay duty on them,' she said.

'Do,' Claire said, smiling, straightening her mother's collar, wanting to say something endearing, something that would atone, without having to go over their differences, word for word.

'No one can say but that you fitted me out well, look at all my style,' the mother said smiling at her image in the glass door of the telephone box. 'And our trip up the river,' she said. 'I think I enjoyed it more than anything.' She was referring to a short trip they'd taken down the Thames to Westminster. They had planned to go in the opposite direction towards the greenness of Kew and Hampton Court but they'd left it—at least Claire had left it—too late and could only go towards the city on a passenger boat that was returning from those green places.

Claire had been miserly with her time and on that particular evening she'd sat at her desk pretending to work, postponing the time until she got up and rejoined her mother, who was downstairs sewing on all the buttons that had fallen off over the years. And now the mother was thanking her, saying it had been lovely. Lovely. They had passed warehouses and cranes brought to their evening standstill yellow and tilted, pylons like floodlit honeycombs in the sky, and boats, and gasworks, and filthy chimneys. The spring evening had been drenched with sewerage smell and yet her mother went on being thankful.

'I hope my mad lady won't be aboard,' the mother said, trying to make a joke out of it now.

'Not likely,' Claire said, but the mother declared that life was full of strange and sad coincidences. They looked at each other, looked away, criticized a man who was wolfing sandwiches from his pocket, looked at the airport clock and compared the time on their watches.

'Sssh . . . ssh . . .' Claire had to say.

'That's it,' they both said then, relieved. As if they had secretly feared the flight number would never be called.

At the barrier they kissed, their damp cheeks touched and stayed for a second like that, each registering the other's sorrow.

'I'll write to you, I'll write oftener,' Claire said, and for a few minutes she stood there waving, weeping, not aware that the visit was over and that she could go back to her own life now, such as it was.

Rape Fantasies

MARGARET ATWOOD
(Canadian, 1939–   )

The way they're going on about it in the magazines you'd think it was just invented, and not only that but it's something terrific, like a vaccine for cancer. They put it in capital letters on the front cover and inside they have these questionnaires like the ones they used to have about whether you were a good enough wife or an endomorph or an ectomorph, remember that? with the scoring upside down on page 73, and then these numbered do-it-yourself dealies, you know? RAPE, TEN THINGS TO DO ABOUT IT, like it was ten new hairdos or something. I mean, what's so new about it?

So at work they all have to talk about it because no matter what magazine you open, there it is, staring you right between the eyes, and they're beginning to have it on the television too. Personally I'd prefer a June Allyson movie anytime but they don't make them any more and they don't even have them that much on the Late Show. For instance, day before yesterday, that would be Wednesday, thank god it's Friday as they say, we were sitting around in the women's lunch room—the *lunch* room, I mean you'd think you could get some peace and quiet in there—and Chrissy closes up the magazine she's been reading and says, "How about it, girls, do you have rape fantasies?"

The four of us were having our game of bridge the way we always do, and I had a bare twelve points counting the singleton with not that much of a bid in anything. So I said one club, hoping Sondra would remember about the one club convention, because the time before when I used that she thought I really meant clubs and she bid us up to three, and all I had was four little ones with nothing higher than a six, and we went down two and on top of that we were vulnerable. She is not the world's best bridge player. I mean, neither am I but there's a limit.

Darlene passed but the damage was done. Sondra's head went round like it was on ball bearings and she said, *"What* fantasies?"

"Rape fantasies," Chrissy said. She's a receptionist and she looks like one, she's pretty but cool as a cucumber, like she's been painted all over with nail polish if you know what I mean. Varnished. "It says here all women have rape fantasies."

"For Chrissake, I'm eating an egg sandwich," I said, "and I bid one club and Darlene passed."

"You mean, like some guy jumping you in an alley or something," Sondra said. She was eating her lunch, we all eat our lunches during the game, and she bit into a piece of that celery she always brings and started to chew away on it with this thoughtful expression in her eyes and I knew we might as well pack it in as far as the game was concerned.

"Yeah, sort of like that," Chrissy said. She was blushing a little, you could see it even under her makeup.

"I don't think you should go out alone at night," Darlene said, "you put yourself in a position," and I may have been mistaken but she was looking at me. She's the oldest, she's forty-one though you wouldn't know it and neither does she, but I looked it up in the employees' file. I like to guess a person's age and then look it up to see if I'm right, I let myself have an extra pack of cigarettes if I am, though I'm trying to cut down. I figure it's harmless as long as you don't tell. I mean, not everyone has access to that file, it's more or less confidential. But it's all right if

I tell you, I don't expect you'll ever meet her, though you never know, it's a small world. Anyway.

"For *heaven's* sake, it's only *Toronto,*" Greta said. She worked in Detroit for three years and she never lets you forget it, it's like she thinks she's a war hero or something, we should all admire her just for the fact that she's still walking this earth, though she was really living in Windsor the whole time, she just worked in Detroit. Which for me doesn't really count. It's where you sleep, right?

"Well, do you?" Chrissy said. She was obviously dying to tell us about hers but she wasn't about to go first, she's cautious, that one.

"I certainly don't," Darlene said, and she wrinkled up her nose, like this, and I had to laugh. "I think it's disgusting." She's divorced, I read that in the file too, she never talks about it. It must've been years ago anyway. She got up and went over to the coffee machine and turned her back on us as though she wasn't going to have anything more to do with it.

"Well," Greta said. I could see it was going to be between her and Chrissy. They're both blondes, I don't mean that in a bitchy way but they do try to outdress each other. Greta would like to get out of Filing, she'd like to be a receptionist too so she could meet more people. You don't meet much of anyone in Filing except other people in Filing. Me, I don't mind it so much. I have outside interests.

"Well," Greta said, "I sometimes think about, you know my apartment? It's got this little balcony. I like to sit out there in the summer and I have a few plants out there. I never bother that much about locking the door to the balcony, it's one of those sliding glass ones, I'm on the eighteenth floor for heaven's sake, I've got a good view of the lake and the CN Tower and all. But I'm sitting around one night in my housecoat, watching TV with my shoes off, you know how you do, and I see this guy's feet coming down past the window, and the next thing you know he's standing on the balcony, he's let himself down by a rope with a hook on the end of it from the floor above, that's the nineteenth, and before I can even get up off the chesterfield he's inside the apartment. He's all dressed in black with black gloves on"—I knew right away what show she got the black gloves off because I saw the same one—"and then he, well, you know."

"You know what?" Chrissy said, but Greta said, "And afterwards he tells me that he goes all over the outside of the apartment building like that, from one floor to another, with his rope and his hook . . . and then he goes out to the balcony and tosses his rope, and he climbs up it and disappears."

"Just like Tarzan," I said, but nobody laughed. "Is that all?" Chrissy said. "Don't you ever think about, well, I think about being in the bathtub, with no clothes on . . ."

"So who takes a bath in their clothes?" I said, you have to admit it's stupid when you come to think of it, but she just went on, ". . . . with lots of bubbles, what I use is Vitabath, it's more expensive but it's so relaxing, and my hair pinned up, and the door opens and this fellow's standing there . . ."

"How'd he get in?" Greta said.

"Oh, I don't know, through a window or something. Well, I can't very well get out of the bathtub, the bathroom's too small and besides he's blocking the doorway, so I just *lie* there, and he starts to very slowly take his own clothes off, and then he gets into the bathtub with me."

"Don't you scream or anything?" said Darlene. She'd come back with her cup of coffee, she was getting really interested. "I'd scream like bloody murder."

"Who'd hear me?" Chrissy said. "Besides, all the articles say it's better not to resist, that way you don't get hurt."

"Anyway you might get bubbles up your nose," I said, "from the deep breathing," and I swear all four of them looked at me like I was in bad taste, like I'd insulted the Virgin Mary or something. I mean, I don't see what's wrong with a little joke now and then. Life's too short, right?

"Listen," I said, "those aren't *rape* fantasies. I mean, you aren't getting *raped,* it's just some guy you haven't met formally who happens to be more attractive than Derek Cummins"—he's the Assistant Manager, he wears elevator shoes or at any rate they have these thick soles and he has this funny way of talking, we call him Derek Duck—"and you have a good time. Rape is when they've got a knife or something and you don't want to."

"So what about you, Estelle," Chrissy said, she was miffed because I laughed at her fantasy, she thought I was putting her down. Sondra was miffed too, by this time she'd finished her celery and she wanted to tell about hers, but she hadn't got in fast enough.

"All right, let me tell you one," I said. "I'm walking down this dark street at night and this fellow comes up and grabs my arm. Now it so happens that I have a plastic lemon in my purse, you know how it always says you should carry a plastic lemon in your purse? I don't really do it. I tried it once but the darn thing leaked all over my chequebook, but in this fantasy I have one, and I say to him, "You're intending to rape me, right?" and he nods, so I open my purse to get the plastic lemon, and I can't find it! My purse is full of all this junk, Kleenex and cigarettes and my change purse and my lipstick and my driver's license, you know the kind of stuff; so I ask him to hold out his hands, like this, and I pile all this junk into them and down at the bottom there's the plastic lemon, and I can't get the top off. So I hand it to him and he's very obliging, he twists the top off and hands it back to me, and I squirt him in the eye."

I hope you don't think that's too vicious. Come to think of it, it is a bit mean, especially when he was so polite and all.

"*That's* your rape fantasy?" Chrissy says. "I don't believe it."

"She's a card," Darlene says, she and I are the ones that've been here the longest and she never will forget the time I got drunk at the office party and insisted I was going to dance under the table instead of on top of it, I did a sort of Cossack number but then I hit my head on the bottom of the table—actually it was a desk—when I went to get up, and I knocked myself out cold. She's decided that's the mark of an original mind and she tells everyone new about it and I'm not sure that's fair. Though I did do it.

"I'm being totally honest," I say, I always am and they know it. There's no point in being anything else, is the way I look at it, and sooner or later the truth will out so you might as well not waste the time, right? "You should hear the one about the Easy-Off Oven Cleaner."

But that was the end of the lunch hour, with one bridge game shot to hell, and the next day we spent most of the time arguing over whether to start a new game or play out the hands we had left over from the day before, so Sondra never did get a chance to tell about her rape fantasy.

It started me thinking though, about my own rape fantasies. Maybe I'm abnormal or something, I mean I have fantasies about handsome strangers coming in through the window too, like Mr. Clean, I wish one would, please god somebody without flat feet and big sweat marks on his shirt, and over five feet five, believe me being tall is a handicap though it's getting better, tall guys are starting to like someone whose nose reaches higher than their belly button. But if you're being totally honest you can't count those as rape fantasies. In a real rape fantasy, what you should feel is this anxiety, like when you think about your apartment building catching on fire and whether you should use the elevator or the stairs or maybe just stick your head under a wet towel, and you try to remember everything you've read about what to do but you can't decide.

For instance, I'm walking along this dark street at night and this short, ugly fellow comes up and grabs my arm, and not only is he ugly, you know, with a sort of puffy nothing face, like those fellows you have to talk to in the bank when your account's overdrawn—of course I don't mean they're all like that—but he's absolutely covered in pimples. So he gets me pinned against the wall, he's short but he's heavy, and he starts to undo himself and the zipper gets stuck. I mean, one of the most significant moments in a girl's life, it's almost like getting married or having a baby or something, and he sticks the zipper.

So I say, kind of disgusted, "Oh for Chrissake," and he starts to cry. He tells me he's never been able to get anything right in his entire life, and this is the last straw, he's going to go jump off a bridge.

"Look," I say, I feel so sorry for him, in my rape fantasies I always end up feeling sorry for the guy, I mean there has to be something *wrong* with them, if it was Clint Eastwood it'd be different but worse luck it never is. I was the kind of little girl who buried dead robins, know what I mean? It used to drive my mother nuts, she didn't like me touching them, because of the germs I guess. So I say, "Listen, I know how you feel. You really should do something about those pimples, if you got rid of them you'd be quite good looking, honest; then you wouldn't have to go around doing stuff like this. I had them myself once," I say, to comfort him, but in fact I did, and it ends up I give him the name of my old dermatologist, the one I had in high school, that was back in Leamington, except I used to go to St. Catherines for the dermatologist. I'm telling you, I was really lonely when I first came here; I thought it was going to be such a big adventure and all, but it's a lot harder to meet people in a city. But I guess it's different for a guy.

Or I'm lying in bed with this terrible cold, my face is all swollen up, my eyes are red and my nose is dripping like a leaky tap, and this fellow comes in through the window and *he* has a terrible cold too, it's a new kind of flu that's been going around. So he says, "I'b goig do rabe you"— I hope you don't mind me holding my nose like this but that's the way I imagine it—and he lets out this terrific sneeze, which slows him down a bit, also I'm no object of beauty myself, you'd have to be some kind of pervert to want to rape someone with a cold like mine, it'd be like raping a bottle of LePage's Mucilage the way my nose is running. He's looking wildly around the room, and I realize it's because he doesn't have a piece of Kleenex! "Id's ride here," I say, and I pass him the Kleenex, god knows why he even bothered to get out of bed, you'd think if you were going to go around climbing in windows you'd wait till you were healthier, right? I mean, that takes a certain amount of energy. So I ask him why doesn't he let me fix him a Neo-Citran and scotch, that's what I always take, you still have the cold but you don't feel it, so I do and we end up watching the Late Show together. I mean, they aren't all sex maniacs, the rest of the time they must lead a normal life. I figure they enjoy watching the Late Show just like anybody else.

I do have a scarier one though . . . where the fellow says he's hearing angel voices that're telling him he's got to kill me, you know, you read about things like that all the time in the papers. In this one I'm not in the apartment where I live now, I'm back in my mother's house in Leamington and the fellow's been hiding in the cellar, he grabs my arm when I go downstairs to get a jar of jam and he's got hold of the axe too, out of the garage, that one is really scary. I mean, what do you say to a nut like that?

So I start to shake but after a minute I get control of myself and I say, is he sure the angel voices have got the right person, because I hear the same angel voices and they've been telling me for some time that I'm going to give birth to the reincarnation of St. Anne who in turn has the Virgin Mary and right after that comes Jesus Christ and the end of the world, and he wouldn't want to interfere with that, would he? So he gets confused and listens some more, and then he asks for a sign and I show him my vaccination mark, you can see it's sort of an odd-shaped one, it got infected because I scratched the top off, and that does it, he apologizes and climbs out of the coal chute again, which is how he got in in the first place, and I say to myself there's some advantage in having been brought up a Catholic even though I haven't been to church since they changed the service into English, it just isn't the same, you might as well be a Protestant. I must write to Mother and tell her to nail up that coal chute, it always has bothered me. Funny, I couldn't tell you at all what this man looks like but I know exactly what kind of shoes he's wearing, because that's the last I see of him, his shoes going up the coal chute, and they're the old-fashioned kind that lace up the ankles, even though he's a young fellow. That's strange, isn't it?

Let me tell you though I really sweat until I see him safely out of there and I go upstairs right away and make myself a cup of tea. I don't think about that one much. My mother always said you shouldn't dwell on unpleasant things and I generally agree with that, I mean, dwelling on them doesn't make them go away. Though not dwelling on them doesn't make them go away either, when you come to think of it.

Sometimes I have these short ones where the fellow grabs my arm but I'm really a Kung-Fu expert, can you believe it, in real life I'm sure it would just be a conk on the head and that's that, like getting your tonsils out, you'd wake up and it would be all over except for the sore places, and you'd be lucky if your neck wasn't broken or something, I could never even hit the volleyball in gym and a volleyball is fairly large, you know?—and I just go *zap* with my fingers into his eyes and that's it, he falls over, or I flip him against a wall or something. But I could never really stick my fingers in anyone's eyes, could you? It would feel like hot Jello and I don't even like cold Jello, just thinking about it gives me the creeps. I feel a bit guilty about that one, I mean how would you like walking around knowing someone's been blinded for life because of you?

But maybe it's different for a guy.

The most touching one I have is when the fellow grabs my arm and I say, sad and kind of dignified, "You'd be raping a corpse." That pulls him up short and I explain that I've just found out I have leukemia and the doctors have only given me a few months to live. That's why I'm out pacing the streets alone at night, I need to think, you know, come to terms with myself. I don't really have leukemia but in the fantasy I do, I guess I chose that particular disease because a girl in my grade four class died of it, the whole class sent her flowers when she was in the hospital. I didn't understand then that she was going to die and I wanted to have leukemia too so I could get flowers. Kids are funny, aren't they? Well, it turns out that he has leukemia himself, and *he* only has a few months to live, that's why he's going around raping people, he's very bitter because he's so young and his life is being taken from him before he's really lived it. So we walk along gently under the street lights, it's spring and sort of misty, and we end up going for coffee, we're happy we've found the only other person in the world who can understand what we're going through, it's almost like fate, and after a while we just sort of look at each other and our hands touch, and he comes back with me and moves into my apartment and we spend our last months together before we die, we just sort of don't wake up in the morning, though I've never decided which one of us gets to die first. If it's him I have to go on and fantasize about the funeral, if it's me I don't have to worry about that, so it just about depends on how tired I am at the time. You may not believe this but sometimes I even start crying. I cry at the ends of movies, even the ones that aren't all that sad, so I guess it's the same thing. My mother's like that too.

The funny thing about these fantasies is that the man is always someone I don't know, and the statistics in the magazines, well, most of them anyway, they say it's often someone you do know, at least a little bit, like your boss or something—I mean, it wouldn't be *my* boss, he's over sixty and I'm sure he couldn't rape his way out of a paper bag, poor old thing, but it might be someone like Derek Duck, in his elevator shoes, perish the thought—or someone you just met, who invites you up for a drink, it's getting so you can hardly be sociable any more, and how are you supposed to meet people if you can't trust them even that basic amount? You can't spend your whole life in the Filing Department or cooped up in your own apartment with all the doors and windows locked and the shades down. I'm not what you would call a drinker but I like to get out now and then for a drink or two in a nice place, even if I am by myself, I'm with Women's Lib on that even though I can't agree with a lot of other things they say. Like here for instance, the waiters all know me and if anyone you know, bothers me. . . . I don't know why I'm telling you all this, except I think it helps you get to know a person, especially at first, hearing some of the things they think about. At work they call me the office worry wart, but it isn't so much like worrying, it's more like figuring out what you should do in an emergency, like I said before.

Anyway, another thing about it is that there's a lot of conversation, in fact I spend most of my time, in the fantasy that is, wondering what I'm going to say and what he's going to say. I think it would be better if you could get a conversation going. Like, how could a fellow do that to a person he's just had a long conversation with, once you let them know you're human, you have a life too, I don't see how they could go ahead with it, right? I mean, I know it happens but I just don't understand it. That's the part I really don't understand.

The Courtship of Mr. Lyon

ANGELA CARTER
(English, 1940–)

Outside her kitchen window, the hedgerow glistened as if the snow possessed a light of its own; when the sky darkened towards evening, an unearthly, reflected pallor remained behind upon the winter's landscape, while still the soft flakes floated down. This lovely girl, whose skin possesses that same inner light so you would have thought she, too, was made all of snow, pauses in her chores in the mean kitchen to look out at the country road. Nothing has passed that way all day; the road is white and unmarked as a spilled bolt of bridal satin.

Father said he would be home before nightfall.

The snow brought down all the telephone wires; he couldn't have called, even with the best of news.

The roads are bad. I hope he'll be safe.

But the old car stuck fast in a rut, wouldn't budge an inch; the engine whirred, coughed and died and he was far from home. Ruined once; then ruined again, as he had learned from his lawyers that very morning; at the conclusion of the lengthy, slow attempt to restore his fortunes, he had turned out his pockets to find the cash for petrol to take him home. And not even enough money left over to buy his Beauty, his girl child, his pet, the one white rose she said she wanted; the only gift she wanted, no matter how the case went, how rich he might once again be. She had asked for so little and he had not been able to give it to her. He cursed the useless car, the last straw that broke his spirit; then, nothing for it but to fasten his old sheepskin coat around him, abandon the heap of metal and set off down the snow-filled lane to look for help.

Behind wrought-iron gates, a short, snowy drive performed a reticent flourish before a miniature, perfect, Palladian house that seemed to hide itself shyly behind snow-laden skirts of an antique cypress. It was almost night; that house, with its sweet, retiring, melancholy grace, would have seemed deserted but for a light that flickered in an upstairs window, so vague it might have been the reflection of a star, if any stars could have penetrated the snow that whirled yet more thickly. Chilled through, he pressed the latch of the gate and saw, with a pang, how, on the withered ghost of a tangle of thorns, there clung, still, the faded rag of a white rose.

The gate clanged loudly shut behind him; too loudly. For an instant, that reverberating clang seemed final, emphatic, ominous, as if the gate, now closed, barred all within it from the world outside the walled, wintry garden. And, from a distance, though from what distance he could not tell, he heard the most singular sound in the world: a great roaring, as of a beast of prey.

In too much need to allow himself to be intimidated, he squared up to the mahogany door. This door was equipped with a knocker in the shape of a lion's head, with a ring through the nose; as he raised his hand towards it, it came to him this lion's head was not, as he had thought at first, made of brass, but, instead, of solid gold. Before, however, he could announce his presence, the door swung silently inward on well-oiled hinges and he saw a white hall where the candles of a great chandelier cast their benign light upon so many, many flowers in great, free-standing jars of crystal that it seemed the whole of spring drew him into its warmth with a profound intake of perfumed breath. Yet there was no living person in the hall.

The door behind him closed as silently as it had opened, yet, this time, he felt no fear although he knew by the pervasive atmosphere of a suspension of reality that he had entered a place of privilege where all the laws of the world he knew need not necessarily apply, for the very rich are often very eccentric and the house was plainly that of an exceedingly wealthy man. As it was, when nobody came to help him with his coat, he took it off himself. At that, the crystals of the chandelier tinkled a little, as if emitting a pleased chuckle, and the door of a cloakroom opened of its own accord. There were, however, no clothes at all in this cloakroom, not even the statutory country house garden mackintosh to greet his own squirearchal sheepskin, but when he emerged again into the hall, he found a greeting waiting for him at last—there was, of all things, a liver-and-white King Charles spaniel crouched, with head intelligently cocked, on the Kelim runner. It gave him further, comforting proof of his unseen host's wealth and eccentricity to see the dog wore, in place of a collar, a diamond necklace.

The dog sprang to its feet in welcome and busily shepherded him (how amusing!) to a snug little leather-paneled study on the first floor, where a low table was drawn up to a roaring log fire. On the table, a silver tray; round the neck of the whisky decanter, a silver tag with the legend *Drink me,* while the cover of the silver dish was engraved with the exhortation *Eat me,* in a flowing hand. This dish contained sandwiches of thick-cut roast beef, still bloody. He drank the one with soda and ate the other with some excellent mustard thoughtfully provided in a stoneware pot, and when the spaniel saw to it he had served himself, she trotted off about her own business.

All that remained to make Beauty's father entirely comfortable was to find, in a curtained recess, not only a telephone, but the card of a garage that advertised a twenty-four-hour rescue service; a couple of calls later and he had confirmed, thank God, there was no serious trouble, only the car's age and the cold weather. . . . Could he pick it up from the village in an hour? And directions to the village, but half a mile away, were supplied, in a new tone of deference, as soon as he described the house from where he was calling.

And he was disconcerted but, in his impecunious circumstances, relieved to hear the bill would go on his hospitable if absent host's account; no question, assured the mechanic. It was the master's custom.

Time for another whisky as he tried, unsuccessfully, to call Beauty and tell her he would be late; but the lines were still down, although, miraculously, the storm had cleared as the moon rose and now a glance between the velvet curtains revealed a landscape as of ivory with an inlay of silver. Then the spaniel appeared again, with his hat in her careful mouth, prettily wagging her tail, as if to tell him it was time to be gone, that this magical hospitality was over.

As the door swung to behind him, he saw the lion's eyes were made of agate.

Great wreaths of snow now precariously curded the rose trees, and when he brushed against a stem on his way to the gate, a chill armful softly thudded to the ground to reveal, as if miraculously preserved beneath it, one last, single, perfect rose that might have been the last rose left living in all the white winter, and of so intense and yet delicate a fragrance it seemed to ring like a dulcimer on the frozen air.

How could his host, so mysterious, so kind, deny Beauty her present?

Not now distant but close at hand, close as that mahogany front door, rose a mighty, furious roaring; the garden seemed to hold its breath in apprehension. But still, because he loved his daughter, Beauty's father stole the rose.

At that, every window of the house blazed with furious light and a fugal baying, as of a pride of lions, introduced his host.

There is always a dignity about great bulk, an assertiveness, a quality of being more *there* than most of us are. The being who now confronted Beauty's father seemed to him, in his confusion, vaster than the house he owned, ponderous yet swift, and the moonlight glittered on his great, mazy head of hair, on the eyes green as agate, on the golden hairs of the great paws that grasped his shoulders so that their claws pierced the sheepskin as he shook him like an angry child shakes a doll.

This leonine apparition shook Beauty's father until his teeth rattled and then dropped him sprawling on his knees while the spaniel, darting from the open door, danced round them, yapping distractedly, like a lady at whose dinner party blows have been exchanged.

"My good fellow—" stammered Beauty's father; but the only response was a renewed roar.

"Good fellow? I am no good fellow! I am the Beast, and you must call me Beast, while I call you Thief!"

"Forgive me for robbing your garden, Beast!"

Head of a lion; mane and mighty paws of a lion; he reared on his hind legs like an angry lion yet wore a smoking jacket of dull red brocade and was the owner of that lovely house and the low hills that cupped it.

"It was for my daughter," said Beauty's father. "All she wanted, in the whole world, was one white, perfect rose."

The Beast rudely snatched the photograph her father drew from his wallet and inspected it, first brusquely, then with a strange kind of wonder, almost the dawning of surmise. The camera had captured a certain look she had, sometimes, of absolute sweetness and absolute gravity, as if her eyes might pierce appearances and see your soul. When he handed the picture back, the Beast took good care not to scratch the surface with his claws.

"Take her her rose, then, but bring her to dinner," he growled; and what else was there to be done?

Although her father had told her of the nature of the one who waited for her, she could not control an instinctual shudder of fear when she saw him, for a lion is a lion and a man is a man, and though lions are more beautiful by far than we are, yet they belong to a different order of beauty and, besides, they have no respect for us; why should they? Yet wild things have a far more rational fear of us than is ours of them, and some kind of sadness in his agate eyes, that looked almost blind, as if sick of sight, moved her heart.

He sat, impassive as a figurehead, at the top of the table; the dining room was Queen Anne, tapestried, a gem. Apart from an aromatic soup kept hot over a spirit lamp, the food, though exquisite, was cold—a cold bird, a cold soufflé, cheese. He asked her father to serve them from a buffet and, himself, ate nothing. He grudgingly admitted what she had already guessed, that he disliked the presence of servants because, she thought, a constant human presence would remind him too bitterly of his otherness, but the spaniel sat at his feet throughout the meal, jumping up from time to time to see that everything was in order.

How strange he was. She found his bewildering difference from herself almost intolerable; its presence choked her. There seemed a heavy, soundless pressure upon her in his house, as if it lay under water, and when she saw the great paws lying on the arm of his chair, she thought: They are the death of any tender herbivore. And such a one she felt herself to be, Miss Lamb, spotless, sacrificial.

Yet she stayed, and smiled, because her father wanted her to do so; and when the Beast told her how he would aid her father's appeal against the judgment, she smiled with both her mouth and her eyes. But when, as they sipped their brandy, the Beast, in the diffuse, rumbling purr with which he conversed, suggested, with a hint of shyness, of fear of refusal, that she should stay here, with him, in comfort, while her father returned to London to take up the legal cudgels again, she forced a smile. For she knew with a pang of dread, as soon as he spoke, that it would be so and her visit to the Beast must be, on some magically reciprocal scale, the price of her father's good fortune.

Do not think she had no will of her own; only, she was possessed by a sense of obligation to an unusual degree and, besides, she would gladly have gone to the ends of the earth for her father, whom she loved dearly.

Her bedroom contained a marvelous glass bed; she had a bathroom, with towels thick as fleece and vials of suave unguents; and a little parlor of her own, the walls of which were covered with an antique paper of birds of paradise and Chinamen, where there were precious books and pictures and the flowers grown by invisible gardeners in the Beast's hothouses. Next morning, her father kissed her and drove away with a renewed hope about him that made her glad, but all the same, she longed for the shabby home of their poverty. The unaccustomed luxury about her she found poignant, because it gave no pleasure to its possessor, and himself she did not see all day as if, curious reversal, she frightened him, although the spaniel came and sat with her, to keep her company. Today the spaniel wore a neat choker of turquoises.

Who prepared her meals? Loneliness of the Beast; all the time she stayed there, she saw no evidence of another human presence but the trays of food that arrived on a dumbwaiter inside a mahogany cupboard in her parlor. Dinner was eggs Benedict and grilled veal; she ate it as she browsed in a book she had found in the rosewood revolving bookcase, a collection of courtly and elegant French fairy tales about white cats who were transformed princesses and fairies who were birds. Then she pulled a sprig of muscat grapes from a fat bunch for her dessert and found herself yawning; she discovered she was bored. At that, the spaniel took hold of her skirt with its velvet mouth and gave it a firm but gentle tug. She allowed the dog to trot before her to the study in which her father had been entertained and there, to her well-disguised dismay, she found her host, seated beside the fire with a tray of coffee at his elbow from which she must pour.

The voice that seemed to issue from a cave full of echoes, his dark, soft rumbling growl—after her day of pastel-colored idleness, how could she converse with the possessor of a voice that seemed an instrument created to inspire the terror that the chords of great organs bring? Fascinated, almost awed, she watched the firelight play on the gold fringes of his mane; he was irradiated, as if with a kind of halo, and she thought of the first great beast of the Apocalypse, the winged lion with his paw upon the Gospel, Saint Mark. Small talk turned to dust in her mouth; small talk had never, at the best of times, been Beauty's forte, and she had little practice at it.

But he, hesitantly, as if he himself were in awe of a young girl who looked as though she had been carved out of a single pearl, asked after her father's law case; and her dead mother; and how they, who had been so rich, had come to be so poor. He forced himself to master his shyness, which was that of a wild creature, and so she contrived to master her own—to such effect that soon she was chattering away to him as if she had known him all her life. When the little cupid in the gilt clock on the mantelpiece struck its miniature tambourine, she was astonished to discover it did so twelve times.

"So late! You will want to sleep," he said.

At that, they both fell silent, as if these strange companions were suddenly overcome with embarrassment to find themselves together, alone, in that room in the depths of the winter's night. As she was about to rise, he flung himself at her feet and buried his head in her lap. She stayed stock-still, transfixed; she felt his hot breath on her fingers, the stiff bristles of his muzzle grazing her skin, the rough lapping of his tongue, and then, with a flood of compassion, understood: All he is doing is kissing my hands.

He drew back his head and gazed at her with his green, inscrutable eyes, in which she saw her face repeated twice, as small as if it were in bud. Then, without another word, he sprang from the room and she saw, with an indescribable shock, he went on all fours.

Next day, all day, the hills on which the snow still settled echoed with the Beast's rumbling roar. Has master gone a-hunting? Beauty asked the spaniel. But the spaniel growled, almost bad-temperedly, as if to say that she would not have answered, even if she could have.

Beauty would pass the day in her suite reading or, perhaps, doing a little embroidery; a box of colored silks and a frame had been provided for her. Or, well wrapped up, she wandered in the walled garden, among the leafless roses, with the spaniel at her heels, and did a little raking and rearranging. An idle, restful time; a holiday. The enchantment of that bright, sad, pretty place enveloped her and she found that, against all her expectations, she was happy there. She no longer felt the slightest apprehension at her nightly interviews with the Beast. All the natural laws of the world were held in suspension here, where an army of invisibles tenderly waited on her, and she would talk with the lion, under the patient chaperonage of the brown-eyed dog, on the nature of the moon and its borrowed light, about the stars and the substances of which they were made, about the variable transformations of the weather. Yet still his strangeness made her shiver; and when he helplessly fell before her to kiss her hands, as he did every night when they parted, she would retreat nervously into her skin, flinching at his touch.

The telephone shrilled; for her. Her father. Such news!

The Beast sunk his great head on his paws. You will come back to me? It will be lonely here, without you.

She was moved almost to tears that he should care for her so. It was in her heart to drop a kiss upon his shaggy mane, but though she stretched out her hand towards him, she could not bring herself to touch him of her own free will, he was so different from herself. But, yes, she said; I will come back. Soon, before the winter is over. Then the taxi came and took her away.

You are never at the mercy of the elements in London, where the huddled warmth of humanity melts the snow before it has time to settle; and her father was as good as rich again, since his hirsute friend's lawyers had the business so well in hand that his credit brought them nothing but the best. A resplendent hotel; the opera, theaters; a whole new wardrobe for his darling, so she could step out on his arm to parties, to receptions, to restaurants, and life was as she had never known it, for her father had ruined himself before her birth killed her mother.

Although the Beast was the source of the new-found prosperity and they talked of him often, now that they were so far away from the time-less spell of his house it seemed to possess the radiant and finite quality of dream and the Beast himself, so monstrous, so benign, some kind of spirit of good fortune who had smiled on them and let them go. She sent him flowers, white roses in return for the ones he had given her; and when she left the florist, she experienced a sudden sense of perfect freedom, as if she had just escaped from an unknown danger, had been grazed by the possibility of some change but, finally, left intact. Yet, with this exhilaration, a desolating emptiness. But her father was waiting for her at the hotel; they had planned a delicious expedition to buy her furs and she was as eager for the treat as any girl might be.

Since the flowers in the shop were the same all the year round, nothing in the window could tell her that winter had almost gone.

Returning late from supper after the theater, she took off her earrings in front of the mirror: Beauty. She smiled at herself with satisfaction. She was learning, at the end of her adolescence, how to be a spoiled child and that pearly skin of hers was plumping out, a little, with high living and compliments. A certain inwardness was beginning to transform the lines around her mouth, those signatures of the personality, and her sweetness and her gravity could sometimes turn a mite petulant when things went not quite as she wanted them to go. You could not have said that her freshness was fading, but she smiled at herself in mirrors a little too often these days, and the face that smiled back was not quite the one she had seen contained in the Beast's agate eyes. Her face was acquiring, instead of beauty, a lacquer of the invincible prettiness that characterizes certain pampered, exquisite, expensive cats.

The soft wind of spring breathed in from the nearby park through the open windows; she did not know why it made her want to cry.

There was a sudden, urgent, scrabbling sound, as of claws, at her door.

Her trance before the mirror broke; all at once, she remembered everything perfectly. Spring was here and she had broken her promise. Now the Beast himself had come in pursuit of her! First, she was frightened of his anger; then, mysteriously joyful, she ran to open the door. But it was his liver-and-white spotted spaniel who hurled herself into the girl's arms in a flurry of little barks and gruff murmurings, of whimpering and relief.

Yet where was the well-brushed, jeweled dog who had sat beside her embroidery frame in the parlor with birds of paradise nodding on the walls? This one's fringed ears were matted with mud, her coat was dusty and snarled, she was thin as a dog that has walked a long way, and if she had not been a dog, she would have been in tears.

After that first, rapturous greeting, she did not wait for Beauty to order her food and water; she seized the chiffon hem of her evening dress, whimpered and tugged. Threw back her head, howled, then tugged and whimpered again.

There was a slow, late train that would take her to the station where she had left for London three months ago. Beauty scribbled a note for her father, threw a coat round her shoulders. Quickly, quickly, urged the spaniel soundlessly; and Beauty knew the Beast was dying.

In the thick dark before dawn, the stationmaster roused a sleepy driver for her. Fast as you can.

It seemed December still possessed his garden. The ground was hard as iron, the skirts of the dark cypress moved on the chill wind with a mournful rustle and there were no green shoots on the roses, as if, this year, they would not bloom. And not one light in any of the windows, only, in the topmost attic, the faintest smear of radiance on a pane, the thin ghost of a light on the verge of extinction.

The spaniel had slept a little, in her arms, for the poor thing was exhausted. But now her grieving agitation fed Beauty's urgency, and as the girl pushed open the front door, she saw, with a thrust of conscience, how the golden door knocker was thickly muffled in black crepe.

The door did not open silently, as before, but with a doleful groaning of the hinges and, this time, onto perfect darkness. Beauty clicked her gold cigarette lighter; the tapers in the chandelier had drowned in their own wax and the prisms were wreathed with drifting arabesques of cobwebs. The flowers in the glass jars were dead, as if nobody had had the heart to replace them after she was gone. Dust, everywhere; and it was cold. There was an air of exhaustion, of despair, in the house and, worse, a kind of physical disillusion, as if its glamour had been sustained by a cheap conjuring trick and now the conjurer, having failed to pull the crowds, had departed to try his luck elsewhere.

Beauty found a candle to light her way and followed the faithful spaniel up the staircase, past the study, past her suite, through a house echoing with desertion up a little back staircase dedicated to mice and spiders, stumbling, ripping the hem of her dress in her haste.

What a modest bedroom! An attic, with a sloping roof, they might have given the chambermaid if the Beast had employed staff. A night light on the mantelpiece, no curtains at the windows, no carpet on the floor and a narrow, iron bedstead on which he lay, sadly diminished, his bulk scarcely disturbing the faded patchwork quilt, his mane a grayish rat's nest and his eyes closed. On the stick-backed chair where his clothes had been thrown, the roses she had sent him were thrust into the jug from the washstand, but they were all dead.

The spaniel jumped up on the bed and burrowed her way under the scanty covers, softly keening.

"Oh, Beast," said Beauty. "I have come home."

His eyelids flickered. How was it she had never noticed before that his agate eyes were equipped with lids, like those of a man? Was it because she had only looked at her own face, reflected there?

"I'm dying, Beauty," he said in a cracked whisper of his former purr. "Since you left me, I have been sick. I could not go hunting, I found I had not the stomach to kill the gentle beasts, I could not eat. I am sick and I must die; but I shall die happy because you have come to say goodbye to me."

She flung herself upon him, so that the iron bedstead groaned, and covered his poor paws with her kisses.

"Don't die, Beast! If you'll have me, I'll never leave you."

When her lips touched the meat-hook claws, they drew back into their pads and she saw how he had always kept his fists clenched but now, painfully, tentatively, at last began to stretch his fingers. Her tears fell on his face like snow and, under their soft transformation, the bones showed through the pelt, the flesh through the wide, tawny brow. And then it was no longer a lion in her arms but a man, a man with an unkempt mane of hair and, how strange, a broken nose, such as the noses of retired boxers, that gave him a distant, heroic resemblance to the handsomest of all the beasts.

"Do you know," said Mr. Lyon, "I think I might be able to manage a little breakfast today, Beauty, if you would eat something with me."

Mr. and Mrs. Lyon walk in the garden; the old spaniel drowses on the grass, in a drift of fallen petals.

Secrets

BERNARD MACLAVERTY
(Irish, 1942–   )

He had been called to be there at the end. His Great Aunt Mary had been dying for some days now and the house was full of relatives. He had just left his girlfriend's home—they had been studying for 'A' levels together—and had come back to the house to find all the lights spilling onto the lawn and a sense of purpose which had been absent from the last few days.

He knelt at the bedroom door to join in the prayers. His knees were on the wooden threshold and he edged them forward onto the carpet. They had tried to wrap her fingers around a crucifix but they kept loosening. She lay low on the pillow and her face seemed to have shrunk by half since he had gone out earlier in the night. Her white hair was damped and pushed back from her forehead. She twisted her head from side to side, her eyes closed. The prayers chorused on, trying to cover the sound she was making deep in her throat. Someone said about her teeth and his mother leaned over her and said, 'That's the pet', and took her dentures from her mouth. The lower half of her face seemed to collapse. She half opened her eyes but could not raise her eyelids enough and showed only crescents of white.

'Hail Mary full of grace . . .' the prayers went on. He closed his hands over his face so that he would not have to look but smelt the trace of his girlfriend's handcream from his hands. The noise, deep and guttural, that his aunt was making became intolerable to him. It was as if she were drowning. She had lost all the dignity he knew her to have. He got up from the floor and stepped between the others who were kneeling and went into her sitting-room off the same landing.

He was trembling with anger or sorrow, he didn't know which. He sat in the brightness of her big sitting-room at the oval table and waited for something to happen. On the table was a cut-glass vase of irises, dying because she had been in bed for over a week. He sat staring at them. They were withering from the tips inward, scrolling themselves delicately, brown and neat. Clearing up after themselves. He stared at them for a long time until he heard the sounds of women weeping from the next room.

His aunt had been small—her head on a level with his when she sat at her table—and she seemed to get smaller each year. Her skin fresh, her hair white and waved and always well washed. She wore no jewelry except a cameo ring on the third finger of her right hand and, around her neck, a gold locket on a chain. The white classical profile on the ring was almost worn through and had become translucent and indistinct. The boy had noticed the ring when she had read to him as a child. In the beginning fairy tales, then as he got older extracts from famous novels, *Lorna Doone, Persuasion, Wuthering Heights* and her favourite extract, because she read it so often, Pip's meeting with Miss Havisham from *Great Expectations.* She would sit with him on her knee, her arms around him and holding the page flat with her hand. When he was bored he would interrupt her and ask about the ring. He loved hearing her tell of how her grandmother had given it to her as a brooch and she had had a ring made from it. He would try to count back to see how old it was. Had her grandmother got it from *her* grandmother? And if so what had she turned it into? She would nod her head from side to side and say, 'How would I know a thing like that?' keeping her place in the closed book with her finger.

'Don't be so inquisitive,' she'd say. 'Let's see what happens next in the story.'

One day she was sitting copying figures into a long narrow book with a dip pen when he came into her room. She didn't look up but when he asked her a question she just said, 'Mm?' and went on writing. The vase of irises on the oval table vibrated slightly as she wrote.

'What is it?' She wiped the nib on blotting paper and looked up at him over her reading glasses.

'I've started collecting stamps and Mamma says you might have some.'

'Does she now—?'

She got up from the table and went to the tall walnut bureau-bookcase standing in the alcove. From a shelf of the bookcase she took a small wallet of keys and selected one for the lock. There was a harsh metal shearing sound as she pulled the desk flap down. The writing area was covered with green leather which had dog-eared at the corners. The inner part was divided into pigeon holes, all bulging with papers. Some of them, envelopes, were gathered in batches nipped at the waist with elastic bands. There were postcards and bills and cashbooks. She pointed to the postcards.

'You may have the stamps on those,' she said. 'But don't tear them. Steam them off.'

She went back to the oval table and continued writing. He sat on the arm of the chair looking through the picture postcards—torchlight processions at Lourdes, brown photographs of town centres, dull black and whites of beaches backed by faded hotels. Then he turned them over and began to sort the stamps. Spanish, with a bald man, French with a rooster, German with funny jerky print, some Italian with what looked like a chimney-sweep's bundle and a hatchet.

'These are great,' he said. 'I haven't got any of them.'

'Just be careful how you take them off.'

'Can I take them downstairs?'

'Is your mother there?'

'Yes.'

'Then perhaps it's best if you bring the kettle up here.'

He went down to the kitchen. His mother was in the morning room polishing silver. He took the kettle and the flex upstairs. Except for the dipping and scratching of his Aunt's pen the room was silent. It was at the back of the house overlooking the orchard and the sound of traffic from the main road was distant and muted. A tiny rattle began as the kettle warmed up, then it bubbled and steam gushed quietly from its spout. The cards began to curl slightly in the jet of steam but she didn't seem to be watching. The stamps peeled moistly off and he put them in a saucer of water to flatten them.

'Who is Brother Benignus?' he asked. She seemed not to hear. He asked again and she looked over her glasses.

'He was a friend.'

His flourishing signature appeared again and again. Sometimes Bro Benignus, sometimes Benignus and once Iggy.

'Is he alive?'

'No, he's dead now. Watch the kettle doesn't run dry.'

When he had all the stamps off he put the postcards together and replaced them in the pigeon-hole. He reached over towards the letters but before his hand touched them his aunt's voice, harsh for once, warned.

'A-A-A,' she moved her pen from side to side. 'Do-not-touch,' she said and smiled. 'Anything else, yes! That section, no!' She resumed her writing.

The boy went through some other papers and found some photographs. One was of a beautiful girl. It was very old-fashioned but he could see that she was beautiful. The picture was a pale brown oval set on a white square of card. The edges of the oval were misty. The girl in the photograph was young and had dark, dark hair scraped severely back and tied like a knotted rope on the top of her head—high arched eyebrows, her nose straight and thin, her mouth slightly smiling, yet not smiling—the way a mouth is after smiling. Her eyes looked out at him dark and knowing and beautiful.

'Who is that?' he asked.

'Why? What do you think of her?'

'She's all right.'

'Do you think she is beautiful?' The boy nodded.

'That's me,' she said. The boy was glad he had pleased her in return for the stamps.

Other photographs were there, not posed ones like Aunt Mary's but Brownie snaps of laughing groups of girls in bucket hats like German helmets and coats to their ankles. They seemed tiny faces covered in clothes. There was a photograph of a young man smoking a cigarette, his hair combed one way by the wind against a background of sea.

'Who is that in the uniform?' the boy asked.

'He's a soldier,' she answered without looking up.

'Oh,' said the boy. 'But who is he?'

'He was a friend of mine before you were born,' she said. Then added, 'Do I smell something cooking? Take your stamps and off you go. That's the boy.'

The boy looked at the back of the picture of the man and saw in black spidery ink 'John, Aug '15 Ballintoye'.

'I thought maybe it was Brother Benignus,' he said. She looked at him not answering.

'Was your friend killed in the war?'

At first she said no, but then she changed her mind.

'Perhaps he was,' she said, then smiled. 'You are far too inquisitive. Put it to use and go and see what is for tea. Your mother will need the kettle.' She came over to the bureau and helped tidy the photographs away. Then she locked it and put the keys on the shelf.

'Will you bring me up my tray?'

The boy nodded and left.

It was a Sunday evening, bright and summery. He was doing his homework and his mother was sitting on the carpet in one of her periodic fits of tidying out the drawers of the mahogany sideboard. On one side of her was a heap of paper scraps torn in quarters and bits of rubbish, on the other the useful items that had to be kept. The boy heard the bottom stair creak under Aunt Mary's light footstep. She knocked and put her head round the door and said that she was walking to Devotions. She was dressed in her good coat and hat and was just easing her fingers into her second glove. The boy saw her stop and pat her hair into place before the mirror in the hallway. His mother stretched over and slammed the door shut. It vibrated, then he heard the deeper sound of the outside door closing and her first few steps on the gravelled driveway. He sat for a long time wondering if he would have time or not. Devotions could take anything from twenty minutes to three quarters of an hour, depending on who was saying it.

Ten minutes must have passed, then the boy left his homework and went upstairs and into his aunt's sitting room. He stood in front of the bureau wondering, then he reached for the keys. He tried several before he got the right one. The desk flap screeched as he pulled it down. He pretended to look at the postcards again in case there were any stamps he had missed. Then he put them away and reached for the bundle of letters. The elastic band was thick and old, brittle almost and when he took it off its track remained on the wad of letters. He carefully opened one and took out the letter and unfolded it, frail, khaki-coloured.

My dearest Mary, it began. I am so tired I can hardly write to you. I have spent what seems like all day censoring letters (there is a howitzer about

100 yds away firing every 2 minutes). The letters are heartrending in their attempt to express what they cannot. Some of the men are illiterate, others almost so. I know that they feel as much as we do, yet they do not have the words to express it. That is your job in the schoolroom to give us generations who can read and write well. They have . . .

The boy's eye skipped down the page and over the next. He read the last paragraph.

Mary I love you as much as ever—more so that we cannot be together. I do not know which is worse, the hurt of this war or being separated from you. Give all my love to Brendan and all at home.

It was signed, scribbled with what he took to be John. He folded the paper carefully into its original creases and put it in the envelope. He opened another.

My love, it is thinking of you that keeps me sane. When I get a moment I open my memories of you as if I were reading. Your long dark hair—I always imagine you wearing the blouse with the tiny roses, the white one that opened down the back—your eyes that said so much without words, the way you lowered your head when I said anything that embarrassed you, and the clean nape of your neck.

The day I think about most was the day we climbed the head at Ballycastle. In a hollow, out of the wind, the air full of pollen and the sound of insects, the grass warm and dry and you lying beside me your hair undone, between me and the sun. You remember that that was where I first kissed you and the look of disbelief in your eyes that made me laugh afterwards.

It makes me laugh now to see myself savouring these memories standing alone up to my thighs in muck. It is everywhere, two, three feet deep. To walk ten yards leaves you quite breathless.

I haven't time to write more today so I leave you with my feet in the clay and my head in the clouds. I love you, John.

He did not bother to put the letter back into the envelope but opened another.

My dearest, I am so cold that I find it difficult to keep my hand steady enough to write. You remember when we swam the last two fingers of your hand went the colour and texture of candles with the cold. Well that is how I am all over. It is almost four days since I had any real sensation in my feet or legs. Everything is frozen. The ground is like steel.

Forgive me telling you this but I feel I have to say it to someone. The worst thing is the dead. They sit or lie frozen in the position they died. You can distinguish them from the living because their faces are the colour of slate. God help us when the thaw comes . . . This war is beginning to have an effect on me. I have lost all sense of feeling. The only emotion I have experienced lately is one of anger. Sheer white trembling anger. I have no pity or sorrow for the dead and injured. I thank God it is not me but I am enraged that it had to be them. If I live through this experience I will be a different person.

The only thing that remains constant is my love for you.

Today a man died beside me. A piece of shrapnel had pierced his neck as we were moving under fire. I pulled him into a crater and stayed with him until he died. I watched him choke and then drown in his blood.

I am full of anger which has no direction.

He sorted through the pile and read half of some, all of others. The sun had fallen low in the sky and shone directly into the room onto the pages he was reading making the paper glare. He selected a letter from the back of the pile and shaded it with his hand as he read.

Dearest Mary, I am writing this to you from my hospital bed. I hope that you were not too worried about not hearing from me. I have been here, so they tell me, for two weeks and it took another two weeks before I could bring myself to write this letter.

I have been thinking a lot as I lie here about the war and about myself and about you. I do not know how to say this but I feel deeply that I must do something, must sacrifice something to make up for the horror of the past year. In some strange way Christ has spoken to me through the carnage . . .

Suddenly the boy heard the creak of the stair and he frantically tried to slip the letter back into its envelope but it crumpled and would not fit. He bundled them all together. He could hear his aunt's familiar puffing on the short stairs to her room. He spread the elastic band wide with his fingers. It snapped and the letters scattered. He pushed them into their pigeon hole and quickly closed the desk flap. The brass screeched loudly and clicked shut. At that moment his aunt came into the room.

'What are you doing boy?' she snapped.

'Nothing.' He stood with the keys in his hand. She walked to the bureau and opened it. The letters sprung out in an untidy heap.

'You have been reading my letters,' she said quietly. Her mouth was tight with the words and her eyes blazed. The boy could say nothing. She struck him across the side of the face.

'Get out,' she said. 'Get out of my room.'

The boy, the side of his face stinging and red, put the keys on the table on his way out. When he reached the door she called to him. He stopped, his hand on the handle.

'You are dirt,' she hissed, 'and always will be dirt. I shall remember this till the day I die.'

Even though it was a warm evening there was a fire in the large fireplace. His mother had asked him to light it so that she could clear out Aunt Mary's stuff. The room could then be his study, she said. She came in and seeing him at the table said, 'I hope I'm not disturbing you.'

'No.'

She took the keys from her pocket, opened the bureau and began burning papers and cards. She glanced quickly at each one before she flicked it onto the fire.

'Who was Brother Benignus?' he asked.

His mother stopped sorting and said, 'I don't know. Your aunt kept herself very much to herself. She got books from him through the post occasionally. That much I do know.'

She went on burning the cards. They built into strata, glowing red and black. Now and again she broke up the pile with the poker, sending showers of sparks up the chimney. He saw her come to the letters. She took off the elastic band and put it to one side with the useful things and began dealing the envelopes into the fire. She opened one and read quickly through it, then threw it on top of the burning pile.

'Mama,' he said.

'Yes?'

'Did Aunt Mary say anything about me?'

'What do you mean?'

'Before she died—did she say anything?'

'Not that I know of—the poor thing was too far gone to speak, God rest her.' She went on burning, lifting the corners of the letters with the poker to let the flames underneath them.

When he felt a hardness in his throat he put his head down on his books. Tears came into his eyes for the first time since she had died and he cried silently into the crook of his arm for the woman who had been his maiden aunt, his teller of tales, that she might forgive him.

Night in Tunisia

NEIL JORDAN
(Irish, 1951–   )

That year they took the green house again. She was there again, older than him and a lot more venal. He saw her on the white chairs that faced the tennis-court and again in the burrows behind the tennis-court and again still down on the fifteenth hole where the golf-course met the mouth of the Boyne. It was twilight each time he saw her and the peculiar light seemed to suspend her for an infinity, a suspended infinite silence, full of years somehow. She must have been seventeen now that he was fourteen. She was fatter, something of an exhausted woman about her and still something of the girl whom adults called mindless. It was as if a cigarette between her fingers had burnt towards the tip without her noticing. He heard people talking about her even on her first day there, he learnt that underneath her frayed blouse her wrists were marked. She was a girl about whom they would talk anyway since she lived with a father who drank, who was away for long stretches in England. Since she lived in a green corrugated-iron house. Not even a house, a châlet really, like the ones the townspeople built to house summer visitors. But she lived in it all the year round.

They took a green house too that summer, also made of corrugated iron. They took it for two months this time, since his father was playing what he said would be his last stint, since there was no more place for brassmen like him in the world of three-chord showbands. And this time the two small bedrooms were divided differently, his sister taking the small one, since she had to dress on her own now, himself and his father sharing the larger one where two years ago his sister and he had slept. Every night his father took the tenor sax and left for Mosney to play with sixteen others for older couples who remembered what the big bands of the forties sounded like. And he was left alone with his sister who talked less and less as her breasts grew bigger. With the alto saxophone which his father said he could learn when he forgot his fascination for three-chord ditties. With the guitar which he played a lot, as if in spite against the alto saxophone. And with the broken-keyed piano which he played occasionally.

When it rained on the iron roof the house sang and he was reminded of a green tin drum he used to have when he was younger. It was as if he was inside it.

He wandered round the first three days, his sister formal and correct beside him. There was one road made of tarmac, running through all the corrugated houses towards the tennis-court. It was covered always with drifts of sand, which billowed while they walked. They passed her once, on the same side, like an exotic and dishevelled bird, her long yellow cardigan coming down to her knees, covering her dress, if she wore any. He stopped as she passed and turned to face her. Her feet kept billowing up the sand, her eyes didn't see him, they were puffy and covered in black pencil. He felt hurt. He remembered an afternoon three years ago when they had lain on the golf links, the heat, the nakedness that didn't know itself, the grass on their three backs.

'Why don't you stop her?' he asked his sister.

'Because,' she answered. 'Because, because.'

He became obsessed with twilights. Between the hour after tea when his father left and the hour long after dark when his father came home he would wait for them, observe them, he would taste them as he would a sacrament. The tincture of the light fading, the blue that seemed to be sucked into a thin line beyond the sea into what the maths books called infinity, the darkness falling like a stone. He would look at the long shadows of the burrows on the strand and the long shadows of the posts that held the sagging tennis-nets on the tarmac courts. He would watch his sister walking down the road under the eyes of boys that were a little older than him. And since he hung around at twilight and well into the dark he came to stand with them, on the greens behind the clubhouse their cigarette tips and their laughter punctuating the dark. He played all the hits on the honky-tonk piano in the clubhouse for them and this compensated for his missing years. He played and he watched, afraid to say too much, listening to their jokes and their talk about girls, becoming most venal when it centred on her.

He laughed with them, that special thin laugh that can be stopped as soon as it's begun.

There was a raft they would swim out to on the beach. His skin was light and his arms were thin and he had no Adam's apple to speak of, no hair creeping over his togs, but he would undress all the same with them and swim out. They would spend a day on it while the sun browned their backs and coaxed beads of resin from the planks. When they shifted too much splinters of wood shot through their flesh. So mostly they lay inert, on their stomachs, their occasional erections hidden beneath them, watching on the strand the parade of life.

It galled his father what he played.
'What galls me,' he would say, 'is that you could be so good.'
But he felt vengeful and played them incessantly and even sang the tawdry lyrics. Some day soon, he sang, I'm going to tell the Moon about the crying game. And maybe he'll explain, he sang.

'Why don't you speak to her?' he asked his sister when they passed her again. It was seven o'clock and it was getting dark.
'Because,' she said. 'Because I don't.'

But he turned. He saw her down the road, her yellow cardigan making a scallop round her fattening buttocks.

'Rita,' he called. 'Rita.'

She turned. She looked at him blankly for a moment and then she smiled, her large pouting lips curving the invitation she gave to any boy that shouted at her.

He sat at the broken-keyed piano. The light was going down over the golf-links and his sister's paperback novel was turned over on the wooden table. He heard her in her room, her shoes knocking off the thin wooden partition. He heard the rustling of cotton and nylon and when the rustles stopped for a moment he got up quickly from the piano and opened the door. She gave a gasp and pulled the dress from the pile at her feet to cover herself. He asked her again did she remember and she said she didn't and her face blushed with such shame that he felt sorry and closed the door again.

The sea had the movement of cloth but the texture of glass. It flowed and undulated, but shone hard and bright. He thought of cloth and glass and how to mix them. A cloth made of glass fibre or a million woven mirrors. He saw that the light of twilight was repeated or reversed at early morning.

He decided to forget about his sister and join them, the brashness they were learning, coming over the transistors, the music that cemented it. And the odd melancholy of the adulthood they were about to straddle, to ride like a Honda down a road with one white line, pointless and inevitable.

His father on his nights off took out his Selmer, old loved talisman that was even more shining than on the day he bought it. He would sit and accompany while his father stood and played 'That Certain Feeling', 'All the Things You Are', the names that carried their age with them, the embellishments and the filled-in notes that must have been something one day but that he had played too often, that he was too old now to get out of. And to please his father he would close his eyes and play, not knowing how or what he played, and his father would stop and let him play on, listening. And he would occasionally look and catch that look in his listening eyes, wry, sad and loving, his pleasure at how his son played only marred by the knowledge of how little it meant to him. And he would catch the look in his father's eyes and get annoyed and deliberately hit a bum note to spoil it. And the sadness in the eyes would outshine the wryness then and he would be sorry, but never sorry enough.

He soon learned that they were as mistrustful of each other as she was of them and so he relaxed somewhat. He learned to turn his silence into a pose. They listened to his playing and asked about his sister. They lay on the raft, watched women on the strand, their eyes stared so hard that the many shapes on the beach became one, indivisible. It made the sand-dunes and even the empty clubhouse redundant. Lying face down on the warm planks, the sun burning their backs with an aching languor. The blaring transistor, carried over in its plastic bag. Her on the beach, indivisible, her yellow cardigan glaring even on the hottest days. He noticed she had got fatter since he came. Under them on the warm planks the violent motion of their pricks. She who lived in the châlet all the year round.

The one bedroom and the two beds, his father's by the door, his by the window. The rippled metal walls. The moon like water on his hand, the bed beside him empty. Then the front door opening, the sound of the saxophone case laid down. His eyes closed, his father stripping in the darkness, climbing in, long underwear and vest. The body he'd known lifelong, old and somewhat loved, but not like his Selmer, shining. They get better with age, he said about instruments. His breath scraping the air now, scraping over the wash of the sea, sleeping.

The tall thin boy put his mouth to the mouth of the french letter and blew. It expanded, huge and bulbous, with a tiny bubble at the tip.

'It's getting worked up,' he said.

He had dark curling hair and dark shaven cheeks and a mass of tiny pimples where he shaved. The pimples spread from his ears downwards, as if scattered from a pepper-canister. His eyes were dark too, and always a little closed.

'We'll let it float to England,' he said, 'so it can find a fanny big enough for it.'

They watched it bobbing on the waves, brought back and forwards with the wash. Then a gust of wind lifted it and carried it off, falling to skim the surface and rising again, the bubble towards the sky.

He had walked up from the beach and the french letter bound for England. He had seen her yellow cardigan on the tennis-court from a long way off, above the strand. He was watching her play now, sitting on the white wrought-iron seat, his hands between his legs.

She was standing on the one spot, dead-centre of the court, hardly looking at all at her opponent. She was hitting every ball cleanly and lazily and the sound that came from her racquet each time was the taut twang that he knew only came from a good shot. He felt that even a complete stranger would have known, from her boredom, her ease, that she lived in a holiday town with a tennis-court all the year round. The only sign of effort was the beads of sweat round her lips and the tousled blonde curls round her forehead. And every now and then when the man she was playing against managed to send a shot towards the sidelines, she didn't bother to follow it at all. She let the white ball bounce impotent towards the wire mesh.

He watched the small fat man he didn't recognise lose three balls for every ball won. He relished the spectacle of a fat man in white being beaten by a bored teenage girl in sagging high-heels. Then he saw her throw her eyes upwards, throw her racquet down and walk from the court. The white ball rolled towards the wire mesh.

She sat beside him. She didn't look at him but she spoke as if she had known him those three years.

'You play him. I'm sick of it.'

He walked across the court and his body seemed to glow with the heat generated by the slight touch of hers. He picked up the racquet and the ball, placed his foot behind the white line and threw the ball up, his eye on it, white, skewered against the blue sky. Then it came down and he heard the resonant twang as his racquet hit it and it went spinning into the opposite court but there was no one there to take it. He looked up and saw the fat man and her walking towards a small white car. The fat man gesturing her in and she looked behind at him once before she entered.

And as the car sped off toward Mornington he swore she waved.

The car was gone down the Mornington road. He could hear the pop-pop of the tennis-balls hitting the courts and the twang of them hitting the racquets as he walked, growing fainter. He walked along the road, past the tarmac courts and past the grass courts and past the first few holes of the golf-course which angled in a T round the tennis-courts. He walked past several squares of garden until he came to his. It wasn't really a garden, a square of sand and scutch. He walked through the gate and up the path where the sand had been trodden hard to the green corrugated door. He turned the handle in the door, always left open. He saw the small square room, the sand fanning across the line from the doorstep, the piano with the sheet-music perched on the keys. He thought of the midday sun outside, the car with her in the passenger seat moving through it, the shoulders of the figure in the driver's seat. The shoulders hunched and fat, expressing something venal. He thought of the court, the white tennis-ball looping between her body and his. Her body relaxed, vacant and easeful, moving the racquet so the ball flew where she wished. His body worried, worrying the whole court. He felt there was something wrong, the obedient ball, the running man. What had she lost to gain that ease? he wondered. He thought of all the jokes he had heard and of the act behind the jokes that none of those who told the jokes experienced. The innuendos and the charged words like the notes his father played, like the melodies his father willed him to play. The rich full twang as the ball met her racquet at the centre.

He saw the alto saxophone on top of the piano. He took it down, placed it on the table and opened the case. He looked at the keys, remembering the first lessons his father had taught him when it was new-bought, months ago. The keys unpressed, mother-of-pearl on gold, spotted with dust. He took out the ligature and fixed the reed in the mouthpiece. He put it between his lips, settled his fingers and blew. The note came out harsh and childish, as if he'd never learnt. He heard a shifting movement in the inside room and knew that he'd woken his father.

He put the instrument back quietly and made for the tiny bathroom. He closed the door behind him quietly, imagining his father's grey vest rising from the bed to the light of the afternoon sun. He looked into the mirror that closed on the cabinet where the medicine things were kept. He saw his face in the mirror looking at him, frightened, quick glance. Then he saw his face taking courage and looking at him full-on, the brown eyes and the thin fragile jawline. And he began to look at his eyes as directly as they looked at him.

'You were playing,' his father said, in the living-room, in shirt-sleeves, in uncombed afternoon hair, 'the alto—'

'No,' he said, going for the front door, 'you were dreaming.'

And on the raft the fat asthmatic boy, obsessed more than any with the theatre on the strand, talking about 'it' in his lisping, mournful voice, smoking cigarettes that made his breath wheeze more. He had made classifications, rigid as calculus, meticulous as algebra. There were girls, he said, and women, and in between them what he termed lady, the lines of demarcation finely and inexorably drawn. Lady was thin and sat on towels, with high-heels and suntan-lotions, without kids. Woman was fat, with rugs and breasts that hung or bulged, with children. Then there were girls, his age, thin, fat and middling, nyloned, short-stockinged—

He lay on his stomach on the warm wood and listened to the fat boy talking and saw her walking down the strand. The straggling, uncaring walk that, he decided, was one of these or all of these at once. She was wearing flat shoes that went down at the heels with no stockings and the familiar cardigan that hid what could have classified her. She walked to a spot up the beach from the raft and unrolled the bundled towel from under her arm. Then she kicked off her shoes and pulled off her cardigan and wriggled out of the skirt her cardigan had hidden. She lay back on the towel in the yellow bathing suit that was too young for her, through which her body seemed to press like a butterfly already moulting in its chrysalis. She took a bottle then and shook it into her palm and began rubbing the liquid over her slack exposed body.

He listened to the fat boy talking about her—he was local too—about her father who on his stretches home came back drunk and bounced rocks off the tin roof, shouting, 'Hewer.'

'What does that mean?' he asked.

'Just that,' said the asthmatic boy. 'Rhymes with "sure".'

He looked at her again from the raft, her slack stomach bent forward, her head on her knees. He saw her head lift and turn lazily towards the raft and he stood up then, stretching his body upwards, under what he imagined was her gaze. He dived, his body imagining itself suspended in air before it hit the water. Underwater he held his breath, swam through the flux of tiny bubbles, like crotchets before his open eyes.

'What did you say she was?' he asked the fat boy, swimming back to the raft.

'Hewer,' said the fat boy, more loudly.

He looked towards the strand and saw her on her back, her slightly plump thighs towards the sky, her hands shielding her eyes. He swam to the side of the raft then and gripped the wood with one hand and the fat boy's ankle with the other and pulled. The fat boy came crashing into the water and went down and when his head came up, gasping for asthmatic breath, he forced it down once more, though he didn't know what whore meant.

His father was cleaning the alto when he came back.

'What does "hewer" mean?' he asked his father.

His father stopped screwing in the ligature, and looked at him, his old sidesman's eyes surprised, and somewhat moral.

'A woman,' he said, 'who sells her body for monetary gain.'

He stopped for a moment. He didn't understand.

'That's tautology,' he said.

'What's that?' his father asked.

'It repeats,' he said, and went into the toilet.

He heard the radio crackle over the sound of falling water and heard a rapid-fire succession of notes that seemed to spring from the falling water, that amazed him, so much faster than his father ever played, but slow behind it all, melancholy, like a river. He came out of the toilet and stood listening with his father. 'Who is that?' he asked his father. Then he heard the continuity announcer say the name Charlie Parker and saw his father staring at some point between the wooden table and the wooden holiday-home floor.

He played later on the piano in the clubhouse with the dud notes, all the songs, the trivial mythologies whose significance he had never questioned. It was as if he was fingering through the years and as he played he began to forget the melodies of all those goodbyes and heartaches, letting his fingers take him where they wanted to, trying to imitate that sound like a river he had just heard. It had got dark without him noticing and when finally he could just see the keys as question-marks in the dark, he stopped. He heard a noise behind him, the noise of somebody who has been listening, but who doesn't want you to know they are there. He turned and saw her looking at him, black in the square of light coming through the door. Her eyes were on his hands that were still pressing the keys and there was a harmonic hum tiny somewhere in the air. Her eyes rose to his face, unseeing and brittle, to meet his hot, tense stare. He still remembered the rough feel of the tartan blanket over them, three of them, the grass under them. But her eyes didn't, so he looked everywhere but on them, on her small pinched chin, ridiculous under her large face, on the yellow linen dress that was ragged round her throat, on her legs, almost black from so much sun. The tiny hairs on them glistened with the light behind her. He looked up then and her eyes were still on his, keeping his fingers on the keys, keeping the chord from fading.

He was out on the burrows once more, he didn't know how, and he met the thin boy. The thin boy sat down with him where they couldn't be seen and took a condom from his pocket and masturbated among the bushes. He saw how the liquid was caught by the antiseptic web, how the sand clung to it when the thin boy threw it, like it does to spittle.

He left the thin boy and walked down the beach, empty now of its glistening bodies. He looked up at the sky, from which the light was fading, like a thin silver wire. He came to where the beach faded into the mouth of a river. There was a statue there, a Virgin with thin fingers towards the sea, her feet layered with barnacles. There were fishermen looping a net round the mouth. He could see the dim line of the net they pulled and the occasional flashes of white salmon. And as the boat pulled the net towards the shore he saw how the water grew violent with flashes, how the loose shoal of silver-and-white turned into a panting, open-gilled pile. He saw the net close then, the fishermen lifting it, the water falling from it, the salmon laid bare, glutinous, clinging, wet, a little like boiled rice.

He imagined the glistening bodies that littered the beach pulled into a net like that. He imagined her among them, slapping for space, panting for air, he heard transistors blare Da Doi Run Run, he saw suntan-lotion bottles crack and splinter as the Fisher up above pulled harder. He imagined his face like a lifeguard's, dark sidelocks round his muscular jaw, a megaphone swinging from his neck, that crackled.

He saw the thin band of light had gone, just a glow off the sea now. He felt frightened, but forced himself not to run. He walked in quick rigid steps past the barnacled Virgin then and down the strand.

'Ten bob for a touch with the clothes on. A pound without.'

They were playing pontoon on the raft. He was watching the beach, the bodies thicker than salmon. When he heard the phrase he got up and kicked the dirt-cards into the water. He saw the Queen of Hearts face upwards in the foam. As they made for him he dived and swam out a few strokes.

'Cunts,' he yelled from the water. 'Cunts.'

On the beach the wind blew fine dry sand along the surface, drawing it in currents, a tide of sand.

His sister laid the cups out on the table and his father ate with long pauses between mouthfuls. His father's hand paused, the bread quivering in the air, as if he were about to say something. He looked at his sister's breasts across a bowl of apples, half-grown fruits. The apples came from monks who kept an orchard. Across the fields, behind the house. He imagined a monk's hand reaching for the unplucked fruit, white against the swinging brown habit. For monks never sunbathed.

When he had finished he got up from the table and idly pressed a few notes on the piano.

'Why do you play that?' his father asked. He was still at the table, between mouthfuls.

'I don't know,' he said.

'What galls me,' said his father, 'is that you could be good.'

He played a bit more of the idiotic tune that he didn't know why he played.

'If you'd let me teach you,' his father said, 'you'd be glad later on.'

'Then why not wait until later on and teach me then?'

'Because you're young, you're at the age. You'll never learn as well as now, if you let me teach you. You'll never feel things like you do now.'

He began to play again in defiance and then stopped.
'I'll pay you,' his father said.

His father woke him coming in around four. He heard his wheezing
breath and his shuffling feet. He watched the grey, metal-coloured light
filling the room that last night had emptied it. He thought of his father's
promise to pay him. He thought of the women who sold their bodies for
monetary gain. He imagined all of them on the dawn golf-course, waking
in their dew-sodden clothes. He imagined fairways full of them, their
monetary bodies covered with fine drops of water. Their dawn chatter
like birdsong. Where was that golf-course, he wondered? He crept out of
bed and into his clothes and out of the door, very quietly. He crossed the
road and clambered over the wire fence that separated the road from the
golf-course. He walked through several fairways, across several greens,
past several fluttering pennants with the conceit in his mind all the time
of her on one green, asleep and sodden, several pound notes in her closed
fist. At the fourteenth green he stopped and saw that the dull metal
colour had faded into morning, true morning. He began to walk back, his
feet sodden from the dew.

He went in through the green corrugated door and put on a record of the
man whose playing he had first heard two days ago. The man played
'Night in Tunisia', and the web of notes replaced the web that had tightened round his crown. The notes soared and fell, dispelling the world
around him, tracing a series of arcs that seemed to point to a place, or if
not a place, a state of mind. He closed his eyes and let the music fill him
and tried to see that place. He could see a landscape of small hills,
stretching to infinity, suffused in a yellow light that seemed to lap like
water. He decided it was a place you were always in, yet always trying to
reach, you walked towards all the time and yet never got there, as it was
always beside you. He opened his eyes and wondered where Tunisia was
on the atlas. Then he stopped wondering and reached up to the piano and
took down the alto saxophone and placed it on the table. He opened the
case and saw it gleaming in the light, new and unplayed. He knew he was
waking his father from the only sleep he ever got, but he didn't care,
imagining his father's pleasure. He heard him moving in the bedroom
then, and saw him come in, his hair dishevelled, putting his shirt on. His
father sat then, while he stood, listening to the sounds that had dispelled

the world. When it had finished his father turned down the volume controls and took his fingers and placed them on the right keys and told him to blow.

He learned the first four keys that day and when his father took his own instrument and went out to his work in Butlin's he worked out several more for himself. When his father came back, at two in the morning, he was still playing. He passed him in the room, neither said anything, but he could feel his father's pleasure, tangible, cogent. He played on while his father undressed in the bedroom and when he was asleep he put it down and walked out the door, across the hillocks of the golf-course onto the strand, still humid with the warmth of that incredible summer.

He forgot the raft and the games of pontoon and the thin boy's jargon. He stayed inside for days and laboriously transferred every combination of notes he had known on the piano onto the metal keys. He lost his tan and the gold sheen of the instrument became quickly tarnished with sweat, the sweat that came off his fingers in the hot metal room. He fashioned his mouth round the reed till the sounds he made became like a power of speech, a speech that his mouth was the vehicle for but that sprang from the knot of his stomach, the crook of his legs.

As he played he heard voices and sometimes the door knocked. But he turned his back on the open window and the view of the golf-course. Somewhere, he thought, there's a golf-course where bodies are free, not for monetary gain—

He broke his habit twice. Once he walked across the fields to the orchard where the monks plucked fruit with white fingers. He sat on a crumbling wall and watched the darkening and fading shadows of the apple trees. Another night he walked back down the strand to where it faded into the river mouth. He looked at the salmonless water and imagined the lifeguard up above calling through his megaphone. He imagined childhood falling from him, coming off his palms like scales from a fish. He didn't look up, he looked down at his fingers that were forming hard coats at the tips, where they touched the keys.

And then, ten days after it had started, his face in the mirror looked older to him, his skin paler, his chin more ragged, less round. His father got up at half-past three and played the opening bars of 'Embraceable You' and, instead of filling in while his father played, he played while his father filled in. And then they both played, rapidly, in a kind of mutual anger, through all his favourites into that area where there are no tunes, only patterns like water, that shift and never settle. And his father put his instrument away and put several pound notes on the table. He took them, put the case up above the piano and went out the green door.

It was five o'clock as he walked down the road by the golf-course, squinting in the sunlight. He walked down by the tennis-court onto the strand, but it was too late now and the beach was empty and there was no one on the raft.

He walked back with the pound notes hot in his pocket and met the fat boy with two racquets under his arm. The fat boy asked him did he want to play and he said, 'Yes.'

They had lobbed an endless series of balls when the fat boy said, 'Did you hear?' 'Hear what?' he asked and then the fat boy mentioned her name. He told him how the lifeguard had rescued her twice during the week, from a part of the beach too near the shore to drown in by accident. He hit the ball towards the fat boy and imagined her body in the lifeguard's arms, his mouth on her mouth, pushing the breath in. Then he saw her sitting on the iron-wrought seat in a green dress now, vivid against the white metal. The pound notes throbbed in his pocket, but he hadn't the courage to stop playing and go to the seat. Her eyes were following the ball as it went backwards and forwards, listless and vacant. The light gradually became grey, almost as grey as the ball, so in the end he could only tell where it fell by the sound and they missed more than half the volleys. But still she sat on the white chair, her eyes on the ball, following it forwards and back. He felt a surge of hope in himself. He would tell her about that place, he told himself, she doesn't know. When it got totally dark he would stop, he told himself, go to her. But he knew that it never gets totally dark and he just might never stop and she might never rise from the white seat.

He hit the ball way above the fat boy's head into the wire meshing. He let the racquet fall on the tarmac. He walked towards her, looking straight into her eyes so that if his courage gave out he would be forced to say something. Come over to the burrows, he would say. He would tell her about that place, but the way she raised her head, he suspected she knew it.

She raised her head and opened her mouth, her answer already there. She inhabited that place, was already there, her open mouth like it was for the lifeguard when he pressed his hand to her stomach, pushed the salt water out, then put his lips to her lips and blew.

AUTHOR INDEX

TITLE INDEX